PARK CITY

PARK CITY

NEW AND

SELECTED STORIES

BY

ANN BEATTIE

ALFRED A. KNOPF   NEW YORK   1998

THIS IS A BORZOI BOOK
PUBLISHED BY ALFRED A. KNOPF, INC.

www.randomhouse.com

Library of Congress Cataloging-in-Publication Data
Beattie, Ann.
Park City : new and selected stories / by Ann Beattie.
p. cm.
ISBN 0-679-45506-X
1. United States—Social life and customs—20th century—Fiction.
I. Title.
PS3552.E177C66 1998
813'.54—dc21   97-49470
CIP

Manufactured in the United States of America
First Edition

For my mother and father

AUTHOR'S NOTE

The stories here were written over approximately a twenty-five-year period. In selecting them, I noticed that quite a few of the stories have characters with the same name. I intended no linkage from story to story—though there are a few in-jokes, of course.

The first eight stories, in the section "Park City," have never appeared in a book before. The others are from previously published collections:

Distortions (1976)

Secrets and Surprises (1979)

The Burning House (1982)

Where You'll Find Me (1986)

What Was Mine (1991)

CONTENTS

Contents

THE BURNING HOUSE

WHERE YOU'LL FIND ME

WHAT WAS MINE

PARK CITY

COSMOS

Jason is the first to run onto the patio. He takes the side steps and bangs on the French doors, and Carl and I follow grudgingly. We would have preferred the front walkway, but as we have done so many times, we sigh and follow Jason's lead. And there stands Grand-Mam, delighted to see the person she calls "my favorite boy in all the world," no matter which way—or with what war whoops—he has approached the house. In the cement flower urns, cosmos are still blooming in mid-November. Some of the leaves are still on the trees, too, and the Japanese maple is the deep rose-brown of dried blood.

Grand-Mam's dining room is cluttered with things she has bought for us at her neighbor's house sale: rattan chairs; a twin-bed frame; a fireplace screen and andirons; a rolled rug that I think I remember as being too wildly geometric. Jason runs the obstacle course into the kitchen, to get the freshly baked gingerbread squares he heard about on the phone. Estelle—Grand-Mam—calls hello to us over her shoulder. She is on the run, trying to catch Jason so she can tie his shoestring. Jason's shoes don't just come untied; they seem to sprout octopus tentacles, because he prefers his shoelaces extra long. He is very particular about his clothes. He won't wear anything bright. He won't wear knit shirts, or knit anything. He will never wear a raincoat, regardless of how hard it is raining, so Carl sprays his jackets to weatherproof them. He wears a baseball cap turned backward, but forget keeping his ears warm: the brighter they are, the more Jason swears they're—as he calls them—"room temperature." He also insists he is room temperature when he has a fever. He had one two days ago, and I thought for sure we wouldn't be making this trip, but just as the doctor's nurse predicted:

it zoomed up like a strongman's mallet hitting the weight to ring the bell, then subsided with the first dose of Tylenol.

Grand-Mam is no one's grandmother. She did raise Carl, though, after his parents died in the crash of a single-engine plane in Alaska. She was the next-door neighbor, and since there were only tenuous next of kin, she stepped in. By all accounts, she was happy to inherit a ten-year-old boy. This amazes me, since Jason is eight and I cringe to imagine the intensity of his desires and declarations when he is two years older. When I was eight, my parents had my sister, Marge, and overnight my own disposition changed; frantic for attention, I had Jasonesque energy, but instead of running everywhere, I went on talking jags. To this day, my mother is even wary of talking to me on the phone, in case I might start monologuing again, and prefers to write letters. I know they are disappointed that, for the second time, I am living with a man I haven't married. It's not that I'm opposed to marriage, but men now seem to want to observe the women they're considering with the focus of scientists squinting at slides under a microscope. I was judged unworthy of one boyfriend because I didn't carry a spare tire *or* a jack in my trunk. For a while, I almost wavered out of Carl's affections because I drank what he called "girl's drinks": brandy Alexanders and mimosas. I had it out with Carl, pointing out his own deficiencies—for example, that he gripped his beer bottles as if they were grenades he intended to throw—which actually resulted in his grudging respect. According to Carl, he likes women who show gumption. I have lived happily with Carl since Jason was seven. If I decide to give Jason a brother or sister, Carl has said he will marry me. If not, he doesn't see the point. Carl considers this pragmatic. All I can say is that pragmatism is not a quality Carl mentioned in the personals ad I responded to. I have taken to calling him "Fickle Fellow" instead of "Charismatic Carpenter."

By the time I get to the kitchen, there are squares of gingerbread on four plates, and Jason is reaching, with gooey fingers, for another piece. As always, he has removed the napkin from the table, put it on his lap, then brushed it to the floor.

"I had to fire Nonette," Estelle whispers to me. "The money was gone from the green vase." She nods at the vase next to the stove, which holds yellow chrysanthemums. It looks very pretty—much more festive than the Ball jar I pour grease into that sits next to our stove.

"Carl, I hate to tell you this after all the work you did, but I'm afraid the squirrels are back in the attic," Estelle says.

"Let me at 'em," Jason says. "I can karate chop 'em." He pushes his chair back so he can demonstrate a kick, seated. He turns so he is seated on one hip; several times, his left leg flies up, rising higher than you might expect. On the third kick, his foot brushes the edge of the table and everything shakes. "Earthquaaaake!" Jason screams. His whole body trembles, as if the shock waves are going to shake him to death. "I'm sorry!" he says, grabbing the edge as the table tips. There is a landslide of plates and glasses, silverware, stacked newspapers. Jason looks horrified. Across from him, Carl is white-faced, trying to stabilize the table.

"Oh, it was an *accident*," Estelle says. Something else is toppled in the living room, but whatever it is falls with a simple, dull thump. The safety glass on the French doors stops them from shattering as Jason flings one open and runs from the house.

"Things happen in threes," Estelle says. "First the maid steals my petty cash, then the squirrels burrow back in, and then poor Jason has an accident with this silly table."

"What exactly is it that makes the table silly?" Carl says. Since the tornado has whirled through, Carl has decided to take out his hostility, inappropriately, on what remains standing. It's not me, because I'm on all fours, carefully picking up what isn't broken. *Charismatic Carpenter, looking for long term commitment, likes canoeing, candlelight dinners, and cozy evenings by the fire.* What a joke. Carl turns out to be a big Bruce Lee fan, which is what he watches on the VCR while too-wet wood smolders in the fireplace. Candlelight dinners, maybe, if his son hasn't made creative use of the candle holders, and if I cook the dinner. And the canoeing—the canoe fell off the top carrier of his friend Alex's car and what was left might as well have been driftwood. Alex: the same joker who wrote the touchy-feely ad Carl put in the *Washingtonian*: the bait I took, letting him reel me in with promises of glowing candles and gliding boats.

"You get back here, Jason," Carl hollers, staring at the door. Leaves blow in. A strong wind sends bright pink cosmos with the leaves—the flowers Jason apparently uprooted on his way out the door.

"Oh, Carl—" Estelle says.

"Little bastard," Carl says.

"Carl, you *must* not use that language around him," Estelle says.

Carl expresses his frustration by mocking a frustrated person: for a few seconds he pantomimes a gorilla; then his face subsides into a bad actor's tortured Hamlet. By the time he has walked into the living room, Estelle is smiling at his antics. He takes her in his arms and dances one perfect box step.

Unbeknownst to us, Jason has stolen the neighbor boy's bike and is using it as an all-terrain vehicle in the woods behind the house. It will later cost Carl forty dollars—as much as it would cost to buy another similar piece of junk, according to Carl—to have the metal on the bent fender banged out and repainted.

"It's such a delight to see you," Estelle says, curtsying after her dance. "I hope you don't think I'd ever mind anything Jason did, because he is my very favorite boy in all the world, you know."

"That monster is what replaced me in your affections?" Carl says.

"Oh, Carl, no one is *replaced*. . . ."

Meanwhile, the looming tree; the wheels skidding on wet leaves; the crash; the young boy toppled, though he will walk away with only a bruise. He might even flash the trees the victory sign.

My students at Benjamin Franklin Junior High pay little attention to their lessons but suffer exquisitely whenever I make a mistake with my wardrobe (old-lady rubber boots, instead of cool lace-up hiking boots), or when I reveal myself to be ignorant of popular culture (no one cares about Jane's Addiction anymore). They want to know why I do not wear a wedding ring (I have deliberately misled them into thinking that I'm married). I seem to be the only Canadian they are aware of ever having met. One of their mothers, writing me a note explaining her daughter's absence, wanted to know two things: (1) *Do you have a fax? My daughter often has inner ear infections accompanying colds, and it would be easier to explain her absence without having to write a note that she will probably lose on the way to school and* (2) *Did you ever meet Pierre Trudeau? My husband says he was a charming, well-educated man who stood by his wife as long as he could. My husband was picked out of a crowd to dance with Margaret Trudeau up the aisle of Books & Co., in New York City. If you want to know more, we will be at Parent-Teacher night.*

But most of all—more than they pity me for not knowing to wear black-red Morticia lipstick instead of stupid pale pink, or for having my hair blunt cut, rather than layered in a retro Farrah Fawcett style that has recently been welcomed enthusiastically—most of all, they pity me for having chosen to spend my time in school. They feel that I could be making more money working for a corporation, as their fathers and some of their mothers do, or at the very least that I could be a consultant, and therefore have more flexible time. I try to discuss my private life very little, but I am torn between wanting them to like me and my normal adult tendency to withhold unnecessary information from everyone except personal friends, unless I absolutely have to let a telephone salesperson know everything about me so I can order from a catalog. The problem is a little complicated: many of my students are Japanese. Nothing I tell them is really extraneous information, because they are all recent immigrants to the United States, and they don't have a very good sense of how Americans live (although they do have a firm sense of how people should dress and style their hair). I exist for them— for the girls, anyway—somewhere in the limbo between parents and pranksters (American boys at thirteen can be terribly cruel), and as such, I am watched intently for signs that I might be listing one way or the other. Part of their ongoing quiz is a genuine desire to see that I have not shifted ground; another part is curiosity, yet it transcends curiosity, and perhaps should be respected as such.

I started at Benjamin Franklin as a substitute. I went there to replace the history teacher, when her appendix ruptured. She recovered from this, slowly, but was mugged in late September when she left her sickbed, against the doctor's advice, to attend her son's wedding in Detroit. Mrs. Truehall died, and a team of two psychologists was dispatched to Benjamin Franklin to explain that Mrs. Truehall would not be returning: the students would not be seeing her because race relations continued to be a problem in our country, and because drugs such as crack caused senseless violence. It wasn't a very good talk. It was the sort of negative, cover-all-bases talk that was the obverse of the "have a nice day" mentality so rampant in the culture. I had only met Mrs. Truehall once. She clearly adored the students, and they adored her. I was shocked when the principal called me to say that she had died—that the news would be in the next day's paper, but that I should prepare myself for what was sure to be a sad, demanding, and arduous day at Benjamin Franklin. The principal, Darren Luftquist, always explains himself by giving examples in groups of three: when he asked me to finish the term, and I accepted, he was pleased, grateful, and relieved. Not one more thing? I wanted to ask him: not just a *teeny* bit irritated that the students had unanimously said I was the best teacher they'd ever had, except for Mrs. Truehall, when his own *wife* taught social sciences at the school? But I said nothing, and from September until late October I continued to teach history, double-checking my interpretations of certain historical events during pillow talk with Carl, as well as consulting an invaluable yard-sale Toynbee. In November, another problem arose that sprang me from history class and deposited me into what was for me the much-better-known field (and ruts) of English: Howard von der Meiss, the Princeton Ph.D. who had sought the job in order to be close to his boyfriend, who ran the family lumber business ("I was nonjudgmental, open-minded, and supportive"), ran off with a stock boy and sent hate mail to the former lover and to the principal announcing that he had done so, though the letter did not arrive until several days of unexplained absences had passed. I was "rotated" (an apt word; Luftquist's conversation could make a person's head spin) into what had formerly been von der Meiss's seventh-grade classroom. A replacement history teacher had been more quickly found than an English teacher, and Darren Luftquist's wife had reminded her husband that my actual training was in English. She did this not to be truly helpful, but because she was a bitch. She knew that the ten Asian students—all of them girls, by coincidence—had had their own classes suspended, while they attended nonstop English classes, in order to better learn the language. They sat there like a Greek chorus—if you can imagine Japanese teenage girls as a Greek chorus—whispering, and eventually giggling (this was progress?), as the other students trudged through their days, going from classroom to classroom. To the Japanese students, the bell was only a minor annoyance, like hearing someone's cell phone ring in a crowded theater. They shifted in their chairs and chatted as the halls filled with students, then emptied. They knew they had been nicknamed "the Tokyo Toads," though not one of them was from Tokyo, and all ranged from attractive to beautiful. Still, the nickname had traumatized them, separated them from the other students, made them suspicious and self-critical and—when I pressed the point with them—resentful. They were astonished to find out how negative I felt about the boys who had been mean to them. In a private meeting with the girls after school, the braver ones named names, and I threw in a couple of others. I made them all brush their hair off their foreheads, even if they had bangs. I told them that they could do whatever they wanted when they left my classroom, but in the classroom I would expect to see any hair that was not tucked behind their ears held back by headbands and bobby pins, and that they were to sit with space between their chairs and not only look me in the eye, but any boy they felt like staring down. I taught them the word "decondition." I told them that there was a little boy in my own family, and that I dreaded the time when he might go through an awful period in adolescence when he became cruel, and that I was doing everything possible to see that he always treated other people the way he would like to be treated. I discussed with them hormones, insecurity, the male tendency not to ask for directions, and the glass ceiling. Then I explained that men were now in a difficult position because they suddenly found themselves in a different world, which had different expectations. I discussed harmful stereotyping and quoted Oscar Wilde on the war between the sexes. I was a little out of control, but kept going because they were leaning forward, inclining their bodies at exactly the same angle, like the Rockettes—except that of course they were not kicking. I stopped when I found myself passing around my compact so they could look in the mirror and receive makeup hints. Subsequently, they sat taller, pinned back their bangs, wore early–Hillary Rodham Clinton headbands, and asked me privately for advice about everything from easing menstrual cramps to training their family pets.

I came to like the girls so much that I made a mistake. I began to mythologize my own life, though I didn't realize at first that that was what I was doing because I was never the heroine of my stories; instead, like my students, I was a stranger in a strange land (suburbia), expected to play a confusing new role (stepmother; I eventually had to confess my real relationship to Jason, while still fudging about my marital status); soul mate to someone who thought of himself as charismatic—a word I had success in defining by conjuring up Mick Jagger, who seemed to be an excellent cross-cultural reference point for many things—but who was actually quite conservative and demanding. I gave them an example: Carl would manipulate me into going on family outings I wouldn't like by thanking me in advance for being such a trooper. I let Carl remain a little ambiguous to them by making him seem romantic and likable as well as the source of many of my problems, but Jason I simply demonized. I described the dishes sliding off Estelle's table with the fervor of someone who had viewed the devastation at Hiroshima; I made Jason's eating habits interchangeable with those of starving cannibals; I explained his clumsiness in serious psychological terms (disguised aggression), after conjuring up Wile E. Coyote going over a cliff. I told them that if Jason were Superman, he would fly into buildings.

They listened, spellbound. They wanted more and more. Without exactly intending it, I had created a fictional character for them to confront in their imaginations, distracting them from the teenage boys who were their real tormentors. Manic, clumsy Jason was someone they could feel superior to. They liked it that all his adventures were misadventures. They liked it that we had a common bond, that by rejecting Jason, I accepted them; they all became Teacher's Pet, like Cerberus sprouting extra heads.

I miscalculated, though, because I trusted that they would understand, on some level, that I was inventing a larger-than-life Jason. I assumed that my grudging affection for Jason would shine through. I probably even thought that they would intuit that I was in over my head. Moriko Watanabe, however, became all too enthralled with Jason. She begged me to take him shopping somewhere where she could see him; she offered to smuggle me her father's expensive camcorder so I could record him in mid-dash from some calamity. She had a bright-eyed I-Believe-in-Santa expression of such incredulity that it bordered on being obscene; it was really a leer.

One day Moriko, bright-eyed, caught up with me when I was walking to my car. Her friend Miharu was with her.

"Mrs. Woodruff," Moriko said, "Jason reminds me of the story of Susanowo. Have you heard it? He was a god, but the story is really about his sister."

"I don't know that story," I said.

"Well," she said, "it's about a boy just like your son. He messes everything up! He never does what he is supposed to do. He's the storm god, and he's supposed to watch over the sea, but instead, he ruins the land. He destroys everything, and his sister, Ameterasu, becomes frightened of him and goes into a cave. She is gone, and there is no light for anyone." Moriko pauses for effect. "And then there is a huge celebration that some people have, because perhaps if there is a party outside the cave, she will come out."

As she spoke, I noticed how fine her fingers were; how slender her wrists. She waved one hand elegantly, as if she were waving politely to a crowd that admired her. "Then," she said, "when she cannot stand the suspense, she comes all the way out, and a mirror—like the mirror in your compass—"

"Compact," I said.

"Yes. It's held out to her, and she sees her own reflection and is brought all the way out and everyone rejoices because there is light again, and the sun god is among them."

"She was *kunitokotachi*," Miharu broke in to tell me, as I opened my car door. She pronounced the word with reverence. "This means what is unseen. The spirit of the universe."

They both nodded, smiling.

"Good," I said. "She presided again, and everything was okay."

"A rope is stretched across the cave. It stops her, so she cannot go back in even if she wants to," Miharu said.

Moriko nodded. In equal measure, there seemed to be simultaneous confusion and acceptance of what Miharu had just told me.

"I'll see you tomorrow," I told the girls.

Then they became girls again, whispering and giggling together.

Several days later, Moriko began phoning the house. She set a fire in a trash can, probably hoping Jason would run out to smother it.

I knew who the silent caller was because, after many hang-ups, I heard someone call Moriko's name while she was holding the silent phone. It was the neighbor who saw her set the fire and called the police. We were trekking in the Blue Ridge Mountains, several hours away from Carl's house in suburban Washington—an outing made miserable by Jason's having switched the Evian in my bottle for salt water.

Our neighbor, Anthony Diaz, gave chase to Moriko and caught her a few houses away, then dragged her back to his house and called the police when she wouldn't tell him her name. She was taken to the police station, where her parents, Mr. and Mrs. Tomoo Watanabe, were called. There, apparently, a chilling though garbled account was given of our mutual persecution—Moriko's and mine—by a name-calling, xenophobic monster (she remembered the term I had taught her well). I was called by an outraged Tomoo Watanabe at ten o'clock at night (not that he hadn't left plenty of messages earlier). I was guilty of ruining Moriko's life, and of causing her to disgrace the family. In his own fictionalization, my son, Jason, was a person with a mental handicap whom I was badly mistreating. I had tried to throw the boy over a cliff, he informed me. After a lengthy talk with his daughter at the police station, she had informed the police of the same thing. Tomoo Watanabe, Spin Doctor: the wrongly maligned Moriko had set the fire to rescue Jason.

Let it be known that when all this first began to unfold I had been home alone with Jason because message 1 of our filled-up message tape had been from Estelle, saying that Nonette's son had threatened her and that she had left her house and gone to a Holiday Inn and didn't know what to do next.

Jason hid under his bed when the police came, late at night, to the house, and when I tried to drag him out to corroborate that I had never tried to throw him over a cliff, he kicked and screamed (he was angry that his father had spanked him on the trail when the salt-water switch was discovered) and told them I wasn't his mother. Fortunately, he was too out of control to be believed, and I have the open, honest face of any woman who has not been totally steamrollered by life. When Jason provided no further specifics, the police officers became more sympathetic and even relaxed enough to accept a cup of tea. They sat at the kitchen table. I tried to be very calm and slightly world-weary (no problem there) as I communicated that I was bemused by what one of my silly young students had done. Both of the police officers had children. They seemed to sympathize and hurried through their written report. One took lavender honey with her tea. Fortunately, they left before I had to explain Carl's absence in any detail (he was "visiting a friend who was having something of a crisis"), but I didn't get off the hook as easily with "my husband" when he arrived home. With him, too, I tried to act bemused about Moriko's folly. I could not very well explain that I had created a cartoon demon in Moriko's mind by caricaturing his son, though, so Moriko's actions ended up seeming random and bizarre, and the more I tried to insist that a fire in a trash can was nothing, the more Carl presented it as our neighbor had to the police: the little bitch was dangerous, and furthermore, he had advised against my taking a permanent teaching job to begin with, and here was an example of how kids that age would do anything for a teacher's attention—by implication, Helter Skelter was next—and what he really needed was a mother for his son (snoring on top of the bed, by the time Dad returned; if someone could be smug in sleep, Jason was) and a mother for the daughter he so dearly desired.

Carl and I stand looking into his sleeping son's room. A poster of King Kong, holding tiny Jessica Lange, is taped to the wall above his bed. Legos are scattered on the floor like rice in a church driveway. Carl is taking the opportunity to conjure up for me his wedding: the four-months-pregnant Beatrice in her white velvet dress, with "something blue" the half-slip she wore, embroidered by her with a small depiction of a tiny, big-headed embryo of the child she was carrying—a sort of latter-day Hester (if Hester had worn her *A* on the inside), a little personal reminder, a little symbolic nod toward the future, no more likely to be seen—or, if seen, recognized—than the clean underwear so many people's mothers urge them to wear when taking a trip. The sleeping Jason has provoked a trip down memory lane for Carl that even has him describing his former wife's undergarments, as well as the amount, the sheer amount, of rice that was once thrown in a church driveway in his behalf. Do I, or do I not, want a daughter? he demands.

"What would you do if it turned out to be another son?" I ask, trying to be reasonable, not shitty, but it sets him off.

He asked a serious and logical question, okay. But consider it from my perspective: I had been looking for romance, not family life, when I responded to his misleading ad. It could not be said that Jason and I have become soul mates. It could also not be said that Carl and I are a match made in heaven, because he is old-fashioned in thinking that women should not work, except to take care of the home and the family. Does he seriously, really and truly, think that I should hang around the house, sweeping up dust, sweeping problems under the rug, growing a baby belly just so he can pursue his relentless desire to be normal, average, and in that way somehow cosmically make up for the fact that his parents were thrill-seeking adventurers who left him orphaned?

We climb into bed—my favorite moment of the day—and he tells me the story of Estelle, hiding from Nonette's son, Tyrone Jr., but not so nervous she didn't make an appointment for a hair styling and facial at the Holiday Inn's new spa. It seems Tyrone Jr. did not actually threaten her, but used language not fit for a lady to hear. He insisted that his mother had taken no money, and that furthermore, their minister would attest to her honesty. The minister was apparently in a bar with Tyrone Jr. when he called, and Estelle obviously panicked as much to think they might pay a late-night call and expect her to pray with them— Estelle is not a religious woman—as that Tyrone Jr. might come to the house and deck her. It was Nonette's dishonesty that offended Estelle, not the missing money. As Carl talked, I could almost hear her simpering.

Carl resumes the discussion of Moriko Watanabe, and, sleepy, I find myself doing the same thing to Carl that I did to Moriko. I begin to think aloud—the way so many bedtime stories come into being—and to create a story in which Moriko is acting out her hostility because too much is expected of her.

How exactly did this cause her to set a fire in our trash can?

I sidestep this. "It wasn't exactly the Feds storming Ruby Ridge." What Moriko did was more analogous to Brownies gathered around the campfire, roasting marshmallows: just a little fire; just a little danger. "She's my favorite student," I say to Carl, having just decided that. "Her real problem is with her parents."

"She can be the flower girl at our wedding," Carl says, sliding a hand under my nightgown.

"She's too old to be a flower girl."

"Matron of honor," he says, sliding his hand higher.

"Stop pretending to be sex crazed and insensitive."

He sits up and reaches below the bed and comes up with my bedroom slipper. It is blue terry cloth: the stretchy kind, with a small blue bow. "You are not my true love if this shoe doesn't fit," he says. He cradles it in his hand, drawing out the moment when he will slip it on my foot.

"Oh, Carl, give it a break," I say.

"You're not going to find anybody better than me, because you're not perfect yourself," he says.

"When did I say I was? I'm sulky and I don't respect myself for being too easily manipulated, and I have no idea what I'd really like to work at, but I do know that I have to refuse to be an incubator for you and a stepmother to a boy who doesn't like me very much."

"He's jealous," Carl says. "He used to have my undivided attention."

We jump when the phone rings. It is Tomoo Watanabe, even more incensed after receiving whatever call he has by now received from the police. This man wanted body parts to be found, I am certain.

"Listen, buddy boy," Carl says, grabbing the phone. "It's bedtime. You have some respect for our customs. You've got the juvenile delinquent daughter. She could have burned our house down."

"Not my daughter!" Tomoo Watanabe shouts.

Carl hangs up on him and turns off the ringer. He also makes it downstairs in time to hear only one ring from Mr. Watanabe's next call before he turns off that ringer, too.

"Marry me," he says, coming back into the bedroom and thudding onto the bed. "It's the only way. What are you going to do, keep auditioning guys? They'll all tell you a good story and then turn out to be just as disappointing as me."

"You haven't been disappointing. I just don't agree with many of your ideas."

"I don't agree with all of them myself," he says. "It was once my idea to marry a woman who kept a half-pint of Jack Daniel's floating in the toilet tank and jars of candied cherries hidden in her underwear drawer."

"You were young," I say.

"Tins of anchovies hidden in the umbrella stand," he says.

"Stop punishing yourself."

"Anchovies," he repeats, after a pause.

I turn off the clip-on light on my side of the headboard.

"I realize there isn't much of anywhere for this conversation to go after bringing up my bulimic former wife," Carl says glumly.

Beatrice advertised for a new companion while still married to Carl. When a new relationship worked out, she left the man's ad taped to the bathroom mirror, with a big lipsticked check mark beside it. To begin immediately: Carl's further dependency on Estelle + a cycle of nannies. Then—inspired by Beatrice's boldness and determined to prove that some good always comes of adversity—Carl's own ad, so transparently downbeat that his best friend rewrote it. Then: me. A conventional girl from a conventional family, a nice Canadian with a red maple leaf pin on her lapel and a charm bracelet that advertised her conflict: it dangled a miniature typewriter, an artist's palette, a baby shoe, a Scottie dog, and a shovel, which a former boyfriend maintained was actually a coke spoon. Back in my days at Humber College, I had had exactly eight dates: five with a boy who left school to go to England to study acting (I lived with him the summer before he left, so I stopped counting the days as "dates"), one with a boy from Hamilton, New York, who wanted to participate in the space program, and two with my English-lit professor, who made me read his whole 1,200-page novel before he admitted he was married. I was twenty-four when I met Carl, who is the one true love of my life: thirty-four, six feet tall, handsome, with a Roman nose that often has an eternal adolescent pimple on one side. He is exactly the age his father was when the plane he was piloting smashed into trees in Anchorage. It was a dark, well-kept secret, until her obituary ran, that his wife, Carl's mother, was seven years older than her husband. Even Estelle didn't know.

"What do you think made her float the bourbon bottle?" I say.

No answer. I turn onto one hip and consider my future. Except for my students, I am out of touch with almost everybody. My best friend, Cora Kelley, moved with her husband to Ann Arbor. I hardly know Darren Luftquist or his wife, and none of the other teachers seems very interested in being friendly. Even my parents have faded away, because I see them so infrequently, and when I do see them, Carl and Jason are the Subject Not to Be Discussed—my mother does not approve of women and men cohabiting and thinks this would present a bad example to my little sister. With the exception of my mother's unwillingness to discuss the love of my life, my parents, like most Canadians, are relentlessly neutral about almost everything. According to them, my sister and older brothers are all prospering, the boys happily married, everyone hormonally well balanced. And maybe they are: I had enough of them when we were growing up in the same house.

"I admire Moriko for what she did," I suddenly hear myself say.

He snorts. I knew he wasn't asleep.

"You know what I mean. The Japanese don't value girls very highly. Moriko was expressing her discontent."

"Go to sleep," he says.

"Estelle doesn't have a very clear sense of self-worth," I say. "That probably got communicated to you, and it gave you the message that women aren't very forceful. Think about it. She thought Nonette's son was going to cause her trouble, and instead of calling the police or something, she checked into a Holiday Inn. That's what a Canadian would do, for chrissake. And feel guilty that maybe somebody else needed the room."

"You've lost your mind."

"I haven't. I'm just saying that I don't understand my countrymen."

"I can't believe this is who I'm lying in bed with," Carl says.

"Well, you are. You advertised for it, and here it is."

" 'Wanted: Woman who does not understand her own kind. Maternal instincts unnecessary, but should be expansive in thinking about the virtues of pyromaniacs. Prolonged bedtime banter a plus.' "

"You actually have a very good sense of humor, Carl. Why didn't you write your own ad and mention your sense of humor?"

I think long and hard about it. Carl does not. He falls asleep.

The following day, Moriko does not attend school. The other nine girls have heard what has happened. I know they know: they let their hair flop in their faces and draw close again. They regard me sullenly. I am the person responsible for their friend's absence. What do they think? I can guess, all too easily. They assume I reported her to the police. They think, at the very least, that even if I might be a victim, I am still, as an adult, somehow capable of undoing the damage. They see me in a new light—see right through me, actually—and think I provoked her. They see what Moriko did as bold, and therefore very American. They see that now that someone has learned my lessons about necessary aggression and has taken action, the instigator has retreated into the shadows.

Tomoo Watanabe and his lawyer—a short, grimacing man in a Johnnie Cochran tie—and Darren Luftquist march grim-faced to my office at the end of the school day. I am more than willing to let bygones be bygones, but Mr. Watanabe will not have it. He speaks animatedly to the lawyer, in Japanese, moving in his seat like a warming jumping bean before I finish my sentences. I try to suggest that we forget what is surely a slight transgression and move forward. Unless that means inching toward me anxiously in his chair, he isn't about to. Neither does he seem able to let go of the idea of Jason-the-Monster.

Mr. Watanabe speaks. The lawyer says: "Jason may make you fatigued. He stays up all night, dirties his room, throws his toys everywhere. You come to school tired. How can you direct students toward academic excellence if you are tired?"

"Frankly, that is not my only goal," I say. "School is—"

"She is an excellent teacher!" Luftquist says huffily.

Mr. Watanabe speaks. The lawyer says: "This is his niece. His brother died in a tragic accident. An avalanche. He married the widow. Moriko is Takayo's daughter with his deceased brother, and he does not think it would be correct to adopt her. Mr. Watanabe was never before married, and would not be married now except for extenuating circumstances."

"That's very sad," Luftquist says, "but I don't—"

Mr. Watanabe gives a jumping-bean jerk. He speaks to the lawyer.

"I must tell you about his position at Samaya, U.S.," the lawyer says. "Mr. Watanabe is CEO of Samaya, U.S. The company currently employs over forty people. He must get a good night's sleep, every night, to be excellent in his job. As a word from myself, personally, he is excellent in his job. I, too, work at Samaya, U.S." The lawyer reaches in his jacket pocket and holds out a piece of paper: "Mr. Watanabe's curriculum vitae."

"We have no doubt Mr.—"

The lawyer: "Forgive me. Mr. Watanabe wished me to say, previously, as well, that Westerners may not understand the importance of sleep, because they think Japanese people work all the time. This is not so for Mr. Watanabe, who sleeps seven hours each night but who has also taken a cruise with his niece and his wife on the *Q.E. Two*."

"Very bad voyage on the *Q.E. Two*. Money is to be refunded," Mr. Watanabe says.

"What, really, is your point here, sir?" Luftquist says. Confused about who to converse with, he looks at the space between their heads.

Mr. Watanabe speaks. The lawyer turns to me. "Mr. Watanabe extends his good wishes for your ability to have a good night's sleep. I must not continue to interject my own thoughts, or we will never finish. Mr. Watanabe wants to know if you consider Moriko to be of superior intelligence."

"Superior?" Mr. Watanabe echoes, edgily.

"After approximately two and a half months in our school, there is no way that—"

"Excellent or not," Luftquist says, "she saw fit to start a fire."

"Let's not get into that again," I say.

Mr. Watanabe stands up suddenly. He speaks to the lawyer. The lawyer looks puzzled. Again, he holds out the curriculum vitae to Luftquist. Luftquist looks at me as if I am the one being unusually persistent. "Mr. Watanabe's credentials are not in question. Ms. Woodruff—"

"Fire!" Mr. Watanabe says, so loud that he fools me, and I look around. His arm waves through the air. Then, frowning, he takes his curriculum vitae from the lawyer and looks it over.

Luftquist stands. Following his lead, so do I. The lawyer quickly gets to his feet. Mr. Watanabe says to me: "In Japan, this would be impossible. No fires in trash cans. No fires."

Mr. Watanabe extends his hand. Luftquist shakes Mr. Watanabe's hand. The lawyer faces first me, and bows, then Luftquist, to whom he bows more deeply. Luftquist bows back. Mr. Watanabe speaks to the lawyer.

The lawyer says: "Moriko will return to school. Mr. Watanabe understands that you wish the students to strive for academic excellence. In Japan, though, Moriko would not set a fire in a trash can." The translator adds, sotto voce: "He feels."

"I am happy this has been clarified," Luftquist says. "Gentlemen, good day."

"Goodbye," the translator says, bowing slightly. Mr. Watanabe walks ahead of the translator. The janitor, polishing the floors, makes way. He is wearing jade-green pants with a sleeveless T-shirt tucked inside and a cap with BOBBY BROWN ATLANTA 1993 written across the front. DO WE DANCE? is written on the back.

"What do you suppose all that was about?" Luftquist whispers.

"He was implying that I am deficient as a teacher and as a parent."

"You have to be kidding," Luftquist says. "*That's* what you think that was about?"

"Well, what did you think?"

"I'm sure I did not understand, did not care to persevere, and do not really sympathize with the conversational modes of the Japanese."

"What do you think his deepest thoughts are?" I say as we pass the janitor.

"The building maintenance person? His wife and my wife are volunteers at Forward, the women's shelter," Luftquist says, as if he has answered the question. There is a long silence, but it feels chummier than my previous long silences with Luftquist. I am headed for my car. I don't know where Luftquist is headed. "If I may say," Luftquist says. "If I may, what I want to say is that, number one, I hope I was supportive of you, because I was trying to communicate that you are a valued member of our staff, and that whatever happened with that silly girl, that niece, or whatever she is, we all do value you here, and we don't—we don't think you have it easy. Who has it easy, of course? But you shouldn't think that I haven't taken notice of the way you have worked with the Japanese girls. I hope you don't think that your efforts go unappreciated. In spite of the fact that one of them started that fire at your house, I mean."

"Thank you," I say.

"You're welcome," he says.

We walk awhile, and near the front door to the school he says: "God knows, it's a relief to say something to you and to be understood, instead of trying to express my thoughts to Mr. Watanabe and that lawyer."

"Did you think you would be a principal?" I say.

"No. I planned to be a biologist," Luftquist says.

"You knew that Carl and I met through the personals listing, right?"

He stops. "How might I know that?"

"The party at your house before the start of school. Carl told me he told you."

"Perhaps he told Doris," Luftquist says. "At any rate: superior job you've been doing, very commendable you've extended yourself as you have to the Japanese girls, glad the rotation worked out so successfully."

"He didn't tell you that? He really didn't tell you?"

"If you think that I think life makes any more sense than you do, you're wrong," Luftquist says.

"Thank you," I say again.

"Welcome," he says, reaching around me to push open the door.

"Carl," I say.

XXXXX

"Come on. Listen to me."

XX

"Carl, I have something to say."

"What?"

"I think we've unfairly pigeonholed Luftquist."

"Bake him some Christmas cookies," Carl says sleepily.

"You always say something sarcastic. You thought Moriko should be a flower girl at our wedding. You think I should bake cookies for Luftquist. All right, I'm a little stressed out lately. But the thing is, I'm rethinking things. The fire in the trash has made me look at things in a different way. It seems to me that Luftquist finds his job difficult. He intended to be a biologist."

"That lunkhead?"

"Carl, be serious. I'm beginning to think that we all drift into things."

"Like snow," he says.

"Not like snow. That we drift sort of *unnaturally*."

"Okay," he says, turning on his light.

"My finding you was just chance. My becoming a teacher because of some scores I got on an aptitude test, and because of the coincidence of my moving in with you, and then hearing at some stupid party about the opening at Benjamin Franklin."

"Are you saying I'm just some random guy?" Carl says.

"What would make you think that? I feel closer to you than I've felt to anyone, ever. But the thing is, I have a confession to make: I told them certain stories. I made my life . . . I made it the opposite of glamorous. I sort of sacrificed Jason, actually. I used to joke about how wild he was, and how disorderly, and Moriko somehow didn't quite get the drift of it. She sort of got fascinated by Jason. She tried to get me to bring him to school. She's a very imaginative girl, and she got very excited about meeting him. Then when I wouldn't come through, she got desperate."

Carl doubles up the pillow behind his head. He looks at me blankly and turns off his light, so we are in the dark again.

?

X

??

"All right," he says. "What exactly happened with you and Moriko? Just cut to the chase. Why, exactly, did she set a fire in our trash can?"

"God, Carl, there aren't exact, one hundred percent verifiable reasons for these things."

He grunts.

"Okay," I say, taking a deep breath. "Moriko probably feels persecuted, and I was being cute and insinuating that I did, too, by my son—they assume he's my son—I acted like maybe what he did was upsetting, like when he stole the bike and crashed into a tree, because actually it was upsetting to me. The thing is, she's just a kid, and I guess I thought I was being funny, you know, wry, and she thought I was really *complaining*, and I guess I was, but there wasn't anything I expected her to do, because, I mean, she doesn't know anything about our country, even, she just got here in August, so she probably misunderstood . . . she's literal minded, and she thought I had a problem, and she got very interested in my problem, and she wanted to see it, so to speak. She wanted to meet Jason, and of course I'm not going to trot him out to be observed, I'm not going to put him on display like Dr. Hannibal Lecter . . . you aren't asleep, are you?"

"I keep feeling like she's prowling around out there," Carl says.

"Well, she isn't."

"I rely on you to see things clearly," Carl says.

"You just want to end the discussion." I sit up in bed. "Carl," I say, "do you think I'm an awful person?"

"No," Carl says. He is silent again, but then he surprises me by sitting up and turning on the light on his side of the bed. In a split second, in the too-bright room, I see our clothes strewn on the floor, the broken slat of the venetian blind, the rug pad protruding from one end of the rug—all the usual chaos of daily life. It's not only Jason, and his tossed toys and ticktacktoe of shoes gradually filling the house; it's the sprawl created by the adults' holding pattern of possessions, things owned by people overgifted and overly acquisitive, who've forgotten to discard the old as they've brought in the new. The rattan chair, which would look much better on the porch we don't have, sits in the far corner, draped with my brassiere and checkmated by Carl's Jockey shorts. The bureau drawers are ajar. Dried flowers in a glass vase—why even pretend that real ones, untended, would last any time at all? My mother would be horrified. My mother believes in order and cleanliness, which she managed in spite of the fact that she had such a big family: everything in its place; order in the house bringing order to the soul. In this, as in so many things, I resisted her teachings. Estelle is also very orderly, but Carl is more like me. Maybe not quite as haphazard, but still hardly organized. Misplacing keys is one thing, but misplacing your tool belt is another. Our house is enough to make me yearn for the Zen-like simplicity of a single stone on a tabletop, one flower in a vase. Which brings me back to thinking about Moriko. It seems to me, tonight, that my playing Scheherazade with the students was such a *Western* way of relating. Such a selfish way of communicating with them: spinning tales to save myself even though I was never in any danger, just engaging in narcissistic fantasies, really, while poor Moriko tried to grasp their common threads in order to have something to hang on to.

The next day, though Mr. Watanabe said Moriko would be in school, she is not. Her friends regard me coolly. Thick, newly cut bangs flop forward onto Kyoko Iida's forehead. I feel that I have done something bad. I intuit that Moriko's day is not going well. I drop the chalk, drop the eraser. Before class is over, I trip on a bit of chalk and barely retain my balance. The Japanese girls bring their heads together for a moment of quiet bobbing, as if they are birds clustered at a tiny suet ball.

Jason brings home his friend's ferret without asking us first if it's okay to keep the ferret while his friend has his tonsils removed. It gets loose and runs through the house. Carl curses, and Jason echoes him. "Fuck!" Jason screams. In case we didn't hear: "Fuck, fuck, fuck, fuck, fuck!"

"I am not a good parent," I say to Carl, through clenched teeth, when he comes into the kitchen and deliberately collides with me to stop me from bringing the telephone book down on the ferret's head. (In my fury, I am convinced I can smoosh it the second it darts out from under the refrigerator.)

"No!" Jason wails.

"Honey—it really is only a ferret," Carl says.

"Murderer!" Jason screams, as if the ferret's bashed-in brains are a done deal.

"Let's all take a long, deep breath," Carl says, holding out his hand for the telephone book.

"Grand-Mam's going to buy me an aquarium with baby barracudas!" Jason says, grabbing the pile of paper napkins on the table and throwing them up in the air. "I can live with Grand-Maaaaaaaaaaam!" Then he's gone, out the back door, slamming it behind him.

Carl pulls out a kitchen chair and sinks down, elbows on the table-top, head in his hands.

"I'm sorry," I say. "It . . . the thing looks like a mouse."

"No Disney World for you," Carl mutters. "Apparently you're going to have to be a little more mature before we take you to Disney World."

This makes me laugh. As I laugh, the ferret streaks into the living room. Would this happen in Japan, in a *ryokan*? If not, could I go there to live, with my one rock on a table?

"Things are out of control," I say.

"It's just a ferret," Carl says.

"Jason ran out the back door in the freezing cold. Without a coat."

"That means he'll be back soon."

"Are you having a day of being unflappable just to get my goat?"

"I'm going to be fired if I don't get over to the Wrights' house to install their cabinets," he says. "I promised them I'd work tonight, to make up for lost time. The plumber's fault, not mine," he adds.

"So what am I supposed to do? Go around wringing my hands, waiting for Jason's return?"

"You could probably use a soak in a hot bath," Carl says. "Why don't you take a bath?"

"I'd start screaming, like Frances Farmer."

"Who's Frances Farmer?" he says.

"Jessica Lange," I say.

An hour or so after Jason's departure, Mrs. Kniessel calls to say that Jason is at her house, watching *Bram Stoker's Dracula* with Jake's older brother. Jake's surgery was successful. She thanks me for suggesting to Jason that he pay a courtesy call. He is a very nice boy who has gone to their house to console them while their son, the owner of the ferret that is now at large, is in the hospital. Am I aware, she asks, that Jason is without a coat? She says this with exaggerated tactfulness, as if she were asking if I am aware that Jason has wings. I mutter something about children refusing to acknowledge winter and say that Carl will pick Jason up when he returns from work. "Such long hours!" Mrs. Kniessel says. ("What wings!") It is eight o'clock.

Then I do it: I screw up my courage and call the home of Moriko Watanabe. I'm not at all sure what tone to strike if she's there. Should I be angry that she's been absent? Chide her, tell her to return to class? A little pleading—how much her friends miss her? Should I simply sound as abject as I feel and apologize?

The lawyer answers the phone: "Good evening. Watanabe residence. This is their lawyer speaking. How may I help you?"

"Hello," I bring myself to say, after a pause long enough to have offered him every opportunity to hang up. "This is Alison Woodruff, Moriko's teacher."

"Ms. Woodruff. Hello. You are calling Mr. Watanabe?"

"No, actually I'm calling for Moriko."

This produces a long silence. In the background, I hear the television. "Thank you for calling," the lawyer says. "I will get Mr. Watanabe."

He comes to the phone. The lawyer explains that he will remain on the extension. In the background, Niles archly responds to something Frasier has said.

"Thank you very much for your concern for my niece's academic excellence," Mr. Watanabe says.

Why did I call? Why did I do this?

"I was hoping to speak to Moriko directly," I say.

"Moriko is studying," Mr. Watanabe says.

"But she hasn't been in school. I don't want you to think that there is any problem about her returning to school."

He says nothing.

"In fact," I say, "she has to come back to school."

He says nothing.

"It's the law," I say.

"She must study very hard to catch up," Mr. Watanabe says.

"Mr. Watanabe, do you understand what I'm saying? I'm not angry about the fire. Adolescents go through these periods. Moriko hasn't stayed out of school because she's embarrassed to come back, has she?"

Silence.

"The law requires that Moriko be in school. Is she going to be there tomorrow?"

"Snow tomorrow," the lawyer says. It is the briefest mention of the weather I have heard in years.

"Is Mrs. Watanabe there?" I ask.

"Mrs. Watanabe does not speak English," Mr. Watanabe says.

"Mr. Watanabe, you understand English very well, don't you?"

"Mr. Watanabe has an excellent understanding," the lawyer says.

"The reason for my call is to apologize"—now that I've said it, I realize the reason for my call—"and to say that I may have overstepped my bounds in relating so many personal things about my life to the students. To Moriko," I add. It is slowly coming clearer to me: the distinct possibility that Moriko, who is apparently kept hostage by the men in the house, not even allowed to come to the telephone, might well have tried to be my knight in shining armor. Maybe she wasn't only trying to get a glimpse of Jason; maybe she was trying to smoke him out.

"Mr. Watanabe, please let me speak to your niece," I say, starting all over again.

"This would not happen in Japan," Mr. Watanabe says. "There is no burning of trash outside a person's home. There are vandals. There are some problems. But not this."

"It doesn't matter," I say. I am getting totally worn down. "The only important thing is that Moriko knows I'm not angry with her, and that she return to school. She can pursue academic excellence at school," I add, not caring if he hears the sarcasm in my voice.

"Thank you very much," Mr. Watanabe says.

"Thank you for calling," the lawyer says. Someone hangs up.

"Hello?" I say to the person remaining on the line.

"You say goodbye and I say goodbye and hang up next," the lawyer says.

"Please put Moriko on. I'm worried about Moriko."

"She has promised to work very hard," the lawyer says. "Goodbye."

"Goodbye," I say.

He hangs up.

I turn on the TV. Frasier is in his recording studio, with his earphones on. "Good morning, Seattle," he says. In the adjacent glass cubicle, Roz gestures wildly. I turn the TV off. I am afraid, irrationally, that the lawyer will reappear on *Frasier*, and that the show will quickly spin off into perplexing exchanges that go nowhere.

Carl does not return, and does not return. Neither does Jason. He's probably watching *Dracula* a second time, absorbing new tricks. Even the ferret stays hidden. At ten o'clock, though—it is a school night, after all—I get in the car and drive to the Kniessels' house to round up Jason. He is just a little boy, I remind myself. I am the mature, responsible adult. I should not have tried to kill the ferret. I will apologize for losing my temper. We may discuss why women are afraid of rodents. He is probably afraid to come home, but when he sees me, he will be relieved to know that all is forgiven. He treats me fine when Carl isn't around to impress. We have a better relationship, he and I, when neither one of us is vying for Carl's attention.

Mrs. Kniessel's house is picture-perfect. There is even an orchid blooming. From upstairs, I hear chilling noises. Downstairs, Brahms is playing quietly. Mr. Kniessel stands when I come into the living room. He is wearing leather slippers and a white shirt and dark pants. He shakes my hand and asks whether we ever took the trip to the Grand Canyon we were considering. I tell him we didn't. This disappoints all three of us, it seems.

"Jason, dear," Mrs. Kniessel calls.

He comes to the top of the stairs. He looks down at me. I look up and smile. It is not an entirely sincere smile, but truly: I don't mean to give him any more trouble. He studies my face. He smiles back, slightly. He has rolled up his pant legs, for some reason. He also has on red kneesocks. As he prepares to leave the den of Dracula, Mrs. Kniessel explains that he slipped on his way to their house. He refused to relinquish his pants so she could wash and dry them, but he accepted a pair of red kneesocks. She is also giving him a dirty white jacket, what she calls "a spare parka—just an old thing" to wear home. Zipped into it, he looks like the Pillsbury Doughboy in lederhosen. Amid thanks and wishes for their son's speedy recovery, we start down the walk.

"You find it?" he says, when we are both seated in the car.

"No, but it can't go anywhere," I say. "Listen: I want to apologize. Sometimes adults get upset about things they can't articulate themselves, and tonight when—"

"What's 'articulate'?" he says.

"It just means to speak. But what I'm trying to say is that sometimes people don't know themselves what's bothering them, and they—"

"It's okay," he says. "We've got to find Freddie, though. I didn't tell them he got out."

"Well, that was good you didn't upset them," I say.

"I slid the door back and he jumped out."

I nod. It doesn't matter how the ferret got out.

"Where's Dad?" he says.

"He's installing kitchen cabinets for those people who had their house renovated. The English lady who leaves those long phone messages we always roll our eyes over."

"Oh yeah," he says. "The lady who says, 'One feels.' " His English accent isn't bad. "Hey, why don't we go over there?" he says. "I want to see what it looks like."

Without further discussion, we head for the big Tudor. It's only five minutes away, but it's up a private drive, not visible from the street. I remember where it is because there's an organic nursery next to it, where I bought herbs in the spring.

"Hey, that movie was really cool," he says.

"I wouldn't tell your father that you were watching *Dracula* until ten-thirty," I say.

"I wouldn't either," he says.

I look at him. He often responds to things instantly, with a very adult tone. But he's eight years old. Still: it must have been traumatic to have his mother walk out on them. Even with Estelle to rely on, it must have been devastating.

"Listen," I say, overcome with sympathy for him. "You like me, don't you?"

"Yeah," he says warily. "So what?"

"A couple of things. One is that I'm glad you like me, but I wish you wouldn't play so many tricks on me. It makes me feel bad sometimes. Like in the Blue Ridge."

He looks out the window.

"The other thing," I say, trying to lighten my voice, "is that I have a student at school who'd like to meet you. To see how neat you really are, I mean. Because I do think you're neat. You do things you want to do without asking permission all the time. That can cause problems, but I also have to admire the way you have an idea, and you act on it."

"Freddie," he says.

"Right. Like taking Freddie."

We are almost to the top of the hill, and I have been so distracted talking to him that only now do I realize that the big house in front of us is dark. It's a big shape against the sky. Unlit.

"He's already left," I say. "We must have crossed paths."

"Damn," Jason says.

"Jason—I know your father and I slip up, too, but you should really try to stop cursing."

If Carl were present, I know my comment would elicit an outpouring of curses from Jason. Jason taps the toes of his shoes together. He says nothing.

I go around the circular driveway and start down the hill. "Anyway," I say. "Moriko. You figure in this story, actually. It's because I did something silly. I told her things about our family, and I made all of us funny. You know how that is, when you're exaggerating so you tell a better story? I exaggerated, but I'm afraid she believed every word of it, and it . . . it sort of excited her. You know that book called *Eloise?*"

"She lives at the Plaza."

"Right. Well—I was trying to explain American life to some of my students, because they're from Japan, and Moriko got very interested in things I told her about you. Like the time you took the bike and raced it through the woods."

"Is that an example of my thinking up something and just doing it?"

"It certainly is."

"Are you gonna start in about the bike again?"

"No. No, I'm not. Actually, what I'm trying to say is that we all can be sort of cartoonish, at times, if we look at ourselves a particular way. But the truth of it is, I didn't say enough about me and your father, and I said too much about you. She wanted to meet you. And that's why she set that fire last weekend, I think. Because she was really intent on meeting you."

"She wants to meet me *that* much?" he says. "Isn't she old?"

"Old? What do you mean?"

"Don't you teach big kids?"

"Oh, right. Yes, she's thirteen, I think. It's not like . . . she doesn't want to meet you to get together with you, or anything."

He looks at me. "Stupid girl," he finally says.

"No, really, she isn't. She's quite nice, and it's very difficult to be in a foreign country, and to tell you the truth, she has very strict parents. Her stepfather makes her study all the time. I think I made our family sound very interesting, and very exciting, compared to the way she has to live. She sort of overreacted to you . . . to the stories about you . . . it was more like responding to an idea than to a real person, if you see what I mean. I mean, it's not like you think Batman is a real person, but you think he's a neat character, right?"

"Where does Batman come in?"

"He doesn't . . . he doesn't actually have anything to do with what we're talking about. He's just an example. What I'm saying is that in her mind, you're sort of like Eloise, or sort of like Batman."

"I'll be Batman," he says instantly.

"But, you know," I rush on, "when you're a child, you don't want to know that there's some teenager inside the rabbit suit, or whatever. You believe the rabbit is real. But when you get older—as old as Moriko is—if you *still* think it's a real rabbit, it's better if someone—"

"Goodbye, Santa Claus," he says, bringing his hand to his throat and pretending to cut it.

"Right," I say hesitantly.

"Then what do you want me to do with this dumb girl?" he says.

"First of all, I wouldn't want you to do anything to hurt her feelings. My idea is that if she could meet you, she'd see that you were a real boy, and that would burst the bubble. Do you know what I mean by that?"

"I'm supposed to just be there? Where? School?"

"No, not school. Some place—" How would I ever arrange it? "Some place where we could have a Coke, or maybe she could come over to our house to watch a TV show with all of us, or something."

"*Dracula,*" he whispers, spreading his fingers and pointing them downward.

"Would you do that for me?" I say.

He shrugs. "Sure. No big deal."

"Thank you," I say. "That is really very, very nice of you."

We turn onto our street. Our house, unlike the Tudor, is ablaze with light. I must have left most of the lights on in the rooms when I was cleaning. Carl's car is not in the driveway. Where is he? Could he possibly have been so kind as to stop at the grocery store? Whatever he's doing, he's avoiding dealing with Jason. Carl is tired of disciplining him and then waiting for the other shoe to fall; he told me that the night before. He is tired of being the heavy; he is tired of never really making any progress with his willful son.

If my own life were a fairy tale, what happens next could have been anticipated from the first. We go down the side path from the driveway to the front door, and I see—I am frightened to see—that the door is ajar. I reach out and clamp a hand on Jason's big, down-stuffed shoulder. He sees the open door, too, and stops. How could the door be open? If the door is open, the last thing we should do is walk in—walk into who knows what: a robbery in progress; punks vandalizing the house. An instant headache spreads behind my eyes. "Don't go in there!" I whisper harshly. I lunge at him and we almost topple to the lawn: Jason, who has already fallen once tonight, and the big, brave adult who is supposedly in charge.

"Let go!" he says, struggling. "I'm coming with you!"

Then I see, as the door seems to open in slow motion, a small person standing in the doorway. I see—my brain swarming with fear and confusion—that it is Moriko. What can she possibly . . . how can she possibly have been in my house? Is she crazier than I thought?

"That's her," I manage to whisper.

"Who?" Jason says, frowning at me.

"Moriko. It's the girl I was telling you about."

"What's she doing in our house?"

Moriko calls, "Mrs. Woodruff?" Her voice is quavery. I am glad Jason is here, or I would swear this could not really be happening. As we approach, Moriko retreats into the brightness. By now, Jason and I are relieved—relieved, and intensely curious.

"The door wasn't locked," she says. She looks at Jason. A long look. He drops his eyes. "I came to explain," she says. It is Moriko, in a blue wool pleated skirt and a white turtleneck with a group of big-footed, embroidered forest animals cavorting on the front. She wears running shoes and navy-blue kneesocks. She stares at Jason's kneesocks; he studies hers.

"Moriko, this is Jason. Jason, Moriko," I say.

"How do you do?" he says.

"I left the door unlocked?" I say, dazed. "You mean you just happened to be coming here, and you found the door unlocked?"

"Mr. Hamachi brought me when my uncle went to sleep. My mother is waiting for word of our visit. We were worried that your house was open. Mr. Hamachi said you must have gone on an errand."

Jason stands at my side. I am not sure if he is clinging, or if he is being proprietary.

"Mr. Hamachi pushed on it when he knocked, and your door opened. I begged him to let me stay. He's driving around the block."

"It's cold in here," Jason says. "Turn up the thermostat."

"Won't you . . . come into the living room, Moriko. Is everything all right?"

"My uncle is very mad. He was mad before I set the fire. I must explain to you that it wasn't to be bad. I was smoking a cigarette"—she hangs her head—"I was waiting for you, and I had brought you some poems I had written. Then I got embarrassed and ripped them up and put them in your trash. I only wanted to talk to you and to say that I read the books you suggest. I read every night, but no one can read enough to please my uncle. I shook an ash in the trash can, and the things inside went up in flames. I know that it's wrong to smoke. I'll never smoke again."

This is heartfelt, but I'm not entirely sure I believe it. Then again, think of what I asked her to believe: I asked her to believe in a Superman who would fly into buildings.

"Your mother is a very good teacher," Moriko says to Jason.

I wait for him to tell her what he told the police—to explain that I am not his mother. Instead, he says nothing.

"Please. That is the way it happened," she says. "My uncle doesn't believe me. My mother believes me."

"And Mr. Hamachi," I say. "He must believe you, if he drove you here."

"He only thinks it's unreasonable that my uncle won't let me talk on the telephone."

"Ah," I say.

"Mr. Hamachi says that's very American. American people hate the telephone."

The ferret runs from under the sofa. It goes into the hallway and disappears into the glare.

"I appreciate your coming to explain," I say. "But why couldn't you explain at school? You're coming to school tomorrow, aren't you?"

Outside, I see car headlights. At first I think it's Carl, and I think how daunting it's going to be to explain all this to him, but it isn't Carl; it's Mr. Hamachi, who taps his horn. Moriko rushes to the door and waves him away. He lingers.

"My uncle will punish me by keeping me home all week. He's very mad at me."

"I'm impulsive, too," Jason says.

Moriko looks at him. She waits for his story. He says nothing, though. He looks over his shoulder, hoping the ferret will reappear. He is acting very proper. Very mature. She must see that he is not the holy terror I described him as; she must wonder why I caricatured him. Everyone in the room seems poised but me.

"I'm sure your uncle is overly protective of you because he has your best interests at heart. I know that doesn't make it any easier to take, but I know he's concerned about you."

"Because when my father died, he was very kind to join my mother and me," Moriko says, almost as if she's prompting me.

Jason looks at her, and there is an instant connection. "She did that," he says. "My mom left us, and then she came," Jason says, pointing at me.

Moriko looks interested, but when the car reappears outside the window, she jumps up. "Please believe I had no bad idea in mind," she says, pulling on her coat. "I'll see you at school, and you are always my favorite teacher."

Moriko rushes out to the car. The car door on the passenger's side is pushed open. The two conspirators—an unlikely duo—pull away into the night.

"She likes you," Jason says.

"Yes. And I appreciate your being so gracious. That was very nice of you, to talk to her and to stay in the room and be so nice."

"No problem," he says. "One thing I wanted to ask, though. Would you do me a favor, too? It's something I did wrong, and I want you to fix it."

"What's that?" I say. It has been a long, exhausting day. At this point, I think I'm prepared for almost anything.

"It's pretty bad," he says.

I wince. "What is it?" I say quietly.

"It's not so, so bad, but it's not good."

"Just tell me," I say.

"Tell me you'll fix it before I tell you," he says.

I look at him, hearing myself making the same request when I was a child. Trying to get my brother to say he'd do anything for me, since I knew my parents would never bite. Such a large, all-encompassing request, but why not try? To have an automatic guarantee, no matter what, that the other person would do what you wanted. . . . After childhood, who would dare ask?

He looks me in the eye. "I stole money," he says.

"*Money?* Where did you steal *money?*"

"Estelle's."

My shock is partly because of what he answers, partly because I've never heard him call Estelle anything but Grand-Mam.

"Come on," he says. "You saw, didn't you?" He speaks more urgently: "In the flower pot. Underneath the *flowers*."

"Go slower," I say. "I don't know what you're talking about."

"Those flowers outside her door. Outside. I buried it in the flower pot."

"Oh, my God," I say. "You took the money from the vase? You took the money, not Nonette?"

He puts his face in his hands. He mumbles something I don't understand. I've drawn back, shocked, but the shock quickly subsides, and I find I've put my hand on his back. I rub up and down his spine. "Well, at least you know you did wrong," I say.

"She can have it back," he says. "But do I have to tell her it was me? Can't you pretend you discovered it?"

"Honey—" I falter. "Honey, what would I be doing digging around Estelle's urn? And if I did find it, what would that prove? Somebody would still have had to put it there. Nonette could have put it there."

"Nonette would not," he says, exasperated, rebuking me.

"Jason, the very best thing, I promise you, is to tell Grand-Mam what you did and to say how sorry you are. She's made mistakes, too. She'll forgive you. I'll go with you." My mind is racing: Nonette—what can ever be done to make it up to Nonette?

"You do it. You tell her," he says.

"All right," I say. "As long as you're there with me, I'll tell her."

"Then come on," he says.

"Now? We can't go there now. Estelle's in bed. We'll have to do it tomorrow."

"Shhh!" he says. Carl's car has just pulled in beside mine, in the driveway. It's almost eleven-thirty. He will not be happy to see Jason up so long past his bedtime. I whisper: "Just forget about *Dracula* and all the rest of it."

Carl comes in, under a carapace of cold air. He sees his son sitting on the sofa, dangling his feet, trying to look casual, and raises an eyebrow. His eyes widen, as he looks at his watch.

"We were talking," I say. "I kept him up too late."

Jason races past me. At first I think he's going to throw himself into his father's arms, but it's not that: he's seen Freddie the ferret, and this time he means to get it.

"That was one hellacious job, but just now it all got finished," he says. "The kitchen is finito. The electrician was there—everybody working overtime." He looks at me. "The plumber came, too," he throws in for good measure.

I bite my tongue. Jason is listening with one ear, as he chases after the ferret. In the doorway he looks at me, confused, but when I turn my expressionless face toward him, he, too, adjusts his expression. "Here, fella," he calls softly to the ferret, in a quiet, pleasant little voice I know is put on, but that Carl probably doesn't even register. Only in a Walt Disney animation would the ferret make a U-turn and run to his ankles. Jason waits a few seconds, then tiptoes after the ferret. He's overacting, making his escape from his lying father, wise enough not to chance staying in the room in case there's a fight.

Later, when Jason is tucked in (I wink, as if whatever happened is not of any great consequence; he's too smart to be fooled, but his hesitant smile lets me know he appreciates the gesture), I pick up Carl's discarded clothes from the bedroom chair and hold the shirt against my nose. You'd think the thing was a scratch-n-sniff strip in a glossy magazine, it's so permeated with perfume. Just like that. Another woman. Some—as Jason would say—"stupid girl." I smell it and smell it again. Then I drop it on the chair. I turn back the covers and climb into bed. I have an image of Jason, in his twin bed, stretched out on his favorite sheets patterned with cowboys galloping on horses. A little boy with lassos twirling all around him. What's it going to be like for Jason, out on that vast open range?

Gloomily, I turn off my light. Just a couple of nights before, I had considered becoming Carl's wife. Agreeing to a child. Marrying the charismatic carpenter. The odor of the woman's perfume is still in my nose. It lingers, and I can't quite manage a sneeze. I sniff, instead, but my lone tear can't be inhaled. I wipe it away and turn on my side.

"Quite a job," Carl says, coming back into the bedroom, a towel wrapped around him.

"You weren't at that house," I say. "Jason and I went there, and the place was dark."

The silence is as deafening as if I'd smacked cymbals together, then thrown them to the floor. Considering the usual messiness of the bedroom, they would also be just one more thing.

"I saw an old high school girlfriend. I thought you'd be jealous, so I didn't tell you where I was going."

"You just made that up," I say.

"What do you mean? You don't think I'm telling you the truth? You don't think it's possible that I was sparing your feelings because you might have misunderstood what was going on?"

"What might I have misunderstood?"

He is sitting on the side of the bed. From the alcohol I can smell on his breath, I have at least part of my answer, anyway. He says nothing.

"You know, I know it from your perspective," I say. "I know why you think your marriage ended. But what would your wife say? That you were a devoted husband, and she was just catting around?"

"She would have said I was a womanizer," he says. "That's what that drunken, bulimic bitch would have said. That was then, and this is now. But in terms of what she would have said, that's what she would have said. Satisfied?" he asks, but he's not looking my way. He's staring straight across the room, to the closed dresser drawers, to the venetian blind lowered to hang straight across, its slats in place. Order, order. Like water, water everywhere, but not a drop to drink. That old paradox always presented with a bit of malevolence to children. I say it again, silently, to myself. Strange, the silly things that come to you when you're convinced your life has ended.

"Dear me," Estelle says, rushing to open the door. "To come on such a snowy day as this! I'm so happy to see you, but I can't imagine why. . . ."

"I'm your favorite boy in all the world," Jason says, mocking the concept—how inappropriate that whole concept is soon going to be—though Grand-Mam doesn't yet know it.

"We have a confession to make," I say, wasting no time.

"Please, come in and warm yourselves. We can certainly discuss whatever you would like to discuss in one short moment, but right now, wouldn't someone like hot chocolate? Mint tea?"

Jason looks at me. I unbutton my coat and relinquish it. He unzips the dirty white ski parka, which I have yet to return to the Kniessels. Estelle holds it so close to her face that it seems to me for a moment she might be sniffing it. My heart sinks, as if she were me, about to make a terrible discovery.

"Estelle," I say, following her to the coatrack. "Estelle, we've got some unpleasant business to discuss that I know you're going to be sad to hear."

"You're not leaving?" she says. It comes out so fast, she clamps her hand over her mouth immediately afterward, as if she can push the words back inside.

Am I? I wonder. A person with any pride would. Then again, a person who cared about the young person she'd spent a year with wouldn't just waltz out the door, would she? But her question has rattled me. I sit on her two-seat sofa, in the kitchen, and don't know what to say. Jason looks miserable. He squirms against my side like a baby.

"Goodness!" Estelle says. "Well, out with it. What is it?"

"Jason made a mistake. He took the money out of your vase by the stove," I say, gesturing to the vase, which still holds dried flowers. "He feels awful about it, and he knows it was a very bad thing to do."

"You *did*?" Estelle says. Her voice is so high-pitched, it almost squeals. "Why did you do such a thing? Wouldn't I give you anything you wanted?"

"Not a trail bike," he says bitterly. The suddenness, the intensity with which he speaks, almost paralyzes me. He wanted a trail bike very much, I realize for the first time.

"This is the sort of news that might provoke a heart attack," Estelle says. "Here I open my home to you and offer you anything I can give you, and in return. . . ." Tears come to her eyes. "I don't want to see you for some time," Estelle says. "You must go home now."

At this, Jason starts to cry. It's harsher than what I imagined; Jason has deeply disappointed Estelle, but he's a child. And he's come to apologize.

Estelle walks out of the room. She sideswipes his coat and it falls off the coatrack. It lies on the floor, but she doesn't look back. I hear her bedroom door slam shut. This is not what I imagined.

"It took her aback," I say lamely. "You know how it is when you're not expecting something."

He makes fists and rubs his eyes, hard.

"We'll give her some time alone, and later I'm sure—"

"We have to dig it up!" he says. "I want to give it back to her. Come on."

Dig it up. I had never thought about that part. It must still be right where he buried it, in her cement urn.

In the kitchen, I find a spoon that isn't a good spoon. I hand it to Jason. We proceed grimly to the back door, and as we approach I remember the rattan chair Estelle got for us. The andirons. The dizzying rug. Her kind offerings. She put her trust in us, and at the moment it has not worked out very well.

A squirrel jumps off the stone wall, something clamped in its teeth. A male cardinal flashes by, a small plume of red. Everything is quiet, except for the rustle of wind through the snow-covered branches. Jason walks to the urn on the right. He moves like an animal trainer approaching a dangerous beast for the first time, trying to appear self-confident at the same time he intuits he should hesitate. The cosmos have become a mass of frost-frozen stems with congealed flower heads. They grew tall before the frost bit them, though; now, they are tangled and deflated: seaweed washed ashore; fallen scaffolding.

He tries to dig with the spoon, but the soil is frozen. He tries to dig with his hands, but the soil is too solid. I pitch in to help, lowering the urn from the pedestal, turning it on its side and chipping away at the soil with the heel of my boot. Big, white snowflakes fall. Our breath clouds the air.

To my surprise, my heel makes some progress. After a few minutes, a big clump of roots drops out, trailing bits of rock and clotted dirt. Something that looks like a taproot—but what would that be, since cosmos are always delicately rooted?—stretches out, and I see that it is the dirt-smeared paper bag Jason apparently rolled tight and stuffed in the urn. We lift it together, withdrawing it slowly. Inside is the money. I clasp the bag to me, doubling over as if protecting it, somehow, racing back into the house, trailing dirt.

"That's it," he says. "That's all of it."

"Let's clean up a bit," I say. "Let's clean this whole part of the house, as a matter of fact."

I look for Estelle's vacuum in the hall closet, find it, and wheel it out. Jason stands holding the money, relieved but still ashamed. His bright pink cheeks are not only the result of windburn, it seems to me. He's learned something about how difficult it is to undo a wrong. He is still learning all the time I vacuum.

"Knock on her door. Tell her again that you're sorry, and that we're leaving it on the kitchen counter," I say.

He shakes his head no. I can tell that he is sincere: he cannot bring himself to do this. I walk away from him, feeling gradually calmer as I make my way down the corridor. Calmer, or more resigned. "Estelle," I say. "I know you don't want to see us now, but please think about talking to us later on the phone. I'll call you."

Nothing from her room. No tears, nothing.

"He's sorry," I whisper. "I am, too." I put my head against the door. Silence. I take my head away.

When we are almost to the car, she opens the front door. She has taken off her wig, the too-brown wig with what Carl calls her Mamie Eisenhower bangs. The top of her head is hazed with long strands of hair, like a balding man's. The hair is a mixture of brown and gray, with gray predominating. She has no bangs of her own. There is only her high, bony forehead. She is wearing glasses, instead of her contact lenses. It is the first time I have ever seen Estelle with her own hair, without her contacts. She stands on the walkway defiantly, and then she speaks: "Maybe you wouldn't know what it's like to find yourself with a child to raise because you were a stay-at-home and your glamorous neighbors took off into the wild blue yonder," she says. "You know what it was? It was hard work and sacrifice. My life changed. I hope you never know what it's like to have your own life changed that drastically." She stares at us, hard, then turns and walks back to the house, the wan glare from the sun illuminating shiny skin visible through thin wisps of hair streaming down the back of her head.

"She's never going to forgive me, is she," Jason says in a tiny voice. He isn't asking a question; he's telling me.

"You know what she's upset about, don't you?" I say, once we're seated in the car.

"The money," he says.

"Well, yes, but she's upset because she expected something nobody ever gets. She thought that because she did certain things—that because she was a good person—things would turn out well."

Whether he understands this or not, he nabs his bottom lip with his front tooth and turns and stares out the window. It's a snow day, or we wouldn't have been able to make the visit until school let out. But it's still only eleven in the morning: there's the chance of brighter sun as the day goes on.

"Why did she ask if you were leaving?" he says.

For once, the answer is as clear to me as a fissure in a crystal ball. No, I am not. I am not, under any circumstances, leaving. And I tell him so.

As we come near our house, Jason asks another question. "What does 'cosmos' mean?" he says.

Inside, I read to him from the dictionary. I do this because I have no idea why the flower is named what it's named, and also because I don't want to guess wrong one more time—if not forever, at least for the rest of the day.

"Cosmos" is Greek, meaning "the universe." I read: "the universe as a manifestation of order; any orderly whole developed from complex parts; any—" I stop, and paraphrase: "Bright flowers. 'Showy flowers' is how it's actually put."

Today, with the world so whited out, it is difficult to conjure up the flowers' bright pinks and electric lavenders, but as soon as I stop trying, another image appears: Carl's parents . . . what could it have been like, to fall out of the sky over Anchorage, Alaska, into endless drifts of snow? For a few seconds there must have been such color in the air: the engine sparking; detritus blown like confetti, far and wide; a free fall of bright winter clothes.

Jason, at the sink, may or may not have taken in my recitation from the dictionary. After turning on the water, he's preoccupied, totally involved in the moment: here is the chance, again, to be the good boy, the vigilant boy, who carefully washes his hands. I stand behind him and put my own dirty hands under the water. Down the sink the dirt goes, his hands turning cleaner and cleaner, even the grit embedded under his fingernails eventually washing away, so that his hands become, again, unblemished little boy's hands; my clasping them, as I quickly move my thumb back and forth, is done only out of habit.

SECOND QUESTION

There we were, in the transfusion room at the end of the corridor at Bishopgate Hospital: Friday morning, the patients being dripped with blood or intravenous medicine so they could go home for the weekend. It was February, and the snow outside had turned the gritty gray of dirty plaster. Ned and I stood at the window, flanking a card table filled with desserts: doughnuts, cakes, pies, brownies, cookies. Some plastic forks and knives were piled in stacks, others dropped pick-up-sticks style between the paper plates. Ned surveyed the table and took a doughnut. In his chair, Richard was sleeping, chin dropped, breathing through his mouth. Half an hour into the transfusion, he always fell asleep. He was one of the few who did. A tall, redheaded man, probably in his mid-fifties, was hearing from a nurse about the hair loss he could expect. "Just remember, honey, Tina Turner wears a wig," she said.

Outside, bigger snowflakes fell, like wadded-up tissues heading for the trash. Which was what I had turned away from when I went to the window: the sight of a nurse holding a tissue for a young woman to blow her nose into. The woman was vomiting, with her nose running at the same time, but she refused to relinquish the aluminum bowl clamped under her thumbs. "Into the tissue, honey," the nurse was still saying, not at all distracted by her posturing colleague's excellent imitation of Tina Turner. I'd stopped listening, too, but I'd stuck on the phrase "Gonna break every rule."

Richard was dying of AIDS. Ned, his ex-lover and longtime business associate, found that instead of reading scripts, typing letters, and making phone calls, his new job description was to place organically grown vegetables in yin/yang positions inside a special steamer, below which we boiled Poland Spring water. A few months earlier, in that period before Richard's AZT had to be discontinued so that he could enter an experimental outpatient-treatment program at Bishopgate, Ned had always slept late. He couldn't call the West Coast before two in the afternoon, anyway—or maybe an hour earlier, if he had the unlisted number of an actor or of a director's car phone. All of the people Richard and Ned did business with worked longer hours than nine-to-fivers, and it was a standing joke among us that I was never busy—I had no real job, and when I did work I was paid much more than was reasonable. Ned joked with me a lot, an edge in his voice, because he was a little jealous of the sudden presence of a third person in Richard's apartment. Richard and I had met in New York when we were seated in adjacent chairs at a cheapo haircutter's on Eighth Avenue. He thought I was an actress in an Off Broadway play he'd seen the night before. I was not, but I'd seen the play. As we talked, we discovered that we often ate at the same restaurants in Chelsea. His face was familiar to me, as well. Then began years of our being neighbors—a concept more important to New Yorkers than to people living in a small town. The day we met, Richard took me home with him so I could shower.

That year, my landlord on West Twenty-seventh Street remained unconcerned that hot water rarely made it up to my top-floor apartment. After I met Richard it became a habit with me to put on my sweatsuit and jog to his apartment, three blocks east and one block over. Richard's own landlord, who lived in the other second-floor apartment, could never do enough for him, because Richard had introduced him to some movie stars and invited him to so many screenings. He would sizzle with fury over the abuse I had to endure, working himself up to what Richard (who made *café filtre* for the three of us) swore was a caffeine-induced sexual high, after which he'd race around doing building maintenance. Now, in the too-bright transfusion room, it was hard for me to believe that only a few months ago I'd been sitting in Richard's dining alcove, with the cluster of phones that rested on top of *Variety* landslides and formed the centerpiece of the long tavern table, sipping freshly ground Jamaica Blue Mountain as my white-gloved hands curved around the pleasant heat of a neon-colored coffee mug. The gloves allowed the lotion to sink in as long as possible. I make my living as a hand model. Every night, I rub on a mixture of Dal Raccolta olive oil with a dash of Kiehl's moisturizer and the liquid from two vitamin E capsules. It was Richard who gave me the nickname "Rac," for "Raccoon." My white, pulled-on paws protect me from scratches, broken nails, chapped skin. Forget the M.B.A.: as everyone knows, real money is made in strange ways in New York.

I turned away from the snowstorm. On a TV angled from a wall bracket above us, an orange-faced Phil Donahue glowed. He shifted from belligerence to incredulity as a man who repossessed cars explained his life philosophy. Hattie, the nicest nurse on the floor, stood beside me briefly, considering the array of pastry on our table as if it were a half-played chess game. Finally, she picked up one of the plastic knives, cut a brownie in half, and walked away without raising her eyes to look at the snow.

Taking the shuttle to Boston every weekend had finally convinced me that I was never going to develop any fondness for Beantown. To be fair about it, I didn't have much chance to see Boston as a place where anyone might be happy. Ned and I walked the path between the apartment (rented by the month) and the hospital. Once or twice I took a cab to the natural-food store, and one night, as irresponsible as the babysitters of every mother's nightmare, we had gone to a bar and then to the movies, while Richard slept a drug-induced sleep, with the starfish night-light Hattie had brought him from her honeymoon in Bermuda shining on the bedside table. In the bar, Ned had asked me what I'd do if time could stop: Richard wouldn't get any better and he wouldn't get any worse, and the days we'd gone through—with the crises, the circumlocutions, the gallows humor, the perplexity, the sudden, all-too-clear medical knowledge—would simply persist. Winter, also, would persist: intermittent snow, strong winds, the harsh late-afternoon sun we couldn't stand without the filter of a curtain. I was never a speculative person, but Ned thrived on speculation. In fact, he had studied poetry at Stanford, years ago, where he had written a series of "What If" poems. Richard, visiting California, answering questions onstage after one of the movies he'd produced had been screened, had suddenly found himself challenged by a student whose questions were complex and rhetorical. In the following fifteen years, they had been lovers, enemies, and finally best friends, associated in work. They had gone from Stanford to New York, New York to London, then from Hampstead Heath back to West Twenty-eighth Street, with side trips to gamble in Aruba and to ski in Aspen at Christmas.

"You're breaking the rules," I said. "No what-ifs."

"What if we went outside and flowers were blooming, and there were a car—a convertible—and we drove to Plum Island," he went on. "Moon on the water. Big Dipper in the sky. Think about it. Visualize it and your negative energy will be replaced by helpful, healing energy."

"Is there such a place as Plum Island or did you make it up?"

"It's famous. Banana Beach is there. Bands play at night in the Prune Pavilion."

"There is a Plum Island," the man next to me said. "It's up by

Newburyport. It's full of poison ivy in the summer, so you've got to be careful. I once got poison ivy in my lungs from some asshole who was burning the stuff with his leaves. Two weeks in the hospital, and me with a thousand-dollar deductible."

Ned and I looked at the man.

"Buy you a round," he said. "I just saved a bundle. The hotel I'm staying at gives you a rate equal to the temperature when you check in. It's a come-on. I've got a queen-size bed, an honor bar, and one of those showers you can adjust so it feels like needles shooting into you, all for sixteen dollars. I could live there cheaper than heating my house."

"Where you from?" Ned asked.

"Hope Valley, Rhode Island," the man said, his arm shooting in front of me to shake Ned's hand. "Harvey Milgrim," he said, nodding at my face. "Captain, United States Army Reserve."

"Harvey," Ned said, "I don't think you have any use for guys like me. I'm homosexual."

The man looked at me. I was surprised, too; it wasn't like Ned to talk about this with strangers. Circumstance had thrown me together with Ned; fate precipitated our unlikely bonding. Neither of us could think of life without Richard. Richard opened up to very few people, but when he did he made it a point to be indispensable.

"He's kidding," I said. It seemed the easiest thing to say.

"Dangerous joke," Harvey Milgrim said.

"He's depressed because I'm leaving him," I said.

"Well, now, I wouldn't rush into a thing like that," Harvey said. "I'm Bud on draft. What are you two?"

The bartender walked over the minute the conversation shifted to alcohol.

"Stoli straight up," Ned said.

"Vodka tonic," I said.

"Switch me to Jim Beam," Harvey said. He rolled his hand with the quick motion of someone shaking dice. "Couple of rocks on the side."

"Harvey," Ned said, "my world's coming apart. My ex-lover is also my boss, and his white-blood-cell count is sinking too low for him to stay alive. The program he's in at Bishopgate is his last chance. He's a Friday-afternoon vampire. They pump blood into him so he has enough energy to take part in an experimental study and keep his outpatient status, but do you know how helpful that is? Imagine he's driving the Indy. He's in the lead. He screeches in for gas, and what does the pit crew do but blow him a kiss? The other cars are still out there, whipping past. He starts to yell, because they're supposed to fill the car with gas, but the guys are nuts or something. They just blow air kisses."

Harvey looked at Ned's hand, the fingers fanned open, deep Vs of space between them. Then Ned slowly curled them in, kissing his fingernails as they came to rest on his bottom lip.

The bartender put the drinks down, one-two-three. He scooped a few ice cubes into a glass and put the glass beside Harvey's shot glass of bourbon. Harvey frowned, looking from glass to glass without saying anything. Then he threw down the shot of bourbon and picked up the other glass, lifted one ice cube out, and slowly sucked it. He did not look at us or speak to us again.

The night after Ned and I snuck off to the bar, Richard started to hyperventilate. In a minute his pajamas were soaked, his teeth chattering. It was morning, 4 a.m. He was holding on to the door frame, his feet in close, his body curved away, like someone windsurfing. Ned woke up groggily from his sleeping bag on the floor at the foot of Richard's bed. I was on the foldout sofa in the living room, again awakened by the slightest sound. Before I'd fallen asleep, I'd gone into the kitchen to get a drink of water, and a mouse had run under the refrigerator. It startled me, but then tears sprang to my eyes because if Richard knew there were mice—mice polluting the environment he was trying to purify with air ionizers, and humidifiers that misted the room with mineral water—he'd make us move. The idea of gathering up the piles of holistic-health books, the pamphlets on meditation, the countless jars of vitamins and chelated minerals and organically grown grains, the eye of God that hung over the stove, the passages he'd made Ned transcribe from Bernie Siegel and tape to the refrigerator—we'd already moved twice, neither time for any good reason. Something couldn't just scurry in and make us pack it all up again, could it? And where was there left to go anymore? He was too sick to be in a hotel, and I knew there was no other apartment anywhere near the hospital. We would have to persuade him that the mouse existed only in his head. We'd tell him he was hallucinating; we'd talk him out of it, in the same way we patiently tried to soothe him by explaining that the terror he was experiencing was only a nightmare. He was not in a plane that had crashed in the jungle; he was tangled in sheets, not weighed down with concrete.

When I got to the bedroom, Ned was trying to pry Richard's fingers off the door frame. He was having no luck, and looked at me with an expression that had become familiar: fear, with an undercurrent of intense fatigue.

Richard's robe dangled from his bony shoulders. He was so wet that

I thought at first he might have blundered into the shower. He looked in my direction but didn't register my presence. Then he sagged against Ned, who began to walk him slowly in the direction of the bed.

"It's cold," Richard said. "Why isn't there any heat?"

"We keep the thermostat at eighty," Ned said wearily. "You just need to get under the covers."

"Is that Hattie over there?"

"It's me," I said. "Ned is trying to get you into the bed."

"Rac," Richard said vaguely. He said to Ned, "Is that my bed?"

"That's your bed," Ned said. "You'll be warm if you get into bed, Richard."

I came up beside Richard and patted his back, and walked around and sat on the edge of the bed, trying to coax him forward. Ned was right: it was dizzyingly hot in the apartment. I got up and turned back the covers, smoothing the contour sheet. Ned kept Richard's hand, but turned to face him as he took one step backward, closer to the bed. The two of us pantomimed our pleasure at the bed's desirability. Richard began to walk toward it, licking his lips.

"I'll get you some water," I said.

"Water," Richard said. "I thought we were on a ship. I thought the bathroom was an inside cabin with no window. I can't be where there's no way to see the sky."

Ned was punching depth back into Richard's pillows. Then he made a fist and punched the center of the bed. "All aboard the S.S. *Fucking A*," he said.

It got a fake laugh out of me as I turned into the kitchen, but Richard only began to whisper urgently about the claustrophobia he'd experienced in the bathroom. Finally he did get back in his bed and immediately fell asleep. Half an hour later, still well before dawn, Ned repeated Richard's whisperings to me as if they were his own. Though Ned and I were very different people, our ability to imagine Richard's suffering united us. We were sitting in wooden chairs we'd pulled away from the dining-room table to put by the window so Ned could smoke. His cigarette smoke curled out the window.

"Ever been to Mardi Gras?" he said.

"New Orleans," I said, "but never Mardi Gras."

"They use strings of beads for barter," he said. "People stand up on the balconies in the French Quarter—women as well as men, some-times—and they holler down for people in the crowd to flash 'em: you give them a thrill, they toss down their beads. The more you show, the more you win. Then you can walk around with all your necklaces and everybody will know you're real foxy. *Real* cool. You do a bump-and-grind, you can get the good ole boys—the men, that is—and the transvestites all whistling together and throwing down the long necklaces. The real long ones are the ones everybody wants. They're like having a five-carat-diamond ring." He opened the window another few inches so he could stub out his cigarette. One-fingered, he flicked it to the ground. Then he lowered the window, not quite pushing it shut. This wasn't one of Ned's wild stories; I was sure what he'd just told me was true. Sometimes I thought Ned told me certain stories to titillate me, or perhaps to put me down in some way: to remind me that I was straight and he was gay.

"You know what I did one time?" I said suddenly, deciding to see if I could shock him for once. "When I was having that affair with Harry? One night we were in his apartment—his wife was off in Israel—and he was cooking dinner, and I was going through her jewelry box. There was a pearl necklace in there. I couldn't figure out how to open the clasp, but finally I realized I could just drop it over my head carefully. When Harry hollered for me, I had all my clothes off and was lying on the rug, in the dark, with my arms at my side. Finally he came after me. He put on the light and saw me, and then he started laughing and sort of dove onto me, and the pearl necklace broke. He raised up and said, 'What have I done?' and I said, 'Harry, it's your wife's necklace.' He didn't even know she had it. She must not have worn it. So he started cursing, crawling around to pick up the pearls, and I thought, No, if he has it restrung at least I'm going to make sure it won't be the same length."

Ned and I turned our heads to see Richard, his robe neatly knotted in front, kneesocks pulled on, his hair slicked back.

"What are you two talking about?" he said.

"Hey, Richard," Ned said, not managing to disguise his surprise.

"I don't smell cigarette smoke, do I?" Richard said.

"It's coming from below," I said, closing the window.

"We weren't talking about you," Ned said. His voice was both kind and wary.

"I didn't say you were," Richard said. He looked at me. "May I be included?"

"I was telling him about Harry," I said. "The story about the pearls." More and more, it seemed, we were relying on stories.

"I never liked him," Richard said. He waved a hand toward Ned. "Open that a crack, will you? It's too hot in here."

"You already know the story," I said to Richard, anxious to include him. "You tell Ned the punch line."

Richard looked at Ned. "She ate them," he said. "When he wasn't looking she ate as many as she could."

"I didn't want them to fit anymore if she tried to put them over her head," I said. "I wanted her to know something had happened."

Richard shook his head, but fondly: a little gesture he gave to indicate that I was interchangeable with some gifted, troublesome child he never had.

"One time, when I was on vacation with Sander, I picked up a trick in Puerto Rico," Ned said. "We were going at it at this big estate where the guy's employer lived, and suddenly the guy, the employer, hears something and starts up the stairs. So I ran into the closet—"

"He played football in college," Richard said.

I smiled, but I had already heard this story. Ned had told it at a party one night long ago, when he was drunk. It was one of the stories he liked best, because he appeared a little wild in it and a little cagey, and because somebody got his comeuppance. His stories were not all that different from those stories boys had often confided in me back in my college days—stories about dates and sexual conquests, told with ellipses to spare my delicate feelings.

"So I grabbed whatever was hanging behind me—just grabbed down a wad of clothes—and as the guy comes into the room, I throw open the door and spring," Ned was saying. "Buck naked, I start out running, and here's my bad luck: I slam right into him and knock him out. Like it's a cartoon or something. I know he's out cold, but I'm too terrified to think straight, so I keep on running. Turns out what I've grabbed is a white pleated shirt and a thing like a—what do you call those jackets the Japanese wear? Comes halfway down my thighs, thank God."

"These are the things he thanks God for," Richard said to me.

Ned got up, growing more animated. "It's *all* like a cartoon. There's a dog in the yard that sets out after me, but the thing is on a *chain*. He reaches the end of the chain and just rises up in the air, baring his teeth, but he can't go anywhere. So I stand right there, inches in front of the dog, and put on the shirt and tie the jacket around me, and then I stroll over to the gate and slip the latch, and about a quarter of a mile later I'm outside some hotel. I go in and go to the men's room to clean up, and that's the first time I realize I've got a broken nose."

Although I had heard the story before, this was the first mention of Ned's broken nose. For a few seconds he seemed to lose steam, as if he himself were tired of the story, but then he started up again, revitalized.

"And here's the rest of my good luck: I come out and the guy on the desk is a fag. I tell him I've run into a problem and will he please call my boyfriend at the hotel where we're staying, because I don't even have a coin to use the pay phone. So he looks up the number of the hotel, and he dials it and hands me the phone. They connect me with Sander, who is sound asleep, but he snaps to right away, screaming, 'Another night on the town with a prettyboy? Suddenly the bars close and Ned realizes his wallet's back at the hotel? And do you think I'm going to come get you, just because you and some pickup don't have money to pay the bill?' "

Eyes wide, Ned turned first to me, then to Richard, playing to a full house. "While he was ranting, I had time to think. I said, 'Wait a minute, Sander. You mean they didn't get anything? You mean I left my wallet at the hotel?' " Ned sank into his chair. "Can you believe it? I'd actually left my fuckin' wallet in our room, so all I had to do was pretend to Sander that I'd gotten mugged—sons of bitches made me strip and ran off with my pants. Then I told him that the guy at the hotel gave me the kimono to put on." He clicked his fingers. "That's what they're called: 'kimonos.' "

"He didn't ask why a kimono?" Richard said wearily. He ran his hand over the stubble of his beard. His feet were tucked beside him on the sofa.

"Sure. And I tell him it's because there's a Japanese restaurant in the hotel, and if you want to wear kimonos and sit on the floor Japanese style, they let you. And the bellboy thought they'd never miss a kimono."

"He believed you?" Richard said.

"Sander? He grew up in L.A. and spent the rest of his life in New York. He knew you had to believe everything. He drives me back to the hotel saying how great it is that the scum that jumped me didn't get any money. The sun's coming up, and we're riding along in the rental car, and he's holding my hand." Ned locked his thumbs together. "Sander and I are like *that* again."

In the silence, the room seemed to shrink around us. Sander died in 1985.

"I'm starting to feel cold," Richard said. "It comes up my body like somebody's rubbing ice up my spine."

I got up and sat beside him, half hugging him, half massaging his back.

"There's that damn baby again," Richard said. "If that's their first baby, I'll bet they never have another one."

Ned and I exchanged looks. The only sound, except for an intermittent hiss of steam from the radiator, was the humming of the refrigerator.

"What happened to your paws, Rac?" Richard said to me.

I looked at my hands, thumbs pressing into the muscles below his shoulders. For the first time in as long as I could remember, I'd forgotten to put on the lotion and the gloves before going to sleep. I was also reflexively doing something I'd trained myself not to do years ago. My insurance contract said I couldn't use my hands that way: no cutting with a knife, no washing dishes, no making the bed, no polishing the furniture. But I kept pressing my thumbs in Richard's back, rubbing them back and forth. Even after Ned dropped the heavy blanket over Richard's trembling shoulders, I kept pressing some resistance to his hopeless dilemma deep into the bony ladder of Richard's spine.

"It's crazy to hate a baby for crying," Richard said, "but I really hate that baby."

Ned spread a blanket over Richard's lap, then tucked it around his legs. He sat on the floor and bent one arm around Richard's blanketed shins. "Richard," he said quietly, "there's no baby. We've gone through the building floor by floor, to humor you. That noise you get in your ears when your blood pressure starts to drop must sound to you like a baby crying."

"Okay," Richard said, shivering harder. "There's no baby. Thank you for telling me. You promised you'd always tell me the truth."

Ned looked up. "Truth? From the guy who just told the Puerto Rico story?"

"Or maybe you're hearing something in the pipes, Richard," I said. "Sometimes the radiators make noise."

Richard nodded hard, in agreement. But he didn't quite hear me. That was what Ned and I had found out about people who were dying: their minds always raced past whatever was being said, and still the pain went faster, leapfrogging ahead.

Two days later, Richard was admitted to the hospital with a high fever, and went into a coma from which he never awoke. His brother flew to Boston that night, to be with him. His godson, Jerry, came, too, getting there in time to go with us in the cab. The experimental treatment hadn't worked. Of course, we still had no way of knowing—we'll never know—whether Richard had been given the polysyllabic medicine we'd come to call "the real stuff," or whether he'd been part of the control group. We didn't know whether the priest from Hartford was getting the real stuff, either, though it was rumored among us that his flushed face was a good sign. And what about the young veterinarian who always had something optimistic to say when we ran into each other in the transfusion room? Like Clark Kent, with his secret "S" beneath his shirt, the vet wore a T-shirt with a photograph reproduced on the front, a snapshot of him hugging his Border collie on the day the dog took a blue ribbon. He told me he wore it every Friday for good luck, as he sat in oncology getting the I.V. drip that sometimes gave him the strength to go to a restaurant with a friend that night.

Ned and I, exhausted from another all-nighter, took the presence of Richard's brother and godson as an excuse to leave the hospital and go get a cup of coffee. I felt light-headed, though, and asked Ned to wait for me in the lobby while I went to the bathroom. I thought some cold water on my face might revive me.

There were two teenage girls in the bathroom. As they talked, it turned out they were sisters and had just visited their mother, who was in the oncology ward down the hall. Their boyfriends were coming to pick them up, and there was a sense of excitement in the air as one sister teased her hair into a sort of plume, and the other took off her torn stockings and threw them away, then rolled her knee-length skirt up to make it a micromini. "Come on, Mare," her sister, standing at the mirror, said, though she was taking her time fixing her own hair. Mare reached into her cosmetic bag and took out a little box. She opened it and began to quickly streak a brush over the rectangle of color inside. Then, to my amazement, she began to swirl the brush over both knees, to make them blush. As I washed and dried my face, a fog of hair spray filtered down. The girl at the mirror fanned the air, put the hair spray back in her purse, then picked up a tube of lipstick, opened it, and parted her lips. As Mare straightened up after one last swipe at her knees, she knocked her sister's arm, so that the lipstick shot slightly above her top lip.

"Jesus! You feeb!" the girl said shrilly. "Look what you made me *do*."

"Meet you at the car," her sister said, grabbing the lipstick and tossing it into her makeup bag. She dropped the bag in her purse and almost skipped out, calling back, "Soap and water's good for that!"

"What a bitch," I said, more to myself than to the girl who remained.

"Our mother's dying, and she doesn't care," the girl said. Tears began to well up in her eyes.

"Let me help you get it off," I said, feeling more light-headed than I had when I'd come in. I felt as if I were sleepwalking.

The girl faced me, mascara smudged in half-moons beneath her eyes, her nose bright red, one side of her lip more pointed than the other. From the look in her eyes, I was just a person who happened to be in the room. The way I had happened to be in the room in New York the day Richard came out of the bathroom, one shirtsleeve rolled up, frowning, saying, "What do you think this rash is on my arm?"

"I'm all right," the girl said, wiping her eyes. "It's not your problem."

"I'd say she does care," I said. "People get very anxious in hospitals. I came in to throw some water on my face because I was feeling a little faint."

"Do you feel better now?" she said.

"Yes," I said.

"We're not the ones who are dying," she said.

It was a disembodied voice that came from some faraway, perplexing place, and it disturbed me so deeply that I needed to hold her for a moment—which I did, tapping my forehead lightly against hers and slipping my fingers through hers to give her a squeeze before I walked out the door.

Ned had gone outside and was leaning against a lamppost. He pointed the glowing tip of his cigarette to the right, asking silently if I wanted to go to the coffee shop down the block. I nodded, and we fell into step.

"I don't think this is a walk we're going to be taking too many more times," he said. "The doctor stopped to talk, on his way out. He's run out of anything optimistic to say. He also took a cigarette out of my fingers and crushed it under his heel, told me I shouldn't smoke. I'm not crazy about doctors, but there's still something about that one that I like. Hard to imagine I'd ever warm up to a guy with tassels on his shoes."

It was freezing cold. At the coffee shop, hot air from the electric heater over the door smacked us in the face as we headed for our familiar seats at the counter. Just the fact that it wasn't the hospital made it somehow pleasant, though it was only a block and a half away. Some of the doctors and nurses went there, and of course people like us— patients' friends and relatives. Ned nodded when the waitress asked if we both wanted coffee.

"Winter in Boston," Ned said. "Never knew there was anything worse than winter where I grew up, but I think this is worse."

"Where did you grow up?"

"Kearney, Nebraska. Right down Route Eighty, about halfway between Lincoln and the Wyoming border."

"What was it like, growing up in Nebraska?"

"I screwed boys," he said.

It was either the first thing that popped into his head, or he was trying to make me laugh.

"You know what the first thing fags always ask each other is, don't you?" he said.

I shook my head no, braced for a joke.

"It's gotten so the second thing is 'Have you been tested?' But the first thing is still always 'When did you know?' "

"Okay," I said. "Second question."

"No," he said, looking straight at me. "It can't happen to me."

"Be serious," I said. "That's not a serious answer."

He cupped his hand over mine. "How the hell do you think I got out of Kearney, Nebraska?" he said. "Yeah, I had a football scholarship, but I had to hitchhike to California—never been to another state but Wyoming—hitched with whatever I had in a laundry bag. And if a truck driver put a hand on my knee, you don't think I knew that was a small price to pay for a ride? Because luck was with me. I always knew that. Just the way luck shaped those pretty hands of yours. Luck's always been with me, and luck's with you. It's as good as anything else we have to hang on to."

He lifted his hand from mine, and yes, there it was: the perfect hand, with smooth skin, tapered fingers, and nails curved and shining under the gloss of a French manicure. There was a small, dark smudge across one knuckle. I licked the middle finger of the other hand to see if I could gently rub it away, that smudge of mascara that must have passed from the hand of the girl in the bathroom to my hand when our fingers interwove as we awkwardly embraced. The girl I had been watching, all the time Ned and I sat talking. She was there in the coffee shop with us— I'd seen them come in, the two sisters and their boyfriends—her hair neatly combed, her eyes sparkling, her makeup perfectly stroked on. Though her sister tried to get their attention, both boys hung on her every word.

GOING HOME WITH UCCELLO

Three weeks into the trip to Italy she'd given up wearing anything but comfortable shoes and clothes. The brassiere had been replaced by Teddy's mistakenly shrunken undershirt; her linen pants were left in the hotel room—where, draped over a chair, they would probably continue to wrinkle on their own—and she wore, instead, her sweatpants. Running shoes instead of hiking boots. Teddy's navy-blue pullover, unadorned. Of course, anyone would take her for a tourist: not even simple earrings or a bright scarf. They wouldn't have to hear her speak to know she was American.

Teddy was English. She enjoyed making fun of him, saying that he represented his culture by carrying his umbrella everywhere. Men were lucky: their shoes always fit comfortably. He had on black-and-white bucks with pink rubber soles. He was wearing his jeans, and a cashmere sweater his sister had given him for Christmas. Men were lucky: dark circles under *their* eyes were sexy. Unkempt hair made them look casual, not disheveled. She had it in for Teddy a little, though she hated to admit it. (She usually pretended even to herself that she had it in for all men.) She wished so many feminists hadn't become shrill. Or clownish, like Camille Paglia. She also wished she had a job, and that she could decide whether or not to move to London and live with Teddy and his son, Nigel.

As a little child, the boy had bitten her. Buying him sweets was really the only way to keep him on your side. That and coming to his rescue, explaining homework assignments he didn't understand, or being able to sort out what the teacher probably told the class to bring to school, in spite of the cryptic abbreviations Nigel had written down: "Be—wax." Could the teacher possibly have wanted beeswax from everyone?

No, it was beads and some special thread, waxed thread, Nigel suddenly remembered, for Thursday's crafts class. But why did Nigel have to tell her these things late at night? Why not earlier, when she could send his father out to get them? Amazingly, she had been able to provide the beads, because she'd kept a broken necklace in an envelope in her make-up bag for years. The bracelet Nigel finally made went that weekend to Mum, in Kensington. So Mum was now wearing a beaded bracelet fashioned from a broken necklace she had swiped from an ex-lover's apartment in New York City. On the night table, she'd found a cigarette stubbed out in an ashtray that usually served only as a dish under a plant, and under the unsteady ashtray a necklace of tiny green beads. She had pocketed the necklace and turned the ashtray upside down so her ex-lover might notice that she had noticed it.

What a way to think about people: ex-this, ex-that. Maybe she thought of him as her ex-lover because it was a way of putting a big X through him, the way Zorro had slashed his Z through the air on TV. A bit of implicit violence there—but if she ever parted from Teddy, she couldn't imagine feeling any way but sorrowful. Teddy, who had insisted her friend Moira see an acupuncturist and who had driven her fifty miles each way every Monday for months, until she died. "Maybe I should have taken her to somebody who practiced voodoo," he had said. It had taken her a while to register what he meant, and then to realized that he was serious: half angry at life's cruelty, and half self-deprecating.

Now, in the museum gift shop, she flipped through a rack of reproductions of paintings she and Teddy were about to see. The museum wouldn't open for another ten minutes—in Italian time, perhaps half an hour. She was wondering idly about the nationality of other people who browsed with her. She played little games she often played, spinning suddenly to look at Teddy and trying to imagine what she would think if she were seeing him for the first time, or standing near another couple and trying to see him through their eyes—if they saw him at all. It was amazing how many people did not seem to see him. He was handsome enough, though slight. He looked like a nice man. She decided that was true: he looked benevolent, and his graying sideburns could even seem dashing. His shoes must be meant to be funny, yes? Because he was too old for such shoes, and a man in a cashmere sweater would know they were rather funny-looking.

There was a woman, a woman five feet ten to six feet tall, her auburn hair clipped back, bending to peer into a glass case. Only, she didn't care what she saw. She only meant to be standing next to Teddy. She edged him away, a bit, and when he was about to step sideways, she apologized—in English, with a French accent—and drew him back by placing her hand on his wrist. Her long bangs fell free of the clip and scooped forward. "That bookmark," the woman said. "Do you know what that could be?" And to her complete surprise, Teddy, drawing close, said, "A detail of a painting by Uccello, I should think."

Uccello? It was as if the windows had been thrown open and a breeze had blown into the room. It was the experience one had hearing music shift from major to minor. She frowned, wondering how he would know the work of a painter she'd never heard of. She watched them. Then Teddy moved away, flipping through the box of postcards, stepping away from the Frenchwoman's side. How long will she wait before moving close to him again? she found herself thinking, while a man the same height as the woman came into the shop and put his hand on her upper arm and said something to her, quietly. He was followed in by a towheaded boy of four or five, who ran to the man and butted his head against the back of his knees, hugging his legs from behind. The boy wore glasses. By the way he ran, which was more like loping, you could tell something was wrong. When she looked again, she saw a brace—something like a temporary cast—strapped around the outside of his pants. He was wearing some doctor-rigged contraption on his right leg, and he was hugging his father from behind, embracing him with as much force as he could muster, which in an adult would have brought the man down. Instead, the man carefully lifted him onto his shoulders, and from up above, with the best possible view of the shop, the boy began to survey the scene. How interesting that his eyes, like his mother's, settled on Teddy.

Teddy was looking at a framed reproduction of a painting. The original must have been five or six panels, because on closer inspection you could see the seams. It was rosy and gold, about four feet long and five or six inches high. Now at his side, she looked with him. Something terrible was depicted: men breaking down a door as blood flowed from the room. Midway across the painting was a hovering angel, as predictable as a star in the night sky. Golden salvation: a painting with a message. She looked from left to right, trying to read the story. Finally, she said, "Uccello."

He looked at her, startled. "Yes," he said. "How did you know that?"

She sidestepped the question. "It's obviously not Mantegna," she said, shrugging in the direction of a portrait she did know, framed near the corner, "so I figured it might be Uccello."

"Yes," he said. "I remember it from art-history class, all those years ago. The Jews have taken the Host, I think, and the Christians are trying to get it back. I think it's very strange and wonderful. We must take this home."

Whose home went unsaid. At the end of this trip, it was up to her to decide where she was going to live. Her lease in New York would be up October 1. Though she rarely occupied the apartment, she had kept it during the two years she had been with Teddy. Today was September 8. The Virgin Mary's birthday, as he'd told her at the *pensione* that morning. Had he found that out from the *Herald-Tribune* or from his datebook, or had he just known? Her mouth foaming with toothpaste, shivering naked beneath his white-turned-gray bathrobe, she had ducked her head around and asked him. "To tell the truth," he said, "I know from my school days." As toothpaste suds swirled down the basin, he said, "Because I always remember Molly Bloom's birthday. And Joyce had her born on the birthday of the Virgin."

She had listened as she dried her mouth on the hem of the robe. Only one small towel had been provided with the room, and they'd dampened that the night before, sloshing water on themselves and making the best of a room without a bath—just the bath down the hall, which had overflowed and couldn't be entered. On top of that, the proprietor had turned off the lights at 11 p.m. and the two of them, reading in bed, had found themselves in total darkness. Somehow it had seemed very funny, their being reproached for their late-night ways. As had the one little towel, earlier—like trying to dry off with a handkerchief after a rainstorm.

She turned to Teddy, who was still staring at the painting. In her peripheral vision, she could see the man and the little boy leaving the shop, the woman staring studiously, as if registering sudden changes beneath a microscope instead of viewing objects in a glass case. Suddenly, the Frenchwoman began speaking Italian, asking to see something. Then, much to her surprise, Teddy went to the woman's side and said, "Excuse me. You speak Italian as well as English. Could you ask for me if they have the Uccello, you know, rolled up? Not laminated and framed?"

Teddy hadn't been wrong: The woman behind the counter only stared at him, puzzled. So the Frenchwoman nodded and asked his question. She watched while the woman gestured. Then the woman behind the counter shook her head no. The Frenchwoman said to

Teddy, "She doesn't. So if you want to be able to pack your things flat, maybe you should settle for one of the lovely bookmarks."

"But I want to hang the Uccello above a doorway, you see," Teddy said. "And I'm not a character in *Alice in Wonderland*; I'm a poor sod who lives near Hampstead Heath, where everything has to be its real size. Or at the very least, the size someone else has decided on for a reproduction, and certainly nothing so small as a bookmark."

As he finished his sentence, she had an insight: most things could be reduced to a joke with Teddy; he could be self-deprecating and call himself a "sod," though he had far more money than she did; he could approach strangers with ease because he had such faith in his own charm. People who approached others the way Teddy approached the Frenchwoman were recognizable: safe, part of a club. All those jokes about people picking up other people in fern bars in New York—what was the difference between that much-joked-about courting ritual and what Teddy was doing now? This going-with-your-sometimes-girlfriend to beautiful Italia for a romantic rendezvous in the fall and flirting with whoever got your attention in a shop that sold reproductions of the old masters?

He settled for the laminated, framed reproduction. Which doorway did he mean to adorn? In Teddy's house, the molding extended, in graduated layers, from the high ceilings to within a few inches of the door tops. He had such interest in getting the painting back to London, but what about the fact that he'd refused, utterly refused, to carry back on the plane any plates or bowls? "Any wine you want, darling, but we must drink it in Italy. And buy Italian pottery in London. No breakables." He had said that, a week or so before, kissing her forehead, as they walked through a tantalizing wine shop that stocked extra-virgin olive oil in breathtakingly beautiful bottles—bottles closed with gold twine and sealing wax, the labels illustrated by artists who could render a single grape as luminous as a rainbow. This way, not that way, darling. At the end of it we fly home. Your home as well as mine, unless you're crazy and don't think there's enough cashmere to warm you through English winters, unless you don't trust me to be a magician who can provide anything you want.

She envisioned Teddy, the night before, holding out the wrung-out towel as if it had mysteriously dried at his fingertips. This was something he was adept at, something he knew about: if you made yourself the subject of the joke, the other person, by default, would become your audience. And those times you were serious about something, it was best to let the other person know, subtly but quickly, that you were entitled to whatever you might want; to make mention, say, of what a proper neighborhood you lived in.

In Italy, they usually let you carry your packages into the museums. She had been amazed to see women carrying little dogs in their arms, or people sipping from a cup of coffee. Teddy carried the Uccello, wrapped in brown paper, under his arm. The museum was filled with small rooms that they went into, one after another. From time to time, the Frenchwoman and her family would come into the room where they stood, though she and her husband seemed to take things in quickly and leave. Finally, the French couple preceded them by several rooms, so it was only toward the end of the corridor that they caught up with them. She could overhear snippets of conversation, see them walk arm in arm to the window, where they looked down into the courtyard, their child always letting go of his parents' hands, intent upon being where his parents were not. As she and Teddy passed them, moving toward the end of the hallway, Teddy slipped his arm around her waist, and she thought how strange it was: if she and Teddy had been taller, and if Nigel had been with them, they might be a mirror image of the French family.

At the roped-off staircase to the second floor, a guard was posted, sitting on a fold-down stool. About a dozen people congregated around him, waiting for the clock to click through the last few minutes so that they might ascend. The guard did not make eye contact with anyone, and he did not slip the hook at the tip of the velvet rope from its eye until the hands of the clock moved to exactly 2 p.m. Then, as if sleepwalking, he stood slowly and unhooked the rope, eyes cast down as people rushed around him.

Her eyes, too, were downcast; in avoiding looking at the Frenchwoman, she had seen, as if the marble floor were a crystal ball, a vision not of the future but of the recent past: Teddy, standing in the museum shop, all but being asked whether he wasn't a tourist—the woman had talked about "packing things flat"—and then Teddy, letting her know by his answer where he lived. Where she might find him. As they'd passed her in the corridor, the woman had repositioned her hair clip, her loosened hair the sign that something had transpired between them. Well, then: Teddy must have taken her on this trip to Italy not so much to show her a wonderful time and persuade her to join him and Nigel in London forever after; he must have wanted, instead, to persuade himself that he loved her so much that no one else could be a distraction—that no other woman could come between them.

She climbed the stairs slowly, the Frenchwoman's husband in the lead; his wife, with her lovely, flowing hair and her deeply kick-pleated skirt, walking behind; they were followed by several other couples and then by Teddy, who had reached behind and taken her hand to try to hurry her along. At the landing, the man bent down to hoist his son atop his shoulders again. Then the two of them sprinted ahead, the boy leaning forward, craning his neck toward whatever mysterious realm would next be explored.

As the people ascended, the guard, from below, threw a switch, sending up a loud buzzing noise, as if a swarm of mosquitoes had flown into electric coils. And there it was: the Uccello, lit spottily and much too brightly, so that some of the paint glowed firelike while other areas were cast in shadow. With an abrupt click, the lights went off. For further viewing, it was necessary to deposit two hundred lire. Annoyed, Teddy plunged his hand in his pocket, but the Frenchwoman, who knew the way things worked and who must have already been holding the coins, got to the box to deposit the money first. The Uccello lit up again, under its weird illumination. As the woman turned to receive the appreciation of the crowd, Teddy took one small step forward, smiling.

THE SIAMESE TWINS
GO SNORKELING

Harry DeKroll, house-sitting for Ames and Alice Albright, began enacting the daily rituals: today, seeing which of the plants needed watering; double-checking to make sure the refrigerator was spotless inside;
checking the answering machine, which was programmed to give an
outgoing message saying that the Albrights could be reached in New
York at the following number, and that messages should not be left for
them on the Key West machine. (When did that ever stop some enthusiastic, drunken friend or business acquaintance from leaving a piña
colada–inspired message about meeting for drinks on the Sunset Deck,
or how about dinner at blah blah?)

Nine blossoms and three buds on the *Streptocarpus X hybridus*—a
plant with flowers as purple as Liz Taylor's eye shadow in the sixties.
Pinkie into the soil to test for wetness—a wiggle that suggested soli-
darity with mothers everywhere, testing infants' diapers. (Indeed: mod-
erately wet.) The refrigerator: a small smudge of applesauce on the
bottom shelf. Mopped up, with a sponge dunked under hot tap water
and wrung out so that just enough moisture remained to allow for a
careful cleanup. God help him if Alice ever again found the refrigerator
anything less than pristine. Then the machine: sure enough, somebody
named Buzz, calling from Islamorada, "just on the chance you two
might be there, but I guess you're back in the city. Okay, try you again
tonight." Information about Buzz's rented LeBaron convertible (preferable to Buzz's wife's Jeep in terms of fun; not as smooth as Buzz's
BMW). "Hey, if you get this message, Alice, call Betsy about whether
that benefit for the kids' hospital is in March or April, will you?"

Harry's friend Nance had given him, for his birthday, a telephone
that, with the push of a button, allowed for many options in disguising

your voice. One made him sound like a baritone; another made him sound very fey (useful for reserving good tables in certain restaurants; not that he ate at them, but when the Albrights came into town, they asked him to call ahead to reserve); another provided a credible imitation of a young girl. If there had been a phone number left by Buzz, in Islamorada, he would have selected that one to leave a return message, saying that the Albrights should be called directly, in New York. Alice had asked him, recently, why people assumed they weren't really talking to their house sitter. Several people had commented that it sounded like a child had returned their call, or . . . He'd assured her the people were either imagining things, or perhaps—how would he know? sounded fine on his end—there was something strange about the connection. He stashed the machine under his bed, in the downstairs guest bedroom he had come to prefer. It was still painted a muted green, untouched by the interior decorator's sponge-and-glaze frenzy upstairs. It was a testament to how much he liked the machine that he so often got down on his knees to drag it out and plug it in, then shove it back under. Alice had been known, on rare occasions, to appear at the Ashe Street house like Mary Poppins, plop, right out of the sky. Brought by USAir, but unannounced. And oh: the time she found the Spanish champagne, forgotten, become a dripping fountain in the freezer, the yellowish spillover spoiling the purity of the white, white shelf.

A little Leonard Cohen from the CD player. Cohen nouveau—a treat that arrived with the springtime, exported *par avion* by his friend Goldman, to be enjoyed quickly. Much better than Leonard Cohen's old shit. *The Future:* Cohen's voice rattling along like tires riding over singing gravel. That, for a little morning cheer, plus an English, the crumbs from which would later be dumped into the garbage disposal. An English, with no-sugar-added grape jelly. Glass of Citrucel, big heaping tablespoon, fill the Flipper glass half full with water, stir madly, add a few ice cubes, a dollop of guava nectar, from the Cubano grocery. Then out for a morning stroll, a *con leche*, maybe the paper if the headlines suggested any real mayhem among warring Conchs and tourists, or further irreversible destruction of the Keys.

And so, to the morning. Roll up blue plastic pool cover to allow for weekly cleaning by pool service. Not that they wouldn't do it—just a friendly thing to do, a little Save-John-the-Poolman-Three-Minutes gesture. Lock the gate. Give the street the once-over: tourists consulting a map; Mrs. Lolliso's blue parrot out in its cage on the front porch—once it gets used to a person, no more trying to please with a "good morning," all hope of a cracker abandoned. Silence from the Man in Blue. *Walk on by,* as the song goes. Black Pig (tanned Conch) riding a Harley.

Kittens still hanging out around the back tires of the tarped Ford—
someone put out dishes of food. One bold kitten coming out to mew,
standing in close proximity to empty dish. *Con leche grande: Sí, un azú-
car.* Just another day in paradise.

Key West had been more fun in the old days, when the reef was still
more alive than dead, when drugs were plentiful and everybody was
young enough to still enjoy them, before people with money started
moving into the houses and fixing them up, putting pools in the backyards, shooing out the roosters. He and Alice would go snorkeling off
Billy G's catamaran, float by the hour in their wet-suit vests, studying
the parrot fish and the blue tangs and the triggerfish and the barracudas. They drank a lot of Mount Gay and agreed with each other that
this was the great escape: no shoveling snow; no heavy winter clothes;
you could take your dog right into most restaurants.

He had first gotten to Key West in the late seventies, just a few
months before Ron, Alice's first husband, sniffed out the Southernmost
Point as being ripe for making money. Ron was a builder, a master reno-
vator, and he had connections up the wazoo from West Palm. Harry had
been bartending at Tropics back then, an exile from Amesbury, Mas-
sachusetts, himself, and when Ron ordered a Corona and asked about
recommendations of good carpenters, Harry had reconsidered his long-
held position that he was out of the building biz and made tentative
noises about perhaps, just maybe, volunteering his own services on the
days he wasn't working—which in those days meant four days a week.
Midway through job number 1, Ron had shown up with a tall, thin
woman with flaxen hair, wearing black wraparounds and a hard hat: an
artist, no less, and he was married to her, it turned out, and what she
did with her days was sketch people in motion and then make what she
had sketched abstract, enlarging the sketches on enormous sheets of
paper six or seven feet high, which she reportedly sold for large amounts
of money to interior decorators, who framed them in Plexiglas and put
them in stairwells, or some such thing. To this day, he couldn't remember how it had been explained to him, except that all his life he thought
you were supposed to look at an abstraction and see in it various
things—that it looked like two people hugging, or something—but what
Alice would do was sketch two people hugging and manage to make
them look very lifelike, and then she'd do another version that would
look like a brick wall half demolished, or people transformed into enormous palm fronds. Anyway: Alice came with the territory. She had a

folding stool and her big sketch pad and her box of stuff, and every day she'd sit out of the way and sketch Ron and Harry and the Black Pig, who worked harder than two other people, plus his sidekick, Lazy, who worked about half as much as most guys, though he was a teetotaler and extremely dependable. Lazy didn't even take off on his birthday and would have been happy to work on Christmas. The only time he took off—this was pre-VCR—was to watch the Jerry Lewis Telethon, which he told you he was going to do the minute you started interviewing him, so most people thought they'd be getting a major nutcase, and usually found other reasons not to hire him. Once, for Lazy's birthday, Harry had made him a foldout birthday card, folding a piece of paper the way his grandmother had taught him years before, folding and folding and cutting just so until presto! Four people holding hands stretched out. Harry penciled in pinwheel eyes and *Jaws* teeth and wavy horizontal lines to indicate deep wrinkles and wrote HAPPY BIRTHDAY TO LAZY across their chests. He had been showing off for Alice—showing off and perhaps putting her down a bit, too, in making the paper dolls. Years ago, all of that, and just think: Lazy, whose greatest pleasures in life seemed to be doing work in slow motion, drinking Cokes, and watching Jerry Lewis go batshit, and he was found in the early eighties with his throat slit ear to ear, washed up on the shore of Big Coppitt, no idea who did it, no idea why.

By then, Harry was no longer in touch with Ron. Ron and Alice had gotten divorced after she found him in bed with a three-hundred-pound transsexual, story went, though, as people said at the time, who *was* this three-hundred-pounder? Even in Key West, such a person would be noticed before long, because come on: people went to the trouble of going all the way to Key West in order to strut their stuff, but no one had ever seen him/her except Alice.

Harry's friendship with Alice began after Ron sold the business, renovated the last eyebrow house (symbolic; after the transsexual, everyone's eyebrows were raised), got a quickie divorce, and moved to Costa Rica. Though just recently, word was, on good authority (the Black Pig's girlfriend), Ron had moved again, to San Miguel de Allende. His friendship with Alice . . . Several years before, she called him one night after Ron had been gone a week or so and she asked him if he was working for the new guy. He wasn't, as it happened. The new guy was an asshole, and he was tired of doing construction, anyway. Tired of even seeing all those backyards bulldozed for pools while he was ripping out dry rot and the termites were swarming. Was there a chance she could buy him a drink and talk over something with him? she wanted to know. When he missed a beat, she answered his unasked question: No funny stuff—she wanted to talk to him about continuing her project: drawing him. As they chatted, he found out she knew a guy with a catamaran, and that when she wasn't sketching, she was floating over the reef, snorkeling. It sounded like fun—fascinating, the way she talked about it; it sounded like she didn't want to see the fish and later make them into squares and rectangles and have them falling through space, she just *appreciated* them. He remembered being almost hypnotized by the way she'd described the fishes' colors, and how silvery and surprising everything looked down there, so that first he agreed to go out on Billy G's boat, then he said—yeah, he probably said—that if she wanted to come into the bar and sketch while he worked—he was working four days a week when the construction job ended—that would be fine with him, as long as she realized a bunch of drunken fools would try to pick her up because she was an artist. Or just because she'd be sitting there, actually.

The snorkeling outings got to be a regular thing, or at least as regular as anything got to be in Key West: most Mondays, except for bad weather, except for anything unavoidable that came up. Also, Alice almost always showed up when he was working. It got so he'd leave a message if his schedule changed. But except for seeing her on the boat or, more often, seeing her shadow floating near him, seeing her black flippers, feeling, almost, her fascination with the fish encircling them as they both swished through the water—except for that, he never saw her unless it was in Tropics. Didn't even run into her at the store. Didn't see her walking around town. Therefore, after eight, nine months or so, why had he been so surprised to hear from her that she was remarrying? Sitting and sketching at the bar, the rare times things were slow, he'd learned a little about her marriage to Ron. The big transsexual hadn't been the first—Ron had a taste for exotica. And he didn't want kids, and she thought she did. Maybe she should have married the guy she intended to marry years ago, because she'd heard he was still pining away for her, even though he was living with somebody else, in White Plains. She seemed to think it was as confusing and pointless—all of it— as he did, and she hadn't really been asking for advice. She knew he was seeing a girl named Lucia, because when he told her about his weekends, Lucia's name usually came up. And after that, she knew he was seeing Nance Goodwin, and that it was top secret because Nance would lose her alimony if she lived with anybody, and every time Nance even hung out with a guy for a long time, her ex would have her tailed— usually for considerably longer than the guy lasted. So Alice knew those things, but he never talked about his feelings (yeah, yeah: everybody always said men didn't), and he had to guess at hers vis-à-vis the man in White Plains. He was pretty surprised when she called him early one Sunday morning, either drunk or weepy or both, and asked him if he would do her an enormous favor. She called him at three in the morning, but then, she'd been in the bar until two, and she knew—because he'd told her so—that he was going home when he got off at three, because Nance was being followed again.

The big favor was that Ames Albright, Mr. White Plains, was coming to Key West a week from Monday, and she wanted him to have dinner with them. In fact, if there was any way he could spare the time, she would also like it if he would go to the airport to pick him up with her, but she realized that was asking a lot. He was surprised she asked, and he also didn't want to do it, but he didn't know exactly how to get out of it.

"Please," she said. She sounded urgent.

"What do you want me to meet him for?" he said. He realized this sounded uncharitable, but why *did* she want him to meet the man?

"It doesn't have to be *for* anything, does it?"

"But Alice, you know—we don't hang out," he said.

There was a long moment of silence, during which he reflected that what he had just said was not very charitable, but he also felt that in spite of the snorkeling, and in spite of their fragmented conversations as she sat on a bar stool at Tropics, he had spoken the truth.

"You're not my friend?" she said, her voice very quiet.

That one got him. "Of course," he said. "You want me to meet the guy, I'll meet the guy."

"You have time to come to the airport?"

"No," he lied, "but you name the place for dinner and I'll be there."

"Well, at the house," she said. "You know, come by at seven o'clock."

He had never been to her house. Ron had said many times that he was going to have everybody over for a barbecue, but the one time he'd asked them, it had gotten rained out. The house was on Frances, five blocks or so from where he was renting a room.

"Will do," he said.

"You're supposed to say, 'What can I bring?' " she said, "so I can say, 'Just bring yourself.' "

"That's all I was bringing," he said. Three-thirty in the morning, ex-boss's ex-wife wanting him to come to some pointless dinner with some guy from New York. For what? Which was the way he thought in those days. Work all the time—for what? Get married—for what? Mortgage?

Sniveling kids? Support another person? Play the Man's game—for what? So you can be like every other ungratified, overworked chump? He put on Jim Morrison—this many years later, he could remember putting on Dead Jim, stretching out on the futon, falling asleep looking at the palm fronds blowing outside his window: his version of venetian blinds.

She didn't come to the bar on Sunday evening, but she'd missed a couple of Sundays. She and a girlfriend had started to check out lawn sales and flea markets farther up the Keys. But she didn't come the next night, either, and he decided that if he didn't see her on Wednesday, when he worked next, he'd call. Naturally, she wasn't there, though once he looked up and saw a woman who resembled her, in a scarf, and he was surprised how relieved he felt for a split second. He phoned her from the bar but only got her answering machine. "Hey—let me know if anything's wrong. Got used to your being here," he said. It wasn't until he'd hung up that he realized that if something was wrong—say, if somebody'd broken in and knocked her out or tied her up—she could hardly return the message. But how likely was that? He decided to walk by, to see if everything looked okay. And he did, when he got off, but it was late, and there were no lights. The front door was closed. The moon seemed to be shining directly over the roof. Very nice cacti on the front lawn, plus the inevitable two or three cats. Hers? He walked home and watched TV for a while, hoping she might call. Before he went to bed, he left a second message, because he couldn't remember exactly what he'd said on the first: "Hey, listen, last time I called I got the machine, and then I worried that if something was wrong, and you couldn't get back to me for some reason . . . I wanted to say that I'm here tonight, if you want to talk about anything. I'm assuming everything's okay. Call me if there's any change in plans. About the dinner, I mean."

He hung up and wondered why he hadn't told her to call him, period.

He didn't hear from her or see her in the bar. The last night he worked that week, Friday, he didn't expect to see her, and he didn't. A couple of underage kids with fake IDs tried to hassle him, but he grabbed one by the wrist and made it clear he could do damage, and they both ran out of the bar afterward, screaming insults over their shoulders, but what did that matter? Down the bar, an older guy was putting the make on a dyed blond in a low-cut dress who feigned great interest in what he was saying. The guy kept asking for more peanuts and scooping them up like he was thirsty and drinking water from a stream. Like he'd come a long way, but finally, at long last, he'd arrived at the peanut dish.

On Monday, late in the afternoon, he went to Fausto's and got a bottle of wine and an Entenmann's crumb cake, thinking that it would be funny to take something, after all. He got a box of devil's food cookies and opened it and ate as he walked home. He was eating nervously, he realized. He had not been able to shake the thought that she might not be there that night, especially after he'd called twice and gotten neither her nor the machine. He thought about going by the house again, but decided that would be pointless, because he felt entirely sure she wouldn't be there. Maybe she would have left for the airport, but even if she hadn't, he still felt sure she wouldn't be home.

By the time it was time to leave, he'd eaten almost all the cookies and wasn't very hungry. He'd also cut himself shaving, because he'd done it in a hurry, realizing at the last minute that he'd forgotten to shave. He wore his favorite khaki shirt—the one Nance had given him for Valentine's Day, with one of those peel-off metallic hearts above the pocket. He'd been relieved the thing hadn't been sewn onto the shirt. That was long gone. Valentine's Day was long gone. Nance was, herself: gone back to Mother in Buffalo, New York, to ditch the guy tailing her. Nobody her ex-husband hired lasted long in the winter in Buffalo.

Alice opened the door before he even knocked. She said "Hi!" and reached out her arms. He hugged her one-armed, because he was carrying the Fausto's bag.

"Something for the hostess," he said, indicating with a small downward turn of his lip that he meant it wryly. But she took it, exclaiming as if he'd brought some wonderful gift.

He was surprised at the living room. It was quite striking, all done in black and white, with a green rug and very healthy palms growing out of big brass containers. There were spotlights beaming down from the ceiling on the palms. There was a black leather sofa, and two black and two gray chairs. A big aquarium, freestanding, was at the side of the room, where you might expect a wall to divide the living room from the kitchen. Ames Albright stood to the left of the aquarium. He had risen from one of the gray chairs, and he was walking forward, with his hand extended. He had a very pleasant face, but he was winter pale, and as Harry grasped his hand, both he and the man seemed to instantly realize how different they were. Also, the man must be fifty, fifty-five.

He was handsome, with thick hair, black streaked with gray. He was wearing a shirt with cufflinks, khakis with pleats at the waist, and loafers. He was like nobody who ever came into Tropics, and like nobody Harry had seen personally for years. One of those guys you'd see with a cotton sweater tied around his shoulders, up on the Sunset Deck at Pier House, being serenaded by white boys playing reggae on their Rhythm Ace as sailboats passed by and seagulls swooped: a rich guy on vacation, waiting for sunset.

"Ames, this is my good friend Harry. Harry, Ames."

She sounded nervous. He wasn't exactly comfortable himself. In this context, the boxed cake and the bottle of wine looked quite strange sitting next to a large geode on a marble-topped table. He had also apparently lost a devil's food cookie in the bottom of the bag as he ate. She had taken it out and looked at it, puzzled.

"Those are very special. I just brought you one to try," he said.

"Oh," she said. "Well, thank you. Thank you very much."

"Flight get in all right?" he asked Ames, sitting in a chair next to Ames's.

"There was some delay in Miami, but it worked out all right."

"Have you been to Key West before?"

"No. Never have. Went fishing years ago off Key Largo with my brother, but we didn't make it down this far."

"It's really special," Alice said. "I love being here."

"I'm trying to persuade her to move to New York," Ames said. He smiled at Harry.

"You are?" Harry said.

"Well—keep a place here and live in New York, too."

He looked at her, but he couldn't read her expression. She got up and went into the kitchen and came back with a bottle of champagne.

"Here," he said, reaching for the bottle.

"Thanks," she said. "And I guess I should get glasses—"

"Can I help with anything, darling?" Ames said.

Darling?

"No," she said, over her shoulder. "They're right here."

"So I understand you're a fisherman yourself," Ames said.

"Oh, I used to do some fishing. Not too much these days, though. I'm a bartender," he said, hoping the information would fall like a lead balloon.

"Yes, I heard that. But Alice says—oh, sorry: I know what it is she told me. She said the two of you liked to snorkel. Not quite the same thing as fishing."

"No, not exactly," he said. He reached for a champagne flute. He had begun to feel like a minor character in a 1940s movie. He also felt extraneous, antisocial, and confused.

"So then," Ames said, raising his glass, "here's to possibility."

"Possibility," Alice said, raising her glass.

Harry raised his glass, silently, then sipped.

"Alice says you're her muse," Ames said.

"She draws me when I'm tending bar. Yeah," Harry said.

"Yes, she said," Ames said. "I hope I'm not taking you away from your work tonight."

"No," he said, "I wasn't scheduled." He wasn't trying hard enough. Why wasn't he? Because he was exasperated with Alice. Because he'd worried for so long that something might be the matter. Because she was someone's *darling*, so what was he there for?

"Alice and I were engaged years ago," Ames said. "I was awfully happy she decided to call, after my letter finally found its way to her. The thing is, if she thought you liked me, I think my chances would be significantly improved. I'm afraid you're here to approve of me, but because of the way I appear, I doubt that you do. Not that I feel you need to approve, but Alice cares very much."

Talk about odd fish. This guy had the brain of a needlefish, if he was willing to hang around to be auditioned in front of someone else. Of course they didn't like each other. How could she have thought they would?

Harry frowned. He put his glass on the table. He saw that Alice had put her hands over her face.

"You understand that I used to be on her husband's construction team, right? That she and I have in common snorkeling and a fondness for this place. That it's been fine with me if she's wanted to draw me while I'm working, but that's it. Right?"

"Oh, right, absolutely," Ames said. "I hope I didn't in any way suggest that she—"

"Oh God," Alice sighed.

"Well, I don't see—I don't see what's wrong with our conversation, really," Ames said. "I don't see anything to be upset about. I just thought I'd put my cards on the table, so to speak."

"With the Entenmann's?" Harry said.

"He's never been here before. He brought that to be funny," Alice said. "I twisted his arm to come, and the Entenmann's is his retaliation."

Harry looked at Alice. "I wish I'd heard from you this week. I was worried something had happened to you."

"Oh God," Alice said again. "I couldn't work. I tried to draw, and I was too nervous. I painted this whole room so it would look nice, and

I borrowed the furniture. I thought if it looked nice, I could persuade you to maybe be with me in Key West, Ames, instead of my moving to New York. And then some part of me thought—I wanted to test and see if Harry was really my friend, if there was even any reason to stay, because what's the point in staying if I don't even have one really good friend, just Janey that I go to lawn sales with sometimes, and the Black Pig's girlfriend."

"The Black Pig?" Ames said.

"Black Pig worked construction with us," Harry said.

"It's really quite colorful here, isn't it?" Ames said. He turned to Alice. "But tell me, you didn't paint the room just for me, did you?"

"Why wouldn't you think I was your friend?" Harry said, paying no attention to the fact that Ames was talking to Alice. "You were punishing me for not being friendly enough by refusing to answer any of my messages?"

"Those spotlights weren't in the ceiling until yesterday," Alice sniffled.

"Well—they're really quite lovely," Ames said. "I don't know what to say. It would never have occurred to me that you would have painted or changed the house in any way and, you know, borrowed furniture."

"Who did you borrow this stuff from?" Harry said.

"Cheryl and Dieter Hals," Alice said.

"Who are they?" Harry said.

"Dieter is opening a restaurant down here. Louis Quatorze sold them two of my drawings, and they came over to see what I was working on, and one thing led to another because their furniture was going to have to be put in storage because the house wasn't finished, and I asked if I could put it in the living room."

"Louis Quatorze?" Harry said.

"You know who he is, don't pretend you don't. The interior decorator in Back Bay. *Louis.* Everybody calls him Louis Quatorze behind his back."

"No relation to the Black Pig, I trust?" Ames said.

"I like you better," Harry said to Ames.

"Thank you. I knew I was losing ground," Ames said.

"I'm so embarrassed I could die," Alice said.

"She's quite levelheaded. You should be flattered she brought in this trendy furniture for you," Harry said.

"I'm glad to hear that. I've always thought of Alice as very practical."

"Stop talking about me like I'm not here," she said.

"Shouldn't you be in the kitchen cooking?" Harry said.

"Who cares? Why can't we have your cake and finish this champagne?" Ames said.

"See! That's what I love about Ames. He's completely serious when he says that," Alice said.

"I'd marry a man with such sterling qualities," Harry said.

"You see! He likes me so well he thinks you should marry me," Ames said.

"Then I will."

"Really?" Harry said. But now he liked Ames, and he suddenly realized that of course she would—he should have known that. It remained a rhetorical question only because neither Ames nor Alice could answer it. She had jumped into Ames's lap and was kissing him. This was the first "dinner"—the first nonpotluck, nonbarbecue—he had been to in so many years he couldn't remember the last dinner he had attended, unless he included the dinner at the Methodist church that he and Nance got stoned and went off to: ham and beans and jars of mustard the size of umbrella stands. No such middle-class ritual ever figured into his life in Key West. He also probably wasn't getting dinner.

Today's scenario: Have one last, final, no matter what happens and no matter how desperately you desire it no more going back to the Cubano grocery *con leche*. Go home, shoot the shit with the poolman, see if Nance finished the Dutch detective novel she borrowed and whether she had a clue in hell about who did it. Then a bit of pacing, working up to the chores and choices of the day: a little daytime TV that could be turned off when the first person on *Sally* or *Oprah* or whoever it was hung her blow-dried head and cried. *Señor Leonard Cohen, sí!* Maybe a phone call to Goldman in Chicagoland, see how the computer programs he's been writing are going. Continue work on Great American Novel about drifters in Key West; *yes, it will have been written before, but ne'er so well expressed.* Check in with Alice about projected arrival time at Key West International, call Ames at his office to let him know the Mapplethorpe sale seemed to have gone through, according to the oblique FedEx letter from the madman collector in Gallup, New Mexico. Then the late-afternoon funeral of the florist, interment preceded by marching band, as per deathbed request, plus small gathering after service to drink tequila sunrises "until the first person becomes genuinely morose."

Through the garden gate, high on caffeine, depressed about the Plague.

Sage advice for poolman: Let the boy toy go to South Beach; he'll see soon enough what he's missing and come crawling—or tangoing—back.

Horoscope: Success! Love! Fortune!

Real horoscope: You're always bouncing off the walls. What do you think you are? A ball?

Telephone call to Nance (malevolent ex-husband dead; remarried to guy who tailed her to Buffalo): No idea who did it. A total surprise. Price of avocados ridiculous. O.J. murdered Nicole. Aromatherapy the best thing for tension headaches, foot reflexology the best thing for salt and/or sugar cravings. Husband, on business trip, has departed a day early to see Kitaj exhibit in New York. Amniocentesis reveals fetus is boy.

Response to news of friend's amniocentesis results, the sad death of the florist, a man in his midthirties, who never hurt a soul, + pool man's problems with younger lover (sexual identity omitted) who wants to become a model, as phone is held up to senile mother's ear at rest home in Flemington, New Jersey: "Walk on through the wind, and the same for the rain. Mama always loved you best, Harry."

Harry has gotten to the part of his manuscript where he has to describe the evening his main character, a charismatically irresponsible yet somewhat romantic drifter named Wylie, agrees, as a favor, to attend a dinner in which the not conventionally beautiful but nevertheless quirkily beautiful love interest, a photographer instead of a painter—and boy, did that take a lot of research, finding out all the chemicals those people plunge their hands into regularly. . . . Anyway: the quirkily beautiful photog suddenly comes apart, realizing she loves Wylie, not her suitor. The suitor has to be credible, both sympathetic but also possessing enough negative qualities that the reader will increasingly side with the woman, named Alicia, and Wylie. So he names the suitor Liam. Makes him a Brit. The guy is rather inhibited and arch and sometimes silly. All buttoned up, as those Brits can be. Older than our hero, but still viable. Still a hurdle to be jumped.

Blah, blah, blah: dialogue with increasing subtext.

Props: champagne; trendy leather furniture to establish how cosmopolitan is our Alice/Alicia.

From there on, he can tell the truth, though every time he would write "drawing," he simply writes "photograph." The three of them have their bottle of champagne and then it turns out there is a second bottle, which the Brit opens, calling the woman "Darling."

They went/go from the living room into her studio—just another bedroom, really, but the wall had been knocked down so that two adjoining bedrooms were opened up to provide a large space in which she could work. And then she gave/gives a sort of tour, though Wylie's eyes went/go to the end of the line of artwork almost immediately. At first Alicia had been working abstractly, taking photographs that couldn't easily be deciphered, because they were close-ups of parts of Wylie's body: his knuckles, say, quite blurry and enlarged, so that the sense of proportion further threw off the viewer, and it was difficult to puzzle out what you were seeing. But toward the end she began to move away from abstraction, and that is how he knew/knows she's in love with him: much larger photographs, but expressive in a different way than the abstract ones; close-ups that show his expressions, so that you have no doubt this is him, not her; this is not a case of the artist projecting onto the subject.

What Harry had actually seen, that night, was himself. The way Alice had hung the drawings evoked a sort of Humpty-Dumpty in reverse, so that first you saw the breakage, and then you moved into the present, which was highly detailed, and very realistic. No more indecipherable shapes falling down. For years she had seen him as a shape, turning, and then something had happened and she had begun to draw him as he was, drawn him full figure, in precise detail, and clearly with great feeling. After all that time of being interested in how he might come apart, she had started to be interested in the way he was put together.

When he returned to the house to look at them more carefully, he saw that they were dated, as well as signed. The realistic drawings had begun soon after Ron left town. Ron disappeared; Harry suddenly became a person. Bizarrely, there had been that strange moment when she watched him understand this. When they had stood there with the wealthy, older man between them—Ames had been standing there between them—there the silly Brit had stood, understanding nothing.

Five days after the dinner, when curiosity got the better of him and he went back to the house, she was gone. He knew she would be. It was her day for lawn sales and flea markets. As he thought, the bathroom window was easily shoved open. He climbed in and listened for a second, just to make sure. Silence. Then he splashed water on his face and wiped his face and hands on a towel. That made him think of having dipped his fingers in the holy water before Nance's wedding at St. Mary Star of the Sea—something he hadn't done since he was ten or eleven, which was when he put his foot down and stopped attending church.

Alice's house had been as quiet as the inside of a church, and the quiet caused him to walk gently. He picked up a key on a table, thought what trouble he might be able to cause by taking it, held it in his hand for a few seconds, then put it back.

In the rooms she used as her studio, the drawings were still pinned to the wall. He stood back to survey them again. He had quite a few conflicting thoughts. The most recent drawings were quite good, as he'd remembered. She knew him very well. His expressions. What lay behind the expressions also showed through. If he'd known that was what she was doing, would he have let her draw him? He would have been uncomfortable, probably. And she also probably guessed that, so she'd said nothing. Clever. She hadn't misrepresented herself. It was his mistake if he thought the process was always the same. That the reality of whoever and whatever he was would forever be only in the service of some abstraction.

He found a piece of paper on a pad by the telephone. On it, he wrote: *I came back for a longer look. I think you have an amazing talent. You really captured me. Is this about art, though, or is this about something else? Don't get me wrong. I know you're marrying Ames. I never wanted a wife, a family, any of that stuff. I don't now. But why not stick together? Think of us as two floaters on the surface of life. Think of me—as I think of you—as my friend.* It was heartfelt, though he wasn't sure, himself, exactly what he meant. But he was proud of himself for writing the note, and amused that he thought to tape it to the wall at the end of the series, the way a teacher might comment at the end of a student's essay.

Before he left, he went into the kitchen to see if she had something cold he could take with him—a Coke, a beer, whatever. He walked by the aquarium, still attuned for any sound, not so much worried that she'd come back and find him as that his presence might initially frighten her. He passed the aquarium the way he'd circumvent a room divider, but opening a can of ginger ale as he passed it a second time, he stopped. The aquarium was bubbling, but almost empty: a few neons; one black molly. What the fish swam over, which at first looked curiously like a diving bell, was, on closer inspection, her white hard hat, sunk in the middle of the tank. As he watched, the little fish darted over it. There was one clump of seaweed, frizzy and anemic, that had drifted into a corner. How very curious. Did it mean that she was done with being on construction sites for all time, and what the hell: Maybe the fish would like the hat? Had she done it in anger, the way a frustrated warrior might plunge his sword in soil? The three neons stayed together, swimming left and right. The water was slightly cloudy. The world inside the tank didn't look too pleasant. Which was what made him think of a final possibility: the destruction of the reef. The hard hat as garbage, possibly—Alice's version of a sunken tire—the coral ruined, the reef sparse and dying, the fish mostly gone. It might be that the aquarium stood there, brackish and bubbling, nearly empty of fish, as a sort of symbolic reminder.

He tapped the glass, but it was only an idle gesture, nothing he thought would register with the fish. He trailed his fingertips down the glass, then went back to the kitchen, dumped the rest of the too-sweet ginger ale down the drain. He looked around and found scissors on the counter by the phone. Then he went to the sink and picked up the sponge, a slightly wet, blue, rectangular sponge, that had been leaning against the dish drainer. He folded it and began to carefully cut, seeing what would emerge even before he stopped snipping and unfolded it. And *pop!* There it was: two figures, joined at the hip, one with a left arm raised above its head, the other with its right arm raised. He considered his handiwork and shaved a little off one of the figure's heads, giving the male figure short hair. Then he turned on the water and held the sponge under the faucet and watched it puff up. He had done quite a nice job. He took it to the aquarium and put it on the surface of the water. The black molly rose for it instantly, assuming it was food, but when the fish saw that it was not, it veered away and darted into the seaweed. He tapped his fingers on the glass gently, one more time, then turned and walked down the hallway, past three brass Chinese characters hung vertically on the wall, stopping when he came to her bedroom. There was a queen-size bed against the far wall: no headboard, no bedspread. At the foot of the bed was a quilt, a patchwork quilt, that looked old. Family heirloom or, more likely, a flea market find? He squatted and touched his cheek to the material, which felt slightly rough because of the way it was channel-stitched. On the bureau, there was a dresser set: comb, brush, mirror. He ran his hands through the brush and put the little wad of hair he pulled out in his pocket. Then he picked up the mirror, but quickly replaced it before he turned it over, having no desire to see himself close-up, at all. In a small glass bottle was an iris, long dead. Wood shutters were open on one window, closed on another. He looked out both windows—to the side yard, and, opening the shutters, to a cement birdbath in the backyard—then went back to the bathroom, stood on the lid of the toilet, and exited through the window. He dropped to the ground and stood up, his legs a little shaky from the impact. Behind him was Alice's house, Alice's museum, of sorts, to which he'd just added his own little contribution. Such a long time had elapsed between her doing the drawings of him and his seeing them. How long would it take her to discover the floating figures?

In this odd but pleasant arrangement that has come to be his life, on this day of March 1995, fired by *con leche* and impelled by his quest to get it all down, in writing, like McGuane and Sanchez before him, yes, yes, but ne'er so well expressed, to make a little poem . . . in his quest to define a time and a place for everyone who was somewhere else, he nevertheless takes time out to go to the florist's funeral before meeting Alice's plane at five-fifteen. He is a sort of servant, he supposes—but who among us cannot see himself as that, from time to time, if not with depressing regularity? On the days when he's feeling particularly cynical, he thinks that what he lacks is a good drug connection—he's nostalgic for the old days, the old ways, but to be realistic, he couldn't handle the drugs anymore, even if he had access. Most days, he'd admit—though he's never asked—that what he lacks is a settled life and an affectionate companion, but look where everyone's significant others seem to be disappearing these days—into the cemetery; into the coral limestone.

After the funeral, some tourists on pink motor scooters stop to look at the spectacle passing by: a six-man brass band, led by a high-stepping bugle player, followed by other musicians and oddly dressed people clasping the florist's favorites, birds-of-paradise, like big candles. The strutting marching band and its entourage include gays, straight people, blacks, whites, and a dog in a wagon, who has bells fastened on his collar and paws, and whose every attempt to steady himself results in his own contribution of a jingle.

Alice found the note he left for her years ago—he is sure of it—but never once referred to that, or to the floating blue spongepeople, directly. He realized that it had registered, though, the minute Ames called and stumbled through the recitation of a rather bizarre "idea": having Harry house-sit and "take care of things" while they were away, though of course as his wife's muse and as his own friend, he must feel a member of the household, not some—some—

"Floater," Harry had filled in.

And then, hearing the obvious put to him so simply, Ames had gone into almost as much of a dither as the black tuba player was in at this very moment, desperate to finish his short riff before the cortege turned into the cemetery, swearing that was not what he had meant at all, not what he intended to say.

ZALLA

Recently, I had reason to think about Thomas Kurbell—Little Thomas, as the family always called him. Little Thomas fooled the older members of the family for a while because he was so polite as a child—almost obsequious—and because his father, Thomas Sr., had been a genuinely nice man. Ours was an urban family, based in Philadelphia and Washington, D.C., and Little Thomas's father's death reinforced every bit of paranoia everyone had about life in the country. No matter that he actually died of complications of pneumonia, which he had contracted in the hospital as he was lying in traction, recovering from a broken leg, shattered ankle, and patched-together pelvis, suffered after falling from a hay wagon. Legend had it that he'd died instantly from the fall, and this was always invoked as a cautionary warning to any youngster in the family who took an interest in skiing or sailing or even hiking. For the sake of storytelling, Thomas Sr.'s death often dovetailed into the long-ago death of his cousin Pete, who had been struck by lightning when he got out to investigate a backup on the Brooklyn Bridge: wham! With Thomas still sliding out of the hay wagon, there was a sudden bolt of electricity, and Pete, moved to New York City, was struck dead, lit up for such a quick second it seemed somebody was just taking a picture with a flash. I suppose it's true in many families that some things get to be lumped together for effect, and others to obscure some issue. I was thirty years old before I got the chronology of the two deaths correct. It's just the way people in our family tell stories: it wasn't done to mislead Little Thomas.

Little Thomas was a sneaky child. He'd sneak around for no good reason, padding through the house in his socks, sometimes scaring his mother and his sister Lilly when they turned a corner and found him standing there like a statue. His mother always said Little Thomas had no radar. No instinct for avoiding people and things. His going around in his socks made things worse, because if you were frightened and yelped he would become frightened, too, and burst into tears or topple something from a table in his fright. But he wouldn't wear shoes in the house—to get even with his mother, he said, for making him wear boots to school on days when it wasn't even raining, only damp—and no amount of pleading or punishment could make him change his ways. As he got older, he deliberately frightened his sister from time to time, because he loved to see her jump, but most of the scares with his mother were unintentional, he later maintained.

Little Thomas's mother was named Etta Sue. She was five years older than my mother, Alice Dawn Rose. There was a brother in between, who had died of rheumatic fever. Though Etta Sue married a man named Thomas Kurbell, she maintained that Little Thomas was named not for him but for her dead brother, Thomas Wyatt. Little Thomas's middle name was Nathaniel. "She put that name in because she wanted to include everybody, even the milkman," Thomas Sr. used to say. Apparently, the milkman was a subject of fond kidding between them: she really did like the milkman, and he became a family friend. He'd push open the back door, come in, and wipe off the milk bottles before putting them on the top shelf of the refrigerator, and then pour himself some tea and sit and talk to whoever happened to be in the kitchen— Thomas Sr.; my mother, on a visit; me. He was Nat the Milkman. One time when I wasn't there, Little Thomas jumped out of the broom closet and startled Nat the Milkman, and Nat grabbed him and flipped him over, holding him upside down by his ankles for a good long while. This was the reason Little Thomas hated him.

As well as slipping around in his stocking feet, Little Thomas was quiet and rarely could be coaxed into a conversation. He was quiet and troubled—that much the family would finally allow, though they refused to admit that there were any *real* problems. It was said he was troubled because he'd had to wear glasses as a child. Or because his father was so personable that he'd presented his son with a hard act to follow. Later, Little Thomas's asthma was blamed, and then his guilt over the fact that Punkin Puppy, the family's russet-colored mutt, had to be given away because of Little Thomas's allergies. Growing up, I heard these things over and over. The reasons were like a mantra, or like the stages of grief being explained—the steps from denial to acceptance. By the time he was a teenager, it was no longer a question just of his being troubled but of his actively troubling others. Garden hoses were turned on in the neighbors' gardens late at night, washing their flowers away in great landslides of mud; brown bags filled with dog excrement were set burning on some neighbor's porch, so whoever opened the door would be ankle deep in dog shit when he stomped out the flames. Things got worse, and then Little Thomas was sent away to a special school.

Yesterday I visited my mother in her new apartment in Alexandria. She was afraid of crime in downtown Washington and thought she should relocate. Her nurse-companion came with her, a kindhearted woman named Zalla, who attended the school of nursing at American University two nights a week and every summer. When she got her nursing degree, Zalla intended to return to her home, Belize, where she was going to work in a hospital. The hospital was still under construction. Building had to be stopped when the architect was accused of embezzling; then the hurricane struck. But Zalla had faith that the hospital would be completed, that she would eventually graduate from nursing school, and that—though this went unsaid—she would not be with my mother forever. My mother has emphysema and diabetes, and needs someone with her. Zalla cooks and washes and does any number of things no one expects her to do, and during the day she's never off her feet. At night she watches James Bond movies over and over on my mother's VCR. My mother sits in the TV room with her, rereading Dickens. She says the James Bond movies provide wonderful soundtracks for the stories. Carly Simon singing "Nobody Does It Better" in *The Spy Who Loved Me* as my mother's reading about Mr. Pickwick.

Anyway, what happened was in no way Zalla's fault, but she was tortured by guilt. Days after the incident I'm going to tell about, which I heard of when I visited, Zalla was still upset.

That Monday, my mother had checked into Sibley Hospital for a day of tests. In the afternoon, there was a knock on the door and Zalla looked out of the peephole and saw Little Thomas. She'd met him several times through the years, so of course she let him in. He said he was there to return some dishes my mother had let him borrow when he was setting up housekeeping. He also wanted to say goodbye, because he was moving out of the apartment he'd been sharing with other people in Landover, Maryland, and was headed down to the Florida Keys to tend bar. Then he worked the conversation around to asking Zalla for a loan: fifty dollars, which he'd send back as soon as he got to Key West and opened a bank account and deposited some checks. She had thirty-some dollars and gave him everything she had, minus the bus fare she needed to get to Sibley Hospital that evening. He asked for a sheet of paper so he could write a goodbye note to my mother, and Zalla

found him a notepad. He sat at the kitchen table, writing. It didn't occur to her to stand over him. She unpacked the dishes and loaded them
into the dishwasher, and then tidied up in the TV room. He wrote and
wrote. He was writing my mother a nasty note, telling her that through
therapy he had come to realize that the family perpetuated harmful
myths, and that no one had ever chosen to "come clean" about his
father's death, because his father had actually died of pneumonia, not
from the fall off a wagon. He told her how horrifying it had been to
see his father slipping away in the hospital, and he blamed her and Etta
Sue for always discussing Cousin Pete's last moments when they talked
about his father's death. "Fact is, lightning impressed you more than
simple pneumonia," he wrote. He also thought they should have talked
more to him about his father's accomplishments. He thought they should
have told about his father's love for him. He made no mention of his sister Lilly, from whom he was estranged. He folded the note and put it
under the saltshaker, and then he mixed himself a cup of instant cocoa
and left, taking the mug he was drinking from.

Zalla was nervous. She thought he might have been drinking,
though his breath didn't smell of alcohol. He'd gone to the bathroom
while he was there, so Zalla went into the bathroom to make sure everything was all right. It was, but she still had an uneasy feeling. It wasn't
until that evening, when she left for the hospital to escort my mother
home, that she saw the black felt-pen graffiti on the wall in the downstairs hallway: stick people with corkscrew hair like Martians' anten-
nae, and a quickly scrawled SCREW YOU BLOWING THIS JOINT. She was
horrified, and at first she thought she'd keep quiet about Little Thomas's
visit—just pretend it was all a mystery—but she knew that was wrong
and she'd have to make a full disclosure.

By the time I heard the story, Zalla and my mother had agreed he
was probably drunk—or, worse, on drugs—and that he was a coward
to pretend to confront my mother, when all he did was write a note. He
also hadn't had the nerve to face his own mother, who was still living
on Twentieth Street, and tell her that he was moving away. Zalla kept
quiet about the thirty dollars, but the next morning she confessed that,
too. In with the dishes he'd brought back were several strange, gold-
bordered plates my mother had not given him; neither she nor Zalla
knew exactly what to make of that. Both feared, irrationally, that someone would now come for the plates. They seemed to understand, though,
that Little Thomas was gone and wouldn't be heard from for some time,
if ever. Zalla remained afraid of him, in the abstract. She said he'd crept
around like a burglar. That gave my mother and me a good laugh,
because he'd been sneaky all his life. Good that he spared Mother's

bathroom wall, I joked: bad enough that they'd had to call the management to apologize and to arrange to have the hallway repainted.

While Zalla watched *Goldfinger*, my mother led me into her bedroom and told me one of the Dark Secrets she'd never before revealed. It turned out she had always feared Little Thomas would do something really awful, because he had done something very bad as a child. My mother had been furious, but she had never told on him, because she was embarrassed at her own fury, and also because she felt that Little Thomas's demons tortured him enough.

She asked whether I remembered the silhouettes. I did remember them, vaguely, though I had to be reminded that they'd once hung on a satin ribbon in Etta Sue's living room. I remembered them from later on, when they'd hung below the light above the bed in my mother's bedroom, attached to the same ribbon. There had also been one of Lilly, as a baby, and another of Punkin Puppy, in separate frames. The three framed silhouettes on the ribbon had been of Thomas Sr., Etta Sue, and the man who, Etta Sue told my mother, had cut the silhouettes. Etta Sue explained this somewhat humorous fact by saying that the silhouette cutter was going to throw his self-portrait away—he probably did it the way secretaries practice their typing, or something—and that she had rescued it from the trash. Little Thomas had destroyed *his* silhouette before it got into the frame, and though Etta Sue always meant to have another one cut, Little Thomas wouldn't sit still a second time. My mother shook her head. She said that she supposed the silhouette cutter's self-portrait was sort of like Alfred Hitchcock's including himself in his own films, though that wasn't a good comparison, because Etta Sue had hung it up, not the man himself.

When Etta Sue was forced to move out of her house and into the Twentieth Street apartment after Thomas Sr.'s death, she had to discard many things. The furniture my mother could understand, but parting with so many personal possessions had seemed to her a mistake. When the ribbon with the framed silhouettes went into the trash, my mother grabbed it out and said she would keep it for Etta Sue until she felt better. And Etta Sue had given her the strangest look. First shocked, then sad, my mother thought. And in all the years my mother had the silhouettes hung in her bedroom, Etta Sue never mentioned them, although she did eventually ask for Thomas Sr.'s shaving mug back, and for the framed picture of herself and her husband taken at a Chinese restaurant on their first anniversary.

But the point of the story, my mother said, was this: One weekend a few months after Thomas Sr.'s death, she was taking care of Little Thomas and Lilly, and Little Thomas had gone into the bedroom while all the rest of us were in the backyard and he had taken the silhouettes out of the frames and cut the noses off. Then he slipped them all back into their frames and rehung them. It was days before my mother noticed—everyone with his or her nose chopped off, plus Punkin Puppy, earless.

She hurried right over to Little Thomas's school and waited for him to get out. He walked home, but that day he didn't go anywhere before she confronted him. By her own account, she grabbed the tip of his nose and squeezed it, asking him how he thought he'd like being without his nose. Then she grabbed his ears and asked him if he thought he might like to spend the rest of his life not hearing, too. She crouched and made him look her in the eye and tell her why he'd done it. It was amazing that someone didn't notice her making such a scene and come over, she said. Little Thomas gasped when she pulled him around and shook him by his shoulders, but he never cried.

He had done it, he told her, because the faces in the frames were miniature black ghosts, there to haunt people. He disfigured them because they were ghost monsters with special powers of sneaking inside people. If he got rid of the black ghosts, cut them up a little, they would become white ghosts, with no special power.

My mother was so horrified she couldn't stand. He had given a quite specific, terribly upsetting answer, and she had no idea what response to make, because if he really thought those things he was mad. That would make it the first incidence of real madness in the family. She was 90 percent sure he was telling her what he really believed, but she also thought there was some small chance he might be having her on. She stayed there quite a while, weak in the knees, staring into his face, looking for more information.

"You think I'd care if I didn't have a nose?" he said. "*I* wouldn't care if I didn't have a nose or a mouth or eyes. I wish the sperm had never gone into the egg. I wouldn't mind if there was no me, and you wouldn't either."

My mother remembered being surprised that he knew about sex—that he knew such words as "sperm" and "egg." She didn't remember what she said to him next, but it had something to do with how she understood that he was very upset that his father was dead and had disappeared, but that he mustn't confuse that with thinking his father didn't love him.

Little Thomas broke away from her. "You stupid fool," he said. She remembered that distinctly: "You stupid fool."

After Little Thomas's father's death, my mother now suddenly reminded me, someone courted Etta Sue for a bit, but eventually faded away. In retrospect, my mother said, she thought it might quite possibly have been ("Now, don't laugh," she said) the milkman. Because, come to think of it, why else—unless she was a little embarrassed—would Etta Sue refuse to let anyone in the family know whom she was seeing? Also, Nat the Milkman had been a Sunday painter, so perhaps he had also cut silhouettes.

"Say nothing of this to Zalla," my mother said. It was something she had begun to say increasingly, as an afterthought, in recent years—or perhaps as an end to each of her stories, not as an afterthought, really.

I kissed her cheek and gave her hand a squeeze, turning off her bed-side lamp with my free hand. It was early evening and dark. We were in autumn, the season when Thomas Sr. had slipped from high atop the mounded hay—slipped in slow motion, compared to the way his cousin Pete had been struck by lightning.

That was the past. I imagined the future: the graffiti figures that had already disappeared in the downstairs hallway, whited out by a paint roller. Then I thought about the hospital in Belize, to which for all intents and purposes that paint roller could travel like a comet, to whiten the drywall that had at long last been installed in the corridors of the new hospital. Zalla would be standing there, her starched white nurse's uniform contrasting with her dark skin, and in a blink my mother would be dead, quite unexpectedly—gone from her white-sheeted bed to the darkness, as Zalla paused in her busy day to remember us, a nice American family.

ED AND DAVE VISIT
THE CITY

Luis had never seen anything like New York City. Though he had lived
in crowded, metropolitan La Paz for thirteen years (he had just cele-
brated his fourteenth birthday in Weston, Connecticut, with the Winstons, whose house he was living in as an exchange student), New York
continued to amaze him. He had visited from Connecticut three times:
once for the lighting of the tree at Rockefeller Center; once to see *Phan-
tom of the Opera*; and once to SoHo to have cappuccino and to look at
large paintings—grids and blocks of color that made him think of children's toys filled with helium, quickly floating away.

Today Luis was in New York with Harold, the Winstons' oldest son.
Harold—known to everyone as Har—was separated from his wife and
children in Ann Arbor. He had stopped to see his parents on his way
south to visit his former college roommate. The night before, the
Winstons had gone to bed early, after Har demanded that pictures of his
wife and children be put away. Har had pointed to the picture of the
two of them on their wedding day and said, "You think that's an angel.
You think I'm the devil. I've got news for you: this isn't a medieval
morality play. It's a comedy of manners. I only married her because I
was on the rebound, and then what happened but her old flame showed
up, and high hilarity ensued. He moved right into the house—but what
else could be done, because he'd had—get this—brain surgery, and no
one else was available to nurse him back to health. Roll the drums!
Bring on the feather dusters and the ladies in crinoline!" Mrs. Winston
went directly upstairs after Har's outburst. Mr. Winston followed.
When they left the room, Har suggested he and Luis might go to the
store and rent a couple of videos. They decided on *Dreamchild* and

Down and Out in Beverly Hills. The next morning, returning the tapes, Har suggested they keep driving into New York.

It was a hot day, and the air conditioning was broken in the car. As Har drove, they talked about music. Har was very enthusiastic about U2. Luis learned that Joshua Tree was a place in the desert. Then, somehow, they began to talk about the terrain of Bolivia. Luis remembered, with nostalgia, the Andes: the snowcapped peaks, white even in summer. Har said that his soon-to-be-ex-wife liked to ski.

In the city, Har parked in an enormous lot on the West Side. He stopped at a phone to call a woman he knew on Twentieth Street. Her outgoing message said she would be out of town until Sunday night. Har shrugged; he said to Luis that since it was Sunday, she might be back soon.

Several blocks later, he stopped at another phone. "Here," Har said, taking a quarter out of his pocket. "You listen to the message, and when it's time to leave a message, say you're my friend, and that we'll call later."

"Why can't you do it?" Luis said.

Har picked up the phone, deposited a quarter, dialed, and handed the phone to Luis.

"Hello?" a woman's voice said.

In his surprise, Luis blurted, "Hello?"

"Who is this?" the woman said.

"Har's friend," he said. "I'm calling for Har."

"Harold?" the woman said. "What about him?"

Luis looked quickly over his shoulder. Har was watching a hunchbacked woman driving by in a little motorized car. Her white scarf blew in the wind. "Take it!" Luis whispered, holding out the phone. "Har— she's on the phone!"

"I was just thinking," Har said. "The last time we got together, dinner was supposed to be on her, and she stuck me with the bill."

Luis put the phone to his ear. The woman had hung up; all he heard was the dial tone.

"Who was she?" Luis said, frowning as he hung up.

"Just somebody I knew in college. She calls herself an actress. Did a play at Long Wharf and a detergent commercial. As far as I know, that's her career."

"My mother's best friend is an actress," Luis said.

"Speaking of which—do you miss them? How come you wanted to come to the U.S. of A.?"

"My parents thought my uncle was moving to Buffalo," Luis said, hurrying to keep up with Har. "And then when he didn't go, my father found out about the student exchange program."

"You know," Har said, "some adults buddy up to kids and ask them personal questions, but I've never liked that. I've been along when a guy asks the kid if he's had sex, or fooled around with drugs. What he drinks. That kind of stuff. But I don't think that's anybody's business. The same way you're not supposed to needle somebody about their religion. If they bring it up, fine. But that's another matter."

"I'm Catholic," Luis said.

Har looked at him. "I think I knew that," he said. "I think my parents mentioned going to some Christmas Eve service with you."

"I don't go every Sunday," Luis said. "My mother, I would say, is the only devoutly religious member of our family."

They had been walking crosstown, on a block where men stood in baggy pants and T-shirts, playing their radios, or clustered to play cards. Har saw a man cleaning his knife blade. He hailed the first cab that passed.

"Tower Records. Near there. I'll tell you," Har said to the driver.

"Tower o' power," the cabbie said. "Wish I owned stock."

"Been in a New York cab before?" Har asked Luis.

"Yes. I've taken cabs with your parents every time I've been here," Luis said.

"Yeah, they're getting old. My father used to make it a point of honor to ride the subway. He knows them like the back of his hand. But you get old and tired, it doesn't matter what you know. That's when you do what you want, instead of what you know about."

At the next light, Har told the driver to stop. He gave the driver several wadded-up dollar bills and told him to keep the change. When they got out, they were in front of a store with black mannequins wearing pillbox hats and mannequins painted bright green standing inside piles of hula hoops. Inside, Har headed for the shirt rack. "Look," he said to Luis. "Every one of these has a name sewn somewhere. These were a big thing in the fifties. You can pick who you want to be." He pulled a shirt off the rack. ED was sewn over the pocket, and MANDELL'S PLUMBING was stitched in big letters across the back. It was a two-tone shirt, with red in front and white and red stripes in back. "Size large," Har said. "Looks like I've found one right off the bat."

"Off the bat," Luis echoed, flipping through the shirts. The one he liked was aqua, with white piping around the sleeves and DAVE sewn with gray thread over the front pocket. DAWSON'S LAWN SERVICE it said on the back.

Har paid for the shirts. Outside, they stuffed the shirts they'd been wearing in the bag. Each bit off the other's price tag. Har nodded his approval, and they continued their walk.

"I've got a friend on East Seventh," Har said. "His name is Allen Purvis. He's an actor, too. His show got canceled. Last I heard, he was living on unemployment and writing a novel about an unemployed actor."

As they turned onto East Seventh, they crossed the street. Har went into a store that sold lingerie. He took a pair of underpants off a hanger and dangled them from his thumb, considering them. They were lavender lace. Har raised his eyebrows and smiled. The saleswoman took his money and wrapped them in pink tissue paper, then put them in a tiny bag. They were the fanciest panties Luis had ever seen.

A few buildings past the store, they crossed the street again. Luis followed Har up the steps of a brownstone. He rang the buzzer. There was no intercom, so their first sight of Allen Purvis was at the door. He was wearing white shorts and rubber thongs. "Son of a bitch!" he said, throwing the door open. Har spread his arms wide; he kept them above his head as Allen embraced him.

"What have we here?" Allen said. "We have Ed and Dave, I see, come for a visit." He smiled at Luis.

"This is my adopted son," Har said. "We thought we'd come by and become characters in your book."

"Full of surprises, this life," Allen said. "Do come in."

They followed him down a corridor to another door, which was already open. "Unbelievable," Allen said. "What are you doing in town, Har?"

The phone rang. Allen ignored it, clapping Har on the back and steering him toward the front of the apartment. As Luis trailed behind, he saw that Allen's shorts were split. They had been sewn with red thread.

"Sit down, gentlemen," he said. "I happen to have a bottle of champagne, courtesy of Mrs. Perry, upstairs, who was deeply indebted to me for watering her plants for two weeks while they cut out half her stomach. Please: sit down and prepare yourselves for pleasure." Allen turned and almost ran to the kitchen. As he went through the glass beads, he kicked one foot high in the air behind him.

Luis looked at Har. He had expected some sign when Allen went into the kitchen—a wink, or something. Instead, Har sank into a chair, dropping the bag and pushing it aside with his foot. "I seem to be a bit tired," Har said to Luis.

As Allen returned with a bottle of champagne and three stacked water glasses, Har said, "You know, my friend here is actually an exchange student from Bolivia. He's been living with my parents in Weston."

"Really?" Allen said. "Then let's have a toast to him. You make the toast, Har."

Har sighed. He watched Allen pop the cork. "In fact, I don't even have a marriage anymore, let alone an adopted son. Susan's reunited with her former love. No kidding: he came to Michigan to court her again, got a brain tumor, and we spent three weeks in the hospital, sleeping in chairs. Man is very, very sick. This made clear to her her love for him."

"To good health," Allen said, raising his glass.

The phone rang again. This time, Allen went over to where it sat on the floor and turned up the volume control. "Juliette!" he said, pouncing on the phone. "Juliette, my most darling. You're back from the beach early."

"The person we called earlier?" Luis said to Har.

"The very," Har said.

"Juliette. There is a surprise for you, if you come right over," Allen said.

Har looked at Luis. He rolled his eyes. "I don't know," he said. "Maybe it's time to take off if Juliette's coming over."

"But you were going to see her," Luis said.

"No, darling. Not recruiting you to play bridge with the woman upstairs. Just inviting you to a celebration, of sorts."

"Maybe we should get a pizza," Har said, getting out of his chair. "I'm pretty hungry. How about you?"

"Sure," Luis said.

"No, darling," Allen said into the phone. "Nothing nasty at all. A pleasant surprise."

Outside, a bum asked for a quarter, and Har gave it to him. "It's none of my business," Har said, "but what do you want to be, Luis?"

"I think I'd like to be an illustrator."

"Illustrations? Didn't my mother say something about your going to medical school?"

"My father wants me to be a doctor, but I want to draw. I want to draw things for books. I'm interested in botany."

"Really?" Har said. "I'll bet my mother likes that. Nobody in her family is at all visual. She likes Toulouse-Lautrec. Did you know that?"

"Oh, yes."

"Those damn paintings were nightmares to me when I was a kid.

That one of the woman with the blue face? She couldn't have hung a three-headed monster and scared me more."

"Whaddya want?" the counterman said. He had on a white shirt and a gold chain with a silver cross dangling from it. There was cross-hatching on the silver. Many people in Bolivia wore such crosses.

"Cheese, sausage, and still more cheese," Har said.

"Sure you don't want a fondue?" the counterman said.

Luis leaned against the counter, like Har. "The mother of one of the girls in my drawing group says that a great depression is coming," Luis said. "She's a very good watercolorist. She told me that when she was my age, both her parents died, and she was raised by an aunt. The aunt hit her if she saw her drawing, because she thought drawing was a waste of her mind."

"Some days, I don't know how anybody survives," Har sighed.

"Being hit for drawing still makes her very mad," Luis said.

When their pizza was ready, the man slid it into a box and taped the top closed. Har paid for it, and they walked outside. The man who had asked for a quarter before asked for another. "No can do," Har said.

"Fuck you!" the man shouted.

The doughy smell of the pizza, mixed with the smell of gasoline as someone tried to start his car at the curb, made Luis a little light-headed. He hurried to keep up with Har.

"You see those beads over Allen's kitchen door?" Har said, as they walked up the steps to the brownstone. Luis rang the bell. "That's because when he didn't have any money, back in the days when he was waiting for calls from his agent, Juliette offered him ten bucks for the door, and he sold it to her. He found the beads in the trash later that week, on Avenue A." Har shook his head, as if baffled by something. He said: "She wanted to turn her bathtub into a table. She had one of those claw-footed numbers in her kitchen, and she wanted to turn the tub into a table when she wasn't using it, so she bought the door so she could have a table."

Luis nodded. Allen Purvis threw open the door.

"Remember Juliette's table?" Har said to Allen.

"Do I remember the table? I mean, if not for my generosity, there would have been no table," Allen said.

"She painted the door green, and there were blue Fiestaware plates. It was very fashionable. And she made sushi before anyone ever heard of it. Boy—those were some strange times."

They went back to the front room. Allen had put out plates and folded squares of paper towels. A Swiss Army knife sat on one of the plates. Allen clicked out a blade and offered it to Har to cut the pizza.

They were finishing their first slices when Juliette rang the door-bell. She came in carrying a bottle of wine and a loaf of French bread. "Harold!" she screamed, when she saw Har. "*What* is going on here? No word from Harold Winston for two years at *least*, and here he is in New York City, and . . . with another gentleman I don't believe I've been introduced to."

"His adopted son," Luis said, extending his hand.

"Harold!" Juliette said. "Why do you keep such news from old friends?"

Har shrugged. Outside, someone passed by with a radio. Michael Jackson was squealing. A car screeched away from the curb, and the gasoline fumes began to waft through the window. Reaching for another slice of pizza, Luis thought: I am going to remember this day. Not because it was a typical day, or because anything very important was happening, but because of the way they all seemed to be drifting, as if they, too, were part of the breeze. This day had nothing to do with the way people visited and talked in La Paz; there, people spoke more formally, as if they were interviewing one another.

"This is the last thing I would have expected," Juliette said, sitting near Har's feet. "Harold Winston back in town, with his son, and me, sitting by his side."

"This is the very woman who asked Allen to take his door off the hinges and sell it to her for ten dollars when she lived next door," Har said to Luis.

"Five," Juliette said. "I got it on the cheap."

"You paid me ten," Allen said.

"Well!" Juliette said, reaching up for Har's champagne glass. He gave it to her. She took a sip. "Another surprise," she said. "That Allen, who speaks so often about how cheap I am when my back is turned, tonight asserts that I offered twice the money I did for his kitchen door."

"We've got to get going," Har said abruptly, as Juliette handed his glass up to him.

"Oh, Harold," Juliette said. "Isn't that just like you? So mercurial. So let's-drop-in-and-stir-up-the-waters."

Har stood. With great mock seriousness, he said, "Then . . . can you get along without me?"

As he watched, Luis had a crazy thought. It was only half formed when he reached for the champagne bottle, shook it hard with his thumb over the top, then pointed it at Juliette and let the champagne fly, the white foam shooting out with more force than he would have thought possible.

"Oh God, he *is* your son," Allen laughed.

"Apparently," Juliette said. She was angry, but she looked at Har, not at Luis. "Do you know what this proves?" she said. "It proves that whenever more than one man is present, there's always competition for my affection. I thought the trouble might only be between you and Allen, Harold, but I see your son has added himself as another potential candidate."

Luis tried to look as unsurprised as Allen and Har as Juliette slowly unbuttoned her soaked blouse, then let it drop to the floor. She stood there in a white brassiere and a pearl necklace, looking at all of them in turn. She stared at Har until he dropped his eyes, and then she turned to Allen. "What I just said makes a lot of sense, doesn't it, Allen?" she said, and then he, too, looked away. Luis was the last one to be gazed upon, and in the moments before she shifted her attention to him, he had had time to think. She turned to him, and he reached forward, dipping his hand into the bag and carefully extracting the little package wrapped in pink tissue paper. "For you, Juliette," he said.

She was so surprised, she took it from his hand and opened it. In the few seconds it took her to remove the lavender pants from the tissue paper, and before she burst into wild laughter, Har thought: Oh, what the hell. What was the chance of its working, anyway? The reconciliation with his wife.

THE FOUR-NIGHT FIGHT

The four-night fight began on Father's Day, June 20, but had nothing to do with the day. Her father had been dead for almost fifteen years; his father had left his mother and moved to Santa Barbara to spend his remaining years—so far, twelve had passed—golfing. Henry was not himself a father.

It had been a beautiful, sunny day. Lavender geraniums were in bloom, bordering the back porch. Inside the porch, yellow and red begonias blossomed, their flowers as large as their leaves. In one of the pots, a plastic parrot's one moving wing rotated as the wind blew. The summer before, Henry had gotten the other wing going, but this year he'd done nothing. Neither had he brought home plants for the porch, nor helped weed the geranium bed, to which he had added, against her objections, a dozen blue-black tulips, planting the bulbs the previous fall as she slept. First he refused to enlarge the flower bed. Then, when she did that, he "borrowed" bricks from the border to brace a rickety bookshelf. Then he ordered red tulips, was sent the bruise-colored ones instead, shrugged, ignored her dismay, and planted them while she was asleep. None of these things had anything to do with the fight.

The fight began in early evening, so that properly speaking, it was a four-night, three-day fight. The fight reminded her of hotel package deals: four nights, five days, in sunny Bermuda—but after you struggled to the hotel the pleasure of the first day would inevitably be shot: plane late; luggage delayed; rainstorm slowing the car to the hotel; a long line for check-in. They had taken a trip to Bermuda in October, to celebrate their anniversary. She had wanted to stay in a small hotel, he had insisted on staying at a sprawling resort. Like his father, he loved to golf. She had gone around on her moped alone, while he golfed, and though that might have made her feel bad, it had not, so why pretend to hold a grudge when actually she had quite enjoyed her freedom? She didn't pretend to hold a grudge. Nothing that happened in Bermuda had anything to do with the fight.

In fact, the reason the fight was so bad was that it snuck up on her. In the seconds preceding the fight, she had been perfectly happy, scooping the center out of a cantaloupe. Henry had become diabetic, so they no longer had cookies for dessert, only fruit. She kept a package of Chips Ahoy hidden behind boxes of Tide in the laundry room, but she'd lost her taste for sweets, suddenly. Or maybe not so suddenly: she'd lost it when the cookies somehow absorbed, like a sponge, the smell of Tide. When she was a child, her mother had put milk of magnesia in chocolate milk to disguise the taste, but all it had done was make her cringe at the thought of plain chocolate milk, and also chocolate ice cream, or chocolate milk shakes. She was even wary of chocolate cake, and sniffed skeptically at Hershey bars. No matter: cookies and chocolate could easily be done without, and a person would be healthier because of it. So there she had been, scooping out the melon, looking forward to a made-for-TV movie the listing had said would be good, when suddenly Henry was standing in the kitchen doorway, looking at her in a peculiar way, contributing nothing toward fixing their dessert, having said not a word about the dinner she had just served. . . . Well: the thing was, the fight, in his mind, had already begun, but she had been slow to understand his sulking, mistaking it for simple fatigue, since before dinner he'd hauled out the trash and sprayed the lid with Clorox so that during the night the raccoon couldn't simply saunter up to the can and with a swipe of its paw crash the top of the trash can to the ground. Also, he had sawed off the broken limb of the lilac and dragged it into the woods, then gone inside and called his mother to give her some information she needed to pay her taxes. His mother was not the world's most pleasant person. Also, since it was Father's Day, she was in a bleaker mood than usual, despising Henry's father for leaving her and spending his retirement golfing in California. Maybe his mother's bad mood was contagious. Maybe Henry had done one too many chores. Maybe he harbored a grudge that she had made him spray the trash can with Clorox, which he continued to call "ridiculous," though it was the one thing that had ever deterred the tenacious, fat, garbage-can-toppling raccoon.

Standing in the kitchen doorway, he had said to her: "Sometimes I think this is all a huge fucking joke. Sometimes I think we're ants, and here in our anthill we scurry around, moving the dirt, building the anthill higher, eating our food, shitting it out, doing our humble chores for the fucking Queen Ant, foraging and accumulating, bringing things in, piling things up, moving the piles around, and all the while, in our little specks of ant brain, we hope a big rainstorm doesn't come and pound the whole fucking anthill into the ground, that we don't get washed down the hill, that we don't drown in the flood, but what would it matter if we did? What the fuck would it matter?"

It was so unexpected. So typical of Henry, though, who while having finally admitted, one night in Bermuda, as the sky was brightening from rose to crimson, that his obsessing about the deterioration of the ozone layer was really a way of not focusing on more immediate, personal problems that he might do something about . . . well: going on with this line of thought would give the mistaken impression that she had been assessing the situation, seeing in it the seeds of similar situations—Christ! Did he think she'd gone to college to scoop the insides of melons into a garbage disposal? Could he really have thought that she would appreciate such a barrage of adolescent, ridiculous despair . . . had he been standing in the doorway with his weight thrown on one hip, in his loafers with their mashed-down backs, and his thumb hooked through a belt loop . . . was this miserable sight, this person she'd for some unfathomable reason married, so stupid as to think she'd appreciate being compared to an ant as she stood scooping pulp and seeds and fiber into the sink so that his diabetes wouldn't rage out of control . . . had they had what they agreed would be their last discussion of the ozone layer only to have him recast everything in terms of their pointless life inside an anthill?

"You're really insane," she said.

"I'm insane?" he said. And then he said something she didn't get—something about the Clorox. That didn't surprise her at all, because whenever she gave him a helpful hint he derided her or ignored it. The use of Clorox as a repellent hadn't been her own epiphany, by the way: it was something she'd read flipping through a tabloid in the supermarket, which was where she spent half her life, half of her pointless ant life, gathering food for Henry, because maybe Henry himself was the Ant King? After all, who was standing in the doorway, the picture of casualness, while her hair had fallen from her barrette to tickle her nose as she peered down into the messy abortion of melon pulp in the sink. . . .

She had apparently thrown the phone book at him. She saw that she had, because his hands flew up to protect his head, and certainly the phone book had not just animated itself to join in the fracas, surely she must have thrown it, accelerating the fight, which by that time had been going on for perhaps five minutes, of screaming and accusations, suspended only for troubled sleep, to resume the next morning.

The day after the fight he did not go to work, which did trouble her. If he had called to say he would not be at work, he would have had to do it while she slept—he didn't mind planting ugly tulips while she slept, for all she knew he had a complete private life. He told her about deficiencies in her character as he toasted an English muffin—one only; none for her—blaming her for trying to infantilize him with her air of superiority, banging his fist on the kitchen island and sending the nondairy creamer crashing to the floor, whatever he was saying about Clorox drowned out by the crashing glass. Then, insanely, completely insanely, as the muffin lodged in the toaster and began to burn, though it would be a cold day in hell if she ever again rescued any of his food, let him forage for it himself, ant that he was . . . Henry began to pick up the shards of glass and throw them, claiming the bits of glass were ants, or like ants—whatever he was saying. He was saying that he was scattering the anthill. Really, he was just a bully, uncivilized and out of control, wanting to lash out at who knew what, who could know who the designated Queen Ant was that morning, in his paranoia and rage. Black smoke poured from the toaster, and again the telephone book was animated, sailing through the air, smeared with cantaloupe juice, crashing way off course into the wall. She had wanted to paint the kitchen walls green; Henry had wanted them yellow. They had compromised on peach, which was good, considering the melon juice that was now smeared on the wall, though she resolutely did not care about that, did not care if the whole toaster erupted, did not care what he did with the rest of his day, did not care if he stood forever making analogies between broken glass and anthills, because he was cynical and unbalanced, she was not, she was—he was saying again—superior. Then he kicked the phone book as if he were making a final goal and looked around crazily, as if she represented a whole team who would cheer him. Looking over his shoulder, he asked if she had ever had a kind thought about his mother in her life. It did not deserve an answer.

The next day, he was gone when she woke up, but he was so agitated that he had left a message—a rant, really—on the answering machine. At the beginning, he taunted her by daring her to listen to the message all the way through, which she did intend to do, sitting at the kitchen counter, the air still redolent with the smell of burned bread, bits of glass scattered underfoot. "I did what the raccoon couldn't do," he screamed on the tape. "I turned over your fucking garbage can that the fucking garbage truck neglected to empty because they do not give a flying fuck if the whole world festers and deteriorates, if they can shorten their working day by ignoring the cans on the route. I turned it over and I was within one second, one millionth of an inch, of taking the lid and ramming it through the side window of your car. . . ."

At this, she got slowly off the stool and went out to the driveway, his voice fading in the background. She walked as if in a trance, but she was not really in a trance, she was just practicing being in a trance. What if he had really traumatized her, so that she had become a zombie? What if at this moment she was a zombie, looking at chicken bones, food-stained newspapers, all the detritus of their lives scattered in the street—not by the raccoon, but by the wild beast that was her husband? No: she would not let him drive her crazy. It was reasonable to be superior, and not a zombie. She could shuffle along, traumatized, and become what he would like her to become, but it was better simply to sidestep his expectations, just as she sidestepped the garbage. That night, a neighbor's boy would stuff most of it back in the can. She would see that from the bathroom window, getting up from the closed toilet seat where she was reading a mystery, preferring to be locked in the bathroom rather than downstairs, where Henry was silently watching the long-ago resignation of Richard Nixon on TV. It was not true that all teenagers were destructive and self-absorbed. The boy picked up almost everything, including soup cans with jagged edges and soggy coffee filters, then put the lid firmly on the trash can again. He could have been Sir Lancelot, he shone so in her imagination as what a man could be. Downstairs, she heard gunshots, and for a horrifying second she was so on edge that she had rewritten history and imagined Nixon being shot, then realized that Henry must have begun shooting at the teenager! Henry having a gun. Did he have a gun? Of course he didn't have a gun. And if he did have a gun, then she hoped he would use it on himself.

No, she didn't. She tried thinking that, to see how it would feel. It felt wrong. She was afraid she was beginning to forgive him. In saying she wanted him shot when she did not want him shot, she had begun to forgive him. And she might have, too, if he hadn't glared at her so coldly before pulling off the comforter and going to sleep on the sofa. Such histrionics, when there was a guest room. He was really out of control. Maybe he was actually cracking up. She tossed in bed half the night, and when she went down in the morning he was still there, the cover over the top of his body, including his head, his bare legs sticking out, one on the sofa arm, one on the floor. It was like finding the Elephant Man in a casual moment. She stood in the doorway, so fatigued she decided to forgive him, to try to get things back on track. If nothing else, he would certainly have to go back to his job soon. Perhaps he hadn't gone back yesterday. Perhaps she had assumed, incorrectly, that the hysterical message of the day before had been left from work—but how likely was that? He had probably not sat at his desk and simply raged, spitting his irrational thoughts into a telephone. He had probably called from . . . "Henry," she said, trying to keep her voice calm, "were you at work yesterday when you left that ridiculous message?"

He jumped up, tossing off the comforter with such force that she jumped back. He stood there, glowering at her, the comforter puddled around him like a collapsed parachute. His wild eyes made her think of someone who had just crashed into a dangerous jungle. He might have been wondering: Could this native be friendly? She tried to look friendlier by smiling, but the attempt to alter the expression of her mouth, she could tell, was only resulting in narrowed eyes. She could not smile. She did manage to unknot the frown that creased between her eyes. They stood there that way, gazing at each other, she barefoot in her long nightgown patterned with blue morning glories, he wearing a white sleeveless undershirt and nothing else, his knock-knees pathetic, his penis curved like a tiny fountain spout, and—she had been blocking it out because she really did not want to focus on it—on his arm, on his biceps, a terrible bruise, a terrible swelling: from doing battle with the trash can? From . . . God, it was a tattoo. It was a tattoo, and he saw that she saw it. Even the fountain spout seemed to recoil in dismay. Henry was standing there, staring at her with the We Are Ants expression on his face, and on his upper arm, the part of his arm she had clasped so many times as they made love, was MOM in red-inked script, and a circle inscribing it, a circle, she saw, upon closer inspection, that was not a conglomerate of ants, but swirls of small hearts and flowers, interspersed with skin puckered into scabs, an outer rim of flesh around the circle swollen and flecked with what seemed to be broken veins.

"Hurts," he said.

"Hurts?" she echoed. She was becoming the zombie whose role she had tried on for size. Numb. Unblinking. Who could blink looking at such a thing?

"I went drinking with Jim Cavalli, made a bet, guy couldn't pay up, we went to his tattoo studio, I got to choose from the fifty-dollar possibilities."

"Henry," she said, "what is this about your mother?"

"Cavalli chose."

"Cavalli had your arm tattooed MOM?"

"Cavalli wanted to beat him up. I was the one who agreed to settle on a tattoo."

"Cavalli . . . ," she said, searching her mind for a visual image of the man. The new, gawky kid from Princeton? Pink shirt, drank a lot of Dos Equis at the company picnic? Though she was not aware she'd been speaking, Henry began to respond to her sharpening mental image of Cavalli. "Went off the wagon himself because his Princeton girlfriend left him for her analyst," Henry said.

"So . . . what?" she said. "You and Cavalli went to a bar, and he told you his girlfriend had left him, you told him the human race, or you and I, how should I know? You told him we were ants, and then some guy who worked at a tattoo parlor sat down and you bet him . . . you bet what?"

"That the guy on TV would miss the shot."

"You bet that a guy would miss a shot, he said the guy would make it, the guy missed, and you ended up with MOM in majesty on your arm?"

"Hurts," he said quietly.

"Well, Jesus," she said. "I think we should go to the doctor and see if he can treat it, because I think your arm is infected." A headache came up inside her like rolling thunderclouds spreading across the sky. By the time she finished her sentence, electricity was crackling through her brain, a tooth-chattering wind had begun.

It was as if her pain made her transparent. Suddenly, he looked at her as if he could see the rain clouds inside. The pain piercings sinking into her jaw like lightning. "Your name is Angelina," he said. Her head hurt so much that she didn't mind this simple, neutral observation at all. Indeed she was Angelina. So true. He continued: "While I admit I hated you in that moment, it did occur to me that if I hadn't been angry, if I hadn't been angry when I was getting the tattoo, I could have had a tattoo of my wife's name, except that only three letters could be had for fifty dollars, because Cavalli was insisting on scrollwork. The part around the word is called scrolling. It's generic hearts and flowers and stuff."

This was too much to take in. Her head was pounding.

"They do it the way people doodle on a notepad when they're on the telephone, I guess." He had sunk into the sofa, pulling the comforter over himself. He looked like an ill, miserable child. He looked at her expectantly.

"I think we should go to the doctor," she said. She had begun to worry about the tattooist's needles. Why would Henry have done such a thing, when everyone was so worried about AIDS? How could he have been sure the needles were clean? Needles—Jesus Christ. He had let someone take needles and scratch dye into his flesh. He had gone with some self-pitying moron named Cavalli. And yet, she was on the sofa beside him, snuggled under his good arm, the comforter around them both feeling soft and sheltering. At that moment, the last thing she was thinking about was the fight. He had become, in her mind, a victim. Someone who had received far worse punishment than he deserved. Someone who needed medical attention, understanding, forgiveness. She envisioned herself driving him to the doctor's office—never mind that the doctor was sure to be horrified—going there, getting a prescription for antibiotics, perhaps topical creams, perhaps . . . perhaps the doctor would see that Henry was unbalanced and think of something to do. Though the more she thought about it, the more she disbelieved it. Unless she could walk right into the doctor's office with him, he would probably present it as regrettable, drunken madness. She would have to go in and be a Greek chorus: *No, no, he was comparing life to being in an anthill; he's never cared if flowers are atrocious colors, he just plants them anyway, like flowers that would bloom in hell; his mother upsets him, complaining about his father; our fight began on Father's Day, which can't be insignificant—either it's resentment of his own father spilling over into our life, or he's angry that people are procreating: he sees all these things as a personal affront, whether it's the holes in the ozone layer or clear-cutting the forest or people giving birth to a child. He's in a state of madness and despair, I tell you. He doesn't go to work anymore. Come to think of it, for days I haven't seen him eat.* She would have to say those things; no sitting in the waiting room reading *Good Housekeeping.* No information, today, about Kathie Lee's thoughts on how to parent. Cheese dips be damned.

The fight began again when, to her complete surprise, he refused to see the doctor. It was feeling better already, he suddenly said. He thought he had a bit of a fever, though, so he would—if she did not mind—nap for a bit.

"You're going to the doctor," she said.

"No," he said. "I am not."

Thus began a new day of fighting, which she had not been prepared for at all, having begun to forgive him. And, like anyone dragged into something unexpectedly, her reactions were not the best. Instead of focusing on his obviously infected arm, she found herself demanding an explanation of how, exactly, he would keep the raccoon out of the trash if he did not want to use her method. She twisted up her mouth and marched like a martinet, imitating his expression and his quick exit from the living room when the phone rang. The phone: news from the outside world. The doctor, by telepathic message having realized he should call? When she picked it up, it was Cavalli. The nerve! What did he want, she asked: to know if Henry would meet him for more drinks and then go out to a whorehouse? "No," Cavalli said evenly. "To know if he's coming to work." She hung up on him. Then the fight really swung into full gear. She was emasculating him again, it appeared. Again, he threatened her car windows. Couldn't he think of anything more original than that? Or, at the very least, admit that he wanted to hit *her*? "You'd like that, wouldn't you?" he said. It was not until three in the afternoon that she looked out and realized that neither of them had brought in the paper.

That night, he ate nothing. He sat with the remote control, flipping through channels, sentence fragments and incomplete sounds no doubt echoing the chaos of his brain. Once, he ran out the front door with the still-rolled newspaper, threatening a cat digging near a bush. He could have been heard miles away. If he did become violent, no one in the neighborhood would be surprised. Yes, they'd say, that guy was really nuts. Nuts but wounded. She couldn't get the image of his infected arm out of her mind. It was as if the pain throbbed in her own head. Of course, it was next to impossible to sleep. And when she was at last almost asleep, what did he do but tear off in the car, going who knew where, dressed—as she later found out—in the only clothes he could find downstairs: a pair of madras bermudas with a ripped zipper he'd taken from her sewing room and his flip-flops with the thongs he'd glued back together in the basement, and her blouse. The nice navy-blue blouse she'd ironed before the fight began and never taken upstairs. He had left after cramming his body into her navy-blue blouse.

She went downstairs and turned off the answering machine because she did not want to hear whatever vicious message he might leave. She did, though, make sure the ringer on the phone was on, so that if he— or the police, God forbid—needed to reach her, they could. The only phone call came from his mother, who had no sense of time, wanting him to install a new bathroom sink for her at what she called "your convenience." Wait until she saw the MOM tattoo. Let the two of them discuss that.

Was he, in fact, headed for his mother's—and should she have warned the woman that might be the case? Or to Cavalli's? Back to the bar? Who knew where. Who knew how this was going to end, if it ever did end. It was the longest fight she had ever been involved in, and it was exhausting her and making her feel crazy herself. She took aspirin and went back to bed.

In the morning, when she awoke, he was lying next to her. It was not a dream, he was really there. The blue blouse was on the floor, the madras bermudas discarded amid the thongs, his eyes squeezed shut so tightly she wondered if he was only pretending to sleep. At first, barely distinguishable in the tangle of white sheets, she didn't realize there was a large gauze bandage on his arm. It was a thick pad of gauze, wrapped entirely around his arm, and near the top were black stitches—no: there was writing. On the gauze bandage, he had written, as best he could, left-handed, because the tattoo was on his right arm, the scratchy letters S O R R Y. There it was: the white flag of surrender, and an added apology lest she mistake it. Propped on one elbow, she frowned as she considered it: the wobbly O like a bubble being blown from a bubble wand; the Y like a sprouting seed. It seemed to her the sweetest thing he had ever done. Though he had done so many sweet things in the time they'd been together. The four-night fight must have been worse for him than for her, because he hated to carry a grudge. "Let him golf. Forget him if you can't forgive him," he always said to his mother. "Buy more flowers if that's what you want, honey," he had said to her when the garden bloomed that spring with its strange blossoms. She stared at the bandage. It was professionally done. He must have gone to the emergency room. On the night table she saw a glass of water and a bottle of medicine. It seemed to her a real salvation: the antibiotics that would cure the wound's infection, protecting his precious arm, that arm that had curled around her so many times, guiding her through crowds, protectively placed when he introduced her to a stranger. She stayed there, propped up, observing him, the way a person will look out a window and study the land after a storm, everything seeming greener, lighter, suddenly distinct. The familiar landscape was all there: from chin stubble to chest hair, from navel to knee, it was Henry, slumbering after the great storm. Henry, simply, no scrollwork needed to establish his importance, because when she saw him small hearts and flowers invisibly surrounded him always, an embellished border around the valentine of affection that was her love. What couple does not occasionally fight?

PARK CITY

For a week, possibly a week and a half, I'm stringing along to Utah with my half sister, Janet, more or less looking after Janet's boyfriend's daughter, Lyric (fourteen), who is in turn looking after Janet's child, my niece, Nell (three): Nell the Bell, Nell from Hell, Bad Smell Nell. Nell is the youngest child—in fact, there are only two others I've seen, so far—in the building. Unfortunately, one is a pudgy girl of about ten, who will not reveal her own name and who is obviously jealous that Nell is pretty, petite, and doted upon. She has taken to making up nasty names for Nell. Fortunately, the ten-year-old has in-line skates, so she's gone a lot. We usually only encounter her in the morning, and then again in the evening, when she hangs around eating ice-cream cones with her father, who has a Clint Eastwood squint and therefore the look of someone who wouldn't enjoy hearing anything negative about his child's behavior. Where's the mother? Where's anyone except the run-amok girl who races through the breakfast area as if imitating Pee-wee Herman might be appreciated by real people.

Janet and Damon are renting a unit on the second floor of the Ski Galaxy condo. Lyric and Nell and I share an oddly configured first-floor suite that is laid out like half a spider. There are five corridors leading to five bedrooms, all with their own bathrooms. The central room is a half circle with a big bay window curving around one side that contains many floor cushions silk-screened with pictures of prairie dogs, moose, elk, and—this we don't get—gored bulls. There is a large rear-projection television flanked by deer heads. There is an orange leather sofa that we avoid. It looks like furniture recovering from a chemical peel. We've been here for three days. Settling in, as always, has to do with clothes strewn all over and shoes that get mysteriously separated from their mates.

Each morning an odd spread is put out at one end of the lobby by the resident manager, a Vietnamese lady who, in addition to her care-taking duties, gives something called "deep tissue massage." She is also a would-be chanteuse (so far, the only job she's landed is accompanying herself singing with the Rhythm Ace at the Mexican restaurant on Friday nights those times the owner's nephew has been too high to go on). Each morning, Nguyen ("Nikki") Williams, widow of P.F.C. Theo-dore Roosevelt Williams, sets out her version of a continental breakfast, which invariably consists of hard-boiled eggs she has dyed pink; blue-berry toaster tarts she arranges on the tabletop like carefully laid tiles; Waldorf salad (she told me that's what it is) that is essentially whipped cream and miniature marshmallows amid a few flecks of fruit; and halved bagels with a choice of Kraft grape jelly or I Can't Believe It's Not Butter spray. I stick to a plain bagel, myself, and always wrap an extra bagel for Nell to eat later, and then, before we go back upstairs and change into our swimsuits and ride the free bus over to the big pool at Wasatch Mountain Center, I spritz Nell's hair in a fairly hopeless effort to untangle it before the water does another day's damage, then put in whatever Third World–motif barrette appeals to her that day: the brown farmer with his brown cow; tiny women balancing baskets on their heads. There is also a Pocahontas barrette and there are some ridiculous butterfly barrettes we never use that Lyric has clipped to the rim of the pot containing a red amaryllis that blooms profusely on the shelf above the Jacuzzi in one of our many bathrooms. During the win-ter, the condo is a ski resort. Off-season, they rent to L.A. burnouts, people who are on vacation or (Nikki has confided to me, with a wink) having "trysts," and conference attendees.

Nell's mother, my older half sister, Janet, is enrolled in a weeklong screenwriting course team-taught by her current love interest: a profes-sor from Cornell who quit his job teaching film theory to experience total immersion in The Industry. For two years, he has had full custody of Lyric, after some incident that is only obliquely referred to, if at all. He and his wife went to Amsterdam when a private detective located their missing twelve-year-old, after which the wife decided to stay on and begin living the life of a man in preparation for a sex-change opera-tion. Come to think of it, references to that trip are not so much oblique as quickly dismissed by Janet, who inevitably begins to fan her face as if smoke were coming at her when any mention of the ex lasts more than ten seconds. Lyric never mentions her mother and rarely mentions

Amsterdam, except to say that it was cool to run away and pass as an eighteen-year-old, and that it was a good place to hang out and chill, which is what she prefers to do wherever she is. This means, in part, that she strikes up conversations with random men, and that she watches MTV and paints either her toenails or her fingernails daily. She alternates between being quite talkative and completely silent, and I alternate between relating to her easily and thinking she's a Martian. Nell is a nice child, slightly precocious, entirely predictable in her demands, and, like most children, she doesn't like her hair combed.

Right now, Nell pulls her hair around to one side, pokes her nose in, and breathes deeply. "Stop smelling yourself, Nelly the Smelly," Lyric says. She has picked up the malevolent ten-year-old's way of taunting, which she gets away with because she imitates the fat girl at the same time she says nasty things to her possibly new stepsister-to-be. Nell appreciates my being along on this trip, I know: it provides her with someone who will be reflexively sympathetic when she's made fun of, and it spares her a real babysitter—the sort who phone their boyfriends constantly on their cellular phones and watch TV shows about daughters who pray for the salvation of their mothers who are addicted to body piercing, or priests who battle bulimia. The sitters all assume Nell will love pizza, but actually she's burned out on the pizza-for-dinner routine, and she thinks the trendy ones, like Hawaiian, should be sent back to Hawaii. Recently, she crayoned a picture of a slice of pizza with golden wings, headed in the direction of a large black shape I'm sure was a volcano. Neither is she fond of pineapple pureed into "virgin" drinks, though Janet is, so at the end of her long, hard days we often sit with her at the café outside the Mexican restaurant and watch her sipping through pastel foam, lifting out cherries and pineapple wedges, which Nell does like. Lyric and I stick to Diet Coke, which is always available, especially if you're willing to compromise for Diet Pepsi.

There are five TVs in the five bedrooms, though one is set into the wood headboard of the king-size waterbed I often sprawl out on with Lyric, and it can't be budged, so we watch from the foot of the bed, which has been made from largish tree trunks. Nell's TV is on a glass-topped column that culminates in a flattened plaster cow skull, which she has had us help her wheel around to the side of the bed, close to her pillow. In our adjacent rooms, the shows war with each other: Jay Leno drives through a fast-food drive-in and orders tons of food to give the clerk ample time to notice it's him; Catherine Deneuve, looking classy and scintillating at the same time, seduces someone in *Belle de Jour*. The night before, we all eventually channel surfed to CNN to get stereophonic news about the hurricane that had just started to pound the Carolina coast. The reporter looked like he was ready for liftoff, right there on the scene, holding on to a rope, or whatever it was flapping in his hand as he screamed into his microphone. People were shown nailing plywood to their windows. A roof blew off. There was much screaming on the reporter's part about windsurfers who were out earlier who either went home or drowned, though all we could see was rain pelting the camera lens.

So here I am, in Park City, to—as Lyric would have it—hang and chill with Janet and the gang until approximately the eighteenth of July, give or take a few L.A. minutes, or days. The day when the screenwriting course ends is ambiguously described in the brochure. As best we can make out, it may end on different days for people with different astrological signs. I'm along because even Janet burned out on the babysitters, and she also thought it would be a good idea to get my mind off my former fiancé, Hale Dowd, who didn't so much leave me at the altar as leave *to acquire* altars. Altar gathering in the Southwest; I kid you not. Not that he has a religious bone in his body: it was about procuring altars (sometimes, quite easily; other times, major bribes required; occasionally, an indignant turndown when he genuinely offended the padre). Rich people in L.A. now want altars as additions to their entranceways and as frames for their wet bars. Two months ago, Hale traded his leased BMW for a Ford pickup, his taste in music mutated with no transitions from early Brian Eno to Lyle Lovett all in one trip to Tower Records, and he tried to persuade me to give up my job as a Clinique salesperson so that I could drive around with him and eat *chiles verdes* and help him sweet-talk priests. It wasn't like I'd ever envisioned picket fences, and he'd had a vasectomy, so we weren't going to be a mommy-and-daddy-and-baby family or anything like that, but I did sometimes think about growing herbs and having a dog, though when I think of it, that does seem pretty pathetic. When we broke up, Janet drove over to Silver Lake with a big bottle of Sapporo, a trowel, some rosemary in a tub and some basil in a punch-out six-pack, and a cardboard dog that looked exactly like a perky terrier, and we had some beer and planted the plants and put the dog in among them and backed up and looked, and of course it made us laugh. That night it rained, and that was it for the dog, although I can still see the little assemblage so perfectly that it wasn't a waste of Janet's money at all.

Right now, 10:10 a.m., Lyric is tying the laces of her espadrilles around her shapely ankles. It doesn't matter that we're only going swimming: she doesn't own a pair of crappy shoes. It's her theory that if you have noticeable shoes, you'll get instant respect and admiration, however else you look. I slip into my plastic flip-flops and pull a sleeveless T-shirt size XXL—I barely remember the days of buying T-shirts in my size—over my suit as Lyric teases her hair into an Ivana. She never actually swims at the pool; the most she'll do is sit at the shallow end and dangle her feet in the water while Nell splashes around.

Nell is plopped in the middle of the lumber bed, watching cartoons. A bear peeks into a beehive and is swarmed by bees. Scrambling to right himself, he trips over an alligator and is eaten, headfirst. I watch the cartoon to see the bear regurgitated. Nothing happens. The bees spiral and fly away: a black tornado that is really inconsequential, compared to Hurricane Bertha. The alligator gulps several times and, its sides bulging and its back looking more like it swallowed a camel, slithers into some bushes.

"Turn that off. It's awful," I say.

"She might as well learn the way of the world," Lyric says to me.

Nell takes this as confirmation that she can continue watching. At long last, the wet, exhausted bear reappears, stumbling out of the woods. It slams down into two enormous poles that turn out to be . . . dinosaur legs. This is definitely not a day in the life of Teddy Ruxpin. The dinosaur snatches up the bear. From the woods, the terrible sounds continue—I'm hearing the alligator, right?—as the bear disappears down the escalator-length throat of the dinosaur.

"I wonder if that cute guy will be there again," Lyric says, dotting my Clinique lipstick on her cheeks and rubbing it in. "The guy with the Euro boner," she says, anticipating my "Which one?" question. She means the Frenchman who was walking around displaying his anatomy in little striped briefs. I saw him later in the day reading *GQ*, wearing those half glasses that accountants and gynecologists always peer over, and any curiosity I had about him instantly vanished.

"He was old," I say. "Forty-five, at least," I say, anticipating her "How old?"

"I don't want the fat girl to be there," Nell says, as the now-sopping bear makes another escape, popping out the dinosaur's nostril.

"She's never there. She's a condo rat. She stays here and stuffs her fat face all day and then Rollerblades around until her precious Daddy comes home, and then they stuff themselves with ice cream," Lyric says to Nell. "Give it a break with the anxiety."

"What did she say?" Nell says to me.

"Let's go to the pool," I say. "Come on, Nell. Turn off the TV. Come on, Lyric. Stop preening."

"I swear to God, I think I am getting this spider vein on my throat," she says, her head turned away from the mirror.

Nell gets off the bed with both hands on top of her head, to protect it from my attempts to comb her hair, and runs past me.

"Your suit's on the towel rack," I call after her.

"I don't want to wear my suit," she calls back. Every day, the same thing.

"There are no other girls your age without a swimsuit," I say, with as much solemnity as possible. "You'd be the only one."

"I'm not a girl," she says.

"What are you?"

"A mermaid," she says. I hear the toilet flush. When she returns, she has the suit on. One shoulder strap flops under her armpit. "I want shoes like hers," Nell says.

"These are super-chic shoes made only for people with a minimum shoe size of six," Lyric says, standing on one foot and turning the other foot from side to side, admiringly. "Do you know how much these shoes cost?"

"I want ones like that!" Nell says to me. She looks desperate.

"They cost so much that when you start getting paid for doing chores—when your mom starts quartering you and fifty-centing you for dumping your cruddy clothes in the hamper instead of on the floor, you would have to save for approximately . . ."

"Mommy can buy me shoes like that!" Nell says to me, her voice rising.

"Talk to Mommy about it later," I say, trying to dodge the whole issue.

"Where's Mommy?" Nell says, her eyes clouding with tears.

"Mommy's at her seminar," I say. "You know where Mommy is. She kissed you goodbye."

"I was asleep," Nell says.

There seems no good answer to that. Also, if truth be told, I'm pretty sure it was only Damon who came into the suite this morning, to look at all three of us to make sure we were where we were supposed to be. He walks hard, and it sounded like just one set of footsteps, but it was too early to bother opening my eyes and to possibly risk a conversation. Janet, I know, is not used to rising early, and having to be in class at 9 a.m. is really a struggle for her.

Nell chooses the Pocahontas barrette and I clip it in a clump of hopelessly frizzed curls. Her swimsuit is pink polka dots, with a ruffle bisecting her belly. She's got her mother's pigeon toes and squared shoulders.

She looks at once robotically durable and mysteriously frail. Her father is a famous actor who has set up a trust fund for her, in addition to paying monthly child support. This, in an agreement his lawyer made with Janet's lawyer that he would never have to see the child or otherwise participate in her upbringing, and that Janet agree not to tell his wife or to write about their relationship—which lasted all of a month and a half, including the three weeks when she didn't know she was pregnant. We happened to see him on TV a couple of nights ago, and Nell paid less attention to him than to the bear, which I suppose was only natural, since she had no idea he was her father. He was just another guy plotting a crime.

"Are we ready?" I ask. Lyric clips her Walkman to her fanny pack, which she wears pouch forward. She puts on the earphones and turns on the music and does a few dance steps in silent acknowledgment of my question. "I want you to carry me," Nell says, reaching up. This is because she's afraid of encountering the fat girl; she usually hates to be carried. Still, I heft all forty-two pounds of her, shift her to one arm, and with my other hand pick up the sack I've packed with the daily bagel, the *USA Today* Nikki always leaves outside our door, with a photocopied note stapled to it reminding us that she does deep tissue massage "by appointment or even on spur moments," sunblock in two strengths, Evian water in a thermal bottle, Nell's coloring book and crayons. Janet—my father's child of his youth, while I was the child of his old age, and don't I sympathize today, schlepping around a forty-two-pounder . . . my sister, as I think of her more simply, is in an air-conditioned room at something called the Yarrow, learning how to perfect her screenplay about Sally Hemmings, servant to, and alleged lover of, Thomas Jefferson. Originally, the screenplay began in the present day, with the mounted heads of the animal trophies brought back by Lewis and Clark that were hung on the walls at Monticello talking to each other about the odd goings-on at night, but when I lost it entirely and almost died laughing, she was forced to see what she'd written in a new light. I know she's changed the beginning, though she's refused to ever show it to me again. P.O.V. moose. That's my perspective for the day: P.O.V. moose. You can imagine how strange that makes Park City look, as we exit the condo.

But it's just a place: yuppified, restored, renovated, repainted, recast. One shop dips perfectly good Oreo cookies into dark chocolate and sells them for a markup that might make simple Oreo fanciers faint. At another store you can have your picture taken by a camera attached to a computer, after which it's put through another machine that fragments the image, then sends it through a tube, and when it emerges, it's been altered into one of those optical-trick pictures. You have to stare at the maze of indecipherable pattern and let your eyes go out of focus until you see a three-dimensional version of yourself. I had one made my first day in Park City, which I intended to send to Hale, back in the nano-second of sentimentality when I thought we should probably still stay in touch, but it turned out so frightening that I only showed it to Nikki for corroboration of how awful it was (when it came into—or is it out of?—focus, she put her hands over her mouth and inhaled sharply). The thought occurred to me that an enterprising businessperson might realize that small ones might make excellent, repellent business cards. The picture was of me as I was dressed that day, in a baseball cap turned backward. Giggly Nell had painted a cross on my forehead with the zinc oxide I'd applied to her nose, and I'd forgotten about it when I got in front of the camera, so I looked like some deranged cult person or, at the very least, someone making an untimely protest against Ash Wednesday. As the background, I selected rockets being fired, but when you first looked at the picture it seemed to be just nice abstract shades of red and yellow in a sort of herringbone pattern. I apparently selected some other element I didn't realize I was choosing, because when I saw the picture, all the rockets were rising as a maze, and I was above the maze, floating *2001*-ish, tipped slightly forward. I ended up looking like some monstrous apparition with weird war paint that had already descended from space while the rockets were wasting their time going exploring.

"Check it out," Lyric says to me from her lounge. Above us, a woman in white and a man are floating in a big balloon. The balloon has descended enough that we can see it's a bride. She's cake-ornament small, but I swear: you can see her smile. The dark, tiny groom stands next to her. There they go, borne on the breezes of optimism.

"Do you think they got married in the air?" Lyric says.

"People get married on cruise ships all the time. I suppose they could have," I say.

"I mean, who's supposed to throw confetti? The angels?"

She lowers the back of her chaise and turns onto her stomach. She reaches back and unties the string of her bikini top. On the other lounge, Nell has fallen asleep clasping the bagel half near her lips like a big pacifier. Fortunately, I slathered her with sunblock before she fell asleep. The curls that have escaped the barrette blow in the breeze, while the painted Pocahontas kneels resolutely, braced for anything.

Someone's beeper goes off.

A waitress passes by carrying a tray with two bowls of salad on it with little state-of-Utah flags stuck in them and two bottles of beer. She exaggerates the swing of her hips. That's because Euro boner is back today, and it turns out he's a big tipper. She almost swooned a while ago when he said, "Keep the change."

In Utah, it seems to be a rule that bartenders can only pour five ounces of wine at a time—enough to intoxicate Thumbelina, but a modest half glass for the rest of us—though it seems they can serve a person an entire bottle of beer, which is curious.

A screenplay about Sally Hemmings. Janet's sincere plan for an organizing principle for the rest of her life seems to be completing this screenplay.

Someone is reading a tabloid. Margaux Hemingway, who has died, is depicted on the cover. Her lips are deep pink, her eyebrows penciled dark. She definitely did not strive for the Clinique natural look.

"May you build a ladder to the stars and climb on every rung," Dylan sings. I'm actually hearing the song, not just remembering it. It's floating on the breeze—from where? From somewhere distant.

But oh, Bobecito, we are already no longer young. Which might not be so bad in itself, except that the world doesn't seem young any longer, either. I mean, self-absorption aside, who thought both things would happen simultaneously? The world really seems to be slipping: global warming; the population explosion. What compounds the problem is that once any group starts to be condescended to in the guise of being catered to—once yuppies say yes, and buy the yuppified Oreos they're offered—it's all over. They're taking the bait, they're eating saltpeter, they're becoming impervious to excess, and to surprise. They're just more people trying to keep up the excitement level by having adventure weddings, adventure honeymoons, adventure babies.

This is the way Janet would prefer I not talk when I can be overheard by anyone who might influence her destiny. Meaning: Damon. She's every bit as cynical as I am—haven't we been hearing that heredity explains almost everything?—but she would prefer that I be silent, and that my silence be mistaken for judiciousness. I am, after all, in charge of her most precious possession. I'm her dependable sister whose life has never bottomed out, the slightly introverted, interesting blond counterpart to her extroversion, her slightly horsey, Andie MacDowell–ish beauty. Her looks come from her Brazilian mother: the high cheekbones; the dark, cascading hair. Janet's mother was so beautiful that my own mother never minded the painting of her that hung over my father's desk. Of course, the woman in the painting was dead and was therefore no threat, unless someone was far more neurotic than my mother and thought that the painting was hung because he was still in love with his first wife. My mother didn't think that. All she wondered was whether he ever loved anyone except himself. For a long time in the seventies, it was fashionable for women to think about their husbands that way, though; after a few years of marriage, it came upon them almost the way people get colds when the seasons change.

Lyric turns on her side. "Are you always thinking?" she says.

"What do you mean?"

"Do you have, like, these deep inner thoughts?" She turns sideways, propping herself on an elbow.

"Does something make you think I do?"

"I wish I had them," she says. "Do you like, get them when you get older? Damon"—she calls her father by his first name: none of that "Daddy" stuff—"it's like he's always trying to come down from sensory overload without totally crashing, you know? He calls it brain buzz. Have you ever heard a buzz?"

"No."

"Maybe it's like those diseases that are stored in your nerve cells and they reappear. If you have chicken pox, it can stay dormant for years, and then you might get shingles. But maybe if it's something inside your brain, the stored stuff gets tired of waiting to break out and it starts to rumble, or something."

"Run that by me again," I say.

"You seem, like, really bright. It seems like you're always thinking. Because, I mean, if people are talkative, they're not necessarily thinking, they're just talking, you know? And you don't seem to be a very talkative person."

"I was thinking about my father. He died last year," I say. "While I was sitting here, I heard some music that made me sad. It made me think of him."

"Ooh," she says. "I do this all the time. I go fishing, and then I don't know what to do when I catch a fish."

"I guess you can put it back in the water," I say.

She smiles. "You have an interesting way of talking," she says. "You should talk more."

Is she right about my not being talkative? If so, I realize for the first time why that might be. "Don't take this wrong, but part of the problem might be that while I'm very fond of the people I hang out with, I'm thirty-one and you're fourteen. And Nell is three, and your father is fifty, and my sister is thirty-nine."

"The age thing is what you think it is? I mean, like, I don't have any problem talking to people because of what age they are."

"You're very gregarious. You talk to everybody."

"It comes from being self-involved," she says. "What I'm really doing is projecting my anxiety."

I look at her, surprised.

"He sent me to a psychologist after the Amsterdam thing," she says.

"Oh," I say.

"But you know another thing," she says. "When you do talk, you probably really want to connect with people. I think I just like to talk."

"You're being too hard on yourself," I say.

"No. I've thought about it."

I consider what she's said. "Well, if you're on to yourself, you've got a chance to change," I say.

"I get discouraged, because my limitations all seem to have sorted themselves out while I was sleeping, or something. I mean, I live with Damon, and unless I run away again and he finds me again, I'm going to be living with him until I go to college—right? That's a joke. I do not envision college. But what I'm saying is that Damon's never going to change, is he?"

"People are pretty much the way they're going to be at that age," I say.

"Right. So I'm going to have to watch him bait your sister and then send her flying," she says. "A year from now, no chance I'll know you people."

I look at her, startled.

"What?" she says. "You said you had trouble talking to people who weren't your age, so I'm trying to talk seriously to you."

"Well . . . what exactly are you saying?"

"Don't you know? He's got a violent temper. He scares the shit out of women. He scared my mother so much and he made her feel so powerless that she decided the only thing she could do was get away from him and also become a man for safe measure. I know that sounds funny, but she used to talk to me about it. She'd be lifting weights she kept hidden under her bed, and she'd talk about him through clenched teeth, with the bedroom door closed."

"What did he . . . he has a violent temper?" I shift onto one hip, leaning toward her. "Has he ever hurt you?"

"No," she says. "I've got what's-it-called. I've got immunity. So far, at least, and there have been more than a few times when I've really pushed his buttons."

"But you're not saying he'd do anything to really hurt Janet, are you?"

"He's more a bully than a hitter," Lyric says.

"A hitter? Did he hit your mother?"

"They used to have shoving matches. He didn't really hit her, I don't think. But she always lost. He could stay solid as a sandbag, but the energy would just drain right out of her."

"Jesus. That's horrible," I say.

She waves her hand at me dismissively. "You even get upset by violent cartoons."

My thoughts are bottlenecking; how exactly should I bring this up with Janet? If Lyric was wondering what was going on inside my head, I was naive not to wonder what was going on inside hers.

"He's been that way with women other than your mother?" I say weakly.

"Yeah, he's always that way, eventually," she says.

"I don't suppose it's something you've ever tried to talk to him about? I mean, I guess you wouldn't get very far, being fourteen years old."

"I wouldn't get very far if I was sixty years old, and he was a hundred and ten. You've seen how he shuts down conversation about anything he doesn't want to hear."

In fact, I have. When I was complaining about how the fate of Park City indicated the downward spiral of the modern world, I could see from the way he looked right through me that such observations were not appreciated. I close my eyes and envision my sister just the way Lyric described her: small and snagged on a fishhook. Then I see her spiral out, across choppy water. I immediately open my eyes, and all the people around the pool seem very particular, very distinct, very real.

"I've had girlfriends who've had boyfriends or fathers, or whatever, who've really gotten rough with them. I testified against one girl's stepfather. Some guy came to the house and I gave a deposition. It's not that unusual. I mean, it's a lot more likely that one of those lawyer guys, or whatever they are, are going to show up than that they'll ring your doorbell because you've won the Publishers Clearing House sweepstakes."

"I don't think I know anybody personally who was ever beaten up. But it's so prevalent. It must have happened to someone I know, but no one ever told me that."

"You seem pretty observant," Lyric says. "I mean, you seem like the sort of person who'd put two and two together if a friend said she walked into a wall. Just think about Nicole. I mean, no one with half a brain ever had any doubt about whether he really beat up Nicole, right?"

"Right," I say.

"I don't want to go so far as to say that Damon's a Bruno Magli man," Lyric says.

"But still," I say.

She sighs again. "You're right," she says. " 'But still.' "

"I want ice cream," Nell says, touching my arm. I'm so much in another world that when she touches me, I jump. I look at her and think how vulnerable she is. How vulnerable we all are. How long has she been listening?

"Because this bagel got all sweaty, and it tastes like lotion, and I'm tired of bagels, too," she says. That's Nell: always developing her thoughts fully in order to convince you. I smile at her fondly.

"If I give you the money, can you go get it yourself?" I say.

She looks at me, perturbed. "I'm not big enough that they can see me," she says. She looks over at the bar, which is not where she'd go for an ice cream. That's where she'd go for five ounces of wine, if she were my age. And in need of a drink, which I think I might be.

"No, sweetie, you don't go to that window. You just ask the waitress."

"*You* do it," she says.

"When the waitress comes by, we'll get you an ice cream. What kind do you want?"

"Pink," she says.

"If they don't have strawberry, what's the next choice?"

"Find out if they have it!" she says.

"Hel-*lo*? Am I a ghost?" Lyric says.

"Oh," I say. "Sorry. What kind do you want?"

"I want pink, too," she says.

"And I don't suppose you have a backup if they don't have pink?"

"Green," she says.

Great: the alternative is pistachio.

When the waitress does appear, Nell is sitting on the edge of her lounge, like the relative of someone in an operating room, frantic for news. The flavors are: Cherry Garcia (pink with cherries and chocolate, I explain: she'll like it); Swiss almond fudge; and nonfat banana yogurt. I order a Corona, which the man next to Lyric is drinking. Lyric decides on Swiss almond fudge. I cancel my beer and order banana yogurt. Nell, still squinting as she assimilates the information about Cherry Garcia, looks like the doctor has just explained the patient's condition in language too technical to understand. "Does it have coconut?" she says, worrying aloud. "No," the waitress and I say in unison. "Jerry Garcia was only about the greatest musician who ever lived," Lyric says. "I mean, I can understand being a total, absolute Deadhead."

"What does she say is in it?" Nell says to me.

"No coconut. Believe me, you'll like it."

"Okay," Nell says hesitantly.

"Hey, Cindy, let me have another one of these," the man next to Lyric says, holding up his empty bottle. The waitress takes his bottle without comment and walks away, not sashaying a bit.

"It is like so weird to be in a state where almost nobody drinks," Lyric says. "I mean, it's against their religious beliefs to drink, but at the same time, they think stuff that people with the D.T.'s think, like that there are spirit babies floating around in heaven they've got to round up and find a way to give birth to."

"What?" Nell says. Before I can answer, she says, "I'm not going to be floating when Mommy comes home, am I?"

Lyric bursts into laughter. I give her a dirty look.

"No. Why would you think you'd be floating around?" I ask.

"Because that lady in a balloon."

"I thought you were asleep when that went over," I say.

"A bride edging closer to her spirit babies," Lyric says.

This is too much for Nell. She just ignores her. But the man next to Nell has gotten interested. I see him looking at her. I see that she is aware she's being overheard. She adjusts the top of her bikini and looks straight ahead.

The man next to Lyric turns his head. "Here on vacation?" he says.

"No," Lyric says slowly. "This is all work related."

There's a pause.

"May I ask what kind of work you do?" the man asks.

"I work with computers. I set up programs to monitor the way vineyards are run."

This exchange all happens quickly, and Lyric sounds so calm and reasonable, that I'm stunned into silence. Not that the man was flirting with me, in the first place.

"There are vineyards in Utah?"

"I'm here to meet with a client from Sonoma, who's on vacation."

"Really?" the man says. The longer Lyric keeps it up, the more you can see him questioning his perceptions. She might be some sort of prodigy, for all he knows.

"And what about you?" she says.

"I'm one of those people writing the great American novel," he says. "I'm retired from Dow Corning."

"Dow Corning! You know, when I was in my midtwenties, I had breast implants," Lyric says, raising one leg and resting the calf of the other leg on her knee. She looks at me. "Did you hear that? This man is responsible for the money I'm soon going to receive." She turns to the man. "Those implants were responsible for causing me more than a bit of trouble."

"I wasn't a scientist," the man says. "I worked in bookkeeping."

"I was thanking you," Lyric says. "Don't feel defensive."

"Are you . . . are you all in the wine business?" he says to me. I can tell he doubts this highly.

"Who is that man?" Nell says to me.

Lyric answers for me: "It's not that we're in the wine business, per se; we're developmental people, responsible for setting up creative programs that monitor—"

"The little girl, too?" he says.

"I'm a mermaid!" she says.

The man laughs slightly.

"Have you met Jacques?" Lyric says. "He's in a snit today, because we shot down one of his ideas, so he's sulking over there across the pool."

She points to the Frenchman in his little bathing suit. He is reading a magazine.

"I haven't met him," the man says.

"Lyric," I say. She ignores me. I see the waitress approaching. She moves to the man's lounge and gives him a bottle of beer, with a plastic cup turned upside down on the neck. Our three cones stand upright in a metal holder. They are wrapped with napkins absorbing the melting ice cream.

"So here's to great financial settlements!" Lyric says, raising her cone as if to toast him.

"Lyric," I say again. "Give it a rest. Please."

I pay the waitress money for the cones and tell her to keep the change. It might be a lot, it might be a little. Lyric is making me very uncomfortable. From the waitress's "Thank you" I can't tell how I tipped.

There is awkward silence as we lick our cones. For the rest of the time we're there—another half hour or so—the man avoids looking our way, and Lyric loses interest entirely in her game. From her fanny pack, she takes a bottle of nail polish and redoes her toes. It's a big day for ballooning; several others float by, like big, colorful insects. Nell requests her coloring book and crayons and obliterates a picture of a rose garden with wide blue strokes. Before we leave, I take her to the ladies' room to pee. She shrugs her bathing suit to her ankles and jumps backward on the toilet, bracing herself with both hands.

"Don't watch," she says, and I turn and face the door of the stall. I don't hear anything, but in a few seconds she hops off and says, "Flush when I leave," and quickly unlocks the door and rushes out, clutching her half-pulled-up bathing suit, before I hit the handle. She has no fear of flushing a toilet where we live, but she is terrified of flushing toilets in public places.

What a handful Lyric is, I think, following Nell out of the bathroom. Damon has obviously not had an easy time, but I don't even want to look at him, let alone hear his point of view, after what Lyric told me. I wonder how many women there have been, then decide that might be the way to open the discussion with Janet. If she knows. But if she doesn't know, if she hasn't wanted to hear about his past, she's really not going to want to hear my bad news.

Ahead of me, Nell is running back to three empty lounges. Lyric is nowhere in sight, and neither is the man. I see his beer bottle, empty, beside his lounge, and my heart stops for a second; it's like finding a missing person's watch deep in the woods. I look all around. It doesn't help that Nell asks, "Where's Lyric?" The man is nowhere. And then he is somewhere: he's coming out of a telephone booth, walking slowly in our direction, returning to his lounge. Not long afterward, I see Lyric's head break the surface of the water—she never swims!—and she pulls herself onto the rim of the pool, very close to where "Jacques" sits. She sits with her back to him, swishing her legs in the pool. Then she turns sideways, pretending to want to catch the sun on her face. She has Jacques' attention. I go and get her. If it were necessary to take her by the hand and pull her, I would. But she can see from my expression that she's gone as far as she can go. She hops up and skitters toward me, giving me a wet hug.

"Admit it. I was pretty good," she says.

Back at the condo, there's a message on the answering machine. Tom Selleck is paying an unscheduled visit to the seminar; Janet and Damon won't be back until after dinner. We should get dinner on our own. "Jillie Mack is already in the hotel," Janet adds, as if this would matter. But it does matter to Janet: she's decided on a new direction for her life, and Tom Selleck, and even his wife, are beacons. She ends her message by asking, "Who does Mommy love most? Bye."

"It's me," Nell says triumphantly, standing on tiptoe, as if that will bring her closer to her mother, whose voice has been playing from the telephone-answering machine mounted on the kitchen wall.

"To save this message, press one," an automated voice says.

"Press. Press!" Nell says.

I lift her up and let her press it herself.

"Play it again," Nell says.

"Press the replay button," I say, pointing to it. Janet begins to speak again. "Hi, everybody, it's me. Listen, we're going to be late getting home because Tom Selleck is flying in to talk to us. I already saw"—she lowers her voice—"Jillie Mack is in the hotel, and she is *tiny*. I saw her by the Coke machine. There was some rumor that Robert Redford was going to show up and it was like Fantasy Island: somebody who worked at the hotel started pointing to a helicopter and saying it was him, and everybody ran out of the building and stood around, but the thing never landed. I'm not exactly sure what he's going to be doing—Selleck, I mean—but you should get dinner because there's some reception for him at some lodge a friend of Damon's is renting after the talk he's giving, or whatever it is. Anyway: love you all, and I'll see you soon, and I want my dear sister to give a special kiss to Nell if Nell can correctly answer the question: Who does Mommy love most? Bye."

Nell turns in my arms to look at me. "What do I get for a special kiss?" she says.

"Top of the head," I say, kissing her lightly before setting her on the floor.

"I'm not going to take a bath," Nell says. She calls over her shoulder: "I don't have to."

Lyric and I get iced decaf cappuccinos from the store next to the condo. We get an Orangina for Nell. Basically, she likes the bottle. She ate almost no dinner, sulking because Janet didn't come back. In the living room of the condo, when we returned earlier that afternoon, was a green glass vase filled with red roses—a totally unexpected hello (that's all the card said) from Hale. There was also a note:

> *These delivered approx. 1 p.m. Delivery person upset because he was sent to Yarrow House, where they knew where you were. V. upset when he got here, then I heard he had dropped roses and broken vase—had to come back a second time. I left them in an ice bucket in my sink until he returned, and I cleaned up the broken glass. I noticed that there were eleven roses only and suspected they had counted wrong. Had him phone the florist, who he says told him only eleven were ordered, one dozen bad luck, 13 bad luck, therefore rather under. I will be playing Friday night, because the boy is already too sick. Please come! Hope you are enjoying your stay!*

Remember that I am always available for deep tissue massage.—Nikki

"So, like, would you consider going back with him?" Lyric says, flopping on the strange-colored sofa.

"I don't know that I should jump to conclusions, when all the card says is 'Hello,' " I say.

"You could send him flowers, too, and let him make the next move," Lyric says.

"I don't know where he is. He's driving around the Southwest."

"So how did he know where you were?"

I think about it a minute. "I had the brochure for this conference lying around the house in Silver Lake for a long time," I say.

"Do you think that maybe he went back there and saw the brochure and missed you?"

"Since when do you have this romantic impulse to get everybody together?" I say.

"I'm meddlesome," she says. "Isn't that a great word? Damon said it about me. Not when I was trying to get him back together with somebody—just when I was putting some decent stuff into the grocery cart."

From Nell's bedroom, we hear the TV. She's channel surfing.

"Please put your nightgown on, Nell, even if you aren't going to bathe," I call out to her.

"I think it was nice of him to send you roses," Lyric says, touching her toes to the edge of the vase. "What was your biggest problem, or was it nothing but problems?"

I'm scanning the *USA Today* I didn't read at the pool. "He was a mechanic when I first met him. Then suddenly he and a guy he worked with started going to Mexico on the weekends and bringing chests back. Chests, chairs, all kinds of stuff. The other guy got a storefront and was selling it in Santa Monica. I thought it was sort of nuts, going to Mexico all the time, but the money was great, and I guess I didn't want to ask questions. Then one night we had the volume control up on the phone by mistake, and in the middle of the night I heard a voice shouting that Hale should stay away, not come anywhere near the store, that it was better to let them do Helter Skelter. He jumped out of bed and took the call. The cops had gone into the store in the middle of the night. They apparently took the door off the hinges and walked in and started axing chair legs off and prying up the bottoms of the chests, or whatever they were doing, looking for drugs. Which they didn't find, but they ended up arresting the other guy. When they didn't find drugs, the stuff suddenly became priceless antiquities, and the other guy got hauled out of his house in the middle of the night, but he never said anything about Hale, and he also got word to his lawyer to tell Hale to stay away. I was *stunned* to realize that a lawyer was calling in the middle of the night, that hysterical."

"Wow," Lyric says. "But I don't get it. Were they smuggling drugs?"

"Hale didn't think so. They didn't find any," I say.

"Yeah, but were they?"

"I don't know," I say.

"So why did you break up?"

"Things hadn't been great before Helter Skelter. We had separate friends, he wanted to move away from L.A. and I didn't. But the week after the phone call was terrible. We got so paranoid we thought people were watching the house."

"Looks like he wants to apologize," Lyric says.

"I wouldn't get back together with him," I say, surprising myself by how suddenly I speak. "I always had an uneasy feeling that he was up to a lot of stuff I didn't know about. I don't want to be with somebody I'd hesitate to ask questions of."

"That's very sensible," Lyric says. "That's a good way of looking at things. I hope I remember that."

I look at her to see if she's mocking me. She isn't. Furthermore, she does me the favor of calling out to Nell to change the channel, so I don't have to be the heavy.

"No! I'm watching!" Nell hollers back.

"You know, if I don't get to hang with you down the line, maybe we could still talk on the phone," Lyric says.

"Sure," I say.

"But you don't know where you'll be living, right?"

"No. I've got to be out of the house by the end of the month. But I know where you are, so I can call you."

"Can you keep a secret?" she says.

"I don't want to," I say, raising my hands as if she's announced a stickup.

"Are you kidding?" she says.

I look at her and suddenly am so self-conscious about my expression that I realize I must look the way Nell did, much earlier, hearing the contents of Cherry Garcia.

"I'm moving to Brooklyn," she says. "He was with this very nice woman before he started going out with Janet. I mean, she was *ex-*

tremely nice. When she got away from him, she got a job in New York, and just like she said she would, she kept in touch with me. I'm actually a better person to talk to on the phone than in person, because when I'm not looking right at a person, I tend to have more complex thoughts."

I pick up a pillow and hold it against my stomach, listening.

"The job she got in New York was way below her, but she's waiting for a job in book publishing. She's at one of those brides' magazines right now. I mean, she has a master's degree in history. Did Janet tell you anything about her? Sharon Oglethorpe?"

I shake my head no.

"Well, promise you won't tell. Except that you can tell Janet—you *have to* tell Janet—because it's really important that he doesn't think he can get away with this stuff for all time. But if you tell her all the particulars, and she tells him, he's going to know where she got the information. If that happens, I will not have immunity, I assure you." She slides to the edge of the sofa. "I sort of deemphasized what I said before," she says. "He slapped her one time. Sharon. And she got a detached retina. It was unbelievably awful. But anyway, she was out of there. She filed a complaint with the cops—she did all this stuff that really made him nervous. It ended up with her calling off the cops and with him giving her some money. When she got to New York, she called me, and she said if I'd promise to attend school, I could live with her. And that New York was way cooler than California. Which I'm thinking might not be such a bad change. So the thing is, she's going to send me a plane ticket at my best friend's, and I'm going to do it. If he tries to cause any problems, we're both going to lie and say he pushed me around all the time. Get this: she's *living* with a lawyer."

This is almost too much to take in at one time. I find myself only nodding. She gets up, goes into the other room, and comes back with her fanny pack. From inside one of the zippered pouches she takes a small piece of paper and holds it out. It's a business card, already imprinted with her name, telephone number, and Park Slope address. She says: "So when you land wherever, call me, and that way we can be in touch."

"This is pretty unbelievable," I say. "You're fourteen years old."

"I never think about that," she says. Then she says it again, but the second time, instead of sounding cryptic, she sounds wistful: "It's true," she says. "I never think about that."

Nell skitters through the room, naked. She gets a banana from the kitchen counter and runs back into the bedroom, to the TV.

"If you're going—" I say. I start again: "If you were going to live with her, how come you came to Park City?"

"She's at a spa this week," Lyric says. "And anyway: Who'd miss this?"

We both look around the condo and shake our heads. "I'm with you," Lyric says. "If this is what the Wild West has become, fuck it." She scoots back and leans against the sofa. "Damon had all this stuff from the tourist board about white-water rafting and all this cool stuff I thought I'd gear up to do, but I don't seem to have done it," she says. "You don't seem like somebody who wishes she was out riding horses or shooting the rapids, either."

"No," I say.

"I'd actually say there's something deenergizing about this place. But that's true of any place that seems artificial, I guess," she says.

"Maybe at the very least we should go up by the miniature golf course and get on one of the rides before we leave," I say.

"You scared me," she says. "I thought for a minute you were suggesting miniature golf."

I start slow with Janet. The night before, I put a note under her door telling her it was very important that we talk, alone, and that she had to meet me in the lobby at eight. I don't know what time she got back, but from the circles under her eyes, I'd say it was late.

"Why don't we take the bus down?" I say. "We can get coffee and talk at the Yarrow."

She stands sulkily at the bus stop beside me, more like a pouting little girl than my older sister. She says nothing. In two or three minutes the bus comes, opening its doors for just the two of us.

"If you're going to say anything critical of me, I don't want to hear it," Janet says. She sits in a single seat that faces sideways. I sit down in a two-seater right behind her that faces forward.

"Why don't you give me a little credit for having something I really want to talk to you about?" I say.

"You're not pregnant, are you?" she says, looking right at me.

"No," I say. "What would make you think that?"

"Because I am," she says. "That's why I've been such a bitch."

"*What?*"

"Well, just because you aren't doesn't mean other people can't be," she says.

"*Janet! No!*"

She pats my shoulder idly. Then she drops her hand in her lap as if it's made of lead. "I found out in the ladies' room of the Yarrow, on lunch break," she says. "But I knew I was, even before I took the test. I just knew I was."

"Have you told anybody?"

"This bus is making me nauseated," she says.

"Is it really making you sick?" I say, rising to my feet—as if by rushing to her I can do anything about the way her stomach feels. I loom over her, unsteadily. I grab the metal bar and sink back into my seat.

"I told Damon," she says. "Damon, wouldn't you know, is delighted. He's excited about having a second chance to do it right."

"What's wrong with Lyric?" I say.

She raises an eyebrow and lets it sink slowly. "I appreciate your devotion to the child," she says, "but we're not talking about a National Merit Scholar."

"That's not the only way to judge people," I say. "She's very bright."

This time Janet looks at me without the raised eyebrow. First she looks into my eyes, then she drops her eyes when they well with tears. "Oh hell," she says.

"You're upset about this," I say.

Janet nods her head yes. "Or as your friend might say: 'All I wanted to do was hang and chill.' "

"Janet, really, she hasn't had an easy time of it."

"My God, if you're so nuts about her, maybe you could join our little family unit and pal around with her, while I take care of Nell and the baby."

What I know is that there is not going to be any such family unit. But the idea that my sister might be having a baby by a man who knocks women around . . . it's too awful to contemplate.

"He's delighted," she says again. "And then the day after he finds out, who shows up but Selleck, saying that his daughter is the most wonderful thing in his life. Except for his teeny tiny little wife, of course. Who doesn't dance anymore, as far as I know."

"You don't have to do this!" I say urgently.

"My mother was a Catholic," she says. "You don't know about Catholic guilt."

"Janet! That can't seriously be a deciding factor—"

Janet pulls her silver cross out from beneath her T-shirt.

"That's . . . let's not argue about jewelry, Janet. Please. Please. I mean—"

The bus turns the corner and opens its doors to two boys wearing

Rollerblades. "In the back and sit down for the duration of the ride," the driver says mechanically. The boys zoom to the back of the bus and start laughing. I look in the rearview mirror and see the bus driver's look of disapproval. It takes me a minute to realize that he's scrutinizing the whole bus, though: he's heard what I've been saying, as well as hearing the boys' silliness. I realize that he's probably a Mormon. Which makes me think of spirit babies, which in turn makes me look upward. I see the ceiling of the bus.

At the Yarrow, we disembark. I get off first and reach back for Janet's hand, as if she's already hugely pregnant. She takes my hand without noticing my odd gentility. She also doesn't drop it as we walk across the circular drive to the hotel. "Okay," she says, taking a deep breath as we walk in the front door. "This is fine. I can deal with this." She walks a slight bit faster. We're going in the direction of the restaurant. Someone says hello and she says hello back. The restaurant is almost empty.

"I don't suppose black coffee has been helping me to feel less nauseous," she says, when we're seated.

"You just got together with Damon," I say. "Don't you think—"

"Not only that, but I already have a three-year-old and a highly evolved Valley Girl stepchild, to say nothing of the fact that he's got a cat I'm allergic to."

"Are you going to let him keep the cat?" I say.

She studies my face. I don't mind meeting her gaze at all. I've got to stand my ground. "No," she says. "I'm going to suggest he get rid of the cat."

She looks at the menu again. When the waitress comes to the table, Janet says, "No coffee for me. Iced tea, if you have it. And the granola with fruit."

"I'll have an English muffin and grapefruit juice," I say. "Coffee with milk, please."

Janet reaches across the table and takes my hand. "I don't know," she says. "I don't know anything."

"That's why we're here," I say. "I have to tell you something."

"Right," she says. "Excuse me for sidetracking you. What is it you wanted to tell me?"

"Janet, please don't be business-like."

"I'm not trying to be business-like. I'm trying to allow you to tell me whatever is so important."

"You're going to have trouble hearing this, because you don't like Lyric."

She starts to say something, then stops. "I've been exaggerating," she says. "Lyric's an easy person to make fun of. I've picked up her father's reservations about her, and I realize that isn't fair. If you say she's intelligent, I'm sure she's intelligent."

The waitress brings the iced tea and juice. She goes to a station and gets a coffee mug and brings it to the table, with the coffeepot and two little plastic containers of milk that she takes out of her apron pocket. We thank her. She says, "You're welcome," and goes away.

"Do you know anything about the woman Damon was involved with before he met you?" I say.

She looks surprised. "A few things. Yes," she says.

"Do you know anything about women—you know—before that?"

"That he's quite a womanizer. Yes," she says slowly.

"But about the women," I say.

"Tell me what you're getting at," she says. "I'm not about to give a recitation of random facts about a bunch of women I've never met."

"He's been physically abusive," I say.

She looks at me. To my surprise, she says: "Once."

"Once?"

"That's what I said. Once. I know about that. Yes. Is that what Lyric told you that you had to tell me?"

"Janet, I don't believe it was just once."

She shifts in her chair. "Well, that's what he told me," she said. "And it flipped him out so much that he was in counseling for a year." She takes the lemon out of her iced tea. Instead of squeezing it, she looks at it, then puts it on the tablecloth. "I realize that once is once too often," she says. "Toward the end, when he had that job he really hated in Ithaca, he was drinking too much. I'm not saying that's an excuse. Just that he doesn't touch alcohol now, as you know. He made a mistake. He told me about it."

I persist: "Do you know about the detached retina?"

"God," she says, "this is so painful. Yes I do. I wish you didn't, because I honestly think he realized that his drinking had gotten out of hand, and I'm entirely certain he regrets it and that he'd never do a thing like that again."

"Listen to yourself. That's the way women who'll let themselves be abused always defend the man."

"He's not 'the man.' He's Damon. He's never hurt me, and he told me about what happened with that other woman. Can we drop the subject now? Please?"

"He shoved Lyric's mother around. The way Lyric described it was that her mother would just get drained of energy, and that he stayed as solid as a bag of sand."

She looks at the floor. She looks back at me. "Why do you believe her?" she says. "There's quite a bit of animosity between them. Maybe what looked to a little child—"

"Listen to yourself!" I say.

She stops talking. "That's what she told you?" she says, finally.

"She's told me more than that."

Janet looks very pale. "She didn't say he hit her, did she?"

"She said he didn't. But come to think of it, I'm not sure I believe her. She might have found it possible to tell me about the others, but not about herself."

"Isn't that a little paranoid?"

"Maybe."

" 'Maybe,' " Janet echoes. "So we have for breakfast a big, looming 'maybe' on the table." The waitress is coming our way with a tray. "Why don't we tackle it piece by piece," Janet says. "You eat a bite of muffin, I'll have a spoonful of cereal."

"It wasn't easy to say these things to you."

"I'm sure it wasn't," she says.

"Please don't sound business-like," I say, as the waitress puts my plate in front of me.

"What is my alternative? To sound all screwed up and vulnerable? I'm rattled by what you said, okay? It worked. It's made me very nervous. I'm going to have to think about this."

"You've already got a three-year-old. You've only lived with him for a few months. You don't know what it would be like to live with him for years and years. You've got to do your screenplay."

"Are you serious?" she says.

"Sally Hemmings."

"Thank you. I don't need prompting to remember what my screenplay is about." She takes another bite of cereal. "Nobody's ever going to unravel the truth about that," she says. "Jefferson either did, or he didn't."

On the last day of the conference, which comes, sure enough, a day earlier than the brochure seemed to indicate, Lyric, Nell, and I decide to buy tickets and ride on the Alpine Slide. I don't know about Janet, but I'm ready to go home—even if all that means is that I'll have to start packing boxes. From time to time, I've thought about Janet's sarcastic suggestion that I move in with her, but what she doesn't know is that Lyric isn't going to be around any time at all, and the prospect of daily life with Nell . . . I adore her, but I don't want to spend all my spare time with a three-year-old. What's this living with other people when you're an adult, anyway? Camping out for six days in Park City has been all I can manage. The second bouquet from Hale didn't bring me around any, either; if anything, it reinforced my resolve to keep away from somebody who so little wanted to express enthusiasm for me that he twice sent flowers with a card that simply said, "Hello."

"I don't know why a pretty girl like you has any trouble finding a fellow," Nikki says to me. She's dunking little tubes in the hot tub, then dropping different chemicals in them with an eyedropper. What happens with each one, which is not discernible to my eye, seems to please her. "Maybe you don't talk enough," she says. "You have to put out some give to get some take."

"You're the second person this week who's told me I'm not very talkative," I say.

"If you were talkative, you'd say who the other person was!" Nikki says. She puts her testing kit on a shelf below the redwood floor and closes the little trapdoor. She wipes her hands on her legs. "Probably the teenager, because she can talk up a storm."

"Lyric," I say.

"Real name Linda," Nikki says.

"It is?"

"Yeah, sure. We traded information a few mornings back. She adopted the name Lyric when she was in grade one to make herself special. I know what she feels like, thinking you've got to have the right name. I could not be in Park City, Utah, and always be Nguyen, you know?"

She goes to the control panel on a small redwood column and turns the dial. The water starts to bubble. "Aah," she says, sitting down, swinging her feet into the water. "Just for a minute. You, too," she says.

"I don't like very hot water," I say.

"Relaxing. Try it," Nikki says. She slowly lowers her legs into the water. Then she pulls them up again. "She could be a real beautician," Nikki says, holding one foot high in the air. "How come if Lyric painted my toenails, you don't have painted toenails?" Nikki says.

"I didn't want them painted."

"You," she says. "You're more fun than you want to let on."

"I doubt it," I say.

"Hey, nobody else got two bouquets here this week," she says, lowering her feet again. The water bubbles close to the hem of her white bermuda shorts.

I sit beside her, cross-legged. Then I change my mind, swing my legs around, and lower them into the water. For a second they sting, then they tingle.

"You know I'm fun, right?" Nikki says.

"What do you mean?"

"Girls know what other girls mean when they talk about fun," she says. "Don't tell me you don't. I talked to Lyric about fun. She guessed something and I said it was right."

A chill goes up my spine. I don't know what I anticipate, but I'm sure it's nothing good. I didn't know Lyric had spent any time with Nikki, let alone that she'd painted her toenails.

"I have been a widow for twelve years. Something has to happen, right?"

"What do you mean?" I say again.

"You know. Fun in bed," Nikki says.

I drop my mouth open. At first, I think she's saying she went to bed with Lyric. She sees my mouth agape, and looks puzzled. She even says, "What's wrong?"

"I'm not following what you're saying," I say.

"I swore her to secrecy, now I swear you," Nikki says. "Just one afternoon. When he scheduled deep tissue massage. There wasn't any. You understand?"

I don't know if I'm relieved or dismayed. This was not a discussion I expected to be having when I took two Tylenols and went out on the deck to get some air.

"He loves your sister," Nikki says. "It doesn't mean anything but that two people had fun. You don't tell her, though, because she doesn't need to know. That would not please anyone."

"You're serious?" I say. "He slept with you?"

"Yeah," she says, giving my shoulder a playful shove. "Lyric had a hunch, from the way he looked at me. She asked me, and I swore her to secrecy. I'm thinking maybe I shouldn't have admitted it, because it was her father, but she's so grown-up," Nikki says. "If women aren't honest with other women, there will be no honesty, right?"

"What?" I say, dazed.

"Because the men are not going to be honest! No!" Nikki says.

"Oh, man," I say. "Oh man. I don't believe this."

"You're more surprised than she was!" Nikki says.

"This has been a tough week," I say. "I'm getting tired of being surprised."

"If people weren't willing to be surprised, they'd still think the earth was flat. They wouldn't have tested, right?"

I watch a golden wasp come near the surface of the water and lift off just before it's lapped in. The wasp circles around to buzz behind me and reapproach the water. This time the water gets it, and I watch it wash toward the far end of the whirlpool, where the blue plastic cover is neatly rolled. "Desert rose," Nikki says, lifting her foot to admire it. She looks at me. "If he wasn't nice-looking, I wouldn't have. You can tell when somebody is a nice man."

"Because of the way they look?"

"No, not just looks. Deeper than looks. Some people look at you and let you see inside their soul."

"And he was . . ." I falter. "He was a nice man?"

"Mmmm," Nikki says.

What did I expect? Violence, during the half hour when he was ostensibly getting deep tissue massage? In my imagination, he has become so monstrous I've been assuming he couldn't contain his terrible impulses.

"I like it rough," Nikki whispers. Then she looks to the side, embarrassed.

"Oh no," I say. "Oh no, he didn't do anything to you, did he?"

"When there is real passion, I like it rough," she says again.

"What?" I say. "Nikki, please. What, exactly?"

"Hey, I found a way to get you to talk," Nikki says. When she speaks, though, she sounds more nervous than triumphant.

"Nikki," I say, putting my hand on her elbow. "Nikki, let me level with you. I've been worried that he might do something to my sister. Do you know from Lyric that he's done violent things to women?"

"I was just talking about fun," Nikki says. She looks at my hand clasping her elbow. I remove it. I put my hand on my thigh, spread my fingers, and look at the light circle of skin—much lighter than the rest, in spite of almost a week of tanning—where for years I wore the silver band Hale gave me.

"I don't want to tell," she says, her voice barely audible above the bubbling water. "Too personal."

We sit in silence for a long time. Eventually, extraneously, Nikki says in a very quiet voice: "Don't tell your sister."

To my surprise, when I go downstairs—my headache worse than when I set out—Damon is sprawled on the orange sofa, clicking through channels with the remote.

"There she is!" Nell hollers, jumping off his lap. "Lyric went looking for you!" she squeals.

"Hey—where've you been?" Damon says to me. On the TV screen, there is a shot of Joan Collins, on the witness stand. "Why are they airing old news?" he says, clicking the remote.

"Where's Janet?" I say.

"Mommy has a headache," Nell says.

"Yeah, well, her sister does, too," I say, sitting in a fake-zebra-hide chair.

"What's up with you two? Janet said she was too sick to make it to the last session. You getting sympathetic pains?" Damon says.

"How are we going to find Lyric?" Nell says. "You stay here, and I'll find her."

"No, sweetie," I say. "Just sit here another minute and she'll come back."

"She will come in *one* minute?"

"She definitely will, and if she doesn't, curse me for a fool," I say. I rub my hand over my face. My fingers smell slightly of chlorine.

"We can leave a note for her and go on the ride!" Nell says.

"How would you like it if you went to look for one of us, and when you got back, we'd gone without you?"

"No," Nell says, climbing into my lap. She turns around and puts her thumb in her mouth. She never sucks her thumb.

"You wouldn't like it a bit, would you?" I say. I bounce her slightly on my knees. She is staring at Damon. She continues to suck her thumb.

"Sometimes there are things I sure don't like one bit, either," Damon says. "Like, for instance, one person who will tell another person how she should live her life." He gives me a quick look, then looks back at the TV. "Such as"—he spells—"a-b-o-r-t-i-o-n."

This is not lost on Nell. She looks at me but, surprisingly, does not say, "What did he say?" I jiggle her a little harder on my knees.

"If Lyric goes out to the deck looking for me, Nikki will tell her where I am," I say. Damon shoots me another look, this one much quicker than the last. When he looks away, he looks out the window, not back at the TV. "Because I was up by the hot tub talking to Nikki," I say to Nell, as if she asked to be informed. "She and I were t-a-l-k-i-n-g."

"Tell me!" Nell says. "What did you spell?"

"Talking," I say. "T-a-l-k-i-n-g."

Damon turns off the TV, tosses the remote onto the sofa cushion with obvious disgust, and starts down one of the corridors.

"What's he doing?" Nell says.

"Honey, I can't read his mind. I guess he's going to pee."

"I want the TV back on," Nell says, jumping off my lap.

"No you don't, you want to ride on the fabulous Alpine Slide," Lyric says, coming through the front door. She flops down near my feet. "So now that I've made the entire run of the building, including waking up your sister, who looks totally wasted, I'm sorry to say, I find you in our own cozy living room."

"I didn't realize everybody was ready to leave," I say.

"We are ready!" Nell says, beginning to march in a circle. "We are ready! We are ready!"

"Gee, but the question is: Is Nell ready?" Lyric says.

"Yessssss!" Nell says, crouching and jumping.

"She's perfecting her Ed McMahon imitation," Lyric says to me.

"I am *ready*! I am *ready*!" Nell says.

"So am I! So am I!" Damon says, coming back into the room, tucking his shirt into his jeans. "So is this it? We go have some fun now?"

This is the way he's decided to deal with the information I just gave him. He's going to make me look sulky and strange if I don't get in the swing of things. But the mood is false; it's too put-on, too euphoric, too sudden. What should I believe? That he got happy peeing?

"Do you want to go on the merry-go-round, sweetheart?" he says to Nell.

"No! I want Alpine Slide!"

"Can she go on that?" Damon says. He looks at Lyric. "Is that okay for children?"

"I don't know, Daddy," she says, answering him with a voice as false as his own. "We'll have to go up there and see."

"Yes! I'm going!" Nell says, with the same panic and desire with which she announced, a few days earlier, that her mother would buy her espadrilles. I wonder if she even remembered to ask Janet for them. I wonder when she and Janet last had any real time together. Maternal feelings begin to overwhelm me. Although I'd know better than to do it, some part of me wonders whether Janet might have been half serious about my moving in. Worse, even, than his hurting Janet, if he ever touched a hair on Nell's head. . . .

We ride down together in the elevator. I watch the way Lyric moves closer to the control panel, away from her father. I keep Nell in my arms, but when we reach the lobby, she won't be contained; she kicks free and races for the front door. As fate would have it, the fat girl is coming in at the same time. She's taken off her skates and is walking in her thick brown socks. She's limping, actually. She sees us and looks like she wants to run, but obviously she can't: we're a wall of people coming jaggedly toward her. Damon goes first, taking up so much of the center of the hallway that the girl has to move aside. I go next, not looking at her, holding Nell's hand, which she has backtracked to put in mine. I sense that Nell is looking at the floor.

"Hey, you scuzzes, you might see if you could help me, since I've probably got a broken ankle," the girl says. It stops me in my tracks. I turn around and see her sidling up to the side wall of the hallway. One sock is unrolled almost to her ankle. As I look down, I see blood on it. I'm about to go to her, in spite of how much I dislike her, and in spite of how nastily she spoke to us, when I see her begin to fall. Lyric has hung behind to topple her, hard. I watch in horror as she reaches out and pokes her fingers in the falling girl's chest. "Fuck you," Lyric says. "You're not a human being." I'm stunned. Stunned. I look for Damon, as if, being the oldest, he'll surely do something, but he's already made it out the door.

"Lyric," I gasp. "What did you do?" But I don't stop to find out. Coward that I am—or maybe because I'm so numb I've become robotic—I grab Nell's hand tightly and keep walking. Maybe I just imagined that all that happened. It happened in about six seconds, didn't it? Could I really be hearing the girl, wailing, way back behind the closed door?

"Listen: in this world, you've got to do what you've got to do," Lyric says as she stalks past me, tossing her hair to one side. When she catches up with Damon, she slips her hand into his. He picks up the beat automatically when he takes her hand. Together, they go quickly up the stairs to the next level.

Nell's thumb is back in her mouth. She lags behind, keeping pace with me, while I try to catch my breath. Ahead of us, I see Damon and Lyric stopping at the ticket kiosk. There are a lot of people clustered around, but they don't seem to be in line. They're standing and staring, I see, as we come closer, at a blond girl in a bustier and short-shorts, and her biker boyfriend. A flashbulb goes off. They're movie stars, apparently. But which movie stars? I suddenly feel old and disconnected and—I've felt this since Lyric first confided in me—discouraged and depressed. The man has long, dirty hair, so dark it must be dyed black, and wears boots with spurs and a torn black T-shirt with a heavy chain around the middle. His arms are covered with tattoos. The girl's diamond earrings flash in the sun. "They look just like them," a woman holding a little boy's hand says to me, as I edge nearer.

"Tom Selleck?" Nell says, getting the drift of what's going on. Recently, she's heard Tom Selleck's name mentioned a lot.

The woman looks taken aback. "No. Pamela Anderson and Tommy Lee," she says in a stage whisper. "But they're not really them. They've just made themselves up to look like them."

"The tatts are fake, man," a teenage boy says to his friend. "You can always tell." The boy he speaks to has a tattoo of a coiling serpent that is certainly not fake on his biceps. They stand there, shaking their heads at the impostors. Pamela Anderson has on the brightest pink lipstick I have ever seen. Tommy Lee's boots are made from reptile's skin: some reptile with big, black scales. Meanwhile, Damon and Lyric begin to walk away. Damon drops his arm over Lyric's shoulder. In his other hand, he clasps our tickets.

"That little girl thought Tommy Lee was Tom Selleck," I overhear the woman saying to her son, as we walk away. "Can you imagine that?"

Several Rollerbladers make a path around us, going in the direction of the steps. I keep walking without looking back, but by now there's no wailing: only the sound of wheels receding, and of the breeze. It gets much cooler in Park City about six o'clock. You need a jacket, which I forgot to wear. Nell, too, has hunched her shoulders in the cold. Lyric has on a cotton V-neck sweater over her khakis. Damon has on his leather jacket, which he snatched off the antler coat hook on our way out the front door.

Nell skips ahead as we get closer to the ride. The ski lifts that take passengers to the top are rising. Far in the distance, a few riders on little toboggan-like slides come down a track cut into the mountain. There's almost no line. A group of kids runs into line ahead of us, and a middle-aged man and his gray-haired wife, expressing great doubt about going on the ride, get in line next. The woman is saying exactly what I'm thinking: that she isn't that fond of height; that it looks like a long way up the mountain. Her husband chides her; she'll be fine. Didn't she ride the roller coaster at Coney Island and survive? "They don't make these things so people will get hurt and sue them," the man says, patting his wife's bottom.

"Three to a lift," a teenage boy calls out to the man and woman in front of Lyric and Damon. He stands where the ski lifts round the bend and slow slightly.

"You mean we go with one of them?" the man says to the attendant.

"Not you, them," the attendant hollers, grabbing a car and slowing it ever so slightly for the children to jump on. "Three to a car! No doubles!" he hollers again.

When everyone from their squirmy, excited group is gone, there is one extra boy. He rushes toward the next car and tries to jump on, but a second attendant, in the field, shouts something I can't understand, and the teenage boy puts his arm out, forcing the little boy back in line.

"Step forward! Stand in the footprints!" the attendant says, darting forward to tap his toe on one of three pairs of yellow feet lined up on the mat. He jerks his leg back just before his knee is sideswiped. The boy hesitates, not sure what to do.

"Do we go together?" the middle-aged man says, but before there is any answer, the boy has boarded the lift, sinking in so heavily that it swings wildly from side to side, and the attendant is urging the man into the car, as the man tugs his wife's hand. "Slow it up, okay, open it up again," the attendant hollers. "Oh! My!" I hear the woman exclaim, and then the couple and the boy begin to rise.

So how is it going to work out with four of us? Lyric is already standing soldier-straight in the yellow footprints, but Damon, having heard all the shouting about three to a car, looks over his shoulder at us. "Get in, move!" the attendant says, and suddenly Lyric and Damon are swinging in front of us, being lifted away, the pulley rolling them up the cables. I see Damon put his arm around Lyric. I see her hair float backward. I am, frankly, mesmerized by the sight of the two of them, so that I don't see what's happening with the circling ski lifts, and when the next one comes around, it almost hits me in the head. I duck, and it gets away without either of us in it. Nell is suddenly pulling hard on my hand. What does she want? If she's saying anything, I can't hear her because of the escalating exchange between the two attendants. "Get 'em in! No more empties!" the boy who is farther away hollers, and suddenly I find myself pushed from behind, resting precariously on one hip in the rising lift, scrambling to hold on to the dangling Nell, who is facing me, her belly on the lift, her legs dangling as we rise above the receding green field. "Wait!" I scream hysterically. She seems to weigh twice what she normally does, and I know I'll pitch too far forward myself if I release my grip on the pole on my side of the swaying lift. Suddenly, having leaped an amazing height from the ground, a young man is in our car, pulling—he's got Nell by her waistband at the same time I'm seizing her arm, and he is making good progress in getting her turned forward and seated, though she is screaming so much she can't hear anything he says. At first I think one of the attendants must have jumped on, but when I catch my breath enough to look at the man I see he's just another visitor to the park: a geeky guy in glasses and a baseball cap whose concern seems to be as much about me as about Nell. He is telling me that if the height is bothering me, not to look down. I immediately look down. Someone says, "I don't like height very much," but it's not my voice, it's a little voice inside my head. The ground is bubbling like the hot tub. Some tiny animal zigzags far below. Except for the echo of the little voice, it is preternaturally quiet as we ascend: a swarming, all-enveloping silence. Black specks rise in front of my eyes, like mist. Tears are pouring from my eyes. "Hey, have you ever been on one of these rides before?" the man asks, trying to make light of my near swoon and trying to calm Nell at the same time. "Sit down, honey. We're all taking a ride up the mountain," the man says, reasonably. I see the man's arm tightly around Nell, hooking a seat belt across our car with his free hand. They don't even put seat belts on down there? They didn't even stop the ride when a three-year-old child. . . . But that's it, and then it's blackout. When I come to, I'm lying on the ground at the top of the mountain and people are staring down at me. My hand hurts. I pull it from underneath me and the young man touches my wrist, frowning, then delicately places my hand on my stomach. He continues fanning me, demanding that everyone step back. Nell. Where's Nell? Where is Nell?

Then I see her, in Damon's arms. He's taken off his leather jacket and is holding her in the big black bunting, as she alternately rubs her eyes and struggles to run to my side. She almost died. The kids who run the ride are crazy. What if my reflexes hadn't been as good as they were? What if the man hadn't jumped in the car?

"Jeez, I guess you weren't kidding when you said you didn't like height," the man says to me. People peer over his shoulder. Aspen leaves rustle behind their heads in the breeze: first green, then silver, then green. I see the cloudless, dark-blue evening sky. I don't even want to think of how I'll get off the mountain. Not by riding the Alpine Slide down, that's for sure. My face is wet with tears and perspiration. Lyric is looking deep enough into my eyes to see her own reflection. Remembering what Nikki said to me, I try to look deep into hers, but she wavers out of focus. "You scared me," she says, cupping her hand over my painful wrist.

"We're even," I say.

The ski lifts dangle going down the mountain like big black spiders. The silence, except for the people's whispered voices, is astonishing. The near crisis has slowed everything down, and everyone on top of the mountain, me among them, is temporarily stranded in the cold and silence. Nell bounces in Damon's arms, stretching one hand toward me. He holds her tight. Is it possible, I wonder hazily, that he only made one mistake, one time? And also: Is it possible that he, too, might love Nell?

The man—my savior; our savior—can't disguise his worry. He is adding to the breeze by fanning me more. It's as if he's enacting some weird ritual. He leans close, and I'm sure he's going to confide in me what it is he's really doing: that he's exorcising demons, or keeping away ghosts. "Next time, remember to ask for a slow start," he says. He has stopped fanning and has decided to try to warm me, instead. "I know right this minute you don't think you'll ever be on it again, but believe me, eventually you will. And the one thing you've got to remember"— he lowers his voice, his lips almost touching my ear—"the one thing you've got to remember next time is to request a slow start."

DISTORTIONS

VERMONT

Noel is in our living room shaking his head. He refused my offer and then David's offer of a drink, but he has had three glasses of water. It is absurd to wonder at such a time when he will get up to go to the bathroom, but I do. I would like to see Noel move; he seems so rigid that I forget to sympathize, forget that he is a real person. "That's not what I want," he said to David when David began sympathizing. Absurd, at such a time, to ask what he does want. I can't remember how it came about that David started bringing glasses of water.

Noel's wife, Susan, has told him that she's been seeing John Stillerman. We live on the first floor, Noel and Susan on the second, John on the eleventh. Interesting that John, on the eleventh, should steal Susan from the second floor. John proposes that they just rearrange—that Susan move up to the eleventh, into the apartment John's wife only recently left, that they just . . . John's wife had a mastectomy last fall, and in the elevator she told Susan that if she was losing what she didn't want to lose, she might as well lose what she did want to lose. She lost John— left him the way popcorn flies out of the bag on the roller coaster. She is living somewhere in the city, but John doesn't know where. John is a museum curator, and last month, after John's picture appeared in a newsmagazine, showing him standing in front of an empty space where a stolen canvas had hung, he got a one-word note from his wife: "Good." He showed the note to David in the elevator. "It was tucked in the back of his wallet—the way all my friends used to carry rubbers in high school," David told me.

"Did you guys know?" Noel asks. A difficult one; of course we didn't *know*, but naturally we guessed. Is Noel able to handle such semantics? David answers vaguely. Noel shakes his head vaguely, accepting David's vague answer. What else will he accept? The move upstairs? For now, another glass of water.

David gives Noel a sweater, hoping, no doubt, to stop his shivering. Noel pulls on the sweater over pajamas patterned with small gray fish. David brings him a raincoat, too. A long white scarf hangs from the pocket. Noel swishes it back and forth listlessly. He gets up and goes to the bathroom.

"Why did she have to tell him when he was in his pajamas?" David whispers.

Noel comes back, looks out the window. "I don't know why I didn't know. I can tell you guys knew."

Noel goes to our front door, opens it, and wanders off down the hallway.

"If he had stayed any longer, he would have said, 'Jeepers,' " David says.

David looks at his watch and sighs. Usually he opens Beth's door on his way to bed, and tiptoes in to admire her. Beth is our daughter. She is five. Some nights, David even leaves a note in her slippers, saying that he loves her. But tonight he's depressed. I follow him into the bedroom, undress, and get into bed. David looks at me sadly, lies down next to me, turns off the light. I want to say something but don't know what to say. I could say, "One of us should have gone with Noel. Do you know your socks are still on? You're going to do to me what Susan did to Noel, aren't you?"

"Did you see his poor miserable pajamas?" David whispers finally. He throws back the covers and gets up and goes back to the living room. I follow, half asleep. David sits in the chair, puts his arms on the armrests, presses his neck against the back of the chair, and moves his feet together. "Zzzz," he says, and his head falls forward.

Back in bed, I lie awake, remembering a day David and I spent in the park last August. David was sitting on the swing next to me, scraping the toes of his tennis shoes in the loose dirt.

"Don't you want to swing?" I said. We had been playing tennis. He had beaten me every game. He always beats me at everything—precision parking, three-dimensional ticktacktoe, soufflés. His soufflés rise as beautifully curved as the moon.

"I don't know how to swing," he said.

I tried to teach him, but he couldn't get his legs to move right. He stood the way I told him, with the board against his behind, gave a little jump to get on, but then he couldn't synchronize his legs. "Pump!" I called, but it didn't mean anything. I might as well have said, "Juggle dishes." I still find it hard to believe there's anything I can do that he can't do.

He got off the swing. "Why do you act like everything is a goddamn contest?" he said, and walked away.

"Because we're always having contests and you always win!" I shouted.

I was still waiting by the swings when he showed up half an hour later.

"Do you consider it a contest when we go scuba diving?" he said.

He had me. It was stupid of me last summer to say how he always snatched the best shells, even when they were closer to me. That made him laugh. He had chased me into a corner, then laughed at me.

I lie in bed now, hating him for that. But don't leave me, I think—don't do what Noel's wife did. I reach across the bed and gently take hold of a little wrinkle in his pajama top. I don't know if I want to yank his pajamas—do something violent—or smooth them. Confused, I take my hand away and turn on the light. David rolls over, throws his arm over his face, groans. I stare at him. In a second he will lower his arm and demand an explanation. Trapped again. I get up and put on my slippers.

"I'm going to get a drink of water," I whisper apologetically.

Later in the month, it happens. I'm sitting on a cushion on the floor, with newspapers spread in front of me, repotting plants. I'm just moving the purple passion plant to a larger pot when David comes in. It is late in the afternoon—late enough to be dark outside. David has been out with Beth. Before the two of them went out, Beth, confused by the sight of soil indoors, crouched down beside me to ask, "Are there ants, Mommy?" I laughed. David never approved of my laughing at her. Later, that will be something he'll mention in court, hoping to get custody: I laugh at her. And when that doesn't work, he'll tell the judge what I said about his snatching all the best seashells.

David comes in, coat still buttoned, blue silk scarf still tied (a Christmas present from Noel, with many apologies for losing the white one), sits on the floor, and says that he's decided to leave. He is speaking very reasonably and quietly. That alarms me. It crosses my mind that he's mad. And Beth isn't with him. He has killed her!

No, no, of course not. I'm mad. Beth is upstairs in her friend's apartment. He ran into Beth's friend and her mother coming into the building. He asked if Beth could stay in their apartment for a few minutes. I'm not convinced: What friend? I'm foolish to feel reassured as soon as he names one—Louisa. I feel nothing but relief. It might be more accurate to say that I feel nothing. I would have felt pain if she were dead, but David says she isn't, so I feel nothing. I reach out and begin stroking the plant's leaves. Soft leaves, sharp points. The plant I'm repotting is a cutting from Noel's big plant that hangs in a silver ice bucket in his window (a wedding gift that he and Susan had never used). I helped him put it in the ice bucket. "What are you going to do with the top?" I asked. He put it on his head and danced around.

"I had an uncle who got drunk and danced with a lampshade on his head," Noel said. "That's an old joke, but how many people have actually *seen* a man dance with a lampshade on his head? My uncle did it every New Year's Eve."

"What the hell are you smiling about?" David says. "Are you listening to me?"

I nod and start to cry. It will be a long time before I realize that David makes me sad and Noel makes me happy.

Noel sympathizes with me. He tells me that David is a fool; he is better off without Susan, and I will be better off without David. Noel calls or visits me in my new apartment almost every night. Last night he suggested that I get a babysitter for tonight, so he could take me to dinner. He tries very hard to make me happy. He brings expensive wine when we eat in my apartment and offers to buy it in restaurants when we eat out. Beth prefers it when we eat in; that way, she can have both Noel and the toy that Noel inevitably brings. Her favorite toy, so far, is a handsome red tugboat pulling three barges, attached to one another by string. Noel bends over, almost doubled in half, to move them across the rug, whistling and calling orders to the imaginary crew. He does not just bring gifts to Beth and me. He has bought himself a new car, and pretends that this is for Beth and me. ("Comfortable seats?" he asks me. "That's a nice big window back there to wave out of," he says to Beth.) It is silly to pretend that he got the car for the three of us. And if he did, why was he too cheap to have a radio installed, when he knows I love music? Not only that but he's bowlegged. I am ashamed of myself for thinking bad things about Noel. He tries so hard to keep us cheerful. He can't help the odd angle of his thighs. Feeling sorry for him, I decided that a cheap dinner was good enough for tonight. I said that I wanted to go to a Chinese restaurant.

At the restaurant I eat shrimp in black bean sauce and drink a Heineken and think that I've never tasted anything so delicious. The waiter brings two fortune cookies. We open them; the fortunes make no sense. Noel summons the waiter for the bill. With it come more fortune cookies—four this time. They are no good either: talk of travel and money. Noel says, "What bloody rot." He is wearing a gray vest and a white shirt. I peek around the table without his noticing and see that he's wearing gray wool slacks. Lately it has been very important for me to be able to see everything. Whenever Noel pulls the boats out of sight, into another room, I move as quickly as Beth to watch what's going on.

Standing behind Noel at the cash register, I see that it has started to rain—a mixture of rain and snow.

"You know how you can tell a Chinese restaurant from any other?" Noel asks, pushing open the door. "Even when it's raining, the cats still run for the street."

I shake my head in disgust.

Noel stretches the skin at the corners of his eyes. "Sorry for honorable joke," he says.

We run for the car. He grabs the belt of my coat, catches me, and half lifts me with one arm, running along with me dangling at his side, giggling. Our wool coats stink. He opens my car door, runs around, and pulls his open. He's done it again; he has made me laugh.

We start home.

We are in heavy traffic, and Noel drives very slowly, protecting his new car.

"How old are you?" I ask.

"Thirty-six," Noel says.

"I'm twenty-seven," I say.

"So what?" he says. He says it pleasantly.

"I just didn't know how old you were."

"Mentally, I'm neck and neck with Beth," he says.

I'm soaking wet, and I want to get home to put on dry clothes. I look at him inching through traffic, and I remember the way his face looked that night he sat in the living room with David and me.

"Rain always puts you in a bad mood, doesn't it?" he says. He turns the windshield wipers on high. Rubber squeaks against glass.

"I see myself dead in it," I say.

"You see yourself dead in it?"

Noel does not read novels. He reads *Moneysworth*, the *Wall Street*

Journal, Commentary. I reprimand myself; there must be fitting ironies in the *Wall Street Journal.*

"Are you kidding?" Noel says. "You seemed to be enjoying yourself at dinner. It was a good dinner, wasn't it?"

"I make you nervous, don't I?" I say.

"No. You don't make me nervous."

Rain splashes under the car, drums on the roof. We ride on for blocks and blocks. It is too quiet; I wish there were a radio. The rain on the roof is monotonous, the collar of my coat is wet and cold. At last we are home. Noel parks the car and comes around to my door and opens it. I get out. Noel pulls me close, squeezes me hard. When I was a little girl, I once squeezed a doll to my chest in an antique shop, and when I took it away the eyes had popped off. An unpleasant memory. With my arms around Noel, I feel the cold rain hitting my hands and wrists.

A man running down the sidewalk with a small dog in his arms and a big black umbrella over him calls, "Your lights are on!"

It is almost a year later—Christmas—and we are visiting Noel's crazy sister, Juliette. After going with Noel for so long, I am considered one of the family. Juliette phones before every occasion, saying, "You're one of the family. Of course you don't need an invitation." I should appreciate it, but she's always drunk when she calls, and usually she starts to cry and says she wishes Christmas and Thanksgiving didn't exist. Jeanette, his other sister, is very nice, but she lives in Colorado. Juliette lives in New Jersey. Here we are in Bayonne, New Jersey, coming in through the front door—Noel holding Beth, me carrying a pumpkin pie. I tried to sniff the pie aroma on the way from Noel's apartment to his sister's house, but it had no smell. Or else I'm getting another cold. I sucked chewable vitamin C tablets in the car, and now I smell of oranges. Noel's mother is in the living room, crocheting. Better, at least, than David's mother, who was always discoursing about Andrew Wyeth. I remember with satisfaction that the last time I saw her I said, "It's a simple fact that Edward Hopper was better."

Juliette: long, whitish-blond hair tucked in back of her pink ears, spike-heel shoes that she orders from Frederick's of Hollywood, dresses that show her cleavage. Noel and I are silently wondering if her husband will be here. At Thanksgiving he showed up just as we were starting dinner, with a black-haired woman who wore a dress with a plunging neckline. Juliette's breasts faced the black-haired woman's breasts across the table (tablecloth crocheted by Noel's mother). Noel doesn't like me to criticize Juliette. He thinks positively. His other sister is a musician. She has a husband and a weimaraner and two rare birds that live in a bird-cage built by her husband. They have a lot of money and they ski. They have adopted a Korean boy. Once, they showed us a film of the Korean boy learning to ski. Wham, wham, wham—every few seconds he was groveling in the snow again.

Juliette is such a liberal that she gives us not only the same bedroom but a bedroom with only a single bed in it. Beth sleeps on the couch.

Wedged beside Noel that night, I say, "This is ridiculous."

"She means to be nice," he says. "Where else would we sleep?"

"She could let us have her double bed and she could sleep in here. After all, he's not coming back, Noel."

"Shh."

"Wouldn't that have been better?"

"What do you care?" Noel says. "You're nuts about me, right?"

He slides up against me and hugs my back.

"I don't know how people talk anymore," he says. "I don't know any of the current lingo. What expression do people use for 'nuts about'?"

"I don't know."

"I just did it again! I said 'lingo.' "

"So what? Who do you want to sound like?"

"The way I talk sounds dated—like an old person."

"Why are you always worried about being old?"

He snuggles closer. "You didn't answer before when I said you were nuts about me. That doesn't mean that you don't like me, does it?"

"No."

"You're big on the one-word answers."

"I'm big on going to sleep."

" 'Big on.' See? There must be some expression to replace that now."

I sit in the car, waiting for Beth to come out of the building where the ballet school is. She has been taking lessons, but they haven't helped. She still slouches forward and sticks out her neck when she walks. Noel suggests that this might be analyzed psychologically; she sticks her neck out, you see, not only literally but . . . Noel thinks that Beth is waiting to get it. Beth feels guilty because her mother and father have just been divorced. She thinks that she played some part in it and therefore she deserves to get it. It is worth fifty dollars a month for ballet lessons to disprove Noel's theory. If it will only work.

. . .

I spend the day in the park, thinking over Noel's suggestion that I move in with him. We would have more money. . . . We are together so much anyway. . . . Or he could move in with me, if those big windows in my place are really so important. I always meet reasonable men.

"But I don't love you," I said to Noel. "Don't you want to live with somebody who loves you?"

"Nobody has ever loved me and nobody ever will," Noel said. "What have I got to lose?"

I am in the park to think about what I have to lose. Nothing. So why don't I leave the park, call him at work, say that I have decided it is a very sensible plan?

A chubby little boy wanders by, wearing a short jacket and pants that are slipping down. He is holding a yellow boat. He looks so damned pleased with everything that I think about accosting him and asking, "Should I move in with Noel? Why am I reluctant to do it?" The young have such wisdom—some of the best and worst thinkers have thought so: Wordsworth, the followers of the Guru Maharaj Ji . . . "Do the meditations, or I will beat you with a stick," the guru tells his followers. Tell me the answer, kid, or I will take away your boat.

I sink down onto a bench. Next, Noel will ask me to marry him. He is trying to trap me. Worse, he is not trying to trap me but only wants me to move in so we can save money. He doesn't care about me. Since no one has ever loved him, he can't love anybody. Is that even true?

I find a phone booth and stand in front of it, waiting for a woman with a shopping bag to get out. She mouths something I don't understand. She has lips like a fish; they are painted bright orange. I do not have any lipstick on. I have on a raincoat, pulled over my nightgown, and sandals and Noel's socks.

"Noel," I say on the phone when I reach him, "were you serious when you said that no one ever loved you?"

"Jesus, it was embarrassing enough just to admit it," he says. "Do you have to question me about it?"

"I have to know."

"Well, I've told you about every woman I ever slept with. Which one do you suspect might have loved me?"

I have ruined his day. I hang up, rest my head against the phone. "Me," I mumble. "I do." I reach in the raincoat pocket. A Kleenex, two pennies, and a pink rubber spider put there by Beth to scare me. No more dimes. I push open the door. A young woman is standing there waiting for me. "Do you have a few moments?" she says.

"Why?"

"Do you have a moment? What do you think of this?" she says. It is a small stick with the texture of salami. In her other hand she holds a clipboard and a pen.

"I don't have time," I say, and walk away. I stop and turn. "What is that, anyway?" I ask.

"Do you have a moment?" she asks.

"No. I just wanted to know what that thing was."

"A dog treat."

She is coming after me, clipboard outstretched.

"I don't have time," I say, and quickly walk away.

Something hits my back. "Take the time to stick it up your ass," she says.

I run for a block before I stop and lean on the park wall to rest. If Noel had been there, she wouldn't have done it. My protector. If I had a dime, I could call back and say, "Oh, Noel, I'll live with you always if you'll stay with me so people won't throw dog treats at me."

I finger the plastic spider. Maybe Beth put it there to cheer me up. Once, she put a picture of a young, beautiful girl in a bikini on my bedroom wall. I misunderstood, seeing the woman as all that I was not. Beth just thought it was a pretty picture. She didn't understand why I was so upset.

"Mommy's just upset because when you put things on the wall with Scotch tape, the Scotch tape leaves a mark when you remove it," Noel told her.

Noel is wonderful. I reach in my pocket, hoping a dime will suddenly appear.

Noel and I go to visit his friends Charles and Sol, in Vermont. Noel has taken time off from work; it is a vacation to celebrate our decision to live together. Now, on the third evening there, we are all crowded around the hearth—Noel and Beth and I, Charles and Sol and the women they live with, Lark and Margaret. We are smoking and listening to Sol's stereo. The hearth is a big one. It was laid by Sol, made out of slate he took from the side of a hill and bricks he found dumped by the side of the road. There is a mantel that was made by Charles from a section of an old carousel he picked up when a local amusement park closed down; a gargoyle's head protrudes from one side. Car keys have been draped over the beast's eyebrows. On top of the mantel there is an L. L. Bean catalog, Margaret's hat, roaches and a roach clip, a can of peaches, and an incense burner that holds a small cone in a puddle of lavender ashes.

Noel used to work with Charles in the city. Charles quit when he heard about a big house in Vermont that needed to be fixed up. He was told that he could live in it for a hundred dollars a month, except in January and February, when skiers rented it. The skiers turned out to be nice people who didn't want to see anyone displaced. They suggested that the four stay on in the house, and they did, sleeping in a side room that Charles and Sol fixed up. Just now, the rest of the house is empty; it has been raining a lot, ruining the skiing.

Sol has put up some pictures he framed—old advertisements he found in a box in the attic (after Charles repaired the attic stairs). I study the pictures now, in the firelight. The Butter Lady—a healthy coquette with pearly skin and a mildewed bottom lip—extends a hand offering a package of butter. On the wall across from her, a man with oil-slick black hair holds a shoe that is the same color as his hair.

"When you're lost in the rain in Juarez and it's Eastertime, too," Dylan sings.

Margaret says to Beth, "Do you want to come take a bath with me?"

Beth is shy. The first night we were here, she covered her eyes when Sol walked naked from the bathroom to the bedroom.

"I don't have to take a bath while I'm here, do I?" she says to me.

"Where did you get that idea?"

"Why do I have to take a bath?"

But she decides to go with Margaret, and runs after her and grabs on to her wool sash. Margaret blows on the incense stick she has just lit, and fans it in the air, and Beth, enchanted, follows her out of the room. She already feels at ease in the house, and she likes us all and wanders off with anyone gladly, even though she's usually shy. Yesterday, Sol showed her how to punch down the bread before putting it on the baking sheet to rise once more. He let her smear butter over the loaves with her fingers and then sprinkle cornmeal on the top.

Sol teaches at the state university. He is a poet, and he has been hired to teach a course in the modern novel. "Oh, well," he is saying now. "If I weren't a queer and I'd gone into the army, I guess they would have made me a cook. That's usually what they do, isn't it?"

"Don't ask me," Charles says. "I'm queer, too." This seems to be an old routine.

Noel is admiring the picture frames. "This is such a beautiful place," he says. "I'd love to live here for good."

"Don't be a fool," Sol says. "With a lot of fairies?"

Sol is reading a student's paper. "This student says, 'Humbert is just like a million other Americans,' " he says.

"Humbert?" Noel says.

"You know—that guy who ran against Nixon."

"Come on," Noel says. "I know it's from some novel."

"*Lolita,*" Lark says, all on the intake. She passes the joint to me.

"Why don't you quit that job?" Lark says. "You hate it."

"I can't be unemployed," Sol says. "I'm a faggot and a poet. I've already got two strikes against me." He puffs twice on the roach, lets it slip out of the clip to the hearth. "And a drug abuser," he says. "I'm as good as done for."

"I'm sorry you feel that way, dear," Charles says, putting his hand gently on Sol's shoulder. Sol jumps. Charles and Noel laugh.

It is time for dinner—moussaka, and bread, and wine that Noel brought.

"What's moussaka?" Beth asks. Her skin shines, and her hair has dried in small narrow ridges where Margaret combed it.

"Made with mice," Sol says.

Beth looks at Noel. Lately, she checks things out with him. He shakes his head no. Actually, she is not a dumb child; she probably looked at Noel because she knows it makes him happy.

Beth has her own room—the smallest bedroom, with a fur rug on the floor and a quilt to sleep under. As I talk to Lark after dinner, I hear Noel reading to Beth: "*The Trout Fishing Diary of Alonso Hagen.*" Soon Beth is giggling.

I sit in Noel's lap, looking out the window at the fields, white and flat, and the mountains—a blur that I know is mountains. The radiator under the window makes the glass foggy. Noel leans forward to wipe it with a handkerchief. We are in winter now. We were going to leave Vermont after a week—then two, now three. Noel's hair is getting long. Beth has missed a month of school. What will the Board of Education do to me? "What do you think they're going to do?" Noel says. "Come after us with guns?"

Noel has just finished confiding in me another horrendous or mortifying thing he would never, never tell anyone and that I must swear not to repeat. The story is about something that happened when he was eighteen. There was a friend of his mother's whom he threatened to strangle if she didn't let him sleep with her. She let him. As soon as it was over, he was terrified that she would tell someone, and he threatened to strangle her if she did. But he realized that as soon as he left she could talk, and that he could be arrested, and he got so upset that he broke down and ran back to the bed where they had been, pulled the covers over his head, and shook and cried. Later, the woman told his mother that Noel seemed to be studying too hard at Princeton—perhaps he needed some time off. A second story was about how he tried to kill himself when his wife left him. The truth was that he couldn't give

David his scarf back because it was stretched from being knotted so many times. But he had been too chicken to hang himself and he had swallowed a bottle of drugstore sleeping pills instead. Then he got frightened and went outside and hailed a cab. Another couple, huddled together in the wind, told him that they had claimed the cab first. The same couple was in the waiting room of the hospital when he came to.

"The poor guy put his card next to my hand on the stretcher," Noel says, shaking his head so hard that his beard scrapes my cheek. "He was a plumber. Eliot Raye. And his wife, Flora."

A warm afternoon. "Noel!" Beth cries, running across the soggy lawn toward him, her hand extended like a fisherman's with his catch. But there's nothing in her hand—only a little spot of blood on the palm. Eventually he gets the story out of her: she fell. He will bandage it. He is squatting, his arm folding her close like some giant bird. A heron? An eagle? Will he take my child and fly away? They walk toward the house, his hand pressing Beth's head against his leg.

We are back in the city. Beth is asleep in the room that was once Noel's study. I am curled up in Noel's lap. He has just asked to hear the story of Michael again.

"Why do you want to hear that?" I ask.

Noel is fascinated by Michael, who pushed his furniture into the hall and threw his small possessions out the window into the backyard and then put up four large, connecting tents in his apartment. There was a hot plate in there, cans of Franco-American spaghetti, bottles of good wine, a flashlight for when it got dark. . . .

Noel urges me to remember more details. What else was in the tent?

A rug, but that just happened to be on the floor. For some reason, he didn't throw the rug out the window. And there was a sleeping bag. . . .

What else?

Comic books. I don't remember which ones. A lemon-meringue pie. I remember how disgusting that was after two days, with the sugar ooz-ing out of the meringue. A bottle of Seconal. There was a drinking glass, a container of warm juice . . . I don't remember.

We used to make love in the tent. I'd go over to see him, open the front door, and crawl in. That summer he collapsed the tents, threw them in his car, and left for Maine.

"Go on," Noel says.

I shrug. I've told this story twice before, and this is always my stop-ping place.

"That's it," I say to Noel.

He continues to wait expectantly, just as he did the two other times he heard the story.

One evening, we get a phone call from Lark. There is a house near them for sale—only thirty thousand dollars. What Noel can't fix, Charles and Sol can help with. There are ten acres of land, a waterfall. Noel is wild to move there. But what are we going to do for money, I ask him. He says we'll worry about that in a year or so, when we run out. But we haven't even seen the place, I point out. But this is a fabulous find, he says. We'll go see it this weekend. Noel has Beth so excited that she wants to start school in Vermont on Monday, not come back to the city at all. We will just go to the house right this minute and live there forever.

But does he know how to do the wiring? Is he sure it can be wired?

"Don't you have any faith in me?" he says. "David always thought I was a chump, didn't he?"

"I'm only asking whether you can do such complicated things."

My lack of faith in Noel has made him unhappy. He leaves the room without answering. He probably remembers—and knows that I re-member—the night he asked David if he could see what was wrong with the socket of his floor lamp. David came back to our apartment laugh-ing. "The plug had come out of the outlet," he said.

In early April, David comes to visit us in Vermont for the weekend with his girlfriend, Patty. She wears blue jeans, and has kohl around her eyes. She is twenty years old. Her clogs echo loudly on the bare floorboards. She seems to feel awkward here. David seems not to feel awkward, al-though he looked surprised when Beth called him David. She led him through the woods, running ahead of Noel and me, to show him the waterfall. When she got too far ahead, I called her back, afraid, for some reason, that she might die. If I lost sight of her, she might die. I suppose I had always thought that if David and I spent time together again it would be over the hospital bed of our dying daughter—something like that.

Patty has trouble walking in the woods; the clogs flop off her feet in the brush. I tried to give her a pair of my sneakers, but she wears size $8^1/_2$ and I am a 7. Another thing to make her feel awkward.

David breathes in dramatically. "Quite a change from the high-rise we used to live in," he says to Noel.

Calculated to make us feel rotten?

"You used to live in a high-rise?" Patty asks.

He must have just met her. She pays careful attention to everything he says, watches with interest when he snaps off a twig and breaks it in little pieces. She is having trouble keeping up. David finally notices her difficulty in keeping up with us, and takes her hand. They're city people; they don't even have hiking boots.

"It seems as if that was in another life," David says. He snaps off a small branch and flicks one end of it against his thumb.

"There's somebody who says that every time we sleep we die; we come back another person, to another life," Patty says.

"Kafka as realist," Noel says.

Noel has been reading all winter. He has read Brautigan, a lot of Borges, and has gone from Dante to García Márquez to Hilma Wolitzer to Kafka. Sometimes I ask him why he is going about it this way. He had me make him a list—this writer before that one, which poems are early, which late, which famous. Well, it doesn't matter. Noel is happy in Vermont. Being in Vermont means that he can do what he wants to do. Freedom, you know. Why should I make fun of it? He loves his books, loves roaming around in the woods outside the house, and he buys more birdseed than all the birds in the North could eat. He took a Polaroid picture of our salt lick for the deer when he put it in, and admired both the salt lick ("They've been here!") and his picture. Inside the house there are Polaroids of the woods, the waterfall, some rabbits—he tacks them up with pride, the way Beth hangs up the pictures she draws in school. "You know," Noel said to me one night, "when Gatsby is talking to Nick Carraway and he says, 'In any case, it was just personal'—what does that mean?"

"When did you read *Gatsby*?" I asked.

"Last night, in the bathtub."

As we turn to walk back, Noel points out the astonishing number of squirrels in the trees around us. By David's expression, he thinks Noel is pathetic.

I look at Noel. He is taller than David but more stooped; thinner than David, but his slouch disguises it. Noel has big hands and feet and a sharp nose. His scarf is gray, with frayed edges. David's is bright red, just bought. Poor Noel. When David called to say he and Patty were coming for a visit, Noel never thought of saying no. And he asked me how he could compete with David. He thought David was coming to his house to win me away. After he reads more literature he'll realize that is too easy. There will have to be complexities. The complexities will protect him forever. Hours after David's call, he said (to himself, really—not to me) that David was bringing a woman with him. Surely that meant he wouldn't try anything.

Charles and Margaret come over just as we are finishing dinner, bringing a mattress we are borrowing for David and Patty to sleep on. They are both stoned, and are dragging the mattress on the ground, which is white with a late snow. They are too stoned to hoist it.

"Eventide," Charles says. A circular black barrette holds his hair out of his face. Margaret lost her hat to Lark some time ago and never got around to borrowing another one. Her hair is dusted with snow. "We have to go," Charles says, weighing her hair in his hands, "before the snow woman melts."

Sitting at the kitchen table late that night, I turn to David. "How are you doing?" I whisper.

"A lot of things haven't been going the way I figured," he whispers.

I nod. We are drinking white wine and eating cheddar-cheese soup. The soup is scalding. Clouds of steam rise from the bowl, and I keep my face away from it, worrying that the steam will make my eyes water, and that David will misinterpret.

"Not really things. People," David whispers, bobbing an ice cube up and down in his wineglass with his index finger.

"What people?"

"It's better not to talk about it. They're not really people you know."

That hurts, and he knew it would hurt. But climbing the stairs to go to bed I realize that, in spite of that, it's a very reasonable approach.

Tonight, as I do most nights, I sleep with long johns under my night-gown. I roll over on top of Noel for more warmth and lie there, as he has said, like a dead man, like a man in the Wild West, gunned down in the dirt. Noel jokes about this. "Pow, pow," he whispers sleepily as I lower myself on him. "Poor critter's deader 'n a doornail." I lie there warming myself. What does he want with me?

"What do you want for your birthday?" I ask.

He recites a little list of things he wants. He whispers: a bookcase, an aquarium, a blender to make milk shakes in.

"That sounds like what a ten-year-old would want," I say.

He is quiet too long; I have hurt his feelings.

"Not the bookcase," he says finally.

I am falling asleep. It's not fair to fall asleep on top of him. He doesn't have the heart to wake me and has to lie there with me sprawled on top of him until I fall off. Move, I tell myself, but I don't.

"Do you remember this afternoon, when Patty and I sat on the rock to wait for you and David and Beth?"

I remember. We were on top of the hill, Beth pulling David by his hand, David not very interested in what she was going to show him, Beth ignoring his lack of interest and pulling him along. I ran to catch up, because she was pulling him so hard, and I caught Beth's free arm and hung on, so that we formed a chain.

"I knew I'd seen that before," Noel says. "I just realized where—when the actor wakes up after the storm and sees Death leading those people winding across the hilltop in *The Seventh Seal*."

Six years ago. Seven. David and I were in the Village, in the winter, looking in a bookstore window. Tires began to squeal, and we turned around and were staring straight at a car, a ratty old blue car that had lifted a woman from the street into the air. The fall took much too long; she fell the way snow drifts—the big flakes that float down, no hurry at all. By the time she hit, though, David had pushed my face against his coat, and while everyone was screaming—it seemed as if a whole chorus had suddenly assembled to scream—he had his arms around my shoulders, pressing me so close that I could hardly breathe and saying, "If anything happened to you . . . If anything happened to you . . ."

When they leave, it is a clear, cold day. I give Patty a paper bag with half a bottle of wine, two sandwiches, and some peanuts to eat on the way back. The wine is probably not a good idea; David had three glasses of vodka and orange juice for breakfast. He began telling jokes to Noel—dogs in bars outsmarting their owners, constipated whores, talking fleas. David does not like Noel; Noel does not know what to make of David.

Now David rolls down the car window. Last-minute news. He tells me that his sister has been staying in his apartment. She aborted herself and has been very sick. "Abortions are legal," David says. "Why did she do that?" I ask how long ago it happened. A month ago, he says. His hands drum on the steering wheel. Last week, Beth got a box of wooden whistles carved in the shape of peasants from David's sister. Noel opened the kitchen window and blew softly to some birds on the feeder. They all flew away.

Patty leans across David. "There are so many animals here, even in the winter," she says. "Don't they hibernate anymore?"

She is making nervous, polite conversation. She wants to leave. Noel walks away from me to Patty's side of the car, and tells her about the deer who come right up to the house. Beth is sitting on Noel's shoulders. Not wanting to talk to David, I wave at her stupidly. She waves back.

David looks at me out the window. I must look as stiff as one of those wooden whistles, all carved out of one piece, in my old blue ski jacket and blue wool hat pulled down to my eyes and my baggy jeans.

"*Ciao*," David says. "Thanks."

"Yes," Patty says. "It was nice of you to do this." She holds up the bag.

It's a steep driveway, and rocky. David backs down cautiously—the way someone pulls a zipper after it's been caught. We wave, they disappear. That was easy.

WOLF DREAMS

When Cynthia was seventeen she married Ewell W. G. Peterson. The initials stood for "William Gordon"; his family called him William, her parents called him W.G. (letting him know that they thought his initials were pretentious), and Cynthia called him Pete, which is what his army buddies called him. Now she had been divorced from Ewell W. G. Peterson for nine years, and what he had been called was a neutral thing to remember about him. She didn't hate him. Except for his name, she hardly remembered him. At Christmas, he sent her a card signed "Pete," but only for a few years after the divorce, and then they stopped. Her second husband, whom she married when she was twenty-eight, was named Lincoln Divine. They were divorced when she was twenty-nine and a half. No Christmas cards. Now she was going to marry Charlie Pinehurst. Her family hated Charlie—or perhaps just the idea of a third marriage—but what she hated was the way Charlie's name got mixed up in her head with Pete's and Lincoln's. Ewell W. G. Peterson, Lincoln Divine, Charlie Pinehurst, she kept thinking, as if she needed to memorize them. In high school her English teacher had made her memorize poems that made no sense. There was no way you could remember what came next in those poems. She got Ds all through high school, and she didn't like the job she got after she graduated, so she was happy to marry Pete when he asked her, even if it did mean leaving her friends and her family to live on an army base. She liked it there. Her parents had told her she would never be satisfied with anything; they were surprised when it turned out that she had no complaints about living on the base. She got to know all the wives, and they had a diet club, and she lost twenty pounds, so that she got down to what she weighed when she started high school. She also worked at the local radio station, re-

cording stories and poems—she never knew why they were recorded—
and found that she didn't mind literature if she could just read it and not
have to think about it. Pete hung around with the men when he had
time off; they never really saw much of each other. He accused her of
losing weight so she could attract "a khaki lover." "One's not enough
for you?" he asked. But when he was around, he didn't want to love her;
he'd work out with the barbells in the spare bedroom. Cynthia liked
having two bedrooms. She liked the whole house. It was a frame row
house with shutters missing downstairs, but it was larger than her parents' house inside. When they moved in, all the army wives said the
same thing—that the bedroom wouldn't be spare for long. But it stayed
empty, except for the barbells and some kind of trapeze that Pete hung
from the ceiling. It was nice living on the base, though. Sometimes she
missed it.

With Lincoln, Cynthia lived in an apartment in Columbus, Ohio.
"It's a good thing you live halfway across the country," her father wrote
her, "because your mother surely does not want to see that black man,
who claims his father was a Cherappy Indian." She never met Lincoln's
parents, so she wasn't sure herself about the Indian thing. One of
Lincoln's friends, who was always trying to be her lover, told her that
Lincoln Divine wasn't even his real name—he had made it up and got
his old name legally changed when he was twenty-one. "It's like believ-
ing in Santa Claus," the friend told her. "There is no Lincoln Divine."

Charlie was different from Pete and Lincoln. Neither of them paid
much attention to her, but Charlie was attentive. During the years, she
had regained the twenty pounds she lost when she was first married and
added twenty-five more on top of that. She was going to have to get in
shape before she married Charlie, even though he wanted to marry her
now. "I'll take it as is," Charlie said. "Ready-made can be altered."
Charlie was a tailor. He wasn't really a tailor, but his brother had a
shop, and to make extra money Charlie did alterations on the weekends. Once, when they were both a little drunk, Cynthia and Charlie
vowed to tell each other a dark secret. Cynthia told Charlie she had had
an abortion just before she and Pete got divorced. Charlie was really
shocked by that. "That's why you got so fat, I guess," he said. "Happens when they fix animals, too." She didn't know what he was talking
about, and she didn't want to ask. She'd almost forgotten it herself.
Charlie's secret was that he knew how to run a sewing machine. He
thought it was "woman's work." She thought that was crazy; she had
told him something important, and he had just said he knew how to run
a sewing machine.

"We're not going to live in any apartment," Charlie said. "We're going to live in a house." And "You're not going to have to go up and down stairs. We're going to find a split-level." And "It's not going to be any neighborhood that's getting worse. Our neighborhood is going to be getting better." And "You don't have to lose weight. Why don't you marry me now, and we can get a house and start a life together?"

But she wouldn't do it. She was going to lose twenty pounds and save enough money to buy a pretty wedding dress. She had already started using more makeup and letting her hair grow, as the beauty-parlor operator had suggested, so that she could have curls that fell to her shoulders on her wedding day. She'd been reading brides' magazines, and long curls were what she thought was pretty. Charlie hated the magazines. He thought the magazines had told her to lose twenty pounds—that the magazines were responsible for keeping him waiting.

She had nightmares. A recurring nightmare was one in which she stood at the altar with Charlie, wearing a beautiful long dress, but the dress wasn't quite long enough, and everyone could see that she was standing on a scale. What did the scale say? She would wake up peering into the dark and get out of bed and go to the kitchen.

This night, as she dipped potato chips into cheddar-cheese dip, she reread a letter from her mother: "You are not a bad girl, and so I do not know why you would get married three times. Your father does not count that black man as a marriage, but I have got to, and so it is three. That's too many marriages, Cynthia. You are a good girl and know enough now to come home and settle down with your family. We are willing to look out for you, even your dad, and warn you not to make another dreadful mistake." There was no greeting, no signature. The letter had probably been dashed off by her mother when she, too, had insomnia. Cynthia would have to answer the note, but she didn't think her mother would be convinced by anything she could say. If she thought her parents would be convinced she was making the right decision by seeing Charlie, she would have asked him to meet her parents. But her parents liked people who had a lot to say, or who could make them laugh ("break the monotony," her father called it), and Charlie didn't have a lot to say. Charlie was a very serious person. He was also forty years old, and he had never been married. Her parents would want to know why that was. You couldn't please them: they hated people who were divorced and they were suspicious of single people. So she had never suggested to Charlie that he meet her parents. Finally, he suggested it himself. Cynthia thought up excuses, but Charlie saw through them. He thought it was all because he had confessed to her that he sewed. She was ashamed of him—that was the real reason she was putting off the wedding, and why she wouldn't introduce him to her parents. "No," she said. "No, Charlie. No, no, no." And because she had said it so many times, she was convinced. "Then set a date for the wedding," he told her. "You've got to say when." She promised to do that the next time she saw him, but she couldn't think right, and that was because of the notes that her mother wrote her, and because she couldn't get any sleep, and because she got depressed by taking off weight and gaining it right back by eating at night.

As long as she couldn't sleep, and there were only a few potato chips left, which she might as well finish off, she decided to level with herself the same way she and Charlie had the night they told their secrets. She asked herself why she was getting married. Part of the answer was that she didn't like her job. She was a typer—a *typist*, the other girls always said, correcting her—and also she was thirty-two, and if she didn't get married soon she might not find anybody. She and Charlie would live in a house, and she could have a flower garden, and, although they had not discussed it, if she had a baby she wouldn't have to work. It was getting late if she intended to have a baby. There was no point in asking herself more questions. Her head hurt, and she had eaten too much and felt a little sick, and no matter what she thought she knew she was still going to marry Charlie.

Cynthia would marry Charlie on February the tenth. That was what she told Charlie, because she hadn't been able to think of a date and she had to say something, and that was what she would tell her boss, Mr. Greer, when she asked if she could be given her week's vacation then.

"We would like to be married the tenth of February, and, if I could, I'd like to have the next week off."

"I'm looking for that calendar."

"What?"

"Sit down and relax, Cynthia. You can have the week off if that isn't the week when—"

"Mr. Greer, I could change the date of the wedding."

"I'm not asking you to do that. Please sit down while I—"

"Thank you. I don't mind standing."

"Cynthia, let's just say that week is fine."

"Thank you."

"If you like standing, what about having a hot dog with me down at the corner?" he said to Cynthia.

That surprised her. Having lunch with her boss! She could feel the heat of her cheeks. A crazy thought went through her head: Cynthia Greer. It got mixed up right away with Peterson, Divine, and Pinehurst.

At the hot-dog place, they stood side by side, eating hot dogs and french fries.

"It's none of my business," Mr. Greer said to her, "but you don't seem like the most excited bride-to-be. I mean, you do seem excited, but . . ."

Cynthia continued to eat.

"Well?" he asked. "I was just being polite when I said it was none of my business."

"Oh, that's all right. Yes, I'm very happy. I'm going to come back to work after I'm married, if that's what you're thinking."

Mr. Greer was staring at her. She had said something wrong.

"I'm not sure that we'll go on a honeymoon. We're going to buy a house."

"Oh? Been looking at some houses?"

"No. We might look for houses."

"You're very hard to talk to," Mr. Greer said.

"I know. I'm not thinking quickly. I make so many mistakes typing."

A mistake to have told him that. He didn't pick it up.

"February will be a nice time to have off," he said pleasantly.

"I picked February because I'm dieting, and by then I'll have lost weight."

"Oh? My wife is always dieting. She's eating fourteen grapefruit a week on this new diet she's found."

"That's the grapefruit diet."

Mr. Greer laughed.

"What did I do that was funny?"

She sees Mr. Greer is embarrassed. A mistake to have embarrassed him.

"I don't think right when I haven't had eight hours' sleep, and I haven't even had close to that. And on this diet I'm always hungry."

"Are you hungry? Would you like another hot dog?"

"That would be nice," she says.

He orders another hot dog and talks more as she eats.

"Sometimes I think it's best to forget all this dieting," he says. "If so many people are fat, there must be something to it."

"But I'll get fatter and fatter."

"And then what?" he says. "What if you did? Does your fiancé like thin women?"

"He doesn't care if I lose weight or not. He probably wouldn't care."

"Then you've got the perfect man. Eat away."

When she finishes that hot dog, he orders another for her.

"A world full of food, and she eats fourteen grapefruit a week."

"Why don't you tell her not to diet, Mr. Greer?"

"She won't listen to me. She reads those magazines, and I can't do anything."

"Charlie hates those magazines, too. Why do men hate magazines?"

"I don't hate all magazines. I don't hate *Newsweek*."

She tells Charlie that her boss took her to lunch. At first he is impressed. Then he seems let down. Probably he is disappointed that his boss didn't take him to lunch.

"What did you talk about?" Charlie asks.

"Me. He told me I could get fat—that it didn't matter."

"What else did he say?"

"He said his wife is on the grapefruit diet."

"You aren't very talkative. Is everything all right?"

"He said not to marry you."

"What did he mean by that?"

"He said to go home and eat and eat and eat but not to get married. One of the girls said that before she got married he told her the same thing."

"What's that guy up to? He's got no right to say that."

"She got divorced, too."

"What are you trying to tell me?" Charlie says.

"Nothing. I'm just telling you about the lunch. You asked about it."

"Well, I don't understand all this. I'd like to know what's behind it."

Cynthia does not feel that she has understood, either. She feels sleep coming on, and hopes that she will drop off before long. Her second husband, Lincoln, felt that she was incapable of understanding anything. He had a string of Indian beads that he wore under his shirt, and on their wedding night he removed the beads before they went to bed and held them in front of her face and shook them and said, "What's this?" It was the inside of her head, Lincoln told her. She understood that she was being insulted. But why had he married her? She had not understood Lincoln, and, like Charlie, she didn't understand what Mr. Greer was up to. "Memorize," she heard her English teacher saying. "Anyone can memorize." Cynthia began to go over past events. I married Pete and Lincoln and I will marry Charlie. Today I had lunch with Mr. Greer. Mrs. Greer eats grapefruit.

"Well, what are you laughing about?" Charlie asked. "Some private joke with you and Greer, or something?"

Cynthia saw an ad in the newspaper. "Call Crisis Center," it said. "We Care." She thinks that a crisis center is a good idea, but she isn't having a crisis. She just can't sleep. But the idea of it is very good. If I were having a crisis, what would I do? she wonders. She has to answer her mother's note. Another note came today. Now her mother wants to meet Charlie: "As God is my witness, I tried to get through to you, but perhaps I did not say that you would really be welcome at home and do not have to do this foolish thing you are doing. Your dad feels you are never going to find true happiness when you don't spend any time thinking between one husband and the next. I know that love makes us do funny things, but your dad has said to tell you that he feels you do not really love this man, and there is nothing worse than just doing something funny with not even the reason of love driving you. You probably don't want to listen to me, and so I keep these short, but if you should come home alone we would be most glad. If you bring this new man with you, we will also come to the station. Let us at least look him over before you do this thing. Your dad has said that if he had met Lincoln it never would have been."

Cynthia takes out a piece of paper. Instead of writing her mother's name at the top, though, she writes, "If you are still at that high school, I want you to know I am glad to be away from it and you and I have forgotten all those lousy poems you had me memorize for nothing. Sincerely, Cynthia Knight." On another piece of paper she writes, "Are you still in love with me? Do you want to see me again?" She gets another piece of paper and draws two parallel vertical lines with a horizontal line joining them at the bottom—Pete's trapeze. "Ape man," she prints. She puts the first into an envelope and addresses it to her teacher at the high school. The second is for Lincoln. The next goes to Pete, care of his parents. She doesn't know Lincoln's address, so she rips up that piece of paper and throws it away. This makes her cry. Why is she crying? One of the girls at work says it's the times they are living in. The girl campaigned for George McGovern. Not only that, but she wrote letters against Nixon. Cynthia takes another piece of paper from the box and writes a message to President Nixon: "Some girls in my office won't write you because they say that's crank mail and their names will get put on a list. I don't care if I'm on some list. You're the crank. You've got prices so high I can't eat steak." Cynthia doesn't know what else to say to the president. "Tell your wife she's a stone face," she writes. She addresses the envelope and stamps it and takes the mail to the mailbox before she goes to bed. She begins to think that it's Nixon's fault—all of it. Whatever that means. She is still weeping. Damn you, Nixon, she thinks. Damn you.

Lately, throughout all of this, she hasn't been sleeping with Charlie. When he comes to her apartment, she unbuttons his shirt, rubs her hands across his chest, up and down his chest, and undoes his belt.

She writes more letters. One is to Jean Nidetch, of Weight Watchers. "What if you got fat again, if you couldn't stop eating?" she writes. "Then you'd lose all your money! You couldn't go out in public or they'd see you! I hope you get fatter and fatter and die." The second letter (a picture, really) is to Charlie—a heart with "Cynthia" in it. That's wrong. She draws another heart and writes "Charlie" in it. The last letter is to a woman she knew when she was married to Pete. "Dear Sandy," she writes. "Sorry I haven't written in so long. I am going to get married the tenth of February. I think I told you that Lincoln and I got divorced. I really wish I had you around to encourage me to lose weight before the wedding! I hope everything is well with your family. The baby must be walking now. Everything is fine with me. Well, got to go. Love, Cynthia."

They are on the train, on the way to visit her parents before the wedding. It is late January. Charlie has spilled some beer on his jacket and has gone to the men's room twice to wash it off, even though she told him he got it all out the first time. He has a tie folded in his jacket pocket. It is a red tie with white dogs on it that she bought for him. She has been buying him presents, to make up for the way she acts toward him sometimes. She has been taking sleeping pills, and now that she's more rested she isn't nervous all the time. That's all it was—no sleep. She even takes half a sleeping pill with her lunch, and that keeps her calm during the day.

"Honey, do you want to go to the other car, where we can have a drink?" Charlie asks her.

Cynthia didn't want Charlie to know she had been taking the pills, so when she had a chance she reached into her handbag and shook out a whole one and swallowed it when he wasn't looking. Now she is pretty groggy.

"I think I'll come down later," she says. She smiles at him.

As he walks down the aisle, she looks at his back. He could be anybody. Just some man on a train. The door closes behind him.

A young man sitting across the aisle from her catches her eye. He has long hair. "Paper?" he says.

He is offering her his paper. She feels her cheeks color, and she takes it, not wanting to offend him. Some people wouldn't mind offending somebody who looks like him, she thinks self-righteously, but you are always polite.

"How far you two headed?" he asks.

"Pavo, Georgia," she says.

"Gonna eat peaches in Georgia?" he asks.

She stares at him.

"I'm just kidding," he says. "My grandparents live in Georgia."

"Do they eat peaches all day?" she asks.

He laughs. She doesn't know what she's done right.

"Why, lordy lands, they do," he says with a thick drawl.

She flips through the paper. There is a comic strip of President Nixon. The president is leaning against a wall, being frisked by a policeman. He is confessing to various sins.

"Great, huh?" the man says, smiling, and leans across the aisle.

"I wrote Nixon a letter," Cynthia says quietly. "I don't know what they'll do. I said all kinds of things."

"You did? Wow. You wrote Nixon?"

"Did you ever write him?"

"Yeah, sure, I write him all the time. Send telegrams. It'll be a while before he's really up against that wall, though."

Cynthia continues to look through the paper. There are full-page ads for records by people she has never heard of, singers she will never hear. The singers look like the young man.

"Are you a musician?" she asks.

"Me? Well, sometimes. I play electric piano. I can play classical piano. I don't do much of it."

"No time?" she says.

"Right. Too many distractions."

He takes a flask out from under his sweater. "If you don't feel like the long walk to join your friend, have a drink with me."

Cynthia accepts the flask, quickly, so no one will see. Once it is in her hands, she doesn't know what else to do but drink from it.

"Where you coming from?" he asks.

"Buffalo."

"Seen the comet?" he asks.

"No. Have you?"

"No," he says. "Some days I don't think there is any comet. Propaganda, maybe."

"If Nixon said there was a comet, then we could be sure there wasn't," she says.

The sound of her own voice is strange to her. The man is smiling. He seems to like talk about Nixon.

"Right," he says. "Beautiful. President issues bulletin comet *will* appear. Then we can all relax and know we're not missing anything."

She doesn't understand what he has said, so she takes another drink. That way, she has no expression.

"I'll drink to that, too," he says, and the flask is back with him.

Because Charlie is apparently going to be in the drinking car for a while, the man, whose name is Peter, comes and sits next to her.

"My first husband was named Pete," she says. "He was in the army. He didn't know what he was doing."

The man nods, affirming some connection.

He nods. She must have been right.

Peter tells her that he is on his way to see his grandfather, who is recovering from a stroke. "He can't talk. They think he will, but not yet."

"I'm scared to death of getting old," Cynthia says.

"Yeah," Peter says. "But you've got a way to go."

"And then other times I don't care what happens, I just don't care what happens at all."

He nods slowly. "There's plenty happening we're not going to be able to do anything about," he says.

He holds up a little book he has been looking through. It is called *Know What Your Dreams Mean*.

"Ever read these things?" he asks.

"No. Is it good?"

"You know what it is—right? A book that interprets dreams."

"I have a dream," she says, "about being at an altar in a wedding dress, only instead of standing on the floor I'm on a scale."

He laughs and shakes his head. "There's no weird stuff in here. It's all the usual Freudian stuff."

"What do you mean?" she asks.

"Oh—you dream about your teeth crumbling; it means castration. That sort of stuff."

"But what do you think my dream means?" she asks.

"I don't even know if I half believe what I read in the book," he says, tapping it on his knee. He knows he hasn't answered her question. "Maybe the scale means you're weighing the possibilities."

"Of what?"

"Well, you're in a wedding dress, right? You could be weighing the possibilities."

"What will I do?" she says.

He laughs. "I'm no seer. Let's look it up in your horoscope. What are you?"

"Virgo."

"Virgo," he says. "That would figure. Virgos are meticulous. They'd be susceptible to a dream like the one you were talking about."

Peter reads from the book: "Be generous to friends, but don't be taken advantage of. Unexpected windfall may prove less than you expected. Loved one causes problems. Take your time."

He shrugs. He passes her the flask.

It's too vague. She can't really understand it. She sees Lincoln shaking the beads, but it's not her fault this time—it's the horoscope's fault. It doesn't say enough.

"That man I'm with wants to marry me," she confides to Peter. "What should I do?"

He shakes his head and looks out the window. "Don't ask me," he says, a little nervously.

"Do you have any more books?"

"No," he says. "All out."

They ride in silence.

"You could go to a palmist," he says after a while. "They'll tell you what's up."

"A palmist? Really?"

"Well, I don't know. If you believe half they say . . ."

"You don't believe them?"

"Well, I fool around with stuff like this, but I sort of pay attention to what I like and forget what I don't like. The horoscope told me to delay travel yesterday, and I did."

"Why don't you believe them?" Cynthia asks.

"Oh, I think most of them don't know any more than you or me."

"Then let's do it as a game," she says. "I'll ask questions, and you give the answer."

Peter laughs. "Okay," he says. He lifts her hand from her lap and stares hard at it. He turns it over and examines the other side, frowning.

"Should I marry Charlie?" she whispers.

"I see . . ." he begins. "I see a man. I see a man . . . in the drinking car."

"But what am I going to do?" she whispers. "Should I marry him?"

Peter gazes intently at her palm, then smooths his fingers down hers. "Maybe," he says gravely when he reaches her fingertips.

Delighted with his performance, he cracks up. A woman in the seat in front of them peers over the back of her chair to see what the noise is about. She sees a hippie holding a fat woman's hand and drinking from a flask.

"Coleridge," Peter is saying. "You know—Coleridge, the poet? Well, he says that we don't, for instance, dream about a wolf and then get scared. He says it's that we're scared to begin with, see, and therefore we dream about a wolf."

Cynthia begins to understand, but then she loses it. It is the fault of the sleeping pill and many drinks. In fact, when Charlie comes back, Cynthia is asleep on Peter's shoulder. There is a scene—or as much of a scene as a quiet man like Charlie can make. Charlie is also drunk, which makes him mellow instead of really angry. Eventually, brooding, he sits down across the aisle. Late that night, when the train slows down for the Georgia station, he gazes out the window as if he noticed nothing. Peter helps Cynthia get her bag down. The train has stopped at the station, and Charlie is still sitting, staring out the window at a few lights that shine along the tracks. Without looking at him, without knowing what will happen, Cynthia walks down the aisle. She is the last one off. She is the last one off before the train pulls out, with Charlie still on it.

Her parents watch the train go down the track, looking as if they are visitors from an earlier century, amazed by such a machine. They had expected Charlie, of course, but now they have Cynthia. They were not prepared to be pleasant, and there is a strained silence as the three watch the train disappear.

That night, lying in the bed she slept in as a child, Cynthia can't sleep. She gets up, finally, and sits in the kitchen at the table. What am I trying to think about, she wonders, closing her hands over her face for deeper concentration. It is cold in the kitchen, and she is not so much hungry as empty. Not in the head, she feels like shouting to Lincoln, but in the stomach—somewhere inside. She clasps her hands in front of her, over her stomach. Her eyes are closed. A picture comes to her—a high, white mountain. She isn't on it, or in the picture at all. When she opens her eyes she is looking at the shiny surface of the table. She closes her eyes and sees the snow-covered mountain again—high and white, no trees, just mountain—and she shivers with the coldness of it.

DWARF HOUSE

"Are you happy?" MacDonald says. "Because if you're happy I'll leave you alone."

MacDonald is sitting in a small gray chair, patterned with grayer leaves, talking to his brother, who is standing in a blue chair. Mac-Donald's brother is four feet six and three-quarter inches tall, and when he stands in a chair he can look down on MacDonald. MacDonald is twenty-eight years old. His brother, James, is thirty-eight. There was a brother between them, Clem, who died of a rare disease in Panama. There was a sister also, Amy, who flew to Panama to be with her dying brother. She died in the same hospital, one month later, of the same disease. None of the family went to the funeral. Today MacDonald, at his mother's request, is visiting James to find out if he is happy. Of course James is not, but standing on the chair helps, and the twenty-dollar bill that MacDonald slipped into his tiny hand helps too.

"What do you want to live in a dwarf house for?"

"There's a giant here."

"Well it must just depress the hell out of the giant."

"He's pretty happy."

"Are you?"

"I'm as happy as the giant."

"What do you do all day?"

"Use up the family's money."

"You know I'm not here to accuse you. I'm here to see what I can do."

"She sent you again, didn't she?"

"Yes."

"Is this your lunch hour?"

"Yes."

"Have you eaten? I've got some candy bars in my room."

"Thank you. I'm not hungry."

"Place make you lose your appetite?"

"I do feel nervous. Do you like living here?"

"I like it better than the giant does. He's lost twenty-five pounds. Nobody's supposed to know about that—the official word is fifteen—but I overheard the doctors talking. He's lost twenty-five pounds."

"Is the food bad?"

"Sure. Why else would he lose twenty-five pounds?"

"Do you mind . . . if we don't talk about the giant right now? I'd like to take back some reassurance to Mother."

"Tell her I'm as happy as she is."

"You know she's not happy."

"She knows I'm not, too. Why does she keep sending you?"

"She's concerned about you. She'd like you to live at home. She'd come herself . . ."

"I know. But she gets nervous around freaks."

"I was going to say that she hasn't been going out much. She sent me, though, to see if you wouldn't reconsider."

"I'm not coming home, MacDonald."

"Well, is there anything you'd like from home?"

"They let you have pets here. I'd like a parakeet."

"A bird? Seriously?"

"Yeah. A green parakeet."

"I've never seen a green one."

"Pet stores will dye them any color you ask for."

"Isn't that harmful to them?"

"You want to please the parakeet or me?"

"How did it go?" MacDonald's wife asks.

"That place is a zoo. Well, it's worse than a zoo—it's what it is: a dwarf house."

"Is he happy?"

"I don't know. I didn't really get an answer out of him. There's a giant there who's starving to death, and he says he's happier than the giant. Or maybe he said he was as happy. I can't remember. Have we run out of vermouth?"

"Yes. I forgot to go to the liquor store. I'm sorry."

"That's all right. I don't think a drink would have much effect anyway."

"It might. If I had remembered to go to the liquor store."

"I'm just going to call Mother and get it over with."

"What's that in your pocket?"

"Candy bars. James gave them to me. He felt sorry for me because I'd given up my lunch hour to visit him."

"Your brother is really a very nice person."

"Yeah. He's a dwarf."

"What?"

"I mean that I think of him primarily as a dwarf. I've had to take care of him all my life."

"Your mother took care of him until he moved out of the house."

"Yeah, well it looks like he found a replacement for her. But you might need a drink before I tell you about it."

"Oh, tell me."

"He's got a little sweetie. He's in love with a woman who lives in the dwarf house. He introduced me. She's three feet eleven. She stood there smiling at my knees."

"That's wonderful that he has a friend."

"Not a friend—a fiancée. He claims that as soon as he's got enough money saved up he's going to marry this other dwarf."

"He is?"

"Isn't there some liquor store that delivers? I've seen liquor trucks in this neighborhood, I think."

His mother lives in a high-ceilinged old house on Newfield Street, in a neighborhood that is gradually being taken over by Puerto Ricans. Her phone has been busy for almost two hours, and MacDonald fears that she, too, may have been taken over by Puerto Ricans. He drives to his mother's house and knocks on the door. It is opened by a Puerto Rican woman, Mrs. Esposito.

"Is my mother all right?" he asks.

"Yes. She's okay."

"May I come in?"

"Oh, I'm sorry."

She steps aside—not that it does much good, because she's so wide that there's still not much room for passage. Mrs. Esposito is wearing a dress that looks like a jungle: tall streaks of green grass going every which way, brown stumps near the hem, flashes of red around her breasts.

"Who were you talking to?" he asks his mother.

"Carlotta was on the phone with her brother, seeing if he'll take her in. Her husband put her out again."

Mrs. Esposito, hearing her husband spoken of, rubs her hands in anguish.

"It took two hours?" MacDonald says good-naturedly, feeling sorry for her. "What was the verdict?"

"He won't," Mrs. Esposito answers.

"I told her she could stay here, but when she told him she was going to do that he went wild and said he didn't want her living just two doors down."

"I don't think he meant it," MacDonald says. "He was probably just drinking again."

"He had joined Alcoholics Anonymous," Mrs. Esposito says. "He didn't drink for two weeks, and he went to every meeting, and one night he came home and said he wanted me out."

MacDonald sits down, nodding nervously. The chair he sits in has a child's chair facing it, which is used as a footstool. When James lived with his mother it was his chair. His mother still keeps his furniture around—a tiny child's glider, a mirror in the hall that is knee-high.

"Did you see James?" his mother asks.

"Yes. He said that he's very happy."

"I know he didn't say that. If I can't rely on you I'll have to go myself, and you know how I cry for days after I see him."

"He said he was pretty happy. He said he didn't think you were."

"Of course I'm not happy. He never calls."

"He likes the place he lives in. He's got other people to talk to now."

"Dwarfs, not people," his mother says. "He's hiding from the real world."

"He didn't have anybody but you to talk to when he lived at home. He's got a new part-time job that he likes better, too, working in a billing department."

"Sending unhappiness to people in the mail," his mother says.

"How are you doing?" he asks.

"As James says, I'm not happy."

"What can I do?" MacDonald asks.

"Go to see him tomorrow and tell him to come home."

"He won't leave. He's in love with somebody there."

"Who? Who does he say he's in love with? Not another social worker?"

"Some woman. I met her. She seems very nice."

"What's her name?"

"I don't remember."

"How tall is she?"

"She's a little shorter than James."

"Shorter than James?"

"Yes. A little shorter."

"What does she want with him?"

"He said they were in love."

"I heard you. I'm asking what she wants with him."

"I don't know. I really don't know. Is that sherry in that bottle? Do you mind . . ."

"I'll get it for you," Mrs. Esposito says.

"Well, who knows what anybody wants from anybody," his mother says. "Real love comes to naught. I loved your father and we had a dwarf."

"You shouldn't blame yourself," MacDonald says. He takes the glass of sherry from Mrs. Esposito.

"I shouldn't? I have to raise a dwarf and take care of him for thirty-eight years and then in my old age he leaves me. Who should I blame for that?"

"James," MacDonald says. "But he didn't mean to offend you."

"I should blame your father," his mother says, as if he hasn't spoken. "But he's dead. Who should I blame for his early death? God?"

His mother does not believe in God. She has not believed in God for thirty-eight years.

"I had to have a dwarf. I wanted grandchildren, and I know you won't give me any because you're afraid you'll produce a dwarf. Clem is dead, and Amy is dead. Bring me some of that sherry, too, Carlotta."

At five o'clock MacDonald calls his wife. "Honey," he says, "I'm going to be tied up in this meeting until seven. I should have called you before."

"That's all right," she says. "Have you eaten?"

"No. I'm in a meeting."

"We can eat when you come home."

"I think I'll grab a sandwich, though. Okay?"

"Okay. I got the parakeet."

"Good. Thank you."

"It's awful. I'll be glad to have it out of here."

"What's so awful about a parakeet?"

"I don't know. The man at the pet store gave me a Ferris wheel with it, and a bell on a chain of seeds."

"Oh yeah? Free?"

"Of course. You don't think I'd buy junk like that, do you?"

"I wonder why he gave it to you."

"Oh, who knows. I got gin and vermouth today."

"Good," he says. "Fine. Talk to you later."

MacDonald takes off his tie and puts it in his pocket. At least once a week he goes to a run-down bar across town, telling his wife that he's in a meeting, putting his tie in his pocket. And once a week his wife remarks that she doesn't understand how he can get his tie wrinkled. He takes off his shoes and puts on sneakers, and takes an old brown corduroy jacket off a coat hook behind his desk. His secretary is still in her office. Usually she leaves before five, but whenever he leaves looking like a slob she seems to be there to say good night to him.

"You wonder what's going on, don't you?" MacDonald says to his secretary.

She smiles. Her name is Betty, and she must be in her early thirties. All he really knows about his secretary is that she smiles a lot and that her name is Betty.

"Want to come along for some excitement?" he says.

"Where are you going?"

"I knew you were curious," he says.

Betty smiles.

"Want to come?" he says. "Like to see a little low life?"

"Sure," she says.

They go out to his car, a red Toyota. He hangs his jacket in the back and puts his shoes on the backseat.

"We're going to see a Japanese woman who beats people with figurines," he says.

Betty smiles. "Where are we really going?" she asks.

"You must know that businessmen are basically depraved," MacDonald says. "Don't you assume that I commit bizarre acts after hours?"

"No," Betty says.

"How old are you?" he asks.

"Thirty," she says.

"You're thirty years old and you're not a cynic yet?"

"How old are you?" she asks.

"Twenty-eight," MacDonald says.

"When you're thirty you'll be an optimist all the time," Betty says.

"What makes you optimistic?" he asks.

"I was just kidding. Actually, if I didn't take two kinds of pills, I couldn't smile every morning and evening for you. Remember the day I fell asleep at my desk? The day before I had had an abortion."

MacDonald's stomach feels strange—he wouldn't mind having a couple kinds of pills himself, to get rid of the strange feeling. Betty lights a cigarette, and the smoke doesn't help his stomach. But he had the strange feeling all day, even before Betty spoke. Maybe he has stomach cancer. Maybe he doesn't want to face James again. In the glove compartment there is a jar that Mrs. Esposito gave his mother and that his mother gave him to take to James. One of Mrs. Esposito's relatives sent it to her, at her request. It was made by a doctor in Puerto Rico. Supposedly, it can increase your height if rubbed regularly on the soles of the feet. He feels nervous, knowing that it's in the glove compartment. The way his wife must feel having the parakeet and the Ferris wheel sitting around the house. The house. His wife. Betty.

They park in front of a bar with a blue neon sign in the window that says IDEAL CAFÉ. There is a larger neon sign above that that says SCHLITZ. He and Betty sit in a back booth. He orders a pitcher of beer and a double order of spiced shrimp. Tammy Wynette is singing "D-I-V-O-R-C-E" on the jukebox.

"Isn't this place awful?" he says. "But the spiced shrimp are great."

Betty smiles.

"If you don't feel like smiling, don't smile," he says.

"Then all the pills would be for nothing."

"Everything is for nothing," he says.

"If you weren't drinking you could take one of the pills," Betty says. "Then you wouldn't feel that way."

"Did you see *Esquire*?" James asks.

"No," MacDonald says. "Why?"

"Wait here," James says.

MacDonald waits. A dwarf comes into the room and looks under his chair. MacDonald raises his feet.

"Excuse me," the dwarf says. He turns cartwheels to leave the room.

"He used to be with the circus," James says, returning. "He leads us in exercises now."

MacDonald looks at *Esquire*. There has been a convention of dwarfs at the Oakland Hilton, and *Esquire* got pictures of it. Two male dwarfs are leading a delighted female dwarf down a runway. A baseball team of dwarfs. A group picture. Someone named Larry—MacDonald does not look back up at the picture to see which one he is—says, "I haven't had so much fun since I was born." MacDonald turns another page. An article on Daniel Ellsberg.

"Huh," MacDonald says.

"How come *Esquire* didn't know about our dwarf house?" James asks. "They could have come here."

"Listen," MacDonald says, "Mother asked me to bring this to you. I don't mean to insult you, but she made me promise I'd deliver it. You know she's very worried about you."

"What is it?" James asks.

MacDonald gives him the piece of paper that Mrs. Esposito wrote instructions on in English.

"Take it back," James says.

"No. Then I'll have to tell her you refused it."

"Tell her."

"No. She's miserable. I know it's crazy, but just keep it for her sake."

James turns and throws the jar. Bright yellow liquid runs down the wall.

"Tell her not to send you back here either," James says. MacDonald thinks that if James were his size he would have hit him instead of only speaking.

"Come back and hit me if you want," MacDonald hollers. "Stand on the arm of this chair and hit me in the face."

James does not come back. A dwarf in the hallway says to Mac-Donald, as he is leaving, "It was a good idea to be sarcastic to him."

MacDonald and his wife and mother and Mrs. Esposito stand amid a cluster of dwarfs and one giant waiting for the wedding to begin. James and his bride are being married on the lawn outside the church. They are still inside with the minister. His mother is already weeping. "I wish I had never married your father," she says, and borrows Mrs. Esposito's handkerchief to dry her eyes. Mrs. Esposito is wearing her jungle dress again. On the way over she told MacDonald's wife that her husband had locked her out of the house and that she only had one dress. "It's lucky it was such a pretty one," his wife said, and Mrs. Esposito shyly protested that it wasn't very fancy, though.

The minister and James and his bride come out of the church onto the lawn. The minister is a hippie, or something like a hippie: a tall, white-faced man with stringy blond hair and black motorcycle boots. "Friends," the minister says, "before the happy marriage of these two people, we will release this bird from its cage, symbolic of the new free-dom of marriage, and of the ascension of the spirit."

The minister is holding the cage with the parakeet in it.

"MacDonald," his wife whispers, "that's the parakeet. You can't release a pet into the wild."

His mother disapproves of all this. Perhaps her tears are partly disapproval, and not all hatred of his father.

The bird is released: it flies shakily into a tree and disappears into the new spring foliage.

The dwarfs clap and cheer. The minister wraps his arms around himself and spins. In a second the wedding ceremony begins, and just a few minutes later it is over. James kisses the bride, and the dwarfs swarm around them. MacDonald thinks of a piece of Hershey bar he dropped in the woods once on a camping trip, and how the ants were all over it before he finished lacing his boot. He and his wife step forward, followed by his mother and Mrs. Esposito. MacDonald sees that the bride is smiling beautifully—a smile no pills could produce—and that the sun is shining on her hair so that it sparkles. She looks small, and bright, and so lovely that MacDonald, on his knees to kiss her, doesn't want to get up.

SNAKES' SHOES

The little girl sat between her uncle Sam's legs. Alice and Richard, her parents, sat next to them. They were divorced, and Alice had remarried. She was holding a ten-month-old baby. It had been Sam's idea that they all get together again, and now they were sitting on a big flat rock not far out into the pond.

"Look," the little girl said.

They turned and saw a very small snake coming out of a crack between two rocks on the shore.

"It's nothing," Richard said.

"It's a snake," Alice said. "You have to be careful of them. Never touch them."

"Excuse me," Richard said. "Always be careful of everything."

That was what the little girl wanted to hear, because she didn't like the way the snake looked.

"You know what snakes do?" Sam asked her.

"What?" she said.

"They can tuck their tail into their mouth and turn into a hoop."

"Why do they do that?" she asked.

"So they can roll down hills easily."

"Why don't they just walk?"

"They don't have feet. See?" Sam said.

The snake was still; it must have sensed their presence.

"Tell her the truth now," Alice said to Sam.

The little girl looked at her uncle.

"They have feet, but they shed them in the summer," Sam said. "If you ever see tiny shoes in the woods, they belong to the snakes."

"Tell her the truth," Alice said again.

"Imagination is better than reality," Sam said to the little girl.

The little girl patted the baby. She loved all the people who were sitting on the rock. Everybody was happy, except that in the back of their minds the grown-ups thought that their being together again was bizarre. Alice's husband had gone to Germany to look after his father, who was ill. When Sam learned about this, he called Richard, who was his brother. Richard did not think that it was a good idea for the three of them to get together again. Sam called the next day, and Richard told him to stop asking about it. But when Sam called again that night, Richard said sure, what the hell.

They sat on the rock looking at the pond. Earlier in the afternoon a game warden had come by and he let the little girl look at the crows in the trees through his binoculars. She was impressed. Now she said that she wanted a crow.

"I've got a good story about crows," Sam said to her. "I know how they got their name. You see, they all used to be sparrows, and they annoyed the king, so he ordered one of his servants to kill them. The servant didn't want to kill all the sparrows, so he went outside and looked at them and prayed, 'Grow. Grow.' And miraculously they did. The king could never kill anything as big and as grand as a crow, so the king and the birds and the servant were all happy."

"But why are they called crows?" the little girl said.

"Well," Sam said, "long, long ago, a historical linguist heard the story, but he misunderstood what he was told and thought that the servant had said 'crow,' instead of 'grow.' "

"Tell her the truth," Alice said.

"That's the truth," Sam said. "A lot of our vocabulary is twisted around."

"Is that true?" the little girl asked her father.

"Don't ask me," he said.

Back when Richard and Alice were engaged, Sam had tried to talk Richard out of it. He told him that he would be tied down; he said that if Richard hadn't gotten used to regimentation in the air force he wouldn't even consider marriage at twenty-four. He was so convinced that it was a bad idea that he cornered Alice at the engagement party (there were heart-shaped boxes of heart-shaped mints wrapped in paper printed with hearts for everybody to take home) and asked her to back down. At first Alice thought this was amusing. "You make me sound like a vicious dog," she said to Sam. "It's not going to work out," Sam said. "Don't do it." He showed her the little heart he was holding. "Look at these goddamned things," he said.

"They weren't my idea. They were your mother's," Alice said. She walked away. Sam watched her go. She had on a lacy beige dress. Her shoes sparkled. She was very pretty. He wished she would not marry his brother, who had been kicked around all his life—first by their mother, then by the air force ("Think of me as you fly into the blue," their mother had written Richard once. Christ!)—and now would be watched over by a wife.

The summer Richard and Alice married, they invited Sam to spend his vacation with them. It was nice that Alice didn't hold grudges. She also didn't hold a grudge against her husband, who burned a hole in an armchair and who tore the mainsail on their sailboat beyond repair by going out on the lake in a storm. She was a very patient woman. Sam found that he liked her. He liked the way she worried about Richard out in a boat in the middle of the storm. After that, Sam spent part of every summer vacation with them, and went to their house every Thanksgiving. Two years ago, just when Sam was convinced that everything was perfect, Richard told him that they were getting divorced. The next day, when Sam was alone with Alice after breakfast, he asked why.

"He burns up all the furniture," she said. "He acts like a madman with that boat. He's swamped her three times this year. I've been seeing someone else."

"Who have you been seeing?"

"No one you know."

"I'm curious, Alice. I just want to know his name."

"Hans."

"Hans. Is he a German?"

"Yes."

"Are you in love with this German?"

"I'm not going to talk about it. Why are you talking to me? Why don't you go sympathize with your brother?"

"He knows about this German?"

"His name is Hans."

"That's a German name," Sam said, and he went outside to find Richard and sympathize with him.

Richard was crouching beside his daughter's flower garden. His daughter was sitting on the grass across from him, talking to her flowers.

"You haven't been bothering Alice, have you?" Richard said.

"Richard, she's seeing a goddamned German," Sam said.

"What does that have to do with anything?"

"What are you talking about?" the little girl asked.

That silenced both of them. They stared at the bright orange flowers.

"Do you still love her?" Sam asked after his second drink.

They were in a bar, off a boardwalk. After their conversation about the German, Richard had asked Sam to go for a drive. They had driven thirty or forty miles to this bar, which neither of them had seen before and neither of them liked, although Sam was fascinated by a conversation now taking place between two blond transvestites on the bar stools to his right. He wondered if Richard knew that they weren't really women, but he hadn't been able to think of a way to work it into the conversation, and he started talking about Alice instead.

"I don't know," Richard said. "I think you were right. The air force, Mother, marriage—"

"They're not real women," Sam said.

"What?"

Sam thought that Richard had been staring at the two people he had been watching. A mistake on his part; Richard had just been glancing around the bar.

"Those two blonds on the bar stools. They're men."

Richard studied them. "Are you sure?" he said.

"Of course I'm sure. I live in N.Y.C., you know."

"Maybe I'll come live with you. Can I do that?"

"You always said you'd rather die than live in New York."

"Well, are you telling me to kill myself, or is it okay if I move in with you?"

"If you want to," Sam said. He shrugged. "There's only one bedroom, you know."

"I've been to your apartment, Sam."

"I just wanted to remind you. You don't seem to be thinking too clearly."

"You're right," Richard said. "A goddamned German."

The barmaid picked up their empty glasses and looked at them.

"This gentleman's wife is in love with another man," Sam said to her.

"I overheard," she said.

"What do you think of that?" Sam asked her.

"Maybe German men aren't as creepy as American men," she said. "Do you want refills?"

.   .   .

After Richard moved in with Sam he began bringing animals into the apartment. He brought back a dog, a cat that stayed through the winter, and a blue parakeet that had been in a very small cage that Richard could not persuade the pet-store owner to replace. The bird flew around the apartment. The cat was wild for it, and Sam was relieved when the cat eventually disappeared. Once, Sam saw a mouse in the kitchen and assumed that it was another of Richard's pets, until he realized that there was no cage for it in the apartment. When Richard came home he said that the mouse was not his. Sam called the exterminator, who refused to come in and spray the apartment because the dog had growled at him. Sam told this to his brother, to make him feel guilty for his irresponsibility. Instead, Richard brought another cat in. He said that it would get the mouse, but not for a while yet—it was only a kitten. Richard fed it cat food off the tip of a spoon.

Richard's daughter came to visit. She loved all the animals—the big mutt that let her brush him, the cat that slept in her lap, the bird that she followed from room to room, talking to it, trying to get it to land on the back of her hand. For Christmas, she gave her father a rabbit. It was a fat white rabbit with one brown ear, and it was kept in a cage on the night table when neither Sam nor Richard was in the apartment to watch it and keep it away from the cat and the dog. Sam said that the only vicious thing Alice ever did was giving her daughter the rabbit to give Richard for Christmas. Eventually the rabbit died of a fever. It cost Sam one hundred and sixty dollars to treat the rabbit's illness; Richard did not have a job, and could not pay anything. Sam kept a book of IOUs. In it he wrote, "Death of rabbit—$160 to vet." When Richard did get a job, he looked over the debt book. "Why couldn't you just have written down the sum?" he asked Sam. "Why did you want to remind me about the rabbit?" He was so upset that he missed the second morning of his new job. "That was inhuman," he said to Sam. " 'Death of rabbit—$160'—that was horrible. The poor rabbit. God-damn you." He couldn't get control of himself.

A few weeks later, Sam and Richard's mother died. Alice wrote to Sam, saying that she was sorry. Alice had never liked their mother, but she was fascinated by the woman. She never got over her spending a hundred and twenty-five dollars on paper lanterns for the engagement party. After all these years, she was still thinking about it. "What do you think became of the lanterns after the party?" she wrote in her letter of condolence. It was an odd letter, and it didn't seem that Alice was very happy. Sam even forgave her for the rabbit. He wrote her a long letter, saying that they should all get together. He knew a motel out in the country where they could stay, perhaps for a whole weekend. She wrote back, saying that it sounded like a good idea. The only thing that upset her about it was that his secretary had typed his letter. In her letter to Sam, she pointed out several times that he could have written in long-hand. Sam noticed that both Alice and Richard seemed to be raving. Maybe they would get back together.

Now they were all staying at the same motel, in different rooms. Alice and her daughter and the baby were in one room, and Richard and Sam had rooms down the hall. The little girl spent the nights with different people. When Sam bought two pounds of fudge, she said she was going to spend the night with him. The next night, Alice's son had colic, and when Sam looked out his window he saw Richard holding the baby, walking around and around the swimming pool. Alice was asleep. Sam knew this because the little girl left her mother's room when she fell asleep and came looking for him.

"Do you want to take me to the carnival?" she asked.

She was wearing a nightgown with blue bears upside down on it, headed for a crash at the hem.

"The carnival's closed," Sam said. "It's late, you know."

"Isn't anything open?"

"Maybe the doughnut shop. That's open all night. I suppose you want to go there?"

"I love doughnuts," she said.

She rode to the doughnut shop on Sam's shoulders, wrapped in his raincoat. He kept thinking, Ten years ago I would never have believed this. But he believed it now; there was a definite weight on his shoulders, and there were two legs hanging down his chest.

The next afternoon, they sat on the rock again, wrapped in towels after a swim. In the distance, two hippies and an Irish setter, all in bandannas, rowed toward shore from an island.

"I wish I had a dog," the little girl said.

"It just makes you sad when you have to go away from them," her father said.

"I wouldn't leave it."

"You're just a kid. You get dragged all over," her father said. "Did you ever think you'd be here today?"

"It's strange," Alice said.

"It was a good idea," Sam said. "I'm always right."

"You're not always right," the little girl said.

"When have I ever been wrong?"

"You tell stories," she said.

"Your uncle is *imaginative*," Sam corrected.

"Tell me another one," she said to him.

"I can't think of one right now."

"Tell the one about the snakes' shoes."

"Your uncle was kidding about the snakes, you know," Alice said.

"I know," she said. Then she said to Sam, "Are you going to tell another one?"

"I'm not telling stories to people who don't believe them," Sam said.

"Come on," she said.

Sam looked at her. She had bony knees, and her hair was brownish blond. It didn't lighten in the sunshine like her mother's. She was not going to be as pretty as her mother. He rested his hand on the top of her head.

The clouds were rolling quickly across the sky, and when they moved a certain way it was possible for them to see the moon, full and faint in the sky. The crows were still in the treetops. A fish jumped near the rock, and someone said, "Look," and everyone did—late, but in time to see the circles widening where it had landed.

"What did you marry Hans for?" Richard asked.

"I don't know why I married either of you," Alice said.

"Where did you tell him you were going while he was away?" Richard asked.

"To see my sister."

"How is your sister?" he asked.

She laughed. "Fine, I guess."

"What's funny?" Richard asked.

"Our conversation," she said.

Sam was helping his niece off the rock. "We'll take a walk," he said to her. "I have a long story for you, but it will bore the rest of them."

The little girl's knees stuck out. Sam felt sorry for her. He lifted her on his shoulders and cupped his hands over her knees so he wouldn't have to look at them.

"What's the story?" she said.

"One time," Sam said, "I wrote a book about your mother."

"What was it about?" the little girl asked.

"It was about a little girl who met all sorts of interesting animals— a rabbit who kept showing her his pocket watch, who was very upset because he was late—"

"I know that book," she said. "You didn't write that."

"I did write it. But at the time I was very shy, and I didn't want to admit that I'd written it, so I signed another name to it."

"You're not shy," the little girl said.

Sam continued walking, ducking whenever a branch hung low.

"Do you think there are more snakes?" she asked.

"If there are, they're harmless. They won't hurt you."

"Do they ever hide in trees?"

"No snakes are going to get you," Sam said. "Where was I?"

"You were talking about *Alice in Wonderland*."

"Don't you think I did a good job with that book?" Sam asked.

"You're silly," she said.

It was evening—cool enough for them to wish they had more than two towels to wrap around themselves. The little girl was sitting between her father's legs. A minute before, he had said that she was cold and they should go, but she said that she wasn't and even managed to stop shivering. Alice's son was asleep, squinting. Small black insects clustered on the water in front of the rock. It was their last night there.

"Where will we go?" Richard said.

"How about a seafood restaurant? The motel owner said he could get a babysitter."

Richard shook his head.

"No?" Alice said, disappointed.

"Yes, that would be fine," Richard said. "I was thinking more existentially."

"What does that mean?" the little girl asked.

"It's a word your father made up," Sam said.

"Don't tease her," Alice said.

"I wish I could look through that man's glasses again," the little girl said.

"Here," Sam said, making two circles with the thumb and first finger of each hand. "Look through these."

She leaned over and looked up at the trees through Sam's fingers.

"Much clearer, huh?" Sam said.

"Yes," she said. She liked this game.

"Let me see," Richard said, leaning to look through his brother's fingers.

"Don't forget me," Alice said, and she leaned across Richard to peer through the circles. As she leaned across him, Richard kissed the back of her neck.

SECRETS AND
SURPRISES

SECRETS AND SURPRISES

Corinne and Lenny are sitting at the side of the driveway with their shoes off. Corinne is upset because Lenny sat in a patch of strawberries. "Get up, Lenny! Look what you've done!"

Lenny is one of my oldest friends. I went to high school with Lenny and Corinne and his first wife, Lucy, who was my best friend there. Lenny did not know Corinne then. He met her at a party many years later. Corinne remembered Lenny from high school; he did not remember her. The next year, after his divorce from Lucy became final, they married. Two years later their daughter was born, and I was a godmother. Lenny teases me by saying that his life would have been entirely different if only I had introduced him to Corinne years ago. I knew her because she was my boyfriend's sister. She was a couple of years ahead of us, and she would do things like picking us up if we got drunk at a party and buying us coffee before taking us home. Corinne once lied to my mother when she took me home that way, telling her that there was flu going around and that I had sneezed in her car all the way home.

I was ugly in high school. I wore braces, and everything seemed to me funny and inappropriate: the seasons, television personalities, the latest fashions—even music seemed silly. I played the piano, but for some reason I stopped playing Brahms or even listening to Brahms. I played only a few pieces of music myself, the same ones, over and over: a couple of Bach two-part inventions, a Chopin nocturne. I earnestly smoked cigarettes, and all one spring I harbored a secret love for Lenny. I once confessed my love for him in a note I pushed through the slats in his locker in school. Then I got scared and waited by his locker when school was over, talked to him for a while, and when he opened the locker door, grabbed the note back and ran. This was fifteen years ago.

I used to live in the city, but five years ago my husband and I moved up here to Woodbridge. My husband has gone, and now it is only my house. It is my driveway that Lenny and Corinne sit beside. The driveway badly needs to be graveled. There are holes in it that should be filled, and the drainpipe is cracked. A lot of things here need fixing. I don't like to talk to the landlord, Colonel Albright. Every month he loses the rent check I send him and then calls me from the nursing home where he lives, asking for another. The man is eighty-eight. I should consider him an amusing old character, a forgetful old man. I suspect he is persecuting me. He doesn't want a young person renting his house. Or anyone at all. When we moved in, I found some empty clothing bags hanging in the closets, with old dry-cleaning stubs stapled to the plastic: "Col. Albright, 9-8-54." I stared at the stub. I was eleven years old the day Colonel Albright picked up his clothes at the dry cleaner's. I found one of his neckties wound around the base of a lamp in an upstairs closet. "Do you want these things?" I asked him on the phone. "Throw them out, I don't care," he said, "but don't ask me about them." I also do not tell him about things that need to be fixed. I close off one bathroom in the winter because the tiles are cracked and cold air comes through the floor; the heat register in my bedroom can't be set above sixty, so I set the living-room register at seventy-five to compensate. Corinne and Lenny think this is funny. Corinne says that I will not fight with the landlord because I did enough fighting with my husband about his girlfriend and now I enjoy peace; Lenny says that I am just too kind. The truth is that Colonel Albright shouts at me on the phone and I am afraid of him. He is also old and sad, and I have displaced him in his own house. Twice this summer, a friend has driven him from the nursing home back to the house, and he walked around the gardens in the front, tapping his cane through the clusters of sweet peas that are strangling out the asters and azaleas in the flower beds, and he dusted the pollen off the sundial in the back with a white handkerchief.

Almost every weekend Corinne tries to get me to leave Woodbridge and move back to New York. I am afraid of the city. In the apartment on West End Avenue I lived in with my husband when we were first married, I was always frightened. There was a bird in the apartment next to ours which shrieked, "No, no, go away!" I always mistook it for a human voice in the night, and in my sleepy confusion I thought that I was protesting an intruder in our apartment. Once a woman at the laundromat who was about to pass out from the heat took hold of my arm and pulled me to the floor with her. This could have happened anywhere. It happened in New York. I won't go back.

"Balducci's!" Corinne sometimes murmurs to me, and moves her arm through the air to suggest counters spread with delicacies. I imagine tins of anchovies, wheels of Brie, huge cashews, strange greens. But then I hear voices whispering outside my door plotting to break it down, and angry, wild music late at night that is the kind that disturbed, unhappy people listen to.

Now Corinne is holding Lenny's hand. I am lying on my side and peeking through the netting of the hammock, and they don't see me. She stoops to pick a strawberry. He scratches his crotch. They are bored here, I think. They pretend that they make the two-hour drive up here nearly every weekend because they are concerned for my well-being. Perhaps they actually think that living in the country is spookier than living in the city. "You sent your beagle to live in the country, Corinne," I said to her once. "How can you be upset that a human being wants to live where there's room to stretch?" "But what do you do here all alone?" she said.

I do plenty of things. I play Bach and Chopin on a grand piano my husband saved for a year to buy me. I grow vegetables, and I mow the lawn. When Lenny and Corinne come for the weekend, I spy on them. He's scratching his shoulder now. He calls Corinne to him. I think he is asking her to see if he just got a mosquito bite.

Last year when my husband went on vacation without me, I drove from Connecticut to D.C. to visit my parents. They live in the house where I grew up. The crocheted bedspreads have turned yellow now and the bedroom curtains are the same as ever. But in the living room there is a large black plastic chair for my father and a large brown plastic chair for my mother. My brother, Raleigh, who is retarded, lives with them. He has a friend, Ed, who is retarded, and who visits him once a week. And Raleigh visits Ed once a week. Sometimes my mother or Ed's mother takes them to the zoo. Raleigh's chatter often makes more sense than we at first suspected. For instance, he is very fond of Ling-Ling, the panda. He was not imitating the bell the Good Humor man rings when he drives around the neighborhood, as my father once insisted. My father has never been able to understand Raleigh very well. My mother laughs at him for his lack of understanding. She is a bitter woman. For the last ten years, she has made my father adhere to a diet when he is home, and he is not overweight.

When I visited, I drove Raleigh down to Hains Point, and we looked across the water at the lights. In spite of being retarded, he seems very moved by things. He rolled down the window and let the wind blow across his face. I slowed the car almost to a stop, and he put his hand on my hand, like a lover. He wanted me to stop the car entirely so he could look at the lights. I let him look for a long time. On the way home I drove across the bridge into Arlington and took him to Gifford's for ice cream. He had a banana split, and I pretended not to notice when he ate the toppings with his fingers. Then I washed his fingers with a napkin dipped in a glass of water.

One day I found him in the bathroom with Daisy, the dog, combing over her body for ticks. There were six or seven ticks in the toilet. He was concentrating so hard that he never looked up. Standing there, I realized that there was now a small bald spot at the top of his head, and that Daisy's fur was flecked with gray. I reached over him and got aspirin out of the medicine cabinet. Later, when I went back to the bathroom and found Raleigh and Daisy gone, I flushed the toilet so my parents would not be upset. Raleigh sometimes drops pieces of paper into the toilet instead of into the wastebaskets, and my mother goes wild. Sometimes socks are in the toilet. Coins. Pieces of candy.

I stayed for two weeks. On Mondays, before his friend Ed came, Raleigh left the living room until the door had been answered, and then acted surprised to see Ed and his mother. When I took him to Ed's house, Ed did the same thing. Ed held a newspaper in front of his face at first. "Oh—hello," Ed finally said. They have been friends for almost thirty years, and the visiting routine has remained the same all that time. I think that by pretending to be surprised, they are trying to enhance the quality of the experience. I play games like this with Corinne when I meet her in the city for lunch. If I get to our table first, I study the menu until she's right on me; sometimes, if I wait outside the restaurant, I deliberately look at the sidewalk, as if lost in thought, until she speaks.

I had Raleigh come live with my husband and me during the second year of our marriage. It didn't work out. My husband found his socks in the toilet; Raleigh missed my mother's constant nagging. When I took him home, he didn't seem sorry. There is something comforting about that house: the smell of camphor in the silver cabinet, my grandmother's woven rugs, Daisy's smell everywhere.

My husband wrote last week: "Do you miss wonderful me?" I wrote back saying yes. Nothing came of it.

Corinne and Lenny have always come to Woodbridge for visits. When my husband was here, they came once a month. Now they come almost every week. Sometimes we don't have much to say to each other, so we talk about the old days. Corinne teases Lenny for not noticing her back in high school. Our visits are often dull, but I still look forward to their coming because they are my surrogate family. As in all families, there are secrets. There is intrigue. Suspicion. Lenny often calls me, telling me to keep his call a secret, saying that I must call Corinne at once and arrange to have lunch because she is depressed. So I call, and then I go and sit at a table and pretend not to see her until she sits down. She has aged a lot since their daughter's death. Her name was Karen, and she died three years ago, of leukemia. After Karen died I began having lunch with Corinne, to let her talk about it away from Lenny. By the time she no longer needed to talk about it, my husband had left, and Corinne began having lunch with me to cheer me up. We have faced each other across a table for years. (Corinne, I know, tells Lenny to visit me even when she has to work on the weekend. He has come alone a few times. He gives me a few Godiva chocolates. I give him a bag of fresh peas. Sometimes he kisses me, but it goes no further than that. Corinne thinks that it does, and endures it.)

Once Corinne said that if we all lived to be fifty (she works for a state environmental-protection agency, and her expectations are modest), we should have an honesty session the way the girls did in college. Lenny asked why we had to wait until we were fifty. "Okay—what do you really think of me?" Corinne asked him. "Why, I love you. You're my wife," he said. She backed down; the game wasn't going to be much fun.

Lenny's first wife, Lucy, has twice taken the train to visit me. We sat on the grass and talked about the old days: teasing each other's hair to new heights; photo-album pictures of the two of us, each trying to look more grotesque than the other; the first time we puffed a cigarette on a double date. I like her less as time goes by, because things she remembers about that time are true but the tone of wonder in her voice makes the past seem like a lie. And then she works the conversation around to Corinne and Lenny's marriage. Is it unhappy? Both times she visited, she said she was going back to New York on the last train, and both times she got too drunk to go until the next day. She borrowed my nightgowns and drank my gin and played sad music on my piano. In our high school yearbook, Lucy was named best dancer.

I have a lover. He comes on Thursdays. He would come more frequently, but I won't allow it. Jonathan is twenty-one and I am thirty-three, and I know that eventually he will go away. He is a musician too. He comes in the morning and we sit side by side at the piano, humming and playing Bach's B-Flat-Minor Prelude, prolonging the time before we go to bed as long as possible. He drinks diet cola while I drink gin-and-tonic. He tells me about the young girls who are chasing him. He says he only wants me. He asks me each Thursday to marry him, and calls me on Friday to beg me to let him come again before the week is up. He sends me pears out of season and other things that he can't afford. He shows me letters from his parents that bother him; I am usually in sympathy with his parents. I urge him to spend more time sight-reading and playing scales and arpeggios. He allowed a rich woman who had been chasing him since Christmas to buy him a tape deck for his car, and he plays nothing but rock 'n' roll. Sometimes I cry, but not in his presence. He is disturbed enough. He isn't sure what to do with his life, he can't communicate with his parents, too many people want things from him. One night he called and asked if he could come over to my house if he disguised himself. "No," I said. "How would you disguise yourself?" "Cut off my hair. Buy a suit. Put on an animal mask." I make few demands on him, but obviously the relationship is a strain.

After Corinne and Lenny leave, I write a second letter to my husband, pretending that there is a chance that he did not get the other one. In this letter I give him a detailed account of the weekend, and agree with what he said long ago about Corinne's talking too much and Lenny's being too humble. I tell my husband that the handle on the barbecue no longer makes the grill go up and down. I tell him that the neighbors' dog is in heat and that dogs howl all night, so I can't sleep. I reread the letter and tear it up because these things are all jumbled together in one paragraph. It looks as if a crazy person had written the letter. I try again. In one paragraph I describe Corinne and Lenny's visit. In another I tell him that his mother called to tell me that his sister has decided to major in anthropology. In the last paragraph I ask for advice about the car— whether it may not need a new carburetor. I read the letter and it still seems crazy. A letter like this will never make him come back. I throw it away and write him a short, funny postcard. I go outside to put the postcard in the mailbox. A large white dog whines and runs in front of me. I recognize the dog. It is the same one I saw last night, from my bedroom window; the dog was staring at my neighbors' house. The dog runs past me again, but won't come when I call it. I believe the neighbors once told me that the dog's name is Pierre, and that the dog does not live in Woodbridge.

When I was a child I was punished for brushing Raleigh with the dog's brush. He had asked me to do it. It was Easter, and he had on a blue suit, and he came into my bedroom with the dog's brush and got down on all fours and asked for a brushing. I brushed his back. My father saw us and banged his fist against the door. "Jesus Christ, are you *both* crazy?" he said. Now that my husband is gone, I should bring Raleigh here to live—but what if my husband came back? I remember Raleigh's trotting through the living room, punching his fist through the air, chanting "Ling-Ling, Ling-Ling, Ling-Ling."

I play Scriabin's Étude in C Sharp Minor. I play it badly and stop to stare at the keys. As though on cue, a car comes into the driveway. The sound of a bad muffler—my lover's car, unmistakably. He has come a day early. I wince, and wish I had washed my hair. My husband used to wince also when that car pulled into the driveway. My lover (he was not at that time my lover) was nineteen when he first started coming, to take piano lessons. He was obviously more talented than I. For a long while I resented him. Now I resent him for his impetuousness, for showing up unexpectedly, breaking my routine, catching me when I look ugly.

"This is foolish," I say to him. "I'm going into the city to have lunch."

"My car is leaking oil," he says, looking over his shoulder.

"Why have you come?" I say.

"This once-a-week stuff is ridiculous. Once you have me around a little more often you'll get used to it."

"I won't have you around more often."

"I've got a surprise for you," he says. "Two, actually."

"What are they?"

"For later. I'll tell you when you get back. Can I stay here and wait for you?"

A maroon sweater that I gave him for his birthday is tied around his waist. He sits in front of the hearth and strikes a match on the bricks. He lights a cigarette.

"Well," he says, "one of the surprises is that I'm going to be gone for three months. Starting in November."

"Where are you going?"

"Europe. You know that band I've been playing with sometimes? One of the guys has hepatitis, and I'm going to fill in for him on synthesizer. Their agent got us a gig in Denmark."

"What about school?"

"Enough school," he says, sighing.

He pitches the cigarette into the fireplace and stands up and takes off his sweater.

I no longer want to go to lunch. I am no longer sorry he came unannounced. But he hasn't jumped up to embrace me.

"I'm going to investigate that oil leak," he says.

Later, driving into New York, trying to think of what the second surprise might be (taking a woman with him?), I think about the time when my husband surprised me with a six-layer cake he had baked for my birthday. It was the first cake he ever made, and the layers were not completely cool when he stacked and frosted them. One side of the cake was much higher than the other. He had gone out and bought a little plastic figure of a skier, for the top of the cake. The skier held a toothpick with a piece of paper glued to it that said HAPPY BIRTHDAY. "We're going to Switzerland!" I said, clapping my hands. He knew I had always wanted to go there. No, he explained, the skier was just a coincidence. My reaction depressed both of us. It was a coincidence, too, that a year later I was walking down the same street he was walking down and I saw that he was with a girl, holding her hand.

I'm almost in New York. Cars whiz by me on the Hutchinson River Parkway. My husband has been gone for seven months.

While waiting for Corinne, I examine my hands. My gardening has cut and bruised them. In a picture my father took when I was young, my hands are in very sharp focus but the piano keys are a blur of white streaked with black. I knew by the time I was twelve that I was going to be a concert pianist. My father and I both have copies of this picture, and we probably both have the same thoughts about it: it is a shame I have almost entirely given up music. When I lived in New York I had to play softly, so as not to disturb the neighbors. The music itself stopped sounding right. A day would pass without my practicing. My father blamed my husband for my losing interest. My husband listened to my father. We moved to Connecticut, where I wouldn't be distracted. I began to practice again, but I knew that I'd lost ground—or that I would never make it as a concert pianist if I hadn't by this time. I had Raleigh come and live with us, and I spent my days with him. My father blamed my mother for complaining to me about what a burden Raleigh was, for hinting that I take him in. My father always found excuses. I am like him. I pretended that everything was fine in my marriage, that the only problem was the girl.

.   .   .

"I think it's insulting, I really do," Corinne says. "It's a refusal to admit my existence. I've been married to Lenny for years, and when Lucy calls him and I answer the phone, she hangs up."

"Don't let it get to you," I say. "You know by now that Lucy's not going to be civil to you."

"And it upsets Lenny. Every time she calls to say where she's flying off to, he gets upset. He doesn't care where she's going, but you know Lenny and how he is about planes—how he gets about anyone flying."

These lunches are all the same. I discipline myself during these lunches the way I used to discipline myself about my music. I try to calm Corinne, and Corinne gets more and more upset. She only likes expensive restaurants, and she won't eat the food.

Now Corinne eats a cherry tomato from her salad and pushes the salad plate away. "Do you think we should have another child? Am I too old now?"

"I don't know," I say.

"I think the best way to get children is the way you got yours. Just have them drive up. He's probably languishing in your bed right now."

"Twenty-one isn't exactly a child."

"I'm so jealous I could die," Corinne says.

"Of Jonathan?"

"Of everything. You're three years younger than me, and you look ten years younger. Look at those thin women over there. Look at you and your music. *You* don't have to kill the day by having lunch."

Corinne takes a little gold barrette out of her hair and puts it back in. "We don't come to your house almost every weekend to look after you," she says. "We do it to restore ourselves. Although Lenny probably goes so he can pine over you."

"What are you talking about?"

"You don't sense it? You don't think that's true?"

"No," I say.

"Lucy does. She told Lenny that the last time she called. He told me that she said he was making a fool of himself hanging around you so much. When Lenny hung up, he said that Lucy never did understand the notion of friendship. Of course, he always tries to pretend that Lucy is entirely crazy."

She takes out the barrette and lets her hair fall free.

"And I'm jealous of her, going off on all her business trips, sending him postcards of sunsets on the West Coast," Corinne says. "She ran off with a dirty little furrier to Denver this time."

I look at my clean plate, and then at Corinne's plate. It looks as if a wind had blown the food around her plate, or as if a midget army had marched through it. I should not have had two drinks at lunch. I excuse myself and go to a phone and call my lover. I am relieved when he answers the phone, even though I have told him never to do that. "Come into the city," I say. "We can go to Central Park."

"Come home," he says. "You're going to get caught in the rush hour."

My husband sends me a geode. There is a brief note in the package. He says that before he left for Europe he sat at a table next to John Ehrlichman in a restaurant in New Mexico. The note goes on about how fat John Ehrlichman has become. My husband says that he bets my squash are still going strong in the garden. There is no return address. I stand by the mailbox, crying. From the edge of the lawn, the big white dog watches me.

My lover sits beside me on the piano bench. We are both naked. It is late at night, but we have lit a fire in the fireplace—five logs, a lot of heat. The lead guitarist from the band Jonathan plays with now was here for dinner. I had to fix a meatless meal. Jonathan's friend was young and dumb—much younger, it seemed, than my lover. I don't know why he wanted me to invite him. Jonathan has been here for four days straight. I gave in to him and called Lenny and said for them not to visit this weekend. Later Corinne called to say how jealous she was, thinking of me in my house in the country with my curly-haired lover.

I am playing Ravel's *Valses Nobles et Sentimentales*. Suddenly my lover breaks in with "Chopsticks." He is impossible, and as immature as his friend. Why have I agreed to let him live in my house until he leaves for Denmark?

"Don't," I plead. "Be sensible."

He is playing "Somewhere over the Rainbow" and singing.

"Stop it," I say. He kisses my throat.

Another note comes from my husband, written on stationery from the Hotel Eliseo. He got drunk and was hurt in a fight; his nose wouldn't stop bleeding, and in the end he had to have it cauterized.

In a week, my lover will leave. I am frightened at the thought that I will be here alone when he goes. Now I have gotten used to having someone around. When boards creak in the night I can ask "What is it?" and be told. When I was little, I shared a bedroom with Raleigh until I was seven. All night he'd question me about noises. "It's the monster," I'd say in disgust. I made him cry so many nights that my parents built on an addition to the house so I could have my own bedroom.

In his passport photo, my lover is smiling.

Lenny calls. He is upset because Corinne wants to have another child and he thinks they are too old. He hints that he would like me to invite them to come on Friday instead of Saturday this week. I explain that they can't come at all—my lover leaves on Monday.

"I don't mean to pry," Lenny says, but he never says what he wants to pry about.

I pick up my husband's note and take it into the bathroom and reread it. It was a street fight. He describes a church window that he saw. There is one long strand of brown hair in the bottom of the envelope. That just can't be deliberate.

Lying on my back, alone in the bedroom, I stare at the ceiling in the dark, remembering my lover's second surprise: a jar full of lightning bugs. He let them loose in the bedroom. Tiny, blinking dots of green under the ceiling, above the bed. Giggling into his shoulder: how crazy; a room full of lightning bugs.

"They only live a day," he whispered.

"That's butterflies," I said.

I always felt uncomfortable correcting him, as if I were pointing out the difference in our ages. I was sure I was right about the lightning bugs, but in the morning I was relieved when I saw that they were still alive. I found them on the curtains, against the window. I tried to recapture all of them in a jar so I could take them outdoors and set them free. I tried to remember how many points of light there had been.

WEEKEND

On Saturday morning Lenore is up before the others. She carries her baby into the living room and puts him in George's favorite chair, which tilts because its back legs are missing, and covers him with a blanket. Then she lights a fire in the fireplace, putting fresh logs on a few embers that are still glowing from the night before. She sits down on the floor beside the chair and checks the baby, who has already gone back to sleep—a good thing because there are guests in the house. George, the man she lives with, is very hospitable and impetuous; he extends invitations whenever old friends call, urging them to come spend the weekend. Most of the callers are his former students—he used to be an English professor—and when they come it seems to make things much worse. It makes *him* much worse, because he falls into smoking too much and drinking and not eating, and then his ulcer bothers him. When the guests leave, when the weekend is over, she has to cook bland food: applesauce, oatmeal, puddings. And his drinking does not taper off easily anymore; in the past he would stop cold when the guests left, but lately he only tapers down from Scotch to wine, and drinks wine well into the week—a lot of wine, perhaps a whole bottle with his meal—until his stomach is much worse. He is hard to live with. Once when a former student, a woman named Ruth, visited them—a lover, she suspected—she overheard George talking to her in his study, where he had taken her to see a photograph of their house before he began repairing it. George had told Ruth that she, Lenore, stayed with him because she was simple. It hurt her badly, made her actually dizzy with surprise and shame, and since then, no matter who the guests are, she never feels quite at ease on the weekends. In the past she enjoyed some of the things she and George did with their guests, but since overhearing what he said to Ruth she feels that all their visitors have been secretly told the same thing about her. To her, though, George is usually kind. But she is sure that is the reason he has not married her, and when he recently remarked on their daughter's intelligence (she is five years old, a girl named Maria) she found that she could no longer respond with simple pride; now she feels spite as well, feels that Maria exists as proof of her own good genes. She has begun to expect perfection of the child. She knows this is wrong, and she has tried hard not to communicate her anxiety to Maria, who is already, as her kindergarten teacher says, "untypical."

At first Lenore loved George because he was untypical, although after she had moved in with him and lived with him for a while she began to see that he was not exceptional but a variation on a type. She is proud of observing that, and she harbors the discovery—her silent response to his low opinion of her. She does not know why he found her attractive—in the beginning he did—because she does not resemble the pretty, articulate young women he likes to invite, with their lovers or girlfriends, to their house for the weekend. None of these young women have husbands; when they bring a man with them at all they bring a lover, and they seem happy not to be married. Lenore, too, is happy to be single—not out of conviction that marriage is wrong but because she knows that it would be wrong to be married to George if he thinks she is simple. She thought at first to confront him with what she had overheard, to demand an explanation. But he can weasel out of any corner. At best, she can mildly fluster him, and later he will only blame it on Scotch. Of course she might ask why he has all these women come to visit, why he devotes so little time to her or the children. To that he would say that it was the quality of the time they spent together that mattered, not the quantity. He has already said that, in fact, without being asked. He says things over and over so that she will accept them as truths. And eventually she does. She does not like to think long and hard, and when there is an answer—even his answer—it is usually easier to accept it and go on with things. She goes on with what she has always done: tending the house and the children and George, when he needs her. She likes to bake and she collects art postcards. She is proud of their house, which was bought cheaply and improved by George when he was still interested in that kind of work, and she is happy to have visitors come there, even if she does not admire them or even like them.

Except for teaching a night course in photography at a junior college once a week, George has not worked since he left the university two years ago, after he was denied tenure. She cannot really tell if he is unhappy working so little, because he keeps busy in other ways. He listens to classical music in the morning, slowly sipping herbal teas, and on fair afternoons he lies outdoors in the sun, no matter how cold the day. He takes photographs, and walks alone in the woods. He does errands for her if they need to be done. Sometimes at night he goes to the library or goes to visit friends; he tells her that these people often ask her to come too, but he says she would not like them. This is true—she would not like them. Recently he has done some late-night cooking. He has always kept a journal, and he is a great letter writer. An aunt left him most of her estate, ten thousand dollars, and said in her will that he was the only one who really cared, who took the time, again and again, to write. He had not seen his aunt for five years before she died, but he wrote regularly. Sometimes Lenore finds notes that he has left for her. Once, on the refrigerator, there was a long note suggesting clever Christmas presents for her family that he had thought of while she was out. Last week he Scotch-taped a slip of paper to a casserole dish that contained leftover veal stew, saying: "This was delicious." He does not compliment her verbally, but he likes to let her know that he is pleased.

A few nights ago—the same night they got a call from Julie and Sarah, saying they were coming for a visit—she told him that she wished he would talk more, that he would confide in her.

"Confide what?" he said.

"You always take that attitude," she said. "You pretend that you have no thoughts. Why does there have to be so much silence?"

"I'm not a professor anymore," he said. "I don't have to spend every minute *thinking*."

But he loves to talk to the young women. He will talk to them on the phone for as much as an hour; he walks with them through the woods for most of the day when they visit. The lovers the young women bring with them always seem to fall behind; they give up and return to the house to sit and talk to her, or to help with the preparation of the meal, or to play with the children. The young women and George come back refreshed, ready for another round of conversation at dinner.

A few weeks ago one of the young men said to her, "Why do you let it go on?" They had been talking lightly before that—about the weather, the children—and then, in the kitchen, where he was sitting shelling peas, he put his head on the table and said, barely audibly, "Why do you let it go on?" He did not raise his head, and she stared at him, thinking that she must have imagined his speaking. She was surprised—surprised to have heard it, and surprised that he said nothing after that, which made her doubt that he had spoken.

"Why do I let what go on?" she said.

There was a long silence. "Whatever this sick game is, I don't want to get involved in it," he said at last. "It was none of my business to ask. I understand that you don't want to talk about it."

"But it's really cold out there," she said. "What could happen when it's freezing out?"

He shook his head, the way George did, to indicate that she was beyond understanding. But she wasn't stupid, and she knew what might be going on. She had said the right thing, had been on the right track, but she had to say what she felt, which was that nothing very serious could be happening at that moment because they were walking in the woods. There wasn't even a barn on the property. She knew perfectly well that they were talking.

When George and the young woman had come back, he fixed hot apple juice, into which he trickled rum. Lenore was pleasant, because she was sure of what had not happened; the young man was not, because he did not think as she did. Still at the kitchen table, he ran his thumb across a pea pod as though it were a knife.

This weekend Sarah and Julie are visiting. They came on Friday evening. Sarah was one of George's students—the one who led the fight to have him rehired. She does not look like a troublemaker; she is pale and pretty, with freckles on her cheeks. She talks too much about the past, and this upsets him, disrupts the peace he has made with himself. She tells him that they fired him because he was "in touch" with everything, that they were afraid of him because he was so in touch. The more she tells him the more he remembers, and then it is necessary for Sarah to say the same things again and again; once she reminds him, he seems to need reassurance—needs to have her voice, to hear her bitterness against the members of the tenure committee. By evening they will both be drunk. Sarah will seem both agitating and consoling, Lenore and Julie and the children will be upstairs, in bed. Lenore suspects that she will not be the only one awake listening to them. She thinks that in spite of Julie's glazed look she is really very attentive. The night before, when they were all sitting around the fireplace talking, Sarah made a gesture and almost upset her wineglass, but Julie reached for it and stopped it from toppling over. George and Sarah were talking so energetically that they did not notice. Lenore's eyes met Julie's as Julie's hand shot out.

Lenore feels that she is like Julie: Julie's face doesn't betray emotion, even when she is interested, even when she cares deeply. Being the same kind of person, Lenore can recognize this.

Before Sarah and Julie arrived Friday evening, Lenore asked George if Sarah was his lover.

"Don't be ridiculous," he said. "You think every student is my lover? Is Julie my lover?"

She said, "That wasn't what I said."

"Well, if you're going to be preposterous, go ahead and say that," he said. "If you think about it long enough, it would make a lot of sense, wouldn't it?"

He would not answer her question about Sarah. He kept throwing Julie's name into it. Some other women might then think that he was protesting too strongly—that Julie really was his lover. She thought no such thing. She also stopped suspecting Sarah, because he wanted that, and it was her habit to oblige him.

He is twenty-one years older than Lenore. On his last birthday he was fifty-five. His daughter from his first marriage (his *only* marriage; she keeps reminding herself that they are not married, because it often seems that they might as well be) sent him an Irish country hat. The present made him irritable. He kept putting it on and pulling it down hard on his head. "She wants to make me a laughable old man," he said. "She wants me to put this on and go around like a fool." He wore the hat all morning, complaining about it, frightening the children. Eventually, to calm him, she said, "She intended *nothing*." She said it with finality, her tone so insistent that he listened to her. But having lost his reason for bitterness, he said, "Just because you don't think doesn't mean others don't think." Is he getting old? She does not want to think of him getting old. In spite of his ulcer, his body is hard. He is tall and handsome, with a thick mustache and a thin black goatee, and there is very little gray in his kinky black hair. He dresses in tight-fitting blue jeans and black turtleneck sweaters in the winter, and old white shirts with the sleeves rolled up in the summer. He pretends not to care about his looks, but he does. He shaves carefully, scraping slowly down each side of his goatee. He orders his soft leather shoes from a store in California. After taking one of his long walks—even if he does it twice a day—he invariably takes a shower. He always looks refreshed, and very rarely admits any insecurity. A few times, at night in bed, he has asked, "Am I still the man of your dreams?" And when she says yes he always laughs, turning it into a joke, as if he doesn't care. She knows he does. He pretends to have no feeling for clothing, but actually he cares so strongly about his turtlenecks and shirts (a few are Italian silk) and shoes that he will have no others. She has noticed that the young women who visit are always vain. When Sarah arrived, she was wearing a beautiful silk scarf, pale as conch shells.

Sitting on the floor on Saturday morning, Lenore watches the fire she has just lit. The baby, tucked in George's chair, smiles in his sleep, and Lenore thinks what a good companion he would be if only he were an adult. She gets up and goes into the kitchen and tears open a package of yeast and dissolves it, with sugar and salt, in hot water, slushing her fingers through it and shivering because it is so cold in the kitchen. She will bake bread for dinner—there is always a big meal in the early evening when they have guests. But what will she do for the rest of the day? George told the girls the night before that on Saturday they would walk in the woods, but she does not really enjoy hiking, and George will be irritated because of the discussion the night before, and she does not want to aggravate him. "You are unwilling to challenge anyone," her brother wrote her in a letter that came a few days ago. He has written her for years—all the years she has been with George—asking when she is going to end the relationship. She rarely writes back because she knows that her answers sound too simple. She has a comfortable house. She cooks. She keeps busy and she loves her two children. "It seems unkind to say *but*," her brother writes, "but . . ." It is true; she likes simple things. Her brother, who is a lawyer in Cambridge, cannot understand that.

Lenore rubs her hand down the side of her face and says good morning to Julie and Sarah, who have come downstairs. Sarah does not want orange juice; she already looks refreshed and ready for the day. Lenore pours a glass for Julie. George calls from the hallway, "Ready to roll?" Lenore is surprised that he wants to leave so early. She goes into the living room. George is wearing a denim jacket, his hands in the pockets.

"Morning," he says to Lenore. "You're not up for a hike, are you?"

Lenore looks at him, but does not answer. As she stands there, Sarah walks around her and joins George in the hallway as he holds the door open for her. "Let's walk to the store and get Hershey bars to give us energy for a long hike," George says to Sarah. They are gone. Lenore finds Julie still in the kitchen, waiting for the water to boil. Julie says that she had a bad night and she is happy not to be going with George and Sarah. Lenore fixes tea for them. Maria sits next to her on the sofa, sipping orange juice. The baby likes company, but Maria is a very private child; she would rather that she and her mother were always alone.

She has given up being possessive about her father. Now she gets out a cardboard box and takes out her mother's collection of postcards, which she arranges on the floor in careful groups. Whenever she looks up, Julie smiles nervously at her; Maria does not smile, and Lenore doesn't prod her. Lenore goes into the kitchen to punch down the bread, and Maria follows. Maria has recently gotten over chicken pox, and there is a small new scar in the center of her forehead. Instead of looking at Maria's blue eyes, Lenore lately has found herself focusing on the imperfection.

As Lenore is stretching the loaves onto the cornmeal-covered baking sheet, she hears the rain start. It hits hard on the garage roof.

After a few minutes Julie comes into the kitchen. "They're caught in this downpour," Julie says. "If Sarah had left the car keys, I could go get them."

"Take my car and pick them up," Lenore says, pointing with her elbow to the keys hanging on a nail near the door.

"But I don't know where the store is."

"You must have passed it driving to our house last night. Just go out of the driveway and turn right. It's along the main road."

Julie gets her purple sweater and takes the car keys. "I'll be right back," she says.

Lenore can sense that she is glad to escape from the house, that she is happy the rain began.

In the living room Lenore turns the pages of a magazine, and Maria mutters a refrain of "Blue, blue, dark blue, green-blue," noticing the color every time it appears. Lenore sips her tea. She puts a Michael Hurley record on George's stereo. Michael Hurley is good rainy-day music. George has hundreds of records. His students used to love to paw through them. Cleverly, he has never made any attempt to keep up with what is currently popular. Everything is jazz or eclectic: Michael Hurley, Keith Jarrett, Ry Cooder.

Julie comes back. "I couldn't find them," she says. She looks as if she expects to be punished.

Lenore is surprised. She is about to say something like "You certainly didn't look very hard, did you?" but she catches Julie's eyes. She looks young and afraid, and perhaps even a little crazy.

"Well, we tried," Lenore says.

Julie stands in front of the fire, with her back to Lenore. Lenore knows she is thinking that she is dense—that she does not recognize the implications.

"They might have walked through the woods instead of along the road," Lenore says. "That's possible."

"But they would have gone out to the road to thumb when the rain began, wouldn't they?"

Perhaps she misunderstood what Julie was thinking. Perhaps it has never occurred to Julie until now what might be going on.

"Maybe they got lost," Julie says. "Maybe something happened to them."

"Nothing happened to them," Lenore says. Julie turns around and Lenore catches that small point of light in her eye again. "Maybe they took shelter under a tree," she says. "Maybe they're screwing. How should I know?"

It is not a word Lenore often uses. She usually tries not to think about that at all, but she can sense that Julie is very upset.

"Really?" Julie says. "Don't you care, Mrs. Anderson?"

Lenore is amused. There's a switch. All the students call her husband George and her Lenore; now one of them wants to think there's a real adult here to explain all this to her.

"What am I going to do?" Lenore says. She shrugs.

Julie does not answer.

"Would you like me to pour you tea?" Lenore asks.

"Yes," Julie says. "Please."

George and Sarah return in the middle of the afternoon. George says that they decided to go on a spree to the big city—it is really a small town he is talking about, but calling it the big city gives him an opportunity to speak ironically. They sat in a restaurant bar, waiting for the rain to stop, George says, and then they thumbed a ride home. "But I'm completely sober," George says, turning for the first time to Sarah. "What about you?" He is all smiles. Sarah lets him down. She looks embarrassed. Her eyes meet Lenore's quickly, and jump to Julie. The two girls stare at each other, and Lenore, left with only George to look at, looks at the fire and then gets up to pile on another log.

Gradually it becomes clear that they are trapped together by the rain. Maria undresses her paper doll and deliberately rips a feather off its hat. Then she takes the pieces to Lenore, almost in tears. The baby cries, and Lenore takes him off the sofa, where he has been sleeping under his yellow blanket, and props him in the space between her legs as she leans back on her elbows to watch the fire. It's her fire, and she has the excuse of presiding over it.

"How's my boy?" George says. The baby looks, and looks away.

It gets dark early, because of the rain. At four-thirty George uncorks a bottle of Beaujolais and brings it into the living room, with four glasses pressed against his chest with his free arm. Julie rises nervously to extract the glasses, thanking him too profusely for the wine. She gives a glass to Sarah without looking at her.

They sit in a semicircle in front of the fire and drink the wine. Julie leafs through magazines—New Times, National Geographic—and Sarah holds a small white dish painted with gray-green leaves that she has taken from the coffee table; the dish contains a few shells and some acorn caps, a polished stone or two, and Sarah lets these objects run through her fingers. There are several such dishes in the house, assembled by George. He and Lenore gathered the shells long ago, the first time they went away together, at a beach in North Carolina. But the acorn caps, the shiny turquoise and amethyst stones—those are there, she knows, because George likes the effect they have on visitors; it is an expected unconventionality, really. He has also acquired a few small framed pictures, which he points out to guests who are more important than worshipful students—tiny oil paintings of fruit, prints with small details from the Unicorn Tapestries. He pretends to like small, elegant things. Actually, when they visit museums in New York he goes first to El Grecos and big Mark Rothko canvases. She could never get him to admit that what he said or did was sometimes false. Once, long ago, when he asked if he was still the man of her dreams, she said, "We don't get along well anymore." "Don't talk about it," he said—no denial, no protest. At best, she could say things and get away with them; she could never get him to continue such a conversation.

At the dinner table, lit with white candles burning in empty wine bottles, they eat off his grandmother's small flowery plates. Lenore looks out a window and sees, very faintly in the dark, their huge oak tree. The rain has stopped. A few stars have come out, and there are glints on the wet branches. The oak tree grows very close to the window. George loved it when her brother once suggested that some of the bushes and trees should be pruned away from the house so it would not always be so dark inside; it gave him a chance to rave about the beauty of nature, to say that he would never tamper with it. "It's like a tomb in here all day," her brother had said. Since moving here, George has learned the names of almost all the things that are growing on the land: he can point out abelia bushes, spirea, laurels. He subscribes to National Geographic (although she rarely sees him looking at it). He is at last in touch, he says, being in the country puts him in touch. He is saying it now to Sarah, who has put down her ivory-handled fork to listen to him. He gets up to change the record. Side 2 of the Telemann record begins softly.

Sarah is still very much on guard with Lenore; she makes polite conversation with her quickly when George is out of the room. "You people are so wonderful," she says. "I wish my parents could be like you."

"George would be pleased to hear that," Lenore says, lifting a small piece of pasta to her lips.

When George is seated again, Sarah, anxious to please, tells him, "If only my father could be like you."

"Your father," George says. "I won't have that analogy." He says it pleasantly, but barely disguises his dismay at the comparison.

"I mean, he cares about nothing but business," the girl stumbles on. The music, in contrast, grows lovelier.

Lenore goes into the kitchen to get the salad and hears George say, "I simply won't let you girls leave. Nobody leaves on a Saturday."

There are polite protests, there are compliments to Lenore on the meal—there is too much talk. Lenore has trouble caring about what's going on. The food is warm and delicious. She pours more wine and lets them talk.

"Godard, yes, I know . . . panning that row of honking cars *so* slowly, that long line of cars stretching on and on."

She has picked up the end of George's conversation. His arm slowly waves out over the table, indicating the line of motionless cars in the movie.

"That's a lovely plant," Julie says to Lenore.

"It's Peruvian ivy," Lenore says. She smiles. She is supposed to smile. She will not offer to hack shoots off her plant for these girls.

Sarah asks for a Dylan record when the Telemann finishes playing. White wax drips onto the wood table. George waits for it to solidify slightly, then scrapes up the little circles and with thumb and index finger flicks them gently toward Sarah. He explains (although she asked for no particular Dylan record) that he has only Dylan before he went electric. And *Planet Waves*—"because it's so romantic. That's silly of me, but true." Sarah smiles at him. Julie smiles at Lenore. Julie is being polite, taking her cues from Sarah, really not understanding what's going on. Lenore does not smile back. She has done enough to put them at ease. She is tired now, brought down by the music, a full stomach, and again the sounds of rain outside. For dessert there is homemade vanilla ice cream, made by George, with small black vanilla-bean flecks in it. He is still drinking wine, though; another bottle has been opened. He sips wine and then taps his spoon on his ice cream, looking at Sarah.

Sarah smiles, letting them all see the smile, then sucks the ice cream off her spoon. Julie is missing more and more of what's going on. Lenore watches as Julie strokes her hand absently on her napkin. She is wearing a thin silver choker and—Lenore notices for the first time—a thin silver ring on the third finger of her right hand.

"It's just terrible about Anna," George says, finishing his wine, his ice cream melting, looking at no one in particular, although Sarah was the one who brought up Anna the night before, when they had been in the house only a short time—Anna dead, hit by a car, hardly an accident at all. Anna was also a student of his. The driver of the car was drunk, but for some reason charges were not pressed. (Sarah and George have talked about this before, but Lenore blocks it out. What can she do about it? She met Anna once: a beautiful girl, with tiny, childlike hands, her hair thin and curly—wary, as beautiful people are wary.) Now the driver has been flipping out, Julie says, and calling Anna's parents, wanting to talk to them to find out why it has happened.

The baby begins to cry. Lenore goes upstairs, pulls up more covers, talks to him for a minute. He settles for this. She goes downstairs. The wine must have affected her more than she realizes; otherwise, why is she counting the number of steps?

In the candlelit dining room, Julie sits alone at the table. The girl has been left alone again; George and Sarah took the umbrellas, decided to go for a walk in the rain.

It is eight o'clock. Since helping Lenore load the dishes into the dishwasher, when she said what a beautiful house Lenore had, Julie has said very little. Lenore is tired, and does not want to make conversation. They sit in the living room and drink wine.

"Sarah is my best friend," Julie says. She seems apologetic about it. "I was so out of it when I came back to college. I was in Italy, with my husband, and suddenly I was back in the States. I couldn't make friends. But Sarah wasn't like the other people. She cared enough to be nice to me."

"How long have you been friends?"

"For two years. She's really the best friend I've ever had. We understand things—we don't always have to talk about them."

"Like her relationship with George," Lenore says.

Too direct. Too unexpected. Julie has no answer.

"You act as if you're to blame," Lenore says.

"I feel strange because you're such a nice lady."

A nice lady! What an odd way to speak. Has she been reading Henry James? Lenore has never known what to think of herself, but she certainly thinks of herself as being more complicated than a "lady."

"Why do you look that way?" Julie asks. "You *are* nice. I think you've been very nice to us. You've given up your whole weekend."

"I always give up my weekends. Weekends are the only time we socialize, really. In a way, it's good to have something to do."

"But to have it turn out like this. . . ." Julie says. "I think I feel so strange because when my own marriage broke up I didn't even suspect. I mean, I couldn't act the way you do, anyway, but I—"

"For all I know, nothing's going on," Lenore says. "For all I know, your friend is flattering herself, and George is trying to make me jealous." She puts two more logs on the fire. When these are gone, she will either have to walk to the woodshed or give up and go to bed. "Is there something . . . *major* going on?" she asks.

Julie is sitting on the rug, by the fire, twirling her hair with her finger. "I didn't know it when I came out here," she says. "Sarah's put me in a very awkward position."

"But do you know how far it has gone?" Lenore asks, genuinely curious now.

"No," Julie says.

No way to know if she's telling the truth. Would Julie speak the truth to a lady? Probably not.

"Anyway," Lenore says with a shrug. "I don't want to think about it all the time."

"I'd never have the courage to live with a man and not marry," Julie says. "I mean, I wish I had, that we hadn't gotten married, but I just don't have that kind of . . . I'm not secure enough."

"You have to live somewhere," Lenore says.

Julie is looking at her as if she does not believe that she is sincere. Am I? Lenore wonders. She has lived with George for six years, and sometimes she thinks she has caught his way of playing games, along with his colds, his bad moods.

"I'll show you something," Lenore says. She gets up, and Julie follows. Lenore puts on the light in George's study, and they walk through it to a bathroom he has converted to a darkroom. Under a table, in a box behind another box, there is a stack of pictures. Lenore takes them out and hands them to Julie. They are pictures that Lenore found in his darkroom last summer; they were left out by mistake, no doubt, and she found them when she went in with some contact prints he had left in their bedroom. They are high-contrast photographs of George's face. In all of them he looks very serious and very sad; in some of them his eyes seem to be narrowed in pain. In one, his mouth is open. It is an excellent photograph of a man in agony, a man about to scream.

"What are they?" Julie whispers.

"Pictures he took of himself," Lenore says. She shrugs. "So I stay," she says.

Julie nods. Lenore nods, taking the pictures back. Lenore has not thought until this minute that this may be why she stays. In fact, it is not the only reason. It is just a very demonstrable, impressive reason. When she first saw the pictures, her own face had become as distorted as George's. She had simply not known what to do. She had been frightened and ashamed. Finally she put them in an empty box, and put the box behind another box. She did not even want him to see the horrible pictures again. She does not know if he has ever found them, pushed back against the wall in that other box. As George says, there can be too much communication between people.

Later, Sarah and George come back to the house. It is still raining. It turns out that they took a bottle of brandy with them, and they are both drenched and drunk. He holds Sarah's finger with one of his. Sarah, seeing Lenore, lets his finger go. But then he turns—they have not even said hello yet—and grabs her up, spins her around, stumbling into the living room, and says, "I am in love."

Julie and Lenore watch them in silence.

"See no evil," George says, gesturing with the empty brandy bottle to Julie. "Hear no evil," George says, pointing to Lenore. He hugs Sarah closer. "I speak no evil. I speak the truth. I am in love!"

Sarah squirms away from him, runs from the room and up the stairs in the dark.

George looks blankly after her, then sinks to the floor and smiles. He is going to pass it off as a joke. Julie looks at him in horror, and from upstairs Sarah can be heard sobbing. Her crying awakens the baby.

"Excuse me," Lenore says. She climbs the stairs and goes into her son's room, and picks him up. She talks gently to him, soothing him with lies. He is too sleepy to be alarmed for long. In a few minutes he is asleep again, and she puts him back in his crib. In the next room Sarah is crying more quietly now. Her crying is so awful that Lenore almost joins in, but instead she pats her son. She stands in the dark by the crib and then at last goes out and down the hallway to her bedroom. She takes off her clothes and gets into the cold bed. She concentrates on breathing normally. With the door closed and Sarah's door closed, she can hardly hear her. Someone taps lightly on her door.

"Mrs. Anderson," Julie whispers. "Is this your room?"

"Yes," Lenore says. She does not ask her in.

"We're going to leave. I'm going to get Sarah and leave. I didn't want to just walk out without saying anything."

Lenore just cannot think how to respond. It was really very kind of Julie to say something. She is very close to tears, so she says nothing.

"Okay," Julie says, to reassure herself. "Good night. We're going."

There is no more crying. Footsteps. Miraculously, the baby does not wake up again, and Maria has slept through all of it. She has always slept well. Lenore herself sleeps worse and worse, and she knows that George walks much of the night, most nights. She hasn't said anything about it. If he thinks she's simple, what good would her simple wisdom do him?

The oak tree scrapes against the window in the wind and rain. Here on the second floor, under the roof, the tinny tapping is very loud. If Sarah and Julie say anything to George before they leave, she doesn't hear them. She hears the car start, then die out. It starts again—she is praying for the car to go—and after conking out once more it rolls slowly away, crunching gravel. The bed is no warmer; she shivers. She tries hard to fall asleep. The effort keeps her awake. She squints her eyes in concentration instead of closing them. The only sound in the house is the electric clock, humming by her bed. It is not even midnight.

She gets up, and without turning on the light, walks downstairs. George is still in the living room. The fire is nothing but ashes and glowing bits of wood. It is as cold there as it was in the bed.

"That damn bitch," George says. "I should have known she was a stupid little girl."

"You went too far," Lenore says. "I'm the only one you can go too far with."

"Damn it," he says, and pokes the fire. A few sparks shoot up. "Damn it," he repeats under his breath.

His sweater is still wet. His shoes are muddy and ruined. Sitting on the floor by the fire, his hair matted down on his head, he looks ugly, older, unfamiliar.

She thinks of another time, when it was warm. They were walking on the beach together, shortly after they met, gathering shells. Little waves were rolling in. The sun went behind the clouds and there was a momentary illusion that the clouds were still and the sun was racing ahead of them. "Catch me," he said, breaking away from her. They had been talking quietly, gathering shells. She was so surprised at him for breaking away that she ran with all her energy and did catch him, putting her hand out and taking hold of the band of his swimming trunks as he veered into the water. If she hadn't stopped him, would he really have run far out into the water, until she couldn't follow anymore? He turned on her, just as abruptly as he had run away, and grabbed her and hugged her hard, lifted her high. She had clung to him, held him close. He had tried the same thing when he came back from the walk with Sarah, and it hadn't worked.

"I wouldn't care if their car went off the road," he says bitterly.

"Don't say that," she says.

They sit in silence, listening to the rain. She slides over closer to him, puts her hand on his shoulder and leans her head there, as if he could protect her from the awful things he has wished into being.

A VINTAGE THUNDERBIRD

Nick and Karen had driven from Virginia to New York in a little under six hours. They had made good time, keeping ahead of the rain all the way, and it was only now, while they were in the restaurant, that the rain began. It had been a nice summer weekend in the country with their friends Stephanie and Sammy, but all the time he was there Nick had worried that Karen had consented to go with him only out of pity; she had been dating another man, and when Nick suggested the weekend she had been reluctant. When she said she would go, he decided that she had given in for old time's sake.

The car they drove was hers—a white Thunderbird convertible. Every time he drove the car, he admired it more. She owned many things that he admired: a squirrel coat with a black taffeta lining, a pair of carved soapstone bookends that held some books of poetry on her night table, her collection of Louis Armstrong 78s. He loved to go to her apartment and look at her things. He was excited by them, the way he had been spellbound, as a child, exploring the playrooms of schoolmates.

He had met Karen several years before, soon after he came to New York. Her brother had lived in the same building he lived in then, and the three of them met on the volleyball courts adjacent to the building. Her brother moved across town within a few months, but by then Nick knew Karen's telephone number. At her suggestion, they had started running in Central Park on Sundays. It was something he looked forward to all week. When they left the park, his elation was always mixed with a little embarrassment over his panting and his being sweaty on the street, but she had no self-consciousness. She didn't care if her shirt stuck to her body, or if she looked unattractive with her wet, matted hair. Or perhaps she knew that she never looked really unattractive;

men always looked at her. One time, on Forty-second Street, during a light rain, Nick stopped to read a movie marquee, and when he turned back to Karen she was laughing and protesting that she couldn't take the umbrella that a man was offering her. It was only when Nick came to her side that the man stopped insisting—a nicely dressed man who was only offering her his big black umbrella, and not trying to pick her up. Things like this were hard for Nick to accept, but Karen was not flirtatious, and he could see that it was not her fault that men looked at her and made gestures.

It became a routine that on Sundays they jogged or went to a basketball court. One time, when she got frustrated because she hadn't been able to do a simple hook shot—hadn't made a basket that way all morning—he lifted her to his shoulders and charged the backboard so fast that she almost missed the basket from there too. After playing basketball, they would go to her apartment and she would make dinner. He would collapse, but she was full of energy and she would poke fun at him while she studied a cookbook, staring at it until she knew enough of a recipe to begin preparing the food. His two cookbooks were dog-eared and sauce stained, but Karen's were perfectly clean. She looked at recipes, but never followed them exactly. He admired this—her creativity, her energy. It took him a long while to accept that she thought he was special, and later, when she began to date other men, it took him a long while to realize that she did not mean to shut him out of her life. The first time she went away with a man for the weekend—about a year after he first met her—she stopped by his apartment on her way to Pennsylvania and gave him the keys to her Thunderbird. She left so quickly—the man was downstairs in his car, waiting—that as he watched her go he could feel the warmth of her hand on the keys.

Just recently Nick had met the man she was dating now: a gaunt psychology professor, with a black-and-white tweed cap and a thick mustache that made him look like a sad-mouthed clown. Nick had gone to her apartment not knowing for certain that the man would be there—actually, it was Friday night, the beginning of the weekend, and he had gone on the hunch that he finally would meet him—and had drunk a vodka collins that the man mixed for him. He remembered that the man had complained tediously that Paul McCartney had stolen words from Thomas Dekker for a song on the *Abbey Road* album, and that the man said he got hives from eating shellfish.

In the restaurant now, Nick looked across the table at Karen and said, "That man you're dating is a real bore. What is he—a scholar?"

He fumbled for a cigarette and then remembered that he no longer smoked. He had given it up a year before, when he went to visit an old girlfriend in New Haven. Things had gone badly, they had quarreled, and he had left her to go to a bar. Coming out, he was approached by a tall black round-faced teenager and told to hand over his wallet, and he had mutely reached inside his coat and pulled it out and given it to the boy. A couple of people came out of the bar, took in the situation, and walked away quickly, pretending not to notice. The boy had a small penknife in his hand. "And your cigarettes," the boy said. Nick had reached inside his jacket pocket and handed over the cigarettes. The boy pocketed them. Then the boy smiled and cocked his head and held up the wallet, like a hypnotist dangling a pocket watch. Nick stared dumbly at his own wallet. Then, before he knew what was happening, the boy turned into a blur of motion: he grabbed his arm and yanked hard, like a judo wrestler, and threw him across the sidewalk. Nick fell against a car that was parked at the curb. He was so frightened that his legs buckled and he went down. The boy watched him fall. Then he nodded and walked down the sidewalk past the bar. When the boy was out of sight, Nick got up and went into the bar to tell his story. He let the bartender give him a beer and call the police. He declined the bartender's offer of a cigarette, and had never smoked since.

His thoughts were drifting, and Karen still had not answered his question. He knew that he had already angered her once that day, and that it had been a mistake to speak of the man again. Just an hour or so earlier, when they got back to the city, he had been abrupt with her friend Kirby. She kept her car in Kirby's garage, and in exchange for the privilege she moved into his brownstone whenever he went out of town and took care of his six declawed chocolate-point cats. Actually, Kirby's psychiatrist, a Dr. Kellogg, lived in the same house, but the doctor had made it clear he did not live there to take care of cats.

From his seat Nick could see the sign of the restaurant hanging outside the front window. STAR THROWER CAFÉ, it said, in lavender neon. He got depressed thinking that if she became more serious about the professor—he had lasted longer than any of the others—he would only be able to see her by pretending to run into her at places like the Star Thrower. He had also begun to think that he had driven the Thunderbird for the last time. She had almost refused to let him drive it again after the time, two weeks earlier, when he tapped a car in front of them on Sixth Avenue, making a dent above the left headlight. Long ago she had stopped letting him use her squirrel coat as a kind of blanket. He used to like to lie naked on the tiny balcony outside her apartment in the autumn, with the Sunday *Times* arranged under him for padding and the coat spread on top of him. Now he counted back and came up with the figure: he had known Karen for seven years.

"What are you thinking?" he said to her.

"That I'm glad I'm not thirty-eight years old, with a man putting pressure on me to have a baby." She was talking about Stephanie and Sammy.

Her hand was on the table. He cupped his hand over it just as the waiter came with the plates.

"What are *you* thinking?" she said, withdrawing her hand.

"At least Stephanie has the sense not to do it," he said. He picked up his fork and put it down. "Do you really love that man?"

"If I loved him, I suppose I'd be at my apartment, where he's been waiting for over an hour. If he waited."

When they finished she ordered espresso. He ordered it also. He had half expected her to say at some point that the trip with him was the end, and he still thought she might say that. Part of the problem was that she had money and he didn't. She had had money since she was twenty-one, when she got control of a fifty-thousand-dollar trust fund her grandfather had left her. He remembered the day she had bought the Thunderbird. It was the day after her birthday, five years ago. That night, laughing, they had driven the car through the Lincoln Tunnel and then down the back roads in Jersey, with a stream of orange crepe paper blowing from the radio antenna, until the wind ripped it off.

"Am I still going to see you?" Nick said.

"I suppose," Karen said. "Although things have changed be-tween us."

"I've known you for seven years. You're my oldest friend."

She did not react to what he said, but much later, around midnight, she called him at his apartment. "Was what you said at the Star Thrower calculated to make me feel bad?" she said. "When you said that I was your oldest friend?"

"No," he said. "You are my oldest friend."

"You must know somebody longer than you've known me."

"You're the only person I've seen regularly for seven years."

She sighed.

"Professor go home?" he said.

"No. He's here."

"You're saying all this in front of him?"

"I don't see why there has to be any secret about this."

"You could put an announcement in the paper," Nick said. "Run a little picture of me with it."

"Why are you so sarcastic?"

"It's embarrassing. It's embarrassing that you'd say this in front of that man."

He was sitting in the dark, in a chair by the phone. He had wanted to call her ever since he got back from the restaurant. The long day of driving had finally caught up with him, and his shoulders ached. He felt the black boy's hands on his arm, felt his own body folding up, felt himself flying backward. He had lost sixty-five dollars that night. The day she bought the Thunderbird, he had driven it through the tunnel into New Jersey. He had driven, then she had driven, and then he had driven again. Once he had pulled into the parking lot of a shopping center and told her to wait, and had come back with the orange crepe paper. Years later he had looked for the road they had been on that night, but he could never find it.

The next time Nick heard from her was almost three weeks after the trip to Virginia. Since he didn't have the courage to call her, and since he expected not to hear from her at all, he was surprised to pick up the phone and hear her voice. Petra had been in his apartment—a woman at his office whom he had always wanted to date and who had just broken off an unhappy engagement. As he held the phone clamped between his ear and shoulder, he looked admiringly at Petra's profile.

"What's up?" he said to Karen, trying to sound very casual for Petra.

"Get ready," Karen said. "Stephanie called and said that she was going to have a baby."

"What do you mean? I thought she told you in Virginia that she thought Sammy was crazy to want a kid."

"It happened by accident. She missed her period just after we left."

Petra shifted on the couch and began leafing through *Newsweek*.

"Can I call you back?" he said.

"Throw whatever woman is there out of your apartment and talk to me now," Karen said. "I'm about to go out."

He looked at Petra, who was sipping her drink. "I can't do that," he said.

"Then call me when you can. But call back tonight."

When he hung up, he took Petra's glass but found that he had run out of Scotch. He suggested that they go to a bar on West Tenth Street.

When they got to the bar, he excused himself almost immediately. Karen had sounded depressed, and he could not enjoy his evening with Petra until he made sure everything was all right. Once he heard her voice, he knew he wanted to be with her and not Petra. He told her that he was going to come to her apartment when he had finished having a drink, and she said that he should come over immediately or not at all, because she was about to go to the professor's. She was so abrupt that he wondered if she could be jealous.

He went back to the bar and sat on the stool next to Petra and picked up his Scotch-and-water and took a big drink. It was so cold that it made his teeth ache. Petra had on blue slacks and a white blouse. He rubbed his hand up and down her back, just below the shoulders. She was not wearing a brassiere.

"I have to leave," he said.

"You have to leave? Are you coming back?"

He started to speak, but she put up her hand. "Never mind," she said. "I don't want you to come back." She sipped her margarita. "Whoever the woman is you just called, I hope the two of you have a splendid evening."

Petra gave him a hard look, and he knew that she really wanted him to go. He stared at her—at the little crust of salt on her bottom lip—and then she turned away from him.

He hesitated for just a second before he left the bar. He went outside and walked about ten steps, and then he was jumped. They got him from behind, and in his shock and confusion he thought that he had been hit by a car. He lost sense of where he was, and although it was a dull blow, he thought that somehow a car had hit him. Looking up from the sidewalk, he saw them—two men, younger than he was, picking at him like vultures, pushing him, rummaging through his jacket and his pockets. The crazy thing was he was on West Tenth Street; there should have been other people on the street, but there were not. His clothes were tearing. His right hand was wet with blood. They had cut his arm, the shirt was bloodstained, he saw his own blood spreading out into a little puddle. He stared at it and was afraid to move his hand out of it. Then the men were gone and he was left half sitting, propped up against a building where they had dragged him. He was able to push himself up, but the man he began telling the story to, a passerby, kept coming into focus and fading out again. The man had on a sombrero, and he was pulling him up but pulling too hard. His legs didn't have the power to support him—something had happened to his legs—so that when the man loosened his grip he went down on his knees. He kept blinking to stay conscious. He blacked out before he could stand again.

Back in his apartment, later that night, with his arm in a cast, he felt confused and ashamed—ashamed for the way he had treated Petra, and ashamed for having been mugged. He wanted to call Karen, but he was too embarrassed. He sat in the chair by the phone, willing her to call him. At midnight the phone rang, and he picked it up at once, sure that his telepathic message had worked. The phone call was from Stephanie, at La Guardia. She had been trying to reach Karen and couldn't. She wanted to know if she could come to his apartment.

"I'm not going through with it," Stephanie said, her voice wavering. "I'm thirty-eight years old, and this was a goddamn accident."

"Calm down," he said. "We can get you an abortion."

"I don't know if I could take a human life," she said, and she began to cry.

"Stephanie?" he said. "You okay? Are you going to get a cab?"

More crying, no answer.

"Because it would be silly for me to get a cab just to come get you. You can make it here okay, can't you, Steph?"

The cabdriver who took him to La Guardia was named Arthur Shales. A small pink baby shoe was glued to the dashboard of the cab. Arthur Shales chain-smoked Picayunes. "Woman I took to Bendel's today, I'm still trying to get over it," he said. "I picked her up at Madison and Seventy-fifth. Took her to Bendel's and pulled up in front and she said, 'Oh, screw Bendel's.' I took her back to Madison and Seventy-fifth."

Going across the bridge, Nick said to Arthur Shales that the woman he was going to pick up was going to be very upset.

"Upset? What do I care? Neither of you are gonna hold a gun to my head, I can take anything. You're my last fares of the night. Take you back where you came from, then I'm heading home myself."

When they were almost at the airport exit, Arthur Shales snorted and said, "Home is a room over an Italian grocery. Guy who runs it woke me up at six this morning, yelling so loud at his supplier. 'You call these tomatoes?' he was saying. 'I could take these out and bat them on the tennis court.' Guy is always griping about tomatoes being so unripe."

Stephanie was standing on the walkway, right where she had said she would be. She looked haggard, and Nick was not sure that he could cope with her. He raised his hand to his shirt pocket for cigarettes, forgetting once again that he had given up smoking. He also forgot that he couldn't grab anything with his right hand because his arm was in a cast.

"You know who I had in my cab the other day?" Arthur Shales said, coasting to a stop in front of the terminal. "You're not going to believe it. Al Pacino."

.　.　.

For more than a week, Nick and Stephanie tried to reach Karen. Stephanie began to think that Karen was dead. And although Nick chided her for calling Karen's number so often, he began to worry too. Once he went to her apartment on his lunch hour and listened at the door. He heard nothing, but he put his mouth close to the door and asked her to please open the door, if she was there, because there was trouble with Stephanie. As he left the building he had to laugh at what it would have looked like if someone had seen him—a nicely dressed man, with his hands on either side of his mouth, leaning into a door and talking to it. And one of the hands in a cast.

For a week he came straight home from work, to keep Stephanie company. Then he asked Petra if she would have dinner with him. She said no. As he was leaving the office, he passed by her desk without looking at her. She got up and followed him down the hall and said, "I'm having a drink with somebody after work, but I could meet you for a drink around seven o'clock."

He went home to see if Stephanie was all right. She said that she had been sick in the morning, but after the card came in the mail—she held out a postcard to him—she felt much better. The card was addressed to him; it was from Karen, in Bermuda. She said she had spent the afternoon on a sailboat. No explanation. He read the message several times. He felt very relieved. He asked Stephanie if she wanted to go out for a drink with him and Petra. She said no, as he had known she would.

At seven he sat alone at a table in the Blue Bar, with the postcard in his inside pocket. There was a folded newspaper on the little round table where he sat, and his broken right wrist rested on it. He sipped a beer. At seven-thirty he opened the paper and looked through the theater section. At quarter to eight he got up and left. He walked over to Fifth Avenue and began to walk downtown. In one of the store windows there was a poster for Bermuda tourism. A woman in a turquoise-blue bathing suit was rising out of blue waves, her mouth in an unnaturally wide smile. She seemed oblivious of the little boy next to her who was tossing a ball into the sky. Standing there, looking at the poster, Nick began a mental game that he had sometimes played in college. He invented a cartoon about Bermuda. It was a split-frame drawing. Half of it showed a beautiful girl, in the arms of her lover, on the pink sandy beach of Bermuda, with the caption: "It's glorious to be here in Bermuda." The other half of the frame showed a tall tired man looking into the window of a travel agency at a picture of the lady and her lover. He would have no lines, but in a balloon above his head he would be wondering if, when he went home, it was the right time to urge an abortion to the friend who had moved into his apartment.

When he got home, Stephanie was not there. She had said that if she felt better, she would go out to eat. He sat down and took off his shoes and socks and hung forward, with his head almost touching his knees, like a droopy doll. Then he went into the bedroom, carrying the shoes and socks, and took off his clothes and put on jeans. The phone rang and he picked it up just as he heard Stephanie's key in the door.

"I'm sorry," Petra said, "I've never stood anybody up before in my life."

"Never mind," he said. "I'm not mad."

"I'm very sorry," she said.

"I drank a beer and read the paper. After what I did to you the other night, I don't blame you."

"I like you," she said. "That was why I didn't come. Because I knew I wouldn't say what I wanted to say. I got as far as Forty-eighth Street and turned around."

"What did you want to say?"

"That I like you. That I like you and that it's a mistake, because I'm always letting myself in for it, agreeing to see men who treat me badly. I wasn't very flattered the other night."

"I know. I apologize. Look, why don't you meet me at that bar now and let me not walk out on you. Okay?"

"No," she said, her voice changing. "That wasn't why I called. I called to say I was sorry, but I know I did the right thing. I have to hang up now."

He put the phone back and continued to look at the floor. He knew that Stephanie was not even pretending not to have heard. He took a step forward and ripped the phone out of the wall. It was not a very successful dramatic gesture. The phone just popped out of the jack, and he stood there, holding it in his good hand.

"Would you think it was awful if I offered to go to bed with you?" Stephanie asked.

"No," he said. "I think it would be very nice."

Two days later he left work early in the afternoon and went to Kirby's. Dr. Kellogg opened the door and then pointed toward the back of the house and said, "The man you're looking for is reading." He was wearing baggy white pants and a Japanese kimono.

Nick almost had to push through the half-open door because the psychiatrist was so intent on holding the cats back with one foot. In the kitchen Kirby was indeed reading—he was looking at a Bermuda travel brochure and listening to Karen.

She looked sheepish when she saw him. Her face was tan, and her eyes, which were always beautiful, looked startlingly blue now that her face was so dark. She had lavender-tinted sunglasses pushed on top of her head. She and Kirby seemed happy and comfortable in the elegant, air-conditioned house.

"When did you get back?" Nick said.

"A couple of days ago," she said. "The night I last talked to you, I went over to the professor's apartment, and in the morning we went to Bermuda."

Nick had come to Kirby's to get the car keys and borrow the Thunderbird—to go for a ride and be by himself for a while—and for a moment now he thought of asking her for the keys anyway. He sat down at the table.

"Stephanie is in town," he said. "I think we ought to go get a cup of coffee and talk about it."

Her key ring was on the table. If he had the keys, he could be heading for the Lincoln Tunnel. Years ago, they would be walking to the car hand in hand, in love. It would be her birthday. The car's odometer would have five miles on it.

One of Kirby's cats jumped up on the table and began to sniff at the butter dish there.

"Would you like to walk over to the Star Thrower and get a cup of coffee?" Nick said.

She got up slowly.

"Don't mind me," Kirby said.

"Would you like to come, Kirby?" she asked.

"Not me. No, no."

She patted Kirby's shoulder, and they went out.

"What happened?" she said, pointing to his hand.

"It's broken."

"How did you break it?"

"Never mind," he said. "I'll tell you when we get there."

When they got there it was not yet four o'clock, and the Star Thrower was closed.

"Well, just tell me what's happening with Stephanie," Karen said impatiently. "I don't really feel like sitting around talking because I haven't even unpacked yet."

"She's at my apartment, and she's pregnant, and she doesn't even talk about Sammy."

She shook her head sadly. "How did you break your hand?" she said.

"I was mugged. After our last pleasant conversation on the phone—the time you told me to come over immediately or not at all. I didn't make it because I was in the emergency room."

"Oh, Christ," she said. "Why didn't you call me?"

"I was embarrassed to call you."

"Why? Why didn't you call?"

"You wouldn't have been there anyway." He took her arm. "Let's find someplace to go," he said.

Two young men came up to the door of the Star Thrower. "Isn't this where David had that great Armenian dinner?" one of them said.

"I *told* you it wasn't," the other said, looking at the menu posted to the right of the door.

"I didn't really think this was the place. *You* said it was on this street."

They continued to quarrel as Nick and Karen walked away.

"Why do you think Stephanie came here to the city?" Karen said.

"Because we're her friends," Nick said.

"But she has lots of friends."

"Maybe she thought we were more dependable."

"Why do you say that in that tone of voice? I don't have to tell you every move I'm making. Things went very well in Bermuda. He almost lured me to London."

"Look," he said. "Can't we go somewhere where you can call her?"

He looked at her, shocked because she didn't understand that Stephanie had come to see her, not him. He had seen for a long time that it didn't matter to her how much she meant to him, but he had never realized that she didn't know how much she meant to Stephanie. She didn't understand people. When he found out she had another man, he should have dropped out of her life. She did not deserve her good looks and her fine car and all her money. He turned to face her on the street, ready to tell her what he thought.

"You know what happened there?" she said. "I got sunburned and had a terrible time. He went on to London without me."

He took her arm again and they stood side by side and looked at some sweaters hanging in the window of Countdown.

"So going to Virginia wasn't the answer for them," she said. "Remember when Sammy and Stephanie left town, and we told each other what a stupid idea it was—that it would never work out? Do you think we jinxed them?"

They walked down the street again, saying nothing.

"It would kill me if I had to be a good conversationalist with you," she said at last. "You're the only person I can rattle on with." She stopped and leaned into him. "I had a rotten time in Bermuda," she said. "Nobody should go to a beach but a sand flea."

"You don't have to make clever conversation with me," he said.

"I know," she said. "It just happened."

Late in the afternoon of the day that Stephanie had her abortion, Nick called Sammy from a street phone near his apartment. Karen and Stephanie were in the apartment, but he had to get out for a while. Stephanie had seemed pretty cheerful, but perhaps it was just an act for his benefit. With him gone, she might talk to Karen about it. All she had told him was that it felt like she had caught an ice pick in the stomach.

"Sammy?" Nick said into the phone. "How are you? It just dawned on me that I ought to call and let you know that Stephanie is all right."

"She has called me herself, several times," Sammy said. "Collect. From your phone. But thank you for your concern, Nick." He sounded brusque.

"Oh," Nick said, taken aback. "Just so you know where she is."

"I could name you as corespondent in the divorce case, you know?"

"What would you do that for?" Nick said.

"I wouldn't. I just wanted you to know what I could do."

"Sammy—I don't get it. I didn't ask for any of this, you know."

"Poor Nick. My wife gets pregnant, leaves without a word, calls from New York with a story about how you had a broken hand and were having bad luck with women, so she went to bed with you. Two weeks later I get a phone call from you, all concern, wanting me to know where Stephanie is."

Nick waited for Sammy to hang up on him.

"You know what happened to you?" Sammy said. "You got eaten up by New York."

"What kind of dumb thing is that to say?" Nick said. "Are you try-ing to get even or something?"

"If I wanted to do that, I could tell you that you have bad teeth. Or that Stephanie said you were a lousy lover. What I was trying to do was tell you something important, for a change. Stephanie ran away when I tried to tell it to her, you'll probably hang up on me when I say the same thing to you: you can be happy. For instance, you can get out of New York and get away from Karen. Stephanie could have settled down with a baby."

"This doesn't sound like you, Sammy, to give advice."

He waited for Sammy's answer.

"You think I ought to leave New York?" Nick said.

"Both. Karen *and* New York. Do you know that your normal expression shows pain? Do you know how much Scotch you drank the weekend you visited?"

Nick stared through the grimy plastic window of the phone booth.

"What you just said about my hanging up on you," Nick said. "I was thinking that you were going to hang up on me. When I talk to people, they hang up on me. The conversation just ends that way."

"Why haven't you figured out that you don't know the right kind of people?"

"They're the only people I know."

"Does that seem like any reason for tolerating that sort of rudeness?"

"I guess not."

"Another thing," Sammy went on. "Have you figured out that I'm saying these things to you because when you called I was already drunk? I'm telling you all this because I think you're so numbed out by your lousy life that you probably even don't know I'm not in my right mind."

The operator came on, demanding more money. Nick clattered quarters into the phone. He realized that he was not going to hang up on Sammy, and Sammy was not going to hang up on him. He would have to think of something else to say.

"Give yourself a break," Sammy said. "Boot them out. Stephanie included. She'll see the light eventually and come back to the farm."

"Should I tell her you'll be there? I don't know if—"

"I told her I'd be here when she called. All the times she called. I just told her that I had no idea of coming to get her. I'll tell you another thing. I'll bet—I'll *bet*—that when she first turned up there she called you from the airport, and she wanted you to come for her, didn't she?"

"Sammy," Nick said, staring around him, wild to get off the phone. "I want to thank you for saying what you think. I'm going to hang up now."

"Forget it," Sammy said. "I'm not in my right mind. Goodbye."

"Goodbye," Nick said.

He hung up and started back to his apartment. He realized that he hadn't told Sammy that Stephanie had had the abortion. On the street he said hello to a little boy—one of the neighborhood children he knew.

He went up the stairs and up to his floor. Some people downstairs were listening to Beethoven. He lingered in the hallway, not wanting to go back to Stephanie and Karen. He took a deep breath and opened the door. Neither of them looked too bad. They said hello silently, each raising one hand.

It had been a hard day. Stephanie's appointment at the abortion clinic had been at eight in the morning. Karen had slept in the apartment with them the night before, on the sofa. Stephanie slept in his bed, and he slept on the floor. None of them had slept much. In the morning they all went to the abortion clinic. Nick had intended to go to work in the afternoon, but when they got back to the apartment he didn't think it was right for him to leave Stephanie. She went back to the bedroom, and he stretched out on the sofa and fell asleep. Before he slept, Karen sat on the sofa with him for a while, and he told her the story of his second mugging. When he woke up, it was four o'clock. He called his office and told them he was sick. Later they all watched the television news together. After that, he offered to go out and get some food, but nobody was hungry. That's when he went out and called Sammy.

Now Stephanie went back into the bedroom. She said she was tired and she was going to work on a crossword puzzle in bed. The phone rang. It was Petra. She and Nick talked a little about a new apartment she was thinking of moving into. "I'm sorry for being so cold-blooded the other night," she said. "The reason I'm calling is to invite myself to your place for a drink, if that's all right with you."

"It's not all right," he said. "I'm sorry. There are some people here now."

"I get it," she said. "Okay. I won't bother you anymore."

"You don't understand," he said. He knew he had not explained things well, but the thought of adding Petra to the scene at his apartment was more than he could bear, and he had been too abrupt.

She said goodbye coldly, and he went back to his chair and fell in it, exhausted.

"A girl?" Karen said.

He nodded.

"Not a girl you wanted to hear from."

He shook his head no. He got up and pulled up the blind and looked out to the street. The boy he had said hello to was playing with a hula hoop. The hula hoop was bright blue in the twilight. The kid rotated his hips and kept the hoop spinning perfectly. Karen came to the window and stood next to him. He turned to her, wanting to say that they should go and get the Thunderbird, and as the night air cooled, drive out of the city, smell honeysuckle in the fields, feel the wind blowing.

But the Thunderbird was sold. She had told him the news while they were sitting in the waiting room of the abortion clinic. The car had needed a valve job, and a man she met in Bermuda who knew all about cars had advised her to sell it. Coincidentally, the man—a New York architect—wanted to buy it. Even as Karen told him, he knew she had been set up. If she had been more careful, they could have been in the car now, with the key in the ignition, the radio playing. He stood at the window for a long time. She had been conned, and he was more angry than he could tell her. She had no conception—she had somehow never understood—that Thunderbirds of that year, in good condition, would someday be worth a fortune. She had told him this way: "Don't be upset, because I'm sure I made the right decision. I sold the car as soon as I got back from Bermuda. I'm going to get a new car." He had moved in his chair, there in the clinic. He had had an impulse to get up and hit her. He remembered the scene in New Haven outside the bar, and he understood now that it was as simple as this: he had money that the black boy wanted.

Down the street the boy picked up his hula hoop and disappeared around the corner.

"Say you were kidding about selling the car," Nick said.

"When are you going to stop making such a big thing over it?" Karen said.

"That creep cheated you. He talked you into selling it when nothing was wrong with it."

"Stop it," she said. "How come your judgments are always right and my judgments are always wrong?"

"I don't want to fight," he said. "I'm sorry I said anything."

"Okay," she said and leaned her head against him. He draped his right arm over her shoulder. The fingers sticking out of the cast rested a little above her breast.

"I just want to ask one thing," he said, "and then I'll never mention it again. Are you sure the deal is final?"

Karen pushed his hand off her shoulder and walked away. But it was his apartment, and she couldn't go slamming around in it. She sat on the sofa and picked up the newspaper. He watched her. Soon she put it down and stared across the room and into the dark bedroom, where Stephanie had turned off the light. He looked at her sadly for a long time, until she looked up at him with tears in her eyes.

"Do you think maybe we could get it back if I offered him more than he paid me for it?" she said. "You probably don't think that's a sensible suggestion, but at least that way we could get it back."

SHIFTING

The woman's name was Natalie, and the man's name was Larry. They had been childhood sweethearts; he had first kissed her at an ice-skating party when they were ten. She had been unlacing her skates and had not expected the kiss. He had not expected to do it, either—he had some notion of getting his face out of the wind that was blowing across the iced-over lake, and he found himself ducking his head toward her. Kissing her seemed the natural thing to do. When they graduated from high school he was named "class clown" in the yearbook, but Natalie didn't think of him as being particularly funny. He spent more time than she thought he needed to studying chemistry, and he never laughed when she joked. She really did not think of him as funny. They went to the same college, in their hometown, but he left after a year to go to a larger, more impressive university. She took the train to be with him on weekends, or he took the train to see her. When he graduated, his parents gave him a car. If they had given it to him when he was still in college, it would have made things much easier. They waited to give it to him until graduation day, forcing him into attending the graduation exercises. He thought his parents were wonderful people, and Natalie liked them in a way, too, but she resented their perfect timing, their careful smiles. They were afraid that he would marry her. Eventually, he did. He had gone on to graduate school after college, and he set a date six months ahead for their wedding so that it would take place after his first-semester final exams. That way he could devote his time to studying for the chemistry exams.

When she married him, he had had the car for eight months. It still smelled like a brand-new car. There was never any clutter in the car. Even the ice scraper was kept in the glove compartment. There was not even a sweater or a lost glove in the backseat. He vacuumed the car every weekend, after washing it at the car wash. On Friday nights, on their way to some cheap restaurant and a dollar movie, he would stop at the car wash, and she would get out so he could vacuum all over the inside of the car. She would lean against the metal wall of the car wash and watch him clean it.

It was expected that she would not become pregnant. She did not. It had also been expected that she would keep their apartment clean, and keep out of the way as much as possible in such close quarters while he was studying. The apartment was messy, though, and when he was studying late at night she would interrupt him and try to talk him into going to sleep. He gave a chemistry-class lecture once a week, and she would often tell him that overpreparing was as bad as underpreparing. She did not know if she believed this, but it was a favorite line of hers. Sometimes he listened to her.

On Tuesdays, when he gave the lecture, she would drop him off at school and then drive to a supermarket to do the week's shopping. Usually she did not make a list before she went shopping, but when she got to the parking lot she would take a tablet out of her purse and write a few items on it, sitting in the car in the cold. Even having a few things written down would stop her from wandering aimlessly in the store and buying things that she would never use. Before this, she had bought several pans and cans of food that she had not used, or that she could have done without. She felt better when she had a list.

She would drop him at school again on Wednesdays, when he had two seminars that together took up all the afternoon. Sometimes she would drive out of town then, to the suburbs, and shop there if any shopping needed to be done. Otherwise, she would go to the art museum, which was not far away but hard to get to by bus. There was one piece of sculpture in there that she wanted very much to touch, but the guard was always nearby. She came so often that in time the guard began to nod hello. She wondered if she could ever persuade the man to turn his head for a few seconds—only that long—so she could stroke the sculpture. Of course she would never dare ask. After wandering through the museum and looking at least twice at the sculpture, she would go to the gift shop and buy a few postcards and then sit on one of the museum benches, padded with black vinyl, with a Calder mobile hanging overhead, and write notes to friends. (She never wrote letters.) She would tuck the postcards in her purse and mail them when she left the museum. But before she left, she often had coffee in the restaurant: she saw mothers and children struggling there, and women dressed in fancy clothes talking with their faces close together, as quietly as lovers.

On Thursdays he took the car. After his class he would drive to visit his parents and his friend Andy, who had been wounded in Vietnam. About once a month she would go with him, but she had to feel up to it. Being with Andy embarrassed her. She had told him not to go to Vietnam—told him that he could prove his patriotism in some other way—and finally, after she and Larry had made a visit together and she had seen Andy in the motorized bed in his parents' house, Larry had agreed that she need not go again. Andy had apologized to her. It embarrassed her that this man, who had been blown sky-high by a land mine and had lost a leg and lost the full use of his arms, would smile up at her ironically and say, "You were right." She also felt as though he wanted to hear what she would say now, and that now he would listen. Now she had nothing to say. Andy would pull himself up, relying on his right arm, which was the stronger, gripping the rails at the side of the bed, and sometimes he would take her hand. His arms were still weak, but the doctors said he would regain complete use of his right arm with time. She had to make an effort not to squeeze his hand when he held hers because she found herself wanting to squeeze energy back into him. She had a morbid curiosity about what it felt like to be blown from the ground—to go up, and to come crashing down. During their visit Larry put on the class-clown act for Andy, telling funny stories and laughing uproariously.

Once or twice Larry had talked Andy into getting in his wheelchair and had loaded him into the car and taken him to a bar. Larry called her once, late, pretty drunk, to say that he would not be home that night—that he would sleep at his parents' house. "My God," she said. "Are you going to drive Andy home when you're drunk?" "What the hell else can happen to him?" he said.

Larry's parents blamed her for Larry's not being happy. His mother could only be pleasant with her for a short while, and then she would veil her criticisms by putting them as questions. "I know that one thing that helps enormously is good nutrition," his mother said. "He works so hard that he probably needs quite a few vitamins as well, don't you think?" Larry's father was the sort of man who found hobbies in order to avoid his wife. His hobbies were building model boats, repairing clocks, and photography. He took pictures of himself building the boats and fixing the clocks, and gave the pictures, in cardboard frames, to Natalie and Larry for Christmas and birthday presents. Larry's mother was very anxious to stay on close terms with her son, and she knew that Natalie did not like her very much. Once she had visited them during the week, and Natalie, not knowing what to do with her, had taken her to the museum. She had pointed out the sculpture, and his mother had glanced at it and then ignored it. Natalie hated her for her bad taste. She had bad taste in the sweaters she gave Larry, too, but he wore them. They made him look collegiate. That whole world made her sick.

When Natalie's uncle died and left her his 1965 Volvo, they immediately decided to sell it and use the money for a vacation. They put an ad in the paper, and there were several callers. There were some calls on Tuesday, when Larry was in class, and Natalie found herself putting the people off. She told one woman that the car had too much mileage on it, and mentioned body rust, which it did not have; she told another caller, who was very persistent, that the car was already sold. When Larry returned from school she explained that the phone was off the hook because so many people were calling about the car and she had decided not to sell it after all. They could take a little money from their savings account and go on the trip if he wanted. But she did not want to sell the car. "It's not an automatic shift," he said. "You don't know how to drive it." She told him that she could learn. "It will cost money to insure it," he said, "and it's old and probably not even dependable." She wanted to keep the car. "I know," he said, "but it doesn't make sense. When we have more money, you can have a car. You can have a newer, better car."

The next day she went out to the car, which was parked in the driveway of an old lady next door. Her name was Mrs. Larsen and she no longer drove a car, and she told Natalie she could park their second car there. Natalie opened the car door and got behind the wheel and put her hands on it. The wheel was covered with a flaky yellow-and-black plastic cover. She eased it off. A few pieces of foam rubber stuck to the wheel. She picked them off. Underneath the cover, the wheel was a dull red. She ran her fingers around and around the circle of the wheel. Her cousin Burt had delivered the car—a young opportunist, sixteen years old, who said he would drive it the hundred miles from his house to theirs for twenty dollars and a bus ticket home. She had not even invited him to stay for dinner, and Larry had driven him to the bus station. She wondered if it was Burt's cigarette in the ashtray or her dead uncle's. She could not even remember if her uncle smoked. She was surprised that he had left her his car. The car was much more comfortable than Larry's, and it had a nice smell inside. It smelled a little the way a field smells after a spring rain. She rubbed the side of her head back and forth against the window and then got out of the car and went in to see Mrs. Larsen. The night before, she had suddenly thought of the boy who brought the old lady the evening newspaper every night; he looked old enough to drive, and he would probably know how to shift. Mrs. Larsen agreed with her—she was sure that he could teach her. "Of course, everything has its price," the old lady said.

"I know that. I meant to offer him money," Natalie said, and was surprised, listening to her voice, that she sounded old too.

She took an inventory and made a list of things in their apartment. Larry had met an insurance man one evening while playing basketball at the gym who told him that they should have a list of their possessions, in case of theft. "What's worth anything?" she said when he told her. It was their first argument in almost a year—the first time in a year, anyway, that their voices were raised. He told her that several of the pieces of furniture his grandparents gave them when they got married were antiques, and the man at the gym said that if they weren't going to get them appraised every year, at least they should take snapshots of them and keep the pictures in a safe-deposit box. Larry told her to photograph the pie safe (which she used to store linen), the piano with an inlaid mother-of-pearl decoration on the music rack (neither of them knew how to play), and the table with hand-carved wooden handles and a marble top. He bought her an Instamatic camera at the drugstore, with film and flashbulbs. "Why can't you do it?" she said, and an argument began. He said that she had no respect for his profession and no understanding of the amount of study that went into getting a master's degree in chemistry.

That night he went out to meet two friends at the gym, to shoot baskets. She put the little flashcube into the top of the camera, dropped in the film and closed the back. She went first to the piano. She leaned forward so that she was close enough to see the inlay clearly, but she found that when she was that close the whole piano wouldn't fit into the picture. She decided to take two pictures. Then she photographed the pie safe, with one door open, showing the towels and sheets stacked inside. She did not have a reason for opening the door, except that she remembered a *Perry Mason* show in which detectives photographed everything with the doors hanging open. She photographed the table, lifting the lamp off it first. There were still eight pictures left. She went to the mirror in their bedroom and held the camera above her head, pointing down at an angle, and photographed her image in the mirror. She took off her slacks and sat on the floor and leaned back, aiming the camera down at her legs. Then she stood up and took a picture of her feet, leaning over and aiming down. She put on her favorite record: Stevie Wonder singing "For Once in My Life." She found herself wondering what it would be like to be blind, to have to feel things to see them. She thought about the piece of sculpture in the museum—the two elongated mounds, intertwined, the smooth gray stone as shiny as sea pebbles. She photographed the kitchen, bathroom, bedroom, and living room. There was one picture left. She put her left hand on her thigh, palm up, and with some difficulty—with the camera nestled into her neck like a violin—snapped a picture of it with her right hand. The next day would be her first driving lesson.

He came to her door at noon, as he had said he would. He had on a long maroon scarf, which made his deep-blue eyes very striking. She had only seen him from her window when he carried the paper in to the old lady. He was a little nervous. She hoped that it was just the anxiety of any teenager confronting an adult. She needed to have him like her. She did not learn about mechanical things easily (Larry had told her that he would have invested in a "real" camera, except that he did not have the time to teach her about it), so she wanted him to be patient. He sat on the footstool in her living room, still in coat and scarf, and told her how a stick shift operated. He moved his hand through the air. The motion he made reminded her of the salute spacemen gave to earthlings in a science-fiction picture she had recently watched on late-night television. She nodded. "How much—" she began, but he interrupted and said, "You can decide what it was worth when you've learned." She was surprised and wondered if he meant to charge a great deal. Would it be her fault and would she have to pay him if he named his price when the lessons were over? But he had an honest face. Perhaps he was just embarrassed to talk about money.

He drove for a few blocks, making her watch his hand on the stick shift. "Feel how the car is going?" he said. "Now you shift." He shifted. The car jumped a little, hummed, moved into gear. It was an old car and didn't shift too easily, he said. She had been sitting forward, so that when he shifted she rocked back hard against the seat—harder than she needed to. Almost unconsciously, she wanted to show him what a good teacher he was. When her turn came to drive, the car stalled. "Take it easy," he said. "Ease up on the clutch. Don't just raise your foot off of it like that." She tried it again. "That's it," he said. She looked at him when the car was in third. He sat in the seat, looking out the window. Snow was expected. It was Thursday. Although Larry was going to visit his parents and would not be back until late Friday afternoon, she decided she would wait until Tuesday for her next lesson. If he came home early, he would find out that she was taking lessons, and she didn't want him to know. She asked the boy, whose name was Michael, whether he thought she would forget all he had taught her in the time between lessons. "You'll remember," he said.

When they returned to the old lady's driveway, the car stalled going up the incline. She had trouble shifting. The boy put his hand over hers and kicked the heel of his hand forward. "You'll have to treat this car a little roughly, I'm afraid," he said. That afternoon, after he left, she made spaghetti sauce, chopping little pieces of pepper and onion and mushroom. When the sauce had cooked down, she called Mrs. Larsen and said that she would bring over dinner. She usually ate with the old lady once a week. The old lady often added a pinch of cinnamon to her food, saying that it brought out the flavor better than salt, and that since she was losing her sense of smell, food had to be strongly flavored for her to taste it. Once she had sprinkled cinnamon on a knockwurst. This time, as they ate, Natalie asked the old lady how much she paid the boy to bring the paper.

"I give him a dollar a week," the old lady said.

"Did he set the price, or did you?"

"He set the price. He told me he wouldn't take much because he has to walk this street to get to his apartment anyway."

"He taught me a lot about the car today," Natalie said.

"He's very handsome, isn't he?" the old lady said.

She asked Larry, "How were your parents?"

"Fine," he said. "But I spent almost all the time with Andy. It's almost his birthday, and he's depressed. We went to see Mose Allison."

"I think it stinks that hardly anyone else ever visits Andy," she said.

"He doesn't make it easy. He tells you everything that's on his mind, and there's no way you can pretend that his troubles don't amount to much. You just have to sit there and nod."

She remembered that Andy's room looked like a gymnasium. There were handgrips and weights scattered on the floor. There was even a psychedelic-pink hula hoop that he was to put inside his elbow and then move his arm in circles wide enough to make the hoop spin. He couldn't do it. He would lie in bed with the hoop in back of his neck and, holding the sides, lift his neck off the pillow. His arms were barely strong enough to do that, really, but he could raise his neck with no trouble, so he just pretended that his arms pulling the loop were raising it. His parents thought that it was a special exercise that he had mastered.

"What did you do today?" Larry said now.

"I made spaghetti," she said. She had made it the day before, but she thought that since he was mysterious about the time he spent away from her ("in the lab" and "at the gym" became interchangeable), she did not owe him a straight answer. That day she had dropped off the film and then she had sat at the drugstore counter to have a cup of coffee. She bought some cigarettes, though she had not smoked since high school. She smoked one mentholated cigarette and then threw the pack away in a garbage container outside the drugstore. Her mouth still felt cool inside.

He asked if she had planned anything for the weekend.

"No," she said.

"Let's do something you'd like to do. I'm a little ahead of myself in the lab right now."

That night they ate spaghetti and made plans, and the next day they went for a ride in the country, to a factory where wooden toys were made. In the showroom he made a bear marionette shake and twist. She examined a small rocking horse, rhythmically pushing her finger up and down on the back rung of the rocker to make it rock. When they left they took with them a catalog of toys they could order. She knew that they would never look at the catalog again. On their way to the museum he stopped to wash the car. Because it was the weekend there were quite a few cars lined up waiting to go in. They were behind a blue Cadillac that seemed to inch forward of its own accord, without a driver. When the Cadillac moved into the washing area, a tiny man hopped out. He stood on tiptoe to reach the coin box to start the washing machine. She doubted if he was five feet tall.

"Look at that poor son of a bitch," he said.

The little man was washing his car.

"If Andy could get out more," Larry said. "If he could get rid of that feeling he has that he's the only freak . . . I wonder if it wouldn't do him good to come spend a week with us."

"Are you going to take him in the wheelchair to the lab with you?" she said. "I'm not taking care of Andy all day."

His face changed. "Just for a week was all I meant," he said.

"I'm not doing it," she said. She was thinking of the boy, and of the car. She had almost learned how to drive the car.

"Maybe in the warm weather," she said. "When we could go to the park or something."

He said nothing. The little man was rinsing his car. She sat inside when their turn came. She thought that Larry had no right to ask her to take care of Andy. Water flew out of the hose and battered the car. She thought of Andy, in the woods at night, stepping on the land mine, being blown into the air. She wondered if it threw him in an arc, so he ended up somewhere away from where he had been walking, or if it just blasted him straight up, if he went up the way an umbrella opens. Andy had been a wonderful ice skater. They all envied him his long sweeping turns, with his legs somehow neatly together and his body at the perfect angle. She never saw him have an accident on the ice. Never once. She had known Andy, and they had skated at Parker's pond, for eight years before he was drafted.

The night before, as she and Larry were finishing dinner, he had asked her if she intended to vote for Nixon or McGovern in the election. "McGovern," she said. How could he not have known that? She knew then that they were farther apart than she had thought. She hoped that on Election Day she could drive herself to the polls—not go with him and not walk. She planned not to ask the old lady if she wanted to come along because that would be one vote she could keep Nixon from getting.

At the museum she hesitated by the sculpture but did not point it out to him. He didn't look at it. He gazed to the side, above it, at a Francis Bacon painting. He could have shifted his eyes just a little and seen the sculpture, and her, standing and staring.

After three more lessons she could drive the car. The last two times, which were later in the afternoon than her first lesson, they stopped at the drugstore to get the old lady's paper, to save him from having to make the same trip back on foot. When he came out of the drugstore with the paper, after the final lesson, she asked him if he'd like to have a beer to celebrate.

"Sure," he said.

They walked down the street to a bar that was filled with college students. She wondered if Larry ever came to this bar. He had never said that he did.

She and Michael talked. She asked why he wasn't in high school. He told her that he had quit. He was living with his brother, and his brother was teaching him carpentry, which he had been interested in all along. On his napkin he drew a picture of the cabinets and bookshelves he and his brother had spent the last week constructing and installing in the house of two wealthy old sisters. He drummed the side of his thumb against the edge of the table in time with the music. They each drank beer, from heavy glass mugs.

"Mrs. Larsen said your husband was in school," the boy said. "What's he studying?"

She looked up, surprised. Michael had never mentioned her husband to her before. "Chemistry," she said.

"I liked chemistry pretty well," he said. "Some of it."

"My husband doesn't know you've been giving me lessons. I'm just going to tell him that I can drive the stick shift, and surprise him."

"Yeah?" the boy said. "What will he think about that?"

"I don't know," she said. "I don't think he'll like it."

"Why?" the boy said.

His question made her remember that he was sixteen. What she had said would never have provoked another question from an adult. The adult would have nodded or said, "I know."

She shrugged. The boy took a long drink of beer. "I thought it was funny that he didn't teach you himself, when Mrs. Larsen told me you were married," he said.

They had discussed her. She wondered why Mrs. Larsen wouldn't have told her that, because the night she ate dinner with her she had talked to Mrs. Larsen about what an extraordinarily patient teacher Michael was. Had Mrs. Larsen told him that Natalie talked about him?

On the way back to the car she remembered the photographs and went back to the drugstore and picked up the prints. As she took money out of her wallet she remembered that today was the day she would have to pay him. She looked around at him, at the front of the store, where he was flipping through magazines. He was tall and he was wearing a very old black jacket. One end of his long thick maroon scarf was hanging down his back.

"What did you take pictures of?" he said when they were back in the car.

"Furniture. My husband wanted pictures of our furniture, in case it was stolen."

"Why?" he said.

"They say if you have proof that you had valuable things, the insurance company won't hassle you about reimbursing you."

"You have a lot of valuable stuff?" he said.

"My husband thinks so," she said.

A block from the driveway she said, "What do I owe you?"

"Four dollars," he said.

"That's nowhere near enough," she said and looked over at him. He had opened the envelope with the pictures in it while she was driving. He was staring at the picture of her legs. "What's this?" he said.

She turned into the driveway and shut off the engine. She looked at the picture. She could not think what to tell him it was. Her hands and heart felt heavy.

"Wow," the boy said. He laughed. "Never mind. Sorry. I'm not looking at any more of them."

He put the pack of pictures back in the envelope and dropped it on the seat between them.

She tried to think what to say, of some way she could turn the pictures into a joke. She wanted to get out of the car and run. She wanted to stay, not to give him the money, so he would sit there with her. She reached into her purse and took out her wallet and removed four one-dollar bills.

"How many years have you been married?" he asked.

"One," she said. She held the money out to him. He said "Thank you" and leaned across the seat and put his right arm over her shoulder and kissed her. She felt his scarf bunched up against their cheeks. She was amazed at how warm his lips were in the cold car.

He moved his head away and said, "I didn't think you'd mind if I did that." She shook her head no. He unlocked the door and got out.

"I could drive you to your brother's apartment," she said. Her voice sounded hollow. She was extremely embarrassed, but she couldn't let him go.

He got back in the car. "You could drive me and come in for a drink," he said. "My brother's working."

When she got back to the car two hours later she saw a white parking ticket clamped under the windshield wiper, flapping in the wind. When she opened the car door and sank into the seat, she saw that he had left the money, neatly folded, on the floor mat on his side of the car. She did not pick up the money. In a while she started the car. She stalled it twice on the way home. When she had pulled into the driveway she looked at the money for a long time, then left it lying there. She left the car unlocked, hoping the money would be stolen. If it disappeared, she could tell herself that she had paid him. Otherwise she would not know how to deal with the situation.

When she got into the apartment, the phone rang. "I'm at the gym to play basketball," Larry said. "Be home in an hour."

"I was at the drugstore," she said. "See you then."

She examined the pictures. She sat on the sofa and laid them out, the twelve of them, in three rows on the cushion next to her. The picture of the piano was between the picture of her feet and the picture of herself that she had shot by aiming into the mirror. She picked up the four pictures of their furniture and put them on the table. She picked up the others and examined them closely. She began to understand why she had taken them. She had photographed parts of her body, fragments of it, to study the pieces. She had probably done it because she thought so much about Andy's body and the piece that was gone—the leg, below the knee, on his left side. She had had two bourbon-and-waters at the boy's apartment, and drinking always depressed her. She felt very depressed looking at the pictures, so she put them down and went into the bedroom. She undressed. She looked at her body—whole, not a bad figure—in the mirror. It was an automatic reaction with her to close the curtains when she was naked, so she turned quickly and went to the window and did that. She went back to the mirror; the room was darker now and her body looked better. She ran her hands down her sides, wondering if the feel of her skin was anything like the way the sculpture would feel. She was sure that the sculpture would be smoother—her hands would move more quickly down the slopes of it than she wanted—that it would be cool, and that somehow she could feel the grayness of it. Those things seemed preferable to her hands lingering on her body, the imperfection of her skin, the overheated apartment. If she were the piece of sculpture and if she could feel, she would like her sense of isolation.

This was in 1972, in Philadelphia.

THE LAWN PARTY

I said to Lorna last night, "Do you want me to tell you a story?" "No," she said. Lorna is my daughter. She is ten and a great disbeliever. But she was willing to hang around my room and talk. "Regular dry cleaning won't take that out," Lorna said when she saw the smudges on my suede jacket. "Really," she said. "You have to take it somewhere special." In her skepticism, Lorna assumes that everyone else is also skeptical.

According to the Currier & Ives calendar hanging on the back of the bedroom door, and according to my watch, and according to my memory, which would be keen without either of them, Lorna and I have been at my parents' house for three days. Today is the annual croquet game that all our relatives here in Connecticut gather for (even some from my wife's side). It's the Fourth of July, and damn hot. I have the fan going. I'm sitting in a comfortable chair (moved upstairs, on my demand, by my father and the maid), next to the window in my old bedroom. There is already a cluster of my relatives on the lawn. Most of them are wearing little American flags pinned somewhere on their shirts or blouses or hanging from their ears. A patriotic group. Beer (forgive them: Heineken) and wine (Almadén Chablis) drinkers. My father loves this day better than his own birthday. He leans on his mallet and gives instructions to my sister Eva on the placement of the posts. Down there, he can see the American flags clearly. But if he is already too loaded to stick the posts in the ground, he probably isn't noticing the jewelry.

Lorna has come into my room twice in the last hour—once to ask me when I am coming down to join what she calls "the party," another time to say that I am making everybody feel rotten by not joining them.

A statement to be dismissed with a wave of the hand, but I have none. No right arm, either. I have a left hand and a left arm, but I have stopped valuing them. It's the right one I want. In the hospital, I rejected suggestions of a plastic arm or a claw. "Well, then, what do you envision?" the doctor said. "Air," I told him. This needed amplification. "Air where my arm used to be," I said. He gave a little "ah, so" bow of the head and left the room.

I intend to sit here at the window all day, watching the croquet game. I will drink the Heineken Lorna has brought me, taking small sips because I am unable to wipe my mouth after good foamy sips. My left hand is there to wipe with, but who wants to set down his beer bottle to wipe his mouth?

Lorna's mother has left me. I think of her now as Lorna's mother because she has made it clear that she no longer wants to be my wife. She has moved to another apartment with Lorna. She, herself, seems to be no happier for having left me and visits me frequently. Mention is no longer made of the fact that I am her husband and she is my wife. Recently Mary (her name) took the ferry to the Statue of Liberty. She broke in on me on my second day here in the room, explaining that she would not be here for the croquet game, but with the news that she had visited New York yesterday and had taken the ferry to the Statue of Liberty. "And how was the city?" I asked. "Wonderful," she assured me. She went to the Carnegie Delicatessen and had cheesecake. When she does not visit, she writes. She has a second sense about when I have left my apartment for my parents' house. In her letters she usually tells me something about Lorna, although no mention is made of the fact that Lorna is my child. In fact, she once slyly suggested in a bitter moment that Lorna was not—but she backed down about that one.

Lorna is a great favorite with my parents, and my parents are rich. This, Mary always said jokingly, was why she married me. Actually, it was my charm. She thought I was terrific. If I had not fallen in love with her sister, everything would still be fine between us. I did it fairly; I fell in love with her sister before the wedding. I asked to have the wedding delayed. Mary got drunk and cried. Why was I doing this? How could I do it? She would leave me, but she wouldn't delay the wedding. I asked her to leave. She got drunk and cried and would not. We were married on schedule. She had nothing more to do with her sister. I, on the other hand—strange how many things one cannot say anymore—saw her whenever possible. Patricia—that was her name—went with me on business trips, met me for lunches and dinners, and was driving my car when it went off the highway.

When I came to, Mary was standing beside my hospital bed, her face distorted, looking down at me. "My sister killed herself and tried to take you with her," she said.

I waited for her to throw herself on me in pity.

"You deserved this," she said, and walked out of the room.

I was being fed intravenously in my left arm. I looked to see if my right arm was hooked up to anything. It hurt to move my head. My right arm was free—how free I didn't know at the time. I swear I saw it, but it had been amputated when I was unconscious. The doctor spoke to me at length about this later, insisting that there was no possibility that my arm was there when my wife was in the room and gone subsequently—gone when she left. No, indeed. It was amputated at once, in surgery, and when I saw my wife I was recovering from surgery. I tried to get at it another way, leaving Mary out of it. Wasn't I conscious before Mary was there? Didn't I see the arm? No, I was unconscious and didn't see anything. No, indeed. The physical therapist, the psychiatrist, and the chaplain the doctor had brought with him nodded their heads in fast agreement. But soon I would have an artificial arm. I said that I did not want one. It was then that we had the discussion about air.

Last Wednesday was my birthday. I was unpleasant to all. Mrs. Bates, the cook, baked me chocolate-chip cookies with walnuts (my favorite), but I didn't eat any until she went home. My mother gave me a red velour shirt, which I hinted was unsatisfactory. "What's wrong with it?" she said. I said, "It's got one too many arms." My former student Banks visited me in the evening, not knowing that it was my birthday. He is a shy, thin, hirsute individual of twenty—a painter, a true *artiste*. I liked him so well that I had given him the phone number at my parents' house. He brought with him his most recent work, a canvas of a nude woman, for my inspection. While we were all gathered around the birthday cake, Banks answered my question about who she was by saying that she was a professional model. Later, strolling in the backyard, he told me that he had picked her up at a bus stop, after convincing her that she did not want to spend her life waiting for buses, and brought her to his apartment, where he fixed a steak dinner. The woman spent two days there, and when she left, Banks gave her forty dollars, although she did not want any money. She thought the painting he did of her was ugly, and wanted to be reassured that she wasn't really that heavy around the hips. Banks told her that it was not a representational painting; he said it was an impressionist painting. She gave him her phone number. He called; there was no such number. He could not understand it. He went back to the bus stop, and eventually he found her again. She told him to get away or she'd call the police.

Ah, Banks. Ah, youth—to be twenty again, instead of thirty-two. In class, Banks used to listen to music on his cassette player through earphones. He would eat candy bars while he nailed frames together. Banks was always chewing food or mouthing songs. Sometimes he would forget and actually sing in class—an eerie wail, harmonizing with something none of the rest of us heard. The students who did not resent Banks's talent resented his chewing or singing or his success with women. Banks had great success with Lorna. He told her she looked like Bianca Jagger and she was thrilled. "Why don't you get some platform shoes like hers?" he said, and her eyes shriveled with pleasure. He told her a couple of interesting facts about Copernicus; she told him about the habits of gypsy moths. When he left, he kissed her hand. It did my heart good to see her so happy. I never delight her at all, as Mary keeps telling me.

They have written me from the college where I work, saying that they hope all is well and that I will be back teaching in the fall. It is not going to be easy to teach painting, with my right arm gone. Still, one remembers Matisse in his last years. Where there's a will, et cetera. My department head has sent flowers twice (mixed and tulips), and the dean himself has written a message on a get-well card. There is a bunny on the card, looking at a rainbow. Banks is the only one who really tempts me to go back to work. The others, Banks tells me, are "full of it."

Now I have a visitor. Danielle, John's wife, has come up to see me. John is my brother. She brings an opened beer and sets it on the windowsill without comment. Danielle is wearing a white dress with small porpoises on it, smiling as they leap. Across that chest, no wonder.

"Are you feeling blue today or just being rotten?" she asks.

The beginnings of many of Danielle's sentences often put me in mind of trashy, romantic songs. Surely someone has written a song called "Are You Feeling Blue?"

"Both," I say. I usually give Danielle straight answers. She tries to be nice. She has been nice to my brother for five years. He keeps promising to take her back to France, but he never does.

She sits on the rug, next to my chair. "Their rotten lawn parties," she says. Danielle is French, but her English is very good.

"Pull up a chair and watch the festivities," I say.

"I have to go back," she says, pouting. "They want you to come back with me."

Champagne glasses clinking, white tablecloth, single carnation, key of A: "They Want You Back with Me."

"Who sent you?" I ask.

"John. But I think Lorna would like it if you were there."

"Lorna doesn't like me anymore. Mary's turned her against me."

"Ten is a difficult age," Danielle says.

"I thought the teens were difficult."

"How would I know? I don't have children."

She has a drink of beer, and then puts the bottle in my hand instead of back on the windowsill.

"You have beautiful round feet," I say.

She tucks them under her. "I'm embarrassed," she says.

"Our talk is full of the commonplace today," I say, sighing.

"You're insulting me," she says. "That's why John wouldn't come up. He says he gets tired of your insults."

"I wasn't trying to be insulting. You've got beautiful feet. Raise one up here and I'll kiss it."

"Don't make fun of me," Danielle says.

"Really," I say.

Danielle moves her leg, unstraps a sandal and raises her right foot. I take it in my hand and bend over to kiss it across the toes.

"Stop it," she says, laughing. "Someone will come in."

"They won't," I say. "John isn't the only one tired of my insults."

I have been taking a little nap. Waking up, I look out the window and see Danielle below. She is sitting in one of the redwood chairs, accepting a drink from my father. One leg is crossed over the other, her beautiful foot dangling. They all know I am watching, but they refuse to look up. Eventually my mother does. She makes a violent sweep with her arm—like a coach motioning the defensive team onto the field. I wave. She turns her back and rejoins the group—Lorna, John, Danielle, my aunt Rosie, Rosie's daughter Elizabeth, my father, and some others. Wednesday was also Elizabeth's birthday—her eighteenth. My parents called and sang to her. When Janis Joplin died Elizabeth cried for six days. "She's an emotional child," Rosie said at the time. Then, forgetting that, she asked everyone in the family why Elizabeth had gone to pieces. "Why did you feel so bad about Janis, Elizabeth?" I said. "I don't know," she said. "Did her death make you feel like killing yourself?" I said. "Are you unhappy the way she was?" Rosie now speaks to me only perfunctorily. On her get-well card to me (no visit) she wrote: "So sorry." They are all sorry. They have been told by the doctor to ignore my gloominess, so they ignore me. I ignore them because even before the accident I was not very fond of them. My brother, in particular, bores me. When we were kids, sharing a bedroom, John would talk to me at night. When I fell asleep he'd come over and shake my mattress. One night my father caught him doing it and hit him. "It's not my fault," John hollered. "He's a goddamn snob." We got separate bedrooms. I was eight and John was ten.

Danielle comes back, looking sweatier than before. Below, they are playing the first game. My father's brother Ed pretends to be a majorette and struts with his mallet, twirling it and pointing his knees.

"Nobody sent me this time," Danielle says. "Are you coming down to dinner? They're grilling steaks."

"He's so cheap he'll serve Almadén with them," I say. "You grew up in France. How can you drink that stuff?"

"I just drink one glass," she says.

"Refuse to do it," I say.

She shrugs. "You're in an awful mood," she says.

"Give back that piggy," I say.

She frowns. "I came to have a serious discussion. Why aren't you coming to dinner?"

"Not hungry."

"Come down for Lorna."

"Lorna doesn't care."

"Maybe you're mean to her."

"I'm the same way I always was with her."

"Be a little extra nice, then."

"Give back that piggy," I say, and she puts her foot up. I unbuckle her sandal with my left hand. There are strap marks on the skin. I lick down her baby toe and kiss it, at the very tip. In turn, I kiss all the others.

It's evening, and the phone is ringing. I think about answering it. Finally someone else in the house picks it up. I get up and then sit on the bed and look around. My old bedroom looks pretty much the way it looked when I left for college, except that my mother has added a few things that I never owned, which seem out of place. Two silver New Year's Eve hats rest on the bedposts, and a snapshot of my mother in front of a Mexican fruit stand (I have never been to Mexico) that my father took on their "second honeymoon" is on my bureau. I pull open a drawer and take out a pack of letters. I pull out one of the letters at random and read it. It is from an old girlfriend of mine. Her name was Alison, and she once loved me madly. In the letter she says she is giving up smoking so that when we are old she won't be repulsive to me. The year I graduated from college, she married an Indian and moved to India. Maybe now she has a little red dot in the middle of her forehead.

I try to remember loving Alison. I remember loving Mary's sister, Patricia. She is dead. That doesn't sink in. And she can't have meant to die, in spite of what Mary said. A woman who meant to die wouldn't buy a big wooden bowl and a bag of fruit, and then get in the car and drive it off the highway. It is a fact, however, that as the car started to go sideways I looked at Patricia, and she was whipping the wheel to the right. Maybe I imagined that. I remember putting my arm out to brace myself as the car started to turn over. If Patricia were alive, I'd have to be at the croquet game. But if she were alive, she and I could disappear for a few minutes, have a kiss by the barn.

I said to Lorna last night that I would tell her a story. It was going to be a fairy tale, all about Patricia and me but disguised as the prince and the princess, but she said no, she didn't want to hear it, and walked out. Just as well. If it had ended sadly it would have been an awful trick to pull on Lorna, and if it had ended happily, it would have depressed me even more. "There's nothing wrong with coming to terms with your depression," the doctor said to me. He kept urging me to see a shrink. The shrink came, and urged me to talk to him. When he left, the chaplain came in and urged me to see *him*. I checked out.

Lorna visits a third time. She asks whether I heard the phone ringing. I did. She says that—well, she finally answered it. "When you were first walking, one of your favorite things was to run for the phone," I said. I was trying to be nice to her. "Stop talking about when I was a baby," she says, and leaves. On the way out, she says, "It was your friend who came over the other night. He wants you to call him. His number is here." She comes back with a piece of paper, then leaves again.

"I got drunk," Banks says on the phone, "and I felt sorry for you."

"The hell with that, Banks," I say, and reflect that I sound like someone talking in *The Sun Also Rises*.

"Forget it, old Banks," I say, enjoying the part.

"You're not loaded too, are you?" Banks says.

"No, Banks," I say.

"Well, I wanted to talk. I wanted to ask if you wanted to go out to a bar with me. I don't have any more beer or money."

"Thanks, but there's a big rendezvous here today. Lorna's here. I'd better stick around."

"Oh," Banks says. "Listen. Could I come over and borrow five bucks?"

Banks does not think of me in my professorial capacity.

"Sure," I say.

"Thanks," he says.

"Sure, old Banks. Sure," I say, and hang up.

Lorna stands in the doorway. "Is he coming over?" she asks.

"Yes. He's coming to borrow money. He's not the man for you, Lorna."

"You don't have any money either," she says. "Grandpa does."

"I have enough money," I say defensively.

"How much do you have?"

"I make a salary, you know, Lorna. Has your mother been telling you I'm broke?"

"She doesn't talk about you."

"Then why did you ask how much money I had?"

"I wanted to know."

"I'm not going to tell you," I say.

"They told me to come talk to you," Lorna says. "I was supposed to get you to come down."

"Do you want me to come down?" I ask.

"Not if you don't want to."

"You're supposed to be devoted to your daddy," I say.

Lorna sighs. "You won't answer any of my questions, and you say silly things."

"What?"

"What you just said—about my daddy."

"I am your daddy," I say.

"I know it," she says.

There seems nowhere for the conversation to go.

"You want to hear that story now?" I ask.

"No. Don't try to tell me any stories. I'm ten."

"I'm thirty-two," I say.

My father's brother William is about to score a victory over Elizabeth. He puts his foot on the ball, which is touching hers, and knocks her ball down the hill. He pretends he has knocked it an immense distance and cups his hand over his brow to squint after it. William's wife will not play croquet; she sits on the grass and frowns. She is a dead ringer for the woman behind the cash register in Edward Hopper's *Tables for Ladies*.

"How's it going?" Danielle asks, standing in the doorway.

"Come on in," I say.

"I just came upstairs to go to the bathroom. The cook is in the one downstairs."

She comes in and looks out the window.

"Do you want me to get you anything?" she says. "Food?"

"You're just being nice to me because I kiss your piggies."

"You're horrible," she says.

"I tried to be nice to Lorna, and all she wanted to talk about was money."

"All they talk about down there is money," she says.

She leaves and then comes back with her hair combed and her mouth pink again.

"What do you think of William's wife?" I ask.

"I don't know, she doesn't say much." Danielle sits on the floor, with her chin on her knees. "Everybody always says that people who only say a few dumb things are sweet."

"What dumb things has she said?" I say.

"She said, 'Such a beautiful day,' and looked at the sky."

"You shouldn't be hanging out with these people, Danielle," I say.

"I've got to go back," she says.

Banks is here. He is sitting next to me as it gets dark. I am watching Danielle out on the lawn. She has a red shawl that she winds around her shoulders. She looks tired and elegant. My father has been drinking all afternoon. "Get the hell down here!" he hollered to me a little while ago. My mother rushed up to him to say that I had a student with me. He backed down. Lorna came up and brought us two dishes of peach ice cream (handmade by Rosie), giving the larger one to Banks. She and Banks discussed *The Hobbit* briefly. Banks kept apologizing to me for not leaving, but said he was too strung out to drive. He went into the bathroom and smoked a joint and came back and sat down and rolled his head from side to side. "You make sense," Banks says now, and I am flattered until I realize that I have not been talking for a long time.

"It's too bad it's so dark," I say. "That woman down there in the black dress looks just like somebody in an Edward Hopper painting. You'd recognize her."

"Nah," Banks says, head swaying. "Everything's basically different.

I get so tired of examining things and finding out they're different. This crappy nature poem isn't at all like that crappy nature poem. That's what I mean," Banks says.

"Do you remember your accident?" he says.

"No," I say.

"Excuse me," Banks says.

"I remember thinking of *Jules and Jim*."

"Where she drove off the cliff?" Banks says, very excited.

"Umm."

"When did you think that?"

"As it was happening."

"Wow," Banks says. "I wonder if anybody else flashed on that before you?"

"I couldn't say."

Banks sips his iced gin. "What do you think of me as an artist?" he says.

"You're very good, Banks."

It begins to get cooler. A breeze blows the curtains toward us.

"I had a dream that I was a raccoon," Banks says. "I kept trying to look over my back to count the rings of my tail, but my back was too high, and I couldn't count past the first two."

Banks finishes his drink.

"Would you like me to get you another drink?" I ask.

"That's an awful imposition," Banks says, extending his glass.

I take the glass and go downstairs. A copy of *The Hobbit* is lying on the rose brocade sofa. Mrs. Bates is sitting at the kitchen table, reading *People*.

"Thank you very much for the cookies," I say.

"It's nothing," she says. Her earrings are on the table. Her feet are on a chair.

"Tell them we ran out of gin if they want more," I say. "I need this bottle."

"Okay," she says. "I think there's another bottle, anyway."

I take the bottle upstairs in my armpit, carrying a glass with fresh ice in it in my hand.

"You know," Banks says, "they say that if you face things—if you just get them through your head—you can accept them. They say you can accept anything if you can once get it through your head."

"What's this about?" I say.

"Your arm," Banks says.

"I realize that I don't have an arm," I say.

"I don't mean to offend you," Banks says, drinking.

"I know you don't."

"If you ever want me to yell at you about it, just say the word. That might help—help it sink in."

"I already realize it, Banks," I say.

"You're a swell guy," Banks says. "What kind of music do you listen to?"

"Do you want to hear music?"

"No. I just want to know what you listen to."

"Schoenberg," I say. I have not listened to Schoenberg for years.

"Ahh," Banks says.

He offers me his glass. I take a drink and hand it back.

"You know how they always have cars—car ads—you ever notice . . . I'm all screwed up," Banks says.

"Go on," I say.

"They always put the car on the beach?"

"Yeah."

"I was thinking about doing a thing with a great big car in the background and a little beach up front." Banks chuckles.

Outside, the candles have been lit. A torch flames from a metal holder—one of the silliest things I have ever seen—and blue lanterns have been lit in the trees. Someone has turned on a radio, and Elizabeth and some man, not recognizable, dance to "Heartbreak Hotel."

"There's Schoenberg," Banks says.

"Banks," I say, "I want you to take this the right way. I like you, and I'm glad you came over. Why did you come over?"

"I wanted you to praise my paintings." Banks plays church and steeple with his hands. "But also, I just wanted to talk."

"Was there anything particularly—"

"I thought you might want to talk to me."

"Why don't you talk to me, instead?"

"I've got to be a great painter," Banks says. "I paint and then at night I smoke up or go out to some bar, and in the morning I paint. . . . All night I pray until I fall asleep that I will become great. You must think I'm crazy. What do you think of me?"

"You make me feel old," I say.

The gin bottle is in Banks's crotch, the glass resting on the top of the bottle.

"I sensed that," Banks says, "before I got too wasted to sense anything."

"You want to hear a story?" I say.

"Sure."

"The woman who was driving the car I was in—the Princess . . ." I laugh, but Banks only nods, trying hard to follow. "I think the woman must have been out to commit suicide. We had been out buying things. The backseat was loaded with nice antiques, things like that, and we had had a nice afternoon, eaten ice cream, talked about how she would be starting school again in the fall—"

"Artist?" Banks asks.

"A linguistics major."

"Okay. Go on."

"What I'm saying is that all was well in the kingdom. Not exactly, because she wasn't my wife, but she should have been. But for the purpose of the story, what I'm saying is that we were in fine shape, it was a fine day—"

"Month?" Banks says.

"March," I say.

"That's right," Banks says.

"I was going to drop her off at the shopping center, where she'd left her car, and she was going to continue on to her castle and I'd go to mine . . ."

"Continue," Banks says.

"And then she tried to kill us. She did kill herself."

"I read it in the papers," Banks says.

"What do you think?" I ask.

"Banks's lesson," Banks says. "Never look back. Don't try to count your tail rings."

Danielle walks into the room. "I have come for the gin," she says. "The cook said you had it."

"Danielle, this is Banks."

"How do you do," Banks says.

Danielle reaches down and takes the bottle from Banks. "You're missing a swell old time," she says.

"Maybe a big wind will come along and blow them all away," Banks says.

Danielle is silent a moment, then laughs—a laugh that cuts through the darkness. She ducks her head down by my face and kisses my cheek, and turns in a wobbly way and walks out of the room.

"Jesus," Banks says. "Here we are sitting here and then this weird thing happens."

"Her?" I say.

"Yeah."

Lorna comes, very sleepy, carrying a napkin with cookies on it. She obviously wants to give them to Banks, but Banks has passed out, upright, in the chair next to mine. "Climb aboard," I say, offering my lap. Lorna hesitates, but then does, putting the cookies down on the floor without offering me any. She tells me that her mother has a boyfriend.

"What's his name?" I ask.

"Stanley," Lorna says.

"Maybe a big wind will come and blow Stanley away," I say.

"What's wrong with him?" she says, looking at Banks.

"Drunk," I say. "Who's drunk downstairs?"

"Rosie," she says. "And William, and, uh, Danielle."

"Don't drink," I say.

"I won't," she says. "Will he still be here in the morning?"

"I expect so," I say.

Banks has fallen asleep in an odd posture. His feet are clamped together, his arms are limp at his sides, and his chin is jutting forward. The melting ice cubes from the overturned glass have encroached on the cookies.

At the lawn party, they've found a station on the radio that plays only songs from other years. Danielle begins a slow, drunken dance. Her red shawl has fallen to the grass. I stare at her and imagine her dress disappearing, her shoes kicked off, beautiful Danielle dancing naked in the dusk. The music turns to static, but Danielle is still dancing.

COLORADO

Penelope was in Robert's apartment, sitting on the floor, with the newspaper open between her legs. Her boots were on the floor in front of her. Robert had just fixed the zipper of one of the boots. It was the third time he had repaired the boots, and this time he suggested that she buy a new pair. "Why?" she said. "You fix them fine every time." In many of their discussions they came close to arguments, but they always stopped short. Penelope simply would not argue. She thought it took too much energy. She had not even argued with Robert's friend Johnny, whom she had been living with, when he moved out on her, taking twenty dollars of her money. Still, she hated Johnny for it, and sometimes Robert worried that even though he and Penelope didn't argue, she might be thinking badly of him, too. So he didn't press it. Who cared whether she bought new boots or not?

Penelope came over to Robert's apartment almost every evening. He had met her more than a year before, and they had been nearly inseparable ever since. For a while he and Penelope and Johnny and another friend, Cyril, had shared a house in the country, not far from New Haven. They had all been in graduate school then. Now Johnny had gone, and the others were living in New Haven, in different apartments, and they were no longer going to school. Penelope was living with a man named Dan. Robert could not understand this, because Dan and Penelope did not communicate even well enough for her to ask him to fix her boots. She hobbled over to Robert's apartment instead. And he couldn't understand it back when she was living with Johnny, because Johnny had continued to see another girl, and had taken Penelope's money and tried to provoke arguments, even though Penelope wouldn't argue. Robert could understand Penelope's moving in with Dan at first, because she hadn't had enough money to pay her share of the house rent and Dan had an apartment in New Haven, but why had she just stayed there? Once, when he was drunk, Robert had asked her that, and she had sighed and said she wouldn't argue with him when he'd been drinking. He had not been trying to argue. He had just wanted to know what she was thinking. But she didn't like to talk about herself, and saying that he was drunk had been a convenient excuse. The closest he ever got to an explanation was when she told him once that it was important not to waste your energy jumping from one thing to another. She had run away from home when she was younger, and when she returned, things were only worse. She had flunked out of Bard and dropped out of Antioch and the University of Connecticut, and now she knew that all colleges were the same—there was no point in trying one after another. She had traded her Ford for a Toyota, and Toyotas were no better than Fords.

She was flipping through the newspaper, stretched out on her side on the floor, her long brown hair blocking his view of her face. He didn't need to look at her: he knew she was beautiful. It was nice just to have her there. Although he couldn't understand what went on in her head, he was full of factual information about her. She had grown up in Iowa. She was almost five feet nine inches tall, and she weighed a hundred and twenty-five pounds, and when she was younger, when she weighed less, she had been a model in Chicago. Now she was working as a clerk in a boutique in New Haven. She didn't want to model again, because that was no easier than being a salesperson; it was more tiring, even if it did pay better.

"Thanks for fixing my boots again," she said, rolling up her pants leg to put one on.

"Why are you leaving?" Robert said. "Dan's student won't be out of there yet."

Dan was a painter who had lost his teaching job in the South. He moved to New Haven and was giving private lessons to students three times a week.

"Marielle's going to pick me up," Penelope said. "She wants me to help her paint her bathroom."

"Why can't she paint her own bathroom? She could do the whole thing in an hour."

"I don't want to help her paint," Penelope said, sighing. "I'm just doing a favor for a friend."

"Why don't you do me a favor and stay?"

"Come on," she said. "Don't do that. You're my best friend."

"Okay," he said, knowing she wouldn't fight over it anyway. He went to the kitchen table and got her coat. "Why don't you wait till she gets here?"

"She's meeting me at the drugstore."

"You sure are nice to some of your friends," he said.

She ignored him. She did not totally ignore him; she kissed him before she left. And although she did not say that she'd see him the next day, he knew she'd be back.

When Penelope left, Robert went into the kitchen and put some water on to boil. It was his habit since moving to this apartment to have a cup of tea before bed and to look out the window into the brightly lit alley. Interesting things appeared there: Christmas trees, large broken pieces of machinery, and, once, a fireman's uniform, very nicely laid out—a fireman's hat and suit. He was an artist—or, rather, he had been an artist until he dropped out of school—and sometimes he found that he still arranged objects and landscapes, looking for a composition. He sat on the kitchen table and drank his tea. He often thought about buying a kitchen chair, but he told himself that he'd move soon and he didn't want to transport furniture. When he was a child, his parents had moved from apartment to apartment. Their furniture got more and more battered, and his mother had exploded one day, crying that the furniture was worthless and ugly, and threatening to chop it all up with an ax. Since he moved from the country Robert had not yet bought himself a bed frame or curtains or rugs. There were roaches in the apartment, and the idea of the roaches hiding—being able to hide on the underside of curtains, under the rug—disgusted him. He didn't mind them being there so much when they were out in the open.

The Yale catalog he had gotten months before when he first came to New Haven was still on the kitchen table. He had thought about taking a course in architecture, but he hadn't. He was not quite sure what to do. He had taken a part-time job working in a picture-framing store so he could pay his rent. Actually, he had no reason for being in New Haven except to be near Penelope. When Robert lived in the house with Johnny and Cyril and Penelope, he had told himself that Penelope would leave Johnny and become his lover, but it never happened. He had tried very hard to get it to happen; they had often stayed up later than any of the others, and they talked—he had never talked so much to anybody in his life—and sometimes they fixed food before going to bed, or took walks in the snow. She tried to teach him to play the recorder, blowing softly so she wouldn't wake the others. Once in the summer they had stolen corn, and Johnny had asked her about it the next morning. "What if the neighbors find out somebody from this house stole corn?" he said. Robert defended Penelope, saying that he had suggested it. "Great," Johnny said. "The Bobbsey Twins." Robert was hurt because what Johnny said was true—there wasn't anything more between them than there was between the Bobbsey Twins.

Earlier in the week Robert had been sure that Penelope was going to make a break with Dan. He had gone to a party at their apartment, and there had been a strange assortment of guests, almost all of them Dan's friends—some Yale people, a druggist who had a Marlboro cigarette pack filled with reds that he passed around, and a neighbor woman and her six-year-old son, whom the druggist teased. The druggist showed the little boy the cigarette pack full of pills, saying, "Now, how would a person light a cigarette like this? Which end is the filter?" The boy's mother wouldn't protect him, so Penelope took him away, into the bedroom, where she let him empty Dan's piggy bank and count the pennies. Marielle was also there, with her hair neatly braided into tight cornrows and wearing glasses with lenses that darkened to blue. Cyril came late, pretty loaded. "Better late than never" he said, once to Robert and many times to Penelope. Then Robert and Cyril huddled together in a corner, saying how dreary the party was, while the druggist put pills on his tongue and rolled them sensually across the roof of his mouth. At midnight Dan got angry and tried to kick them all out—Robert and Cyril first, because they were sitting closest to him—and that made Penelope angry because she had only three friends at the party, and the noisy ones, the drunk or stoned ones, were all Dan's friends. Instead of arguing, though, she cried. Robert and Cyril left finally and went to Cyril's and had a beer, and then Robert went back to Dan's apartment, trying to get up the courage to go in and insist that Penelope leave with him. He walked up the two flights of stairs to their door. It was quiet inside. He didn't have the nerve to knock. He went downstairs and out of the building, hating himself. He walked home in the cold, and realized that he must have been a little drunk, because the fresh air really cleared his head.

Robert flipped through the Yale catalog, thinking that maybe going back to school was the solution. Maybe all the hysterical letters his mother and father wrote were right, and he needed some order in his life. Maybe he'd meet some other girls in classes. He did not want to meet other girls. He had dated two girls since moving to New Haven, and they had bored him and he had spent more money on them than they were worth.

The phone rang; he was glad, because he was just about to get very depressed.

It was Penelope, sounding very far away, very knocked out. She had left Marielle's because Marielle's boyfriend was there, and he insisted that they all get stoned and listen to *Trout Mask Replica* and not paint the bathroom, so she left and decided to walk home, but then she realized she didn't want to go there, and she thought she'd call and ask if she could stay with him instead. And the strangest thing. When she closed the door of the phone booth just now, a little boy had appeared and tapped on the glass, fanning out a half circle of joints. "Ten dollars," the boy said to her. "Bargain City." *Imagine* that. There was a long silence while Robert imagined it. It was interrupted by Penelope, crying.

"What's the matter, Penelope?" he said. "Of course you can come over here. Get out of the phone booth and come over."

She told him that she had bought the grass, and that it was powerful stuff. It was really the wrong thing to do to smoke it, but she lost her nerve in the phone booth and didn't know whether to call or not, so she smoked a joint—very quickly, in case any cops drove by. She smoked it too quickly.

"Where are you?" he said.

"I'm near Park Street," she said.

"What do you mean? Is the phone booth on Park Street?"

"Near it," she said.

"Okay. I'll tell you what. You walk down to McHenry's and I'll get down there, okay?"

"You don't live very close," she said.

"I can walk there in a hurry. I can get a cab. You just take your time and wander down there. Sit in a booth if you can. Okay?"

"Is it true what Cyril told me at Dan's party?" she said. "That you're secretly in love with me?"

He frowned and looked sideways at the phone, as if the phone itself had betrayed him. He saw that his fingers were white from pressing so hard against the receiver.

"I'll tell you," she said. "Where I grew up, the cop cars had red lights. These green things cut right through you. I think that's why I hate this city—damn green lights."

"Is there a cop car?" he said.

"I saw one when you were talking," she said.

"Penelope. Have you got it straight about walking to McHenry's? Can you do that?"

"I've got some money," she said. "We can go to New York and get a steak dinner."

"Christ," he said. "Stay in the phone booth. Where is the phone booth?"

"I told you I'd go to McHenry's. I will. I'll wait there."

"Okay. Fine. I'm going to hang up now. Remember to sit in a booth.

If there isn't one, stand by the bar. Order something. By the time you've finished it, I'll be there."

"Robert," she said.

"What?"

"Do you remember pushing me in the swing?"

He remembered. It was when they were all living in the country. She had been stoned that day, too. All of them—stoned as fools. Cyril was running around in Penelope's long white bathrobe, holding a handful of tulips. Then he got afraid they'd wilt, so he went into the kitchen and got a jar and put them in that and ran around again. Johnny had taken a few Seconals and was lying on the ground, saying that he was in a hammock, and cackling. Robert had thought that he and Penelope were the only ones straight. Her laughter sounded beautiful, even though later he realized it was wild, crazy laughter. It was the first really warm day, the first day when they were sure that winter was over. Everyone was delighted with everyone else. He remembered very well pushing her in the swing.

"Wait," he said. "I want to get down there. Can we talk about this when I get there? Will you walk to the bar?"

"I'm not really that stoned," she said, her voice changing suddenly. "I think it's that I'm sick."

"What do you mean? How do you feel?"

"I feel too light. Like I'm going to be sick."

"Look," he said. "Cyril lives right near Park. What if you give me the number of the phone booth, and I call Cyril and get him down there, and I'll call back and talk to you until he comes. Will you do that? What's the phone number?"

"I don't want to tell you."

"Why not?"

"I can't talk anymore right now," she said. "I want to get some air." She hung up.

He needed air too. He felt panicked, the way he had the day she was in the swing, when she said, "I'm going to jump!" and he knew it was going much too fast, much too high—the swing flying out over a hill that rolled steeply down to a muddy bank by the creek. He had had the sense to stop pushing, but he only stood there, waiting, shivering in the breeze the swing made.

He went out quickly. Park Street—somewhere near there. Okay, he would find her. He knew he would not. There was a cab. He was in the cab. He rolled down the window to get some air, hoping the driver would figure he was drunk.

"What place you looking for again?" the driver said.

"I'm looking for a person, actually. If you'd go slowly . . ."

The cabdriver drove down the street at ordinary speed, and stopped at a light. A family crossed in front of the cab: a young black couple, the father with a child on his shoulders. The child was wearing a Porky Pig mask.

The light changed and the car started forward. "Goddamn," the driver said. "I knew it."

Steam had begun to rise from under the hood. It was a broken water hose. The cab moved into the next lane and stopped. Robert stuffed two one-dollar bills into the driver's hand and bolted from the cab.

"Piece of junk!" he heard the driver holler, and there was the sound of metal being kicked. Robert looked over his shoulder and saw the cabdriver kicking the grille. Steam was pouring out in a huge cloud. The driver kicked the cab again.

He walked. It seemed to him as if he were walking in slow motion, but soon he was panting. He passed several telephone booths, but all of them were empty. He felt guilty about not helping the cabdriver, and he walked all the way to McHenry's. He thought—and was immediately struck with the irrationality of it—that New Haven was really quite a nice town, architecturally.

Penelope was not at McHenry's. "Am I a black dude?" a black man said to him as Robert wedged his way through the crowd at the bar. "I'm gonna ask you straight, look at me and tell me: Ain't I a black dude?" The black man laughed with real joy. He did not seem to be drunk. Robert smiled at the man and headed toward the back of the bar. Maybe she was in the bathroom. He stood around, looking all over the bar, hoping she'd come out of the bathroom. Time passed. "If I was drunk," the black man said as Robert walked toward the front door, "I might try to put some rap on you, like I'm the king of Siam. I'm not say-ing nothing like that. I'm asking you straight: Ain't I a black dude, though?"

"You sure are," he said and edged away.

He went out and walked to a phone booth and dialed Dan's num-ber. "Dan," he said, "I don't want to alarm you, but Penelope got a little loaded tonight and I went out to look for her and I've lost track of her."

"Is that right?" Dan said. "She told me she was going to sleep over at Marielle's."

"I guess she was. It's a long story, but she left there and she got pretty wrecked, Dan. I was worried about her, so—"

"Listen," Dan said. "Can I call you back in fifteen minutes?"

"What do you mean? I'm at a phone booth."

"Well, doesn't it have a number? I'll be right back with you."

"She's wandering around New Haven in awful shape, Dan. You'd better get down here and—"

Dan was talking to someone, his hand covering the mouthpiece.

"To tell you the truth," Dan said, "I can't talk right now. In fifteen minutes I can talk, but a friend is here."

"What are you talking about?" Robert said. "Haven't you been listening to what I've been saying? If you've got some woman there, tell her to go to the toilet for a minute, for Christ's sake."

"That doesn't cut the mustard anymore," Dan said. "You can't shuffle women off like they're cats and dogs."

Robert slammed down the phone and went back to McHenry's. She was still not there. He left, and out on the corner the black man from the bar walked up to him and offered to sell him cocaine. He politely refused, saying he had no money. The man nodded and walked down the street. Robert watched him for a minute, then looked away. For just a few seconds he had been interested in the way the man moved, what he looked like walking down the street. When he had lived at the house with Penelope, Robert had watched her, too; he had done endless drawings of her, sketched her on napkins, on the corner of the newspaper. But paintings—when he tried to do anything formal, he hadn't been able to go through with it. Cyril told him it was because he was afraid of capturing her. At first he thought Cyril's remark was stupid, but now—standing tired and cold on the street corner—he had to admit that he'd always been a little afraid of her, too. What would he have done tonight if he'd found her? Why had her phone call upset him so much—because she was stoned? He thought about Penelope—about putting his head down on her shoulder, somewhere where it was warm. He began to walk home. It was a long walk, and he was very tired. He stopped and looked in a bookstore window, then walked past a dry cleaner's. The last time he'd looked, it had been a coffee shop. At a red light he heard Bob Dylan on a car radio, making an analogy between time and a jet plane.

She called in the morning to apologize. When she hung up on him the night before, she got straight for a minute—long enough to hail a cab—but she had a bad time in the cab again, and didn't have the money to pay for the ride. . . . To make a long story short, she was with Marielle.

"Why?" Robert asked.

Well, she was going to tell the cabdriver to take her to Robert's place, but she was afraid he was mad. No—that wasn't the truth. She knew he wouldn't be mad, but she couldn't face him. She wanted to talk to him, but she was in no shape.

She agreed to meet him for lunch. They hung up. He went into the bathroom to shave. A letter his father had written him, asking why he had dropped out of graduate school, was taped to the mirror, along with other articles of interest. There was one faded clipping, which belonged to Johnny and had been hung on the refrigerator at the house, about someone called the California Superman who had frozen to death in his Superman suit, in his refrigerator. All of Robert's friends had bizarre stories displayed in their apartments. Cyril had a story about a family that had starved to death in their car at the side of the highway. Their last meal had been watermelon. The clipping was tacked to Cyril's headboard. It made Robert feel old and disoriented when he realized that these awful newspaper articles had replaced those mindless Day-Glo pictures everybody used to have. Also, people in New Haven had begun to come up to him on the street—cops, surely; they had to be cops—swinging plastic bags full of grass in front of his nose, bringing handfuls of ups and downs out of their pockets. Also, the day before, he had got a box from his mother. She sent him a needlepoint doorstop, with a small white-and-gray Scottie dog on it, and a half wreath of roses underneath it. It really got him down.

He began to shave. His cat walked into the bathroom and rubbed against his bare ankle, making him jerk his leg away, and he cut his cheek. He put a piece of toilet paper against the cut, and sat on the side of the tub. He was angry at the cat and angry at himself for being depressed. After all, Dan was out of the picture now. Penelope had been found. He could go get her, the way he got groceries, the way he got a book from the library. It seemed too easy. Something was wrong.

He put on his jeans—he had no clean underwear; forget about that—and a shirt and his jacket, and walked to the restaurant. Penelope was in the first booth, with her coat still on. There was a bottle of beer on the table in front of her. She was smiling sheepishly, and seeing her, he smiled back. He sat next to her and put his arm around her shoulder, hugging her to him.

"Who's the first girl you ever loved?" she said.

Leave it to her to ask something like that. He tried to feel her shoulder beneath her heavy coat, but couldn't. He tried to remember loving anyone but her. "A girl in high school," he said.

"I'll bet she had a tragic end," she said.

The waitress came and took their orders. When she went away,

Penelope continued, "Isn't that what usually happens? People's first loves washing up on the beach in Mexico?"

"She didn't finish high school with me. Her parents yanked her out and put her in private school. For all I know, she did go to Mexico and wash up on the beach."

She covered her ears. "You're mad at me," she said.

"No," he said, hugging her to him. "I wasn't too happy last night, though. What did you want to talk to me about?"

"I wanted to know if I could live with you."

"Sure," he said.

"Really? You wouldn't mind?"

"No," he said.

While she was smiling at the startled look on his face, the waitress put a cheeseburger in front of him. She put an omelette in front of Penelope, and Penelope began to eat hungrily. He picked up his cheeseburger and bit into it. It was good. It was the first thing he had eaten in more than a day. Feeling sorry for himself, he took another bite.

"I just took a few drags of that stuff, and I felt like my mind was filling up with clouds," she said.

"Forget about it," he said. "You're okay now."

"I want to talk about something else, though."

He nodded.

"I slept with Cyril," she said.

"What?" he said. "When did you sleep with Cyril?"

"At the house," she said. "And at his place."

"Recently?" he said.

"A couple of days ago."

"Well," he said. "Why are you telling me?"

"Cyril told Dan," she said.

That explained it.

"What do you expect me to say?" he said.

"I don't know. I wanted to talk about it."

He took another bite of his cheeseburger. He did not want her to talk about it.

"I don't know why I should be all twisted around," she said. "And I don't even know why I'm telling you."

"I wouldn't know," he said.

"Are you jealous?"

"Yes."

"Cyril said you had a crush on me," she said.

"That makes it sound like I'm ten years old," he said.

"I was thinking about going to Colorado," she said.

"I don't know what I expected," he said, slamming his hand down on the table. "I didn't expect that you'd be talking about screwing Cyril and going to Colorado." He pushed his plate away, angry.

"I shouldn't have told you."

"Shouldn't have told me what? What am I going to do about it? What do you expect me to say?"

"I thought you felt the way I feel," she said. "I thought you felt stifled in New Haven."

He looked at her. She had a way of sometimes saying perceptive things, but always when he was expecting something else.

"I have friends in Colorado," she said. "Bea and Matthew. You met them when they stayed at the house once."

"You want me to move out to Colorado because Bea and Matthew are there?"

"They have a big house they're having trouble paying the mortgage on."

"But I don't have any money."

"You have the money your father sent you so you could take courses at Yale. And you could get back into painting in Colorado. You're not a picture framer—you're a painter. Wouldn't you like to quit your lousy job framing pictures and get out of New Haven?"

"Get out of New Haven?" he repeated, to see what it felt like. "I don't know," he said. "It doesn't seem very reasonable."

"I don't feel right about things," she said.

"About Cyril?"

"The last five years," she said.

He excused himself and went to the bathroom. Scrawled above one of the mirrors was a message: TIME WILL SAY NOTHING BUT I TOLD YOU SO. A very literate town, New Haven. He looked at the bathroom window, stared at the ripply white glass. He thought about crawling out the window. He was not able to deal with her. He went back to the booth.

"Come on," he said, dropping money on the table.

Outside, she began to cry. "I could have asked Cyril to go, but I didn't," she said.

He put his arm around her. "You're bats," he said.

He tried to get her to walk faster. By the time they got back to his apartment, she was smiling again, and talking about going skiing in the Rockies. He opened the door and saw a note lying on the floor, written by Dan. It was Penelope's name, written over and over, and a lot of profanity. He showed it to her. Neither of them said anything. He put it back on the table, next to an old letter from his mother that begged him to go back to graduate school.

"I want to stop smoking," she said, handing him her cigarette pack. She said it as if it were a revelation, as if everything, all day, had been carefully leading up to it.

It is a late afternoon in February, and Penelope is painting her toenails. She had meant what she said about moving in with him. She didn't even go back to Dan's apartment for her clothes. She has been borrowing Robert's shirts and sweaters, and wears his pajama bottoms under his long winter coat when she goes to the laundromat so she can wash her one pair of jeans. She has quit her job. She wants to give a farewell party before they go to Colorado.

She is sitting on the floor, and there are little balls of cotton stuck between her toes. The second toe on each foot is crooked. She wore the wrong shoes as a child. One night she turned the light on to show Robert her feet, and said that they embarrassed her. Why, then, is she painting her toenails?

"Penelope," he says, "I have no interest in any damn party. I have very little interest in going to Colorado."

Today he told his boss that he would be leaving next week. His boss laughed and said that he would send his brother around to beat him up. As usual, he could not really tell whether his boss was kidding. Before he goes to bed, he intends to stand a Coke bottle behind the front door.

"You said you wanted to see the mountains," Penelope says.

"I know we're going to Colorado," he says. "I don't want to get into another thing about that."

He sits next to her and holds her hand. Her hands are thin. They feel about an eighth of an inch thick to him. He changes his grip and gets his fingers down toward the knuckles, where her hand feels more substantial.

"I know it's going to be great in Colorado," Penelope says. "This is the first time in years I've been sure something is going to work out. It's the first time I've been sure that doing something was worth it."

"But why Colorado?" he says.

"We can go skiing. Or we could just ride the lift all day, look down on all that beautiful snow."

He does not want to pin her down or diminish her enthusiasm. What he wants to talk about is the two of them. When he asked if she was sure she loved him she said yes, but she never wants to talk about them. It's very hard to talk to her at all. The night before, he asked some questions about her childhood. She told him that her father died when she was nine, and her mother married an Italian who beat her with the lawn-mower cord. Then she was angry at him for making her remember that, and he was sorry he had asked. He is still surprised that she has moved in with him, surprised that he has agreed to leave New Haven and move to Colorado with her, into the house of a couple he vaguely remembers—nice guy, strung-out wife.

"Did you get a letter from Matthew and Bea yet?" he says.

"Oh, yes, Bea called this morning when you were at work. She said she had to call right away to say yes, she was so excited."

He remembers how excited Bea was the time she stayed with them in the country house. It seemed more like nervousness, really, not excitement. Bea said she had been studying ballet, and when Matthew told her to show them what she had learned, she danced through the house, smiling at first, then panting. She complained that she had no grace— that she was too old. Matthew tried to make her feel better by saying that she had only started to study ballet late, and she would have to build up energy. Bea became more frantic, saying that she had no energy, no poise, no future as a ballerina.

"But there's something I ought to tell you," Penelope says. "Bea and Matthew are breaking up."

"What?" he says.

"What does it matter? It's a huge state. We can find a place to stay. We've got enough money. Don't always be worried about money."

He was just about to say that they hardly had enough money to pay for motels on the way to Colorado.

"And when you start painting again—"

"Penelope, get serious," he says. "Do you think that all you have to do is produce some paintings and you'll get money for them?"

"You don't have any faith in yourself," she says.

It is the same line she gave him when he dropped out of graduate school, after she had dropped out herself. Somehow she was always the one who sounded reasonable.

"Why don't we forget Colorado for a while?" he says.

"Okay," she says. "We'll just forget it."

"Oh, we can go if you're set on it," he says quickly.

"Not if you're only doing it to placate me."

"I don't know. I don't want to stick around New Haven."

"Then what are you complaining about?" she says.

"I wasn't complaining. I was just disappointed."

"Don't be disappointed," she says, smiling at him.

He puts his forehead against hers and closes his eyes. Sometimes it is very nice to be with her. Outside he can hear the traffic, the horns blowing. He does not look forward to the long drive west.

In Nebraska they get sidetracked and drive a long way on a narrow road, with holes so big that Robert has to swerve the car to avoid them. The heater is not working well, and the defroster is not working at all. He rubs the front window clear with the side of his arm. By early evening he is exhausted from driving. They stop for dinner at Gus and Andy's Restaurant, and are served their fried-egg sandwiches by Andy, whose name is written in sequins above his shirt pocket. That night, in the motel, he feels too tired to go to sleep. The cat is scratching around in the bathroom. Penelope complains about the electricity in her hair, which she has just washed and is drying. He cannot watch television because her hair dryer makes the picture roll.

"I sort of wish we had stopped in Iowa to see Elaine," she says. Elaine is her married sister.

She drags on a joint, passes it to him.

"You were the one who didn't want to stop," he says. She can't hear him because of the hair dryer.

"We used to pretend that we were pregnant when we were little," she says. "We pulled the pillows off and stuck them under our clothes. My mother was always yelling at us not to mess up the beds."

She turns off the hair dryer. The picture comes back on. It is the news; the sportscaster is in the middle of a basketball report. On a large screen behind him, a basketball player is shown putting a basketball into a basket.

Before they left, Robert had gone over to Cyril's apartment. Cyril seemed to know already that Penelope was living with him. He was very nice, but Robert had a hard time talking to him. Cyril said that a girl he knew was coming over to make dinner, and he asked him to stay. Robert said he had to get going.

"What are you going to do in Colorado?" Cyril asked.

"Get some kind of job, I guess," he said.

Cyril nodded about ten times, the nods growing smaller.

"I don't know," he said to Cyril.

"Yeah," Cyril said.

They sat. Finally Robert made himself go by telling himself that he didn't want to see Cyril's girl.

"Well," Cyril said. "Take care."

"What about you?" he asked Cyril. "What are you going to be up to?"

"Much of the same," Cyril said.

They stood at Cyril's door.

"Seems like we were all together at that house about a million years ago," Cyril said.

"Yeah," he said.

"Maybe when the new people moved in they found dinosaur tracks," Cyril said.

In the motel that night, in his dreams, Robert makes love to Penelope. When the sun comes through the drapes, he touches her shoulder and thinks about waking her. Instead, he gets out of bed and sits by the dresser and lights the stub of the joint. It's gone in three tokes, and he gets back into bed, cold and drowsy. Going to sleep, he chuckles, or thinks he hears himself chuckling. Later, when she tries to rouse him, he can't move, and it isn't until afternoon that they get rolling. He feels tired but still up from the grass. The effect seems not to have worn off with sleep at all.

They are at Bea and Matthew's house. It was cloudy and cold when they arrived, late in the afternoon, and the sides of the roads were heaped high with old snow. Robert got lost trying to find the house and finally had to stop in a gas station and telephone to ask for directions. "Take a right after the feed store at the crossroads," Matthew told him. It doesn't seem to Robert that they are really in Colorado. That evening Matthew insists that Robert sit in their one chair (a black canvas butterfly chair) because Robert must be tired from driving. Robert cannot get comfortable in the chair. There is a large photograph of Nureyev on the wall across from Robert, and there is a small table in the corner of the room. Matthew has explained that Bea got mad after one of their fights and sold the rest of the living-room furniture. Penelope sits on the floor at Robert's side. They have run out of cigarettes, and Matthew and Bea have almost run out of liquor. Matthew is waiting for Bea to drive to town to buy more; Bea is waiting for Matthew to give in. They are living together, but they have filed for divorce. It is a friendly living-together, but they wait each other out, testing. Who will turn the record over? Who will buy the Scotch?

Their dog, Zero, lies on the floor listening to music and lapping apple juice. He pays no attention to the stereo speakers but loves headphones. He won't have them put on his head, but when they are on the floor he creeps up on them and settles down there. Penelope points out that one old Marianne Faithfull record seems to make Zero particularly euphoric. Bea gives him apple juice for his constipation. She and Matthew dote on the dog. That is going to be a problem.

For dinner Bea fixes beef Stroganoff, and they all sit on the floor with their plates. Bea says that there is honey in the Stroganoff. She is ignoring Matthew, who stirs his fork in a circle through his food and puts his plate down every few minutes to drink Scotch. Earlier Bea told him to offer the bottle around, but they all said they didn't want any. A tall black candle burns in the center of their circle; it is dark outside, and the candle is the only light. When they finish eating, there is only one shot of Scotch left in the bottle and Matthew is pretty drunk. He says to Bea, "I was going to move out the night before Christmas, in the middle of the night, so that when you heard Santa Claus, it would have been me instead, carrying away Zero instead of my bag of tricks."

"Bag of *toys*," Bea says. She has on a satin robe that reminds Robert of a fighter's robe, stuffed between her legs as she sits on the floor.

"And laying a finger aside of my nose . . . ," Matthew says. "No, I wouldn't have done that, Bea. I would have given the finger to you." Matthew raises his middle finger and smiles at Bea. "But I speak figuratively, of course. I will give you neither my finger nor my dog."

"I got the dog from the animal shelter, Matthew," Bea says. "Why do you call him your dog?"

Matthew stumbles off to bed, almost stepping on Penelope's plate, calling over his shoulder, "Bea, my lovely, please make sure that our guests finish that bottle of Scotch."

Bea blows out the candle and they all go to bed, with a quarter inch of Scotch still in the bottle.

"Why are they getting divorced?" Robert whispers to Penelope in bed.

They are in a twin bed, narrower than he remembers twin beds being, lying under a brown-and-white quilt.

"I'm not really sure," she says. "She said that he was getting crazier."

"They both seem crazy."

"Bea told me that he gave some of their savings to a Japanese woman who lives with a man he works with, so she can open a gift shop."

"Oh," he says.

"I wish we had another cigarette."

"Is that all he did?" he asks. "Gave money away?"

"He drinks a lot," Penelope says.

"So does she. She drinks straight from the bottle." Before dinner Bea had tipped the bottle to her lips too quickly and the liquor ran down her chin. Matthew called her disgusting.

"I think he's nastier than she is," Penelope says.

"Move over a little," he says. "This bed must be narrower than a twin bed."

"I *am* moved over," she says.

He unbends his knees, lies straight in the bed. He is too uncomfortable to sleep. His ears are still ringing from so many hours on the road.

"Here we are in Colorado," he says. "Tomorrow we'll have to drive around and see it before it's all under snow."

The next afternoon he borrows a tablet and walks around outside, looking for something to draw. There are bare patches in the snow—patches of brown grass. Bea and Matthew's house is modern, with a sundeck across the back and glass doors across the front. For some reason the house seems out of place; it looks Eastern. There are no other houses nearby. Very little land has been cleared; the lawn is narrow, and the woods come close. It is cold, and there is a wind in the trees. Through the woods, in front of the house, distant snow-covered mountains are visible. The air is very clear, and the colors are too bright, like a Maxfield Parrish painting. No one would believe the colors if he painted them. Instead he begins to draw some old fence posts, partially rotted away. But then he stops. Leave it to Andrew Wyeth. He dusts away a light layer of snow and sits on the hood of his car. He takes the pencil out of his pocket again and writes in the sketchbook: "We are at Bea and Matthew's. They sit all day. Penelope sits. She seems to   waiting. This is happening in Colorado. I want to see the state, bu Bea and Matthew have already seen it, and Penelope says that she ca not face one more minute in the car. The car needs new spa plugs. I ll never be a painter. I am not a writer."

Zero wanders up behind him, and he tears off   piece   sketch paper and crumples it into a ball, throws it in the ai ero's e s ligi up. They play ball with the piece of paper—he throws it nigh, and Zero waits for it and jumps. Finally the paper gets too soggy to handle. Zero walks away, then sits and scratches.

Behind the house is a ruined birdhouse, and some strings hang from a branch, with bits of suet tied on. The strings stir in the wind. "Push me in the swing," he remembers Penelope saying. Johnny was lying in the grass, talking to himself. Robert tried to dance with Cyril, but Cyril wouldn't. Cyril was more stoned than any of them, but showing better sense. "Push me," she said. She sat on the swing and he pushed. She weighed very little—hardly enough to drag the swing down. It took off fast and went high. She was laughing—not because she was having fun, but laughing at him. That's what he thought, but he was stoned. She was just laughing. Fortunately, the swing had slowed when she jumped. She didn't even roll down the hill. Cyril, looking at her arm, which had been cut on a rock, was almost in tears. She had landed on her side. They thought her arm was broken at first. Johnny was asleep, and he slept through the whole thing. Robert carried her into the house. Cyril, following, detoured to kick Johnny. That was the beginning of the end.

He walks to the car and opens the door and rummages through the ashtray, looking for the joint they had started to smoke just before they found Bea and Matthew's house. He has trouble getting it out because his fingers are numb from the cold. He finally gets it and lights it, and drags on it walking back to the tree with the birdhouse in it. He leans against the tree.

Dan had called him the day before they left New Haven and said that Penelope would kill him. He asked Dan what he meant. "She'll wear you down, she'll wear you out, she'll kill you," Dan said.

He feels the tree snapping and jumps away. He looks and sees that everything is okay. The tree is still there, the strings hanging down from the branch. "I'm going to jump!" Penelope had called, laughing. Now he laughs, too—not at her, but because here he is, leaning against a tree in Colorado, blown away. He tried speaking, to hear what his speech sounds like. "Blown away," he says. He has trouble getting his mouth into position after speaking.

In a while Matthew comes out. He stands beside the tree and they watch the sunset. The sky is pale blue, streaked with orange, which seems to be spreading through the blue sky from behind, like liquid seeping through a napkin, blood through a bandage.

"Nice," Matthew says.

"Yes," he says. He is never going to be able to talk to Matthew.

"You know what I'm in the doghouse for?" Matthew says.

"What?" he says. Too long a pause before answering. He spit the word out, instead of saying it.

"Having a Japanese girlfriend," Matthew says, and laughs.

He does not dare risk laughing with him.

"And I don't even *have* a Japanese girlfriend," Matthew says. "She lives with a guy I work with. I'm not interested in her. She needed money to go into business. Not a lot, but some. I loaned it to her. Bea changes facts around."

"Where did you go to school?" he hears himself say.

There is a long pause, and Robert gets confused. He thinks he should be answering his own question.

Finally: "Harvard."

"What class were you in?"

"Oh," Matthew says. "You're stoned, huh?"

It is too complicated to explain that he is not. He says, again, "What class?"

"Nineteen sixty-seven," Matthew says, laughing. "Is that your stuff or ours? She hid our stuff."

"In my glove compartment," Robert says, gesturing.

He watches Matthew walk toward his car. Sloped shoulders. Something written across the back of his jacket, being spoken by what looks like a monster blue bird. Can't read it. In a while Matthew comes back smoking a joint, Zero trailing behind.

"They're inside, talking about what a pig I am," Matthew exhales.

"How come you don't have any interest in this Japanese woman?"

"I do," Matthew says, smoking from his cupped hand. "I don't have a chance in the world."

"I don't guess it would be the same if you got another one," he says.

"Another what?"

"If you went to Japan and got another one."

"Never mind," Matthew says. "Never mind bothering to converse."

Zero sniffs the air and walks away. He lies down on the driveway, away from them, and closes his eyes.

"I'd like some Scotch to cool my lungs," Matthew says. "And we don't have any goddamn Scotch."

"Let's go get some," he says.

"Okay," Matthew says.

They stay, watching the colors intensify. "It's too cold for me," Matthew says. He thrashes his arms across his chest, and Zero springs up, leaping excitedly, and almost topples Matthew.

They get to Matthew's car. Robert hears the door close. He notices that he is inside. Zero is in the backseat. It gets darker. Matthew hums. Outside the liquor store Robert fumbles out a ten-dollar bill. Matthew declines. He parks and rolls down the window. "I don't want to walk in there in a cloud of this stuff," he says. They wait. Waiting, Robert gets confused. He says, "What state is this?"

"Are you kidding?" Matthew asks. Matthew shakes his head. "Colorado," he says.

THE BURNING
HOUSE

LEARNING TO FALL

Ruth's house, early morning: a bowl of apples on the kitchen table, crumbs on the checkered tablecloth. "I love you," she says to Andrew. "Did you guess that I loved you?" "I know it," he says. He's annoyed that his mother is being mushy in front of me. He is eager to seem independent, and cranky because he just woke up. I'm cranky, too, even after the drive to Ruth's in the cold. I'm drinking coffee to wake up. If someone said that he loved me at this moment, I'd never believe him; I can't think straight so early in the morning, hate to make conversation, am angry at the long, cold winter. Andrew and I are both frowning at Ruth's table and she—as always—is tolerating us. "More coffee?" Ruth asks me. I nod yes, and let her pour it, although I could easily get up and walk to the stove for the pot. "What about brushing your hair?" she says to Andrew. He gets up and leaves the room, comes back with her wooden brush and begins to brush his hair. "Not over the table, please," she says. He has finished. He puts the brush on the table and looks at me. "We're going to miss the train," he says. "There's plenty of time," Ruth says. Andrew looks at the clock and sighs loudly. Ruth laughs. She rubs her finger around the top of the open honey jar and sucks it. "Come on," I say to Andrew. "You're right. I'd rather be early than late." I ask Ruth: "Anything from the city?" If she did want something, she wouldn't say—she hates to take things, because she has no money to buy things in return. Nor does she want many things around: the kitchen has only a table and four chairs. What furniture she has came with the house. "No, thanks," she says, and turns off the radio. She says again, as we go out the door, "Thanks." She has a hand on each of our backs as I open the door and cold floods into the house.

Once or twice a month, on Wednesdays, Andrew and I take the train from Connecticut to New York, and I walk down the streets and into stores and through museums with him, holding his little hand, which is as tight as a knot. He does not have friends his own age, but he likes me. After eight years, he trusts me.

Today he is wearing his blue jeans with the Superman patch on the knee. If Superman launched himself from Andrew's knee, he would be flying a foot or so off the ground. People would think that small figure in blue was a piece of trash caught by the wind, a stick blowing, something to gather their hems against.

"I'm hungry again," he says.

Andrew knows that I don't eat during the day. He says *again* because he has already had oatmeal at home and a pastry at the fast-food shop across from the train in Westport at ten o'clock, and now it's only twelve—too early to eat another meal—and he knows I'm going to say: *"Again?"*

Andrew. The morning before the night he was born, Ruth and I swam in Hall's Pond. She loved it that she could float, heavy as she was, about to deliver. She loved being pregnant and wanted the child, although the man who was the father begged her to have an abortion and finally left her six months before Andrew was born. On the last day that we swam in Hall's Pond, she was two weeks overdue. There wasn't a sign of the pain yet, but her tension made me as dizzy as the hot sun on my head as I stood in the too-cold water.

And that night: holding her hand, my hand finally moving up her arm, as if she were slipping away from me. "Take my hand," she kept saying, and I would rub my thumb on her knuckles, squeeze her hand as hard as I dared, but I couldn't stop myself from grasping her wrist, the middle of her arm, hanging on to her elbow, as if she were drowning. It was the same thing I would do with the man who became my lover, years later—but then it would be because I was sinking.

Andrew and I are walking downhill in the Guggenheim Museum, and I am thinking about Ray. Neither of us is looking at the paintings. What Andrew likes about the museum is the view, looking down into the pool of blue water speckled with money.

I stand beside him on the curving walkway. "Don't throw coins from up here, Andrew," I say. "You might hurt somebody."

"Just a penny," he says. He holds it up to show me. A penny: no tricks.

"You're not allowed. It could hit somebody in the face. You could hurt somebody, throwing it."

I am asking him to be careful of hurting people. When he would not be born, an impatient doctor used forceps and tugged him out, and there was slight brain damage. That and some small paralysis of his face, at the mouth.

He pockets the penny. His parka has fallen off one shoulder. He doesn't notice.

"We'll get lunch," I say. "Take your pennies and throw them in the pool when we get down there."

He gets there before me. I look down and see him making his wishes. I doubt that he knows yet what to wish for. Other people are throwing money. Andrew is shy and just stands there, eyes closed and squinting, holding his pennies. He likes to do things in private. You can see the disappointment on his face that other people are in the world. He likes to run with his arms out like the wings of a plane; he likes to be in the first seat in the train compartment—to sit with only me where three seats face two seats across from them. He likes to stretch his legs. He hates cigarette smoke, and the smell of perfume. In spring, he sniffs the breeze like an old man sniffing cognac. He is in the third grade at the elementary school, and so far he has had only slight trouble keeping up. His teacher—who has become Ruth's friend—is young and hopeful, and she doesn't criticize Ruth for the notes she writes pretending that Andrew has been ill on the day the two of us were really in New York. Andrew makes going to the city fun, and for that—and because I know him so well, and I pity him—I almost love him.

We go to his favorite place for hamburgers—a tiny shop on Madison Avenue with a couple of tables in the front. The only time we sat at a table was the time that Ray met us there. Andrew liked sitting at a table, but he was shy and wouldn't say much because Ray was there. The man behind the counter knows us. I know that he recognizes us, even though he doesn't say hello. We always order the same thing: I have black coffee (advertised as the world's best); Andrew has a bacon cheeseburger and a glass of milk. Because Ruth has taught him to make sure he looks neat, he wipes the halo of milk off his mouth after every sip. His hands get sticky from the milk-wet napkin.

Today it is bitter cold, and I am remembering that hot and distant summer. I have hardly been swimming in eight years—not since Arthur and I moved downstate, away from Hall's Pond. When we were in graduate school together, Ruth and I would go there to study. She would have her big, thick Russian novels with her, and I was always afraid she would drop one into the water. Such big books, underlined, full of notes, it would have seemed more than an average tragedy if she had lost one. She never did. I lost a gold chain (a real one), and my lighter. One time my grocery list fell out of my book into the water and I saw the letters bleed and haze and disappear as it went under.

We went there earlier in the day than other people—not that many people knew about Hall's Pond then—so we always got to sit on the big rock. Later in the day, people would come and sit on the smaller rock, or stand around on the pier going out to the water. Some of the people swam naked. One time a golden retriever jumped onto our rock, crouched, and threw its head back and howled at the sky, then ran away through the woods, its feet blackening in the wet dirt by the water's edge. Ruth was freaked out by it. She wrote a poem, and in the poem the dog came to give a warning. Not an angel, a dog. I stared at the poem, not quite understanding it. "It's meant to be funny," she said. When the dog ran off, Ruth had put her hands over her mouth. The next summer, when I married Arthur, she wrote a poem about the bouquet I carried. The bouquet had some closed lilies, and in the poem she said they were like candles—as big as Roman candles to her eye, as if my bunch of flowers were going to explode and shower down. I laughed at the poem. It was the wrong reaction. Now, because things have come apart between Arthur and me, it has turned out to be prophetic.

"What's up now?" Andrew says, laying down the cheeseburger. He always eats them the same way, and it is a way I have never seen another child eat one: he bites around the outside, eating until only the circle at the center is left.

I look at my watch. The watch was a Christmas present from Arthur. It's almost touching that he isn't embarrassed to give me such impersonal presents as eggcups and digital watches. To see the time, you have to push in the tiny button on the side. As long as you hold it, the time stays lit, changes. Take away your hand and the watch turns clear red again.

"We're going to Bonnie's studio. She's printed the pictures Ruth wanted. Those pictures she took the Fourth of July—we're finally going to see them."

I feel in my pocket for the check Ruth gave me to pay Bonnie.

"But where are we going?" he says.

"To Spring Street. You remember your mother's friend with the long hair to her waist, don't you? You know where Bonnie lives. You've been there before."

We take the subway, and Andrew sits in the crowded car by squeezing himself onto the seat next to me and sitting on one hip, his left leg thrown over mine so that we must look like a ventriloquist and a dummy. The black woman sitting next to him shifts over a little. He stays squeezed against me.

"If Bonnie offers you lunch, I bet you take it," I say, poking the side of his parka.

"I couldn't eat any more."

"You?" I say.

"String bean," he says to me. He pats his puffy parka. Underneath it, you would be able to see his ribs through the T-shirt. He is lean and would be quite handsome except for the obvious defect of his mouth, which droops at one corner as if he's sneering.

We are riding on the subway, and Ruth is back at the tiny converted carriage house she rents from a surgeon and his wife in Westport. Like everything else in the area, it is overpriced, and she can barely afford it—her little house with not enough light, with plastic taped over the aluminum screens and the screens left in the windows because there are no storm windows. Wood is burning in the stove, and herbs are clumped in a bag of gauze hung in the pot of chicken stock. She is underlining things in books, cutting coupons out of newspapers. On Wednesdays she does not have to go to work at the community college where she teaches. She is waiting for her lover, Brandon, to call or to come over: there's warmth, soup, discoveries about literature, and, if he cares, privacy. I envy him an afternoon with Ruth, because she will cook for him and make him laugh and ask nothing from him. She earns hardly any money at the community college, but her half gallons of wine taste better than the expensive bottles Arthur's business friends uncork. She will reach out and touch you to let you know she is listening when you talk, instead of suggesting that you go out to see some movie for amusement.

Almost every time I take Andrew home Brandon is there. It's rare that he goes there any other day of the week. Sometimes he brings two steaks. On Valentine's Day he brought her a plant that grows well in the dim light of the kitchen. It sits on the windowsill behind the sink and is weaving upward, guided by tacks Ruth has pushed into the window frame. The leaves are thick and small, green and heart shaped. If I were a poet, those green leaves would be envy, closing her in. Like many people, he does envy her. He would like to be her, but he does not want to take her on. Or Andrew.

. . .

The entryway to Bonnie's loft is so narrow, painted bile green, peeling and filthy, that I always nearly panic, thinking I'll never get to the top. I expect roaches to lose their grip on the ceiling and fall on me; I expect a rat to dart out. I run, silently, ahead of Andrew.

Bonnie opens the door wearing a pair of paint-smeared jeans, one of Hal's V-neck sweaters hanging low over her hips. Her loft is painted the pale yellow of the sun through fog. Her photographs are tacked to the walls, her paintings hung. She hugs both of us and wants us to stay. I take off my coat and unzip Andrew's parka and lay it across his legs. The arms stick out from the sides, no hands coming through them. It could be worse; Andrew could have been born without hands or arms. "I'll tell you what I'm sick of," Ruth said to me not long after he was born, one of the few times she ever complained. "I'm sick of hearing how things might have been worse, when they might also have been better. I'm sick of lawyers saying to wait—not to settle until we're sure how much damage has been done. They talk about damage with their vague regret, the way the weatherman talks about another three inches of snow. I'm sick of wind whistling through the house, when it could be warm and dry." She is never sick of Brandon, and the two steaks he brings, although he couldn't come to dinner the night of Andrew's birthday, and she is not bitter that Andrew's father has had no contact with her since before the birth. "Angry?" Ruth said to me once. "I'm angry at myself. I don't often misjudge people that way."

Bonnie fixes Andrew hot chocolate. My hands are about to shake, but I take another cup of coffee anyway, thinking that it might just be because the space heater radiates so little heat in the loft. Andrew and I sit close together, the white sofa spreading away on either side of us. Andrew looks at some of Ruth's photographs, but his attention drifts away and he starts to hum. I fit them back in the manila envelope, between the pieces of cardboard, and tie the envelope closed. He rests his head on my arm, so that it's hard to wind the string to close the envelope. While his eyes are closed, Bonnie whispers to me: "I couldn't. I couldn't take money from her."

She looks at me as if I'm crazy. Now it's my problem: How am I going to give Ruth the check back without offending her? I fold the check and put it in my pocket.

"You'll think of something," Bonnie said softly.

She looks hopeful and sad. She is going to have a baby, too. She knows already that she is going to have a girl. She knows that she is going to name her Ora. What she doesn't know is that Hal gambled and lost a lot of money and is worried about how they will afford a baby. Ruth knows that, because Hal called and confided in her. Is it modesty or self-preservation that makes Ruth pretend that she is not as important to people as she is? He calls, she told me, just because he is one of the few people she has ever known who really enjoys talking on the telephone.

We take the subway uptown, back to Grand Central Station. It is starting to fill up with commuters: men with light, expensive raincoats and heavy briefcases, women carrying shopping bags. In another couple of hours Arthur will be in the station on his way home. The manila envelope is clamped under my arm. Everyone is carrying something. I have the impulse to fold Andrew to me and raise him in my arms. I could do that until he was five, and then I couldn't do it anymore. I settle for taking his hand, and we walk along swinging hands until I let go for a second to look at my watch. I look from my watch to the clock. They don't agree, and of course the clock is right, the watch is not. We have missed the 3:05. In an hour there is another train, but on that train it's going to be difficult to get a seat. Or, worse, someone is going to see that something beyond tiredness is wrong with Andrew, and we are going to be offered a seat, and he is going to know why. He suspects already, the way children of a certain age look a little guilty when Santa Claus is mentioned, but I hope I am not there when some person's eye meets Andrew's and instead of looking away he looks back, knowing.

"We're going to have to wait for the next train," I tell him.

"How come?"

"Because we missed our train."

"Didn't you know it when you looked at your watch at Bonnie's?"

He is getting tired, and cranky. Next he'll ask how old I am. And why his mother prefers to stay with Brandon instead of coming to New York with us.

"It would have been rude to leave earlier. We were only there a little while."

I look at him to see what he thinks. Sometimes his thinking is a little slow, but he is also very smart about what he senses. He thinks what I think—that if I had meant to, we could have caught the train. He stares at me with the same dead-on stare Ray gives me when he thinks I am being childish. And, of course, it is because of Ray that I lingered. I always mean not to call him, but I almost always do. We cross the terminal and I go to a phone and drop in a dime. Andrew backs up and spins on his heel. His parka slips off his shoulder again. And his glove— where is his glove? One glove is on the right hand, but there's no glove in either pocket. I sound disappointed, far away when Ray says hello.

"It's just—he lost his glove," I say.

"Where are you?" he says.

"Grand Central."

"Are you coming in or going out?"

"Going home."

His soft voice: "I was afraid of that."

Silence.

"Ray?"

"What? Don't tell me you're going to concoct some reason to see me—ask me to take him off, man to man, and buy him new gloves?"

It makes me laugh.

"You know what, lady?" Ray says. "I do better amusing you over the phone than in person."

A woman walks by, carrying two black poodles. She has on a long gray fur coat and carries the little dogs, who look as if they're peeking out of a cave of fur, nestled in the crook of each arm. Everything is a Stan Mack cartoon. Another woman walks across the terminal. She has forgotten something, or changed her mind—she shakes her head suddenly and begins to walk the other way. Far away from us, she starts to run. Andrew turns and turns. I reach down to make him be still, but he jerks away, spins again, loses interest, and just stands there, staring across the station.

"Fuck it," Ray says. "Can I come down and buy you a drink?"

More coffee. Andrew has a milk shake. Ray sits across from us, stirring his coffee as if he's mixing something. Last year when I decided that loving Ray made me as confused as disliking Arthur, and that he had too much power over me and that I could not be his lover anymore, I started taking Andrew to the city with me. It hasn't worked out well; it exasperates Ray, and I feel guilty for using Andrew.

"New shoes," Ray says, pushing his leg out from under the table.

He has on black boots, and he is as happy with them as Andrew was with the pennies I gave him this morning. I smile at him. He smiles back.

"What did you do today?" Ray says.

"Went on an errand for Ruth. Went to the Guggenheim."

He nods. I used to sleep with him and then hold his head as if I believed in phrenology. He used to hold my hands as I held his head. Ray has the most beautiful hands I have ever seen.

"Want to stay in town?" he says. "I was going to the ballet. I can probably get two more tickets."

Andrew looks at me, suddenly interested in staying.

"I've got to go home and make dinner for Arthur."

"Milk the cows," Ray says. "Knead the bread. Stoke the stove. Go to bed."

Andrew looks up at him and smiles broadly before he gets self-conscious and puts his hand to the corner of his mouth and looks away.

"You never heard that one before?" Ray says to Andrew. "My grandmother used to say that. Times have changed and times haven't changed." He looks away, shakes his head. "I'm profound today, aren't I? Good it's coffee and not the drink I wanted."

Andrew shifts in the booth, looks at me as if he wants to say something. I lean my head toward him. "What?" I say softly. He starts a rush of whispering.

"His mother is learning to fall," I say.

"What does that mean?" Ray says.

"In her dance class," Andrew says. He looks at me again, shy. "Tell him."

"I've never seen her do it," I say. "She told me about it—it's an exercise or something. She's learning to fall."

Ray nods. He looks like a professor being patient with a student who has just reached an obvious conclusion. You know when Ray isn't interested. He holds his head very straight and looks you right in the eye, as though he is.

"Does she just go plop?" he says to Andrew.

"Not really," Andrew says, more to me than to Ray. "It's kind of slow."

I imagine Ruth bringing her arms in front of her, head bent, an almost penitential position, and then a loosening in the knees, a slow folding downward.

Ray reaches across the table and pulls my arms away from the front of my body, and his touch startles me so that I jump, almost upsetting my coffee.

"Let's take a walk," he says. "Come on. You've got time."

He puts two dollars down and pushes the money and the check to the back of the table. I hold Andrew's parka for him and he backs into it. Ray adjusts it on his shoulders. Ray bends over and feels in Andrew's pockets.

"What are you doing?" Andrew says.

"Sometimes disappearing mittens have a way of reappearing," Ray says. "I guess not."

Ray zips his own green jacket and pulls on his hat. I walk out of the restaurant beside him, and Andrew follows.

"I'm not going far," Andrew says. "It's cold."

I clutch the envelope. Ray looks at me and smiles, it's so obvious that I'm holding the envelope with both hands so I don't have to hold his hand. He moves in close and puts his hand around my shoulder. No hand swinging like children—the proper gentleman and the lady out for a stroll. What Ruth has known all along: what will happen can't be stopped. Aim for grace.

THE CINDERELLA WALTZ

Milo and Bradley are creatures of habit. For as long as I've known him, Milo has worn his moth-eaten blue scarf with the knot hanging so low on his chest that the scarf is useless. Bradley is addicted to coffee and carries a thermos with him. Milo complains about the cold, and Bradley is always a little edgy. They come out from the city every Saturday—this is not habit but loyalty—to pick up Louise. Louise is even more unpredictable than most nine-year-olds; sometimes she waits for them on the front step, sometimes she hasn't even gotten out of bed when they arrive. One time she hid in a closet and wouldn't leave with them.

Today Louise has put together a shopping bag full of things she wants to take with her. She is taking my whisk and my blue pottery bowl, to make Sunday breakfast for Milo and Bradley; Beckett's *Happy Days*, which she has carried around for weeks, and which she looks through, smiling—but I'm not sure she's reading it; and a coleus growing out of a conch shell. Also, she has stuffed into one side of the bag the fancy Victorian-style nightgown her grandmother gave her for Christmas, and into the other she has tucked her octascope. Milo keeps a couple of dresses, a nightgown, a toothbrush, and extra sneakers and boots at his apartment for her. He got tired of rounding up her stuff to pack for her to take home, so he has bought some things for her that can be left. It annoys him that she still packs bags, because then he has to go around making sure that she has found everything before she goes home. She seems to know how to manipulate him, and after the weekend is over she calls tearfully to say that she has left this or that, which means that he must get his car out of the garage and drive all the way out to the house to bring it to her. One time, he refused to take the hour-long drive, because she had only left a copy of Tolkien's *The Two Towers*. The following weekend was the time she hid in the closet.

"I'll water your plant if you leave it here," I say now.

"I can take it," she says.

"I didn't say you couldn't take it. I just thought it might be easier to leave it, because if the shell tips over the plant might get ruined."

"Okay," she says. "Don't water it today, though. Water it Sunday afternoon."

I reach for the shopping bag.

"I'll put it back on my windowsill," she says. She lifts the plant out and carries it as if it's made of Steuben glass. Bradley bought it for her last month, driving back to the city, when they stopped at a lawn sale. She and Bradley are both very choosy, and he likes that. He drinks French-roast coffee; she will debate with herself almost endlessly over whether to buy a coleus that is primarily pink or lavender or striped.

"Has Milo made any plans for this weekend?" I ask.

"He's having a couple of people over tonight, and I'm going to help them make crepes for dinner. If they buy more bottles of that wine with the yellow flowers on the label, Bradley is going to soak the labels off for me."

"That's nice of him," I say. "He never minds taking a lot of time with things."

"He doesn't like to cook, though. Milo and I are going to cook. Bradley sets the table and fixes flowers in a bowl. He thinks it's frustrating to cook."

"Well," I say, "with cooking you have to have a good sense of timing. You have to coordinate everything. Bradley likes to work carefully and not be rushed."

I wonder how much she knows. Last week she told me about a conversation she'd had with her friend Sarah. Sarah was trying to persuade Louise to stay around on the weekends, but Louise said she always went to her father's. Then Sarah tried to get her to take her along, and Louise said that she couldn't. "You could take her if you wanted to," I said later. "Check with Milo and see if that isn't right. I don't think he'd mind having a friend of yours occasionally."

She shrugged. "Bradley doesn't like a lot of people around," she said.

"Bradley likes you, and if she's your friend I don't think he'd mind."

She looked at me with an expression I didn't recognize; perhaps she thought I was a little dumb, or perhaps she was just curious to see if I would go on. I didn't know how to go on. Like an adult, she gave a little shrug and changed the subject.

. . .

At ten o'clock Milo pulls into the driveway and honks his horn, which makes a noise like a bleating sheep. He knows the noise the horn makes is funny, and he means to amuse us. There was a time just after the divorce when he and Bradley would come here and get out of the car and stand around silently, waiting for her. She knew that she had to watch for them, because Milo wouldn't come to the door. We were both bitter then, but I got over it. I still don't think Milo would have come into the house again, though, if Bradley hadn't thought it was a good idea. The third time Milo came to pick her up after he'd left home, I went out to invite them in, but Milo said nothing. He was standing there with his arms at his sides like a wooden soldier, and his eyes were as dead to me as if they'd been painted on. It was Bradley whom I reasoned with. "Louise is over at Sarah's right now, and it'll make her feel more comfortable if we're all together when she comes in," I said to him, and Bradley turned to Milo and said, "Hey, that's right. Why don't we go in for a quick cup of coffee?" I looked into the backseat of the car and saw his red thermos there; Louise had told me about it. Bradley meant that they should come in and sit down. He was giving me even more than I'd asked for.

It would be an understatement to say that I disliked Bradley at first. I was actually afraid of him, afraid even after I saw him, though he was slender, and more nervous than I, and spoke quietly. The second time I saw him, I persuaded myself that he was just a stereotype, but someone who certainly seemed harmless enough. By the third time, I had enough courage to suggest that they come into the house. It was embarrassing for all of us, sitting around the table—the same table where Milo and I had eaten our meals for the years we were married. Before he left, Milo had shouted at me that the house was a farce, that my playing the happy suburban housewife was a farce, that it was unconscionable of me to let things drag on, that I would probably kiss him and say, "How was your day, sweetheart?" and that he should bring home flowers and the evening paper. "Maybe I would!" I screamed back. "Maybe it would be nice to do that, even if we were pretending, instead of you coming home drunk and not caring what had happened to me or to Louise all day." He was holding on to the edge of the kitchen table, the way you'd hold on to the horse's reins in a runaway carriage. "I care about Louise," he said finally. That was the most horrible moment. Until then, until he said it that way, I had thought that he was going through something horrible—certainly something was terribly wrong—but that, in his way, he loved me after all. *You don't love me?* " I had whispered at once. It took us both aback. It was an innocent and pathetic question, and it made him come and put his arms around me in the last hug he ever gave me. "I'm sorry for you," he said, "and I'm sorry for marrying you and causing this, but you know who I love. I told you who I love." "But you were kidding," I said. "You didn't mean it. You were kidding."

When Bradley sat at the table that first day, I tried to be polite and not look at him much. I had gotten it through my head that Milo was crazy, and I guess I was expecting Bradley to be a horrible parody—Craig Russell doing Marilyn Monroe. Bradley did not spoon sugar into Milo's coffee. He did not even sit near him. In fact, he pulled his chair a little away from us, and in spite of his uneasiness he found more things to start conversations about than Milo and I did. He told me about the ad agency where he worked; he is a designer there. He asked if he could go out on the porch to see the brook—Milo had told him about the stream in the back of our place that was as thin as a pencil but still gave us our own watercress. He went out on the porch and stayed there for at least five minutes, giving us a chance to talk. We didn't say one word until he came back. Louise came home from Sarah's house just as Bradley sat down at the table again, and she gave him a hug as well as us. I could see that she really liked him. I was amazed that I liked him, too. Bradley had won and I had lost, but he was as gentle and low-key as if none of it mattered. Later in the week, I called him and asked him to tell me if any freelance jobs opened in his advertising agency. (I do a little freelance artwork, whenever I can arrange it.) The week after that, he called and told me about another agency, where they were looking for outside artists. Our calls to each other are always brief and for a purpose, but lately they're not just calls about business. Before Bradley left to scout some picture locations in Mexico, he called to say that Milo had told him that when the two of us were there years ago I had seen one of those big circular bronze Aztec calendars and I had always regretted not bringing it back. He wanted to know if I would like him to buy a calendar if he saw one like the one Milo had told him about.

Today, Milo is getting out of his car, his blue scarf flapping against his chest. Louise, looking out the window, asks the same thing I am wondering: "Where's Bradley?"

Milo comes in and shakes my hand, gives Louise a one-armed hug.

"Bradley thinks he's coming down with a cold," Milo says. "The dinner is still on, Louise. We'll do the dinner. We have to stop at Gristede's when we get back to town, unless your mother happens to have a tin of anchovies and two sticks of unsalted butter."

"Let's go to Gristede's," Louise says. "I like to go there."

"Let me look in the kitchen," I say. The butter is salted, but Milo says that will do, and he takes three sticks instead of two. I have a brainstorm and cut the cellophane on a leftover Christmas present from my aunt—a wicker plate that holds nuts and foil-wrapped triangles of cheese—and, sure enough: one tin of anchovies.

"We can go to the museum instead," Milo says to Louise. "Wonderful."

But then, going out the door, carrying her bag, he changes his mind. "We can go to America Hurrah, and if we see something beautiful we can buy it," he says.

They go off in high spirits. Louise comes up to his waist, almost, and I notice again that they have the same walk. Both of them stride forward with great purpose. Last week, Bradley told me that Milo had bought a weather vane in the shape of a horse, made around 1800, at America Hurrah, and stood it in the bedroom, and then was enraged when Bradley draped his socks over it to dry. Bradley is still learning what a perfectionist Milo is, and how little sense of humor he has. When we were first married, I used one of our pottery casserole dishes to put my jewelry in, and he nagged me until I took it out and put the dish back in the kitchen cabinet. I remember his saying that the dish looked silly on my dresser because it was obvious what it was and people would think we left our dishes lying around. It was one of the things that Milo wouldn't tolerate, because it was improper.

When Milo brings Louise back on Sunday night they are not in a good mood. The dinner was all right, Milo says, and Griffin and Amy and Mark were amazed at what a good hostess Louise had been, but Bradley hadn't been able to eat.

"Is he still coming down with a cold?" I ask. I was still a little shy about asking questions about Bradley.

Milo shrugs. "Louise made him take megadoses of vitamin C all weekend."

Louise says, "Bradley said that taking too much vitamin C was bad for your kidneys, though."

"It's a rotten climate," Milo says, sitting on the living-room sofa, scarf and coat still on. "The combination of cold and air pollution . . ."

Louise and I look at each other, and then back at Milo. For weeks now, he has been talking about moving to San Francisco, if he can find work there. (Milo is an architect.) This talk bores me, and it makes

Louise nervous. I've asked him not to talk to her about it unless he's actually going to move, but he doesn't seem to be able to stop himself.

"Okay," Milo says, looking at us both. "I'm not going to say anything about San Francisco."

"*California* is polluted," I say. I am unable to stop myself, either.

Milo heaves himself up from the sofa, ready for the drive back to New York. It is the same way he used to get off the sofa that last year he lived here. He would get up, dress for work, and not even go into the kitchen for breakfast—just sit, sometimes in his coat as he was sitting just now, and at the last minute he would push himself up and go out to the driveway, usually without a goodbye, and get in the car and drive off either very fast or very slowly. I liked it better when he made the tires spin in the gravel when he took off.

He stops at the doorway now, and turns to face me. "Did I take all your butter?" he says.

"No," I say. "There's another stick." I point into the kitchen.

"I could have guessed that's where it would be," he says, and smiles at me.

When Milo comes the next weekend, Bradley is still not with him. The night before, as I was putting Louise to bed, she said that she had a feeling he wouldn't be coming.

"I had that feeling a couple of days ago," I said. "Usually Bradley calls once during the week."

"He must still be sick," Louise said. She looked at me anxiously. "Do you think he is?"

"A cold isn't going to kill him," I said. "If he has a cold, he'll be okay."

Her expression changed; she thought I was talking down to her. She lay back in bed. The last year Milo was with us, I used to tuck her in and tell her that everything was all right. What that meant was that there had not been a fight. Milo had sat listening to music on the phonograph, with a book or the newspaper in front of his face. He didn't pay very much attention to Louise, and he ignored me entirely. Instead of saying a prayer with her, the way I usually did, I would say to her that everything was all right. Then I would go downstairs and hope that Milo would say the same thing to me. What he finally did say one night was "You might as well find out from me as some other way."

"Hey, are you an old bag lady again this weekend?" Milo says now, stooping to kiss Louise's forehead.

"Because you take some things with you doesn't mean you're a bag lady," she says primly.

"Well," Milo says, "you start doing something innocently, and before you know it it can take you over."

He looks angry, and acts as though it's difficult for him to make conversation, even when the conversation is full of sarcasm and double entendres.

"What do you say we get going?" he says to Louise.

In the shopping bag she is taking is her doll, which she has not played with for more than a year. I found it by accident when I went to tuck in a loaf of banana bread that I had baked. When I saw Baby Betsy, deep in the bag, I decided against putting the bread in.

"Okay," Louise says to Milo. "Where's Bradley?"

"Sick," he says.

"Is he too sick to have me visit?"

"Good heavens, no. He'll be happier to see you than to see me."

"I'm rooting some of my coleus to give him," she says. "Maybe I'll give it to him like it is, in water, and he can plant it when it roots."

When she leaves the room, I go over to Milo. "Be nice to her," I say quietly.

"I'm nice to her," he says. "Why does everybody have to act like I'm going to grow fangs every time I turn around?"

"You were quite cutting when you came in."

"I was being self-deprecating." He sighs. "I don't really know why I come here and act this way," he says.

"What's the matter, Milo?"

But now he lets me know he's bored with the conversation. He walks over to the table and picks up a *Newsweek* and flips through it. Louise comes back with the coleus in a water glass.

"You know what you could do," I say. "Wet a napkin and put it around that cutting and then wrap it in foil, and put it in water when you get there. That way, you wouldn't have to hold a glass of water all the way to New York."

She shrugs. "This is okay," she says.

"Why don't you take your mother's suggestion," Milo says. "The water will slosh out of the glass."

"Not if you don't drive fast."

"It doesn't have anything to do with my driving fast. If we go over a bump in the road, you're going to get all wet."

"Then I can put on one of my dresses at your apartment."

"Am I being unreasonable?" Milo says to me.

"I started it," I say. "Let her take it in the glass."

"Would you, as a favor, do what your mother says?" he says to Louise.

Louise looks at the coleus, and at me.

"Hold the glass over the seat instead of over your lap, and you won't get wet," I say.

"Your first idea was the best," Milo says.

Louise gives him an exasperated look and puts the glass down on the floor, pulls on her poncho, picks up the glass again and says a sullen goodbye to me, and goes out the front door.

"Why is this my fault?" Milo says. "Have I done anything terrible? I—"

"Do something to cheer yourself up," I say, patting him on the back.

He looks as exasperated with me as Louise was with him. He nods his head yes, and goes out the door.

"Was everything all right this weekend?" I ask Louise.

"Milo was in a bad mood, and Bradley wasn't even there on Saturday," Louise says. "He came back today and took us to the Village for breakfast."

"What did you have?"

"I had sausage wrapped in little pancakes and fruit salad and a rum bun."

"Where was Bradley on Saturday?"

She shrugs. "I didn't ask him."

She almost always surprises me by being more grown-up than I give her credit for. Does she suspect, as I do, that Bradley has found another lover?

"Milo was in a bad mood when you two left here Saturday," I say.

"I told him if he didn't want me to come next weekend, just to tell me." She looks perturbed, and I suddenly realize that she can sound exactly like Milo sometimes.

"You shouldn't have said that to him, Louise," I say. "You know he wants you. He's just worried about Bradley."

"So?" she says. "I'm probably going to flunk math."

"No, you're not, honey. You got a C-plus on the last assignment."

"It still doesn't make my grade average out to a C."

"You'll get a C. It's all right to get a C."

She doesn't believe me.

"Don't be a perfectionist, like Milo," I tell her. "Even if you got a D, you wouldn't fail."

Louise is brushing her hair—thin, shoulder-length, auburn hair. She is already so pretty and so smart in everything except math that I wonder what will become of her. When I was her age, I was plain and serious and I wanted to be a tree surgeon. I went with my father to the park and held a stethoscope—a real one—to the trunks of trees, listening to their silence. Children seem older now.

"What do you think's the matter with Bradley?" Louise says. She sounds worried.

"Maybe the two of them are unhappy with each other right now."

She misses my point. "Bradley's sad, and Milo's sad that he's unhappy."

I drop Louise off at Sarah's house for supper. Sarah's mother, Martine Cooper, looks like Shelley Winters, and I have never seen her without a glass of Galliano on ice in her hand. She has a strong candy smell. Her husband has left her, and she professes not to care. She has emptied her living room of furniture and put up ballet bars on the walls, and dances in a purple leotard to records by Cher and Mac Davis. I prefer to have Sarah come to our house, but her mother is adamant that everything must be, as she puts it, "fifty-fifty." When Sarah visited us a week ago and loved the chocolate pie I had made, I sent two pieces home with her. Tonight, when I left Sarah's house, her mother gave me a bowl of Jell-O fruit salad.

The phone is ringing when I come in the door. It is Bradley.

"Bradley," I say at once, "whatever's wrong, at least you don't have a neighbor who just gave you a bowl of maraschino cherries in green Jell-O with a Reddi-Wip flower squirted on top."

"Jesus," he says. "You don't need me to depress you, do you?"

"What's wrong?" I say.

He sighs into the phone. "Guess what?" he says.

"What?"

"I've lost my job."

It wasn't at all what I was expecting to hear. I was ready to hear that he was leaving Milo, and I had even thought that that would serve Milo right. Part of me still wanted him punished for what he did. I was so out of my mind when Milo left me that I used to go over and drink Galliano with Martine Cooper. I even thought seriously about forming a ballet group with her. I would go to her house in the afternoon, and she would hold a tambourine in the air and I would hold my leg rigid and try to kick it.

"That's awful," I say to Bradley. "What happened?"

"They said it was nothing personal—they were laying off three people. Two other people are going to get the ax at the agency within the next six months. I was the first to go, and it was nothing personal. From twenty thousand bucks a year to nothing, and nothing personal, either."

"But your work is so good. Won't you be able to find something again?"

"Could I ask you a favor?" he says. "I'm calling from a phone booth. I'm not in the city. Could I come talk to you?"

"Sure," I say.

It seems perfectly logical that he should come alone to talk—perfectly logical until I actually see him coming up the walk. I can't entirely believe it. A year after my husband has left me, I am sitting with his lover—a man, a person I like quite well—and trying to cheer him up because he is out of work. ("Honey," my father would say, "listen to Daddy's heart with the stethoscope, or you can turn it toward you and listen to your own heart. You won't hear anything listening to a tree." Was my persistence willfulness, or belief in magic? Is it possible that I hugged Bradley at the door because I'm secretly glad he's down and out, the way I used to be? Or do I really want to make things better for him?)

He comes into the kitchen and thanks me for the coffee I am making, drapes his coat over the chair he always sits in.

"What am I going to do?" he asks.

"You shouldn't get so upset, Bradley," I say. "You know you're good. You won't have trouble finding another job."

"That's only half of it," he says. "Milo thinks I did this deliberately. He told me I was quitting on him. He's very angry at me. He fights with me, and then he gets mad that I don't enjoy eating dinner. My stomach's upset, and I can't eat anything."

"Maybe some juice would be better than coffee."

"If I didn't drink coffee, I'd collapse," he says.

I pour coffee into a mug for him, coffee into a mug for me.

"This is probably very awkward for you," he says. "That I come here and say all this about Milo."

"What does he mean about your quitting on him?"

"He said . . . he actually accused me of doing badly deliberately, so they'd fire me. I was so afraid to tell him the truth when I was fired that I pretended to be sick. Then I really *was* sick. He's never been angry at me this way. Is this always the way he acts? Does he get a notion in his head for no reason and then pick at a person because of it?"

I try to remember. "We didn't argue much," I say. "When he didn't want to live here, he made me look ridiculous for complaining when I knew something was wrong. He expects perfection, but what that means is that you do things his way."

"I *was*. I never wanted to sit around the apartment, the way he says

I did. I even brought work home with me. He made me feel so bad all week that I went to a friend's apartment for the day on Saturday. Then he said I had walked out on the problem. He's a little paranoid. I was listening to the radio, and Carole King was singing 'It's Too Late,' and he came into the study and looked very upset, as though I had planned for the song to come on. I couldn't believe it."

"Whew," I say, shaking my head. "I don't envy you. You have to stand up to him. I didn't do that. I pretended the problem would go away."

"And now the problem sits across from you drinking coffee, and you're being nice to him."

"I know it. I was just thinking we look like two characters in some soap opera my friend Martine Cooper would watch."

He pushes his coffee cup away from him with a grimace.

"But anyway, I like you now," I say. "And you're exceptionally nice to Louise."

"I took her father," he says.

"Bradley—I hope you don't take offense, but it makes me nervous to talk about that."

"I don't take offense. But how can you be having coffee with me?"

"You invited yourself over so you could ask that?"

"Please," he says, holding up both hands. Then he runs his hands through his hair. "Don't make me feel illogical. He does that to me, you know. He doesn't understand it when everything doesn't fall right into line. If I like fixing up the place, keeping some flowers around, therefore I can't like being a working person, too, therefore I deliberately sabotage myself in my job." Bradley sips his coffee.

"I wish I could do something for him," he says in a different voice.

This is not what I expected, either. We have sounded like two wise adults, and then suddenly he has changed and sounds very tender. I realize the situation is still the same. It is two of them on one side and me on the other, even though Bradley is in my kitchen.

"Come and pick up Louise with me, Bradley," I say. "When you see Martine Cooper, you'll cheer up about your situation."

He looks up from his coffee. "You're forgetting what I'd look like to Martine Cooper," he says.

Milo is going to California. He has been offered a job with a new San Francisco architectural firm. I am not the first to know. His sister, Deanna, knows before I do, and mentions it when we're talking on the phone. "It's middle-age crisis," Deanna says sniffily. "Not that I need to tell you." Deanna would drop dead if she knew the way things are. She is scandalized every time a new display is put up in Bloomingdale's window. ("Those mannequins had eyes like an Egyptian princess, and *rags*. I swear to you, they had mops and brooms and ragged gauze dresses on, with whores' shoes—stiletto heels that prostitutes wear.")

I hang up from Deanna's call and tell Louise I'm going to drive to the gas station for cigarettes. I go there to call New York on their pay phone.

"Well, I only just knew," Milo says. "I found out for sure yesterday, and last night Deanna called and so I told her. It's not like I'm leaving tonight."

He sounds elated, in spite of being upset that I called. He's happy in the way he used to be on Christmas morning. I remember him once running into the living room in his underwear and tearing open the gifts we'd been sent by relatives. He was looking for the eight-slice toaster he was sure we'd get. We'd been given two-slice, four-slice, and six-slice toasters, but then we got no more. "Come out, my eight-slice beauty!" Milo crooned, and out came an electric clock, a blender, and an expensive electric pan.

"When are you leaving?" I ask him.

"I'm going out to look for a place to live next week."

"Are you going to tell Louise yourself this weekend?"

"Of course," he says.

"And what are you going to do about seeing Louise?"

"Why do you act as if I don't like Louise?" he says. "I will occasionally come back East, and I will arrange for her to fly to San Francisco on her vacations."

"It's going to break her heart."

"No it isn't. Why do you want to make me feel bad?"

"She's had so many things to adjust to. You don't have to go to San Francisco right now, Milo."

"It happens, if you care, that my own job here is in jeopardy. This is a real chance for me, with a young firm. They really want me. But anyway, all we need in this happy group is to have you bringing in a couple of hundred dollars a month with your graphic work and me destitute and Bradley so devastated by being fired that of course he can't even look for work."

"I'll bet he is looking for a job," I say.

"Yes. He read the want ads today and then fixed a crab quiche."

"Maybe that's the way you like things, Milo, and people respond to you. You forbade me to work when we had a baby. Do you say anything encouraging to him about finding a job, or do you just take it out on him that he was fired?"

There is a pause, and then he almost seems to lose his mind with impatience.

"I can hardly *believe*, when I am trying to find a logical solution to all our problems, that I am being subjected, by telephone, to an unflattering psychological analysis by my ex-wife." He says this all in a rush.

"All right, Milo. But don't you think that if you're leaving so soon you ought to call her, instead of waiting until Saturday?"

Milo sighs very deeply. "I have more sense than to have important conversations on the telephone," he says.

Milo calls on Friday and asks Louise whether it wouldn't be nice if both of us came in and spent the night Saturday and if we all went to brunch together Sunday. Louise is excited. I never go into town with her.

Louise and I pack a suitcase and put it in the car Saturday morning. A cutting of ivy for Bradley has taken root, and she has put it in a little green plastic pot for him. It's heartbreaking, and I hope that Milo notices and has a tough time dealing with it. I am relieved I'm going to be there when he tells her, and sad that I have to hear it at all.

In the city, I give the car to the garage attendant, who does not remember me. Milo and I lived in the apartment when we were first married, and moved when Louise was two years old. When we moved, Milo kept the apartment and sublet it—a sign that things were not going well, if I had been one to heed such a warning. What he said was that if we were ever rich enough we could have the house in Connecticut *and* the apartment in New York. When Milo moved out of the house, he went right back to the apartment. This will be the first time I have visited there in years.

Louise strides in in front of me, throwing her coat over the brass coatrack in the entranceway—almost too casual about being there. She's the hostess at Milo's, the way I am at our house.

He has painted the walls white. There are floor-length white curtains in the living room, where my silly flowered curtains used to hang. The walls are bare, the floor has been sanded, a stereo as huge as a computer stands against one wall of the living room, and there are four speakers.

"Look around," Milo says. "Show your mother around, Louise."

I am trying to remember if I have ever told Louise that I used to live in this apartment. I must have told her, at some point, but I can't remember it.

"Hello," Bradley says, coming out of the bedroom.

"Hi, Bradley," I say. "Have you got a drink?"

Bradley looks sad. "He's got champagne," he says, and looks nervously at Milo.

"No one *has* to drink champagne," Milo says. "There's the usual assortment of liquor."

"Yes," Bradley says. "What would you like?"

"Some bourbon, please."

"Bourbon." Bradley turns to go into the kitchen. He looks different; his hair is different—more wavy—and he is dressed as though it were summer, in straight-legged white pants and black leather thongs.

"I want Perrier water with strawberry juice," Louise says, tagging along after Bradley. I have never heard her ask for such a thing before. At home, she drinks too many Cokes. I am always trying to get her to drink fruit juice.

Bradley comes back with two drinks and hands me one. "Did you want anything?" he says to Milo.

"I'm going to open the champagne in a moment," Milo says. "How have you been this week, sweetheart?"

"Okay," Louise says. She is holding a pale pink, bubbly drink. She sips it like a cocktail.

Bradley looks very bad. He has circles under his eyes, and he is ill at ease. A red light begins to blink on the phone-answering device next to where Bradley sits on the sofa, and Milo gets out of his chair to pick up the phone.

"Do you really want to talk on the phone right now?" Bradley asks Milo quietly.

Milo looks at him. "No, not particularly," he says, sitting down again. After a moment, the red light goes out.

"I'm going to mist your bowl garden," Louise says to Bradley, and slides off the sofa and goes to the bedroom. "Hey, a little toadstool is growing in here!" she calls back. "Did you put it there, Bradley?"

"It grew from the soil mixture, I guess," Bradley calls back. "I don't know how it got there."

"Have you heard anything about a job?" I ask Bradley.

"I haven't been looking, really," he says. "You know."

Milo frowns at him. "Your choice, Bradley," he says. "I didn't ask you to follow me to California. You can stay here."

"No," Bradley says. "You've hardly made me feel welcome."

"Should we have some champagne—all four of us—and you can get back to your bourbons later?" Milo says cheerfully.

We don't answer him, but he gets up anyway and goes to the kitchen. "Where have you hidden the tulip-shaped glasses, Bradley?" he calls out after a while.

"They should be in the cabinet on the far left," Bradley says.

"You're going with him?" I say to Bradley. "To San Francisco?"

He shrugs, and won't look at me. "I'm not quite sure I'm wanted," he says quietly.

The cork pops in the kitchen. I look at Bradley, but he won't look up. His new hairdo makes him look older. I remember that when Milo left me I went to the hairdresser the same week and had bangs cut. The next week, I went to a therapist who told me it was no good trying to hide from myself. The week after that, I did dance exercises with Martine Cooper, and the week after that the therapist told me not to dance if I wasn't interested in dancing.

"I'm not going to act like this is a funeral," Milo says, coming in with the glasses. "Louise, come in here and have champagne! We have something to have a toast about."

Louise comes into the living room suspiciously. She is so used to being refused even a sip of wine from my glass or her father's that she no longer even asks. "How come I'm in on this?" she asks.

"We're going to drink a toast to me," Milo says.

Three of the four glasses are clustered on the table in front of the sofa. Milo's glass is raised. Louise looks at me, to see what I'm going to say. Milo raises his glass even higher. Bradley reaches for a glass. Louise picks up a glass. I lean forward and take the last one.

"This is a toast to me," Milo says, "because I am going to be going to San Francisco."

It was not a very good or informative toast. Bradley and I sip from our glasses. Louise puts her glass down hard and bursts into tears, knocking the glass over. The champagne spills onto the cover of a big art book about the Unicorn Tapestries. She runs into the bedroom and slams the door.

Milo looks furious. "Everybody lets me know just what my insufficiencies are, don't they?" he says. "Nobody minds expressing himself. We have it all right out in the open."

"He's criticizing me," Bradley murmurs, his head still bowed. "It's because I was offered a job here in the city and I didn't automatically refuse it."

I turn to Milo. "Go say something to Louise, Milo," I say. "Do you think that's what somebody who isn't brokenhearted sounds like?"

He glares at me and stomps into the bedroom, and I can hear him talking to Louise reassuringly. "It doesn't mean you'll *never* see me," he says. "You can fly there, I'll come here. It's not going to be that different."

"You lied!" Louise screams. "You said we were going to brunch."

"We are. We are. I can't very well take us to brunch before Sunday, can I?"

"You didn't say you were going to San Francisco. What *is* San Francisco, anyway?"

"I just said so. I bought us a bottle of champagne. You can come out as soon as I get settled. You're going to like it there."

Louise is sobbing. She has told him the truth and she knows it's futile to go on.

By the next morning, Louise acts the way I acted—as if everything were just the same. She looks calm, but her face is small and pale. She looks very young. We walk into the restaurant and sit at the table Milo has reserved. Bradley pulls out a chair for me, and Milo pulls out a chair for Louise, locking his finger with hers for a second, raising her arm above her head, as if she were about to take a twirl.

She looks very nice, really. She has a ribbon in her hair. It is cold, and she should have worn a hat, but she wanted to wear the ribbon. Milo has good taste: the dress she is wearing, which he bought for her, is a hazy purple plaid, and it sets off her hair.

"Come with me. Don't be sad," Milo suddenly says to Louise, pulling her by the hand. "Come with me for a minute. Come across the street to the park for just a second, and we'll have some space to dance, and your mother and Bradley can have a nice quiet drink."

She gets up from the table and, looking long-suffering, backs into her coat, which he is holding for her, and the two of them go out. The waitress comes to the table, and Bradley orders three Bloody Marys and a Coke, and eggs Benedict for everyone. He asks the waitress to wait awhile before she brings the food. I have hardly slept at all, and having a drink is not going to clear my head. I have to think of things to say to Louise later, on the ride home.

"He takes so many *chances*," I say. "He pushes things so far with people. I don't want her to turn against him."

"No," he says.

"Why are you going, Bradley? You've seen the way he acts. You know that when you get out there he'll pull something on you. Take the job and stay here."

Bradley is fiddling with the edge of his napkin. I study him. I don't know who his friends are, how old he is, where he grew up, whether he believes in God, or what he usually drinks. I'm shocked that I know so little, and I reach out and touch him. He looks up.

"Don't go," I say quietly.

The waitress puts the glasses down quickly and leaves, embarrassed because she thinks she's interrupted a tender moment. Bradley pats my hand on his arm. Then he says the thing that has always been between us, the thing too painful for me to envision or think about.

"I love him," Bradley whispers.

We sit quietly until Milo and Louise come into the restaurant, swinging hands. She is pretending to be a young child, almost a baby, and I wonder for an instant if Milo and Bradley and I haven't been playing house, too—pretending to be adults.

"Daddy's going to give me a first-class ticket," Louise says. "When I go to California we're going to ride in a glass elevator to the top of the Fairman Hotel."

"The Fairmont," Milo says, smiling at her.

Before Louise was born, Milo used to put his ear to my stomach and say that if the baby turned out to be a girl he would put her into glass slippers instead of bootees. Now he is the prince once again. I see them in a glass elevator, not long from now, going up and up, with the people below getting smaller and smaller, until they disappear.

JACKLIGHTING

It is Nicholas's birthday. Last year he was alive, and we took him presents: a spiral notebook he pulled the pages out of, unable to write but liking the sound of paper tearing; magazines he flipped through, paying no attention to pictures, liking the blur of color. He had a radio, so we could not take a radio. More than the radio, he seemed to like the sound the metal drawer in his bedside table made, sliding open, clicking shut. He would open the drawer and look at the radio. He rarely took it out.

Nicholas's brother Spence has made jam. For days the cat has batted grapes around the huge homemade kitchen table; dozens of bloody rags of cheesecloth have been thrown into the trash. There is grape jelly, raspberry jelly, strawberry, quince, and lemon. Last month, a neighbor's pig escaped and ate Spence's newly planted *fraise des bois* plants, but overlooked the strawberry plants close to the house, heavy with berries. After that, Spence captured the pig and called his friend Andy, who came for it with his truck and took the pig to his farm in Warrenton. When Andy got home and looked in the back of the truck, he found three piglets curled against the pig.

In this part of Virginia, it is a hundred degrees in August. In June and July you can smell the ground, but in August it has been baked dry; instead of smelling the earth you smell flowers, hot breeze. There is a haze over the Blue Ridge Mountains that stays in the air like cigarette smoke. It is the same color as the eye shadow Spence's girlfriend, Pammy, wears. The rest of us are sunburned, with pink mosquito bites on our bodies, small scratches from gathering raspberries. Pammy has just arrived from Washington. She is winter-pale. Since she is ten years younger than the rest of us, a few scratches wouldn't make her look as if she belonged, anyway. She is in medical school at Georgetown, and

her summer-school classes have just ended. She arrived with leather sandals that squeak. She is exhausted and sleeps half the day, upstairs, with
the fan blowing on her. All weekend the big fan has blown on Spence,
in the kitchen, boiling and bottling his jams and jellies. The small fan
blows on Pammy.

Wynn and I have come from New York. Every year we borrow his
mother's car and drive from Hoboken to Virginia. We used to take the
trip to spend the week of Nicholas's birthday with him. Now we come
to see Spence, who lives alone in the house. He is making jam early,
so we can take jars back with us. He stays in the kitchen because he
is depressed and does not really want to talk to us. He scolds the cat,
curses when something goes wrong.

Wynn is in love. The girl he loves is twenty, or twenty-one. Twenty-
two. When he told me (top down on the car, talking into the wind), I
couldn't understand half of what he was saying. There were enough
facts to daze me; she had a name, she was one of his students, she had
canceled her trip to Rome this summer. The day he told me about her,
he brought it up twice; first in the car, later in Spence's kitchen. "That
was *not* my mother calling the other night to say she got the car tuned,"
Wynn said, smashing his glass on the kitchen counter. I lifted his hand
off the large shard of glass, touching his fingers as gently as I'd touch a
cactus. When I steadied myself on the counter, a chip of glass nicked my
thumb. The pain shot through my body and pulsed in my ribs. Wynn
examined my hands; I examined his. A dust of fine glass coated our
hands, gently touching, late at night, as we looked out the window at
the moon shining on Spence's lemon tree with its one lemon, too heavy
to be growing on the slender branch. A jar of Lipton iced tea was next
to the tub the lemon tree grew out of—a joke, put there by Wynn, to
encourage it to bear more fruit.

Wynn is standing in the field across from the house, pacing, head down,
the bored little boy grown up.

"When wasn't he foolish?" Spence says, walking through the living
room. "What kind of sense does it make to turn against him now for
being a fool?"

"He calls it midlife crisis, Spence, and he's going to be thirty-two in
September."

"I know when his birthday is. You hint like this every year. Last year
at the end of August you dropped it into conversation that the two of
you were doing something or other to celebrate *his birthday*."

"We went to one of those places where a machine shoots baseballs at you. His birthday present was ten dollars' worth of balls pitched at him. I gave him a Red Sox cap. He lost it the same day."

"How did he lose it?"

"We came out of a restaurant and a Doberman was tied by its leash to a stop sign, barking like mad—a very menacing dog. He tossed the cap, and it landed on the dog's head. It was funny until he wanted to get it back, and he couldn't go near it."

"He's one in a million. He deserves to have his birthday remembered. Call me later in the month and remind me." Spence goes to the foot of the stairs. "Pammy," he calls.

"Come up and kill something for me," she says. The bed creaks. "Come kill a wasp on the bedpost. I hate to kill them. I hate the way they crunch."

He walks back to the living room and gets a newspaper and rolls it into a tight tube, slaps it against the palm of his hand.

Wynn, in the field, is swinging a broken branch, batting hickory nuts and squinting into the sun.

Nicholas lived for almost a year, brain damaged, before he died. Even before the accident, he liked the way things felt. He always watched shadows. He was the man looking to the side in Cartier-Bresson's photograph, instead of putting his eye to the wall. He'd find pennies on the sidewalk when the rest of us walked down city streets obliviously, spot the chipped finger on a mannequin flawlessly dressed, sidestep the one piece of glass among shells scattered on the shoreline. It would really have taken something powerful to do him in. So that's what happened: a drunk in a van, speeding, head-on, Nicholas out for a midnight ride without his helmet. Earlier in the day he'd assembled a crazy nest of treasures in the helmet, when he was babysitting the neighbors' four-year-old daughter. Spence showed it to us—holding it forward as carefully as you'd hold a bomb, looking away the way you'd avoid looking at dead fish floating in a once-nice aquarium, the way you'd look at an ugly scar, once the bandages had been removed, and want to lay the gauze back over it. While he was in the hospital, his fish tank overheated and all the black mollies died. The doctor unwound some of the bandages and the long brown curls had been shaved away, and there was a red scar down the side of his head that seemed as out of place as a line dividing a highway out West, a highway that nobody traveled anyway. It could have happened to any of us. We'd all ridden on the Harley, bodies pressed into his back, hair whipped across our faces. How were we going to feel ourselves again, without Nicholas? In the hospital, it was clear that the thin intravenous tube was not dripping life back into him—that was as far-fetched as the idea that the too-thin branch of the lemon tree could grow one more piece of fruit. In the helmet had been dried chrysanthemums, half of a robin's blue eggshell, a cat's-eye marble, yellow twine, a sprig of grapes, a piece of a broken ruler. I remember Wynn actually jumping back when he saw what was inside. I stared at the strangeness such ordinary things had taken on. Wynn had been against his teaching me to ride his bike, but he had. He taught me to trust myself and not to settle for seeing things the same way. The lobster claw on a necklace he made me was funny and beautiful. I never felt the same way about lobsters or jewelry after that. "Psychologists have figured out that infants start to laugh when they've learned to be skeptical of danger," Nicholas had said. Laughing on the back of his motorcycle. When he lowered the necklace over my head, rearranging it, fingers on my throat.

It is Nicholas's birthday, and so far no one has mentioned it. Spence has made all the jam he can make from the fruit and berries and has gone to the store and returned with bags of flour to make bread. He brought the *Daily Progress* to Pammy, and she is reading it, on the side porch where there is no screening, drying her hair and stiffening when bees fly away from the rose-of-Sharon bushes. Her new sandals are at the side of the chair. She has red toenails. She rubs the small pimples on her chin the way men finger their beards. I sit on the porch with her, catcher's mitt on my lap, waiting for Wynn to get back from his walk so we can take turns pitching to each other.

"Did he tell you I was a drug addict? Is that why you hardly speak to me?" Pammy says. She is squinting at her toes. "I'm older than I look," she says. "He says I'm twenty-one, because I look so young. He doesn't know when to let go of a joke, though. I don't like to be introduced to people as some child prodigy."

"What were you addicted to?" I say.

"Speed," she says. "I had another life." She has brought the bottle of polish with her, and begins brushing on a new layer of red, the fingers of her other hand stuck between her toes from underneath, separating them. "I don't get the feeling you people had another life," she says. "After all these years, I still feel funny when I'm around people who've never lived the way I have. It's just snobbishness, I'm sure."

I cup the catcher's mitt over my knee. A bee has landed on the mitt.

This is the most Pammy has talked. Now she interests me; I always like people who have gone through radical changes. It's snobbishness—it shows me that other people are confused, too.

"That was the summer of 'sixty-seven," she says. "I slept with a stockbroker for money. Sat through a lot of horror movies. That whole period's a blur. What I remember about it is being underground all the time, going places on the subway. I only had one real friend in the city. I can't remember where I was going." Pammy looks at the newspaper beside her chair. "Charlottesville, Virginia," she says. "My, my. Who would have thought twitchy little Pammy would end up here?"

Spence tosses the ball. I jump, mitt high above my head, and catch it. Spence throws again. Catch. Again. A hard pitch that lets me know the palm of my hand will be numb when I take off the catcher's mitt. Spence winds up. Pitches. As I'm leaning to get the ball, another ball sails by on my right. Spence has hidden a ball in his pocket all this time. Like his brother, he's always trying to make me smile.

"It's too hot to play ball," he says. "I can't spend the whole day trying to distract you because Wynn stalked off into the woods today."

"Come on," I say. "It was working."

"Why don't we all go to Virginia Beach next year instead of standing around down here smoldering? This isn't any tribute to my brother. How did this get started?"

"We came to be with you because we thought it would be hard. You didn't tell us about Pammy."

"Isn't that something? What that tells you is that you matter, and Wynn matters, and Nicholas mattered, but I don't even think to mention the person who's supposedly my lover."

"She said she had been an addict."

"She probably tried to tell you she wasn't twenty-one, too, didn't she?"

I sidestep a strawberry plant, notice one croquet post stuck in the field.

"It was a lie?" I say.

"No," he says. "I never know when to let my jokes die."

When Nicholas was alive, we'd celebrate his birthday with mint juleps and croquet games, stuffing ourselves with cake, going for midnight skinny-dips. Even if he were alive, I wonder if today would be anything like those birthdays of the past, or whether we'd have bogged down so hopelessly that even his childish enthusiasm would have had little effect. Wynn is sure that he's having a crisis and that it's not the real thing with his student because he also has a crush on Pammy. We are open about everything: he tells me about taking long walks and thinking about nothing but sex; Spence bakes the French bread too long, finds that he's lightly tapping a rock, sits on the kitchen counter, puts his hands over his face, and cries. Pammy says that she does not feel close to any of us—that Virginia was just a place to come to cool out. She isn't sure she wants to go on with medical school. I get depressed and think that if the birds could talk, they'd say that they didn't enjoy flying. The mountains have disappeared in the summer haze.

Late at night, alone on the porch, toasting Nicholas with a glass of wine, I remember that when I was younger, I assumed he'd be our guide: he saw us through acid trips, planned our vacations, he was always there to excite us and to give us advice. He started a game that went on for years. He had us close our eyes after we'd stared at something and made us envision it again. We had to describe it with our eyes closed. Wynn and Spence could talk about the things and make them more vivid than they were in life. They remembered well. When I closed my eyes, I squinted until the thing was lost to me. It kept going backward into darkness.

Tonight, Nicholas's birthday, it is dark and late and I have been try-ing to pay him some sort of tribute by seeing something and closing my eyes and imagining it. Besides realizing that two glasses of wine can make me drunk, I have had this revelation: that you can look at some-thing, close your eyes and see it again, and still know nothing—like star-ing at the sky to figure out the distances between stars.

The drunk in the van that hit Nicholas thought that he had hit a deer.

Tonight, stars shine over the field with the intensity of flashlights. Every year, Spence calls the state police to report that on his property, people are jacklighting.

WAITING

"It's beautiful," the woman says. "How did you come by this?" She wiggles her finger in the mouse hole. It's a genuine mouse hole: sometime in the eighteenth century a mouse gnawed its way into the cupboard, through the two inside shelves, and out the bottom.

"We bought it from an antique dealer in Virginia," I say.

"Where in Virginia?"

"Ruckersville. Outside of Charlottesville."

"That's beautiful country," she says. "I know where Ruckersville is. I had an uncle who lived in Keswick."

"Keswick was nice," I say. "The farms."

"Oh," she says. "The tax write-offs, you mean? Those mansions with the sheep grazing out front?"

She is touching the wood, stroking lightly in case there might be a splinter. Even after so much time, everything might not have been worn down to smoothness. She lowers her eyes. "Would you take eight hundred?" she says.

"I'd like to sell it for a thousand," I say. "I paid thirteen hundred, ten years ago."

"It's beautiful," she says. "I suppose I should try to tell you it has some faults, but I've never seen one like it. Very nice. My husband wouldn't like my spending more than six hundred to begin with, but I can see that it's worth eight." She is resting her index finger on the latch. "Could I bring my husband to see it tonight?"

"All right."

"You're moving?" she says.

"Eventually," I say.

"That would be something to load around." She shakes her head. "Are you going back South?"

"I doubt it," I say.

"You probably think I'm kidding about coming back with my husband," she says suddenly. She lowers her eyes again. "Are other people interested?"

"There's just been one other call. Somebody who wanted to come out Saturday." I smile. "I guess I should pretend there's great interest."

"I'll take it," the woman says. "For a thousand. You probably could sell it for more and I could probably resell it for more. I'll tell my husband that."

She picks up her embroidered shoulder bag from the floor by the corner cabinet. She sits at the oak table by the octagonal window and rummages for her checkbook.

"I was thinking, What if I left it home? But I didn't." She takes out a checkbook in a red plastic cover. "My uncle in Keswick was one of those gentleman farmers," she says. "He lived until he was eighty-six, and enjoyed his life. He did everything in moderation, but the key was that he did *everything*." She looks appraisingly at her signature. "Some movie actress just bought a farm across from the Cobham store," she says. "A girl. I never saw her in the movies. Do you know who I'm talking about?"

"Well, Art Garfunkel used to have a place out there," I say.

"Maybe she bought his place." The woman pushes the check to the center of the table, tilts the vase full of phlox, and puts the corner of the check underneath. "Well," she says. "Thank you. We'll come with my brother's truck to get it on the weekend. What about Saturday?"

"That's fine," I say.

"You're going to have some move," she says, looking around at the other furniture. "I haven't moved in thirty years, and I wouldn't want to."

The dog walks through the room.

"What a well-mannered dog," she says.

"That's Hugo. Hugo's moved quite a few times in thirteen years. Virginia. D.C. Boston. Here."

"Poor old Hugo," she says.

Hugo, in the living room now, thumps down and sighs.

"Thank you," she says, putting out her hand. I reach out to shake it, but our hands don't meet and she clasps her hand around my wrist. "Saturday afternoon. Maybe Saturday evening. Should I be specific?"

"Anytime is all right."

"Can I turn around on your grass or no?"

"Sure. Did you see the tire marks? I do it all the time."

"Well," she says. "People who back into traffic. I don't know. I honk at them all the time."

I go to the screen door and wave. She is driving a yellow Mercedes, an old one that's been repainted, with a license that says RAVE-1. The car stalls. She restarts it and waves. I wave again.

When she's gone, I go out the back door and walk down the driveway. A single daisy is growing out of the foot-wide crack in the concrete. Somebody has thrown a beer can into the driveway. I pick it up and marvel at how light it is. I get the mail from the box across the street and look at it as cars pass by. One of the stream of cars honks a warning to me, although I am not moving, except for flipping through the mail. There is a CL&P bill, a couple of pieces of junk mail, a postcard from Henry in Los Angeles, and a letter from my husband in—he's made it to California. Berkeley, California, mailed four days ago. Years ago, when I visited a friend in Berkeley we went to a little park and some people wandered in walking two dogs and a goat. An African pygmy goat. The woman said it was housebroken to urinate outside and as for the other she just picked up the pellets.

I go inside and watch the moving red band on the digital clock in the kitchen. Behind the clock is an old coffee tin decorated with a picture of a woman and a man in a romantic embrace; his arms are nearly rusted away, her hair is chipped, but a perfectly painted wreath of coffee beans rises in an arc above them. Probably I should have advertised the coffee tin, too, but I like to hear the metal top creak when I lift it in the morning to take the jar of coffee out. But if not the coffee tin, I should probably have put the tin breadbox up for sale.

John and I liked looking for antiques. He liked the ones almost beyond repair—the kind that you would have to buy twenty dollars' worth of books to understand how to restore. When we used to go looking, antiques were much less expensive than they are now. We bought them at a time when we had the patience to sit all day on folding chairs under a canopy at an auction. We were organized; we would come and inspect the things the day before. Then we would get there early the next day and wait. Most of the auctioneers in that part of Virginia were very good. One, named Wicked Richard, used to lace his fingers together and crack his knuckles as he called the lots. His real name was Wisted. When he did classier auctions and there was a pamphlet, his name was listed as Wisted. At most of the regular auctions, though, he introduced himself as Wicked Richard.

I cut a section of cheese and take some crackers out of a container. I put them on a plate and carry them into the dining room, feeling a little sad about parting with the big corner cupboard. Suddenly it seems older and bigger—a very large thing to be giving up.

The phone rings. A woman wants to know the size of the refrigerator that I have advertised. I tell her.

"Is it white?" she says.

The ad said it was white.

"Yes," I tell her.

"This is your refrigerator?" she says.

"One of them," I say. "I'm moving."

"Oh," she says. "You shouldn't tell people that. People read these ads to figure out who's moving and might not be around, so they can rob them. There were a lot of robberies in your neighborhood last summer."

The refrigerator is too small for her. We hang up.

The phone rings again, and I let it ring. I sit down and look at the corner cupboard. I put a piece of cheese on top of a cracker and eat it. I get up and go into the living room and offer a piece of cheese to Hugo. He sniffs and takes it lightly from my fingers. Earlier today, in the morning, I ran him in Putnam Park. I could hardly keep up with him, as usual. Thirteen isn't so old, for a dog. He scared the ducks and sent them running into the water. He growled at a beagle a man was walking, and tugged on his leash until he choked. He pulled almost as hard as he could a few summers ago. The air made his fur fluffy. Now he is happy, slowly licking his mouth, getting ready to take his afternoon nap.

John wanted to take Hugo across country, but in the end we decided that, as much as Hugo would enjoy terrorizing so many dogs along the way, it was going to be a hot July and it was better if he stayed home. We discussed this reasonably. No frenzy—nothing like the way we had been swept in at some auctions to bid on things that we didn't want, just because so many other people were mad for them. A reasonable discussion about Hugo, even if it was at the last minute: Hugo, in the car, already sticking his head out the window to bark goodbye. "It's too hot for him," I said. I was standing outside in my nightgown. "It's almost July. He'll be a hassle for you if campgrounds won't take him or if you have to park in the sun." So Hugo stood beside me, barking his high-pitched goodbye, as John backed out of the driveway. He forgot: his big battery lantern and his can opener. He remembered: his tent, the cooler filled with ice (he couldn't decide when he left whether he was going to stock up on beer or Coke), a camera, a suitcase, a fiddle, and a banjo.

He forgot his driver's license, too. I never understood why he didn't keep it in his wallet, but it always seemed to get taken out for some reason and then be lost. Yesterday I found it leaning up against a bottle in the medicine cabinet.

Bobby calls. He fools me with his imitation of a man with an English accent who wants to know if I also have an avocado-colored refrigerator for sale. When I say I don't, he asks if I know somebody who paints refrigerators.

"Of course not," I tell him.

"That's the most decisive thing I've heard you say in five years," Bobby says in his real voice. "How's it going, Sally?"

"Jesus," I say. "If you'd answered this phone all morning, you wouldn't think that was funny. Where are you?"

"New York. Where do you think I am? It's my lunch hour. Going to Le Relais to get tanked up. A little *le pain et le beurre*, put down a few Scotches."

"Le Relais," I say. "Hmm."

"Don't make a bad eye on me," he says, going into his Muhammad Ali imitation. "Step on my foot and I kick you to the moon. Glad-hand me and I shake you like a loon." Bobby clears his throat. "I got the company twenty big ones today," he says. "Twenty Gs."

"Congratulations. Have a good lunch. Come out for dinner, if you feel like the drive."

"I don't have any gas and I can't face the train." He coughs again. "I gave up cigarettes," he says. "Why am I coughing?" He moves away from the phone to cough loudly.

"Are you smoking grass in the office?" I say.

"Not this time," he gasps. "I'm goddamn dying of something." A pause. "What did you do yesterday?"

"I was in town. You'd laugh at what I did."

"You went to the fireworks."

"Yeah, that's right. I wouldn't hesitate to tell you that part."

"What'd you do?" he says.

"I met Andy and Tom at the Plaza and drank champagne. They didn't. I did. Then we went to the fireworks."

"Sally at the *Plaza*?" He laughs. "What were they doing in town?"

"Tom was there on business. Andy came to see the fireworks."

"It rained, didn't it?"

"Only a little. It was okay. They were pretty."

"The fireworks," Bobby says. "I didn't make the fireworks."

"You're going to miss lunch, Bobby," I say.

"God," he says. "I am. Bye."

I pull a record out from under the big library table, where they're kept on the wide mahogany board that connects the legs. By coincidence, the record I pull out is the Miles Davis Sextet's *Jazz at the Plaza*. At the Palm Court on the Fourth of July, a violinist played "Play Gypsies, Dance Gypsies" and "Oklahoma!" I try to remember what else and can't.

"What do you say, Hugo?" I say to the dog. "Another piece of cheese, or would you rather go on with your siesta?"

He knows the word "cheese." He knows it as well as his name. I love the way his eyes light up and he perks his ears for certain words. Bobby tells me that you can speak gibberish to people, 90 percent of the people, as long as you throw in a little catchword now and then, and it's the same when I talk to Hugo: "Cheese." "Tag." "Out."

No reaction. Hugo is lying where he always does, on his right side, near the stereo. His nose is only a fraction of an inch away from the plant in a basket beneath the window. The branches of the plant sweep the floor. He seems very still.

"Cheese?" I whisper. "Hugo?" It is as loud as I can speak.

No reaction. I start to take a step closer, but stop myself. I put down the record and stare at him. Nothing changes. I walk out into the backyard. The sun is shining directly down from overhead, striking the dark-blue doors of the garage, washing out the color to the palest tint of blue. The peach tree by the garage, with one dead branch. The wind chimes tinkling in the peach tree. A bird hopping by the iris underneath the tree. Mosquitoes or gnats, a puff of them in the air, clustered in front of me. I sink down into the grass. I pick a blade, split it slowly with my fingernail. I close my eyes and count the times I breathe in and out. When I open them, the sun is shining hard on the blue doors.

After a while—maybe ten minutes, maybe twenty—a truck pulls into the driveway. The man who usually delivers packages to the house hops out of the United Parcel truck. He is a nice man, about twenty-five, with long hair tucked behind his ears, and kind eyes.

Hugo did not bark when the truck pulled into the drive.

"Hi," he says. "What a beautiful day. Here you go."

He holds out a clipboard and a pen.

"Forty-two," he says, pointing to the tiny numbered block in which I am to sign my name. A mailing envelope is under his arm.

"Another book," he says. He hands me the package.

I reach up for it. There is a blue label with my name and address typed on it.

He locks his hands behind his back and raises his arms, bowing. "Did you notice that?" he says, straightening out of the yoga stretch, pointing to the envelope. "What's the joke?" he says.

The return address says "John F. Kennedy."

"Oh," I say. "A friend in publishing." I look up at him. I realize that that hasn't explained it. "We were talking on the phone last week. He was—people are still talking about where they were when he was shot, and I've known my friend for almost ten years and we'd never talked about it before."

The UPS man is wiping sweat off his forehead with a handkerchief. He stuffs the handkerchief into his pocket.

"He wasn't making fun," I say. "He admired Kennedy."

The UPS man crouches, runs his fingers across the grass. He looks in the direction of the garage. He looks at me. "Are you all right?" he says.

"Well—" I say.

He is still watching me.

"Well," I say, trying to catch my breath. "Let's see what this is."

I pull up the flap, being careful not to get cut by the staples. A large paperback called *If Mountains Die*. Color photographs. The sky above the Pueblo River gorge in the book is very blue. I show the UPS man.

"Were you all right when I pulled in?" he says. "You were sitting sort of funny."

I still am. I realize that my arms are crossed over my chest and I am leaning forward. I uncross my arms and lean back on my elbows. "Fine," I say. "Thank you."

Another car pulls into the driveway, comes around the truck, and stops on the lawn. Ray's car. Ray gets out, smiles, leans back in through the open window to turn off the tape that's still playing. Ray is my best friend. Also my husband's best friend.

"What are you doing here?" I say to Ray.

"Hi," the UPS man says to Ray. "I've got to get going. Well." He looks at me. "See you," he says.

"See you," I say. "Thanks."

"What am I doing here?" Ray says. He taps his watch. "Lunchtime. I'm on a business lunch. Big deal. Important negotiations. Want to drive down to the Redding Market and buy a couple of sandwiches, or have you already eaten?"

"You drove all the way out here for lunch?"

"Big business lunch. Difficult client. Takes time to bring some clients around. Coaxing. Takes hours." Ray shrugs.

"Don't they care?"

Ray sticks out his tongue and makes a noise, sits beside me, and puts his arm around my shoulder and shakes me lightly toward him and away from him a couple of times. "Look at that sunshine," he says. "Finally. I thought the rain would never stop." He hugs my shoulder and takes his arm away. "It depresses me, too," he says. "I don't like what I sound like when I keep saying that nobody cares." Ray sighs. He reaches for a cigarette. "Nobody cares," he says. "Two-hour lunch. Four. Five."

We sit silently. He picks up the book, leafs through. "Pretty," he says. "You eat already?"

I look behind me at the screen door. Hugo is not here. No sound, either, when the car came up the driveway and the truck left.

"Yes," I say. "But there's some cheese in the house. All the usual things. Or you could go to the market."

"Maybe I will," he says. "Want anything?"

"Ray," I say, reaching my hand up. "Don't go to the market."

"What?" he says. He sits on his heels and takes my hand. He looks into my face.

"Why don't you—there's cheese in the house," I say.

He looks puzzled. Then he sees the stack of mail on the grass underneath our hands. "Oh," he says. "Letter from John." He picks it up, sees that it hasn't been opened. "Okay," he says. "Then I'm perplexed again. Just that he wrote you? That he's already in Berkeley? Well, he had a bad winter. We all had a bad winter. It's going to be all right. He hasn't called? You don't know if he hooked up with that band?"

I shake my head no.

"I tried to call you yesterday," he says. "You weren't home."

"I went into New York."

"And?"

"I went out for drinks with some friends. We went to the fireworks."

"So did I," Ray says. "Where were you?"

"Seventy-sixth Street."

"I was at Ninety-eighth. I knew it was crazy to think I might run into you at the fireworks."

A cardinal flies into the peach tree.

"I did run into Bobby last week," he says. "Of course, it's not really running into him at one o'clock at Le Relais."

"How was Bobby?"

"You haven't heard from him, either?"

"He called today, but he didn't say how he was. I guess I didn't ask."

"He was okay. He looked good. You can hardly see the scar above his eyebrow where they took the stitches. I imagine in a few weeks when it fades you won't notice it at all."

"You think he's done with dining in Harlem?"

"Doubt it. It could have happened anywhere, you know. People get mugged all over the place."

I hear the phone ringing and don't get up. Ray squeezes my shoulder again. "Well," he says. "I'm going to bring some food out here."

"If there's anything in there that isn't the way it ought to be, just take care of it, will you?"

"What?" he says.

"I mean—if there's anything wrong, just fix it."

He smiles. "Don't tell me. You painted a room what you thought was a nice pastel color and it came out electric pink. Or the chairs—you didn't have them reupholstered again, did you?" Ray comes back to where I'm sitting. "Oh, God," he says. "I was thinking the other night about how you'd had that horrible chintz you bought on Madison Avenue put onto the chairs and when John and I got back here you were afraid to let him into the house. God—that awful striped material. Remember John standing in back of the chair and putting his chin over the back and screaming, 'I'm innocent!' Remember him doing that?" Ray's eyes are about to water, the way they watered because he laughed so hard the day John did that. "That was about a year ago this month," he says.

I nod yes.

"Well," Ray says. "Everything's going to be all right, and I don't say that just because I want to believe in one nice thing. Bobby thinks the same thing. We agree about this. I keep talking about this, don't I? I keep coming out to the house, like you've cracked up or something. You don't want to keep hearing my sermons." Ray opens the screen door. "Anybody can take a trip," he says.

I stare at him.

"I'm getting lunch," he says. He is holding the door open with his foot. He moves his foot and goes into the house. The door slams behind him.

"Hey!" he calls out. "Want iced tea or something?"

The phone begins to ring.

"Want me to get it?" he says.

"No. Let it ring."

"Let it ring?" he hollers.

The cardinal flies out of the peach tree and onto the sweeping branch of a tall fir tree that borders the lawn—so many trees so close together that you can't see the house on the other side. The bird becomes a speck of red and disappears.

"Hey, pretty lady!" Ray calls. "Where's your mutt?"

Over the noise of the telephone, I can hear him knocking around in the kitchen. The stuck drawer opening.

"You *honestly* want me not to answer the phone?" he calls.

I look back at the house. Ray, balancing a tray, opens the door with one hand, and Hugo is beside him—not rushing out, the way he usually does to get through the door, but padding slowly, shaking himself out of sleep. He comes over and lies down next to me, blinking because his eyes are not yet accustomed to the sunlight.

Ray sits down with his plate of crackers and cheese and a beer. He looks at the tears streaming down my cheeks and shoves over close to me. He takes a big drink and puts the beer on the grass. He pushes the tray next to the beer can.

"Hey," Ray says. "Everything's cool, okay? No right and no wrong. People do what they do. A neutral observer, and friend to all. Same easy advice from Ray all around. Our discretion assured." He pushes my hair gently off my wet cheeks. "It's okay," he says softly, turning and cupping his hands over my forehead. "Just tell me what you've done."

DESIRE

Bryce was sitting at the kitchen table in his father's house, cutting out a picture of Times Square. It was a picture from a coloring book, but Bryce wasn't interested in coloring; he just wanted to cut out pictures so he could see what they looked like outside the book. This drawing was of people crossing the street between the Sheraton-Astor and F. W. Woolworth. There were also other buildings, but these were the ones the people seemed to be moving between. The picture was round; it was supposed to look as if it had been drawn on a bottle cap. Bryce had a hard time getting the scissors around the edge of the cap, because they were blunt tipped. At home, at his mother's house in Vermont, he had real scissors and he was allowed to taste anything, including alcohol, and his stepsister Maddy was a lot more fun than Bill Monteforte, who lived next door to his father here in Pennsylvania and who never had time to play. But he had missed his father, and he had been the one who called to invite himself to this house for his spring vacation.

His father, B.B., was standing in the doorway now, complaining because Bryce was so quiet and so glum. "It took quite a few polite letters to your mother to get her to let loose of you for a week," B.B. said. "You get here and you go into a slump. It would be a real problem if you had to do anything important, like go up to bat with the bases loaded and two outs."

"Mom's new neighbor is the father of a guy that plays for the Redskins," Bryce said.

The scissors slipped. Since he'd ruined it, Bryce now cut on the diagonal, severing half the people in Times Square from the other half. He looked out the window and saw a squirrel stealing seed from the bird feeder. The gray birds were so tiny anyway, it didn't look as if they needed anything to eat.

"Are we going to that auction tonight, or what?" Bryce said.

"Maybe. It depends on whether Rona gets over her headache."

B.B. sprinkled little blue and white crystals of dishwasher soap into the machine and closed it. He pushed two buttons and listened carefully.

"Remember now," he said, "I don't want you getting excited at the auction if you see something you want. You put your hand up, and that's a *bid*. You have to really, really want something and then ask me before you put your hand up. You can't shoot your hand up. Imagine that you're a soldier down in the trenches and there's a war going on."

"I don't even care about the dumb auction," Bryce said.

"What if there was a Turkish prayer rug you wanted and it had the most beautiful muted colors you'd ever seen in your life?" B.B. sat down in the chair across from Bryce. The back of the chair was in the shape of an upside-down triangle. The seat was a right-side-up triangle. The triangles were covered with aqua plastic. B.B. shifted on the chair. Bryce could see that he wanted an answer.

"Or we'll play Let's Pretend," B.B. said. "Let's pretend a lion is coming at you and there's a tree with a cheetah in it and up ahead of you it's just low dry grass. Would you climb the tree, or start running?"

"Neither," Bryce said.

"Come on. You've either got to run or *something*. There's known dangers and unknown dangers. What would you do?"

"People can't tell what they'd do in a situation like that," Bryce said.

"No?"

"What's a cheetah?" Bryce said. "Are you sure they get in trees?"

B.B. frowned. He had a drink in his hand. He pushed the ice cube to the bottom and they both watched it bob up. Bryce leaned over and reached into the drink and gave it a push, too.

"No licking that finger," B.B. said.

Bryce wiped a wet streak across the red down vest he wore in the house.

"Is that my boy? 'Don't lick your finger,' he takes the finger and wipes it on his clothes. Now he can try to remember what he learned in school from the *Book of Knowledge* about cheetahs."

"What *Book of Knowledge*?"

His father got up and kissed the top of his head. The radio went on upstairs, and then water began to run in the tub up there.

"She must be getting ready for action," B.B. said. "Why does she have to take a bath the minute I turn on the dishwasher? The dishwasher's been acting crazy." B.B. sighed. "Keep those hands on the table," he said. "It's good practice for the auction."

Bryce moved the two half circles of Times Square so that they overlapped. He folded his hands over them and watched the squirrel scare a bird away from the feeder. The sky was the color of ash, with little bursts of white where the sun had been.

"I'm the same as dead," Rona said.

"You're not the same as dead," B.B. said. "You've put five pounds back on. You lost twenty pounds in that hospital, and you didn't weigh enough to start with. You wouldn't eat anything they brought you. You took an intravenous needle out of your arm. I can tell you, you were nuts, and I didn't have much fun talking to that doctor who looked like Tonto who operated on you and thought you needed a shrink. It's water over the dam. Get in the bath."

Rona was holding on to the sink. She started to laugh. She had on tiny green-and-white striped underpants. Her long white nightgown was hung around her neck, the way athletes drape towels around themselves in locker rooms.

"What's funny?" he said.

"You said, 'It's water over the—' Oh, you know what you said. I'm running water in the tub, and—"

"Yeah," B.B. said, closing the toilet seat and sitting down. He picked up a Batman comic and flipped through. It was wet from moisture. He hated the feel of it.

The radio was on the top of the toilet tank, and now the Andrews Sisters were singing "Hold Tight." Their voices were as smooth as toffee. He wanted to pull them apart, to hear distinct voices through the perfect harmony.

He watched her get into the bath. There was a worm of a scar, dull red, to the left of her jutting hipbone, where they had removed her appendix. One doctor had thought it was an ectopic pregnancy. Another was sure it was a ruptured ovary. A third doctor—her surgeon—insisted it was her appendix, and they got it just in time. The tip had ruptured.

Rona slid low in the bathtub. "If you can't trust your body not to go wrong, what can you trust?" she said.

"Everybody gets sick," he said. "It's not your body trying to do you in. The mind's only one place: in your head. Look, didn't Lyndon Johnson have an appendectomy? Remember how upset people were that he pulled up his shirt to show the scar?"

"They were upset because he pulled his dog's ears," she said.

She had a bath toy he had bought for her. It was a fish with a happy smile. You wound it with a key and then it raced around the tub spouting water through its mouth.

He could hear Bryce talking quietly downstairs. Another call to Maddy, no doubt. When the boy was in Vermont, he was on the phone all the time, telling B.B. how much he missed him; when he was here in Pennsylvania, he missed his family in Vermont. The phone bill was going to be astronomical. Bryce kept calling Maddy, and Rona's mother kept calling from New York; Rona never wanted to take the calls because she always ended up in an argument if she wasn't prepared with something to talk about, so she made B.B. say she was asleep, or in the tub, or that a soufflé was in the last stages. Then she'd call her mother back, when she'd gathered her thoughts.

"Would you like to go to that auction tonight?" he said to Rona.

"An auction? What for?"

"I don't know. There's nothing on TV and the kid's never been to an auction."

"The kid's never smoked grass," she said, soaping her arm.

"Neither do you anymore. Why would you bring that up?"

"You can look at his rosy cheeks and sad-clown eyes and know he never has."

"Right," he said, throwing the comic book back on the tile. "*Right.* My kid's not a pothead. *I was talking about going to an auction.* Would you also like to tell me that elephants don't fly?"

She laughed and slipped lower in the tub, until the water reached her chin. With her hair pinned to the top of her head and the foam of bubbles covering her neck, she looked like a lady in Edwardian times. The fish was in a frenzy, cutting through the suds. She moved a shoulder to accommodate it, shifted her knees, tipped her head back.

"There were flying elephants in those books that used to be all over the house when he visited," she said. "I'm so glad he's eight now. All those *crazy* books."

"You were stoned all the time," he said. "Everything looked funny to you." Though he hadn't gotten stoned with her, sometimes things had seemed peculiar to him, too. There was the night his friends Shelby and Charles had given a dramatic reading of a book of Bryce's called *Bertram and the Ticklish Rhinoceros.* Rona's mother had sent her a loofah for Christmas that year. It was before you saw loofahs all over the place.

Vaguely, he could remember six people crammed into the bathroom, cheering as the floating loofah expanded in water.

"What do you say about the auction?" he said. "Can you keep your hands still? That's what I told him was essential—hands in lap."

"Come here," she said, "I'll show you what I can do with my hands."

The auction was in a barn heated with two woodstoves—one in front, one in back. There were also a few electric heaters up and down the aisles. When B.B. and Rona and Bryce came in the back door of the barn, a man in a black-and-red lumberman's jacket closed it behind them, blowing cigar smoke in their faces. A woman and a man and two teenagers were arguing about a big cardboard box. Apparently one of the boys had put it too close to the small heater. The other boy was defending him, and the man, whose face was bright red, looked as if he was about to strike the woman. Someone else kicked the box away while they argued. B.B. looked in. There were six or eight puppies inside, mostly black, squirming.

"Dad, are they in the auction?" Bryce said.

"I can't stand the smoke," Rona said. "I'll wait for you in the car."

"Don't be stupid. You'll freeze," B.B. said. He reached out and touched the tips of her hair. She had on a red angora hat, pulled over her forehead, which made her look extremely pretty but also about ten years old. A child's hat and no makeup. The tips of her hair were still wet from the bathwater. Touching her hair, he was sorry that he had walked out of the bathroom when she said that about her hands.

They got three seats together near the back.

"Dad, I can't see," Bryce said.

"The damn Andrews Sisters," B.B. said. "I can't get their spooky voices out of my head."

Bryce got up. B.B. saw, for the first time, that the metal folding chair his son had been sitting in had PAM LOVES DAVID FOREVER AND FOR ALL TIME written on it with Magic Marker. He took off his scarf and folded it over the writing. He looked over his shoulder, sure that Bryce would be at the stand where they sold hot dogs and soft drinks. He wasn't; he was still inspecting the puppies. One of the boys said something to him, and his son answered. B.B. got up immediately and went over to join them. Bryce was reaching into his pocket.

"What are you doing?" B.B. said.

"Picking up a puppy," Bryce said. He said it as he lifted the animal.

The dog turned and rooted its snout in Bryce's armpit, its eyes closed. With his free hand, Bryce handed the boy some money.

"What are you *doing*?" B.B. said.

"Dime a feel," the boy said. Then, in a different tone, he said, "Week or so, they start eating food."

"I never heard of anything like that," B.B. said. The loofah popped up in his mind, expanded. Their drunken incredulity. The time, as a boy, he had watched a neighbor drown a litter of kittens in a washtub. He must have been younger than Bryce when that happened. And the burial: B.B. and the neighbor's son and another boy who was an exchange student had attended the funeral for the drowned kittens. The man's wife came out of the house, with the mother cat in one arm, and reached in her pocket and took out little American flags on toothpicks and handed them to each of the boys and then went back in the house. Her husband had dug a hole and was shoveling dirt back in. First he had put the kittens in a shoebox coffin, which he placed carefully in the hole he had dug near an abelia bush. Then he shoveled the dirt back in. B.B. couldn't remember the name of the man's son now, or the Oriental exchange student's name. The flags were what they used to give you in your sundae at the ice-cream parlor next to the bank.

"You can hold him through the auction for a quarter," the boy said to Bryce.

"You have to give the dog back," B.B. said to his son.

Bryce looked as if he was about to cry. If he insisted on having one of the dogs, B.B. had no idea what he would do. It was what Robin, his ex-wife, deserved, but she'd probably take the dog to the pound.

"Put it down," he whispered, as quietly as he could. The room was so noisy now that he doubted that the teenage boy could hear him. He thought he had a good chance of Bryce's leaving the puppy if there was no third party involved.

To his surprise, Bryce handed over the puppy, and the teenager lowered it into the box. A little girl about three or four had come to the rim of the box and was looking down.

"I bet you don't have a dime, do you, cutie?" the boy said to the girl.

B.B. reached in his pocket and took out a dollar bill, folded it, and put it on the cement floor in front of where the boy crouched. He took Bryce's hand, and they walked to their seats without looking back.

"It's just a bunch of junk," Rona said. "Can we leave if it doesn't get interesting?"

.   .   .

They bought a lamp at the auction. It had a nice base, and as soon as they found another lampshade it would be just right for the bedside table. Now it had a cardboard shade on it, imprinted with a cracked, fading bouquet.

"What's the matter with you?" Rona said. They were back in their bedroom.

"Actually," B.B. said, holding on to the window ledge, "I feel very out of control."

"What does that mean?"

She put *From Julia Child's Kitchen* on the night table, picked up her comb, and grabbed a clump of her hair. She combed through the snaggled ends, slowly.

"Do you think he has a good time here?" he said.

"Sure. He asked to come, didn't he? You could look at his face and see that he enjoyed the auction."

"Maybe he just does what he's told."

"What's the matter with you?" she said. "Come over here."

He sat on the bed. He had stripped down to his undershorts, and there were goose bumps all over his body. A bird was making a noise outside, screaming as if it were being killed. It stopped abruptly. The goose bumps slowly went away. Whenever he turned up the thermostat he always knew he was going to be sorry along about 5 a.m., when it got too hot in the room but he was too tired to get up and go turn it down. She said that was why they got headaches. He reached across her now for the Excedrin. He put the bottle back on top of the cookbook and gagged down two of them.

"What's he doing?" he said to her. "I don't hear him."

"If you made him go to bed, the way other fathers do, you'd know he was in bed. Then you'd just have to wonder if he was reading under the covers with a flashlight or—"

"Don't say it," he said.

"I wasn't going to say that."

"What were you going to say?"

"I was going to say that he might have taken more Godivas out of the box my mother sent me. I've eaten two. He's eaten a whole row."

"He left a mint and a cream in that row. I ate them," B.B. said.

He got up and pulled on a thermal shirt. He looked out the window and saw tree branches blowing. *The Old Farmer's Almanac* predicted snow at the end of the week. He hoped it didn't snow then; it would make it difficult taking Bryce back to Vermont. There were two miles of unplowed road leading to Robin's house.

He went downstairs. The oval table Bryce sat at was where the dining room curved out. Window seats were built around it. When they rented the house, it was the one piece of furniture left in it that neither of them disliked, so they had kept it. Bryce was sitting in an oak chair, and his forehead was on his arm. In front of him was the coloring book and a box of crayons and a glass vase with different-colored felt-tip pens stuck in it, falling this way and that, the way a bunch of flowers would. There was a pile of white paper. The scissors. B.B. assumed, until he was within a few feet of him, that Bryce was asleep. Then Bryce lifted his head.

"What are you doing?" B.B. said.

"I took the dishes out of the dishwasher and it worked," Bryce said. "I put them on the counter."

"That was very nice of you. It looks like my craziness about the dishwasher has impressed every member of my family."

"What was it that happened before?" Bryce said.

Bryce had circles under his eyes. B.B. had read once that that was a sign of kidney disease. If you bruised easily, leukemia. Or, of course, you could just take a wrong step and break a leg. The dishwasher had backed up, and all the filthy water had come pouring out in the morning when B.B. opened the door—dirtier water than the food-smeared dishes would account for.

"It was a mess," B.B. said vaguely. "Is that a picture?"

It was part picture, part letter, B.B. realized when Bryce clamped his hands over his printing in the middle.

"You don't have to show me."

"How come?" Bryce said.

"I don't read other people's mail."

"You did in Burlington," Bryce said.

"Bryce—that was when your mother cut out on us. That was a letter for her sister. She'd set it up with her to come stay with us, but her sister's as much a space cadet as Robin. Your mother was gone two days. The police were looking for her. What was I supposed to do when I found the letter?"

Robin's letter to her sister said that she did not love B.B. Also, that she did not love Bryce, because he looked like his father. The way she expressed it was: "Let spitting images spit together." She had gone off with the cook at the natural-food restaurant. The note to her sister—whom she had apparently called as well—was written on the back of one of the restaurant's flyers, announcing the menu for the week the cook ran away. Tears streaming down his cheeks, he had stood in the spare bedroom—whatever had made him go in there?—and read the names of desserts: "Tofu-Peach Whip!" "Granola Raspberry Pie!" "Macadamia Bars!"

"It's make-believe anyway," his son said, and wadded up the piece of paper. B.B. saw a big sunflower turn in on itself. A fir tree go under.

"Oh," he said, reaching out impulsively. He smoothed out the paper, making it as flat as he could. The ripply tree sprang up almost straight. Crinkled birds flew through the sky. B.B. read:

> When I'm B.B.'s age I can be with you allways. We can
> live in a house like the Vt. house only not in Vt. no sno.
> We can get married and have a dog.

"Who is this to?" B.B. said, frowning at the piece of paper.

"Maddy," Bryce said.

B.B. was conscious, for the first time, how cold the floorboards were underneath his feet. The air was cold, too. Last winter he had weather-stripped the windows, and this winter he hadn't. Now he put a finger against a pane of glass in the dining-room window. It could have been an ice cube, his finger numbed so quickly.

"Maddy is your stepsister," B.B. said. "You're never going to be able to marry Maddy."

His son stared at him.

"You understand?" B.B. said.

Bryce pushed his chair back. "Maddy's not ever going to have her hair cut again," he said. He was crying. "She's going to be Madeline and I'm going to live with only her and have a hundred dogs."

B.B. reached out to dry his son's tears, or at least to touch them, but Bryce sprang up. She was wrong: Robin was so wrong. Bryce was the image of her, not him—the image of Robin saying, "Leave me alone."

He went upstairs. Rather, he went to the stairs and started to climb, thinking of Rona lying in bed in the bedroom, and somewhere not halfway to the top, adrenaline surged through his body. Things began to go out of focus, then to pulsate. He reached for the railing just in time to steady himself. In a few seconds the first awful feeling passed, and he continued to climb, pretending, as he had all his life, that this rush was the same as desire.

GREENWICH TIME

"I'm thinking about frogs," Tom said to his secretary on the phone. "Tell them I'll be in when I've come up with a serious approach to frogs."

"I don't know what you're talking about," she said.

"Doesn't matter. I'm the idea man, you're the message taker. Lucky you."

"Lucky you," his secretary said. "I've got to have two wisdom teeth pulled this afternoon."

"That's awful," he said. "I'm sorry."

"Sorry enough to go with me?"

"I've got to think about frogs," he said. "Tell Metcalf I'm taking the day off to think about them, if he asks."

"The health plan here doesn't cover dental work," she said.

Tom worked at an ad agency on Madison Avenue. This week, he was trying to think of a way to market soap shaped like frogs—soap imported from France. He had other things on his mind. He hung up and turned to the man who was waiting behind him to use the phone.

"Did you hear that?" Tom said.

"Do what?" the man said.

"Christ," Tom said. "Frog soap."

He walked away and went out to sit across the street from his favorite pizza restaurant. He read his horoscope in the paper (neutral), looked out the window of the coffee shop, and waited for the restaurant to open. At eleven forty-five he crossed the street and ordered a slice of Sicilian pizza, with everything. He must have had a funny look on his face when he talked to the man behind the counter, because the man laughed and said, "You sure? Everything? You even look surprised yourself."

"I started out for work this morning and never made it there," Tom said. "After I wolf down a pizza I'm going to ask my ex-wife if my son can come back to live with me."

The man averted his eyes and pulled a tray out from under the counter. When Tom realized that he was making the man nervous, he sat down. When the pizza was ready, he went to the counter and got it, and ordered a large glass of milk. He caught the man behind the counter looking at him one more time—unfortunately, just as he gulped his milk too fast and it was running down his chin. He wiped his chin with a napkin, but even as he did so he was preoccupied, thinking about the rest of his day. He was heading for Amanda's, in Greenwich, and, as usual, he felt a mixture of relief (she had married another man, but she had given him a key to the back door) and anxiety (Shelby, her husband, was polite to him but obviously did not like to see him often).

When he left the restaurant, he meant to get his car out of the garage and drive there immediately, to tell her that he wanted Ben—that somehow, in the confusion of the situation, he had lost Ben, and now he wanted him back. Instead, he found himself wandering around New York, to calm himself so that he could make a rational appeal. After an hour or so, he realized that he was becoming as interested in the city as a tourist—in the tall buildings; the mannequins with their pelvises thrust forward, almost touching the glass of the store windows; books piled into pyramids in bookstores. He passed a pet store; its front window space was full of shredded newspaper and sawdust. As he looked in, a teenage girl reached over the gate that blocked in the window area and lowered two brown puppies, one in each hand, into the sawdust. For a second, her eye met his, and she thrust one dog toward him with a smile. For a second, the dog's eye also met his. Neither looked at him again; the dog burrowed into a pile of paper, and the girl turned and went back to work. When he and the girl caught each other's attention, a few seconds before, he had been reminded of the moment, earlier in the week, when a very attractive prostitute had approached him as he was walking past the Sheraton Centre. He had hesitated when she spoke to him, but only because her eyes were very bright—wide-set eyes, the eyebrows invisible under thick blond bangs. When he said no, she blinked and the brightness went away. He could not imagine how such a thing was physically possible; even a fish's eye wouldn't cloud over that quickly, in death. But the prostitute's eyes had gone dim in the second it took him to say no.

He detoured now to go to the movies: *Singin' in the Rain*. He left after Debbie Reynolds and Gene Kelly and Donald O'Connor danced onto the sofa and tipped it over. Still smiling about that, he went to a bar. When the bar started to fill up, he checked his watch and was surprised to see that people were getting off work. Drunk enough now to wish for rain, because rain would be fun, he walked to his apartment and took a shower, and then headed for the garage. There was a movie house next to the garage, and before he realized what he was doing he was watching *Invasion of the Body Snatchers*. He was shocked by the dog with the human head, not for the obvious reason but because it reminded him of the brown puppy he had seen earlier. It seemed an omen—a nightmare vision of what a dog would become when it was not wanted.

Six o'clock in the morning: Greenwich, Connecticut. The house is now Amanda's, ever since her mother's death. The ashes of Tom's former mother-in-law are in a tin box on top of the mantel in the dining room. The box is sealed with wax. She has been dead for a year, and in that year Amanda has moved out of their apartment in New York, gotten a quickie divorce, remarried, and moved into the house in Greenwich. She has another life, and Tom feels that he should be careful in it. He puts the key she gave him into the lock and opens the door as gently as if he were disassembling a bomb. Her cat, Rocky, appears, and looks at him. Sometimes Rocky creeps around the house with him. Now, though, he jumps on the window seat as gently, as unnoticeably, as a feather blown across sand.

Tom looks around. She has painted the living-room walls white and the downstairs bathroom crimson. The beams in the dining room have been exposed; Tom met the carpenter once—a small, nervous Italian who must have wondered why people wanted to pare their houses down to the framework. In the front hall, Amanda has hung photographs of the wings of birds.

Driving out to Amanda's, Tom smashed up his car. It was still drivable, but only because he found a tire iron in the trunk and used it to pry the bent metal of the left front fender away from the tire, so that the wheel could turn. The second he veered off the road (he must have dozed off for an instant), the thought came to him that Amanda would use the accident as a reason for not trusting him with Ben. While he worked with the tire iron, a man stopped his car and got out and gave him drunken advice. "Never buy a motorcycle," he said. "They spin out of control. You go with them—you don't have a chance." Tom nodded. "Did you know Doug's son?" the man asked. Tom said nothing. The man shook his head sadly and then went to the back of his car and opened the trunk. Tom watched him as he took flares out of his trunk and began to light them and place them in the road. The man came forward with several flares still in hand. He looked confused that he had so many. Then he lit the extras, one by one, and placed them in a semicircle around the front of the car, where Tom was working. Tom felt like some saint, in a shrine.

When the wheel was freed, he drove the car to Amanda's, cursing himself for having skidded and slamming the car into somebody's mailbox. When he got into the house, he snapped on the floodlight in the backyard, and then went into the kitchen to make some coffee before he looked at the damage again.

In the city, making a last stop before he finally got his car out of the garage, he had eaten eggs and bagels at an all-night deli. Now it seems to him that his teeth still ache from chewing. The hot coffee in his mouth feels good. The weak early sunlight, nearly out of reach of where he can move his chair and still be said to be sitting at the table, feels good where it strikes him on one shoulder. When his teeth don't ache, he begins to notice that he feels nothing in his mouth; where the sun strikes him, he can feel the wool of his sweater warming him the way a sweater is supposed to, even without sun shining on it. The sweater was a Christmas present from his son. She, of course, picked it out and wrapped it: a box enclosed in shiny white paper, crayoned on by Ben. "B E N," in big letters. Scribbles that looked like the wings of birds.

Amanda and Shelby and Ben were upstairs. Through the doorway he can see a digital clock on the mantel in the next room, on the other side from the box of ashes. At seven, the alarm will go off and Shelby will come downstairs, his gray hair, in the sharpening morning light, looking like one of those cheap abalone lights they sell at the seashore. He will stumble around, look down to make sure his fly is closed; he will drink coffee from one of Amanda's mother's bone-china cups, which he holds in the palms of his hands. His hands are so big that you have to look to see that he is cradling a cup, that he is not gulping coffee from his hands the way you would drink water from a stream.

Once, when Shelby was leaving at eight o'clock to drive into the city, Amanda looked up from the dining-room table where the three of them had been having breakfast—having a friendly, normal time, Tom had thought—and said to Shelby, "Please don't leave me alone with him." Shelby looked perplexed and embarrassed when she got up and followed him into the kitchen. "Who gave him the key, sweetheart?" Shelby whispered. Tom looked through the doorway. Shelby's hand was low on her hip—partly a joking sexual gesture, partly a possessive one. "Don't try to tell me there's anything you're afraid of," Shelby said.

Ben sleeps and sleeps. He often sleeps until ten or eleven. Up there in his bed, sunlight washing over him.

Tom looks again at the box with the ashes in it on the mantel. If there is another life, what if something goes wrong and he is reincarnated as a camel and Ben as a cloud and there is just no way for the two of them to get together? He wants Ben. He wants him now.

The alarm is ringing, so loud it sounds like a million madmen beating tin. Shelby's feet on the floor. The sunlight shining a rectangle of light through the middle of the room. Shelby will walk through that patch of light as though it were a rug rolled out down the aisle of a church. Six months ago, seven, Tom went to Amanda and Shelby's wedding.

Shelby is naked, and startled to see him. He stumbles, grabs his brown robe from his shoulder, and puts it on, asking Tom what he's doing there and saying good morning at the same time. "Every goddamn clock in the house is either two minutes slow or five minutes fast," Shelby says. He hops around on the cold tile in the kitchen, putting water on to boil, pulling his robe tighter around him. "I thought this floor would warm up in summer," Shelby says, sighing. He shifts his weight from one side to the other, the way a fighter warms up, chafing his big hands.

Amanda comes down. She is wearing a pair of jeans, rolled at the ankles, black high-heeled sandals, a black silk blouse. She stumbles like Shelby. She does not look happy to see Tom. She looks, and doesn't say anything.

"I wanted to talk to you," Tom says. He sounds lame. An animal in a trap, trying to keep its eyes calm.

"I'm going into the city," she says. "Claudia's having a cyst removed. It's all a mess. I have to meet her there, at nine. I don't feel like talking now. Let's talk tonight. Come back tonight. Or stay today." Her hands through her auburn hair. She sits in a chair, accepts the coffee Shelby brings.

"More?" Shelby says to Tom. "You want something more?"

Amanda looks at Tom through the steam rising from her coffee cup. "I think that we are all dealing with this situation very well," she says. "I'm not sorry I gave you the key. Shelby and I discussed it, and we both felt that you should have access to the house. But in the back of my mind I assumed that you would use the key—I had in mind more . . . emergency situations."

"I didn't sleep well last night," Shelby says. "Now I would like it if I didn't feel that there was going to be a scene to start things off this morning."

Amanda sighs. She seems as perturbed with Shelby as she is with Tom. "And if I can say something without being jumped on," she says to Shelby, "because, yes, you *told* me not to buy a Peugeot, and now the damned thing won't run—as long as you're here, Tom, it would be nice if you gave Inez a ride to the market."

"We saw seven deer running through the woods yesterday," Shelby says.

"Oh, cut it out, Shelby," Amanda says.

"Your problems I'm trying to deal with, Amanda," Shelby says. "A little less of the rough tongue, don't you think?"

Inez has pinned a sprig of phlox in her hair, and she walks as though she feels pretty. The first time Tom saw Inez, she was working in her sister's garden—actually, standing in the garden in bare feet, with a long cotton skirt sweeping the ground. She was holding a basket heaped high with irises and daisies. She was nineteen years old and had just arrived in the United States. That year, she lived with her sister and her sister's husband, Metcalf—his friend Metcalf, the craziest man at the ad agency. Metcalf began to study photography, just to take pictures of Inez. Finally his wife got jealous and asked Inez to leave. She had trouble finding a job, and Amanda liked her and felt sorry for her, and she persuaded Tom to have her come live with them, after she had Ben. Inez came, bringing boxes of pictures of herself, one suitcase, and a pet gerbil that died her first night in the house. All the next day, Inez cried, and Amanda put her arms around her. Inez always seemed like a member of the family, from the first.

By the edge of the pond where Tom is walking with Inez, there is a black dog, panting, staring up at a Frisbee. Its master raises the Frisbee, and the dog stares as though transfixed by a beam of light from heaven. The Frisbee flies, curves, and the dog has it as it dips down.

"I'm going to ask Amanda if Ben can come live with me," Tom says to Inez.

"She'll never say yes," Inez says.

"What do you think Amanda would think if I kidnapped Ben?" Tom says.

"Ben's adjusting," she says. "That's a bad idea."

"You think I'm putting you on? I'd kidnap you with him."

"She's not a bad person," Inez says. "You think about upsetting her too much. She has problems, too."

"Since when do you defend your cheap employer?"

His son has picked up a stick. The dog, in the distance, stares. The dog's owner calls its name: "Sam!" The dog snaps his head around. He bounds through the grass, head raised, staring at the Frisbee.

"I should have gone to college," Inez says.

"College?" Tom says. The dog is running and running. "What would you have studied?"

Inez swoops down in back of Ben, picks him up and squeezes him. He struggles, as though he wants to be put down, but when Inez bends over he holds on to her. They come to where Tom parked the car, and Inez lowers Ben to the ground.

"Remember to stop at the market," Inez says. "I've got to get something for dinner."

"She'll be full of sushi and Perrier. I'll bet they don't want dinner."

"You'll want dinner," she says. "I should get something."

He drives to the market. When they pull into the parking lot, Ben goes into the store with Inez, instead of to the liquor store next door with him. Tom gets a bottle of cognac and pockets the change. The clerk raises his eyebrows and drops them several times, like Groucho Marx, as he slips a flyer into the bag, with a picture on the front showing a blue-green drink in a champagne glass.

"Inez and I have secrets," Ben says, while they are driving home. He is standing up to hug her around the neck from the backseat.

Ben is tired, and he taunts people when he is that way. Amanda does not think Ben should be condescended to: she reads him R. D. Laing, not fairy tales; she has him eat French food, and only indulges him by serving the sauce on the side. Amanda refused to send him to kindergarten. If she had, Tom believes, if he was around other children his age, he might get rid of some of his annoying mannerisms.

"For instance," Inez says, "I might get married."

"Who?" he says, so surprised that his hands feel cold on the wheel.

"A man who lives in town. You don't know him."

"You're dating someone?" he says.

He guns the car to get it up the driveway, which is slick with mud washed down by a lawn sprinkler. He steers hard, waiting for the instant when he will be able to feel that the car will make it. The car slithers a bit but then goes straight; they get to the top. He pulls onto the lawn, by the back door, leaving the way clear for Shelby and Amanda's car to pull into the garage.

"It would make sense that if I'm thinking of marrying somebody I would have been out on a date with him," Inez says.

Inez has been with them since Ben was born, five years ago, and she has gestures and expressions now like Amanda's—Amanda's patient half smile that lets him know she is half charmed and half at a loss that he is so unsophisticated. When Amanda divorced him, he went to Kennedy to pick her up when she returned, and her arms were loaded with pineapples as she came up the ramp. When he saw her, he gave her that same patient half smile.

At eight, they aren't back, and Inez is worried. At nine, they still aren't back. "She did say something about a play yesterday," Inez whispers to Tom. Ben is playing with a puzzle in the other room. It is his bedtime—past it—and he has the concentration of Einstein. Inez goes into the room again, and he listens while she reasons with Ben. She is quieter than Amanda; she will get what she wants. Tom reads the newspaper from the market. It comes out once a week. There are articles about deer leaping across the road, lady artists who do batik who will give demonstrations at the library. He hears Ben running up the stairs, chased by Inez.

Water is turned on. He hears Ben laughing above the water. It makes him happy that Ben is so well adjusted; when he himself was five, no woman would have been allowed in the bathroom with him. Now that he is almost forty, he would like it very much if he were in the bathtub instead of Ben—if Inez were soaping his back, her fingers sliding down his skin.

For a long time, he has been thinking about water, about traveling somewhere so that he can walk on the beach, see the ocean. Every year he spends in New York he gets more and more restless. He often wakes up at night in his apartment, hears the air-conditioners roaring and the woman in the apartment above shuffling away her insomnia in satin slippers. (She has shown them to him, to explain that her walking cannot possibly be what is keeping him awake.) On nights when he can't sleep, he opens his eyes just a crack and pretends, as he did when he was a child, that the furniture is something else. He squints the tall mahogany chest of drawers into the trunk of a palm tree; blinking his eyes quickly, he makes the night-light pulse like a buoy bobbing in the water and tries to imagine that his bed is a boat, and that he is setting sail, as he and Amanda did years before, in Maine, where Perkins Cove widens into the choppy, ink-blue ocean.

Upstairs, the water is being turned off. It is silent. Silence for a long time. Inez laughs. Rocky jumps onto the stairs, and one board creaks as the cat pads upstairs. Amanda will not let him have Ben. He is sure of it. After a few minutes, he hears Inez laugh about making it snow as she holds the can of talcum powder high and lets it sift down on Ben in the tub.

Deciding that he wants at least a good night, Tom takes off his shoes and climbs the stairs; no need to disturb the quiet of the house. The door to Shelby and Amanda's bedroom is open. Ben and Inez are curled on the bed, and she has begun to read to him by the dim light. She lies next to him on the vast blue quilt spread over the bed, on her side with her back to the door, with one arm sweeping slowly through the air: "*Los soldados hicieron alto a la entrada del pueblo. . . .*"

Ben sees him, and pretends not to. Ben loves Inez more than any of them. Tom goes away, so that she will not see him and stop reading.

He goes into the room where Shelby has his study. He turns on the light. There is a dimmer switch, and the light comes on very low. He leaves it that way.

He examines a photograph of the beak of a bird. A photograph next to it of a bird's wing. He moves in close to the picture and rests his cheek against the glass. He is worried. It isn't like Amanda not to come back, when she knows he is waiting to see her. He feels the coolness from the glass spreading down his body. There is no reason to think that Amanda is dead. When Shelby drives, he creeps along like an old man.

He goes into the bathroom and splashes water on his face, dries himself on what he thinks is Amanda's towel. He goes back to the study and stretches out on the daybed, under the open window, waiting for the car. He is lying very still on an unfamiliar bed, in a house he used to visit two or three times a year when he and Amanda were married—a house always decorated with flowers for Amanda's birthday, or smelling of newly cut pine at Christmas, when there was angel hair arranged into nests on the tabletops, with tiny Christmas balls glittering inside, like miraculously colored eggs. Amanda's mother is dead. He and Amanda are divorced. Amanda is married to Shelby. These events are unreal. What is real is the past, and the Amanda of years ago—that Amanda whose image he cannot get out of his mind, the scene he keeps remembering. It had happened on a day when he had not expected to discover anything; he was going along with his life with an ease he would never have again, and, in a way, what happened was so painful that even the pain of her leaving, and her going to Shelby, would later be dulled in comparison. Amanda—in her pretty underpants, in the bedroom of their city apartment, standing by the window—had crossed her hands at the wrists, covering her breasts, and said to Ben, "It's gone now. The milk is gone." Ben, in his diapers and T-shirt, lying on the bed and look-ing up at her. The mug of milk waiting for him on the bedside table—he'd drink it as surely as Hamlet would drink from the goblet of poison. Ben's little hand on the mug, her breasts revealed again, her hand over-lapping his hand, the mug tilted, the first swallow. That night, Tom had moved his head from his pillow to hers, slipped down in the bed until his cheek came to the top of her breast. He had known he would never sleep, he was so amazed at the offhand way she had just done such a powerful thing. "Baby—" he had said, beginning, and she had said, "I'm not your baby." Pulling away from him, from Ben. Who would have guessed that what she wanted was another man—a man with whom she would stretch into sleep on a vast ocean of blue quilted satin, a bed as wide as the ocean? The first time he came to Greenwich and saw that bed, with her watching him, he had cupped his hand to his brow and looked far across the room, as though he might see China.

The day he went to Greenwich to visit for the first time after the divorce, Ben and Shelby hadn't been there. Inez was there, though, and she had gone along on the tour of the redecorated house that Amanda had insisted on giving him. Tom knew that Inez had not wanted to walk around the house with them. She had done it because Amanda had asked her to, and she had also done it because she thought it might make it less awkward for him. In a way different from the way he loved Amanda, but still a very real way, he would always love Inez for that.

Now Inez is coming into the study, hesitating as her eyes accustom themselves to the dark. "You're awake?" she whispers. "Are you all right?" She walks to the bed slowly and sits down. His eyes are closed, and he is sure that he could sleep forever. Her hand is on his; he smiles as he begins to drift and dream. A bird extends its wing with the grace of a fan opening; *los soldados* are poised at the crest of the hill. About Inez he will always remember this: when she came to work on Monday, after the weekend when Amanda had told him about Shelby and said that she was getting a divorce, Inez whispered to him in the kitchen, "I'm still your friend." Inez had come close to him to whisper it, the way a bashful lover might move quietly forward to say "I love you." She had said that she was his friend, and he had told her that he never doubted that. Then they had stood there, still and quiet, as if the walls of the room were mountains and their words might fly against them.

THE BURNING HOUSE

Freddy Fox is in the kitchen with me. He has just washed and dried an avocado seed I don't want, and he is leaning against the wall, rolling a joint. In five minutes, I will not be able to count on him. However: he started late in the day, and he has already brought in wood for the fire, gone to the store down the road for matches, and set the table. "You mean you'd know this stuff was Limoges even if you didn't turn the plate over?" he called from the dining room. He pretended to be about to throw one of the plates into the kitchen, like a Frisbee. Sam, the dog, believed him and shot up, kicking the rug out behind him and skidding forward before he realized his error; it was like the Road Runner tricking Wile E. Coyote into going over the cliff for the millionth time. His jowls sank in disappointment.

"I see there's a full moon," Freddy says. "There's just nothing that can hold a candle to nature. The moon and the stars, the tides and the sunshine—and we just don't stop for long enough to wonder at it all. We're so engrossed in ourselves." He takes a very long drag on the joint. "We stand and stir the sauce in the pot instead of going to the window and gazing at the moon."

"You don't mean anything personal by that, I assume."

"I love the way you pour cream in a pan. I like to come up behind you and watch the sauce bubble."

"No, thank you," I say. "You're starting late in the day."

"My responsibilities have ended. You don't trust me to help with the cooking, and I've already brought in firewood and run an errand, and this very morning I exhausted myself by taking Mr. Sam jogging with me, down at Putnam Park. You're sure you won't?"

"No, thanks," I say. "Not now, anyway."

"I love it when you stand over the steam coming out of a pan and the hairs around your forehead curl into damp little curls."

My husband, Frank Wayne, is Freddy's half brother. Frank is an accountant. Freddy is closer to me than to Frank. Since Frank talks to Freddy more than he talks to me, however, and since Freddy is totally loyal, Freddy always knows more than I know. It pleases me that he does not know how to stir sauce; he will start talking, his mind will drift, and when next you look the sauce will be lumpy, or boiling away.

Freddy's criticism of Frank is only implied. "What a gracious gesture to entertain his friends on the weekend," he says.

"Male friends," I say.

"I didn't mean that you're the sort of lady who doesn't draw the line. I most certainly did not mean that," Freddy says. "I would even have been surprised if you had taken a toke of this deadly stuff while you were at the stove."

"Okay," I say, and take the joint from him. Half of it is left when I take it. Half an inch is left after I've taken two drags and given it back.

"More surprised still if you'd shaken the ashes into the saucepan."

"You'd tell people I'd done it when they'd finished eating, and I'd be embarrassed. You can do it, though. I wouldn't be embarrassed if it was a story you told on yourself."

"You really understand me," Freddy says. "It's moon madness, but I have to shake just this little bit in the sauce. I have to do it."

He does it.

Frank and Tucker are in the living room. Just a few minutes ago, Frank returned from getting Tucker at the train. Tucker loves to visit. To him, Fairfield County is as mysterious as Alaska. He brought with him from New York a crock of mustard, a jeroboam of champagne, cocktail napkins with a picture of a plane flying over a building on them, twenty egret feathers ("You cannot get them anymore—strictly illegal," Tucker whispered to me), and, under his black cowboy hat with the rhinestone-studded chin strap, a toy frog that hopped when wound. Tucker owns a gallery in SoHo, and Frank keeps his books. Tucker is now stretched out in the living room, visiting with Frank, and Freddy and I are both listening.

". . . so everything I've been told indicates that he lives a purely Jekyll-and-Hyde existence. He's twenty years old, and I can see that since he's still living at home he might not want to flaunt his gayness. When he came into the gallery, he had his hair slicked back—just with water, I got close enough to sniff—and his mother was all but holding his hand. So fresh scrubbed. The stories I'd heard. Anyway, when I called, his father started looking for the number where he could be reached on the Vineyard—very irritated, because I didn't know James, and if I'd just phoned James I could have found him in a flash. He's talking to himself, looking for the number, and I say, 'Oh, did he go to visit friends or—' and his father interrupts and says, 'He was going to a gay pig roast. He's been gone since Monday.' *Just like that.*"

Freddy helps me carry the food out to the table. When we are all at the table, I mention the young artist Tucker was talking about. "Frank says his paintings are really incredible," I say to Tucker.

"Makes Estes look like an abstract expressionist," Tucker says. "I want that boy. I really want that boy."

"You'll get him," Frank says. "You get everybody you go after."

Tucker cuts a small piece of meat. He cuts it small so that he can talk while chewing. "Do I?" he says.

Freddy is smoking at the table, gazing dazedly at the moon centered in the window. "After dinner," he says, putting the back of his hand against his forehead when he sees that I am looking at him, "we must all go to the lighthouse."

"If only *you* painted," Tucker says. "I'd want you."

"You couldn't have me," Freddy snaps. He reconsiders. "That sounded halfhearted, didn't it? Anybody who wants me can have me. This is the only place I can be on Saturday night where somebody isn't hustling me."

"Wear looser pants," Frank says to Freddy.

"This is so much better than some bar that stinks of cigarette smoke and leather. Why do I do it?" Freddy says. "Seriously—do you think I'll ever stop?"

"Let's not be serious," Tucker says.

"I keep thinking of this table as a big boat, with dishes and glasses rocking on it," Freddy says.

He takes the bone from his plate and walks out to the kitchen, dripping sauce on the floor. He walks as though he's on the deck of a wave-tossed ship. "Mr. Sam!" he calls, and the dog springs up from the living-room floor, where he had been sleeping; his toenails on the bare wood floor sound like a wheel spinning in gravel. "You don't have to beg," Freddy says. "Jesus, Sammy—I'm just giving it to you."

"I hope there's a bone involved," Tucker says, rolling his eyes to Frank. He cuts another tiny piece of meat. "I hope your brother does understand why I couldn't keep him on. He was good at what he did, but he also might say just *anything* to a customer. You have to believe me that if I hadn't been extremely embarrassed more than once I never would have let him go."

"He should have finished school," Frank says, sopping up sauce on his bread. "He'll knock around a while longer, then get tired of it and settle down to something."

"You think I died out here?" Freddy calls. "You think I can't hear you?"

"I'm not saying anything I wouldn't say to your face," Frank says.

"I'll tell you what I wouldn't say to your face," Freddy says. "You've got a swell wife and kid and dog, and you're a snob, and you take it all for granted."

Frank puts down his fork, completely exasperated. He looks at me.

"He came to work once this stoned," Tucker says. "*Comprenez-vous?*"

"You like me because you feel sorry for me," Freddy says.

He is sitting on the concrete bench outdoors, in the area that's a garden in the springtime. It is early April now—not quite spring. It's very foggy out. It rained while we were eating, and now it has turned mild. I'm leaning against a tree, across from him, glad it's so dark and misty that I can't look down and see the damage the mud is doing to my boots.

"Who's his girlfriend?" Freddy says.

"If I told you her name, you'd tell him I told you."

"Slow down. What?"

"I won't tell you, because you'll tell him that I know."

"He knows you know."

"I don't think so."

"How did you find out?"

"He talked about her. I kept hearing her name for months, and then we went to a party at Garner's, and she was there, and when I said something about her later he said, 'Natalie who?' It was much too obvious. It gave the whole thing away."

He sighs. "I just did something very optimistic," he says. "I came out here with Mr. Sam and he dug up a rock and I put the avocado seed in the hole and packed dirt on top of it. Don't say it—I know: can't grow outside, we'll still have another snow, even if it grew, the next year's frost would kill it."

"He's embarrassed," I say. "When he's home, he avoids me. But it's rotten to avoid Mark, too. Six years old, and he calls up his friend Neal to hint that he wants to go over there. He doesn't do that when we're here alone."

Freddy picks up a stick and pokes around in the mud with it. "I'll bet Tucker's after that painter personally, not because he's the hottest thing since pancakes. That expression of his—it's always the same. Maybe Nixon really loved his mother, but with that expression who could believe him? It's a curse to have a face that won't express what you mean."

"Amy!" Tucker calls. "Telephone."

Freddy waves goodbye to me with the muddy stick. " 'I am not a crook,' " Freddy says. "Jesus Christ."

Sam bounds halfway toward the house with me, then turns and goes back to Freddy.

It's Marilyn, Neal's mother, on the phone.

"Hi," Marilyn says. "He's afraid to spend the night."

"Oh, no," I say. "He said he wouldn't be."

She lowers her voice. "We can try it out, but I think he'll start crying."

"I'll come get him."

"I can bring him home. You're having a dinner party, aren't you?"

I lower my voice. "Some party. Tucker's here. J.D. never showed up."

"Well," she says. "I'm sure that what you cooked was good."

"It's so foggy out, Marilyn. I'll come get Mark."

"He can stay. I'll be a martyr," she says, and hangs up before I can object.

Freddy comes into the house, tracking in mud. Sam lies in the kitchen, waiting for his paws to be cleaned. "Come on," Freddy says, hitting his hand against his thigh, having no idea what Sam is doing. Sam gets up and runs after him. They go into the small downstairs bathroom together. Sam loves to watch people urinate. Sometimes he sings, to harmonize with the sound of the urine going into the water. There are footprints and pawprints everywhere. Tucker is shrieking with laughter in the living room. ". . . he says, he says to the other one, 'Then, dearie, have you ever played *spin* the bottle?' " Frank's and Tucker's laughter drowns out the sound of Freddy peeing in the bathroom. I turn on the water in the kitchen sink, and it drowns out all the noise. I begin to scrape the dishes. Tucker is telling another story when I turn off the water: ". . . that it was Onassis in the Anvil, and nothing would talk him out of it. They told him Onassis was dead, and he thought they were trying to make him think he was crazy. There was nothing to do but go along with him, but, God—he was trying to goad this poor old fag into fighting about Stavros Niarchos. You know—Onassis's *enemy*. He thought it was *Onassis*. In the *Anvil*." There is a sound of a glass breaking. Frank or Tucker puts *John Coltrane Live in Seattle* on the stereo and turns the volume down low. The bathroom door opens. Sam runs into the kitchen and begins to lap water from his dish. Freddy takes his little silver case and his rolling papers out of his shirt pocket. He puts a piece of paper on the kitchen table and is about to sprinkle grass on it, but realizes just in time that the paper has absorbed water from a puddle. He balls it up with his thumb, flicks it to the floor, puts a piece of rolling paper where the table's dry and shakes a line of grass down it. "You smoke this," he says to me. "I'll do the dishes."

"We'll both smoke it. I'll wash and you can wipe."

"I forgot to tell them I put ashes in the sauce," he says.

"I wouldn't interrupt."

"At least he pays Frank ten times what any other accountant for an art gallery would make," Freddy says.

Tucker is beating his hand on the arm of the sofa as he talks, stomping his feet. ". . . so he's trying to feel him out, to see if this old guy with the dyed hair knew *Maria Callas*. Jesus! And he's so out of it he's trying to think what opera singers are called, and instead of coming up with 'diva' he comes up with 'duenna.' At this point, Larry Betwell went up to him and tried to calm him down, and he breaks into song—some aria or something that Maria Callas was famous for. Larry told him he was going to lose his *teeth* if he didn't get it together, and . . ."

"He spends a lot of time in gay hangouts, for not being gay," Freddy says.

I scream and jump back from the sink, hitting the glass I'm rinsing against the faucet, shattering green glass everywhere.

"What?" Freddy says. "Jesus Christ, what is it?"

Too late, I realize what it must have been that I saw: J.D. in a goat mask, the puckered pink plastic lips against the window by the kitchen sink.

"I'm sorry," J.D. says, coming through the door and nearly colliding with Frank, who has rushed into the kitchen. Tucker is right behind him.

"Oooh," Tucker says, feigning disappointment, "I thought Freddy smooched her."

"I'm sorry," J.D. says again. "I thought you'd know it was me."

The rain must have started again, because J.D. is soaking wet. He has turned the mask around so that the goat's head stares out from the back of his head. "I got lost," J.D. says. He has a farmhouse upstate. "I missed the turn. I went miles. I missed the whole dinner, didn't I?"

"What did you do wrong?" Frank asks.

"I didn't turn left onto Fifty-eight. I don't know why I didn't realize my mistake, but I went *miles*. It was raining so hard I couldn't go over twenty-five miles an hour. Your driveway is all mud. You're going to have to push me out."

"There's some roast left over. And salad, if you want it," I say.

"Bring it in the living room," Frank says to J.D. Freddy is holding out a plate to him. J.D. reaches for the plate. Freddy pulls it back. J.D. reaches again, and Freddy is so stoned that he isn't quick enough this time—J.D. grabs it.

"I thought you'd know it was me," J.D. says. "I apologize." He dishes salad onto the plate. "You'll be rid of me for six months, in the morning."

"Where does your plane leave from?" Freddy says.

"Kennedy."

"Come in here!" Tucker calls. "I've got a story for you about Perry Dwyer down at the Anvil last week, when he thought he saw Aristotle Onassis."

"Who's Perry Dwyer?" J.D. says.

"That is not the point of the story, dear man. And when you're in Cassis, I want you to look up an American painter over there. Will you? He doesn't have a phone. Anyway—I've been tracking him, and I know where he is now, and I am *very* interested, if you would stress that with him, to do a show in June that will be *only* him. He doesn't answer my letters."

"Your hand is cut," J.D. says to me.

"Forget it," I say. "Go ahead."

"I'm sorry," he says. "Did I make you do that?"

"Yes, you did."

"Don't keep your finger under the water. Put pressure on it to stop the bleeding."

He puts the plate on the table. Freddy is leaning against the counter, staring at the blood swirling in the sink, and smoking the joint all by himself. I can feel the little curls on my forehead that Freddy was talking about. They feel heavy on my skin. I hate to see my own blood. I'm sweating. I let J.D. do what he does; he turns off the water and wraps his hand around my second finger, squeezing. Water runs down our wrists.

Freddy jumps to answer the phone when it rings, as though a siren just went off behind him. He calls me to the phone, but J.D. steps in front of me, shakes his head no, and takes the dish towel and wraps it around my hand before he lets me go.

"Well," Marilyn says. "I had the best of intentions, but my battery's dead."

J.D. is standing behind me, with his hand on my shoulder.

"I'll be right over," I say. "He's not upset now, is he?"

"No, but he's dropped enough hints that he doesn't think he can make it through the night."

"Okay," I say. "I'm sorry about all of this."

"Six years old," Marilyn says. "Wait till he grows up and gets that feeling."

I hang up.

"Let me see your hand," J.D. says.

"I don't want to look at it. Just go get me a Band-Aid, please."

He turns and goes upstairs. I unwrap the towel and look at it. It's pretty deep, but no glass is in my finger. I feel funny; the outlines of things are turning yellow. I sit in the chair by the phone. Sam comes and lies beside me, and I stare at his black-and-yellow tail, beating. I reach down with my good hand and pat him, breathing deeply in time with every second pat.

"*Rothko?*" Tucker says bitterly, in the living room. "Nothing is great that can appear on greeting cards. Wyeth is that way. Would *Christina's World* look bad on a cocktail napkin? You know it wouldn't."

I jump as the phone rings again. "Hello?" I say, wedging the phone against my shoulder with my ear, wrapping the dish towel tighter around my hand.

"Tell them it's a crank call. Tell them anything," Johnny says. "I miss you. How's Saturday night at your house?"

"All right," I say. I catch my breath.

"Everything's all right here, too. Yes indeed. Roast rack of lamb. Friend of Nicole's who's going to Key West tomorrow had too much to drink and got depressed because he thought it was raining in Key West, and I said I'd go in my study and call the National Weather Service. Hello, Weather Service. How are you?"

J.D. comes down from upstairs with two Band-Aids and stands beside me, unwrapping one. I want to say to Johnny, "I'm cut. I'm bleeding. It's no joke."

It's all right to talk in front of J.D., but I don't know who else might overhear me.

"I'd say they made the delivery about four this afternoon," I say.

"This is the church, this is the steeple. Open the door, and see all the people," Johnny says. "Take care of yourself. I'll hang up and find out if it's raining in Key West."

"Late in the afternoon," I say. "Everything is fine."

"Nothing is fine," Johnny says. "Take care of yourself."

He hangs up. I put the phone down, and realize that I'm still having trouble focusing, the sight of my cut finger made me so light-headed. I don't look at the finger again as J.D. undoes the towel and wraps the Band-Aids around my finger.

"What's going on in here?" Frank says, coming into the dining room.

"I cut my finger," I say. "It's okay."

"You did?" he says. He looks woozy—a little drunk. "Who keeps calling?"

"Marilyn. Mark changed his mind about staying all night. She was going to bring him home, but her battery's dead. You'll have to get him. Or I will."

"Who called the second time?" he says.

"The oil company. They wanted to know if we got our delivery today."

He nods. "I'll go get him, if you want," he says. He lowers his voice. "Tucker's probably going to whirl himself into a tornado for an encore," he says, nodding toward the living room. "I'll take him with me."

"Do you want me to go get him?" J.D. says.

"I don't mind getting some air," Frank says. "Thanks, though. Why don't you go in the living room and eat your dinner?"

"You forgive me?" J.D. says.

"Sure," I say. "It wasn't your fault. Where did you get that mask?"

"I found it on top of a Goodwill box in Manchester. There was also a beautiful old birdcage—solid brass."

The phone rings again. I pick it up. "Wouldn't I love to be in Key West with you," Johnny says. He makes a sound as though he's kissing me and hangs up.

"Wrong number," I say.

Frank feels in his pants pocket for the car keys.

J.D. knows about Johnny. He introduced me, in the faculty lounge, where J.D. and I had gone to get a cup of coffee after I registered for classes. After being gone for nearly two years, J.D. still gets mail at the department—he said he had to stop by for the mail anyway, so he'd drive me to campus and point me toward the registrar's. J.D. taught English; now he does nothing. J.D. is glad that I've gone back to college to study art again, now that Mark is in school. I'm six credits away from an M.A. in art history. He wants me to think about myself, instead of thinking about Mark all the time. He talks as though I could roll Mark out on a string and let him fly off, high above me. J.D.'s wife and son died in a car crash. His son was Mark's age. "I wasn't prepared," J.D. said when we were driving over that day. He always says this when he talks about it. "How could you be prepared for such a thing?" I asked him. "I am now," he said. Then, realizing he was acting very hard-boiled, made fun of himself. "Go on," he said, "punch me in the stomach. Hit me as hard as you can." We both knew he wasn't prepared for anything. When he couldn't find a parking place that day, his hands were wrapped around the wheel so tightly that his knuckles turned white.

Johnny came in as we were drinking coffee. J.D. was looking at his junk mail—publishers wanting him to order anthologies, ways to get free dictionaries.

"You are so lucky to be out of it," Johnny said, by way of greeting. "What do you do when you've spent two weeks on *Hamlet* and the student writes about Hamlet's good friend Horchow?"

He threw a blue book into J.D.'s lap. J.D. sailed it back.

"Johnny," he said, "this is Amy."

"Hi, Amy," Johnny said.

"You remember when Frank Wayne was in graduate school here? Amy's Frank's wife."

"Hi, Amy," Johnny said.

J.D. told me he knew it the instant Johnny walked into the room— he knew that second that he should introduce me as somebody's wife. He could have predicted it all from the way Johnny looked at me.

For a long time J.D. gloated that he had been prepared for what happened next—that Johnny and I were going to get together. It took me to disturb his pleasure in himself—me, crying hysterically on the phone last month, not knowing what to do, what move to make next.

"Don't do anything for a while. I guess that's my advice," J.D. said. "But you probably shouldn't listen to me. All I can do myself is run away, hide out. I'm not the learned professor. You know what I believe. I believe all that wicked fairy-tale crap: your heart will break, your house will burn."

Tonight, because he doesn't have a garage at his farm, J.D. has come to leave his car in the empty half of our two-car garage while he's in France. I look out the window and see his old Saab, glowing in the moonlight. J.D. has brought his favorite book, *A Vision*, to read on the plane. He says his suitcase contains only a spare pair of jeans, cigarettes, and underwear. He is going to buy a leather jacket in France, at a store where he almost bought a leather jacket two years ago.

In our bedroom there are about twenty small glass prisms hung with fishing line from one of the exposed beams; they catch the morning light, and we stare at them like a cat eyeing catnip held above its head. Just now, it is 2 a.m. At six-thirty, they will be filled with dazzling color. At four or five, Mark will come into the bedroom and get in bed with us. Sam will wake up, stretch, and shake, and the tags on his collar will clink, and he will yawn and shake again and go downstairs, where J.D. is asleep in his sleeping bag and Tucker is asleep on the sofa, and get a drink of water from his dish. Mark has been coming into our bedroom for about a year. He gets onto the bed by climbing up on a footstool that horrified me when I first saw it—a gift from Frank's mother: a footstool that says TODAY IS THE FIRST DAY OF THE REST OF YOUR LIFE in needlepoint. I kept it in a closet for years, but it occurred to me that it would help Mark get up onto the bed, so he would not have to make a little leap and possibly skin his shin again. Now Mark does not disturb us when he comes into the bedroom, except that it bothers me that he has reverted to sucking his thumb. Sometimes he lies in bed with his cold feet against my leg. Sometimes, small as he is, he snores.

Somebody is playing a record downstairs. It's the Velvet Underground—Lou Reed, in a dream or swoon, singing "Sunday Morning." I can barely hear the whispering and tinkling of the record. I can only follow it because I've heard it a hundred times.

I am lying in bed, waiting for Frank to get out of the bathroom. My cut finger throbs. Things are going on in the house even though I have gone to bed; water runs, the record plays. Sam is still downstairs, so there must be some action.

I have known everybody in the house for years, and as time goes by I know them all less and less. J.D. was Frank's adviser in college. Frank was his best student, and they started to see each other outside of class. They played handball. J.D. and his family came to dinner. We went there. That summer—the summer Frank decided to go to graduate school in business instead of English—J.D.'s wife and son deserted him in a more horrible way, in that car crash. J.D. has quit his job. He has been to Las Vegas, to Colorado, New Orleans, Los Angeles, Paris twice; he tapes postcards to the walls of his living room. A lot of the time, on the weekends, he shows up at our house with his sleeping bag. Sometimes he brings a girl. Lately, not. Years ago, Tucker was in Frank's therapy group in New York, and ended up hiring Frank to work as the accountant for his gallery. Tucker was in therapy at the time because he was obsessed with foreigners. Now he is also obsessed with homosexuals. He gives fashionable parties to which he invites many foreigners and homosexuals. Before the parties he does TM and yoga, and during the parties he does Seconals and isometrics. When I first met him, he was living for the summer in his sister's house in Vermont while she was in Europe, and he called us one night, in New York, in a real panic because there were wasps all over. They were "hatching," he said—big, sleepy wasps that were everywhere. We said we'd come; we drove all through the night to get to Brattleboro. It was true: there were wasps on the undersides of plates, in the plants, in the folds of curtains. Tucker was so upset that he was out behind the house, in the cold Vermont morning, wrapped like an Indian in a blanket, with only his pajamas on underneath. He was sitting in a lawn chair, hiding behind a bush, waiting for us to come.

And Freddy—"Reddy Fox," when Frank is feeling affectionate toward him. When we first met, I taught him to ice-skate and he taught me to waltz; in the summer, at Atlantic City, he'd go with me on a roller coaster that curved high over the waves. I was the one—not Frank—who would get out of bed in the middle of the night and meet him at an all-night deli and put my arm around his shoulders, the way he put his arm around my shoulders on the roller coaster, and talk quietly to him until he got over his latest anxiety attack. Now he tests me, and I retreat: this man he picked up, this man who picked him up, how it feels to have forgotten somebody's name when your hand is in the back pocket of his jeans and you're not even halfway to your apartment. Reddy Fox—admiring my new red silk blouse, stroking his fingertips down the front, and my eyes wide, because I could feel his fingers on my chest, even though I was holding the blouse in front of me on a hanger to be admired. All those moments, and all they meant was that I was fooled into thinking I knew these people because I knew the small things, the personal things.

Freddy will always be more stoned than I am, because he feels comfortable getting stoned with me, and I'll always be reminded that he's more lost. Tucker knows he can come to the house and be the center of attention; he can tell all the stories he knows, and we'll never tell the story we know about him hiding in the bushes like a frightened dog. J.D. comes back from his trips with boxes full of postcards, and I look at all of them as though they're photographs taken by him, and I know, and he knows, that what he likes about them is their flatness—the unreality of them, the unreality of what he does.

Last summer, I read "The Metamorphosis" and said to J.D., "Why did Gregor Samsa wake up a cockroach?" His answer (which he would have toyed over with his students forever) was "Because that's what people expected of him."

They make the illogical logical. I don't do anything, because I'm waiting, I'm on hold (J.D.); I stay stoned because I know it's better to be out of it (Freddy); I love art because I myself am a work of art (Tucker).

Frank is harder to understand. One night a week or so ago, I thought we were really attuned to each other, communicating by telepathic waves, and as I lay in bed about to speak I realized that the vibrations really existed: they were him, snoring.

Now he's coming into the bedroom, and I'm trying again to think what to say. Or ask. Or do.

"Be glad you're not in Key West," he says. He climbs into bed.

I raise myself up on one elbow and stare at him.

"There's a hurricane about to hit," he says.

"What?" I say. "Where did you hear that?"

"When Reddy Fox and I were putting the dishes away. We had the radio on." He doubles up his pillow, pushes it under his neck. "Boom goes everything," he says. "Bam. Crash. Poof." He looks at me. "You look shocked." He closes his eyes. Then, after a minute or two, he murmurs, "Hurricanes upset you? I'll try to think of something nice."

He is quiet for so long that I think he has fallen asleep. Then he says, "Cars that run on water. A field of flowers, none alike. A shooting star that goes slow enough for you to watch. Your life to do over again." He has been whispering in my ear, and when he takes his mouth away I shiver. He slides lower in the bed for sleep. "I'll tell you something really amazing," he says. "Tucker told me he went into a travel agency on Park Avenue last week and asked the travel agent where he should go to pan for gold, and she told him."

"Where did she tell him to go?"

"I think somewhere in Peru. The banks of some river in Peru."

"Did you decide what you're going to do after Mark's birthday?" I say.

He doesn't answer me. I touch him on the side, finally.

"It's two o'clock in the morning. Let's talk about it another time."

"You picked the house, Frank. They're your friends downstairs. I used to be what you wanted me to be."

"They're your friends, too," he says. "Don't be paranoid."

"I want to know if you're staying or going."

He takes a deep breath, lets it out, and continues to lie very still.

"Everything you've done is commendable," he says. "You did the right thing to go back to school. You tried to do the right thing by find-ing yourself a normal friend like Marilyn. But your whole life you've made one mistake—you've surrounded yourself with men. Let me tell you something. All men—if they're crazy, like Tucker, if they're gay as the Queen of the May, like Reddy Fox, even if they're just six years old—I'm going to tell you something about them. Men think they're Spider-Man and Buck Rogers and Superman. You know what we all feel inside that you don't feel? That we're going to the stars."

He takes my hand. "I'm looking down on all of this from space," he whispers. "I'm already gone."

WHERE YOU'LL
FIND ME

JANUS

The bowl was perfect. Perhaps it was not what you'd select if you faced a shelf of bowls, and not the sort of thing that would inevitably attract a lot of attention at a crafts fair, yet it had real presence. It was as predictably admired as a mutt who has no reason to suspect he might be funny. Just such a dog, in fact, was often brought out (and in) along with the bowl.

Andrea was a real-estate agent, and when she thought that some prospective buyers might be dog lovers, she would drop off her dog at the same time she placed the bowl in the house that was up for sale. She would put a dish of water in the kitchen for Mondo, take his squeaking plastic frog out of her purse and drop it on the floor. He would pounce delightedly, just as he did every day at home, batting around his favorite toy. The bowl usually sat on a coffee table, though recently she had displayed it on top of a pine blanket chest and on a lacquered table. It was once placed on a cherry table beneath a Bonnard still life, where it held its own.

Everyone who has purchased a house or who has wanted to sell a house must be familiar with some of the tricks used to convince a buyer that the house is quite special: a fire in the fireplace in early evening; jonquils in a pitcher on the kitchen counter, where no one ordinarily has space to put flowers; perhaps the slight aroma of spring, made by a single drop of scent vaporizing from a lamp bulb.

The wonderful thing about the bowl, Andrea thought, was that it was both subtle and noticeable—a paradox of a bowl. Its glaze was the color of cream and seemed to glow no matter what light it was placed in. There were a few bits of color in it—tiny geometric flashes—and some of these were tinged with flecks of silver. They were as mysterious as cells seen under a microscope; it was difficult not to study them, because they shimmered, flashing for a split second, and then resumed their shape. Something about the colors and their random placement suggested motion. People who liked country furniture always commented on the bowl, but then it turned out that people who felt comfortable with Biedermeier loved it just as much. But the bowl was not at all ostentatious, or even so noticeable that anyone would suspect that it had been put in place deliberately. They might notice the height of the ceiling on first entering a room, and only when their eye moved down from that, or away from the refraction of sunlight on a pale wall, would they see the bowl. Then they would go immediately to it and comment. Yet they always faltered when they tried to say something. Perhaps it was because they were in the house for a serious reason, not to notice some object.

Once Andrea got a call from a woman who had not put in an offer on a house she had shown her. That bowl, she said—would it be possible to find out where the owners had bought that beautiful bowl? Andrea pretended that she did not know what the woman was referring to. A bowl, somewhere in the house? Oh, on a table under the window. Yes, she would ask, of course. She let a couple of days pass, then called back to say that the bowl had been a present and the people did not know where it had been purchased.

When the bowl was not being taken from house to house, it sat on Andrea's coffee table at home. She didn't keep it carefully wrapped (although she transported it that way, in a box); she kept it on the table, because she liked to see it. It was large enough so that it didn't seem fragile or particularly vulnerable if anyone sideswiped the table or Mondo blundered into it at play. She had asked her husband to please not drop his house key in it. It was meant to be empty.

When her husband first noticed the bowl, he had peered into it and smiled briefly. He always urged her to buy things she liked. In recent years, both of them had acquired many things to make up for all the lean years when they were graduate students, but now that they had been comfortable for quite a while, the pleasure of new possessions dwindled. Her husband had pronounced the bowl "pretty," and he had turned away without picking it up to examine it. He had no more interest in the bowl than she had in his new Leica.

She was sure that the bowl brought her luck. Bids were often put in on houses where she had displayed the bowl. Sometimes the owners, who were always asked to be away or to step outside when the house was being shown, didn't even know that the bowl had been in their house. Once—she could not imagine how—she left it behind, and then she was so afraid that something might have happened to it that she rushed back to the house and sighed with relief when the woman owner opened the door. The bowl, Andrea explained—she had purchased a bowl and set it on the chest for safekeeping while she toured the house with the prospective buyers, and she . . . She felt like rushing past the frowning woman and seizing her bowl. The owner stepped aside, and it was only when Andrea ran to the chest that the lady glanced at her a little strangely. In the few seconds before Andrea picked up the bowl, she realized that the owner must have just seen that it had been perfectly placed, that the sunlight struck the bluer part of it. Her pitcher had been moved to the far side of the chest, and the bowl predominated. All the way home, Andrea wondered how she could have left the bowl behind. It was like leaving a friend at an outing—just walking off. Sometimes there were stories in the paper about families forgetting a child somewhere and driving to the next city. Andrea had only gone a mile down the road before she remembered.

In time, she dreamed of the bowl. Twice, in a waking dream—early in the morning, between sleep and a last nap before rising—she had a clear vision of it. It came into sharp focus and startled her for a moment—the same bowl she looked at every day.

She had a very profitable year selling real estate. Word spread, and she had more clients than she felt comfortable with. She had the foolish thought that if only the bowl were an animate object she could thank it. There were times when she wanted to talk to her husband about the bowl. He was a stockbroker, and sometimes told people that he was fortunate to be married to a woman who had such a fine aesthetic sense and yet could also function in the real world. They were a lot alike, really—they had agreed on that. They were both quiet people—reflective, slow to make value judgments, but almost intractable once they had come to a conclusion. They both liked details, but while ironies attracted her, he was more impatient and dismissive when matters became many sided or unclear. They both knew this, and it was the kind of thing they could talk about when they were alone in the car together, coming home from a party or after a weekend with friends. But she never talked to him about the bowl. When they were at dinner, exchanging their news of the day, or while they lay in bed at night listening to the stereo and murmuring sleepy disconnections, she was often tempted to come right out and say that she thought that the bowl in the living room, the cream-colored bowl, was responsible for her success. But she didn't say it. She couldn't begin to explain it. Sometimes in the morning, she would look at him and feel guilty that she had such a constant secret.

Could it be that she had some deeper connection with the bowl—a relationship of some kind? She corrected her thinking: How could she imagine such a thing, when she was a human being and it was a bowl? It was ridiculous. Just think of how people lived together and loved each other. . . . But was that always so clear, always a relationship? She was confused by these thoughts, but they remained in her mind. There was something within her now, something real, that she never talked about.

The bowl was a mystery, even to her. It was frustrating, because her involvement with the bowl contained a steady sense of unrequited good fortune; it would have been easier to respond if some sort of demand were made in return. But that only happened in fairy tales. The bowl was just a bowl. She did not believe that for one second. What she believed was that it was something she loved.

In the past, she had sometimes talked to her husband about a new property she was about to buy or sell—confiding some clever strategy she had devised to persuade owners who seemed ready to sell. Now she stopped doing that, for all her strategies involved the bowl. She became more deliberate with the bowl, and more possessive. She put it in houses only when no one was there, and removed it when she left the house. Instead of just moving a pitcher or a dish, she would remove all the other objects from a table. She had to force herself to handle them carefully, because she didn't really care about them. She just wanted them out of sight.

She wondered how the situation would end. As with a lover, there was no exact scenario of how matters would come to a close. Anxiety became the operative force. It would be irrelevant if the lover rushed into someone else's arms, or wrote her a note and departed to another city. The horror was the possibility of the disappearance. That was what mattered.

She would get up at night and look at the bowl. It never occurred to her that she might break it. She washed and dried it without anxiety, and she moved it often, from coffee table to mahogany corner table or wherever, without fearing an accident. It was clear that she would not be the one who would do anything to the bowl. The bowl was only handled by her, set safely on one surface or another; it was not very likely that anyone would break it. A bowl was a poor conductor of electricity: it would not be hit by lightning. Yet the idea of damage persisted. She did not think beyond that—to what her life would be without the bowl. She only continued to fear that some accident would happen. Why not, in a world where people set plants where they did not belong, so that visitors touring a house would be fooled into thinking that dark corners got sunlight—a world full of tricks?

She had first seen the bowl several years earlier, at a crafts fair she had visited half in secret, with her lover. He had urged her to buy the bowl. She didn't *need* any more things, she told him. But she had been drawn to the bowl, and they had lingered near it. Then she went on to the next booth, and he came up behind her, tapping the rim against her shoulder as she ran her fingers over a wood carving. "You're still insisting that I buy that?" she said. "No," he said. "I bought it for you." He had bought her other things before this—things she liked more, at first—the child's ebony-and-turquoise ring that fitted her little finger; the wooden box, long and thin, beautifully dovetailed, that she used to hold paper clips; the soft gray sweater with a pouch pocket. It was his idea that when he could not be there to hold her hand she could hold her own—clasp her hands inside the lone pocket that stretched across the front. But in time she became more attached to the bowl than to any of his other presents. She tried to talk herself out of it. She owned other things that were more striking or valuable. It wasn't an object whose beauty jumped out at you; a lot of people must have passed it by before the two of them saw it that day.

Her lover had said that she was always too slow to know what she really loved. Why continue with her life the way it was? Why be two-faced, he asked her. He had made the first move toward her. When she would not decide in his favor, would not change her life and come to him, he asked her what made her think she could have it both ways. And then he made the last move and left. It was a decision meant to break her will, to shatter her intransigent ideas about honoring previous commitments.

Time passed. Alone in the living room at night, she often looked at the bowl sitting on the table, still and safe, unilluminated. In its way, it was perfect: the world cut in half, deep and smoothly empty. Near the rim, even in dim light, the eye moved toward one small flash of blue, a vanishing point on the horizon.

IN THE WHITE NIGHT

"Don't think about a cow," Matt Brinkley said. "Don't think about a river, don't think about a car, don't think about snow. . . ."

Matt was standing in the doorway, hollering after his guests. His wife, Gaye, gripped his arm and tried to tug him back into the house. The party was over. Carol and Vernon turned to wave goodbye, calling back their thanks, whispering to each other to be careful. The steps were slick with snow; an icy snow had been falling for hours, frozen granules mixed in with lighter stuff, and the instant they moved out from under the protection of the Brinkleys' porch the cold froze the smiles on their faces. The swirls of snow blowing against Carol's skin reminded her—an odd thing to remember on a night like this—of the way sand blew up at the beach, and the scratchy pain it caused.

"Don't think about an apple!" Matt hollered. Vernon turned his head, but he was left smiling at a closed door.

In the small, bright areas under the streetlights, there seemed for a second to be some logic to all the swirling snow. If time itself could only freeze, the snowflakes could become the lacy filigree of a valentine. Carol frowned. Why had Matt conjured up the image of an apple? Now she saw an apple where there was no apple, suspended in midair, transforming the scene in front of her into a silly surrealist painting.

It was going to snow all night. They had heard that on the radio, driving to the Brinkleys'. The Don't-Think-About-Whatever game had started as a joke, something long in the telling and startling to Vernon, to judge by his expression as Matt went on and on. When Carol crossed the room near midnight to tell Vernon that they should leave, Matt had quickly whispered the rest of his joke or story—whatever he was saying—into Vernon's ear, all in a rush. They looked like two children, the one whispering madly and the other with his head bent, but something about the inclination of Vernon's head let you know that if you bent low enough to see, there would be a big, wide grin on his face. Vernon and Carol's daughter, Sharon, and Matt and Gaye's daughter, Becky, had sat side by side, or kneecap to kneecap, and whispered that way when they were children—a privacy so rushed that it obliterated anything else. Carol, remembering that scene now, could not think of what passed between Sharon and Becky without thinking of sexual intimacy. Becky, it turned out, had given the Brinkleys a lot of trouble. She had run away from home when she was thirteen, and, in a family-counseling session years later, her parents found out that she had had an abortion at fifteen. More recently, she had flunked out of college. Now she was working in a bank in Boston and taking a night-school course in poetry. Poetry or pottery? The apple that reappeared as the windshield wipers slushed snow off the glass metamorphosed for Carol into a red bowl, then again became an apple, which grew rounder as the car came to a stop at the intersection.

She had been weary all day. Anxiety always made her tired. She knew the party would be small (the Brinkleys' friend Mr. Graham had just had his book accepted for publication, and of course much of the evening would be spent talking about that); she had feared that it was going to be a strain for all of them. The Brinkleys had just returned from the Midwest, where they had gone for Gaye's father's funeral. It didn't seem a time to carry through with plans for a party. Carol imagined that not canceling it had been Matt's idea, not Gaye's. She turned toward Vernon now and asked how the Brinkleys had seemed to him. Fine, he said at once. Before he spoke, she knew how he would answer. If people did not argue in front of their friends, they were not having problems; if they did not stumble into walls, they were not drunk. Vernon tried hard to think positively, but he was never impervious to real pain. His reflex was to turn aside something serious with a joke, but he was just as quick to wipe the smile off his face and suddenly put his arm around a person's shoulder. Unlike Matt, he was a warm person, but when people unexpectedly showed him affection it embarrassed him. The same counselor the Brinkleys had seen had told Carol—Vernon refused to see the man, and she found that she did not want to continue without him—that it was possible that Vernon felt uncomfortable with expressions of kindness because he blamed himself for Sharon's death: he couldn't save her, and when people were kind to him now he felt it was undeserved. But Vernon was the last person who should be punished. She remembered him in the hospital, pretending to misunderstand Sharon when she asked for her barrette, on her bedside table, and picking it up and clipping the little yellow duck into the hair above his own ear. He kept trying to tickle a smile out of her—touching some stuffed animal's button nose to the tip of her nose and then tapping it on her earlobe. At the moment when Sharon died, Vernon had been sitting on her bed (Carol was backed up against the door, for some reason), surrounded by a battlefield of pastel animals.

They passed safely through the last intersection before their house. The car didn't skid until they turned onto their street. Carol's heart thumped hard, once, in the second when she felt the car becoming light, but they came out of the skid easily. He had been driving carefully, and she said nothing, wanting to appear casual about the moment. She asked if Matt had mentioned Becky. No, Vernon said, and he hadn't wanted to bring up a sore subject.

Gaye and Matt had been married for twenty-five years; Carol and Vernon had been married twenty-two. Sometimes Vernon said, quite sincerely, that Matt and Gaye were their alter egos who absorbed and enacted crises, saving the two of them from having to experience such chaos. It frightened Carol to think that some part of him believed that. Who could really believe that there was some way to find protection in this world—or someone who could offer it? What happened happened at random, and one horrible thing hardly precluded the possibility of others happening next. There had been that fancy internist who hospitalized Vernon later in the same spring when Sharon died, and who looked up at him while drawing blood and observed almost offhandedly that it would be an unbearable irony if Vernon also had leukemia. When the test results came back, they showed that Vernon had mononucleosis. There was the time when the Christmas tree caught fire, and she rushed toward the flames, clapping her hands like cymbals, and Vernon pulled her away just in time, before the whole tree became a torch, and she with it. When Hobo, their dog, had to be put to sleep during their vacation in Maine, that awful woman veterinarian, with her cold green eyes, issued the casual death sentence with one manicured hand on the quivering dog's fur and called him Bobo, as though their dog were like some circus clown.

"Are you crying?" Vernon said. They were inside their house now, in the hallway, and he had just turned toward her, holding out a pink padded coat hanger.

"No," she said. "The wind out there is fierce." She slipped her jacket onto the hanger he held out and went into the downstairs bathroom, where she buried her face in a towel. Eventually, she looked at herself in the mirror. She had pressed the towel hard against her eyes, and for a few seconds she had to blink herself into focus. She was reminded of the kind of camera they had had when Sharon was young. There were two images when you looked through the finder, and you had to make the adjustment yourself so that one superimposed itself upon the other and the figure suddenly leaped into clarity. She patted the towel to her eyes again and held her breath. If she couldn't stop crying, Vernon would make love to her. When she was very sad, he sensed that his instinctive optimism wouldn't work; he became tongue-tied, and when he couldn't talk he would reach for her. Through the years, he had knocked over wineglasses shooting his hand across the table to grab hers. She had found herself suddenly hugged from behind in the bathroom; he would even follow her in there if he suspected that she was going to cry—walk in to grab her without even having bothered to knock.

She opened the door now and turned toward the hall staircase, and then realized—felt it before she saw it, really—that the light was on in the living room.

Vernon lay stretched out on the sofa with his legs crossed; one foot was planted on the floor and his top foot dangled in the air. Even when he was exhausted, he was always careful not to let his shoes touch the sofa. He was very tall, and couldn't stretch out on the sofa without resting his head on the arm. For some reason, he had not hung up her jacket. It was spread like a tent over his head and shoulders, rising and falling with his breathing. She stood still long enough to be sure that he was really asleep, and then came into the room. The sofa was too narrow to curl up on with him. She didn't want to wake him. Neither did she want to go to bed alone. She went back to the hall closet and took out his overcoat—the long, elegant camel's-hair coat he had not worn tonight because he thought it might snow. She slipped off her shoes and went quietly over to where he lay and stretched out on the floor beside the sofa, pulling the big blanket of the coat up high, until the collar touched her lips. Then she drew her legs up into the warmth.

Such odd things happened. Very few days were like the ones before. Here they were, in their own house with four bedrooms, ready to sleep in this peculiar double-decker fashion, in the largest, coldest room of all. What would anyone think?

She knew the answer to that question, of course. A person who didn't know them would mistake this for a drunken collapse, but anyone who was a friend would understand exactly. In time, both of them

had learned to stop passing judgment on how they coped with the inevitable sadness that set in, always unexpectedly but so real that it was
met with the instant acceptance one gave to a snowfall. In the white
night world outside, their daughter might be drifting past like an angel,
and she would see this tableau, for the second that she hovered, as a
necessary small adjustment.

HEAVEN ON A SUMMER NIGHT

Will stood in the kitchen doorway. He seemed to Mrs. Camp to be a little tipsy. It was a hot night, but that alone wouldn't account for his shirt, which was not only rumpled but hanging outside his shorts. Pens, a pack of cigarettes, and what looked like the tip of a handkerchief protruded from the breast pocket. Will tapped his fingertips on the pens. Perhaps he was not tapping them nervously but touching them because they were there, the way Mrs. Camp's mother used to run her fingers over the rosary beads she always kept in her apron pocket. Will asked Mrs. Camp if she would cut the lemon pound cake she had baked for the morning. She thought that the best thing to do when a person had had too much to drink was to humor him, so she did. Everyone had little weaknesses, to be sure, but Will and his sister had grown up to be good people. She had known them since they were toddlers, back when she had first come to work for the Wildes here in Charlottesville. Will was her favorite, then and now, although Kate probably loved her more. Will was nineteen now, and Kate twenty. On the wall, above the sink, was a framed poem that Kate had written and illustrated when she was in the fifth grade:

> *Like is a cookie*
> *Love is a cake*
> *Like is a puddle*
> *Love is a lake*

Years later, Will told her that Kate hadn't made up the poem at all. It was something she had learned in school.

Mrs. Camp turned toward Will, who was sitting at the table. "When does school start?" she said.

"There's a fly!" he said, dropping the slice of cake back onto his plate.

"What?" Mrs. Camp said. She had been at the sink, rinsing glasses before loading them into the dishwasher. She left the water running. The steam rose and thinned out as it floated toward the ceiling. "It's a raisin," she said. "You got me all worried about a raisin."

He plucked some more raisins out of the pound cake and then took another bite.

"If you don't want to talk about school, that's one thing, but that doesn't mean you should holler out that there's a fly in the food," Mrs. Camp said.

A year ago, Will had almost flunked out of college, in his sophomore year. His father had talked to the dean by long distance, and Will was allowed to continue. Now, in the summer, Mr. Wilde had hired Will a tutor in mathematics. Mornings and early afternoons, when Will was not being tutored or doing math problems, he painted houses with his friend Anthony Scoresso. Scoreboard and Will were going to drive to Martha's Vineyard to paint a house there at the end of August. The house was unoccupied, and although she was a little hesitant about doing such a thing, Mrs. Camp was going to accept Will's invitation to go with the boys and stay in the house for the week they were painting it. Scoreboard loved her cooking. She had never been to the Vineyard.

Now that they were older, Will and Kate included Mrs. Camp in many things. They had always told her everything. That was the difference between being who she was and being a parent—they knew that they could tell her anything. She never met one of their friends without hearing what Will or Kate called the Truth. That handsome blond boy, Neal, who told the long story about hitchhiking to the West Coast, Will told her later, was such a great storyteller because he was on speed. The girl called Natasha who got the grant to study in Italy had actually been married *and* divorced when she was eighteen, and her parents never even knew it. Rita, whom Mrs. Camp had known since first grade, now slept with a man as old as her father, for money. It pleased Kate and Will when a worried look came over Mrs. Camp's face as she heard these stories. Years ago, when she told them once that she liked that old song by the Beatles, "Lucy in the Sky with Diamonds," Will announced gleefully that the Beatles were singing about a drug.

Kate's car pulled into the driveway as Mrs. Camp was rinsing the last of the dishes. Kate drove a little white Toyota that made a gentle sound, like rain, as the tires rolled over the gravel. Will got up and pulled open the screen door for his sister on his way to the liquor cabinet. He poured some gin into a glass and walked to the refrigerator and added tonic water but no ice. In this sort of situation, Mrs. Camp's mother would have advised keeping quiet and saying a prayer. Mrs. Camp's husband—he was off on a fishing trip on the Chesapeake somewhere—would never advise her to pray, of course. Lately, if she asked him for advice about almost anything, his reply was "Get off my back." She noticed that Will noticed that she was looking at him. He grinned at her and put down his drink so that he could tuck in his shirt. As he raised the shirt, she had a glimpse of his long, tan back and thought of the times she had held him naked as a baby—all the times she had bathed him, all the hours she had held the hose on him in the backyard. Nowadays, he and Scoreboard sometimes stopped by the house at lunchtime. With their sun-browned bodies flecked with paint, they sat at the table on the porch in their skimpy shorts, waiting for her to bring them lunch. They hardly wore any more clothes than Will had worn as a baby.

Kate came into the kitchen and dropped her canvas tote bag on the counter. She had been away to see her boyfriend. Mrs. Camp knew that men were always going to fascinate Kate, the way her tropical fish had fascinated her many summers earlier. Mrs. Camp felt that most men moved in slow motion, and that that was what attracted women. It hypnotized them. This was not the way men at work were. On the job, construction workers sat up straight and drove tractors over piles of dirt and banged through potholes big enough to sink a bicycle, but at home, where the women she knew most often saw their men, they spent their time stretched out in big chairs, or standing by barbecue grills, languidly turning a hamburger as the meat charred.

Kate had circles under her eyes. Her long brown hair was pulled back into a bun at the nape of her neck. She had spent the weekend, as she had every weekend this summer, with her boyfriend, Frank Crane, at his condominium at Ocean City. He was studying for the bar exam. Mrs. Camp asked Kate how his studying was going, but Kate simply shook her head impatiently. Will, at the refrigerator, found a lime and held it up for them to see, very pleased. He cut off a side, squeezed lime juice into his drink, then put the lime back in the refrigerator, cut side down, on top of the butter-box lid. He hated to wrap anything in wax paper: Mrs. Camp knew that.

"Frank did the strangest thing last night," Kate said, sitting down and slipping her feet out of her sandals. "Maybe it wasn't strange. Maybe I shouldn't say."

"That'll be the day," Will said.

"What happened?" Mrs. Camp said. She thought that Frank was too moody and self-absorbed, and she thought that this was another story that was going to prove her right. Kate looked sulky—or maybe just more tired than Mrs. Camp had noticed at first. Mrs. Camp took a bottle of soda water out of the refrigerator and put it on the table, along with the lime and a knife. She put two glasses on the table and sat down across from Kate. "Perrier?" she said. Kate and Will liked her to call everything by its proper name, unless they had given it a nickname themselves. Secretly, she thought of it as bubble water.

"I was in his bedroom last night, reading, with the sheet pulled up," Kate said. "His bathroom is across the hall from the bedroom. He went to take a shower, and when he came out of the bathroom I turned back the sheet on his side of the bed. He just stood there, in the doorway. We'd had a kind of fight about that friend of his, Zack. The three of us had gone out to dinner that night, and Zack kept giving the waitress a hard time about nothing. Sassing a waitress because a dab of ice cream was on the saucer when she brought it. Frank knew I was disgusted. Before he took his shower, he went into a big thing about how I wasn't responsible for his friends' actions, and said that if Zack had acted as bad as I said he did he'd only embarrassed himself."

"If Frank passes the bar exam this time around, you won't have anything to worry about," Will said. "He'll act nice again."

Kate poured a glass of Perrier. "I haven't told the story yet," she said.

"Oh," Will said.

"I thought everything between us was fine. When he stopped in the doorway, I put the magazine down and smiled. Then he said, 'Kate—will you do something for me?' " Kate looked at Mrs. Camp, then dropped her eyes. "We were going to bed, you know," she said. "I thought things would be better after a while." Kate looked up. Mrs. Camp nodded and looked down. "Anyway," Kate went on, "he looked so serious. He said, 'Will you do something for me?' and I said, 'Sure. What?' and he said, 'I just don't know. Can you think of something to cheer me up?' "

Will was sipping his drink, and he spilled a little when he started laughing. Kate frowned.

"You take everything so seriously," Will said. "He was being funny."

"No, he wasn't," Kate said softly.

"What did you do?" Mrs. Camp said.

"He came over to the bed and sat down, finally. I knew he felt awful about something. I thought he'd tell me what was the matter. When he didn't say anything, I hugged him. Then I told him a story. I can't imagine what possessed me. I told him about Daddy teaching me to drive. How he was afraid to be in the passenger seat with me at the wheel, so he pretended I needed practice getting into the garage. Remember how he stood in the driveway and made me pull in and pull out and pull in again? I never had any trouble getting into the garage in the first place." She took another sip of Perrier. "I don't know what made me tell him that," she said.

"He was kidding. You said something funny, too, and that was that," Will said.

Kate got up and put her glass in the sink. It was clear, when she spoke again, that she was talking only to Mrs. Camp. "Then I rubbed his shoulders," she said. "Actually, I only rubbed them for a minute, and then I rubbed the top of his head. He likes to have his head rubbed, but he gets embarrassed if I start out there."

Kate had gone upstairs to bed. *Serpico* was on television, and Mrs. Camp watched with Will for a while, then decided that it was time for her to go home. Here it was August 25 already, and if she started addressing Christmas cards tonight she would have a four-month jump on Christmas. She always bought cards the day after Christmas and put them away for the following year.

Mrs. Camp's car was a 1977 Volvo station wagon. Mr. and Mrs. Wilde had given it to her in May, for her birthday. She loved it. It was the newest car she had ever driven. It was dark, shiny green—a color only velvet could be, the color she imagined Robin Hood's jacket must have been. Mr. Wilde had told her that he was not leaving her anything when he died but that he wanted to be nice to her when he was aboveground. A strange way to put it. Mrs. Wilde gave her a dozen pink Depression-glass wine goblets at the same time they gave her the car. There wasn't one nick in any of the rims; the glasses were all as smooth as sea-washed stones.

As she drove, Mrs. Camp wondered if Will had been serious when he said to Kate that Frank was joking. She was sure that Will slept with girls. (Will was not there to rephrase her thoughts. He always referred to young girls as women.) He must have understood that general anxiety or dread Frank had been feeling, and he must also have known that having sex wouldn't diminish it. It was also possible that Will was only trying to appear uninterested because Kate's frank talk embarrassed him. "Frank talk" was a pun. Those children had taught her so much.

She still felt a little sorry that they had always had to go to stuffy schools that gave them too much homework. She even felt sorry that they had missed the best days of television by being born too late: no *Omnibus,* no *My Little Margie,* no *Our Miss Brooks.* The reruns of *I Love Lucy* meant nothing to them. They thought Eddie Fisher's loud tenor voice was funny, and shook their heads in disbelief when Lawrence Welk, looking away from the camera, told folks how nice the song was that had just been sung. Will and Kate had always found so many things absurd and funny. As children, they were as united in their giggling as they were now in their harsh dismissals of people they didn't care for. But maybe this gave them an advantage over someone like her mother, who always held her tongue, because laughter allowed them to dismiss things; the things were forgotten by the time they ran out of breath.

In the living room, Mr. Camp was asleep in front of the television. *Serpico* was on. She didn't remember the movie exactly, but she would be surprised if Al Pacino ever got out of his dilemma. She dropped her handbag in a chair and looked at her husband. It was the first time she had seen him in almost two weeks. Since his brother retired from the government and moved to a house on the Chesapeake, Mr. Camp hardly came home at all. Tonight, many cigarettes had been stubbed out in the ashtray on the table beside his chair. He had on blue Bermuda shorts and a lighter blue knit shirt, white socks, and tennis shoes. His feet were splayed on the footstool. When they were young, he had told her that the world was theirs, and, considering the world her mother envisioned for her—the convent—he'd been right. He had taught her, all in one summer, how to drive, smoke, and have sex. Later, he taught her how to crack crabs and how to dance a rumba.

It was eight o'clock, and outside the light was as blue-gray as fish scales. She went into the kitchen, tiptoeing. She went to the refrigerator and opened the door to the freezer. She knew what she would find, and of course it was there: bluefish, foil wrapped, neatly stacked to within an inch of the top of the freezer. He had made room for all of them by removing the spaghetti sauce. She closed the door and pulled open the refrigerator door. There were the two containers. The next night, she would make up a big batch of spaghetti. The night after that, they would start eating the fish he'd caught. She opened the freezer door and looked again. The shining rectangles rose up like steep silver steps. The white air blowing off the ice, surrounding them and drifting out, made her squint. It might have been clouds, billowing through heaven. If she could shrink to a fraction of her size, she could walk into the cold, close the door, and start to climb.

She was tired. It was as simple as that. This life she loved so much had been lived, all along, with the greatest effort. She closed the door again. In order to stay still, she held her breath.

SUMMER PEOPLE

The first weekend at their summer house in Vermont, Jo, Tom, and Byron went out for pizza. Afterward, Tom decided that he wanted to go dancing at a roadside bar. Byron had come with his father and Jo grudgingly, enthusiastic about the pizza but fearing that it would be a longer night than he wanted. "They have Pac-Man here," Tom said to his son, as he swung the car into the bar parking strip, and for a couple of seconds it was obvious that Byron was debating whether or not to go in with them. "Nah," he said. "I don't want to hang out with a bunch of drunks while you two dance."

Byron had his sleeping bag with him in the car. The sleeping bag and a pile of comic books were his constant companions. He was using the rolled-up bag as a headrest. Now he turned and punched it flatter, making it more a pillow, and then stretched out to emphasize that he wouldn't go in with them.

"Maybe we should just go home," Jo said, as Tom pulled open the door to the bar.

"What for?"

"Byron—"

"Oh, Byron's overindulged," Tom said, putting his hand on her shoulder and pushing her forward with his fingertips.

Byron was Tom's son from his first marriage. It was the second summer that he was spending with them on vacation in Vermont. He'd been allowed to decide, and he had chosen to come with them. In the school year he lived with his mother in Philadelphia. This year he was suddenly square and sturdy, like the Japanese robots he collected—compact, complicated robots, capable of doing useful but frequently unnecessary tasks, like a Swiss Army knife. It was difficult for Tom to realize that his son was ten years old now. The child he conjured up when he closed his eyes at night was always an infant, the tangled hair still as smooth as peach fuzz, with the scars and bruises of summer erased, so that Byron was again a sleek, seal-like baby.

The band's instruments were piled on the stage. Here and there, amps rose out of tangled wire like trees growing from the forest's tangled floor. A pretty young woman with a blond pompadour was on the dance floor, shaking her puff of hair and smiling at her partner, with her Sony earphones clamped on, so that she heard her own music while the band took a break and the jukebox played. The man stood there shuffling, making almost no attempt to dance. Tom recognized them as the couple who had outbid him on a chain saw he wanted at an auction he had gone to earlier in the day.

On the jukebox, Dolly Parton was doing the speaking part of "I Will Always Love You." Green bottles of Rolling Rock, scattered across the bar top, had the odd configuration of misplaced bowling pins. Dolly Parton's sadness was coupled with great sincerity. The interlude over, she began to sing again, with greater feeling. "I'm not kidding you," a man wearing an orange football jersey said, squeezing the biceps of the burly man who sat next to him. "I says to him, 'I don't understand your question. What is tuna fish *like*? It's tuna fish.' " The burly man's face contorted with laughter.

There was a neon sign behind the bar, with shining bubbles moving through a bottle of Miller. When Tom was with his first wife, back when Byron was about three years old, he had taken the lights off the Christmas tree one year while needles rained down on the bedsheet snowbank they had mounded around the tree stand. He had never seen a tree dry out so fast. He remembered snapping off branches, then going to get a garbage bag to put them in. He snapped off branch after branch, stuffing them inside, feeling clever that he had figured out a way to get the dried-out tree down four flights of stairs without needles dropping everywhere. Byron came out of the back room while this was going on, saw the limbs disappearing into the black bag, and began to cry. His wife never let him forget all the wrong things he had said and done to Byron. He was still not entirely sure what Byron had been upset about that day, but he had made it worse by getting angry and saying that the tree was only a tree, not a member of the family.

The bartender passed by, clutching beer bottles by their necks as if they were birds he had shot. Tom tried to get his eye, but he was gone, involved in some story being told at the far end of the bar. "Let's dance," Tom said, and Jo moved into his arms. They walked to the dance floor and slow-danced to an old Dylan song. The harmonica cut through the air like a party blower, shrilly unrolling.

When they left and went back to the car, Byron pretended to be asleep. If he had really been sleeping, he would have stirred when they opened and closed the car doors. He was lying on his back, eyes squeezed shut a little too tightly, enclosed in the padded blue chrysalis of the sleeping bag.

The next morning, Tom worked in the garden, moving from row to row as he planted tomato seedlings and marigolds. He had a two-month vacation because he was changing jobs, and he was determined to stay ahead of things in the garden this year. It was a very carefully planned bed, more like a well-woven rug than like a vegetable patch. Jo was on the porch, reading *Moll Flanders* and watching him.

He was flattered but also slightly worried that she wanted to make love every night. The month before, on her thirty-fourth birthday, they had drunk a bottle of Dom Pérignon and she had asked him if he was still sure he didn't want to have a child with her. He told her that he didn't, and reminded her that they had agreed on that before they got married. He had thought, from the look on her face, that she was about to argue with him—she was a teacher and she loved debate—but she dropped the subject, saying, "You might change your mind someday." Since then she had begun to tease him. "Change your mind?" she would whisper, curling up next to him on the sofa and unbuttoning his shirt. She even wanted to make love in the living room. He was afraid Byron would wake up and come downstairs for some reason, so he would turn off the television and go upstairs with her. "What *is* this?" he asked once lightly, hoping it wouldn't provoke her into a discussion of whether he had changed his mind about having a child.

"I always feel this way about you," she said. "Do you think I like it the rest of the time, when teaching takes all my energy?"

On another evening, she whispered something else that surprised him—something he didn't want to pursue. She said that it made her feel old to realize that having friends she could stay up all night talking to was a thing of the past. "Do you remember that from college?" she said. "All those people who took themselves so seriously that everything they felt was a fact."

He was glad that she had fallen asleep without really wanting an answer. Byron puzzled him less these days and Jo puzzled him more. He looked up at the sky now; bright blue, with clouds trailing out thinly, so that the ends looked as if kite strings were attached. He was rinsing his hands with the garden hose at the side of the house when a car came up the driveway and coasted to a stop. He turned off the water and shook his hands, walking forward to investigate.

A man in his forties was getting out of the car—clean-cut, pudgy. He reached back into the car for a briefcase, then straightened up. "I'm Ed Rickman!" he called. "How are you today?"

Tom nodded. A salesman, and he was trapped. He wiped his hands on his jeans.

"To get right to the point, there are only two roads in this whole part of the world I really love, and this is one of them," Rickman said. "You're one of the new people—hell, everybody who didn't crash up against Plymouth Rock is new in New England, right? I tried to buy this acreage years ago, and the farmer who owned it wouldn't sell. Made an offer way back then, when money meant something, and the man wouldn't sell. You own all these acres now?"

"Two," Tom said.

"Hell," Ed Rickman said. "You'd be crazy not to be happy here, right?" He looked over Tom's shoulder. "Have a garden?" Rickman said.

"Out back," Tom said.

"You'd be crazy not to have a garden," Rickman said.

Rickman walked past Tom and across the lawn. Tom wanted the visitor to be the one to back off, but Rickman took his time, squinting and slowly staring about the place. Tom was reminded of the way so many people perused box lots at the auction—the cartons they wouldn't let you root around in because the good things thrown on top covered a boxful of junk.

"I never knew this place was up for grabs," Rickman said. "I was given to understand the house and land were an eight-acre parcel, and not for sale."

"I guess two of them were," Tom said.

Rickman ran his tongue over his teeth a few times. One of his front teeth was discolored—almost black.

"Get this from the farmer himself?" he said.

"Real-estate agent, three years ago. Advertised in the paper."

Rickman looked surprised. He looked down at his Top-Siders. He sighed deeply and looked at the house. "I guess my timing was bad," he said. "That or a question of style. These New Englanders are kind of like dogs. Slow to move. Sniff around before they decide what they think." He held his briefcase in front of his body. He slapped it a couple of times. It reminded Tom of a beer drinker patting his belly.

"Everything changes," Rickman said. "Not so hard to imagine that one day this'll all be skyscrapers. Condominiums or what have you." He looked at the sky. "Don't worry," he said. "I'm not a developer. I don't even have a card to leave with you in case you ever change your mind. In my experience, the only people who change their minds are women. There was a time when you could state that view without having somebody jump all over you, too."

Rickman held out his hand. Tom shook it.

"Just a lovely place you got here," Rickman said. "Thank you for your time."

"Sure," Tom said.

Rickman walked away, swinging the briefcase. His trousers were too big; they wrinkled across the seat like an opening accordion. When he got to the car, he looked back and smiled. Then he threw the briefcase onto the passenger seat—not a toss but a throw—got in, slammed the door, and drove away.

Tom walked around to the back of the house. On the porch, Jo was still reading. There was a pile of paperbacks on the small wicker stool beside her chair. It made him a little angry to think that she had been happily reading while he had wasted so much time with Ed Rickman.

"Some crazy guy pulled up and wanted to buy the house," he said.

"Tell him we'd sell for a million?" she said.

"I wouldn't," he said.

Jo looked up. He turned and went into the kitchen. Byron had left the top off a jar, and a fly had died in the peanut butter. Tom opened the refrigerator and looked over the possibilities.

Later that same week, Tom discovered that Rickman had been talking to Byron. The boy said he had been walking down the road just then, returning from fishing, when a car rolled up alongside him and a man pointed to the house and asked him if he lived there.

Byron was in a bad mood. He hadn't caught anything. He propped his rod beside the porch door and started into the house, but Tom stopped him. "Then what?" Tom said.

"He had this black tooth," Byron said, tapping his own front tooth. "He said he had a house around here, and a kid my age who needed somebody to hang out with. He asked if he could bring this dumb kid over, and I said no, because I wouldn't be around after today."

Byron sounded so self-assured that Tom did a double take, wondering where Byron was going.

"I don't want to meet some creepy kid," Byron said. "If the guy comes and asks you, say no—okay?"

"Then what did he say?"

"Talked about some part of the river where it was good fishing. Where the river curved, or something. It's no big deal. I've met a lot of guys like him."

"What do you mean?" Tom said.

"Guys that talk just to talk," Byron said. "Why are you making a big deal out of it?"

"Byron, the guy's nuts," Tom said. "I don't want you to talk to him anymore. If you see him around here again, run and get me."

"Right," Byron said. "Should I scream, too?"

Tom shivered. The image of Byron screaming frightened him, and for a few seconds he let himself believe that he should call the police. But if he called, what would he say—that someone had asked if his house was for sale and later asked Byron if he'd play with his son?

Tom pulled out a cigarette and lit it. He'd drive across town to see the farmer who'd owned the land, he decided, and find out what he knew about Rickman. He didn't remember exactly how to get to the farmer's house, and he couldn't remember his name. The real-estate agent had pointed out the place, at the top of a hill, the summer he showed Tom the property, so he could call him and find out. But first he was going to make sure that Jo got home safely from the grocery store.

The phone rang, and Byron turned to pick it up.

"Hello?" Byron said. Byron frowned. He avoided Tom's eyes. Then, just when Tom felt sure that it was Rickman, Byron said, "Nothing much." A long pause. "Yeah, sure," he said. "I'm thinking about ornithology."

It was Byron's mother.

The real-estate agent remembered him. Tom told him about Rickman. *"De de de de, De de de de,"* the agent sang—the notes of the theme music from *The Twilight Zone*. The agent laughed. He told him the farmer whose land he had bought was named Albright. He didn't have the man's telephone number, but was sure it was in the directory. It was.

Tom got in the car and drove to the farm. A young woman working in a flower garden stood up and held her trowel up like a torch when his car pulled into the drive. Then she looked surprised that he was a stranger. He introduced himself. She said her name. It turned out she was Mr. Albright's niece, who had come with her family to watch the place while her aunt and uncle were in New Zealand. She didn't know anything about the sale of the land; no, nobody else had come around asking. Tom described Rickman anyway. No, she said, she hadn't seen anyone who looked like that. Over on a side lawn, two Irish setters were barking madly at them. A man—he must have been the woman's husband—was holding them by their collars. The dogs were going wild, and the young woman obviously wanted to end the conversation. Tom didn't think about leaving her his telephone number until it was too late, when he was driving away.

That night, he went to another auction, and when he came back to the car one of the back tires was flat. He opened the trunk to get the spare, glad that he had gone to the auction alone, glad that the field was lit up and people were walking around. A little girl about his son's age came by with her parents. She held a one-armed doll over her head and skipped forward. "I don't feel cheated. Why should you feel cheated? I bought the whole box for two dollars and I got two metal sieves out of it," the woman said to the man. He had on a baseball cap and a black tank top and cutoffs, and sandals with soles that curved at the heel and toe like a canoe. He stalked ahead of the woman, box under one arm, and grabbed his dancing daughter by the elbow. "Watch my dolly!" she screamed, as he pulled her along. "That doll's not worth five cents," the man said. Tom averted his eyes. He was sweating more than he should, going through the easy maneuvers of changing a tire. There was even a breeze.

They floated the tire in a pan of water at the gas station the next morning, looking for the puncture. Nothing was embedded in the tire; whatever had made the hole wasn't there. As one big bubble after another rose to the surface, Tom felt a clutch in his throat, as if he himself might be drowning.

He could think of no good reason to tell the officer at the police barracks why Ed Rickman would have singled him out. Maybe Rickman *had* wanted to build a house on that particular site. The policeman made a fist and rested his mouth against it, his lips in the gully between thumb and finger. Until Tom said that, the policeman had seemed concerned—even a little interested. Then his expression changed. Tom hurried to say that of course he didn't believe that explanation, because something funny was going on. The cop shook his head. Did that mean no, of course not, or no, he did believe it?

Tom described Rickman, mentioning the discolored tooth. The cop wrote this information down on a small white pad. He drew cross-hatches on a corner. The cop did not seem quite as certain as Tom that no one could have a grudge against him or anyone in his family. He asked where they lived in New York, where they worked.

When Tom walked out into the sunlight, he felt a little faint. Of course he had understood, even before the cop said it, that there was nothing the police could do at this point. "Frankly," the cop had said, "it's not likely that we're going to be able to keep a good eye out, in that you're on a dead-end road. Not a *route*," the cop said. "Not a *major thoroughfare.*" It seemed to be some joke the cop was having with himself.

Driving home, Tom realized that he could give anyone who asked a detailed description of the cop. He had studied every mark on the cop's face—the little scar (chicken pox?) over one eyebrow, the aquiline nose that narrowed at the tip almost to the shape of a tack. He did not intend to alarm Jo or Byron by telling them where he had been.

Byron had gone fishing again. Jo wanted to make love while Byron was out. Tom knew he couldn't.

A week passed. Almost two weeks. He and Jo and Byron sat in lawn chairs watching the lightning bugs blink. Byron said he had his eye on one in particular, and he went *"Beep-beep, beep-beep"* as it blinked. They ate raw peas Jo had gathered in a bowl. He and Jo had a glass of wine. The neighbors' M.G. passed by. This summer, the neighbors sometimes tapped the horn as they passed. A bird swooped low across the lawn—perhaps a female cardinal. It was a surprise seeing a bird in the twilight like that. It dove into the grass, more like a seagull than a cardinal. It rose up, fluttering, with something in its beak. Jo put her glass on the little table, smiled, and clapped softly.

The bird Byron found dead in the morning was a grackle, not a cardinal. It was lying about ten feet from the picture window, but until Tom examined the bird's body carefully, he did not decide that probably it had just smacked into the glass by accident.

At Rusty's, at the end of summer, Tom ran into the cop again. They were both carrying white paper bags with straws sticking out of them. Grease was starting to seep through the bags. Rickman had never reappeared, and Tom felt some embarrassment about having gone to see the cop. He tried not to focus on the tip of the cop's nose.

"Running into a nut like that, I guess it makes getting back to the city look good," the cop said.

He's thinking, Summer people, Tom decided.

"You have a nice year, now," the cop said. "Tell your wife I sure do envy her her retirement."

"Her retirement?" Tom said.

The cop looked at the blacktop. "I admit, the way you described that guy I thought he might be sent by somebody who had a grudge against you or your wife," he said. "Then at the fire department picnic I got to talking to your neighbor—that Mrs. Hewett—and I asked her if she'd seen anybody strange poking around before you got there. Hadn't. We got to talking. She said you were in the advertising business, and there was no way of knowing what gripes some lunatic might have with that, if he happened to know. Maybe you walked on somebody's territory, so to speak, and he wanted to get even. And your wife being a schoolteacher, you can't realize how upset some parents get when Johnny doesn't bring home the A's. You never can tell. Mrs. Hewett said she'd been a schoolteacher for a few months herself, before she got married, and she never regretted the day she quit. Said your wife was real happy about her own decision, too." The cop nodded in agreement with this.

Tom tried to hide his surprise. Somehow, the fact that he didn't know that Jo had ever exchanged a word with a neighbor, Karen Hewett, privately made the rest of the story believable. They hardly knew the woman. But why would Jo quit? His credibility with the cop must have been good after all. He could tell from the way the cop studied his face that he realized he had been telling Tom something he didn't know.

When the cop left, Tom sat on the hot front hood of his car, took the hamburgers out of the bag, and ate them. He pulled the straw out of the big container of Coke and took off the plastic top. He drank from the cup, and when the Coke was gone he continued to sit there, sucking ice. Back during the winter, Jo had several times brought up the idea of having a baby, but she hadn't mentioned it for weeks now. He wondered if she had decided to get pregnant in spite of his objections. But even if she had, why would she quit her job before she was sure there was a reason for it?

A teenage girl with short hair and triangle-shaped earrings walked by, averting her eyes as if she knew he'd stare after her. He didn't; only the earrings that caught the light like mirrors interested him. In a convertible facing him, across the lot, a boy and girl were eating their sandwiches in the front seat while a golden retriever in the back moved his head between theirs, looking from left to right and right to left with the regularity of a dummy talking to a ventriloquist. A man holding his toddler's hand walked by and smiled. Another car pulled in, with Hall and Oates going on the radio. The driver turned off the ignition, cutting off the music, and got out. A woman got out the other side. As they walked past, the woman said to the man, "I don't see why we've got to eat exactly at nine, twelve, and six." "Hey, it's twelve-fifteen," the man said. Tom dropped his cup into the paper bag, along with his hamburger wrappers and the napkins he hadn't used. He carried the soggy bag over to the trash can. A few bees lifted slightly higher as he stuffed his trash in. Walking back to the car, he realized that he had absolutely no idea what to do. At some point he would have to ask Jo what was going on.

When he pulled up, Byron was sitting on the front step, cleaning fish over a newspaper. Four trout, one of them very large. Byron had had a good day.

Tom walked through the house but couldn't find Jo. He held his breath when he opened the closet door; it was unlikely that she would be in there, naked, two days in a row. She liked to play tricks on him.

He came back downstairs, and saw, through the kitchen window, that Jo was sitting outside. A woman was with her. He walked out. Paper plates and beer bottles were on the grass beside their chairs.

"Hi, honey," she said.

"Hi," the woman said. It was Karen Hewett.

"Hi," he said to both of them. He had never seen Karen Hewett up close. She was tanner than he realized. The biggest difference, though, was her hair. When he had seen her, it had always been long and wind-blown, but today she had it pulled back in a clip.

"Get all your errands done?" Jo said.

It couldn't have been a more ordinary conversation. It couldn't have been a more ordinary summer day.

The night before they closed up the house, Tom and Jo lay stretched out on the bed. Jo was finishing *Tom Jones*. Tom was enjoying the cool breeze coming through the window, thinking that when he was in New York he forgot the Vermont house; at least, he forgot it except for the times he looked up from the street he was on and saw the sky, and its emptiness made him remember stars. It was the sky he loved in the country—the sky more than the house. If he hadn't thought it would seem dramatic, he would have gotten out of bed now and stood at the window for a long time. Earlier in the evening, Jo had asked why he was so moody. He had told her that he didn't feel like leaving. "Then let's stay," she said. It was his opening to say something about her job in the fall. He had hoped she would say something, but he hesitated, and she had only put her arms around him and rubbed her cheek against his cheek. All summer, she had seduced him—sometimes with passion, sometimes so subtly he didn't realize what was happening until she put her hand up under his T-shirt or kissed him on the lips.

Now it was the end of August. Jo's sister in Connecticut was graduating from nursing school in Hartford, and Jo had asked Tom to stop there so they could do something with her sister to celebrate. Her sister lived in a one-bedroom apartment, but it would be easy to find a motel. The following day, they would take Byron home to Philadelphia and then backtrack to New York.

In the car the next morning, Tom felt Byron's gaze on his back and wondered if he had overheard their lovemaking the night before. It was very hot by noontime. There was so much haze on the mountains that their peaks were invisible. The mountains gradually sloped until suddenly, before Tom realized it, they were driving on flat highway. Late that afternoon they found a motel. He and Byron swam in the pool, and Jo, although she was just about to see her, talked to her sister for half an hour on the phone.

By the time Jo's sister turned up at the motel, Tom had shaved and showered. Byron was watching television. He wanted to stay in the room and watch the movie instead of having dinner with them. He said he wasn't hungry. Tom insisted that he come and eat dinner. "I can get something out of the machine," Byron said.

"You're not going to eat potato chips for dinner," Tom said. "Get off the bed—come on."

Byron gave Tom a look that was quite similar to the look an outlaw in the movie was giving the sheriff who had just kicked his gun out of reach.

"You didn't stay glued to the set in Vermont all summer and miss those glorious days, did you?" Jo's sister said.

"I fished," Byron said.

"He caught four trout one day," Tom said, spreading his arms and looking from the palm of one hand to the palm of the other.

They all had dinner together in the motel restaurant, and later, while they drank their coffee, Byron dropped quarters into the machine in the corridor, playing game after game of Space Invaders.

Jo and her sister went into the bar next to the restaurant for a nightcap. Tom let them go alone, figuring that they probably wanted some private time together. Byron followed him up to the room and turned on the television. An hour later, Jo and her sister were still in the bar. Tom sat on the balcony. Long before his usual bedtime, Byron turned off the television.

"Good night," Tom called into the room, hoping Byron would call him in.

"Night," Byron said.

Tom sat in silence for a minute. He was out of cigarettes and felt like a beer. He went into the room. Byron was lying in his sleeping bag, unzipped, on top of one of the beds.

"I'm going to drive down to that 7-Eleven," Tom said. "Want me to bring you anything?"

"No, thanks," Byron said.

"Want to come along?"

"No," Byron said.

He picked up the keys to the car and the room key and went out. He wasn't sure whether Byron was still sulking because he had made him go to dinner or whether he didn't want to go back to his mother's. Perhaps he was just tired.

Tom bought two Heinekens and a pack of Kools. The cashier was obviously stoned; he had bloodshot eyes and he stuffed a wad of napkins into the bag before he pushed it across the counter to Tom.

Back at the motel, he opened the door quietly. Byron didn't move. Tom put out one of the two lights Byron had left on and slid open the glass door to the balcony.

Two people kissed on the pathway outside, passing the pool on the way to their room. People were talking in the room below—muted, but it sounded like an argument. The lights were suddenly turned off at the pool. Tom pushed his heels against the railing and tipped his chair back. He could hear the cars on the highway. He felt sad about something, and realized that he felt quite alone. He finished a beer and lit a cigarette. Byron hadn't been very communicative. Of course, he couldn't expect a ten-year-old boy to throw his arms around him the way he had when he was a baby. And Jo—in spite of her ardor, his memory of her, all summer, was of her sitting with her nose in some eighteenth-century novel. He thought about all the things they had done in July and August, trying to convince himself that they had done a lot and had fun. Dancing a couple of times, auctions, the day on the borrowed raft, four—no, five—movies, fishing with Byron, badminton, the fireworks and the spareribs dinner outside the Town Hall on the Fourth.

Maybe what his ex-wife always said was true: he didn't connect with people. Jo never said such a thing, though. And Byron chose to spend the summer with them.

He drank the other beer and felt its effect. It had been a long drive. Byron probably didn't want to go back to Philadelphia. He himself wasn't too eager to begin his new job. He suddenly remembered his secretary when he confided in her that he'd gotten the big offer—her surprise, the way she hid her thumbs-up behind the palm of her other hand, in a mock gesture of secrecy. "Where are you going to go from there?" she had said. He'd miss her. She was funny and pretty and enthusiastic—no slouch herself. He'd miss laughing with her, miss being flattered because she thought that he was such a competent character.

He missed Jo. It wasn't because she was off at the bar. If she came back this instant, something would still be missing. He couldn't imagine caring for anyone more than he cared for her, but he wasn't sure that he was still in love with her. He was fiddling, there in the dark. He had reached into the paper bag and begun to wrinkle up little bits of napkin, rolling the paper between thumb and finger so that it formed tiny balls. When he had a palmful, he got up and tossed them over the railing. When he sat down again, he closed his eyes and began what would be months of remembering Vermont: the garden, the neon green of new peas, the lumpy lawn, the pine trees and the smell of them at night—and then suddenly Rickman was there, rumpled and strange, but his presence was only slightly startling. He was just a man who'd dropped in on a summer day. "You'd be crazy not to be happy here," Rickman was saying. All that was quite believable now—the way, when seen in the odd context of a home movie, even the craziest relative can suddenly look amiable.

He wondered if Jo was pregnant. Could that be what she and her sister were talking about all this time in the bar? For a second, he wanted them all to be transformed into characters in one of those novels she had read all summer. That way, the uncertainty would end. Henry Fielding would simply step in and predict the future. The author could tell him what it would be like, what would happen, if he had to try, another time, to love somebody.

The woman who had been arguing with the man was quiet. Crickets chirped, and a television hummed faintly. Below him, near the pool, a man who worked at the motel had rolled a table onto its side. He whistled while he made an adjustment to the white metal pole that would hold an umbrella the next day.

SKELETONS

Usually she was the artist. Today she was the model. She had on sweatpants—both she and Garrett wore medium, although his sweatpants fit her better than they did him, because she did not have his long legs—and a Chinese jacket, plum-colored, patterned with blue octagons, edged in silver thread, that seemed to float among the lavender flowers that were as big as the palm of a hand raised for the high five. A *frog*, Nancy thought; that was what the piece was called—the near knot she fingered, the little fastener she never closed.

It was late Saturday afternoon, and, as usual, Nancy Niles was spending the day with Garrett. She had met him in a drawing class she took at night. During the week, he worked in an artists' supply store, but he had the weekends off. Until recently, when the weather turned cold, they had often taken long walks on Saturday or Sunday, and sometimes Kyle Brown—an undergraduate at the University of Pennsylvania, who was the other tenant in the rooming house Garrett lived in, in a run-down neighborhood twenty minutes from the campus—had walked with them. It was Kyle who had told Garrett about the empty room in the house. His first week in Philadelphia, Garrett had been in line to pay his check at a coffee shop when the cashier asked Kyle for a penny, which he didn't have. Then she looked behind Kyle to Garrett and said, "Well, would *you* have a penny?" Leaving, Kyle and Garrett struck up the conversation that had led to Garrett's moving into the house. And now the cashier's question had become a running joke. Just that morning, Garrett was outside the bathroom, and when Kyle came out, wrapped in his towel, he asked, "Well, got a penny *now*?"

It was easy to amuse Kyle, and he had a lovely smile, Nancy thought. He once told her that he was the first member of his family to leave Utah to go to college. It had strained relations with his parents, but they couldn't argue with Kyle's insistence that the English department at Penn was excellent. The landlady's married daughter had gone to Penn, and Kyle felt sure that had been the deciding factor in his getting the room. That and the fact that when the landlady told him where the nearest Episcopal church was, he told her that he was a Mormon. "At least you have *some* religion," she said. When she interviewed Garrett and described the neighborhood and told him where the Episcopal church was, Kyle had already tipped him; Garrett flipped open a notebook and wrote down the address.

Now, as Garrett and Nancy sat talking as he sketched (Garrett cared so much about drawing that Nancy was sure that he was happy that the weather had turned, so he had an excuse to stay indoors), Kyle was frying chicken downstairs. A few minutes earlier, he had looked in on them and stayed to talk. He complained that he was tired of being known as "the Mormon" to the landlady. Not condescendingly, that he could see— she just said it the way a person might use the Latin name for a plant instead of its common one. He showed them a telephone message from his father she had written down, with "Mormon" printed at the top.

Kyle Brown lived on hydroponic tomatoes, fried chicken, and Pepperidge Farm rolls. On Saturdays, Garrett and Nancy ate with him. They contributed apple cider—smoky, with a smell you could taste; the last pressing of the season—and sometimes turnovers from the corner bakery. Above the sputtering chicken Nancy could hear Kyle singing now, in his strong baritone: "The truth is, I *nev*-er left you . . ."

"Sit still," Garrett said, looking up from his sketchbook. "Don't you know your role in life?"

Nancy cupped her hands below her breasts, turned her head to the side, and pursed her lips.

"Don't do that," he said, throwing the crayon stub. "Don't put yourself down, even as a joke."

"Oh, don't analyze everything so seriously," she said, hopping off the window seat and picking up the Conté crayon. She threw it back to him. He caught it one-handed. He was the second person she had ever slept with. The other one, much to her embarrassment now, had been a deliberate experiment.

"Tell your shrink that your actions don't mean anything," he said.

"You hate it that I go to a shrink," she said, watching him bend over the sketchbook again. "Half the world sees a shrink. What are you worried about—that somebody might know something about me you don't know?"

He raised his eyebrows, as he often did when he was concentrating on something in a drawing. "I know a few things he doesn't know," he said.

"It's not a competition," she said.

"*Everything* is a competition. At some very serious, very deep level, every single thing—"

"You already made that joke," she said, sighing.

He stopped drawing and looked over at her in a different way. "I know," he said. "I shouldn't have taken it back. I really do believe that's what exists. One person jockeying for position, another person dodging."

"I can't tell when you're kidding. Now you're kidding, right?"

"No. I'm serious. I just took it back this morning because I could tell I was scaring you."

"Oh. Now are you going to tell me that you're in competition with me?"

"Why do you think I'm kidding?" he said. "It would *kill* me if you got a better grade in any course than I got. And you're so good. When you draw, you make strokes that look as if they were put on the paper with a feather. I'd take your technique away from you if I could. It's just that I know I can't, so I bite my tongue. Really. I envy you so much my heart races. I could never share a studio with you. I wouldn't be able to be in the same room with somebody who can be so patient and so exact at the same time. Compared to you, I might as well be wearing a catcher's mitt when I draw."

Nancy pulled her knees up to her chest and rested her cheek against one of them. She started to laugh.

"Really," he said.

"Okay—*really*," she said, going poker-faced. "I know, darling Garrett. You really do mean it."

"I do," he said.

She stood up. "Then we don't have to share a studio," she said. "But you can't take it back that you said you wanted to marry me." She rubbed her hands through her hair and let one hand linger to massage her neck. Her body was cold from sitting on the window seat. Clasping her legs, she had realized that the thigh muscles ached.

"Maybe all that envy and anxiety has to be burnt away with constant passion," she said. "I mean—I really, *really* mean that." She smiled. "Really," she said. "Maybe you just want to give in to it—like scratching a mosquito bite until it's so sore you cry."

They were within seconds of touching each other, but just at the moment when she was about to step toward him they heard the old oak stairs creaking beneath Kyle's feet.

"This will come as no surprise to you," Kyle said, standing in the doorway, "but I'm checking to make sure that you know you're invited to dinner. I provide the chicken, sliced tomatoes, and bread—right? You bring dessert and something to drink."

Even in her disappointment, Nancy could smile at him. Of course he knew that he had stumbled into something. Probably he wanted to turn and run back down the stairs. It wasn't easy to be the younger extra person in a threesome. When she raised her head, Garrett caught her eye, and in that moment they both knew how embarrassed Kyle must be. His need for them was never masked as well as he thought. The two of them, clearly lovers, were forgoing candlelight and deliberately bumped knees and the intimacy of holding glasses to each other's lips in order to have dinner with him. Kyle had once told Nancy, on one of their late-fall walks, that one of his worst fears had always been that someone might be able to read his mind. It was clear to her that he had fantasies about them. At the time, Nancy had tried to pass it off lightly; she told him that when she was drawing she always sensed the model's bones and muscles, and what she did was stroke a soft surface over them until a body took form.

Kyle wanted to stay close to them—meant to stay close—but time passed, and after they all had moved several times he lost track of them. He knew nothing of Nancy Niles's life, had no idea that in October 1985 she was out trick-or-treating with Garrett and their two-year-old child, Fraser, who was dressed up as a goblin for his first real Halloween. A plastic orange pumpkin, lit by batteries, bobbed in front of her as she walked a few steps ahead of them. She was dressed in a skeleton costume, but she might have been an angel, beaming salvation into the depths of the mines. Where she lived—their part of Providence, Rhode Island—was as grim and dark as an underground labyrinth.

It was ironic that men thought she could lead the way for them, because Nancy had realized all along that she had little sense of direction. She felt isolated, angry at herself for not pursuing her career as an artist, for no longer being in love. It would have surprised her to know that in a moment of crisis, late that night, in Warrenton, Virginia, when leaves, like shadows on an X ray, suddenly flew up and obscured his vision and his car went into a skid, Kyle Brown would see her again, in a vision. *Nancy Niles!* he thought, in that instant of fear and shock.

There she was, for a split second—her face, ghostly pale under the gas-station lights, metamorphosed into brightness. In a flash, she was again the embodiment of beauty to him. As his car spun in a widening circle and then came to rest with its back wheels on an embankment, Nancy Niles the skeleton was walking slowly down the sidewalk. Leaves flew past her like footsteps, quickly descending the stairs.

WHERE YOU'LL FIND ME

Friends keep calling my broken arm a broken wing. It's the left arm, now folded against my chest and kept in place with a blue scarf sling that is knotted behind my neck, and it weighs too much ever to have been winglike. The accident happened when I ran for a bus. I tried to stop it from pulling away by shaking my shopping bags like maracas in the air, and that's when I slipped on the ice and went down.

So I took the train from New York City to Saratoga yesterday, instead of driving. I had the perfect excuse not to go to Saratoga to visit my brother at all, but once I had geared up for it I decided to go through with the trip and avoid guilt. It isn't Howard I mind but his wife's two children—a girl of eleven and a boy of three. Becky either pays no attention to her brother, Todd, or else she tortures him. Last winter she used to taunt him by stalking around the house on his heels, clomping close behind him wherever he went, which made him run and scream at the same time. Sophie did not intervene until both children became hysterical and we could no longer shout over their voices. "I think I like it that they're physical," she said. "Maybe if they enact some of their hostility like this, they won't grow up with the habit of getting what they want by playing mind games with other people." It seems to me that they will not ever grow up but will burn out like meteors.

Howard has finally found what he wants: the opposite of domestic tranquillity. For six years, he lived in Oregon with a pale, passive woman. On the rebound, he married an even paler premed student named Francine. That marriage lasted less than a year, and then, on a blind date in Los Angeles, he met Sophie, whose husband was away on a business trip to Denmark just then. In no time, Sophie and her daughter and infant son moved in with him, to the studio apartment in

Laguna Beach he was sharing with a screenwriter. The two men had been working on a script about Medgar Evers, but when Sophie and the children moved in they switched to writing a screenplay about what happens when a man meets a married woman with two children on a blind date and the three of them move in with him and his friend. Then Howard's collaborator got engaged and moved out, and the screenplay was abandoned. Howard accepted a last-minute invitation to teach writing at an upstate college in New York, and within a week they were all ensconced in a drafty Victorian house in Saratoga. Sophie's husband had begun divorce proceedings before she moved in with Howard, but eventually he agreed not to sue for custody of Becky and Todd in exchange for child-support payments that were less than half of what his lawyer thought he would have to pay. Now he sends the children enormous stuffed animals that they have little or no interest in, with notes that say, "Put this in Mom's zoo." A stuffed toy every month or so—giraffes, a life-size German shepherd, an overstuffed standing bear—and, every time, the same note.

The bear stands in one corner of the kitchen, and people have gotten in the habit of pinning notes to it—reminders to buy milk or get the oil changed in the car. Wraparound sunglasses have been added. Scarves and jackets are sometimes draped on its arms. Sometimes the stuffed German shepherd is brought over and propped up with its paws placed on the bear's haunch, imploring it.

Right now, I'm in the kitchen with the bear. I've just turned up the thermostat—the first one up in the morning is supposed to do that—and am dunking a tea bag in a mug of hot water. For some reason, it's impossible for me to make tea with loose tea and the tea ball unless I have help. The only tea bag I could find was Emperor's Choice.

I sit in one of the kitchen chairs to drink the tea. The chair seems to stick to me, even though I have on thermal long johns and a long flannel nightgown. The chairs are plastic, very 1950s, patterned with shapes that look sometimes geometric, sometimes almost human. Little things like malformed hands reach out toward triangles and squares. I asked. Howard and Sophie got the kitchen set at an auction, for thirty dollars. They thought it was funny. The house itself is not funny. It has four fireplaces, wide-board floors, and high, dusty ceilings. They bought it with his share of an inheritance that came to us when our grandfather died. Sophie's contribution to restoring the house has been transforming the baseboards into *faux marbre*. How effective this is has to do with how stoned she is when she starts. Sometimes the baseboards look like clotted versions of the kitchen-chair pattern, instead of marble. Sophie considers what she calls "parenting" to be a full-time job. When they first moved to Saratoga, she used to give piano lessons. Now she ignores the children and paints the baseboards.

And who am I to stand in judgment? I am a thirty-eight-year-old woman, out of a job, on tenuous enough footing with her sometime lover that she can imagine crashing emotionally as easily as she did on the ice. It may be true, as my lover, Lance, says, that having money is not good for the soul. Money that is given to you, that is. He is a lawyer who also has money, but it is money he earned and parlayed into more money by investing in real estate. An herb farm is part of this real estate. Boxes of herbs keep turning up at Lance's office—herbs in foil, herbs in plastic bags, dried herbs wrapped in cones of newspaper. He crumbles them over omelettes, roasts, vegetables. He is opposed to salt. He insists herbs are more healthful.

And who am I to claim to love a man when I am skeptical even about his use of herbs? I am embarrassed to be unemployed. I am insecure enough to stay with someone because of the look that sometimes comes into his eyes when he makes love to me. I am a person who secretly shakes on salt in the kitchen, then comes out with her plate, smiling, as basil is crumbled over the tomatoes.

Sometimes, in our bed, his fingers smell of rosemary or tarragon. Strong smells. Sour smells. Whatever Shakespeare says, or whatever is written in *Culpeper's Complete Herbal*, I cannot imagine that herbs have anything to do with love. But many brides-to-be come to the herb farm and buy branches of herbs to stick in their bouquets. They anoint their wrists with herbal extracts, to smell mysterious. They believe that herbs bring them luck. These days, they want tubs of rosemary in their houses, not ficus trees. "I got in right on the cusp of the new world," Lance says. He isn't kidding.

For the Christmas party tonight, there are cherry tomatoes halved and stuffed with peaks of cheese, mushrooms stuffed with pureed tomatoes, tomatoes stuffed with chopped mushrooms, and mushrooms stuffed with cheese. Sophie is laughing in the kitchen. "No one's going to notice," she mutters. "No one's going to say anything."

"Why don't we put out some nuts?" Howard says.

"Nuts are so conventional. This is funny," Sophie says, squirting more soft cheese out of a pastry tube.

"Last year we had mistletoe and mulled cider."

"Last year we lost our sense of humor. What happened that we got all hyped up? We even ran out on Christmas Eve to cut a tree—"

"The kids," Howard says.

"That's right," she says. "The kids were crying. They were feeling competitive with the other kids, or something."

"Becky was crying. Todd was too young to cry about that," Howard says.

"Why are we talking about tears?" Sophie says. "We can talk about tears when it's not the season to be jolly. Everybody's going to come in tonight and love the wreaths on the picture hooks and think this food is so *festive*."

"We invited a new Indian guy from the philosophy department," Howard says. "American Indian—not an Indian from India."

"If we want, we can watch the tapes of *Jewel in the Crown*," Sophie says.

"I'm feeling really depressed," Howard says, backing up to the counter and sliding down until he rests on his elbows. His tennis shoes are wet. He never takes off his wet shoes, and he never gets colds.

"Try one of those mushrooms," Sophie says. "They'll be better when they're cooked, though."

"What's wrong with me?" Howard says. It's almost the first time he's looked at me since I arrived. I've been trying not to register my boredom and my frustration with Sophie's prattle.

"Maybe we should get a tree," I say.

"I don't think it's Christmas that's making me feel this way," Howard says.

"Well, snap out of it," Sophie says. "You can open one of your presents early, if you want to."

"No, no," Howard says, "it isn't Christmas." He hands a plate to Sophie, who has begun to stack the dishwasher. "I've been worrying that you're in a lot of pain and you just aren't saying so," he says to me.

"It's just uncomfortable," I say.

"I know, but do you keep going over what happened, in your mind? When you fell, or in the emergency room, or anything?"

"I had a dream last night about the ballerinas at Victoria Pool," I say. "It was like Victoria Pool was a stage set instead of a real place, and tall, thin ballerinas kept parading in and twirling and pirouetting. I was envying their being able to touch their fingertips together over their heads."

Howard opens the top level of the dishwasher and Sophie begins to hand him the rinsed glasses.

"You just told a little story," Howard says. "You didn't really answer the question."

"I don't keep going over it in my mind," I say.

"So you're repressing it," he says.

"Mom," Becky says, walking into the kitchen, "is it okay if Deirdre comes to the party tonight if her dad doesn't drive here to pick her up this weekend?"

"I thought her father was in the hospital," Sophie says.

"Yeah, he was. But he got out. He called and said that it was going to snow up north, though, so he wasn't sure if he could come."

"Of course she can come," Sophie says.

"And you know what?" Becky says.

"Say hello to people when you come into a room," Sophie says. "At least make eye contact or smile or something."

"I'm not Miss America on the runway, Mom. I'm just walking into the kitchen."

"You have to acknowledge people's existence," Sophie says. "Haven't we talked about this?"

"Oh, hel-*lo*," Becky says, curtsying by pulling out the sides of an imaginary skirt. She has on purple sweatpants. She turns toward me and pulls the fabric away from her hipbones. "Oh, hello, as if we've never met," she says.

"Your aunt here doesn't want to be in the middle of this," Howard says. "She's got enough trouble."

"Get back on track," Sophie says to Becky. "What did you want to say to me?"

"You know what you do, Mom?" Becky says. "You make an issue of something and then it's like when I speak it's a big thing. Everybody's listening to me."

Sophie closes the door to the dishwasher.

"Did you want to speak to me privately?" she says.

"Nooo," Becky says, sitting in the chair across from me and sighing. "I was just going to say—and now it's a big deal—I was going to say that Deirdre just found out that that guy she was writing all year is in *prison*. He was in prison all the time, but she didn't know what the P.O. box meant."

"What's she going to do?" Howard says.

"She's going to write and ask him all about prison," Becky says.

"That's good," Howard says. "That cheers me up to hear that. The guy probably agonized about whether to tell her or not. He probably thought she'd hot-potato him."

"Lots of decent people go to prison," Becky says.

"That's ridiculous," Sophie says. "You can't generalize about convicts any more than you can generalize about the rest of humanity."

"So?" Becky says. "If somebody in the rest of humanity had something to hide, he'd hide it, too, wouldn't he?"

"Let's go get a tree," Howard says. "We'll get a tree."

"Somebody got hit on the highway carrying a tree home," Becky says. "Really."

"You really do have your ear to the ground in this town," Sophie says. "You kids could be the town crier. I know everything before the paper comes."

"It happened yesterday," Becky says.

"Christ," Howard says. "We're talking about crying, we're talking about death." He is leaning against the counter again.

"We are not," Sophie says, walking in front of him to open the refrigerator door. She puts a plate of stuffed tomatoes inside. "In your typical fashion, you've singled out two observations out of a lot that have been made, and—"

"I woke up thinking about Dennis Bidou last night," Howard says to me. "Remember Dennis Bidou, who used to taunt you? Dad put me up to having it out with him, and he backed down after that. But I was always afraid he'd come after me. I went around for years pretending not to cringe when he came near me. And then, you know, one time I was out on a date and we ran out of gas, and as I was walking to get a can of gas a car pulled up alongside me and Dennis Bidou leaned out the window. He was surprised that it was me and I was surprised that it was him. He asked me what happened and I said I ran out of gas. He said, 'Tough shit, I guess,' but a girl was driving and she gave him a hard time. She stopped the car and insisted that I get in the back and they'd take me to the gas station. He didn't say one word to me the whole way there. I remembered the way he looked in the car when I found out he was killed in Nam—the back of his head on that ramrod-straight body, and a black collar or some dark-colored collar pulled up to his hair-line." Howard makes a horizontal motion with four fingers, thumb folded under, in the air beside his ear.

"Now you're trying to depress everybody," Sophie says.

"I'm willing to cheer up. I'm going to cheer up before tonight. I'm going up to that Lions Club lot on Main Street and get a tree. Anybody coming with me?"

"I'm going over to Deirdre's," Becky says.

"I'll come with you, if you think my advice is needed," I say.

"For fun," Howard says, bouncing on his toes. "For fun—not advice."

He gets my red winter coat out of the closet, and I back into it, putting in my good arm. Then he takes a diaper pin off the lapel and pins the other side of the coat to the top of my shoulder, easing the pin through my sweater. Then he puts Sophie's poncho over my head. This is the system, because I am always cold. Actually, Sophie devised the system. I stand there while Howard puts on his leather jacket. I feel like a bird with a cloth draped over its cage for the night. This makes me feel sorry for myself, and then I *do* think of my arm as a broken wing, and suddenly everything seems so sad that I feel my eyes well up with tears. I sniff a couple of times. And Howard faced down Dennis Bidou, for my sake! My brother! But he really did it because my father told him to. Whatever my father told him to do he did. He drew the line only at smothering my father in the hospital when he asked him to. That is the only time I know of that he ignored my father's wishes.

"Get one that's tall enough," Sophie says. "And don't get one of those trees that look like a cactus. Get one with long needles that swoops."

"Swoops?" Howard says, turning in the hallway.

"Something with some fluidity," she says, bending her knees and making a sweeping motion with her arm. "You know—something beautiful."

Before the guests arrive, a neighbor woman has brought Todd back from his play group and he is ready for bed, and the tree has been decorated with a few dozen Christmas balls and some stars cut out of typing paper, with paper-clip hangers stuck through one point. The smaller animals in the stuffed-toy menagerie—certainly not the bear—are under the tree, approximating the animals at the manger. The manger is a roasting pan, with a green dinosaur inside.

"How many of these people who're coming do I know?" I say.

"You know . . . you know . . ." Howard is gnawing his lip. He takes another sip of wine, looks puzzled. "Well, you know Koenig," he says. "Koenig got married. You'll like his wife. They're coming separately, because he's coming straight from work. You know the Miners. You know—you'll really like Lightfoot, the new guy in the philosophy department. Don't rush to tell him that you're tied up with somebody. He's a nice guy, and he deserves a chance."

"I don't think I'm tied up with anybody," I say.

"Have a drink—you'll feel better," Howard says. "Honest to God. I was getting depressed this afternoon. When the light starts to sink so early, I never can figure out what I'm responding to. I gray over, like the afternoon, you know?"

"Okay, I'll have a drink," I say.

"The very fat man who's coming is in A.A.," Howard says, taking a glass off the bookshelf and pouring some wine into it. "These were just washed yesterday," he says. He hands me the glass of wine. "The fat guy's name is Dwight Kule. The Jansons, who are also coming, introduced us to him. He's a bachelor. Used to live in the Apple. Mystery man. Nobody knows. He's got a computer terminal in his house that's hooked up to some mysterious office in New York. Tells funny jokes. They come at him all day over the computer."

"Who are the Jansons?"

"You met her. The woman whose lover broke into the house and did caricatures of her and her husband all over the walls after she broke off with him. One amazing artist, from what I heard. You know about that, right?"

"No," I say, smiling. "What does she look like?"

"You met her at the races with us. Tall. Red hair."

"Oh, that woman. Why didn't you say so?"

"I told you about the lover, right?"

"I didn't know she had a lover."

"Well, fortunately she *had* told her husband, and they'd decided to patch it up, so when they came home and saw the walls—I mean, I get the idea that it was rather graphic. Not like stumbling upon hieroglyphics in a cave or something. Husband told it as a story on himself: going down to the paint store and buying the darkest can of blue paint they had to do the painting-over, because he wanted it done with—none of this three-coats stuff." Howard has another sip of wine. "You haven't met her husband," he says. "He's an anesthesiologist."

"What did her lover do?"

"He ran the music store. He left town."

"Where did he go?"

"Montpelier."

"How do you find all this stuff out?"

"Ask. Get told," Howard says. "Then he was cleaning his gun in Montpelier the other day, and it went off and he shot himself in the foot. Didn't do any real damage, though."

"It's hard to think of anything like that as poetic justice," I say. "So are the Jansons happy again?"

"I don't know. We don't see much of them," Howard says. "We're not really involved in any social whirl, you know. You only visit during the holidays, and that's when we give the annual party."

"Oh, hel-*lo*," Becky says, sweeping into the living room from the front door, bringing the cold and her girlfriend Deirdre in with her. Deirdre is giggling, head averted. "My friends! My wonderful friends!"

Becky says, trotting past, hand waving madly. She stops in the doorway, and Deirdre collides with her. Deirdre puts her hand up to her mouth to muffle a yelp, then bolts past Becky into the kitchen.

"I can remember being that age," I say.

"I don't think I was ever that stupid," Howard says.

"A different thing happens with girls. Boys don't talk to each other all the time in quite the same intense way, do they? I mean, I can remember when it seemed that I never talked but that I was always *confiding* something."

"Confide something in me," Howard says, coming back from flipping the Bach on the stereo.

"Girls just talk that way to other girls," I say, realizing he's serious.

"Gidon Kremer," Howard says, clamping his hand over his heart. "God—tell me that isn't beautiful."

"How did you find out so much about classical music?" I say. "By asking and getting told?"

"In New York," he says. "Before I moved here. Before L.A., even. I just started buying records and asking around. Half the city is an unofficial guide to classical music. You can find out a lot in New York." He pours more wine into his glass. "Come on," he says. "Confide something in me."

In the kitchen, one of the girls turns on the radio, and rock and roll, played low, crosses paths with Bach's violin. The music goes lower still. Deirdre and Becky are laughing.

I take a drink, sigh, and nod at Howard. "When I was in San Francisco last June to see my friend Susan, I got in a night before I said I would, and she wasn't in town," I say. "I was going to surprise her, and she was the one who surprised me. It was no big deal. I was tired from the flight and by the time I got there I was happy to have the excuse to check into a hotel, because if she'd been there we'd have talked all night. Acting like Becky with Deirdre, right?"

Howard rolls his eyes and nods.

"So I went to a hotel and checked in and took a bath, and suddenly I got my second wind and I thought what the hell, why not go to the restaurant right next to the hotel—or in the hotel, I guess it was—and have a great dinner, since it was supposed to be such a great place."

"What restaurant?"

"L'Étoile."

"Yeah," he says. "What happened?"

"I'm telling you what happened. You have to be patient. Girls always know to be patient with other girls."

He nods yes again.

"They were very nice to me. It was about three-quarters full. They put me at a table, and the minute I sat down I looked up and there was a man on a banquette across the room from me. He was looking at me, and I was looking at him, and it was almost impossible not to keep eye contact. It just hit both of us, obviously. And almost on the other side of the curve of the banquette was a woman, who wasn't terribly attractive. She had on a wedding ring. He didn't. They were eating in silence. I had to force myself to look somewhere else, but when I did look up he'd look up, or he'd already be looking up. At some point he left the table. I saw that in my peripheral vision, when I had my head turned to hear a conversation on my right and I was chewing my food. Then after a while he paid the check and the two of them left. She walked ahead of him, and he didn't seem to be with her. I mean, he walked quite far behind her. But naturally he didn't turn his head. And after they left I thought, That's amazing. It was really like kinetic energy. Just wham. So I had coffee, and then I paid my check, and when I was leaving I was walking up the steep steps to the street and the waiter came up behind me and said, 'Excuse me. I don't know what I should do, but I didn't want to embarrass you in the restaurant. The gentleman left this for you on his way out.' And he handed me an envelope. I was pretty taken aback, but I just said, 'Thank you,' and continued up the steps, and when I got outside I looked around. He wasn't there, naturally. So I opened the envelope, and his business card was inside. He was one of the partners in a law firm. And underneath his name he had written, 'Who are you? Please call.' "

Howard is smiling.

"So I put it in my purse and I walked for a few blocks, and I thought, Well, what for, really? Some man in San Francisco? For what? A one-night stand? I went back to the hotel, and when I walked in the man behind the desk stood up and said, 'Excuse me. Were you just eating dinner?' and I said, 'A few minutes ago,' and he said, 'Someone left this for you.' It was a hotel envelope. In the elevator on the way to my room, I opened it, and it was the same business card, with 'Please call' written on it."

"I hope you called," Howard says.

"I decided to sleep on it. And in the morning I decided not to. But I kept the card. And then at the end of August I was walking in the East Village, and a couple obviously from out of town were walking in front of me, and a punk kid got up off the stoop where he was sitting and said to them, 'Hey—I want my picture taken with you.' I went into a store, and when I came out the couple and the punk kid were all laughing together, holding these Polaroid snaps that another punk had taken. It was a joke, not a scam. The man gave the kid a dollar for one of the pictures, and they walked off, and the punk sat back down on the stoop. So I walked back to where he was sitting, and I said, 'Could you do me a real favor? Could I have my picture taken with you, too?' "

"What?" Howard says. The violin is soaring. He gets up and turns the music down a notch. He looks over his shoulder. "Yeah?" he says.

"The kid wanted to know why I wanted it, and I told him because it would upset my boyfriend. So he said yeah—his face lit up when I said that—but that he really would appreciate two bucks for more film. So I gave it to him, and then he put his arm around me and really mugged for the camera. He was like a human boa constrictor around my neck, and he did a Mick Jagger pout. I couldn't believe how well the picture came out. And that night, on the white part on the bottom I wrote, 'I'm somebody whose name you still don't know. Are you going to find me?' and I put it in an envelope and mailed it to him in San Francisco. I don't know why I did it. I mean, it doesn't seem like something I'd ever do, you know?"

"But how will he find you?" Howard says.

"I've still got his card," I say, shrugging my good shoulder toward my purse on the floor.

"You don't know what you're going to do?" Howard says.

"I haven't thought about it in months."

"How is that possible?"

"How is it possible that somebody can go into a restaurant and be hit by lightning and the other person is, too? It's like a bad movie or something."

"Of course it can happen," Howard says. "Seriously, what are you going to do?"

"Let some time pass. Maybe send him something he can follow up on if he still wants to."

"That's an amazing story," Howard says.

"Sometimes—well, I hadn't thought about it in a while, but at the end of summer, after I mailed the picture, I'd be walking along or doing whatever I was doing and this feeling would come over me that he was thinking about me."

Howard looks at me strangely. "He probably was," he says. "He doesn't know how to get in touch with you."

"You used to be a screenwriter. What should he do?"

"Couldn't he figure out from the background that it was the Village?"

"I'm not sure."

"If he could, he could put an ad in the *Voice*."

"I think it was just a car in the background."

"Then you've got to give him something else," Howard says.

"For what? You want your sister to have a one-night stand?"

"You make him sound awfully attractive," Howard says.

"Yeah, but what if he's a rat? It could be argued that he was just cocky, and that he was pretty sure that I'd respond. Don't you think?"

"I think you should get in touch with him. Do it in some amusing way if you want, but I wouldn't let him slip away."

"I never had him. And from the looks of it he has a wife."

"You don't know that."

"No," I say. "I guess I don't know."

"Do it," Howard says. "I think you need this," and when he speaks he whispers—just what a girl would do. He nods his head yes. "Do it," he whispers again. Then he turns his head abruptly, to see what I am staring at. It is Sophie, wrapped in a towel after her bath, trailing the long cord of the extension phone with her.

"It's Lance," she whispers, her hand over the mouthpiece. "He says he's going to come to the party after all."

I look at her dumbly, surprised. I'd almost forgotten that Lance knew I was here. He's only been here once with me, and it was clear that he didn't like Howard and Sophie. Why would he suddenly decide to come to the party?

She shrugs, hand still over the mouthpiece. "Come here," she whispers.

I get up and start toward the phone. "If it's not an awful imposition," she says, "maybe he could bring Deirdre's father with him. He lives just around the corner from you in the city."

"Deirdre's father?" I say.

"Here," she whispers. "He'll hang up."

"Hi, Lance," I say, talking into the phone. My voice sounds high, false.

"I miss you," Lance says. "I've got to get out of the city. I invited myself. I assume since it's an annual invitation it's all right, right?"

"Oh, of course," I say. "Can you just hold on for one second?"

"Sure," he says.

I cover the mouthpiece again. Sophie is still standing next to me.

"I was talking to Deirdre's mother in the bathroom," Sophie whispers. "She says that her ex-husband's not really able to drive yet, and that Deirdre has been crying all day. If he could just give him a lift, they could take the train back, but—"

"Lance? This is sort of crazy, and I don't quite understand the logistics, but I'm going to put Sophie on. We need for you to do us a favor."

"Anything," he says. "As long as it's not about Mrs. Joan Wilde-Younge's revision of a revision of a revision of a spiteful will."

I hand the phone to Sophie. "Lance?" she says. "You're about to make a new friend. Be very nice to him, because he just had his gall-bladder out, and he's got about as much strength as seaweed. He lives on Seventy-ninth Street."

I am in the car with Howard, huddled in my coat and the poncho. We are on what seems like an ironic mission. We are going to the 7-Eleven to get ice. The moon is shining brightly, and patches of snow shine like stepping stones in the field on my side of the car. Howard puts on his directional signal suddenly and turns, and I look over my shoulder to make sure we're not going to be hit from behind.

"Sorry," he says. "My mind was wandering. Not that it's the best-marked road to begin with."

Miles Davis is on the tape deck—the very quiet kind of Miles Davis.

"We've got a second for a detour," he says.

"Why are we detouring?"

"Just for a second," Howard says.

"It's freezing," I say, dropping my chin to speak the words so my throat will warm up for a second.

"What you said about kinetic energy made me think about doing this," Howard says. "You can confide in me and I can confide in you, right?"

"What are you talking about?"

"This," he says, turning onto property marked NO TRESPASSING. The road is quite rutted where he turns onto it, but as it begins to weave up the hill it smooths out a little. He is driving with both hands gripping the wheel hard, sitting forward in the seat as if the extra inch, plus the brights, will help him see more clearly. The road levels off, and to our right is a pond. It is not frozen, but ice clings to the sides, like scum in an aquarium. Howard clicks out the tape, and we sit there in the cold and silence. He turns off the ignition.

"There was a dog here last week," he says.

I look at him.

"Lots of dogs in the country, right?" he says.

"What are we doing here?" I say, drawing up my knees.

"I fell in love with somebody," he says.

I had been looking at the water, but when he spoke I turned and looked at him again.

"I didn't think she'd be here," he says quietly. "I didn't even really think that the dog would be here. I just felt drawn to the place, I guess—that's all. I wanted to see if I could get some of that feeling back if I came here. You'd get it back if you called that man, or wrote him. It was real. I could tell when you were talking to me that it was real."

"Howard, did you say that you fell in love with somebody? When?"

"A few weeks ago. The semester's over. She's graduating. She's gone in January. A graduate student—like that? A twenty-two-year-old kid. One of my pal Lightfoot's philosophy students." Howard lets go of the wheel. When he turned the ignition off, he had continued to grip the wheel. Now his hands are on his thighs. We both seem to be examining his hands. At least, I am looking at his hands so I do not stare into his face, and he has dropped his eyes.

"It was all pretty crazy," he says. "There was so much passion, so fast. Maybe I'm kidding myself, but I don't think I let on to her how much I cared. She saw that I cared, but she . . . she didn't know my heart kept stopping, you know? We drove out here one day and had a picnic in the car—it would have been your nightmare picnic, it was so cold—and a dog came wandering up to the car. Big dog. Right over there."

I look out my window, almost expecting that the dog may still be there.

"There were three freezing picnics. This dog turned up at the last one. She liked the dog—it looked like a mutt, with maybe a lot of golden retriever mixed in. I thought it was inviting trouble for us to open the car door, because it didn't look like a particularly friendly dog. But she was right and I was wrong. Her name is Robin, by the way. The minute she opened the door, the dog wagged its tail. We took a walk with it." He juts his chin forward. "Up that path there," he says. "We threw rocks for it. A sure crowd pleaser with your average lost-in-the-woods American dog, right? I started kidding around, calling the dog Spot. When we were back at the car, Robin patted its head and closed the car door, and it backed off, looking very sad. Like we were really ruining its day, to leave. As I was pulling out, she rolled down the window and said, 'Goodbye, Rover,' and I swear its face came alive. I think his name really was Rover."

"What did you do?" I say.

"You mean about the dog, or about the two of us?"

I shake my head. I don't know which I mean.

"I backed out, and the dog let us go. It just stood there. I got to look at it in the rearview mirror until the road dipped and it was out of sight. Robin didn't look back."

"What are you going to do?"

"Get ice," he says, starting the ignition. "But that isn't what you meant, either, is it?"

He backs up, and as we swing around toward our own tire tracks I turn my head again, but there is no dog there, watching us in the moonlight.

Back at the house, as Howard goes in front of me up the flagstone pathway, I walk slower than I usually do in the cold, trying to give myself time to puzzle out what he makes me think of just then. It comes to me at the moment when my attention is diverted by a patch of ice I'm terrified of slipping on. He reminds me of that courthouse figure—I don't know what it's called—the statue of a blindfolded woman holding the scales of justice. Bag of ice in the left hand, bag of ice in the right—but there's no blindfold. The door is suddenly opened, and what Howard and I see before us is Koenig, his customary bandanna tied around his head, smiling welcome, and behind him, in the glare of the already begun party, the woman with red hair holding Todd, who clutches his green dinosaur in one hand and rubs his sleepy, crying face with the other. Todd makes a lunge—not really toward his father but toward wider spaces—and I'm conscious, all at once, of the cigarette smoke swirling and of the heat of the house, there in the entranceway, that turn the bitter-cold outdoor air silver as it comes flooding in. *Messiah*— Sophie's choice of perfect music for the occasion—isn't playing; someone has put on Judy Garland, and we walk in just as she is singing, "That's where you'll find me." The words hang in the air like smoke.

"Hello, hello, hello, hello," Becky calls, dangling one kneesocked leg over the balcony as Deirdre covers her face and hides behind her. "To both of you, just because you're here, from me to you: a million—a trillion—hellos."

WHAT WAS
MINE

THE WORKING GIRL

This is a story about Jeanette, who is a working girl. She sometimes thinks of herself as a traveler, a seductress, a secret gourmet. She takes a one-week vacation in the summer to see her sister in Michigan, buys lace-edged silk underpants from a mail-order catalog, and has improvised a way, in America, to make crème fraîche, which is useful on so many occasions.

Is this another story in which the author knows the main character all too well?

Let's suppose, for a moment, that the storyteller is actually mystified by Jeanette, and only seems to stand in judgment because words come easily. Let's imagine that in real life there is, or once was, a person named Jeanette, and that from a conversation the storyteller had with her, it could be surmised that Jeanette has a notion of freedom, though the guilty quiver of the mouth when she says "Lake Michigan" is something of a giveaway about how she really feels. If the storyteller is a woman, Jeanette might readily confide that she is a seductress, but if the author is a man, Jeanette will probably keep quiet on that count. Crème fraîche is crème fraîche, and not worth thinking about. But back to the original supposition: Let's say that the storyteller is a woman, and that Jeanette discusses the pros and cons of the working life, calling a spade a spade, and greenbacks greenbacks, and if Jeanette is herself a good storyteller, Lake Michigan sounds exciting, and if she isn't, it doesn't. Let's say that Jeanette talks about the romance in her life, and that the storyteller finds it credible. Even interesting. That there are details: Jeanette's lover makes a photocopy of his hand and drops the piece of paper in her in-box; Jeanette makes a copy of her hand and has her trusted friend Charlie hang it in the men's room, where it is allowed to stay until Jeanette's lover sees it, because it means nothing to anyone else. If the storyteller is lucky, they will exchange presents small enough to be put in a breast pocket or the pocket of a skirt. Also a mini-French-English/English-French dictionary (France is the place they hope to visit); a finger puppet; an ad that is published in the personals column, announcing, by his initials, whom he loves (her), laminated in plastic and made useful as well as romantic by its conversion into a key ring. Let's hope, for the sake of a good story, they are wriggling together in the elevator, sneaking kisses as the bubbles rise in the watercooler, and she is tying his shoelaces together at night, to delay his departure in the morning.

Where is the wife?

In North Dakota or Memphis or Paris, let's say. Let's say she's out of the picture even if she isn't out of the picture.

No no no. Too expedient. The wife has to be there: a presence, even if she's gone off somewhere. There has to be a wife, and she has to be either determined and brave, vile and addicted, or so ordinary that with a mere sentence of description, the reader instantly knows that she is a prototypical wife.

There is a wife. She is a pretty, dark-haired girl who married young, and who won a trip to Paris and is therefore out of town.

Nonsense. *Paris?*

She won a beauty contest.

But she can't be beautiful. She has to be ordinary.

It suddenly becomes apparent that she is extraordinary. She's quite beautiful, and she's in Paris, and although there's no reason to bring this up, the people who sponsored the contest do not know that she's married.

If this is what the wife is like, she'll be more interesting than the subject of the story.

Not if the working girl is believable, and the wife's exit has been made credible.

But we know how that story will end.

How will it end?

It will end badly—which means predictably—because either the beautiful wife will triumph, and then it will be just another such story, or the wife will turn out to be not so interesting after all, and by default the working girl will triumph.

When is the last time you heard of a working girl triumphing?

They do it every day. They are executives, not "working girls."

No, not those. This is about a real working girl. One who gets very little money or vacation time, who periodically rewards herself for life's injustices by buying cream and charging underwear she'll spend a year paying off.

All right, then. What is the story?

Are you sure you want to hear it? Apparently you are already quite shaken, to have found out that the wife, initially ordinary, is in fact extraordinary, and has competed in a beauty pageant and won a trip to Paris.

But this was to be a story about the working girl. What's the scoop with her?

This is just the way the people in the office think: the boss wants to know what's going on in his secretary's mind, the secretary wonders if the mail boy is gay, the mail boy is cruising the elevator operator, and every day the working girl walks into this tense, strange situation. She does it because she needs the money, and also because it's the way things are. It isn't going to be much different wherever she works.

Details. Make the place seem real.

In the winter, when the light disappears early, the office has a very strange aura. The ficus trees cast shadows on the desks. The water in the watercooler looks golden—more like wine than water.

How many people are there?

There are four people typing in the main room, and there are three executives, who share an executive secretary. She sits to the left of the main room.

Which one is the working girl in love with?

Andrew Darby, the most recently hired executive. He has prematurely gray hair, missed two days of work when his dog didn't pull through surgery, and was never drafted because of a deteriorating disk which causes him much pain, though it is difficult to predict when the pain will come on. Once it seemed to coincide with the rising of a bubble in the watercooler. The pain shot up his spine as though mimicking the motion of the bubble.

And he's married?

We just finished discussing his wife.

He's really married, right?

There are no tricks here. He's been married for six years.

Is there more information about his wife?

No. You can find out what the working girl thinks of her, but as far as judging for yourself, you can't, because she is in Paris. What good would it do to overhear a phone conversation between the wife and Andrew? None of us generalizes from phone conversations. Other than that, there's only a postcard. It's a close-up of a column, and she says on the back that she loves and misses him. That if love could be embodied in columns, her love for him would be Corinthian.

That's quite something. What is his reaction to that?

He receives the postcard the same day his ad appears in the personals column. He has it in his pocket when he goes to laminate the ad, punch a hole in the plastic, insert a chain, and make a key ring of it.

Doesn't he go through a bad moment?

A bit of one, but basically he is quite pleased with himself. He and Jeanette are going to lunch together. Over lunch, he gives her the key ring. She is slightly scandalized, amused, and touched. They eat sandwiches. He can't sit in a booth because of his back. They sit at a table.

Ten years later, where is Andrew Darby?

Dead. He dies of complications following surgery. A blood clot that went to his brain.

Why does he have to die?

This is just reporting, now. In point of fact, he dies.

Is Jeanette still in touch with him when he dies?

She's his wife. Married men do leave their wives. Andrew Darby didn't have that rough a go of it. After a while, he and his former wife developed a fairly cordial relationship. She spoke to him on the phone the day he checked into the hospital.

What happened then?

At what point?

When he died.

He saw someone beckoning to him. But that isn't what you mean. What happened is that Jeanette was in a cab on her way to the hospital, and when she got there, one of the nurses was waiting by the elevator. The nurse knew that Jeanette was on her way, because she came at the same time every day. Also, Andrew Darby had been on that same floor, a year or so before, for surgery that was successful. That nurse took care of him then, also. It isn't true that the nurse you have one year will be gone the next.

This isn't a story about the working girl anymore.

It is, because she went right on working. She worked during the marriage and for quite a few years after he died. Toward the end, she wasn't working because she needed the money. She wanted the money, but that's different from needing the money.

What kind of a life did they have together?

He realized that he had something of a problem with alcohol and gave it up. She kept her figure. They went to Bermuda and meant to return, but never did. Every year she reordered perfume from a catalog she had taken from the hotel room in Bermuda. She tried to find another scent that she liked, but always ended up reordering the one she was so pleased with. They didn't have children. He didn't have children with his first wife either, so that by the end it was fairly certain that the doctor had been right, and that the problem was with Andrew, although he never would agree to be tested. He had two dogs in his life, and one cat. Jeanette's Christmas present to him, the year he died, was a Rolex. He gave her a certificate that entitled her to twenty free tanning sessions and a monthly massage.

What was it like when she was a working girl?

Before she met him, or afterward?

Before and afterward.

Before, she often felt gloomy, although she entertained more in those days, and she enjoyed that. Her charge-card bills were always at the limit, and if she had been asked, even at the time, she would have admitted that a sort of overcompensation was taking place. She read more before she met him, but after she met him he read the same books, and it was nice to have someone to discuss them with. She was convinced that she had once broken someone's heart: a man she dated for a couple of years, who inherited his parents' estate when they died. He wanted to marry Jeanette and take care of her. His idea was to commute into New York from the big estate in Connecticut. She felt that she didn't know how to move comfortably into someone else's life. Though she tried to explain carefully, he was bitter and always maintained that she didn't marry him because she didn't like the furniture.

Afterward?

You've already heard some things about afterward. Andrew had a phobia about tollbooths, so when they were driving on the highway, he'd pull onto the shoulder when he saw the sign for a tollbooth, and she'd drive through it. On the Jersey Turnpike, of course, she just kept the wheel. They knew only one couple that they liked equally well— they liked the man as well as they liked the woman, that is. They tended to like the same couples.

What was it like, again, in the office?

The plants and the watercooler.

Besides that.

That's really going back in time. It would seem like a digression at this point.

But what about understanding the life of the working girl?

She turned a corner, and it was fall. With a gigantic intake of breath, her feet lifted off the ground.

Explain.

Nothing miraculous happened, but still things did happen, and life changed. She lost touch with some friends, became quite involved in reading the classics. In Bermuda, swimming, she looked up and saw a boat and remembered very distinctly, and much to her surprise, that the man she had been involved with before Andrew had inherited a collection of ships in bottles from his great-great-grandfather. And that day, as she came out of the water, she cut her foot on something. Whatever it was was as sharp as glass, if it was not glass. And that seemed to sum up something. She was quite shaken. She and Andrew sat in the sand, and the boat passed by, and Andrew thought that it was the pain alone that had upset her.

In the office, when the light dimmed early in the day. In the winter. Before they were together. She must have looked at the shadows on her desk and felt like a person lost in the forest.

If she thought that, she never said it.

Did she confide in Charlie?

To some extent. She and Charlie palled around together before she became involved with Andrew. Afterward, too, a little. She was always consulted when he needed to buy a new tie.

Did Charlie go to the wedding?

There was no wedding. It was a civil ceremony.

Where did they go on their honeymoon?

Paris. He always wanted to see Paris.

But his wife went to Paris.

That was just coincidence, and besides, she wasn't there at the same time. By then she was his ex-wife. Jeanette never knew that his wife had been to Paris.

What things did he not know?

That she once lost two hundred dollars in a cab. That she did a self-examination of her breasts twice a day. She hid her dislike of the dog, which they had gotten at his insistence, from the pound. The dog was a chewer.

When an image of Andrew came to mind, what was it?

Andrew at forty, when she first met him. She felt sorry that he had a mole on his cheekbone, but later came to love it. Sometimes, after his death, the mole would fill the whole world of her dream. At least that is what she thought it was—a gray mass like a mountain, seen from the distance, then closer and closer until it became amorphous and she was awake, gripping the sheet. It was a nightmare, obviously, not a dream. Though she called it a dream.

Who is Berry McKenn?

A woman he had a brief flirtation with. Nothing of importance.

Why do storytellers start to tell one story and then tell another?

Life is a speeding train. Storytellers get derailed too.

What did Andrew see when he conjured up Jeanette?

Her green eyes. That startled look, as if the eyes had a life of their own, and were surprised to be bracketing so long a nose.

What else is there to say about their life together?

There is something of an anecdote about the watercooler. It disappeared once, and it was noticeably absent, as if someone had removed a geyser. The surprise on people's faces when they stared at the empty corner of the corridor was really quite astonishing. Jeanette went to meet Andrew there the day the repairman took it away. They made it a point, several times a day, to meet there as if by accident. One of the other girls who worked there—thinking Charlie was her friend, which he certainly was not: he was Jeanette's friend—had seen the watercooler being removed, and she whispered slyly to Charlie that it would be amusing when Jeanette strolled away from her desk, and Andrew left his office moments later with great purpose in his step and holding his blue pottery mug, because they would be standing in an empty corridor, with their prop gone and their cover blown.

What did Charlie say?

Jeanette asked him that too, when he reported the conversation. "They're in love," he said. "You might not want to think it, but a little thing like that isn't going to be a setback at all." He felt quite triumphant about taking a stand, though there's room for skepticism, of course. What people say is one thing, and what they later report they have said is another.

IN AMALFI

On the rocky beach next to the Cobalto, the boys were painting the boats. In June the tourist season would begin, and the rowboats would be launched, most of them rented by the hour to Americans and Swedes and Germans. The Americans would keep them on the water for five or ten minutes longer than the time for which they had been rented. The Swedes, usually thin and always pale, would know they had begun to burn after half an hour and return the boats early. It was difficult to generalize about the Germans. They were often blamed for the beer bottles that washed ashore, although others pointed out that this wasn't likely, because the Germans were such clean, meticulous people. The young German girls had short, spiky hair and wore earrings that looked like shapes it would be difficult to find the right theorem for in a geometry book. The men were more conventional, wearing socks with their sandals, although when they were on the beach they often wore the sandals barefooted and stuffed the socks in their pockets.

What Christine knew about the tourists came from her very inadequate understanding of Italian. This was the second time she had spent a month in Amalfi, and while few of the people were friendly, it was clear that some of them recognized her. The beachboys talked to her about the tourists, as though she did not belong to that category. Two of them (there were usually six to ten boys at the beach, working on the boats, renting chairs, or throwing a Frisbee) had asked some questions about Andrew. They wanted to know if it was her father who sat upstairs in the bar, at the same table every day, feet resting on the scrollwork of the blue metal railing, writing. Christine said that he was not her father. Then another boy punched his friend and said, "I told you he was her *marito*." She shook her head no. A third boy—probably not much interested in what his friends might find out, anyway—said that his brother-in-law was expanding his business. The brother-in-law was going to rent hang gliders, as well as motorcycles, in June. The first boy who had talked to Christine said to her that hang gliders were like lawn chairs that flew through the air, powered by lawn mowers. Everyone laughed at this. Christine looked up at the sky, which was, as it had been for days, blue and nearly cloudless.

She walked up the steep stairs to the second tier of the beach bar. Three women were having toast and juice. The juice was in tall, thin glasses, and paper dangled from the straw of the woman who had not yet begun to sip her drink. The white paper, angled away, looked like a sail. Her two friends were watching some men who were wading out into the water. They moved forward awkwardly, trying to avoid hurting themselves on the stones. The other woman looked in the opposite direction where, on one of the craggiest cliffs, concrete steps curved like the lip of a calla lily around the round facade of the building that served as the bar and restaurant of the Hotel Luna.

Christine looked at the women's hands. None of them had a wedding ring. She thought then—with increasing embarrassment that she had been embarrassed—that she should have just told the boys on the beach that she and Andrew were divorced. What had happened was that—worse than meaning to be mysterious—she had suddenly feared further questioning if she told the truth; she had not wanted to say that she was a stereotype: the pretty, bright girl who marries her professor. But then, Europeans wouldn't judge that the same way Americans would. And why would she have had to explain what role he occupied in her life at all? All the boys really wanted to know was whether she slept with him now. They were like all questioners in all countries.

It occurred to her that the Europeans—who seemed capable of making wonderful comedies out of situations that were slightly off kilter—might make an interesting film about her relationship with Andrew: running off to Paris to marry him when she was twenty, and losing her nerve; marrying him two years later, in New York; having an abortion; leaving; reuniting with him a few months later at the same hotel that they had gone to on the first trip to Paris in 1968, and then divorcing the summer after their reunion; keeping in touch for fifteen years; and then beginning to vacation together. He had married during that time, was now divorced, and had twin boys who lived with their mother in Michigan.

She had been sitting at Andrew's table, quietly, waiting for him to reach a point where he could stop in his writing. She was accustomed to doing this. It no longer irritated her that for seconds or minutes or even for half an hour, she could be no more real to him than a ghost. She was just about to pull her chair into the shade when he looked up.

He told her, with great amusement, that earlier that morning an English couple with their teenage son had sat at the table nearby, and that the Englishwoman, watching him write, had made him a moral example to her son. She thought that he was a man writing a letter home. She had heard him ordering tea, in English, and—he told Christine again, with even more amusement—assumed that he was writing a letter home. "Can you imagine?" Andrew said. "I'd have to have a hell of an original mind to be scribbling away about a bunch of stones and the Mediterranean. Or, to give her credit, maybe she thought I was just overwrought."

She smiled. For anyone to assume that he liked to communicate about anything that might be even vaguely personal was funny itself, in a mordant way, but the funnier thing was that he was so often thrown by people's quite justifiable misperceptions, yet rarely cracked a smile if something was ludicrous. She had noticed early on that he would almost jump for joy when Alfred Hitchcock did his usual routine of passing briefly through his own film, but when she insisted that he watch a tape of Martin Short going into a frenzy as Ed Grimley on *Saturday Night Live*, he frowned like an archaeologist finding something he had no context for and having to decide, rather quickly, whether it was, say, an icon or petrified cow dung.

She had come to realize that what fascinated her about him was his absolute inadequacy when it came to making small talk. He also did not think of one thing as analogous to another. In fact, he thought of most analogies, metaphors, and similes as small talk. Nothing that caught Diane Arbus's eye ever interested him, but he would open a book of Avedon's photographs and examine a group shot of corporate executives as if he were examining a cross section of a chambered nautilus. When something truly interested him, he had a way of curling his fingers as if he could receive a concept in the palm of his hand.

The day before, Andrew's publisher had cabled to see when the book of essays could be expected. For once he was ahead of schedule with his writing, and the cable actually put him in a better mood. There had been some talk, back in the States, of the publisher's coming from Rome, where he had other business, to Atrani, to spend a few days with them. But just as they were leaving the States, Libya had been bombed, flights were canceled, people abandoned their travel plans. In the cable, the publisher made no mention of coming to Italy. There were few Americans anywhere around them: Libya and Chernobyl had obviously kept away those Americans who might have come before the season began.

Christine looked at the sky, wondering how many hang gliders would be up there during the summer. Icarus came to mind, and Auden's poem about the fall of Icarus that she had studied, years ago, in Andrew's poetry class. It was difficult to remember being that person who sat and listened, although she sometimes remembered how happy she had been to feel, for the first time, that she was part of something. Until she went to college and found out that other people were interested in ideas, she had settled for reading hundreds of books and letting her thoughts about what she read pile up silently. In all the years she spent at college in Middletown, she never ceased to be surprised that real voices argued and agreed and debated almost throughout the night. Sometimes, involved as she was, the talk would nonetheless become mere sound—an abstraction, equivalent to her surprise, when she left the city and lived in the suburbs of Connecticut, that the sounds of cicadas would overlap with the cries of cats in the night, and that the wind would meld animal and insect sounds into some weird, theremin-like music. Andrew was probably attracted to her because, while others were very intelligent and very pretty, they showed their excitement, but she had been so stunned by the larger world and the sudden comradeship that she had soaked it in silently. He mistook her stunned silences for composure and the composure for sophistication. And now, in spite of everything they had been through, apparently she was still something of a mystery to him. Or perhaps the mystery was why he had stayed so attached to her.

They had lunch, and she sipped juice through one of the thin red plastic straws, playing a child's game of sipping until the juice was pulled to the top of the straw, then putting her tongue over the top, gradually releasing the pressure until the sucked-up juice ran back into the glass. She looked over the railing and saw that only a few beachboys were still there, sanding the boats. Another sat at a table on a concrete slab above the beach, eating an ice cream. Although she could not hear it from where she sat, he was probably listening to the jukebox just inside the other café—the only jukebox she knew of that had American music on it.

"You've been flirting with them," Andrew said, biting his roll.

"Don't be ridiculous," she said. "They see me every day. We exchange pleasantries."

"They see me every day and look right through me," he said.

"I'm friendlier than you are. That doesn't mean I'm flirting."

"*They're* flirting," he said.

"Well, then, it's harmless."

"For you, maybe. One of them tried to run me down with his motorcycle."

She had been drinking her juice. She looked up at him.

"I'm not kidding. I dropped the *Herald*," he said.

The archness with which he spoke made her smile. "You're sure he did it on purpose?" she said.

"You love to blame me for not understanding simple things," he said, "and here is a perfect example of understanding a simple thing. I have put two and two together: they flirt with my wife and then, when they see me crossing the street, they gun their motorcycles to double the insult, and then I look not only like an old fool but a coward."

He had spoken in such a rush that he seemed not to realize that he had called her "my wife." She waited to see if it would register, but it did not.

"They are very silly boys," he said, and his obvious petulance made her laugh. How childish—how sweet he was, and how silly, too, to let on that he had been so rattled. He was sitting with his arms crossed, like an Indian chief.

"They all drive like fools," he said.

"All of them?" she said. (Years ago he had said to her, "You find this true of *all* Romantic poets?")

"All of them," he said. "You'd see what they did if you came into town early in the morning. They hide in alleyways on their motorcycles and they roar out when I cross, and this morning, when I was on the traffic island with the *Herald*, one of them bent over the handlebars and hunched up his back like a cat and swerved as if he were going to jump the curb."

She made an effort not to laugh. "As you say, they're silly boys, then," she said.

Much to her surprise, he stood, gathered up his books and tablet, and stalked off, saying over his shoulder, "A lot you care."

She frowned as he walked away, sorry, suddenly, that she had not been more compassionate. If one of the boys had really tried to run him down, of course she cared.

Andrew had walked off so fast that he had forgotten his cane.

She watched the sun sparkling on the water. It was so beautiful that it calmed her, and then she slowly surveyed the Mediterranean. There were a few windsurfers—all very far out—and she counted two canoes and at least six paddleboats. She stared, wondering which would criss-cross first across a stretch of water, and then she turned, having realized that someone was staring at her. It was a young woman, who smiled hesitantly. At another table, her friends were watching her expectantly. With a heavy French accent, but in perfect English, the young woman said, "Excuse me, but if you will be here for just a little while, I wonder if you would do me a favor?"

The woman was squinting in the sun. She was in her late twenties, and she had long, tanned legs. She was wearing white shorts and a green shirt and high heels. The shoes were patterned with grapes and grape leaves. In two seconds, Christine had taken it all in: the elegance, the woman's nice manner—her hopefulness about something.

"Certainly," Christine said. And it was not until the woman slipped the ring off her finger and handed it to her that she realized she had agreed to something before she even knew what it was.

The woman wanted her to wear her ring while she and her companions went boating. They would be gone only half an hour, she said. "My fingers have swollen, and in the cold air on the water they will be small again, and I would spend my whole time being nervous that I would lose my favorite thing." The woman smiled.

It all happened so quickly—and the woman's friends swept her off so fast—that Christine did not really examine the ring until after the giggling and jostling between the woman and her friends stopped, and they had run off, down the steep steps of the Cobalto to the beach below.

The ring was quite amazing. It sparkled so brightly in the sun that Christine was mesmerized. It was like the beginning of a fairy tale, she thought—and imagine: a woman giving a total stranger her ring. It was silver—silver or platinum—with a large opal embedded in a dome. The opal was surrounded by tiny rubies and slightly larger diamonds. It was an antique—no doubt about that. The woman had sensed that she could trust Christine. What a crazy chance to take, with such an obviously expensive ring. Even though she was right, the woman had taken a huge risk. When Christine looked down at the beach, she saw the two men and the beachboy holding the boat steady, and the woman climbing in. Then the men jumped in, shouting something to each other that made all of them laugh, and in only a minute they were quite far from shore. The woman, sitting in back, had her back to the beach.

As he passed, the waiter caught her eye and asked if she wanted anything else.

"*Vino bianco,*" she said. She hardly ever drank, but somehow the ring made her nervous—a little nervous and a little happy—and the whole odd encounter seemed to require something new. A drink seemed just the thing.

She watched the boat grow smaller. The voices had already faded away. It was impossible to believe, she thought, as she watched the boat become smaller and smaller on the sparkling water, that in a world as beautiful as this, one country would drop bombs on another to retaliate against terrorism. That fires would begin in nuclear reactors.

Paddleboats zigzagged over water that was now a little choppier than it had been earlier in the afternoon. A baby was throwing rocks into the water. The baby jumped up and down, squealing approval of his every effort. Christine watched two men in straw hats stop to look at the baby and the baby's mother, close by on the rocks. Around the cliff, going toward the swimming pool chiseled out of a cliff behind the Luna bar and restaurant, the boat that Christine thought held the French people disappeared.

The waiter brought the wine, and she sipped it. Wine and juice were usually cold. Sodas, in cans, were almost always room temperature. The cold wine tasted good. The waiter had brought, as well, half a dozen small crackers on a small silver plate.

She remembered, vaguely, reading a story in college about an American woman in Italy, at the end of the war. The woman was sad and refused to be made happy—or at least that was probably what happened. She could remember a great sense of frustration in the story—a frustration on the character's part that carried over into frustrating the reader. The title of the story wouldn't come to her, but Christine remembered two of the things the woman had demanded: silver candlesticks and a cat.

A speedboat passed, bouncing through white foam. Compared with that boat, the paddleboats—more of them, suddenly, now that the heat of the day was subsiding—seemed to float with no more energy than corks.

The wine Christine had just finished was Episcopio, bottled locally. Very little was exported, so it was almost impossible to find Episcopio in the States. That was what people did: went home and looked at photographs, tried to buy the wine they had enjoyed at the restaurant. But usually it could not be found, and eventually they lost the piece of paper on which the name of the wine had been written.

Christine ordered another glass of wine.

The man she had lived with for several years had given up his job on Wall Street to become a photographer. He had wanted to succeed at photography so much that he had convinced her he would. For years she searched magazines for his name—the tiny photo credit she might see just at the fold. There were always one or two credits a year. There were until recently; in the last couple of years there had been none that she knew of. That same man, she remembered, had always surprised her

by knowing when Groundhog Day was and by being sincerely interested in whether the groundhog saw its shadow when it came out. She
and the man had vacationed in Greece, and although she did not really
believe that he liked retsina any better than she did, it was a part of the
Greek meals he prepared for their friends several times a year.

She was worrying that she might be thought of as a predictable type:
an American woman, no longer young, looking out to sea, a glass of
wine half finished sitting on the table in front of her. Ultimately, she
thought, she was nothing like the American woman in the story—but
then, the argument could be made that all women had something invested in thinking themselves unique.

The man who wanted to be a photographer had turned conversations by asking for her opinion, and then—when she gave her opinion
and he acted surprised and she qualified it by saying that she did not
think her opinion was universal—he would suggest that her insistence
on being thought unrepresentative was really a way of asserting her
superiority over others.

God, she thought, finishing the wine. No wonder I love Andrew.

It was five o'clock now, and shade had spread over the table. The
few umbrellas that had been opened at the beach were collapsed and
removed from the poles and wrapped tightly closed with blue twine.
Two of the beachboys, on the way to the storage area, started a mock
fencing match, jumping nimbly on the rocks, lunging so that one umbrella point touched another. Then one of the boys whipped a Z through
the air and continued on his way. The other turned to look at a tall
blond woman in a flesh-colored bikini, who wore a thin gold chain
around her waist and another chain around her ankle.

Christine looked at her watch, then back at the cliffs beyond which
the rowboat had disappeared. On the road above, a tour bus passed by,
honking to force the cars coming toward it to stop and back up. There
was a tinge of pink to the clouds that had formed near the horizon line.
A paddleboat headed for the beach, and one of the boys started down
the rocks to pull it in. She watched as he waded into the surf and pulled
the boat forward, then held it steady.

In the shade, the ring was lavender-blue. In the sun, it had been
flecked with pink, green, and white. She moved her hand slightly and
could see more colors. It was like looking into the sea, to where the sun
struck stones.

She looked back at the water, half expecting, now, to see the French
people in the rowboat. She saw that the clouds were darker pink.

"I paid the lemon man," Andrew said, coming up behind her. "As
usual, he claimed there were whole sacks of lemons he had left against

the gate, and I played the fool, the way I always do. I told him that we asked for, and received, only one sack of lemons, and that whatever happened to the others was his problem."

Andrew sat down. He looked at her empty wineglass. Or he might have been looking beyond that, out to the water.

"Every week," he sighed, "the same thing. He rings, and I take in a sack of lemons, and he refuses to take the money. Then he comes at the end of the week asking for money for two or three sacks of lemons—only one of which was ever put in my hands. The others never existed." Andrew sighed again. "What do you think he would do if I said, 'But what do you mean, Signor Zito, three sacks of lemons? I must pay you for the *ten* sacks of lemons we received. We have had the most wonderful lemonade. The most remarkable lemon custard. We have baked lemon-meringue pies and mixed our morning orange juice with the juice of fresh-squeezed lemons. Let me give you more money. Let me give you everything I have. Let me pay you anything you want for your wonderful lemons.' "

His tone of voice was cold. Frightening. He was too often upset, and sometimes it frightened her. She clamped her hand over his, and he took a deep breath and stopped talking. She looked at him, and it suddenly seemed clear that what had been charming petulance when he was younger was now a kind of craziness—a craziness he did not even think about containing. Or what if he was right, and things were not as simple as she pretended? What if the boys she spoke to every day really did desire her and wish him harm? What if the person who wrote that story had been right, and Americans really were materialistic—so materialistic that they became paranoid and thought everyone was out to cheat them?

"What's that?" Andrew said. She had been so lost in her confusion that she started when he spoke.

"What?" she said.

"That," he said, and pulled his hand out from under hers.

They were both looking at the opal ring.

"From one of the beachboys," she said.

He frowned. "Are you telling me that ring isn't real?"

She put her hand in her lap. "No," she said. "Obviously it's real. You don't think one of the boys would be crazy enough about me to give me a real ring?"

"I assume I was wrong, and it's a cheap imitation," he said. "No. I am not so stupid that I think one of those boys gave you an expensive ring. Although I do admit the possibility that you bought yourself a ring."

He raised a finger and summoned the waiter. He ordered tea with milk. He looked straight ahead, to the beach. It was now deserted, except for the mother and baby. The baby had stopped throwing stones and was being rocked in its mother's arms. Christine excused herself and walked across the wooden planks to the bar at the back of the Cobalto, where the waiter was ordering tea from the bartender.

"Excuse me," she said quietly. "Do you have a pen and a piece of paper?"

The man behind the bar produced a pencil and handed her a business card. He turned and began to pour boiling water into a teapot.

She wondered whether the man thought that a pen and a pencil were interchangeable, and whether a business card was the same as a piece of paper. Was he being perverse, or did he not understand her request very well? All right, she thought: I'll keep it brief.

As she wrote, she reminded herself that it was a calm sea, and that the woman could not possibly be dead. "I had to leave," she wrote. "There is no phone at the villa we are renting. I will be here tomorrow at ten, with your ring." She signed her name, then handed the card to the bartender. "It's very important," she said. "A woman is going to come in, expecting to find me. A Frenchwoman. If you see someone who's very upset—" She stopped, looking at the puzzled expression on the bartender's face. "Very important," she said again. "The woman had two friends. She's very pretty. She's been out boating." She looked at the card she had given the bartender. He held it, without looking at what she had written. "*Grazie,*" she said.

"*Prego,*" he said. He put the card down by the cash register and then—perhaps because she was looking—did something that struck her as appropriately ironic: he put a lemon on top of the card, to weigh it down.

"*Grazie,*" she said again.

"*Prego,*" he said.

She went back to the table and sat, looking not toward the cliff beyond which the French people's boat had disappeared, but in the other direction, toward Positano. They said little, but during the silence she decided—in the way that tourists are supposed to have epiphanies on vacations, at sunset—that there was such a thing as fate, and that she was fated to be with Andrew.

When he finished his tea, they rose together and went to the bar and paid. She did not think she was imagining that the owner nodded his head twice, and that the second nod was a little conspiratorial signal.

· · ·

From the doors that opened onto the balcony outside their bedroom she could see more of the Mediterranean than from the Cobalto; at this vantage point, high above the Via Torricella, it was almost possible to have a bird's-eye view. From here, the Luna pool was only a dark-blue speck. There was not one boat on the Mediterranean. She heard the warning honking of the bus drivers below and the buzzing sound the motorcycles made. The intermittent noise only made her think how quiet it was most of the time. Often, she could hear the breeze rustling the leaves of the lemon trees.

Andrew was asleep in the room, his breathing as steady as the surf rolling in to shore. He went to bed rather early now, and she often stood on the balcony for a while, before going in to read.

Years ago, when they were first together, she had worn a diamond engagement ring in a Tiffany setting, the diamond held in place by little prongs that rose up and curved against it, from a thin gold band. Now she had no idea what had become of the ring, which she had returned to him, tearfully, in Paris. When they later married, he gave her only a plain gold band. It made her feel suddenly old, to remember things she had not thought about in years—to miss them, and to want them back. She had to stop herself, because her impulse was to go into the bedroom and wake him up and ask him what had become of the ring.

She did go in, but she did not disturb him. Instead, she walked quietly to the bed and sat on the side of it, then reached over and turned off the little bedside lamp. Then she carefully stretched out and pulled the covers over her. She began to breathe in time with his breathing, as she often did, trying to see if, by imitation, she could sink into easy sleep.

With her eyes closed, she remembered movement: the birds sailing between high cliffs, boats on the water. It was possible, standing high up, as she often did in Italy, to actually look down on the birds in their flight: small specks below, slowly swooping from place to place. The tiny boats on the sea seemed no more consequential than sunbeams, glinting on the surface of the water.

Unaccustomed to wearing jewelry, she rubbed the band of the ring on her finger as she began to fall asleep. Although it was not a conscious thought, something was wrong—something about the ring bothered her, like a grain of sand in an oyster.

In time, his breathing changed, and hers did. Calm sleep was now a missed breath—a small sound. They might have been two of the birds she so often thought of, flying separately between cliffs—birds whose movement, which might seem erratic, was always private, and so took them where they wanted to go.

WHAT WAS MINE

I don't remember my father. I have only two photographs of him—one
of two soldiers standing with their arms around each other's shoulders,
their faces even paler than their caps, so that it's difficult to make out
their features; the other of my father in profile, peering down at me
in my crib. In that photograph, he has no discernible expression,
though he does have a rather noble Roman nose and thick hair that
would have been very impressive if it hadn't been clipped so short. On
the back of the picture in profile is written, unaccountably, "Guam,"
while the back of the picture of the soldiers says, "Happy with baby:
5/28/49."

Until I was five or six I had no reason to believe that Herb was not
my uncle. I might have believed it much longer if my mother had not
blurted out the truth one night when I opened her bedroom door and
saw Herb, naked from the waist down, crouched at the foot of the bed,
holding out a bouquet of roses much the way teasing people shake a bis-
cuit in front of a sleeping dog's nose. They had been to a wedding earlier that day, and my mother had caught the nosegay. Herb was tipsy,
but I had no sense of that then. Because I was a clumsy boy, I didn't
wonder about his occasionally knocking into a wall or stepping off a
curb a bit too hard. He was not allowed to drive me anywhere, but I
thought only that my mother was full of arbitrary rules she imposed on
everyone: no more than one hour of TV a day; put Bosco in the glass
first, then the milk.

One of the most distinct memories of my early years is of that night
I opened my mother's door and saw Herb lose his balance and fall forward on the bouquet like a thief clutching bread under his shirt.

"Ethan," my mother said, "I don't know what you are doing in here at a time when you are supposed to be in bed—and without the manners to knock—but I think the time has come to tell you that Herbert and I are very close, but not close in the way family members such as a brother and sister are. Herbert is not your uncle, but you must go on as if he were. Other people should not know this."

Herb had rolled onto his side. As he listened, he began laughing. He threw the crushed bouquet free, and I caught it by taking one step forward and waiting for it to land in my outstretched hand. It was the way Herb had taught me to catch a ball, because I had a tendency to overreact and rush too far forward, too fast. By the time I had caught the bouquet, exactly what my mother said had become a blur: manners, Herbert, not family, don't say anything.

Herb rolled off the bed, stood, and pulled on his pants. I had the clear impression that he was in worse trouble than I was. I think that what he said to me was that his affection for me was just what it always had been, even though he wasn't actually my uncle. I know that my mother threw a pillow at him and told him not to confuse me. Then she looked at me and said, emphatically, that Herb was not a part of our family. After saying that, she became quite flustered and got up and stomped out of the bedroom, slamming the door behind her. Herb gave the door a dismissive wave of the hand. Alone with him, I felt much better. I suppose I had thought that he might vanish—if he was not my uncle, he might suddenly disappear—so that his continued presence was very reassuring.

"Don't worry about it," he said. "The divorce rate is climbing, people are itching to change jobs every five minutes. You wait: Dwight Eisenhower is going to be reevaluated. He won't have the same position in history that he has today." He looked at me. He sat on the side of the bed. "I'm your mother's boyfriend," he said. "She doesn't want to marry me. It doesn't matter. I'm not going anywhere. Just keep it between us that I'm not Uncle Herb."

My mother was tall and blond, the oldest child of a German family that had immigrated to America in the 1920s. Herb was dark haired, the only child of a Lebanese father and his much younger English bride, who had considered even on the eve of her wedding leaving the Church of England to convert to Catholicism and become a nun. In retrospect, I realize that my mother's shyness about her height and her having been indoctrinated to believe that the hope of the future lay in her accomplishing great things, and Herb's self-consciousness about his kinky hair, along with his attempt as a child to negotiate peace between his mother and father, resulted in an odd bond between Herb and my mother: she was drawn to his conciliatory nature, and he was drawn to her no-nonsense attitude. Or perhaps she was drawn to his unusual amber eyes, and he was taken in by her inadvertently sexy, self-conscious girlishness. Maybe he took great pleasure in shocking her, in playing to her secret, more sophisticated desires, and she was secretly amused and gratified that he took it as a given that she was highly competent and did not have to prove herself to him in any way whatsoever.

She worked in a bank. He worked in the automotive section at Sears, Roebuck, and on the weekend he played piano, harmonica, and sometimes tenor sax at a bar off Pennsylvania Avenue called the Merry Mariner. On Saturday nights my mother and I would sit side by side, dressed in our good clothes, in a booth upholstered in blue Naugahyde, behind which dangled nets that were nailed to the wall, studded with starfish, conch shells, sea horses, and clamshells with small painted scenes or decals inside them. I would have to turn sideways and look above my mother to see them. I had to work out a way of seeming to be looking in front of me and listening appreciatively to Uncle Herb while at the very same time rolling my eyes upward to take in those tiny depictions of sunsets, rainbows, and ships sailing through the moonlight. Uncle Herb played a slowish version of "Let Me Call You Sweetheart" on the harmonica as I sipped my cherry Coke with real cherries in it: three, because the waitress liked me. He played "As Time Goes By" on the piano, singing so quietly it seemed he was humming. My mother and I always split the fisherman's platter: four shrimp, one crab cake, and a lobster tail, or sometimes two if the owner wasn't in the kitchen, though my mother often wrapped up the lobster tails and saved them for our Sunday dinner. She would slice them and dish them up over rice, along with the tomato-and-lettuce salad she served almost every night.

Some of Uncle Herb's songs would go out to couples celebrating an anniversary, or to birthday boys, or to women being courted by men who preferred to let Uncle Herb sing the romantic thoughts they hesitated to speak. Once during the evening Herb would dedicate a song to my mother, always referring to her as "my own special someone" and nodding—but never looking directly—toward our booth.

My mother kept the beat to faster tunes by tapping her fingers on the shiny varnished tabletop. During the slow numbers she would slide one finger back and forth against the edge of the table, moving her hand so delicately she might have been testing the blade of a knife. Above her blond curls I would see miniature versions of what I thought must be the most exotic places on earth—so exotic that any small reference to them would quicken the heart of anyone familiar with the mountains of Hawaii or the seas of Bora Bora. My mother smoked cigarettes, so that sometimes I would see these places through fog. When the overhead lights were turned from blue to pink as Uncle Herb played the last set, they would be transformed to the most ideal possible versions of paradise. I was hypnotized by what seemed to me their romantic clarity, as Herb sang a bemused version of "Stormy Weather," then picked up the saxophone for "Green Eyes," and finished, always, with a Billie Holiday song he would play very simply on the piano, without singing. Then the lights went to a dusky red and gradually brightened to a golden light that seemed as stupefying to me as the cloud rising at Los Alamos must have seemed to the observers of Trinity. It allowed people enough light to judge their sobriety, pay the bill, or decide to postpone functioning until later and vanish into the darker reaches of the bar at the back. Uncle Herb never patted me on the shoulder or tousled my cowlick. He usually sank down next to my mother—still bowing slightly to acknowledge the applause—then reached over with the same automatic motion my mother used when she withdrew a cigarette from the pack to run his thumb quickly over my knuckles, as if he were testing a keyboard. If a thunderbolt had left his fingertips, it could not have been more clear: he wanted me to be a piano player.

That plan had to be abandoned when I was thirteen. Or perhaps it did not really have to be abandoned, but at the time I found a convenient excuse to let go of the idea. One day, as my mother rounded a curve in the rain, the car skidded into a telephone pole. As the windshield splattered into cubes of glass, my wrist was broken and my shoulder dislocated. My mother was not hurt at all, though when she called Herb at work she became so hysterical that she had to be given an injection in the emergency room before he arrived to take us both away.

I don't think she was ever really the same after the accident. Looking back, I realize that was when everything started to change—though there is every chance that my adolescence and her growing hatred of her job might have changed things anyway. My mother began to seem irrationally angry at Herb and so solicitous of me I felt smothered. I held her responsible, suddenly, for everything, and I had a maniac's ability to transform good things into something awful. The five cherries I began to get in my Cokes seemed an unwanted pollution, and I was sure that my mother had told the waitress to be extra kind. Her cigarette smoke made me cough. Long before the surgeon general warned against the dangers of smoking, I was sure that she meant to poison me. When she drove me to physical therapy, I misconstrued her positive attitude and was sure that she took secret delight in having me tortured. My wrist set wrong, and had to be put in a cast a second time. My mother cried constantly. I turned to Herb to help me with my homework. She relented, and he became the one who drove me everywhere.

When I started being skeptical of my mother, she began to be skeptical of Herb. I heard arguments about the way he arranged his sets. She said that he should end on a more upbeat note. She thought the lighting was too stagy. He began to play—and end—in a nondescript silver glow. I looked at the shells on the netting, not caring that she knew I wasn't concentrating on Herb's playing. She sank lower in the booth, and her attention also drifted: no puffs of smoke carefully exhaled in the pauses between sung phrases; no testing the edge of the table with her fingertip. One Saturday night we just stopped going.

By that time, she had become a loan officer at Riggs Bank. Herb had moved from Sears to Montgomery Ward, where he was in charge of the lawn and leisure-activities section—everything from picnic tables to electric hedge clippers. She served TV dinners. She complained that there wasn't enough money, though she bought expensive high heels that she wore to work. On Wednesday nights Herb played handball with friends who used to be musicians but who were suddenly working white-collar jobs to support growing families. He would come home and say, either with disbelief or with disorientation, that Sal, who used to play in a Latino band, had just had twins, or that Earl had sold his drums and bought an expensive barbecue grill. She read Perry Mason. He read magazine articles about the Second World War: articles, he said, shaking his head, that were clearly paving the way for a reassessment of the times in which we lived.

I didn't have a friend—a real friend—until I was fourteen. That year my soul mate was a boy named Ryuji Anderson, who shared my passion for soccer and introduced me to *Playboy*. He told me to buy Keds one size too large and stuff a sock in the toe so that I could kick hard and the ball would really fly. We both suffered because we sensed that you had to *look* like John F. Kennedy in order to *be* John F. Kennedy. Ryuji's mother had been a war bride, and my mother had lost her husband six years after the war in a freak accident: a painter on scaffolding had lost his footing high up and tumbled backward to the ground, releasing, as he fell, the can of paint that struck my father on the head and killed him. The painter faithfully sent my mother a Christmas card every year, informing her about his own slow recovery and apologizing for my father's death. Uncle Herb met my mother when his mother, dead of leukemia, lay in the room adjacent to my father's room in the funeral home. They had coffee together one time when they both were exiled to the streets, late at night.

It was not until a year later, when he looked her up in the phone book (the number was still listed under my father's name), that he saw her again. That time I went along, and was bought a paper cone filled with french fries. I played cowboy, circling the bench on which they sat with an imaginary lasso. We had stumbled on a carnival. Since it was downtown Washington, it wasn't really a carnival but a small area of the Mall, taken over by dogs who would jump through burning hoops and clowns on roller skates. It became a standing refrain between my mother and Herb that some deliberate merriment had been orchestrated just for them, like the play put on in A Midsummer Night's Dream.

I, of course, had no idea what to make of the world on any given day. My constants were that I lived with my mother, who cried every night; that I could watch only two shows each day on TV; and that I would be put to bed earlier than I wanted, with a night-light left burning. That day my mother and Herb sat on the bench, I'm sure I sensed that things were going to be different, as I inscribed two people destined to be together in an imaginary lassoed magic circle. From then on, we were a threesome.

He moved in as a boarder. He lived in the room that used to be the dining room, which my mother and I had never used, since we ate off TV trays. I remember his hanging a drapery rod over the arch—nailing the brackets in, then lifting up the bar, pushing onto it the brocade curtain my mother had sewn, then lowering the bar into place. They giggled behind it. Then they slid the curtain back and forth, as if testing to see that it would really work. It was like one of the games I had had as a baby: a board with a piece of wood that slid back and forth, exposing first the sun, then the moon.

Of course, late at night they cheated. He would simply push the curtain aside and go to her bed. Since I would have accepted anything, it's a wonder they didn't just tell me. A father, an uncle, a saint, Howdy Doody, Lassie—I didn't have a very clear idea of how any of them truly behaved. I believed whatever I saw. Looking back, I can only assume that they were afraid not so much of what I would think as of what others might think, and that they were unwilling to draw me into their deception. Until I wandered into her bedroom, they simply were not going to blow their cover. They were just going to wait for me. Eventually, I was sure to stumble into their world.

"The secret about Uncle Herb doesn't go any farther than this house," my mother said that night after I found them together. She was quite ashen. We stood in the kitchen. I had followed her—not because I loved her so much, or because I trusted her, but because I was already sure of Herb. Sure because even if he had winked at me, he could not have been clearer about the silliness of the slammed door. She had on a beige nightgown and was backlit by the counter light. She cast a pond-like shadow on the floor. I would like to say that I asked her why she had lied to me, but I'm sure I wouldn't have dared. Imagine my surprise when she told me anyway: "You don't know what it's like to lose something forever," she said. "It will make you do anything—even lie to people you love—if you think you can reclaim even a fraction of that thing. You don't know what 'fraction' means. It means a little bit. It means a thing that's been broken into pieces."

I knew she was talking about loss. All week, I had been worried that the bird at school, with its broken wing, might never fly again and would hop forever in the cardboard box. What my mother was thinking of, though, was that can of paint—a can of paint that she wished had missed my father's head and sailed into infinity.

We looked down at the sepia shadow. It was there in front of her, and in front of me. Of course it was behind us, too.

Many years later, the day Herb took me out for "a talk," we drove aimlessly for quite a while. I could almost feel Herb's moment of inspiration when it finally came, and he went around a traffic circle and headed down Pennsylvania Avenue. It was a Saturday, and on Saturdays the Merry Mariner was open only for dinner, but he had a key, so we parked and went inside and turned on a light. It was not one of those lights that glowed when he played, but a strong, fluorescent light. Herb went to the bar and poured himself a drink. He opened a can of Coke and handed it to me. Then he told me that he was leaving us. He said that he himself found it unbelievable. Then, suddenly, he began to urge me to listen to Billie Holiday's original recordings, to pay close attention to the paintings of Vermeer, to look around me, and to listen. To believe that what to some people might seem the silliest sort of place might be, to those truly observant, a temporary substitute for heaven.

I was a teenager, and I was too embarrassed to cry. I sat on a bar stool and simply looked at him. That day, neither of us knew how my life would turn out. Possibly he thought that so many unhappy moments would have damaged me forever. For all either of us knew, he had been the father figure to a potential hoodlum, or even to a drifter—that was what the game of pretense he and my mother had been involved in might have produced. He shook his head sadly when he poured another drink. Later, I found out that my mother had asked him to go, but that day I didn't even think to ask why I was being abandoned.

Before we left the restaurant he told me—as he had the night I found him naked in my mother's room—how much he cared for me. He also gave me practical advice about how to assemble a world.

He had been the one who suggested that the owner string netting on the walls. First he and the owner had painted the ocean: pale blue, more shine than paint at the bottom, everything larger than it appeared on land. Then gradually the color of the paint changed, rays of light streamed in, and things took on a truer size. Herb had added, on one of the walls, phosphorescence. He had touched the paintbrush to the wall delicately, repeatedly, meticulously. He was a very good amateur painter. Those who sat below it would never see it, though. Those who sat adjacent to it might see the glow in their peripheral vision. From across the room, where my mother and I sat, the highlights were too delicate, and too far away to see. The phosphorescence had never caught my eye when my thoughts drifted from the piano music, or when I blinked my eyes to clear them of the smoke.

The starfish had been bought in lots of a dozen from a store in Chinatown. The clamshells had been painted by a woman who lived in Arlington, in the suburbs, who had once strung them together as necklaces for church bazaars, until the demand dried up and macramé was all the rage. Then she sold them to the owner of the restaurant, who carried them away from her yard sale in two aluminum buckets years before he ever imagined he would open a restaurant. Before Herb and I left the Merry Mariner that day, there wasn't anything about how the place had been assembled that I didn't know.

Fifteen years after that I drove with my fiancée to Herb's cousin's house to get some things he left with her for safekeeping in case anything happened to him. His cousin was a short, unattractive woman who lifted weights. She had converted what had been her dining room into a training room, complete with Nautilus, rowing machine, and barbells. She lived alone, so there was no one to slide a curtain back for. There was no child, so she was not obliged to play at anything.

She served us iced tea with big slices of lemon. She brought out gua-camole and a bowl of tortilla chips. She had called me several days before to say that Herb had had a heart attack and died. Though I would not find out formally until some time later, she also told me that Herb had left me money in his will. He also asked that she pass on to me a large manila envelope. She handed it to me, and I was so curious that I opened it immediately, on the back porch of some muscle-bound woman named Frances in Cold Spring Harbor, New York.

There was sheet music inside: six Billie Holiday songs that I recog-nized immediately as Herb's favorites for ending the last set of the eve-ning. There were several notes, which I suppose you could call love notes, from my mother. There was a tracing, on a food-stained Merry Mariner place mat, of a cherry, complete with stem, and a fancy pencil-drawn frame around it that I vaguely remembered Herb having drawn one night. There was also a white envelope that contained the two pic-tures: one of the soldiers on Guam; one of a handsome young man look-ing impassively at a sleeping young baby. I knew the second I saw it that he was my father.

I was fascinated, but the more I looked at it—the more remote and expressionless the man seemed—the more it began to dawn on me that Herb wanted me to see the picture of my father because he wanted me to see how different he had been from him. When I turned over the pic-ture of my father in profile and read "Guam," I almost smiled. It cer-tainly wasn't my mother's handwriting. It was Herb's, though he had tried to slope the letters so that it would resemble hers. What sweet revenge, he must have thought—to leave me with the impression that my mother had been such a preoccupied, scatterbrained woman that she could not even label two important pictures correctly.

My mother had died years before, of pneumonia. The girl I had been dating at the time had said to me, not unkindly, that although I was very sad about my mother's death, one of the advantages of time passing was sure to be that the past would truly become the past. Words would become suspect. People would seem to be only poor souls struggling to do their best. Images would fade.

Not the image of the wall painted to look like the ocean, though. She was wrong about that. Herb had painted it exactly the way it really looks. I found this out later when I went snorkeling and saw the world underwater for the first time, with all its spooky spots of overexposure and its shimmering irregularities. But how tempting—how reassuring—

to offer people the possibility of climbing from deep water to the surface by moving upward on lovely white nets, gigantic ladders from which no one need ever topple.

On Frances's porch, as I stared at the photographs of my father, I saw him as a young man standing on a hot island, his closest friend a tall broomstick of a man whom he would probably never see again once the war was over. He was a hero. He had served his country. When he got off Guam, he would have a life. Things didn't turn out the way he expected, though. The child he left behind was raised by another man, though it is true that his wife missed him forever and remained faithful in her own strange way by never remarrying. As I continued to look at the photograph, though, it was not possible to keep thinking of him as a hero. He was an ordinary man, romantic in context—a sad young soldier on a tropical island that would soon become a forgotten land. When the war was over he would have a life, but a life that was much too brief, and the living would never really recover from that tragedy.

Herb must also have believed that he was not a hero. That must have been what he was thinking when he wrote, in wispy letters, brief, transposed captions for two pictures that did not truly constitute any legacy at all.

In Cold Spring Harbor, as I put the pictures back in the envelope, I realized that no one had spoken for quite some time. Frances tilted her glass, shaking the ice cubes. She hardly knew us. Soon we would be gone. It was just a quick drive to the city, and she would see us off, knowing that she had discharged her responsibility by passing on to me what Herb had said was mine.

WINDY DAY AT THE RESERVOIR

Fran figured out that the key worked when it was inserted upside down—all the Brunettis had mentioned in the note was that the key had to be turned counterclockwise to open the door.

Chap groped along the wall for the light switch, found it, and said, "There!" triumphantly. On wooden pegs hung above the switch were the family's ski-lift passes: Lou Brunetti, smiling the same way he smiled in his passport picture; Pia, poker-faced, self-consciously touching the ends of her hair; Anthony, cherubic and bemused, no doubt thinking: What is the family into now? Another world that his father intended to master, with books about organic gardening and expensive skis to allow people to streak through the snow.

This would have been a bit much to notice simply from looking at the picture of Anthony, but Chap had seen some of the letters Anthony wrote Fran, who had once been his first-grade teacher. She was a hero to the Brunetti family because she had put them in touch with the doctor who prescribed Ritalin for Anthony. By the time he had taken the drug for a month he had made friends. Dishes no longer toppled from the table. He began to finger-paint with great concentration. That winter, Fran had invited the Brunettis to dinner. The Brunettis had reciprocated by having them over for sweet wine, homemade biscotti, and a slide show of Capri, where they had often vacationed before they emigrated to the States at Lou's insistence. Fran had given them *Mastering the Art of French Cooking*. They had given Fran and Chap a print of the Trevi Fountain, taken from an old book, with so many birds circling the gushing water it seemed a cartoon caption should be under-neath. In late summer, they had gone to the visiting carnival together. Fran had recommended her dermatologist when Anthony's doctor was mystified by a rash behind his knees. Pia had sewn Fran's niece's wed-ding dress. When the Brunettis moved away to Vermont, Fran and Chap put on a brave front and helped pack their dishes. There was much amusement when they gave the Brunettis a bottle of champagne to open in their new home, and the Brunettis gave them a farewell present, too: a kind of amaretto liqueur impossible to buy in the States. The women were teary, and the men shook hands, squeezing with extra pressure. Then they were gone, and after a year or so they wrote more often than they called. There was a May rendezvous in Boston, at a restaurant in the North End, when Anthony sat briefly on Fran's leg even though he otherwise took pride in being a big boy, and talked excitedly to Chap about computers. At the end of the evening, though, in their own car, Fran and Chap agreed that the Brunettis seemed much more re-strained—not with them so much as with one another. Fran wondered whether Pia resented the move. Chap thought a sort of rigidity had set in with Lou: Would he ever before have had such strong opinions on regional politics? He had actually banged the table, reminding Fran of the way Anthony behaved when she first met him. Lou had spoken to the waitress in Italian, tapping the bread and sending it back because the crust was not crisp. Pia, much to Fran and Chap's astonishment, or-dered a martini instead of mineral water before dinner. In the ladies' room, Pia confided to Fran that Lou had been urging her to see a fer-tility doctor because she had had trouble conceiving. She was having trouble, she told Fran, because she was taking birth control pills. Her husband was almost forty-six; she could not imagine why he would want to have more children. Alone at the table with Lou, when Anthony was invited into the kitchen to meet the chef, Chap had learned nothing more than that the natives of Vermont blamed the governor for the mos-quito problem. Before they parted, it was agreed that for their vacation, Fran and Chap would house-sit for the Brunettis, who would be gone in July, visiting a cousin in Atlanta, then continuing to New York City, where at the end of the weekend they would board a cruise to nowhere. "What if the *ship* doesn't ever leave port but the people on it all dis-appear instead?" Anthony had said. His father had chuckled, as Pia frowned with real concern.

Several days later, the key to the Brunettis' house arrived in an enve-lope in the mail, taped to the back of a postcard of cows in a field. "Maybe they know they preside over Heaven on Earth!" Lou had writ-ten underneath the information printed at the top: that there were

450,000 cows in Vermont. Pia's note was warm, thanking them several times for picking up the dinner check. Warmer than she had been in person, Fran said sadly, handing the note to Chap. In the note, Pia told them how to open the door, what to do if the sump pump did not come on during a hard rain, and the peculiarities of one burner on the gas stove. There was a P.S., telling them that mosquitoes bit more when the body was warm. After a dip in the stream behind the house, Pia said, they could sit on the banks for twenty minutes or half an hour without being bitten.

When they began to walk around the house, sensing the shape of lamps and fumbling for buttons or switches to turn them on, they noticed, immediately, that the Brunettis had become collectors: of wooden decoys, hand-tinted photographs, glass insulators, silver candlesticks. It was a big house, but so low-ceilinged it felt constricting, in spite of the four-over-four windows that came almost to the floor. For a while, disoriented, they noticed small things; the house had been added on to so many times, the configuration of rooms was impossible to predict. The long span of shelves in the living room sagged from age, not from the weight of books. Lou's architecture books, many of them oversize, were lined up on the bottom shelves, but the rest of the shelves held only a few paperbacks. As they toured the living room, they found pepper shakers from the fifties: Scottie dogs and pirouetting ballerinas whose craniums poured salt and pepper; seven box cameras in a row; at least a dozen unpaired ladies' shoes, fancy high heels from the forties; hair combs displayed standing upright in shallow bowls filled with sand; Roseville vases; replicas of the Eiffel Tower. The Italian landscapes both of them had always admired were there, clustered now in the hallway that led to the kitchen instead of interspersed throughout the house. *Mastering the Art of French Cooking* was in the kitchen, but Fran could see no other cookbooks; it looked as if the book had been put in the book stand and placed in the center of the counter so Fran wouldn't miss seeing it. More decoys were clustered at the far end of the counter. On the refrigerator, another picture of the intense Anthony stared them in the eye. There was a postcard of the evangelist Matthew (Fran took it off the freezer door and turned it over; it was from a museum in Germany), and several photographs, slightly overlapping, of what was probably the Brunettis' garden: phlox, gladiolas, columbine, twiggy lilacs.

Chap turned on the faucet, filled a coffee mug with water, and glugged it down. He turned the mug upside down and put it in the dish drainer. It was what he did at home—just upended a glass or mug as if he hadn't drunk from it. Fran bit her tongue and turned back toward the refrigerator. There was a picture of an elderly lady she did not recognize. Everything was held in place with magnets shaped like clouds. Droplets of rain fell from the cloud holding the postcard of Matthew to the refrigerator. Four differently shaped clouds not in use were lined up vertically next to the door handle. Fran moved them until they were separated by wider spaces, pushing one higher and another lower, the way clouds would really look in the sky.

"It's certainly not their house in Cambridge, is it?" Chap said.

Outside, moths fluttered against the glass, seeking the light. She saw on the counter a spray can of Yard Guard and another can of Deep Woods Off. A mosquito buzzed her ear. Reflexively, she flinched and ducked. Chap ran toward her, clapping his hands. He was as quick as a snake's tongue. A bug hardly ever escaped him. At home, if a cricket or a lightning bug got in, she would have to holler out quickly so he wouldn't kill it. She always got a glass and the notepad they kept by the kitchen phone so she could capture nice insects and release them outdoors. He chided her. "You let in more than you free," he said. Still, something made her patiently stalk them, and she felt victorious when she pulled her hand back inside after shaking out the glass and finding it empty. That had happened the night before they left for Vermont. "What does your crystal ball say?" Chap had asked, passing by in his pajamas as she was closing the door with her foot and gazing into the bottom of an empty glass. And she had thrown it at him. Not hard—she had more or less tossed it, but it had caught him by surprise; he hadn't ducked, and it had hit him in the shoulder. He winced, more perplexed than angry. Several expressions crossed his face before he pulled his chin in tight to his throat as if to say: What's this?

"It looks like one of those antique shops that's set up to look like somebody's house when actually everything's for sale," she said.

"The decoys must be his," Chap said.

"Jesus," she said. "We don't collect anything. I wonder when they started doing this?"

He leaned against the counter, the moths behind his head like large, durable snowflakes. She thought of Anthony's letter—the one he had sent about Christmastime, telling her about the new lights the college in town had installed so people could cross-country ski at night. Everything the Brunettis wrote made the town sound idyllic. Cows—whether or not they were presiding over heaven—were not dear to Fran's heart, but what she had heard about the horses made her curious to see them, and from the photographs on the refrigerator, she could tell she was going to love the garden. She and Chap had enough sunny land behind their house to garden. She wondered why they never had. She began to fantasize that there would be endless herbs. As a child, she had stood in her grandmother's dill patch, tickling her nose with a stalk of the delightful, feathery stuff, hoping a wind would blow other big stalks her way to touch her legs. She looked again at the picture of the elderly lady on the refrigerator. The woman was eating something from a plate on her lap. It looked like white-frosted cake. Strawberry shortcake? Or a mound of vanilla ice cream? She suddenly wondered if there would be a farmers' market in town; if there might be special dinners at the fire-house, or even some celebratory day. In the town her grandmother had lived in, they had had an annual celebration to commemorate the day the library opened. She had gotten her first kiss in a rowboat on the lake in that town on the seventeenth anniversary of the opening of the library. Her grandmother's next-door neighbor had taught her how to spot the constellations.

"You collect cookbooks," Chap said suddenly. "Isn't that what you always look for in airport bookshops?"

They were on the Brunettis' screened porch. It seemed quite large, but she could not put her finger on the light switch. As her eyes focused a little better in the dark, she went toward a cord dangling from a ceiling light. She pulled it and a breeze started up; it was a fan, not a light. Then Chap found the light switch and two sconces flickered bright on the far side of the porch, at each corner. In a few seconds Chap had also pulled the chain on a table lamp, so the porch was almost as bright as the kitchen.

"The place goes on and on," Chap said.

She looked at him. "A little jealous of the Brunettis' house?" she asked, raising her eyebrows. He shook his head no, walking toward her.

"Well, maybe in the daylight," he said, hugging her.

Feeling his body against hers, and feeling his fingertips pressing into her, she said: "Honey, I don't buy cookbooks for the recipes, you know. I buy them if they have funny old-time illustrations."

In college, she had intended to become an illustrator. One of the things that had drawn her to Pia Brunetti had been Pia's love of drawing. Of course she had been very fond of Anthony and might have become the Brunettis' friend in any case, but one day she had run into Pia at a bookstore when Pia had been staring at a book of Ingres drawings. She did not usually—in fact, ever—run into people in the art section of bookshops. And when Pia began to speak about the drawing she was looking at, running her finger through the air as if lightly shaving a layer from something that could not be seen, she had been moved, and had asked her to join her for coffee after they finished browsing. That was when she found out that Pia was a seamstress, and that she was adept at altering patterns so her creations would be entirely unique. Fran's own career as an illustrator had gotten derailed in college as she began to study biology in order to do biological drawings. Biology itself became so much more interesting. First biology, then medicine. Then the thought of so many years in medical school (she had already met, and was almost engaged to, Chap) gave her cold feet. Somehow—she herself was not quite sure how—she had decided to teach art to children, though when she went to graduate school she had not specialized in that, after all. She had written her thesis on the use of music in early childhood development, and taken exams, the summer she married, for her teacher's certification. She had Anthony in class her second year of teaching. By then, the tests she and Chap had undergone had revealed that it was almost certain he and she could not conceive. A more intense feeling for children—children as a category—came over her. She indulged herself and became quite attached to certain children, even fantasizing that they might be hers, though the fantasizing did not extend beyond scenarios she would imagine as she was falling asleep at night. She had a strange reaction to those late-night imaginings. Or at least she thought it must be a strange reaction: both to wish that they extended into her dreams and to luxuriate in the letdown when her eyes opened in the morning. That was where she really might have had a crystal ball: she could tell quickly—so quickly that she thought of it as intuition—if, and in what way, a child was in distress. Anthony was easy to diagnose. Telling the parents in a way that would not offend or frighten them was the only problem. She had been so good at her job that several private schools had tried to hire her away from Bailey, but she had liked her colleagues, appreciated the fact that few administrative meetings were convened unless there was a real need to bring everyone together. But in the fall of her third year of teaching she had begun to have headaches, and in the morning her eyelids were swollen. Chap finally persuaded her to go to the doctor. She had blood tests, and was diagnosed as having mono. A young person's kissing disease, and her usual outlet of affection, except for kissing Chap, had been hugging the children at school. In fact, although she and Chap made love two or three times a week, they rarely kissed—or only afterward: little kisses she planted on his shoulder; a fond kiss smack in the center of her forehead, before he rolled out of bed. It was his idea, after she spent almost two weeks at home and seemed to enjoy it in spite of her low energy, that she take time off from teaching and indulge her love of drawing. People were too programmed in this society, he said: his salary was quite adequate to support them both. Something persuaded her that he was right. Perhaps she wanted to be flattered and cajoled by the headmaster of Bailey. In the back of her mind she also thought about putting out feelers to other schools—seeing what response she would get if she instigated something, rather than receiving surprise offers. Instead, she walked around the empty house in the day, wearing Chap's bathrobe, which she appropriated, thinking: This is what solitude is. This is what it's like to be childless. She enjoyed the misery this provoked, the way she enjoyed, in part, the disturbing dreams. Word got out in the community that she and Chap had inherited money—that she had quit because they now had a great amount of money and because she wanted to follow other pursuits. It was never a surprise to her that adults fantasized as quickly as children, because the converse was true: speculative children inevitably grounded themselves, after a spell, in reality. It was just too frightening to fly by the seat of their pants for too long. They would begin to paint within the borders. Read from beginning to end.

The white wicker furniture on the porch had an opalescent patina. Pink pillows—pink had always been Pia's favorite color: slightly orangish pinks, or electric pinks—were banked against the back of the settee. Larger pink pillows were propped against the backs of the four white chairs.

She pulled away from Chap and reached up to try to grab a mosquito that had been buzzing behind her head. He bent to scratch his leg. He and Fran were lingering on the porch because it was a sort of annex to the house. Almost at a glance, they had found that the house no longer had anything to do with their conception of how the Brunettis lived. It was still a mystery to both of them that Lou had resigned from private practice and become co-chair of the architecture department at a small-town college. The house itself, with its unevenly spaced floorboards, sinking shelves, and peeling ceiling, needed a lot of work, but Fran supposed that it was the same situation you always found with doctors: they would not treat members of their own family.

Back in the kitchen, she found that one of the cloud magnets had fallen to the floor after she rearranged them. She pressed it back and followed Chap out of the kitchen, frowning. She felt like a burglar, but one who had all the time in the world to really consider what was of interest.

Chap poked his head into Lou's study. Fran turned on the light in the bathroom. A framed print of Monet water lilies hung on the wall beside the claw-footed tub. A vase of lavender flowers, dropping petals, sat on a shelf above the sink.

"Look at this," Chap said.

She walked across the squeaking floorboards and went into Lou's study. Chap was looking at a child's drawing of cubes and pyramids seen from different angles. "The Future," it was titled, and underneath, printed a little lopsidedly, "Anthony Brunetti." She saw, in her own hand—that slightly calligraphic way of writing—the date: May 1, 1985.

(2)

Chap stood in the garden. He had tried it the day before, without spraying himself with bug repellent, and had added eight or ten bites to his quickly spotting body. Today he had sprayed himself from head to toe, intent on gathering enough basil for pesto, some arugula and Boston lettuce for salad. He had not been able to find plastic bags in the kitchen, so he had brought his emptied-out duffel bag in which he had transported his summer reading. If a color could have a smell, basil would be the essence of green. He killed a mosquito on his wrist, then turned like a paranoiac: a bee's buzz had sounded like a tornado of mosquitoes. He did not, of course, try to kill the bee. He bent over and carefully twisted a small head of lettuce from the ground, banging the roots against the duffel bag before dropping it inside. He had been at the Brunettis' house before, though Fran had no idea of that.

The buzzing behind his head this time was a mosquito. He turned and clapped his hands, then flicked the black body from his palm. He looked where it fell and saw that radishes had begun to sprout. He had grown them as a child: radishes and tomatoes, in a big cedar tub on his mother's porch. He suddenly remembered his heartache—heartache!—when, on one of his infrequent visits, his father had pulled up radish after radish, to see if they had formed yet. Only swollen white worms dangled below the leaves. After his father pulled four or five, Chap reached out and put his hand on his father's wrist. His father stopped. His father had been perplexed, as if he had been guaranteed a prize simply for reaching out and pulling, and he had gotten nothing. Chap had been named for his mother's brother, Chaplin J. Anderson—the *J* for "Jerome." His uncle had been his father figure, coming every weekend until he moved to the West Coast when Chap was fifteen or sixteen. Sixteen, it must have been, because Chaplin had been teaching him to drive. He died mountain climbing, when Chap was in his second year of college. After that, his mother was never the same. She turned to a cousin—crazy Cousin Marshall—who suddenly became, in spite of his belief in the spirit world and his railing against Ezra Pound as if the man still lived, a pillar of sanity. And now, since his mother's death, he was saddled with Marshall, because he had been kind to his mother. He arranged to have Marshall's road plowed in winter; sent him thermal underwear. But since Marshall's dogs, Romulus and Remus, died, he had been increasingly sad and bitter. Would he have another dog? No. Would he take a little trip on the weekend—get away from the house with the dog bed and the sad memories? Not even if Chap sent a check for a million dollars. Didn't his belief in the afterlife offer him some consolation? Silence on the telephone. Marshall was now eighty-one years old. He would not move out of his house but would not have it insulated because he thought *all* insulation was poison. Chap would barely have known Marshall if his mother had not sought him out. Now he was often vaguely worried about Marshall's health, his depression, his naïveté, which could well get him into trouble those times he ventured into the big city of Hanover, New Hampshire.

With his bag full of greens, Chap quickened his step as he walked toward the house. He saw that a wasp nest had begun to form next to the drainpipe. Inside, he heard the coffee machine perking. He had always had keen hearing. Passing the open window, he looked through the screen and saw Fran searching through a kitchen drawer. Even at home, she always misplaced the corkscrew, scissors, and apple slicer. Fran had a circular implement that could be placed over an apple and pushed down to core it and separate the apple into sections. She believed in eating an apple a day. Whatever else she believed in these days was a mystery. In saving the rain forest—that was what she believed. In banning pesticides. She also believed in cotton sheets and linen pants, even though they wrinkled.

He opened the door, knowing he was doing her an injustice. She was a very intelligent woman, gifted in more ways than she liked to admit. And, in fact, she was usually the one who took Marshall's calls. She also wrote polite notes when he sent books depicting the archangels.

"Maybe in the daylight," she muttered, still riffling through the drawer. He smiled; it had become a standing joke between them that everything in the house, and by extension everything, period, would come clear in the light of day.

On their third day in the house daylight had revealed one of Anthony's jokes: a piece of rubber shaped and painted to look like a melted chocolate-covered ice-cream bar. Chap had peeked at blueprints rolled up on Lou's drafting table. Fran had put fresh flowers throughout the house. She was reading *War and Peace* and listening to the Brunettis' collection of classical CDs, though earlier in the morning she had been leafing through a *Teenage Mutant Ninja Turtles* comic and listening to an old Lou Reed record. The elderly woman whose picture was on the refrigerator turned out to be a neighbor who cleaned house for the Brunettis once a week. She took an instant liking to Fran, once she saw the flowers set out in vases. She said the photograph on the refrigerator had been taken by Anthony during the strawberry festival the year before. He had wanted to catch her with a beard of whipped cream, but she had licked it away too fast. Chap had seen her—Mrs. Brikel—the other time he visited, and this time he had held his breath, hoping she would not remember their meeting. From the way her eyes flickered, he had thought she was going to say something, then decided against it.

Fran said, as if she had tuned in to his thoughts: "Mrs. Brikel called and said she wants to give us half an apple pie. Wasn't that nice of her? We'll have to think of something to do for her before we leave."

The Brunettis' pictures and postcards on the refrigerator had been joined by two postcards forwarded from Fran and Chap's: a detail of a stained-glass window at the Matisse chapel, sent by a friend of Fran's who was traveling through France, and a picture of her niece's new baby, propped up in her mother's arm, eyes closed.

"Would you mind going over to Mrs. Brikel's?" Fran said. "I said the least we could do would be to walk over and get our share of pie."

He put the bag on the counter. "Drop all this in the sink and splatter it with water," he said. "I'll be back in a flash." He had gone out the door and closed it before he thought to open it again and ask whether Mrs. Brikel lived to the left or the right.

"Right," Fran said, pointing.

He closed the door again. Two or three mosquitoes trailed him, hovering near the center of his body as he cut across the grass. He tried to swat them away, quickening his step. A jogger went by on the road, a big black Lab keeping time with him as he ran. A car honked when it passed, for no reason. He looked after the dog, who reminded him of Romulus, and wondered briefly whether it might be nice to have a dog.

"Could you smell it baking?" Mrs. Brikel asked, opening the door. She was smiling a bright smile. Her eyes were not particularly bright, though, and the smile began to fade when he did not answer instantly.

"There's no breeze," he said. "Isn't there always supposed to be a breeze in Vermont? If we had some wind, those mosquitoes couldn't land the way they do." He flicked one off his elbow. He entered the house quickly, smiling to make up for his lack of cheerfulness a few seconds before.

"I thought I'd bake a pie, and I would have made blueberry, but I came down this morning and saw my son had eaten every one for breakfast," she said. "I usually don't make apple pies except for fall, but your wife said apples were a favorite of hers."

In the gloom of Mrs. Brikel's back room, he saw another person: a tall boy, watching television. The shades were dropped. His feet were propped up on a footstool. Guns exploded. Then he changed the channel. Someone was singing, "What happened to the fire in your voice?" Someone laughed uproariously on a quiz show. The sound of a buzzer obliterated more gunfire.

"What's your favorite pie?" Mrs. Brikel said. She had turned. He followed her into the kitchen. There was a wooden crucifix on the wood panel separating the windows over the sink. There were two rag rugs on the floor. A little fan circulated air. "All the screens are out being repaired," Mrs. Brikel said. "I sure wouldn't open the windows with these mosquitoes."

In the kitchen, the aroma was strong. Chap could actually feel his mouth water as Mrs. Brikel cut into the pie.

"I'd give it all to you, but that it upsets him," Mrs. Brikel said, nodding over her shoulder. Chap turned and looked. There was no one in the doorway. She was referring to the person watching television.

"I was all set to make two, but I ran out of flour," Mrs. Brikel said. "That's always the way: you remember to buy the little things, but you're always running out of the big things like milk and flour."

There were stickers of dancing dinosaurs on the window ledge. He looked at the refrigerator. Long strips of stickers hung there, taped at the top: stickers of birthday cakes and little animals holding umbrellas, pinwheels of color, multicolored star stickers.

"He knows you're taking half the pie," Mrs. Brikel said, tilting the dish. Half the pie slid free, landing perfectly on a plate. "That's what he knows," she said, talking to herself. She opened a drawer, pulled off a length of Saran Wrap, and spread it over the pie, tucking it under the plate.

"This is *very* kind of you, Mrs. Brikel," he said. Without her saying anything directly, he assumed that the person in the living room was her son and that there was something wrong with him. The TV changed from muffled rifle shots to girls singing.

"I love to bake in the winter," Mrs. Brikel said, "but come summer I don't often think of it, except that we have to have our homemade bread. Yes we do," she said, her voice floating off a little. He looked at the half pie. He knew he should thank her again and leave, but instead he leaned against the kitchen counter. "Mrs. Brikel," he said, "do you remember me?"

"Do I what?" she said.

"We met, briefly. It was during the winter. Lou and I were backing out of the driveway and you and your son—or I guess it was your son, walking in front of you—were coming up the driveway . . ."

"In the car with Mr. Brunetti?" Mrs. Brikel said. "You were up here at the end of that big winter storm, then."

"I was pretty surprised to find myself here," he said. "Lou called me when Pia went in for surgery."

"Oh, yes," Mrs. Brikel said, bowing her head. "That was an awful day."

"Not as bad for us as for Pia," he said. He looked at the plate covered in Saran Wrap. He wanted to say something else, but wasn't sure what.

"But now she seems to be coming along well," Mrs. Brikel said.

"My wife doesn't know I was here," he said. "I was quite surprised, to tell you the truth, that Lou asked me to come. I told my wife I was visiting my cousin in New Hampshire."

"Well, you were good to do it," Mrs. Brikel said. She ran her hand along the counter edge. She thumbed away an imaginary spot of dirt.

"My wife doesn't know about the trip because Lou asked me not to tell her," he said. "It's a funny thing, but I guess there are some things women don't want other women to know."

Mrs. Brikel looked slightly perplexed, then dropped her eyes. If he was going to continue, he would have to think of what to say. The TV was changing from station to station in the other room.

"Lou thought Pia wasn't only upset to be losing a breast, but worried that with her breast gone, she'd . . ." He let his voice drift, then started again. "She was worried, Lou thought, that she'd lose stature in my wife's eyes. That's not true, of course. My wife is a very kind woman. Pia apparently worshiped Fran, and she must have thought the operation would . . ." He faltered. "Would distance them," he said.

He had never tried to articulate this before. He had tried, many times, to remember exactly what Lou had said, but even a second after he heard it, it had seemed confusing and puzzling. This was the best paraphrase he could manage: that Pia had taken some crazy notion into her head, in her anxiety. To this day, Pia did not know that he knew she had had a mastectomy. Lou had not wanted him to visit Pia, but to go to the bar with him at night and have a few drinks and shoot pool. On the way back to Fran, he had detoured to Marshall's house in New Hampshire, taken him on errands, left him with a new jack for his car and with new washers on the faucets. He told Fran that he had spent four days there, when really he had spent only one. He had been at the

Brunettis' the other three days. Anthony had been sent to stay with a family friend. At night, Lou had ducked his head through Anthony's bedroom door, though, before turning off the downstairs lights. Chap did not know whether Lou had any other close friends. Until Lou called, he had assumed that of course he did—but maybe they were just acquaintances. Couples in the community.

"It's a strange reaction," he said, pushing away from the counter. He had kept Mrs. Brikel too long, imposed on her by making her listen to a story that wasn't even really a story. He looked at her. "I'm sorry," he said.

"Well, I don't know," Mrs. Brikel said. "I don't have any firsthand knowledge of these matters. I think Pia's doing much better though, now that the treatments she's had have been successful."

He followed Mrs. Brikel to the door. He had not intended to ask any more questions, and was surprised to hear himself asking one more.

"Do they seem happy here?" he said.

She dropped her eyes again. "Anthony loves it," she said. "So much to do in the winter, and all. I don't know Mr. Brunetti very well because we go to bed early around here, and he's a late one coming home. But Pia, you mean? Pia I wouldn't say likes it very much. Of course, she's had a very bad year."

"I'm sorry if I've upset you," he said. "I think I've been upset about the past year myself, and Lou isn't the most talkative man."

"He isn't," Mrs. Brikel said.

"Where's my pie?" a voice called from the dark front room. The TV went silent. There was a long pause, and then it started up again. Mrs. Brikel looked in her son's direction. "Pie's on the counter," she said quietly to Chap, as if he had been the one who asked the question.

"Thank you for your kindness, Mrs. Brikel," he said, holding out his hand.

She shook it and smiled slightly. "Keeps me with something to do while the Wild West is won every day," she said. "I'd relive all the wars and hear nothing but gunfire if I didn't play the kitchen radio and make some pies and bread."

"I sneak cigarettes," he said. "Fran doesn't know it, but after lunch, at work, I light up. One cigarette a day."

This brought a bigger, more genuine smile from Mrs. Brikel.

"Okay, then," she said, as he started down the walkway.

He would tell Fran, if she asked, that he had done some minor repair to help Mrs. Brikel. The coffee would still be hot; he would have some coffee with the apple pie.

What if they never came back? Fran thought. She wrote the question in her notebook. It was a notebook covered with lavender cloth Chap had given her for Valentine's Day; since then, she had been keeping some notes, making a few sketches of things she had seen or done during the day. Like a teenager, she had sketched her face with and without bangs, to see if she should let the wisps continue to grow or have them trimmed. She decided, after looking at what she had drawn, to let the hair grow; soon she would have it all one length—the stark but simple way she liked to see herself.

She thought for a moment about people who had disappeared: Judge Crater; Amelia Earhart; Mrs. Ramsey. Though it was cheating to count Mrs. Ramsey among the missing: she had died—it was just that the reader found out about her death abruptly, and so reacted with great shock.

Fran drew parentheses in her notebook. She stared at the little curving lines for a while, then made quick motions with her pen, zigzagging a connection between the curves until they looked like the vertebrae she had sketched years before in her college anatomy class. She had fallen in love with the teaching assistant in that class. The summer she was twenty they had gone to Key West together, and he had given diving instructions while she waited tables at Pier House. They lived in a room in a guest house owned by one of his former girlfriends. The only other person living there that summer was a man named Ed Jakes, who wrote poetry they thought brilliant at the time, and who introduced them to good wine. She had kept in touch with him. He had become an interior decorator. Recently, she had shown Chap Ed's name in *Architectural Digest*. It meant nothing to him, of course; no one ever really shared another person's sentimental youthful attachments. He had collected canes with carved heads, she suddenly remembered: dog faces, tropical birds in profile. One night, in the courtyard of the guest house, Ed Jakes had held one of his canes higher and higher as she leaped over. When the cane rose to a certain height, her boyfriend had walked away, disgusted. Much later, meaning to hurt her, he had said that he and the woman who owned the guest house had gone to bed during the period they stayed there. It never occurred to her to question the truth of that until another boyfriend asked why she was so sure her previous lover hadn't just been trying to make her jealous. She had learned a lot from that boyfriend, including skepticism. If she had stayed with him, and gone to his classes in method acting, she might have become quite a different person.

Since moving into the Brunettis' house, she had begun to think about their lives. It was only natural. All houses had their owners' personalities. In wandering through the rooms, though, she had not sensed much of Pia's presence. She had even decided that the collections of things on the shelves must belong to Lou—or even that Anthony might have gotten into the act by collecting miniature versions of the Empire State Building. Anthony's room was a shrine to athletes and rock stars. Instead of finding dust, Fran had found footballs—footballs had rolled into three corners. There were weird robots that fascinated Chap (they could be altered to become rockets), and he had chuckled over the violent comic books and the collection of movies: Schwarzenegger; *Ghostbusters*; *RoboCop*. There had been so little evidence of Pia, though, that Fran had had to open the bedroom closet and run her hand along Pia's dresses to conjure up a sense of her. She was puzzled that she could find no bottles of perfume, that the medicine cabinet shelves were almost empty, that the kitchen looked so well scrubbed, as if no one ever cooked there. Take-out menus were tucked in the phone book like bookmarks.

Chap was outside cutting the grass, seated atop Lou's riding mower. He had on a baseball cap and the shorts he had bought in four different colors at the factory outlet they had stopped at on their way up. It was true of many men: their desire to get a bargain won out over their indifference to clothes. Fran thought about the garment bag she had brought—dresses she would probably never wear. All the restaurants allowed you to dress casually. She had removed her fingernail polish and not repainted her nails. Her hair was clipped back on top, to keep her bangs out of her eyes. She looked at Chap, heading down a line of uncut grass, fanning mosquitoes away from his face. He had covered his body with insect repellent before he went out, though his shirt was unbuttoned and he was pouring sweat, so most of it had probably washed away.

She thought of all the things she liked about Chap: his endearing smile when she came upon him and found him staring into space; his insistence that he had total recall, beginning at the age of five, which of course she could not dispute; his myopic concentration as his big fingertips moved over the tiny buttons of the calculator; the way he always pointed out a full moon; his insistence, every time, that at last he had found an honest car mechanic. When women talked about their husbands, there seemed to be no nice, comfortable gray areas of love: women either detested their mates or bragged or implied that they were great lovers, that they spent their nights joyfully enacting sexual fantasies as they jumped and toppled and fucked, like figures perpetually animated in a flip book thumbed through time and again.

As Chap turned the mower and steered down another span of grass, she decided that when he headed back she would call out to him. She opened the refrigerator door and took out the half-empty bottle of red wine they had recorked the night before. She took a sip, then poured some into a wineglass. She would hold the wineglass out to Chap and smile a sly smile. She knew that he liked being propositioned in the afternoon; he acted slightly abashed, but secretly he liked it. Aside from surprises, he preferred morning sex, and she liked sex late at night—later than they usually managed, because he fell asleep by midnight.

As she put the glass on the counter, another thought came to her. She would go upstairs and put on one of Pia's stylish dresses, maybe even Pia's high heels if she could find fancier ones than she had brought herself. Clip on Pia's earrings. Make a more thorough search for the perfume.

Going up the stairs, she felt as excited as a child about to play a sophisticated trick. There were small silhouettes—a series of ten or twelve—rising up the wall as the stairs rose. She wondered if they might be family members, or whether they were just something else that had been collected.

In the bedroom, she pulled the shade, on the off chance Chap might glance up and see her undressing. She opened the closet door and flipped through: such pretty colors; such fine material. Pia sewed her own clothes, using Vogue patterns. Friends in Rome sent her fabric. Everything Pia wore was unique and in the best of taste. From the look of the closet—dress after dress—it seemed she still did not wear pants.

The perfume—several bottles—sat in a wicker container. Fran found them when she lifted the lid. She unscrewed the tops and sniffed each one. She put a drop of Graffiti on the inside of each wrist, tapped another drop on her throat. She touched her fingertip to the bottle again and placed her moist finger behind her knee. Then she screwed the top on tightly and began to take off her clothes. She dropped them on the bed, then decided that she and Chap would be using the bed, so she picked them up and draped them over a chair. It was probably Pia's needlework on the seat: a bunch of flowers, circled by lovebirds—very beautiful.

She took a dress the color of moss out of the closet. It was silk, flecked with silver. It had broad, high shoulder pads. Fran wiggled the dress over her head and felt at once powerful and feminine when the shoulder pads settled on her shoulders. She smoothed the fabric in front, adjusting the waist so the front pleat would be exactly centered. The appeal of the dress was all in the cut and the fabric—a much more provocative dress than some low-cut evening wear. The perfect shoes to go with it, simple patent-leather shoes with very high heels, were only a bit too small for Fran's foot. She twisted her arm and slowly zipped the back zipper. Facing the mirror, she let her hair down and ran her fingers through it, deciding to let it stay a bit messy, only patting it into place. She clipped her bangs back neatly and looked at herself in the mirror. This was the place where Pia often stood studying herself. She smoothed her hands down the sides of the dress, amazed at how perfectly it fit.

Chap came into the house and called for Fran. The timing was too perfect to believe. She would slowly unzip the zipper, let him watch as the dress became a silk puddle on the floor. She would step out of it carefully. Once free, she could run to the bed and he would run after her.

She called to him to come into the hallway and close his eyes.

"I can't," he said. "A goddamn bee bit me."

"Oh no," she said. She checked her impulse to run down the stairs. "Put baking soda on it," she called. "Baking soda and water."

She heard him mutter something. The floorboards creaked. In a second, he hollered something she couldn't understand. She went halfway down the stairs. "Chap?" she said.

"You don't know where she'd have baking soda, do you?" he said, slamming drawers.

"There's some in the refrigerator!" she said suddenly. She had seen an open box in the refrigerator. "Top shelf," she hollered.

"The mosquitoes aren't bad enough, I've got to get a bee bite," he muttered.

"Have you got it?" she said.

He must have, because she heard the water running.

"Do you think taking aspirin would do any good?" he said. "Come in here so I can talk to you, would you?"

She stepped out of the shoes and ran into the kitchen. He was leaning against the counter, frowning, the box of baking soda on the drainboard, the bee bite—he had made a paste and then for some reason clapped his hand over the area—on his biceps. His face was white.

"Sit down," she said, going toward him to lead him to the nearest chair. "It's okay," she said reflexively, deciding to be optimistic. Chap always rallied when someone was optimistic. "It'll be fine," she said, taking his elbow. "Go into the living room and sit down."

"I don't believe this," he said. "I was finished. I'd shut the mower off. It came right at me and bit me, for no reason."

They stepped across a fallen postcard and two cloud magnets he had knocked down as he bent to get the baking soda.

"What are you all dressed up for?" he said, frowning as he sank into a chair.

"Take your hand away," she said. "Let me see."

"I don't think baking soda does anything," he said. He closed his eyes and shook his head. "I haven't had a bee bite since I was about ten years old. How long is this thing going to sting?"

"I don't know," she said. She wiped his sweaty forehead. She dropped her wet hand onto the arm of the chair. She was crouching, looking up at him, wondering if he was just pale from shock.

"What are you doing in that dress?" he said.

"I was going to surprise you," she said. "I got all dressed up to seduce you."

He snorted. He closed his eyes again. In a few seconds he opened his eyes and said, "Is that your dress?"

"It's Pia's."

"Pia's?" he said. "What was the idea? That I'd dress up like Lou and we'd play house?"

She smiled. "I just thought I'd dress up and seduce you."

"Well, when this fucking pain stops—if it ever stops—why don't I put on one of Lou's suits and we can talk about postmodern architecture and politics at the college?"

"And what do I talk about?" she said.

"Whatever Pia would talk about," he said. A little color was coming back to his face. There was a white smear over the bee bite. So far, it hadn't swollen.

She sat on the floor, her hand resting on his knee. "Does it feel at all better?" she said.

"I can't tell," he said. He briefly touched her hand, then clapped his over the bite again.

"I don't know what she'd talk about," Fran said. "She'd say that Anthony wants a new robot. Or she'd tell him about some paper Anthony got a good grade on."

"Couples aren't supposed to always talk about their children," he said.

"But then I don't know what she'd talk about," Fran said, puzzled.

"Hey," he said, "we don't really have to do this. It's just a game."

"I don't think she wears these dresses," Fran said softly, running her hand across the skirt to smooth it. "The minute I opened her closet and saw that long row of dresses hanging there so neatly, I had the feeling that she never wore them anymore."

"What do you think she wears?"

"I don't know, but it wouldn't make sense, would it? Most everywhere you go, you can just go as you are. She always looked so beautiful in the city. Remember that until I found out she sewed, I couldn't understand how she could have so many designer clothes?"

"I always thought you were a little jealous of Pia," he said. "Which is particularly stupid, because you're such different types."

"She's what American girls want to be," Fran said. "Very cosmopolitan. Sophisticated. Simple, but beautiful."

"You're beautiful," he said.

"You know what I mean."

"Take off Pia's dress and we'll go to bed and be sophisticated," he said. "Just let me take a quick shower."

"Is your arm better?" she said, letting him help her up.

"There!" he said. "That's good: that's just what Pia would say in this situation, right?"

She smiled. "I would imagine," she said.

"Then maybe what Lou needs is to be in pain more often. That way his wife will have something to talk to him about."

In the same way it came upon Fran that Pia no longer wore elegant dresses, it dawned on Chap that Lou and Pia no longer communicated.

"I don't want anything to ever happen to you," Chap said, following Fran up the stairs. He stood in the doorway and watched as she shimmied out of the dress.

"I don't either," she said, "but that's not too likely, is it?"

"No," he said.

"The question is just what's going to hit me between the eyes." She stepped out of the dress as carefully as she intended. She was wearing only panties and Pia's black high heels. She gave him a coquettish look.

He knew that she only meant to turn aside what he said, but for a split second, he wanted to say something important, so she would wipe the smile off her face. He wanted to say: "Let me tell you what happened to Pia," though he did not, because Lou had sworn him to secrecy.

They made love before he showered. He closed his eyes tightly and did not open them again until after he climaxed, though the scent of Pia's perfume almost tempted him to look quickly to make sure it was Fran.

Afterward, he looked at Pia's green dress on the floor. He ran his finger lightly down Fran's spine. The smell of sweat intermingled with the perfume. The shade flapped in the breeze, then was sucked against the window screen. How was it that he knew only now—not months before, when he sat beside Lou at the bar or cooked breakfast for him or clapped his arm around his shoulder as he headed off to the hospital—how was it that only now he knew the Brunettis' marriage had caved in?

"I was always jealous of her," Fran said, her voice muffled in the pillow. "You were right when you said that."

(4)

"Mrs. Brikel," Chap said as he rolled down the window on the passenger's side of the car. He had just gotten into the car when he looked out and saw her leaving the Laundromat, carrying a white laundry bag.

"Hello there," she said, raising one elbow instead of waving. The bag was as round as a barrel. Sunglasses were on top of her head. She was squinting in the sun.

"You have a car, I suppose," he said.

"That's a long story," she said, "but my cousin's boy is coming to get me."

"I'd be glad to give you a ride," he said.

"Well, I wonder about that," she said. She moved her elbow again. Her arm moved away from her body like a bird's wing stretching. She looked at her watch: a large digital watch. He noticed also that she was wearing pink running shoes with white tennis socks. The shoes were tied with bright red laces. She shifted from foot to foot as she thought about taking the ride.

"Would you be so kind?" she said. "I can go over there by the hardware store to call and save Jay a trip."

"Go ahead," he said, turning the button to start the air conditioning. He put the fan on 3. "Leave those here," he said, as Mrs. Brikel turned away with her laundry bag.

"I guess I will," Mrs. Brikel said. He pushed open the door and she put the bag on the front seat; as she walked away, he tossed it into the backseat and stood it upright. Looking after her, he wondered if she was as old as he had thought. Perhaps today she looked younger because of her silly shoes, and her slightly disheveled clothes. All the fashions now were supposed to sag and droop. He was glad that except for sleeping in oversize T-shirts, Fran ignored the new look. Fran had always been quite an individual. It was at her insistence that they married, years ago, in a grove of willows. When something stopped being fun, Fran usually found a way to stop doing it. They no longer flew to his brother's house for Christmas, since his brother remarried and his wife had four noisy cats. Fran had been trying to decide what career she would embark on next for quite a while, but he gave her credit: if she was restless, she hid it well, and she did not think her quandaries should be his.

Mrs. Brikel was hurrying back toward the car. She greeted a boy on a skateboard, then ran the last few steps. This time when he pushed open the door it was cool inside. She sank into the seat and said, "Aah. This has got to be my lucky day. I would have had to wait another half hour even if Jay was coming. It's the best luck, running into you."

He decided she was younger than he had thought.

"Today you remember me, right?" he said.

She laughed as if he had made a very good joke. "I guess by now I do," she said.

"Car in for repairs?" he said.

"No, it's a long story. I loaned it to a friend who had to go on a trip. Tomorrow night I'll get it back, but my son was upset he was missing so many clothes, so I headed in to the Laundromat."

"I'm glad I ran into you."

"It works out," she said.

At the rotary, he waited for a sports car to pass in front of him, then quickly accelerated into the circling traffic. Three-quarters of the way around, he turned onto the highway leading to the Brunettis'.

"Small town, I don't guess you've had too much trouble learning your way around," she said.

"I've got a lousy sense of direction, but no—this place hasn't stumped me," he said. He touched his neck. "There certainly are a lot of mosquitoes. We'd have gone out for more walks, but it's impossible."

There was a pause in the conversation.

"The damp did it," she said. "I've lived here most all my life and I've never seen anything like this. Some kinds of bug spray they're all out of, you know." She shifted in the seat. "All that rain's kept my son cooped up for a long time, and that's not good," she said. "You might have noticed he was in a very quiet mood when you were at the house the other day."

"I didn't expect him to make conversation while the TV was on," he said.

"Oh, he does," Mrs. Brikel said. "He gives more of a running commentary than some of those news announcers. When my son starts to think about something, nobody on earth can shut him up. He sees that television as a member of the family—talks back to it, thinks he's in there as part of the picture some of the time. Worst time of day is when he should go to bed, because you know some stations stay on all night now. There never comes a natural time to go to bed."

"I didn't realize that," he said.

"When the rain did stop, there was an accident out on the road one night. Someone put out flares just past our walkway, and it scared him. Two days later he still wouldn't go out of the house."

He thought about the tests he and Fran had gone through, trying to solve their infertility problem. What if she had gotten pregnant and they had been saddled, all their lives, with someone like Mrs. Brikel's son? You put such thoughts out of your mind unless you were confronted with the possibility. Something about the way Mrs. Brikel talked about her son made him feel the boy's presence in the car. His eyes darted to the rearview mirror. The big white laundry bag had tipped over.

Mrs. Brikel knocked her feet together. "He picks out my shoes," she said. "I let him pick out things like that. He found these laces at the Ben Franklin. He's got them in all his shoes, too. Something appeals to him, he never wants to have it change."

He didn't know what to say. He thought that someone more adept would turn the conversation—find a way to move on to something else.

"I know you've been friends of the Brunettis' for some time," she said. "Pia told me she wished she'd planted twice the flower garden when she knew your wife was coming, because your wife was such a lover of flowers."

He looked at her, slightly puzzled. Perhaps Fran did care about flowers: though she never put flowers in their house, she had picked flowers from Pia's garden as soon as they arrived. Did she have a favorite flower? He would have to ask her.

"Pia's coming along real well," Mrs. Brikel said. "With her trouble lifting her arm, I'm surprised she got in as much of a garden as she did. Wouldn't you think she'd plant perennials? But she loves the annuals. If I went to that much trouble, I'd like them to spring up again every year."

"You don't have a garden?" he said.

"Something of one," she said, "but my cousin's boy, Jay, puts in so many things that all summer we eat the overflow."

"It seems pretty idyllic to a city boy."

"Have you been in a city all your life?" she said.

He thought about it. "Pretty much," he said. "Yes. I guess I have."

"When my son was younger I was in cities quite a lot, taking him to doctors. Waiting in doctors' offices. My heart went out to Pia when she had to go so many times for all those examinations and treatments." She looked at Chap. "How does Mr. Brunetti say she is?"

The question surprised him. He had no current information. Except for one call after his visit, when Lou said the doctors had found a drug to lessen the nausea, he hadn't heard anything. The prognosis—or was it just the hope?—was that after she completed the treatments, she would be all right.

"I don't know anything you wouldn't know," he said.

She nodded and looked down. He hoped she didn't think he had cut her off. If he had known anything, he would gladly have told her.

"I was very surprised when he called and wanted me to come to Vermont," he said. "It's also a little awkward. Not being able to tell my wife."

"I would imagine," Mrs. Brikel said.

There was a long silence that made him wish he had put on the radio as they pulled out of the parking lot.

"Of course there's not a soul on earth who doesn't have secrets," she said. "And it's funny how one minute something seems the most important thing imaginable to keep hushed up, and a year later it's something you could tell anyone."

She was looking out the window. Land was being plowed for another new shopping center. The barbershop near where the land was being plowed would probably disappear—that funny little building with the stripes spiraling down the pole out front.

"May I ask why you mentioned it to me?" Mrs. Brikel said.

"What?" he said. He had been lost in thought about urban sprawl. The way roads leading into towns already looked exactly the same.

"I was wondering why you mentioned to me that you'd been here when Pia was sick."

"I don't know why," he said, then contradicted himself. "I thought you might suddenly remember me and say something in front of my wife."

Mrs. Brikel nodded. "You know, I only saw you for a few seconds that day in the snow."

He nodded.

"You were both pretty bundled up. Hats and scarves and all of that."

"I know," he said. "It seems crazy to me now, but I thought you were going to remember me. I thought it was better to say something than take the chance."

"Wouldn't you have just said I was mistaken?"

"Well, yes, I could have," he said. "But if I wasn't thinking quickly . . . I don't know."

"Not that I mind your confidence," Mrs. Brikel said.

"I don't know what made me say that," he said, this time really considering it. "Maybe to acknowledge that I'd really been here. My wife thought I was with my cousin."

"You said that," Mrs. Brikel said.

"Did I startle you when I brought it up? I think I was a little startled myself, to be saying it. Or that I said it because something startled me. That's it: I said it because something startled me."

Mrs. Brikel smiled. "That something wouldn't have been my son, would it?"

"No," he said. It was an instant, immediate response. But then he began to wonder what *had* startled him.

"The reason I was curious is because Mr. Brunetti has also confided some things in me. Things I never would have known if he hadn't brought them up. Things that happened in another town, say. Nowhere I'd ever been." She rubbed her finger on the edge of the dashboard. "If I could say something without you thinking I meant it as personal?"

He nodded. In the rearview mirror, he saw that a car was riding his bumper. He accelerated slightly, but the car stayed with him.

"I've done some substitute teaching at the elementary school," she said. "I couldn't teach subjects, but if the gym teacher or the home economics teacher was out, sometimes they'd give me a call."

He nodded.

"And the gym teacher there was a lady named Mrs. Pepin. She had flu so many times that one fall I was called in every couple of weeks, and I got to like it and the children got to like me. Anyway, the point of my story is that when there was a Parents' Night, Mrs. Pepin told me, she was always asked to bake and serve cookies. She thought some of the other teachers would do it next, but every time the night to have the parents came around the principal would call her in and ask her to please bake and serve cookies. After three years, she asked him why he always asked her, and this man, who was even by Mrs. Pepin's account a quite nice, educated man, said, 'Because French women have a heritage of serving, and they do it so gracefully.' "

"Good God," Chap said.

"Over the years, I've tried to think about this," Mrs. Brikel said. "I don't mean Mrs. Pepin in specific, but the prejudices people have that they never examine. I don't mean to be superior in this matter. I can remember picking on a scrawny girl when I was a child just because she was thin and funny-looking. There are two things that continue to mystify me in this life. Prejudice, and why some people are drawn to other people. Drawn in so they want to tell them things. It comes as a great surprise to me that I seem to be one of those people that other people need to say things to. When our local minister was contemplating a divorce, he told me about it and swore me to secrecy. He said that if he had the courage of his convictions, he'd be gone from town soon enough, and that then he wouldn't care what I said. But for one year, the minister was still in town. It was almost another six months after that before he divorced his wife and moved to Michigan, I think it was. And shortly thereafter Mr. Brunetti moved to town. When he was returning a snow shovel he hinted at some things about his life elsewhere. Eventually he said quite a few things, although I don't consider that we have the sort of relationship that I can even ask how things really are with Mrs. Brunetti." Mrs. Brikel was rubbing her knees with both hands. She saw that he was looking at her hands and stopped. "But I don't mean I don't have some ideas," she said. "As I've thought about it, I think that people see that I've been dealt some problem cards in life, and that here I am, dealing with the situation. To me, that's just the way you have to live—the best way you can. But tell me if I'm wrong here. Do you think that because of my son being something of a trial, people think I've learned something from the experience of raising him, and that I could say something that might help them in times of stress?"

"That makes sense," he said. Once he spoke, he realized he had spoken too quickly. She was going to distrust such an automatic answer. She was going to stop talking to him just when he was trying to formulate something important to say to her. Just when his curiosity was piqued about Lou Brunetti's life.

"Of course," she said, "I can imagine that I'm making it too complicated. It might just be that people see you have one kind of problem, which makes people feel less guilty about presenting you with another one." She dropped her hands to her lap.

"Let's have a cup of coffee," he said.

She took her sunglasses off the top of her head. She looked out the window, as if he hadn't spoken, then gently pushed the arms of the glasses above her ears.

"Let's go on to the next town," she said quietly. "If I'm going to be gone awhile longer from my son, let's go somewhere that's new to me. Someplace where I'll feel like I'm really away from him."

"Who do you talk to?" he said. The car that had been riding his tail passed, cutting sharply in front of him to avoid an oncoming truck.

"Sometimes I talk to my son's father," she said, "but he has a wife and family. I can't quite pick up the phone and talk to him."

"He remarried?" Chap said. He was nervous. Why had he asked a question when he had already been told the facts?

"He's always had a wife and family," Mrs. Brikel said. "There was never a time I was married to the father of my son."

(5)

"You keep looking away," Ben said.

"I was looking at that table over there. Tired tourists not knowing what to eat."

Ordinarily, she did not eat fried food, but Fran loved the fried fish platter at this restaurant. Each time she and Ben returned, she ordered it. "And obviously it feels strange to be seeing you again," she said. She took a sip of iced tea. Before they went on vacation, she had established the lie: that she was being interviewed by a design firm that might want her to handle the graphics for a big new Boston hotel. In fact, she had already gotten a commission to do the artwork for the hotel's brochure. She did not think she would land the large part of the account, though.

"Have you been drawing in Vermont?" he said.

"I've just been batting around the house," she said. "It must seem like a real vacation, though, because my city driving reflexes didn't come back to me. And the air is killing my eyes."

He nodded. His cup of black coffee sat on the table untouched, steaming. His right hand was on the table, a few inches from the saucer, absolutely immobile.

He picked up the cup and took a sip.

"Chap and I are getting along very well," she said.

"I can't see why somebody wouldn't get along well with Chap," he said. "Such an upbeat fellow."

He infuriated her. They had been together only ten minutes, and already he was violating the rule of not criticizing the other person's mate. The four of them had crossed paths half a dozen times over the years. Boston—and the art world—was only a small game in a small town, when you came to think of it.

"I did do a still life," she said, deciding not to let him spark her anger. "I'd hoped the house would have interesting spaces and that things . . ." She frowned in concentration. "That things would call out to be sketched. But the house is strange. A lot of it is empty space, like the kitchen, and when you do find things you might draw, they look too predictable. Like duck decoys. Or the collections of things they have."

"What do they collect?" he said.

"More stuff than you could imagine. I was in his study and closed the door behind me, and there were shelves behind the door holding blue Fiestaware. Imagine finding that behind a door?"

"So you went into his study to snoop, huh?" Ben said. A year before, Ben had been a sort of mentor to her. She had taken one of his classes at night. As a former teacher, she liked the way he was always one step ahead of any student, however advanced the student might be. Now she tended to think that he just didn't listen.

"I went in because I heard a noise somewhere in the house, coming from that direction."

"But if there's a prowler, you're never supposed to close doors behind you," he said. "You haven't watched enough late-night movies." He took another sip of coffee. "What else do they collect?" he said.

"Why are you so interested?"

"Because I'm a visual sort of person," he said. "I like to be able to imagine where you are."

She smiled in spite of herself. When he said he was "visual," he was alluding to a pronouncement someone had made about him at a cocktail party. They had found the drunk's interpretation of Ben's raison d'être particularly funny. They had gone late to the cocktail party, and arrived sober, because they had been making love.

"I used to collect powder horns," he said. "I still collected them when I was in college. They were what my grandfather collected, but after a while I couldn't see the point in buying powder horns and putting them in boxes." He finished his coffee and looked for the waitress. In profile, Ben was the most handsome man Fran had ever known. Though she had met him as a grown woman, she still had something of a schoolgirl's crush on him. The waitress was coming toward them with a pot of coffee. "The way some of them are embossed reminds me of certain drawings of yours," he said. As the waitress poured, he said: "I should dig some of the good ones out and send them to you."

"We're never meeting again?" she said.

"Excuse me," the waitress said. She put the coffeepot on a busboy's cart. "Would you like to order?"

Ben opened his menu. "Do you know what you want?" he said to Fran. Please get some excitement into your voice about the fisherman's platter, he thought. Please get some excitement into your voice about something.

Her eyes lit up a bit when she ordered the fisherman's platter. Coleslaw, not french fries. Yes: another iced tea.

He ordered broiled mackerel. He asked for a Samuel Adams. That satisfied both desires: not to drink, because he might get morose, but to have a beer, because a beer was not a potent mixed drink that would go to his head.

When the waitress walked away, he, too, looked at the tourists. They were pale and slightly overweight. Their teenage son did nothing to disguise his annoyance at being on the trip. One of the things Ben hoped most earnestly was that his three-year-old son would never become sulky and estranged from him. They could change the ground rules entirely when the boy hit puberty, if it came to that. Whatever it took, Ben was willing to do it.

"Well," Ben said, "our rental on the Vineyard fell through. They returned the check last week, when there was no chance in hell of our finding anything else, with a scrawled note that didn't even have our names on it. They said they'd decided to rent the house year-round, and the tenant was already occupying it. We've rented that house for the last six years, and that's the sort of kiss-off we get. Great, huh?"

She gnawed her lip. She felt sure that he was saying something indirectly about the two of them. Obviously, that was why he was so angry.

"We had a signed rental agreement," he said. "If my lawyer wasn't already working on two other things, I'd dump this one on his desk."

"You always talk about Rob as if you hardly know him. 'My lawyer.' He was your college roommate."

He shrugged. "When we're playing handball I think of him as my college roommate, and when I'm pissed, I think of him as my lawyer."

The busboy brought bread and butter. For a second, the white napkin folded over the basket reminded him of his son's diapers. He had been awake at five a.m., changing his diapers.

"You can find a place somewhere on the Cape to rent," she said. "People always cancel at the last minute."

"Maybe we could have your friends' house," he said. "Didn't you tell me they were leaving for a month, but you could only be there two weeks because that was all the vacation time Chap had?"

She looked at him. There was some small chance that he was completely serious.

"It's just a house in the middle of nowhere," she said.

"Aren't you skeptical of my wife for liking flashy things? It might be a way to start deconditioning her."

"I think you and your wife should try to work out your problems on more neutral territory," she said. "I always have thought you should work out your problems."

He surprised her by laughing. He fluttered his eyelids and said, quite archly: "I always have thought you should work out your problems."

The busboy, passing with bread he was carrying to another table, looked down as he heard Ben speaking in falsetto.

Ben saw the boy slow down and could hardly muffle his laughter. Fran, too, began laughing.

"You're lucky he walked by when he did," Fran said. "You'll probably be shocked to hear that I was about to strongly object to your impersonation of me."

" 'Atta girl," he said. "Got to defend yourself in this world."

"You know," she said, "you talk about people in the capacity in which they exist: my wife; my lawyer. You always say 'my son' and 'my tenants,' and the people who live downstairs from you have been there for what? Ten years?"

"I don't get your point," he said. "I hear your voice icing over, but I'm not quite sure what you're getting at."

"You don't use people's names," she said.

The family they had watched earlier got up. The teenage son was the last to leave the table, and he pushed all the chairs back in place, which broke her heart. She could remember being places she had not wanted to be, and acting inappropriately. Tripping over herself in an attempt not to stumble. What equanimity she had now had not even begun until she was in her twenties. What did she still do that communicated things she was oblivious of signaling? Until Ben mentioned the way her voice became detached and cold—icing over, as he called it—she had had no idea of her immediate impulse to withdraw when there was contention. She knew she sometimes lifted her hand to her head and fluffed her hair, but she had not known about the voice change until he pointed it out.

"Ben," she said suddenly, "I don't feel there and I don't feel here. I do think it's a good idea that we be friends, but coming back to the city to meet you, when I was off in the woods on vacation, just makes me feel . . ."

"It makes you feel bad," he said. "You've always been very consistent about saying that. That basically, seeing me under any circumstances makes you feel bad. Why don't you tell me a lie for a change and see if there's some truth in the lie."

"I don't want to lie to you," she said. "I feel peculiar about seeing you. I'm afraid I didn't cancel this lunch because of cowardice. I wanted to fall back on you, in case the vacation turned out to be a disaster."

"Is that true?"

She nodded yes.

"We're friends," he said. "What's wrong with wanting something from me?"

He was astonished when tears began to roll down her cheeks. So surprised that he pushed his chair back, wanting to embrace her. He would have, if she had not held up her hand. What a strange gesture! As if those delicate fingers could stop anything more tangible than a breeze. He thought of the school crossing guard at his son's preschool. The black gloves so large they must have been padded. Yet why would a crossing guard have boxer's mitts? Or was that the way the man's hands had looked, after all? He blinked, remembering his son, early that morning, walking in front of him, the sun striking his ash-blond hair, and the gloved hand at the crossing guard's side, the other hand raised to stop traffic. He thought: The crossing guard was Tony Hightower, taking his turn as a volunteer. Not a crossing guard, *Tony Hightower.*

"You look terrible," she said, drying her cheeks. "I'm sorry. Let's talk about something else. Do you know anything funny?"

He sighed, letting the image go. "I'm sure that's what half the people in the restaurant are doing," he said. "Half of them are recounting disasters, and the other half are telling jokes."

The waitress appeared at Fran's side.

"What do you think?" he said to the waitress, who was lowering a plate. "I just said to my friend that I thought half the people here were yukking it up and the other half were in great distress."

"Whichever way it starts out, they always walk out in the opposite mood," she said. She was standing there with her hands at her sides, like a child reciting. She reached up and touched her earring. "At least, that's usually true," she said. "If they're drunk, it's another thing. But if they're just in a good mood, they'll be sedate when they leave, and if they came in quiet, they'll be talking up a storm when they go out."

Ben was looking at Fran, who was looking at the waitress. It wasn't collusion, Fran knew—there was no way he could have put the waitress up to saying what she'd said. But what had she said, really, that puzzled her so deeply? Just that people changed?

"I don't often stop to think about it," the waitress said, springing into action again and giving Ben his lunch. "Is there anything else I can get for you?"

"You probably see it all in a second, don't you?" Fran said. "You can probably look in their eyes and see what kind of a tip they're going to leave."

"Oh, I don't know about that," the waitress said.

"What their relationship is to one another," Fran said.

"Yes," the waitress said, looking directly into Fran's eyes. "I'm usually right about that."

(6)

Disturbing, Chap thought. Disturbing to get such a self-pitying letter from Marshall, saying that summer would be the ideal time to die. That predictable periphrasis: "Passing on to the Heavenly Kingdom."

Disturbing that the Brunettis' house seemed to intensify Fran's feeling of isolation. Though she had finally perched on one of the wooden kitchen stools to draw a still life of fruit in a wicker basket, her heart hadn't been in it. Things had to speak to Fran—declare their necessity, so she would not feel she was just some zookeeper, capturing them—or drawing became just a chore. Of the several drawings she had done during their stay, the first seemed to him the most complex and . . . well, disturbing. The loose weave of the basket was picked up, or rather made to seem similar to, the grillwork of the Galaxy fan they had brought with them. Once the eye detected the strange similarity between the fan front's splayed metallic regularity and the basket's handwoven symmetry, though, you began to notice what the grillwork hid (amber blades) and what the basket contained (shiny, overripe fruit). That was what artists did. Like poets, they ferreted out strange connections. Though he was not really sure what conclusion could be drawn from what he observed in Fran's drawing. That two dissimilar things were similar? If that was all there was to it, why wouldn't she jumble together any number of similar shapes?

He looked, again, at Anthony Brunetti's drawing he had seen his first night in the house. Naturally Lou would like the fact that his son could think three-dimensionally. That the boy was not put off by the material world, but saw in it shapes that could be exposed, transparent cubes wittily tipped and rectangles into which he could stare.

He remembered seeing *2001* stoned, and how utterly convincing and involving it had seemed. He wondered if there was a video store nearby, and whether he might be able to rent that movie to watch again, although he realized at the same time that in doing so, he would just be opening the floodgates for disappointment.

That word again.

He finished his letter to Marshall a bit more abruptly than he intended. He was afraid that if he went on, and allowed larger issues to intrude, he would never be able to keep Marshall focused on the facts. When a person was in distress, it was not the time for anyone else to question the order of the cosmos. He had written a firm, fond letter to Marshall, enclosing a check and telling him to have the house insulated before winter, or he would be forced to go there and hire somebody to do the job himself.

Of course he realized that Marshall had not wanted the mention of winter's cold to suggest only the temperature of the house. He knew perfectly well what Marshall meant, but except for insisting on his own affection for Marshall, he could not imagine what incentive to go on he might offer.

He was sitting on a kitchen stool. He had pushed it across the floor so it was six feet away from the area where Fran had been drawing. She had her spot, he had his. In her spot, a few tiny gnats spiraled up from the ripe bananas. In his, there was a stain made by the bottom of the coffee mug. He gave it a moment's thought: it was interesting that while the Brunettis liked variety among the things they collected, the kitchen plates and cups were all uniform: mugs in different colors, but exactly the same shape. Simple white plates in graduated sizes.

He was not sure which of Pia's breasts had been removed. But of course that did not matter at all. The fact of having one breast missing was horrible, but undoubtedly something a man could never really understand, just as a woman couldn't really know what it felt like to be kicked in the balls.

The sun was shining on the garden. Butterflies fluttered. For a split second, he allowed a Daliesque scene to shimmer outside the kitchen window, where a naked-torsoed Pia stood behind the garden, like the Virgin presiding over paradise. Just as quickly the image was gone, and he thought, for the second time that day, about LSD. About seeing *2001* stoned, about the chances he had taken, the time he had wasted during that period of his life when he often viewed the world through a drug haze.

He ground fresh coffee. As the water boiled, he thought that skills—things you could do in the world—were likely to help you, but that objects—because they could never be complex enough, and rarely beautiful enough—would almost always disappoint you. Fran was not a skier, so it was difficult to explain to her how the same ski slope could be so involving, day after day. The slope itself was fascinating: varying, even as you rode the lift to descend again. But the further fascination was in your own skill, because you could never tell when chance would intervene, when you would have to compensate for something that was happening. Only an egocentric fool would try to predict his response vis-à-vis chance and as a variable in danger. You just snapped to, even when it already seemed too late, and you found yourself operating automatically.

He turned off the water, deciding that caffeine was the last thing he needed. He even took a deep breath and left the kitchen, suspecting, as Fran did, that the room made him a little crazy. Bad vibes, he would have said in the sixties. Or no vibes at all, which was just as bad.

He, too, discovered the Fiestaware in Lou's study. The window above Lou's drafting table had been left open, and the wind that had begun to blow as the sky clouded over sucked the door closed. When Chap opened the door, he looked for a doorstop and found, instead, the shelf of blue dishes. Marshall's wife had had some of those plates, though he hadn't seen them in years. By now, they were probably all broken.

Lou's room did have good vibrations. The posters from European museums were in good taste; the architectural drawings drew you in. He sat on Lou's high chair and looked out the window. He could imagine being an architect. Which also made him think about Fran, and the decision she was trying to come to about what job to move on to next. When you were an adult, you could not easily try on other professions: no dressing up in a white hat as a nurse; no clomping around in fire-men's boots. It was no longer a matter of how you dressed that trans-ported you, but the possibilities, say, awakened by music, though explaining its direct application would have made you sound like a fool.

He pushed the POWER button on Lou's stereo, then the PLAY but-ton for the tape inside. Whatever it was was unfamiliar. He listened for quite a while, though, liking it—liking being in the room sitting on Lou's drafting chair, his feet dangling because they could not touch the floor—preoccupied by the motion of a wasp examining the outside win-dow frame. It had such a delicate, frightening body, and it was so intent upon what it was doing. Though there was every chance that the wasp was only programmed. That what it was doing had nothing to do with selectivity and everything to do with survival. The wasp flew up, then landed and crawled to the top corner of the outside window frame. It was just a little too far away for him to see it clearly without his glasses. In a minute or two, during which he lowered the window a bit because the breeze was coming much stronger and there was going to be a storm, the music changed. As he was transported, the music changed once again. The tape must have been a compilation of things Lou liked. He pushed EJECT and took out the tape. He had been wrong: it was a tape by a group called Metropolis. They were so good they could play in a variety of musical styles and be utterly convincing. Fran's favorite book by Calvino was on the floor. A book by Richard Rorty was on Lou's drafting table, the charge receipt tucked inside. Another wasp joined the wasp crawling outside the window. The first drops of rain began to fall. He got up, closed the window all the way, and went back to the kitchen, where he stood looking out the screen door. The driveway was deeply rutted. The holes had been filled with muddy water when he and Fran arrived, from so much rain. Mosquitoes hovered outside the screen, wanting to get in. He realized his folly: he was anthropomorphizing again. They were instinctually drawn to the surface of the screen. Who knew what made them hover?

He rubbed his hand over his forehead. The conversation a couple of days before, with Mrs. Brikel, came back to him in snatches, though he remembered more what she looked like, the view from the window of the tiny restaurant, the missing letters on the shop across the street: JOH DEER. As he and Mrs. Brikel talked about things left incomplete, the fragment of the sign above her head, across the street, had riveted his attention. Mrs. Brikel's love affair gone wrong. His insistence, in the face of no opposition from Mrs. Brikel, that he and his wife confided easily in each other.

Hadn't she led him to a chair when the bee bit him?

But what did that have to do with sharing confidences?

He tried to conjure up Fran's presence in the house, but it was slow in coming and vague when it seemed to be there.

"Frannie, Frannie, Frannie," he said aloud, though he had not used her nickname in years.

(7)

He snapped a branch off a bush, threw it to the ground, and walked past the blue clapboard house where the painters had been scraping wood for what seemed like half the summer. The shutters had been removed and were stacked in the carport, the Audi backed out in the driveway. One of the men was getting a drink of water from the hose and made a motion as if to spray him as he walked by.

He waved. It was the house of the woman who sometimes sat with him in the evening, Mrs. Torius. Her name was much longer than that. She was a Greek woman with a name too long to spell and too hard to pronounce, so he called her Mrs. Torius. He had laughed about it when he found out that Spaniards called bulls *toro*. Most of what he knew he had found out from television, although his mother still insisted on reading schoolbooks to him as if he were small. He was five feet ten inches, and twenty-six years old. For twenty years his mother had been thinking over whether he could have another gerbil, because he had killed the first one. He didn't care anymore, but it was something to keep after her about.

"Get on home, Loretta," he squealed. There were many things the Beatles ordered people to do that he liked to hear. "Don't leave me standing here" was another, though he could never get the cadence of that one right, so he just shouted it.

"How ya doin' today, Royce?" the mailman said.

"You've got the mail," Royce said.

The mailman walked on. In the cartoons, dogs bit mailmen.

Royce, after promising he wouldn't go out, had left a note for his mother (he had whirled the yellow crayon around and around in a circle, so she would know he was taking a walk around the neighborhood; it had cut the paper, and he was going to be in trouble for getting crayon marks on the kitchen counter, which was not where he was supposed to color). In his note, he also told her, in purple Magic Marker, that he was going to bring home a fish. He liked fish very much, but his mother would only buy fish sticks because it disgusted her to see the way he chewed and chewed so carefully to make sure there were no bones, which would kill him if he swallowed them.

"Get on home, Loretta," he said again, to a cat crossing his path. The cat could have run away from a Dr. Seuss book. Come to think of it, he could be the man in *The Cat in the Hat* because he had put on a top hat for his stroll. A walk was a stroll if you went slower than you normally walk. He slowed down even more, putting the heel of one red-laced high-topper against the toe of his other shoe, and alternating feet so he moved forward one footstep at a time.

John, his second-favorite Beatle, was dead.

Royce stopped to practice the Heimlich maneuver on an imaginary victim of choking. Then he metamorphosed into Batman and the bad guy fell to the ground, knocked unconscious. He put his arms above his head, knowing full well that he wouldn't disappear like Batman, and he didn't. He had seen *Batman* three times. The first time he saw it he sat through it a second time. He made such a stink that his mother couldn't get him to leave and gave up. The other time he had to promise all day that he would only sit through *Batman* one time, if she allowed him to go. She did not go inside with him, having also made him promise that he would sit alone and not say anything to anybody. His mother was crazy if she thought he always had something to say. He didn't.

His favorite pies were cherry, apple, blueberry, peach. In the order: apple, cherry, peach . . . and he could not at the moment remember the other kind of pie he liked.

He poked his finger in the air to make a decimal point. Ralph Sampson got to it, though, and once his hand touched it, it became a basketball. Score one victory. Jump off the ground and fly it up there, Ralph. Easy come, easy go.

That was what his mother said when he got his footprints on something, like the bedsheets or the dining-room table, which he was forbidden to stand on. *The Cat in the Hat* propped up one side of the recliner chair he sat in to watch TV. The house was old and the living-room floor sloped, but he liked sitting on the most sloping part. And the book made the tilt better. He teased his mother by leaning way over the side of the chair and waving his arms, saying "Whooooooooooo" sometimes, pretending he was falling off the side of a ship. He could always make her ask why he didn't sit elsewhere.

His plan for catching the fish was to puff up his chest and dive into the Mediterranean Sea and get one from one of the frogmen who hunted fish at night with spears. He had just seen a show about night fishing off the coast of Italy. The men put on black suits and floated in shallow water, looking for what they wanted. He intended to see what he wanted by going to the water's edge and peering in. It was very bad to go out when he had promised to stay home, but even worse to go near water. Therefore, he would carefully peer in. At the curb, he tested: he leaned slightly forward, like an elegant, myopic British gentleman about to meet someone of importance. The night before, on television, he had seen a movie in which an Englishman with a monocle eventually reached for some princess's hand. People in that movie had been wearing top hats. His mother had had her father's top hat in a box on the top shelf of the closet for years. He had brought it down with his magnet-vision. He just looked at a thing and it came to him. This only happened when his mother was not at home, though.

One of the boys in his crafts class, where he made belts and pouches and might be allowed to make a pair of moccasins, wore a diaper. A few days before, the boy had unbuttoned his long pants and let them drop around his ankles while the teacher's attention was elsewhere. Mothers always liked buttons better than zippers, because they were harder to undo.

He thought that he had been on the corner long enough. He put one toe in the water. It was dry. He looked both ways. No fish yet. He decided to swim across the stream, but in case anyone came along he wouldn't want to appear to be swimming, because they might tell his mother. What he would do would be look left and right and then hurry across the stream with only his invisible arms swimming.

He did so, and got to the other side.

For almost an hour, Royce walked in the direction of the reservoir. He had gone there years ago with his mother—more than once, actually—but his sense of direction was bad, so it was difficult to say what kept him on course. Walking along in his chinos, with a tie-dyed shirt he had picked out himself and a top hat, he might have fooled anyone whizzing by in a car who didn't notice the expression on his face, because this part of Vermont was still full of hippies. Where the hill dipped, instinct carried him once more down the road, where it forked to the right, and once on it, he was headed directly toward his destination. His mother and father had often walked with him there on summer nights, up until the time he began to scream because he wanted to go in the water. Though he had no memory of it, his screaming when he was two years old had brought his mother to tears, daily. She had taken tranquilizers and considered institutionalizing him. His father stopped coming, because his mother would no longer speak to him. Sometimes, for as much as a week, he and his mother would stay inside the house. In the house, she could run away from him and lock herself behind a door. Some things he did were only the things any baby would do, yet she reacted strongly to them. When he reached for her glasses, she stopped wearing them and functioned in a fog. When he was old enough to pull out her shoelaces, she did not replace them. She had a lock on one small closet that contained clothes she would wear when she took him into Boston to see doctors. Except for those clothes, she would often stay, all day, in her nightgown. Even after his teeth came through, she rubbed his gums with whiskey, hoping he might fall asleep earlier. She would smash delicate things that fascinated him before he had a chance. They drank from paper cups and ate more food than was reasonable with their fingers.

He took off one shoe and sock and left them by a tree, because the little piggy that cried "Wee-wee-wee" all the way home was also telling him it wanted to walk barefoot on the grass. When he took off the shoe, he made a mental note of where to find it again. He had left it at tree number fifty. There were exactly four thousand four hundred and ninety-six trees on this road to the reservoir.

Pale white clouds began to turn luminous, becoming the same yellowish color—something like burnt yellow—as the water in town, where the water was shallow as it fanned out to go over the waterfall. The clouds were quickly overlapping. It was as if blotting paper was soaking up all color. From second to second, more brightness faded as a stronger wind blew up. This was the sort of wind that preceded an alien landing. It could be used to advantage, Royce also knew, by criminals, who would step through broken store windows and steal whatever was to be had. In the distance, he heard sirens.

By now, he could see cars parked off the side of the road and the big green hill that led to the water. He looked down and saw that he had cut his toe. He crossed his arms across his chest and marched bravely on. He only stopped when he felt the wind start to lift his hat. He pulled it lower on his forehead, then ran his fingers along his temples to feel the fringe of mashed-down hair.

Several sirens were wailing at the same time. He looked over his shoulder. Two men were hurrying toward their truck: no fire in the distance, no car through which a toppled tree had crashed. He looked at the front of his shirt and thought that the mottled orange and yellow looked like fire. That made him feel powerful again, and he pulled his foot out of his other sneaker and kicked it high, like a football. It landed in the grass partway up the hill. By now the clouds were dark gray against a pale gray sky, and blowing so they twisted one in front of the other. He was a little out of breath from trying to breathe in such wind. He had to duck his head to breathe easily. When he got to his shoe, he sat down for a minute, enjoying the way the raindrops fell, flicking themselves over his body. He touched his hand to the top of his hat. The rain made the same sound falling on his hat that it did when it fell on the roof. He looked at the trees fringing the flat land on which bright green grass grew, now made dusty green by blowing dirt and a lack of light. The grass was newly mowed; something in the air made him sneeze. He sneezed several times in succession, blessing himself after each explosion, yelling God's name louder each time. His feet were cold, and he thought about going back for the abandoned shoe, but the wind was blowing across the water in the reservoir so enticingly that he was transfixed. It reminded him of what it looked like when his mother peeled Saran Wrap back from a tray of chocolate-frosted brownies.

When the next gust of wind blew the top hat from his head and sent it skipping down the darkening grass, he followed behind, hobbling a bit because of his cut toe. He put his hands over his ears. The sound the wind made, rushing through the trees—a sound like paper being crumpled—muted. The sirens' wail continued. What do fish hear? he thought.

A couple ran past, a sweater or jacket that was too small held over their heads as they laughed, running from the picnic area. They were the last people to see Royce, and later the girl said she believed that she had seen his hat blow in the water, though she had no reason to concentrate on that or anything else in her desperate rush toward shelter.

Maybe the fish said *glug-glug*. Maybe they talked the way fish did in fairy tales, and said something like: Come into the kingdom of the deep. Or maybe the hat itself started to talk, and that was what made Royce edge into the water, looking back as if taunting someone behind him as he advanced.

The reservoir was posted: no swimming, no boating, no water sports of any kind. No no no no no. Just a beautiful body of water that could magnetize people. Picnic tables to eat at while they enjoyed the view. Little paths that worked their way into the woods like shallow veins running down an arm. A place where lovers could stroll.

The hat was found floating, like a hat in one of the comics Royce loved so much. The shoes were found first, then the hat.

(8)

All her life Mrs. Brikel had been struck by the way people and things turned up when they were most needed and least expected. Today, just when she was feeling discouraged because her cold had lingered so long, a flower arrangement had been delivered from the local florist—a thank-you from a professor whose paper she had typed the night before on a moment's notice, staying up until midnight so he could present it today at a conference in Chicago. There were daisies, roses, and three irises in the flower arrangement—a lovely sight to see in midwinter.

Since the publication of Pia Brunetti's book almost a year before, Mrs. Brikel's typing services had been much in demand. The acknowledgment in Pia's book thanked Mrs. Brikel for her dedication and support: when Pia was unable to type for so long after her mastectomy, the entire task of typing the manuscript had fallen to Mrs. Brikel. But who would have done otherwise? It was not as though Pia had not paid her. As well as being an occasion for kindness, it had allowed her to develop her typing skills. She now had a word processor and more work than she had ever imagined. Suddenly she was doing very nicely in terms of income. The previous summer she had planted annuals instead of perennials. The house, if not exactly toasty warm, was quite comfortable since insulation had been blown into the attic and aluminum siding had been installed. If Royce were still alive, it would be much too hot for him in the house. He had sat around in his shirtsleeves even in winter because he was never cold. The house would seem like a sauna bath to Royce.

Recently a health club had opened in town, and she had been hired to type the information that would be included in the brochure. The young woman who managed the health club, Marsha, had invited her, the week before, to use the facilities. She had ridden the stationary bicycle. At first she had laughed and said she was too old for such a thing, but Marsha's husband, who was older than she, had proven her wrong by jumping onto one of the bikes and pedaling a mile, grinning, as she protested that she herself was rather uncoordinated. Bicycling was good for the circulation, and although she would feel silly going out on the street on a bicycle, she saw no point in not using one at the health club. Afterward, she would change into her bathing suit and sink into the hot tub's warm bubbling water, which soothed her shoulder muscles. She had thought about using the sauna, but something about the uncomfortable-looking wood benches and the sharp smell of pine had made her hesitate: perhaps sometime when Marsha had time to join her, she would spend five or ten minutes in the sauna.

It came as no surprise to Mrs. Brikel that the town was changing. Those children she had seen all her life were bound to grow up and have children of their own. Now, instead of rushing off to the city to make their mark, many people wanted to settle into life in a small town. They missed out on something, but they gained something, as well: a sense of the continuity of days; a feeling of belonging.

Chap had written her recently that he was giving serious thought to moving to Vermont. He had always seemed the sort of person who might prosper under the right circumstances. Since his divorce—his wife had run off with another man, at the end of the summer they spent house-sitting for the Brunettis—he had gone through quite a metamorphosis. Now Anthony Brunetti had gone to live with him outside Boston. Lou, after the book's publication and his separation from Pia, had moved to California. And Pia—of course, Pia was now back in Italy and the toast of the town, as well as being a widely respected feminist author in the United States.

As she was looking for her car keys (she had promised Marsha she would drop off a letter to new members Marsha had given her earlier in the week), a word came to Mrs. Brikel's mind: *paradoxically.* Typing Pia's manuscript—or perhaps more exactly, reading the reviews—had provided Mrs. Brikel with quite an education. The reviewer for the *Boston Globe* had said that Pia's book was about the Americanization of an Italian family. The reviewer wrote that *paradoxically,* only when she learned she had cancer and faced the prospect of death did Pia truly come to have a sense of her own individuality and strength. Mrs. Brikel had read the book twice—reading was quite a different thing from typing a manuscript—and on the second reading, with the help of the newspaper reviews, she began to see more clearly why people thought about the book the way they did. On first reading, she had thought that Pia was writing only about the difficulty of having made a specific transition. It seemed to her that a family would naturally have some trouble adapting to life in a new country. A family, like a small town, was a particular thing: you had to give up something in order to gain something. You had to give up some . . . what? Some individuality, for the common good. The only part of the book that still seemed puzzling was the part she had typed last, but that came first: the introduction.

In the introduction, Pia had made public a very surprising secret. Typing it, Mrs. Brikel had been uncomfortable. Imagine allowing the world to know that before going on vacation, she had taken the two special brassieres she had had made after her surgery and hidden them in the attic, in a suitcase inside another suitcase, so there was no chance her friends who were house-sitting would discover them and therefore discover her secret. That was not the most shocking part, however. The shocking part was Pia's admission that she took it for granted her friends would snoop through her house. She spoke of them as if they were burglars looking for silver, or teenagers hunting for the liquor cabinet. Perhaps such things went on more than she knew. She had read letters in Ann Landers from people who claimed to have stumbled upon drug paraphernalia in the apartment of a friend, had overheard girls at school complaining that their mothers read their diaries. Looking through a keyhole had never held any fascination for Mrs. Brikel. Sticking her nose in other people's business (as her own mother had called prying) had never seemed a way to maintain a friendship. Even when you did not ask, you usually heard more than you wanted to, in Mrs. Brikel's experience.

She put on her hat and coat and picked up the keys from the little dish on the table in the hallway. It was not really a dish, but a saucer— a piece of Fiestaware in a dark shade of blue that Mr. Brunetti had given her as a little souvenir. She had gone to the Brunettis' house to return a turkey baster Pia had once loaned her, as Mr. Brunetti had been packing to leave, and he had told her to please just keep the turkey baster. Then he had straightened up—he had been packing things in his study, and his face looked very bad, though perhaps it was just red because he had been bent over for so long—he had straightened up and said he supposed a turkey baster was not really the nicest thing he could think to offer her. Then he had asked what she might really like, and she had understood from the way he looked at her that if she said she would like the living-room sofa, it could have been hers. If she had said that she would like every picture on the wall, or even the china press, and all the china, that would have been hers also. So she had pointed at the closest thing: the piece of unpacked Fiestaware. She was sure that if she did not choose something small, he would insist she take something large and expensive. She tended to like things that were more delicate than Fiestaware, and in fact blue was not her favorite color, but she had been a little unnerved by his expression. So there it was, then—the blue saucer that served quite nicely as a place to keep her keys. As soon as she got a package of Kleenex from the kitchen drawer she would be ready to leave.

But instead of going into the kitchen, she sat down in the living room, luxuriating, for a moment, in the added warmth of her coat in what was finally, after all these years, a perfectly well insulated house. The sun was moving westward. In a couple of hours it would set and sink below the mountains.

She tapped her toes together, and looked at her shoes. They were a new sort of shoe Marsha had told her about that exercised the foot when you walked and resembled a ballet slipper: black cloth, with a small grosgrain bow on top. She liked them so much, and they were so comfortable, that sometimes she forgot where she lived—forgot that outside there was dirty snow, and deep mud where the snow had melted—and she would occasionally start out the door as if she could simply breeze off without a care in the world in her delicate new shoes.

In the spring she would wear them outdoors. She might even ride a bicycle to and from town then, if she built up more strength riding the stationary bike during the winter. What did it matter if you were a little eccentric, if you did not act exactly like everyone else? People were quick to forgive. They forgave you because they were eager to keep things polite and eager to get on with their own lives. On the day of Royce's funeral, everyone had offered their condolences and admired her for what she had done. They spoke about the lightning that had struck the tree, the sudden storm that had blown up—they said everything they could think to say about what a gray, wild, windy day it had been, while saying nothing about the fact that if the sun had been shining, the flowers blooming, and all of nature glistening in the sunlight, Royce would still have wandered away, taken some crazy idea into his head, and drowned. The only difference might have been that if there had been no storm, someone might have been at the reservoir to hear his cries.

But who knew whether he had made a sound? The only sound might have been the slight stirring of water displaced by a body.

It was very hard to be alone in the world. Not alone as in no-one-in-the-house alone, but by yourself, even when you meant to be. Certain people would be drawn to you and would buzz around as if a quiet person, a woman in late middle age, no longer attractive, could provide them with nectar. Years before, her lover—Royce's father—had hovered around that way. He was one of those people who would get as close as she allowed. It seemed not quite real now, all those rendezvous, and those late-night whispered phone conversations with him. Surprising and a bit sad, too, that Mr. Brunetti had wanted to confess first his peccadilloes, then his absolute shame—his feeling that he could never forgive himself for ruining Pia's life. Perhaps when sex was not involved it was easier for people to forgive. It had been years before she first had sex with Royce's father—that had not been the nature of the attraction. And now she was old. Safe, in a way. Though there had been that odd moment the summer Royce died when she and Chap had coffee and the tension between them had been, undeniably, sexual. There was some urge as intimate as sex, though it had nothing to do with sex itself, which had made him confess that she had seen him when he first visited the Brunettis. She would never have remembered. That snowy day, and she had been in such a hurry. But he had wanted her to know that he had been there, a real person, someone she needed to factor into the landscape.

Sitting in the newly upholstered chair, enjoying the colors of the flowers in the fading light, she let her eyes sweep slowly across the floor. After Royce's death, it had taken three men only one afternoon to make it perfectly level. The high polyurethane gloss made the floorboards glisten like water. It looked like a large, calm lake that she could imagine gliding swiftly over. Just looking at it, she could feel the buoyance of her heart.

IMAGINE A DAY AT THE END OF YOUR LIFE

Sometimes I do feel subsumed by them. My wife, Harriet, only wanted two children in the first place. With the third and fourth, I was naturally pressing for a son. The fifth, Michael, was an accident. Jenny was third and Denise was number four. Number one, Carolyn, was always the most intelligent and the most troublesome; Joan was always the one whose talent I thought would pan out, but there's no arguing with what she says: dancers are obsessive, vain people, and many of them have problems with drugs and drink, and it's no fun to watch people disfigure their bodies in the name of art. Jenny was rather plain. She developed a good sense of humor, probably as compensation for not being as attractive or as talented as the older ones. The fourth, Denise, was almost as talented at painting as Joan was at dance, but she married young and gave it up, except for creating her family's Christmas card. Michael is a ski instructor in Aspen—sends those tourists down the slopes with a smile. I think he likes the notion of keeping people at a distance. He has felt overwhelmed all his life.

My wife's idea of real happiness is to have all the family lined up on the porch in their finery, with their spouses and all the children, being photographed like the Royal Family. She's always bustled with energy. She gave the rocking chair to Goodwill last spring because, she said, it encouraged lethargy.

Harriet is a very domestic woman, but come late afternoon she's at the Remington, conjuring up bodies buried in haystacks and mass murderers at masked balls—some of the weirdest stuff you can imagine. She's done quite well financially writing these mysteries, and every couple of years we hire a driver and set off across the United States, stopping to see friends and family. At night, in the motel room, she puts the typewriter on the bureau, piles pillows on one of the chairs, and starts typing. Nothing interferes with her concentration. At home, she might run off after lunch to examine an animal in the zoo, or even march onto a construction site with her tape recorder to ask questions about ditch digging. She has a lot of anecdotes, and that keeps things lively. We get more than our share of invitations to parties. People would have us to breakfast if we'd go.

Harriet says that I'm spoiled by how much fun we have and that it's going to be hard to settle for the way life will be when we're old. At the end of every year we've got a dozen new friends. Policemen who've taken a liking to her, or whoever's new at the local library. Last year a man who imported jumping beans lived with us for a month, when he was down on his luck. Those boxes, out in the hallway, sounded like the popcorn machine at the movies.

Some people undervalue what Harriet does, or don't have sympathy with my having resigned my position on the route, but how many more years are dairies going to deliver, anyway? I got to feeling like a dinosaur, passing the time until the great disaster. I felt like a vanishing breed, is what I mean. And how many people would go on doing what they've been doing if they had the means to do otherwise?

The girls are good-natured about their mother, and I think that Jenny and Denise, in particular, quite admire her. Things didn't ever really come together and take shape for those two, but that's understandable, because no matter how much you try, every parent does have favorites. I was quite taken aback by Carolyn because she was so attractive and intelligent. Maybe instead of saying that she was a real favorite, I should say that she was a real shock. She walked at eight months! Never took time to crawl. One day, outside the playpen, she pulled herself up and took off across the rug. There she went. She married a fool, but she seems happy with his foolishness. Joan is remarried to a very nice man who owns a bank—flat out owns it!—in Michigan. She's recovered well from her bad first marriage, which isn't surprising, considering that she's in her first year of law school and has inherited two daughters. There are three dalmatians, too. Dogs that eat her out of house and home. Jenny works as a buyer for a big department store, and she's pretty close to her younger sister, Denise. All year, Jenny thinks about sweaters, contracts with people to knit sweaters, goes to look at the plants where sweaters are manufactured. That's what we get as gifts: sweaters. She and Denise go on sweater-shopping expeditions in the spring. Harriet and I get postcards telling us what the towns look like, what they ate for dinner, and sometimes anecdotes about how the two of them located some interesting sweater.

Michael, lately, is the problem. That's the way it is: you hope and hope for a particular child and that's the one who's always eluding you. He'll plan a trip home and cancel it at the last minute, send pictures that are too blurry to see his face. Occasionally I get mad and tell him that he neglects his mother and me, but those comments just roll off his back. He says that he doesn't cause us any trouble and that he doesn't ask for anything, which isn't the issue at all. He keeps bringing up that he offered to teach me to ski and that I turned him down. I'm not athletically inclined. He takes that personally. It's so often the way that the position you're in as a parent gets reversed, so that one day you're the one who lags behind. You're the one who won't try anything new. Michael's always been a rather argumentative boy, but I've never believed in fighting fire with fire. Harriet says he's the apple of my eye, but as I said to her: "What does that mean? That when Michael's here, I see red?" With the last three, I think, both she and I slacked off.

Live in the present, Harriet's always telling me. As a joke, she's named the man who runs the morgue in her mysteries, who's a worry-wart, after me. But I never did hold with the notion that you should have children and then cast them to the wind. They're interesting people. Between them, they know seven foreign languages. If I want advice about what stock to buy, I can call one son-in-law, and if I want to criticize the president, I can call another. Naturally, my children don't see eye-to-eye about how to live, and sometimes they don't even speak to one another, or they write letters I'm sure they later regret. Still, I sense great loyalty between them.

The last time the whole family was here was for our fortieth wedding anniversary. The TV ran night and day, and no one could keep on top of the chaos in the kitchen. Jenny and Joan had even given friends the phone number, as if they were going into exile instead of visiting their parents for the weekend. The phone rang off the hook. Jenny brought her dog and Joan brought her favorite dalmatian, and the two got into such an awful fight that Jenny's had to spend the night in the backseat of her car. All night long, inside the house, the other dog paced, wanting to get at it. At the end of the visit, when the last car pulled away, Harriet admitted to me that it had been too much for her. She'd gone into the kitchen and stood a broom upside down in the corner and opened the scissors facing the bristles. She'd interviewed a woman who practiced voodoo, and the woman had told her that that was a surefire way to get rid of guests. Harriet felt a little guilty that it had worked: initially, Denise had said that she was going to leave early Monday morning, but by Sunday noon she was gone—and the last to leave.

. . .

I have in my possession cassettes of music the children thought their mother and I should be aware of, photocopies of grandchildren's report cards, California wine with a label saying that it was bottled especially for Joan, and an ingenious key chain you can always find because when you whistle, it beeps. My anniversary present from Jenny was a photo album, in a very nice, compact size, called a brag book. She has filled it with pictures of the grandchildren and the husbands and cats and dogs, and with some cartoons that she thought were amusing. And then there was another brag book that was empty, with a note inside saying that I could brag about whatever I wanted.

For a long while the albums just stayed on the coffee table, buried under magazines or Harriet's fan mail. Then one day when I was coming up the front walk, I looked down and saw a ginkgo leaf. It was as bright as a jewel. I was amazed, even though the neighbor had had that tree, and the leaves had blown over our property, for years. I put the leaf on the coffee table, and then it occurred to me that I could put it in the brag book—press it between the plastic pages—maybe even add some other leaves.

The next day, I put the leaf underneath the plastic, and then I went out and started to look for other leaves. By the end of the week, the book was filled up. I have no memory of doing anything like that as a child. I did collect stamps for a while, but the leaves were a different thing entirely.

To be truthful, there are a few pages in the book right in the middle that aren't filled, but it's getting cold and the leaves are losing their color fast. It may be next year before it's filled. I worked on the front of the book because I had some sense of how I wanted it to begin, and then I filled the back of the book, because I found the perfect leaf to end with, but I wasn't sure about the rest. I thought there might be some particularly unusual leaves, if I went far enough afield.

So yesterday I drove out to the woods in Batesville, to look. If I'd been looking for birds, there were certainly enough of them. It was the sort of day—with all that blue sky and with the tree bark almost jumping out at you in the strong light—that makes you think: Why don't I do this every day? Why isn't everybody out walking? That's the mystery to me—not that there are so many duplicitous people and so many schemes and crimes, but that out there, in the real world, people are so rarely where they should be. I don't usually think about mortality, but the albums were a present commemorating forty years of marriage, which would put anyone in mind of what had happened, as well as what was inevitable. That day in the woods, I thought: Don't run away from the thought of death. Imagine a day at the end of your life. I wasn't thinking of people who were hospitalized or who saw disaster coming at them on the highway. I was thinking of a day that was calm, that seemed much like other days, when suddenly things speeded up—or maybe slowed down—and everything seemed to be happening with immediacy. The world is going on, and you know it. You're not de-crepit, you're not in pain, nothing dramatic is happening. A sparrow flies overhead, breeze rustles leaves. You're going along and suddenly your feet *feel* the ground. I don't mean that your shoes are comfortable. Or even that the ground is solid and that you have a moment when you realize that you are a temporary person, passing. I mean that it seems possible to feel the ground, solid below you, while at the same time the air reminds you that there's a lightness, and then you soak that in, let it sink down, so that suddenly you know that the next wind might blow you over, and that wouldn't be a bad thing. You might squint in the sun-light, look at a leaf spiraling down, genuinely surprised that you were there to see it. A breeze comes again, rippling the surface of a pond. A bird! A leaf! Clouds elongate and stretch thinly across a silvery sky. Flowers, in the distance. Or, in early evening, a sliver of moon. Then imagine that you aren't there any longer, but at a place where you can touch those things that were always too dazzlingly high or too far in the distance—light-years would have been required to get to them—and suddenly you can pluck the stars from the sky, gather all fallen leaves at once.

A NOTE ON THE TYPE

The text of this book was set in Sabon, a typeface designed by Jan Tschichold (1902–1974), the well-known German typographer. Because it was designed in Frankfurt, Sabon was named for the famous Frankfurt typefounder Jacques Sabon, who died in 1580 while manager of the Egenolff foundry. Based loosely on the original designs of Claude Garamond (c. 1480–1561), Sabon is unique in that it was explicitly designed for hot-metal composition on both the Monotype and Linotype machines as well as for film composition.

Composed by Creative Graphics,
Allentown, Pennsylvania

Printed and bound by Berryville Graphics,
Berryville, Virginia

Typography and binding design
by Dorothy S. Baker